MASTERPIECES
OF
FANTASY
AND
ENCHANTMENT

MASTERPIECES
of
FANTASY
and
ENCHANTMENT

Compiled by

David G. Hartwell

with the assistance of

Kathryn Cramer

Doubleday Book & Music Clubs, Inc.
Garden City, New York

Copyright © 1988 by Doubleday Book & Music Clubs, Inc.
All Rights Reserved
Printed in the United States of America

Published by GuildAmerica ® Books, an imprint and a registered trademark of Doubleday Book & Music Clubs, Inc., Department GB, 401 Franklin Avenue, Garden City, New York 11530.

ISBN: 1-56865-174-0

ACKNOWLEDGMENTS

Grateful acknowledgment is made to the following for permission to reprint their copyrighted material:

"The Rule of Names" by Ursula K. Le Guin. Copyright © 1964, 1975 by Ursula K. Le Guin. Reprinted by permission of the author and the author's agent, Virginia Kidd.

"The Goddess on the Street Corner" by Margaret St. Clair. Copyright © 1953 by Margaret St. Clair. Copyright © renewed 1981 by Margaret St. Clair. Reprinted by permission of McIntosh and Otis, Inc.

ACKNOWLEDGMENTS

"The Root and the Ring" by Wyman Guin. From September 1954 *Beyond*. Copyright © 1954 by Galaxy Publishing Corporation. Reprinted by permission of Larry Sternig Literary Agency.

"The Green Magician" by L. Sprague de Camp and Fletcher Pratt. Copyright © 1954 by Galaxy Publishing Corporation; renewed 1982 by L. Sprague de Camp.

"Our Fair City" by Robert A. Heinlein. Copyright © 1948 by *Weird Tales;* copyright © renewed 1975 by Robert A. Heinlein.

"The Man Who Could Not See Devils" by Joanna Russ. Copyright © Anne McCaffrey 1970, *Alchemy and Academe* (N.Y.: Doubleday) 1970.

"Bird of Prey" by John Collier. Copyright 1941, 1968 by John Collier. Reprinted by permission of Harold Matson Company, Inc.

"The Detective of Dreams" by Gene Wolfe. Copyright © 1980 by Gene Wolfe. Reprinted by permission of the author and the author's agent, Virginia Kidd.

"The Red Hawk" by Elizabeth Lynn. Copyright © 1983 by Elizabeth A. Lynn. Reprinted by permission of Richard Curtis Associates, Inc.

"The Silken-swift" by Theodore Sturgeon. Copyright © 1953 by Fantasy House, Inc.; copyright © renewed 1981 by Mercury Press, Inc.

"Mr. Lupescu" by Anthony Boucher. Copyright © 1945 by *Weird Tales Magazine*, renewed 1972 by Phyllis White. Reprinted by permission of Curtis Brown, Ltd.

"The King of the Cats" by Stephen Vincent Benét. From *The Selected Works of Stephen Vincent Benét*. Published by Holt, Rinehart & Winston, Inc. Copyright 1933 by Stephen Vincent Benét. Copyright renewed © 1963 by Thomas C. Benét, Stephanie B. Mahin, and Rachel Benét Lewis. Reprinted by permission of Brandt & Brandt Literary Agents, Inc.

ACKNOWLEDGMENTS

"Uncle Einar" by Ray Bradbury. Copyright © 1947; renewed 1975 by Ray Bradbury. Reprinted by permission of Don Congdon Associates, Inc.

"Space-Time for Springers" by Fritz Leiber. Copyright © 1958 by Fritz Leiber. Reprinted by permission of Richard Curtis Associates, Inc.

"Great Is Diana" by Avram Davidson. Copyright renewed © 1986 by Avram Davidson. First published in *The Magazine of Fantasy and Science Fiction,* August 1958. Reprinted by permission of the author and the author's agent, Richard D. Grant.

"The King of the Elves" by Philip K. Dick. Copyright © 1953 by Galaxy Publishing Corporation; renewed 1981 by Philip K. Dick. Reprinted by permission of the estate of Philip K. Dick and the author's agents, Scott Meredith Literary Agency, Inc., 845 Third Avenue, New York, New York 10022.

"The Tale of Dragons and Dreamers" by Samuel R. Delany. Copyright © 1979 by Samuel R. Delany. Reprinted by permission of the author and his agents, Henry Morrison Inc. (USA)

"Elric at the End of Time" by Michael Moorcock. Copyright © 1981 by Michael Moorcock. Reprinted by permission of Don Congdon Associates, Inc.

"The Sword of Welleran" by Lord Dunsany. Copyright of the estate of Lord Dunsany 1908 © 1972 by Dover Publications Inc. Reprinted by permission of Curtis Brown Ltd. on behalf of John Child Villiers and Valentine Lamb as literary executors of Lord Dunsany.

"Operation Afreet" by Poul Anderson. Copyright © 1956 by Fantasy House, Inc. Reprinted by permission of the author and the author's agents, Scott Meredith Literary Agency, Inc., 845 Third Avenue, New York, New York 10022.

Contents

INTRODUCTION   xi

Enchantments

THE RULE OF NAMES   3
  Ursula K. Le Guin
THE MAGIC FISHBONE   13
  Charles Dickens
THE GODDESS ON THE STREET CORNER   23
  Margaret St. Clair
FEATHERTOP: A MORALIZED LEGEND   31
  Nathaniel Hawthorne
THE ROOT AND THE RING   49
  Wyman Guin
THE GREEN MAGICIAN   70
  L. Sprague de Camp and Fletcher Pratt
OUR FAIR CITY   128
  Robert A. Heinlein

Wonders

THE MAN WHO COULD NOT SEE DEVILS   149
  Joanna Russ

HIEROGLYPHIC TALES
  Horace Walpole
  A New Arabian Night's Entertainment   162
  The King and His Three Daughters   166
  The Dice-box: A Fairy Tale   169
  The Peach in Brandy: A Milesian Tale   173
  Mi Li: A Chinese Fairy Tale   176
  A True Love Story   182
  The Bird's Nest   185

BIRD OF PREY   189
  John Collier

THE DETECTIVE OF DREAMS   197
  Gene Wolfe

THE BEE-MAN OF ORN   214
  Frank R. Stockton

THE RED HAWK   224
  Elizabeth A. Lynn

THE CANVASSER'S TALE   252
  Mark Twain

Creatures

THE SILKEN-SWIFT . . .   261
  Theodore Sturgeon

THE NEW MOTHER   280
  Lucy Clifford

MR. LUPESCU   291
  Anthony Boucher

THE KING OF THE CATS   296
  Stephen Vincent Benét

UNCLE EINAR   310
  Ray Bradbury

SPACE-TIME FOR SPRINGERS   318
  Fritz Leiber

GREAT IS DIANA   330
   Avram Davidson

THE LAST OF THE HUGGERMUGGERS:
A GIANT STORY   339
   Christopher Pearse Cranch

TOBERMORY   368
   Saki

THE KING OF THE ELVES   375
   Philip K. Dick

Worlds

4 AMERICAN FAIRY TALES
   L. Frank Baum

   The Glass Dog   397
   The Queen of Quok   405
   The Magic Bonbons   413
   The Dummy That Lived   419

THE TALE OF DRAGONS AND DREAMERS   426
   Samuel R. Delany

from PHANTASMION   455
   Sara Coleridge

3 TALES
   Kenneth Morris

   The Sapphire Necklace   465
   The Regent of the North   473
   The Eyeless Dragons: A Chinese Story   483

Adventures

ELRIC AT THE END OF TIME   491
   Michael Moorcock

LINDENBORG POOL   532
   William Morris

CONTENTS

THE MOON POOL   540
   A. Merritt
THE SWORD OF WELLERAN   580
   Lord Dunsany
OPERATION AFREET   593
   Poul Anderson

Introduction

Fantasy promises escape from reality. It is characteristic of stories of fantasy that they take the reader out of the real world of hard facts, hard objects, and hard decisions, into a world of wonders and enchantments, a world that need not be either frivolous or inherently juvenile.

Tales of wonder and the fantastic are as old as recorded human imaginative thought, from the epic of Gilgamesh to the *Odyssey* and the fantastic myths of all cultures. What we recognize today as the fantasy story, however, has a much shorter history. Before the eighteenth century, a significant portion of the reading audience considered what we now read as fantastic literature to be in some way true: the tales of gods and goddesses, witches, voyages to strange lands, knights battling monsters, were all presented as taking place in the real world, or in historical or distant parts of that real world. Cervantes wrote *Don Quixote* in part as a satire upon those who read the romances of chivalry as literally as the miracles of the Bible. One can be sure that not all readers did this, but it was a commonplace-enough attitude among readers of his day for Cervantes to create a classic of world literature attacking it. Many people did not take the tales of Arthur as historical, but still, many others did. We do not read the same stories that way now. We read them as charming fantasies, often embodying wisdom.

The literary fantasy, the prose narrative written with the implicit or explicit declaration that "this story is not real," begins to occur in the English language toward the end of the eighteenth century. The idea of prose fiction as a form of popular entertainment became dominant in the eighteenth century, and consequent to the rise of such classic Gothic fiction as Horace Walpole's *The Castle of Otranto* and the novels of Ann Radcliffe and Clara Reeve, tales filled with supernatural occurrences and set in the medieval past. Some, but not all, of the

Gothic works were fantastic in part. Moreover, the fantastic tales of the Arabian Nights and other such stories were first translated into English during this period, as well as some of the Continental fairy tales. The fairy tales and the children's stories achieved the greatest popularity, leading to the persistent notion that realistic fiction is adult reading matter and fantasy is appropriate only for children or the young.

Many of the finest works of fantasy of the nineteenth and twentieth centuries were published only as children's literature. Indeed, the notion of adult fantasy, written about and for the adult reader but often using children as main characters, did not take hold firmly until the twentieth century, and did not become truly widespread until the last two decades. In spite of the Victorian craze for fairy tales and folk tales and regardless of the popularity of such classics as *Alice in Wonderland,* fantasy remained predominantly children's literature.

The earliest fantasy novel in English, Sara Coleridge's *Phantasmion* (1837), an excerpt of which appears in this collection, was published in a small edition as a children's book. While it is perhaps arguable that William Beckford's *Vathek* (1786), that most fantastic of Gothic novels, set in a magical Arabia, holds precedence, it is not until the 1850s that we find repeated examples of long fantasy works written at least in part for an adult audience [George Meredith's *The Shaving of Shagpat* (1856), in the Oriental tradition of Beckford; William Morris' *The Hollow Land* (1856); George MacDonald's *Phantastes* (1858)], and not until the 1890s is there a proliferation of works. The fairy tale, the folk tale, the ghost story, and the horror story all occurred regularly but only the dark fantasies—frightening or pessimistic tales usually involving vengeance from the past and set in the real world—were adult reading. We have chosen for this volume stories by Charles Dickens, Mark Twain, Frank R. Stockton, and William Morris, which are scarce examples of fantasy for adults from the nineteenth century contributing to what we recognize today as adult fantasy.

The fantasy novel had never been common until the influence of J. R. R. Tolkien's masterpiece, *The Lord of the Rings*—its large scale, carefully built fantasy world, and literary complexity—began to be felt in the late 1950s and early 1960s. The current publishing category of fantasy fiction is an innovation of the 1970s. Hundreds of new works have been published and much of the best long work of the last hundred years has been reprinted in the last fifteen years, without formal distinction between much work originally published for children and current adult fantasy. Fortunately, for our purposes, the fantasy short story for adults has grown and thrived since the turn of this century, and much of it has rarely, if ever, been reprinted during the recent novel boom.

Before 1900, the characteristic form of fantasy fiction was the fairy tale. But by the 1890s, other strains of myth and the supernatural mixed and blended with the traditional form, producing many new variations ranging from the heroic medievalism of William Morris to the haunting inventions of Lord Dunsany, from the animal tales of Rudyard Kipling to the scientific wonders of H. G. Wells and the jungle adventures of H. Rider Haggard, and to L. Frank Baum's American fairy tales of Oz. So the fantasy fiction field was evolving and proliferating adult and children's forms of all sorts.

In the early twentieth century, fantastic adventure fiction became standard in the thriving pulp fiction magazines. Edgar Rice Burroughs's and A. Merritt's works, in the Rider Haggard tradition, first appeared in these magazines, and became so popular that Burroughs and Merritt dominated fantasy fiction for more than two decades, until the end of the 1930s. In the 1940s, such magazines as *Famous Fantastic Mysteries, Fantastic Adventures,* and most important, *Unknown* (which first published Theodore Sturgeon, Anthony Boucher, Fritz Leiber, Fredric Brown, and Robert A. Heinlein fantasy stories, among many others) cultivated the adult fantasy reader. Since the 1940s, many digest-size magazines, particularly *The Magazine of Fantasy & Science Fiction* from 1949 to the present, have been the home for adult short fantasy of generally high quality. Most of the stories in this book are from this rich lode of magazine material from 1940 to the present.

Let us now consider the nature of fantasy fiction, which has grown so in recent decades. It seems to me that the slow building and then rapid rise in popularity of the many forms of fantasy, right alongside the rise and proliferation of science fiction and horror fiction, may constitute a popular reaction against the various modes of literary realism. Fashionable fiction has progressively, since the 1930s, become obsessed with technique and with the nuances and gestures of ordinary characters in ordinary situations. It has particularly exhausted every avenue imaginable to illuminate the inner life of characters. Fantasy, on the other hand, manifests and dramatizes internal and psychological states, images, and struggles as external and concrete, and focuses on the external actions of its characters.

Fantasy stories take the reader clearly out of the world of consensus reality. Sometimes we begin in the "real" world, but it quickly becomes evident that behind the veil of real things and people another world exists, rich and strange and magical. The most easily categorized fantasy works are defined by their specifically magical nature, whether they take place in an imaginary medieval landscape, fairyland, or a contemporary metropolis such as New York City or Seattle: magic works. Someone in the story can do magic, has supernatural powers, or is a supernatural creature. While this is the dominant mode, it has never been exclusively the case. The more general case is that fantasy fiction contains and depends upon the intrusion of at least one clearly fantastic element or event into the real world (such as Mark Twain's echo salesman in "The Canvasser's Tale" and Margaret St. Clair's goddess in "The Goddess on the Street Corner"); or, at the other extreme, one real person into an utterly fantastic landscape (e.g., Alice falling into Wonderland, Dorothy in Oz). In either case we have an entry into the fantastic world through setting or character that we recognize as familiar and comforting in the face of the strange and often disturbingly unfamiliar.

Good and evil are clearly manifest in fantasy literature ordinarily. The fantasy takes place in a world wherein moral coordinates are clear and distinct, in a moral landscape wherein moral qualities are most often embodied in major characters other than the central character (who is usually at first portrayed as an everyman, a fairly ordinary person of no particular consequence in the world). But the central character becomes a crucial figure in a struggle between good and evil, in which evil is initially strong and dominant but in the end loses because of the innate superiority of the forces of good and due to the actions and choices of the central character. Phillip K. Dick's "The King of the Elves" is a fine example.

We should note that the subdivision of fantasy known as Sword and Sorcery or Heroic Fantasy (typified by Conan the Barbarian) operates on quite different but still strict moral coordinates. In an amoral world, the hero triumphs over evil because he is strong and clever, but does not change the world essentially, or its moral balance. Edgar Rice Burroughs's Tarzan, for instance, wins every time, but the jungle remains the same.

INTRODUCTION

The single most influential work of contemporary fantasy is Tolkien's trilogy, as I mentioned earlier, from which most others depart but upon which they depend. Above all else, Tolkien's use of moral allegory seems to have created a paradigm for the whole contemporary field of fantasy, especially at novel or trilogy length (and we have Tolkien to thank for the resurrection of the trilogy form). But this convention (the battle between good and evil in a fantasy world) seems to be wearing thin, in spite of Tolkien's immense and enduring popularity. Too many second-rate trilogies clog the book racks. We've seen a proliferation of novels recounting a relatively easy moral victory (as soon as the hero gets the magic sword, jewel, ring, staff, amulet, or whatnot, and learns to accept his ability to use it against the evil god, wizard, witch, ogre, dragon, etc.), which are barely concealed wish-fulfillment fantasies of a rather shallow variety. Much greater variety exists in short forms.

The tone of popular fantasy fiction is basically optimistic. The world of wonders into which the fantasy reader escapes is a version of pastoral utopia set in a vision of the past colored and often somewhat simplified by a nostalgia for pretechnological civilization. It is a world in which values and rank, usually monarchal, are passed in a hereditary line from generation to generation, and a world in which the central character rises in importance, at least in moral strength, if not in fact politically or socially. This world setting is strongly juxtaposed to the morally ambiguous or indeterminate and generally pessimistic tone of literary adult fiction, which is set in a world of equality of suffering where heroism is no longer an option—an urban, technological world. It is also opposed to the world of impossible sexual hospitality of the torrid bestseller or the romantic utopia of the Harlequin Romance, both equally fantastic but essentially repetitive and unimaginative. So the rising popularity of fantasy fiction seems assured in our time.

This anthology presents selections from among the best tales of the past two hundred years, providing a rich sampling of the diversity and delights of fantasy fiction. I have blithely ignored the artificial barrier between children's and adult fiction (a barrier that, I think, is often disregarded by contemporary readers) and sought out excellences of many varieties. It is my hope that you will be surprised, as well as charmed, to discover some of the selections, many of which have never before been anthologized. In assembling the stories, I've attempted to compile a broad selection of the conventional and the unconventional in fantasy writing, to present to the extent possible in a single volume a wide spectrum of fantasy.

Among the escapes and entertainments included are neglected classics by Horace Walpole and Christopher P. Cranch and Mark Twain, an excerpt from Sara Coleridge's novel *Phantasmion*, and little-known pieces by Nathaniel Hawthorne, Charles Dickens, and L. Frank Baum. But a majority of the writers are contemporary, for as we remarked earlier more fantasy seems to have been published in the latter half of this century than ever before. Thus, from the magical world of Le Guin to the fantastical future of Moorcock, from the prehistoric worlds of Joanna Russ and Samuel R. Delany to the present-day enchantments of Fritz Leiber's kitten or Philip K. Dick's elves, I have filled this book with tales of wonder. It seems likely that if fantasy fiction is to attain full adult status in the eyes of the world, then such a rich collection of tradition and achievement as is represented in this book gives substance and force to the claim for the maturity of fantasy fiction.

David G. Hartwell
Pleasantville, N.Y.

ENCHANTMENTS

Stories of magical workings
in this world and others

In this playful, pleasant tale of dragons, magic, treasure, and a battle between wizards, a mediocre wizard turns out to have surprising powers. This story is part of the genesis of URSULA K. LE GUIN's *famous, award-winning* A Wizard of Earthsea, *the first volume of the Earthsea trilogy, one of the greatest works of fantasy of recent decades. Although primarily known as a writer of science fiction, Le Guin's contributions to the emerging publishing genre of fantasy in the 1960s and 1970s are especially significant. Her essay "From Elfland to Poughkeepsie" has influenced a whole generation of fantasy writers. And the Earthsea books, reinterpreting the conventional fantasy images of wizards, dragons, and magic in a carefully constructed, original fantasy world, using a clear, lucid prose style, although published for children, have become one of the foundations of the contemporary adult field. There is no more distinguished fantasist alive, and so it is appropriate to open this volume with a story by Ursula K. Le Guin.*

The Rule of Names
BY URSULA K. LE GUIN

Mr. Underhill came out from under his hill, smiling and breathing hard. Each breath shot out of his nostrils as a double puff of steam, snow-white in the morning sunshine. Mr. Underhill looked up at the bright December sky and smiled wider than ever, showing snow-white teeth. Then he went down to the village.

"Morning, Mr. Underhill," said the villagers as he passed them in the narrow street between houses with conical, overhanging roofs like the fat red caps of toadstools. "Morning, morning!" he replied to each. (It was of course bad luck to wish anyone a *good* morning; a simple statement of the time of day was quite enough, in a place so permeated with Influences as Sattins Island, where a careless adjective might change the weather for a week.) All of them spoke to him, some with affection, some with affectionate disdain. He was all the little island had in the way of a wizard, and so deserved respect—but how could you respect a little fat man of fifty who waddled along with his toes turned in, breathing steam and smiling? He was no great shakes as a workman either. His fireworks were fairly elaborate but his elixirs were weak. Warts he charmed off frequently reappeared after three days; tomatoes he enchanted grew no bigger than cantaloupes; and those rare times when a strange ship stopped at Sattins Harbor, Mr. Underhill always stayed under his hill—for fear, he explained, of the evil eye. He was, in other words, a wizard the way walleyed Gan was a carpenter: by default. The villagers made do with badly-hung doors and inefficient spells, for this generation, and relieved their annoyance by treating Mr. Underhill quite familiarly, as a mere fellow-villager. They even asked him to dinner. Once he asked some of them to dinner, and served a splendid repast, with silver, crystal, damask, roast goose, sparkling Andrades '639, and plum pudding with hard sauce; but he was so nervous all through the meal that it took the joy out of it, and besides, everybody was hungry again half an hour afterward. He did not like anyone to visit his cave, not even the anteroom, beyond which in fact nobody had ever got. When he saw people approaching the hill he always came trotting out to meet them. "Let's sit out here under the pine trees!" he would say, smiling and waving towards the fir grove, or if it was raining, "Let's go have a drink at the inn, eh?" though everybody knew he drank nothing stronger than well-water.

Some of the village children, teased by that locked cave, poked and pried and made raids while Mr. Underhill was away; but the small door that led into the inner chamber was spell-shut, and it seemed for once to be an effective spell. Once a couple of boys, thinking the wizard was over on the West Shore curing Mrs. Ruuna's sick donkey, brought a crowbar and a hatchet up there, but at the first whack of the hatchet on the door there came a roar of wrath from inside, and a cloud of purple steam. Mr. Underhill had got home early. The boys fled. He did not come out, and the boys came to no harm, though they said you couldn't believe what a huge hooting howling hissing horrible bellow that little fat man could make unless you'd heard it.

His business in town this day was three dozen fresh eggs and a pound of liver; also a stop at Seacaptain Fogeno's cottage to renew the seeing-charm on the old man's eyes (quite useless when applied to a case of detached retina, but Mr. Underhill kept trying), and finally a chat with old Goody Guld, the concertina-maker's widow. Mr. Underhill's friends were mostly old people. He was timid with the strong young men of the village, and the girls were shy of him. "He makes me nervous, he smiles so much," they all said, pouting, twisting silky ringlets round a finger. "Nervous" was a newfangled word, and their mothers all replied grimly, "Nervous my foot, silliness is the word for it. Mr. Underhill is a very respectable wizard!"

After leaving Goody Guld, Mr. Underhill passed by the school, which was being held this day out on the common. Since no one on Sattins Island was literate, there were no books to learn to read from and no desks to carve initials on and no blackboards to erase, and in fact no schoolhouse. On rainy days the children met in the loft of the Communal Barn, and got hay in their pants; on sunny days the schoolteacher, Palani, took them anywhere she felt like. Today, surrounded by thirty interested children under twelve and forty uninterested sheep under five, she was teaching an important item on the curriculum: the Rules of Names. Mr. Underhill, smiling shyly, paused to listen and watch. Palani, a plump, pretty girl of twenty, made a charming picture there in the wintry sunlight, sheep and children around her, a leafless oak above her, and behind her the dunes and sea and clear, pale sky. She spoke earnestly, her face flushed pink by wind and words. "Now you know the Rules of Names already, children. There are two, and they're the same on every island in the world. What's one of them?"

"It ain't polite to ask anybody what his name is," shouted a fat, quick boy, interrupted by a little girl shrieking, "You can't never tell your own name to nobody my ma says!"

"Yes, Suba. Yes, Popi dear, don't screech. That's right. You never ask anybody his name. You never tell your own. Now think about that a minute and then tell me why we call our wizard Mr. Underhill." She smiled across the curly heads and the woolly backs at Mr. Underhill, who beamed, and nervously clutched his sack of eggs.

" 'Cause he lives under a hill!" said half the children.

"But is it his truename?"

"No!" said the fat boy, echoed by little Popi shrieking, "No!"

"How do you know it's not?"

" 'Cause he came here all alone and so there wasn't anybody knew his truename so they couldn't tell us, and *he* couldn't—"

"Very good, Suba. Popi, don't shout. That's right. Even a wizard can't tell his truename. When you children are through school and go through the Passage, you'll leave your childnames behind and keep only your truenames, which you must never ask for and never give away. Why is that the rule?"

The children were silent. The sheep bleated gently. Mr. Underhill answered the question: "Because the name is the thing," he said in his shy, soft, husky voice, "and the truename is the true thing. To speak the name is to control the thing. Am I right, Schoolmistress?"

She smiled and curtseyed, evidently a little embarrassed by his participation. And he trotted off towards his hill, clutching his eggs to his bosom. Somehow the minute spent watching Palani and the children had made him very hungry. He locked his inner door behind him with a hasty incantation, but there must have been a leak or two in the spell, for soon the bare anteroom of the cave was rich with the smell of frying eggs and sizzling liver.

The wind that day was light and fresh out of the west, and on it at noon a little boat came skimming the bright waves into Sattins Harbor. Even as it rounded the point a sharp-eyed boy spotted it, and knowing, like every child on the island, every sail and spar of the forty boats of the fishing fleet, he ran down the street calling out, "A foreign boat, a foreign boat!" Very seldom was the lonely isle visited by a boat from some equally lonely isle of the East Reach, or an adventurous trader from the Archipelago. By the time the boat was at the pier half the village was there to greet it, and fishermen were following it homewards, and cowherds and clamdiggers and herb-hunters were puffing up and down all the rocky hills, heading towards the harbor.

But Mr. Underhill's door stayed shut.

There was only one man aboard the boat. Old Seacaptain Fogeno, when they told him that, drew down a bristle of white brows over his unseeing eyes. "There's only one kind of man," he said, "that sails the Outer Reach alone. A wizard, or a warlock, or a Mage . . ."

So the villagers were breathless hoping to see for once in their lives a Mage, one of the mighty White Magicians of the rich, towered, crowded inner islands of the Archipelago. They were disappointed, for the voyager was quite young, a handsome black-bearded fellow who hailed them cheerfully from his boat, and leaped ashore like any sailor glad to have made port. He introduced himself at once as a sea-peddlar. But when they told Seacaptain Fogeno that he carried an oaken walking-stick around with him, the old man nodded. "Two wizards in one town," he said. "Bad!" And his mouth snapped shut like an old carp's.

As the stranger could not give them his name, they gave him one right away: Blackbeard. And they gave him plenty of attention. He had a small mixed cargo of cloth and sandals and piswi feathers for trimming cloaks and cheap incense and levity stones and fine herbs and great glass beads from Venway—the usual peddlar's lot. Everyone on Sattins Island came to look, to chat with the voyager, and perhaps to buy something—"Just to remember him by!" cackled Goody Guld, who like all the women and girls of the village was smitten with Blackbeard's bold good looks. All the boys hung round him too, to hear him tell of his voyages to far, strange islands of the Reach or describe the great rich islands of the Archipelago, the Inner Lanes, the roadsteads white with ships, and the golden roofs of Havnor. The men willingly listened to his tales; but some of them wondered why a trader should sail alone, and kept their eyes thoughtfully upon his oaken staff.

But all this time Mr. Underhill stayed under his hill.

"This is the first island I've ever seen that had no wizard," said Blackbeard one evening to Goody Guld, who had invited him and her nephew and Palani in for a cup of rushwash tea. "What do you do when you get a toothache, or the cow goes dry?"

"Why, we've got Mr. Underhill!" said the old woman.

"For what that's worth," muttered her nephew Birt, and then blushed purple and spilled his tea. Birt was a fisherman, a large, brave, wordless young man. He loved the schoolmistress, but the nearest he had come to telling her of his love was to give baskets of fresh mackerel to her father's cook.

"Oh, you do have a wizard?" Blackbeard asked. "Is he invisible?"

"No, he's just very shy," said Palani. "You've only been here a week, you know, and we see so few strangers here. . . ." She also blushed a little, but did not spill her tea.

Blackbeard smiled at her. "He's a good Sattinsman, then, eh?"

"No," said Goody Guld, "no more than you are. Another cup, nevvy? keep it in the cup this time. No, my dear, he came in a little bit of a boat, four years ago was it? just a day after the end of the shad run, I recall, for they was taking up the nets over in East Creek, and Pondi Cowherd broke his leg that very morning—five years ago it must be. No, four. No, five it is, 'twas the year the garlic didn't sprout. So he sails in on a bit of a sloop loaded full up with great chests and boxes and says to Seacaptain Fogeno, who wasn't blind then, though old enough goodness knows to be blind twice over, 'I hear tell,' he says, 'you've got no wizard nor warlock at all, might you be wanting one?' 'Indeed, if the magic's white!' says the Captain, and before you could say cuttlefish Mr. Underhill had settled down in the cave under the hill and was charming the mange off Goody Beltow's cat. Though the fur grew in grey, and 'twas an orange cat. Queer-looking thing it was after that. It died last winter in the cold spell. Goody Beltow took on so at that cat's death, poor thing, worse than when her man was drowned on the Long Banks, the year of the long herring-runs, when nevvy Birt here was but a babe in petticoats." Here Birt spilled his tea again, and Blackbeard grinned, but Goody Guld proceeded undismayed, and talked on till nightfall.

Next day Blackbeard was down at the pier, seeing after the sprung board in his boat which he seemed to take a long time fixing, and as usual drawing the taciturn Sattinsmen into talk. "Now which of these is your wizard's craft?" he asked. "Or has he got one of those the Mages fold up into a walnut shell when they're not using it?"

"Nay," said a stolid fisherman. "She's oop in his cave, under hill."

"He carried the boat he came in up to his cave?"

"Aye. Clear oop. I helped. Heavier as lead she was. Full oop with great boxes, and they full oop with books o' spells, he says. Heavier as lead she was." And the stolid fisherman turned his back, sighing stolidly. Goody Guld's nephew, mending a net nearby, looked up from his work and asked with equal stolidity, "Would ye like to meet Mr. Underhill, maybe?"

Blackbeard returned Birt's look. Clever black eyes met candid blue ones for a long moment; then Blackbeard smiled and said, "Yes. Will you take me up to the hill, Birt?"

"Aye, when I'm done with this," said the fisherman. And when the net was mended, he and the Archipelagan set off up the village street towards the high green hill above it. But as they crossed the common Blackbeard said, "Hold on a while, friend Birt. I have a tale to tell you, before we meet your wizard."

"Tell away," says Birt, sitting down in the shade of a live-oak.

"It's a story that started a hundred years ago, and isn't finished yet —though it soon will be, very soon. . . . In the very heart of the Archipelago, where the islands crowd thick as flies on honey, there's a little isle called Pendor. The sealords of Pendor were mighty men, in the old days of war before the League. Loot and ransom and tribute came pouring into Pendor, and they gathered a great treasure there, long ago. Then from somewhere away out in the West Reach, where dragons breed on the lava isles, came one day a very mighty dragon. Not one of those overgrown lizards most of you Outer Reach folk call dragons, but a big, black, winged, wise, cunning monster, full of strength and subtlety, and like all dragons loving gold and precious stones above all things. He killed the Sealord and his soldiers, and the people of Pendor fled in their ships by night. They all fled away and left the dragon coiled up in Pendor Towers. And there he stayed for a hundred years, dragging his scaly belly over the emeralds and sapphires and coins of gold, coming forth only once in a year or two when he must eat. He'd raid nearby islands for his food. You know what dragons eat?"

Birt nodded and said in a whisper, "Maidens."

"Right," said Blackbeard. "Well, that couldn't be endured forever, nor the thought of him sitting on all that treasure. So after the League grew strong, and the Archipelago wasn't so busy with wars and piracy, it was decided to attack Pendor, drive out the dragon, and get the gold and jewels for the treasury of the League. They're forever wanting money, the League is. So a huge fleet gathered from fifty islands, and seven Mages stood in the prows of the seven strongest ships, and they sailed towards Pendor. . . . They got there. They landed. Nothing stirred. The houses all stood empty, the dishes on the tables full of a hundred years' dust. The bones of the old Sealord and his men lay about in the castle courts and on the stairs. And the Tower rooms reeked of dragon. But there was no dragon. And no treasure, not a diamond the size of a poppyseed, not a single silver bead . . . Knowing that he couldn't stand up to seven Mages, the dragon had skipped out. They tracked him, and found he'd flown to a deserted island up north called Udrath; they followed his trail there, and what did they find? Bones again. His bones—the dragon's. But no treasure. A wizard, some unknown wizard from somewhere, must have met him single-handed, and defeated him—and then made off with the treasure, right under the League's nose!"

The fisherman listened, attentive and expressionless.

"Now that must have been a powerful wizard and a clever one, first to kill a dragon, and second to get off without leaving a trace. The lords and Mages of the Archipelago couldn't track him at all, neither where he'd come from nor where he'd made off to. They were about to give up. That was last spring; I'd been off on a three-year voyage up in the North Reach, and got back about that time. And they asked me to help them find the unknown wizard. That was clever of them. Because I'm not only a wizard myself, as I think some of the oafs here have guessed, but I am also a descendant of the Lords of Pendor. That treasure is mine. It's mine, and knows that it's mine. Those fools of the League couldn't find it, because it's not theirs. It belongs to the House of Pendor, and the great emerald, the star of the hoard, Inalkil the

Greenstone, knows its master. Behold!" Blackbeard raised his oaken staff and cried aloud, "Inalkil!" The tip of the staff began to glow green, a fiery green radiance, a dazzling haze the color of April grass, and at the same moment the staff tipped in the wizard's hand, leaning, slanting till it pointed straight at the side of the hill above them.

"It wasn't so bright a glow, far away in Havnor," Blackbeard murmured, "but the staff pointed true. Inalkil answered when I called. The jewel knows its master. And I know the thief, and I shall conquer him. He's a mighty wizard, who could overcome a dragon. But I am mightier. Do you want to know why, oaf? Because I know his name!"

As Blackbeard's tone got more arrogant, Birt had looked duller and duller, blanker and blanker; but at this he gave a twitch, shut his mouth, and stared at the Archipelagan. "How did you . . . learn it?" he asked very slowly.

Blackbeard grinned, and did not answer.

"Black magic?"

"How else?"

Birt looked pale, and said nothing.

"I am the Sealord of Pendor, oaf, and I will have the gold my fathers won, and the jewels my mothers wore, and the Greenstone! For they are mine.—Now, you can tell your village boobies the whole story after I have defeated this wizard and gone. Wait here. Or you can come and watch, if you're not afraid. You'll never get the chance again to see a great wizard in all his power." Blackbeard turned, and without a backward glance strode off up the hill towards the entrance to the cave.

Very slowly, Birt followed. A good distance from the cave he stopped, sat down under a hawthorn tree, and watched. The Archipelagan had stopped; a stiff, dark figure alone on the green swell of the hill before the gaping cave-mouth, he stood perfectly still. All at once he swung his staff up over his head, and the emerald radiance shone about him as he shouted, "Thief, thief of the Hoard of Pendor, come forth!"

There was a crash, as of dropped crockery, from inside the cave, and a lot of dust came spewing out. Scared, Birt ducked. When he looked again he saw Blackbeard still standing motionless, and at the mouth of the cave, dusty and dishevelled, stood Mr. Underhill. He looked small and pitiful, with his toes turned in as usual, and his little bowlegs in black tights, and no staff—he never had had one, Birt suddenly thought. Mr. Underhill spoke. "Who are you?" he said in his husky little voice.

"I am the Sealord of Pendor, thief, come to claim my treasure!"

At that, Mr. Underhill slowly turned pink, as he always did when people were rude to him. But he then turned something else. He turned yellow. His hair bristled out, he gave a coughing roar—and was a yellow lion leaping down the hill at Blackbeard, white fangs gleaming.

But Blackbeard no longer stood there. A gigantic tiger, color of night and lightning, bounded to meet the lion. . . .

The lion was gone. Below the cave all of a sudden stood a high grove of trees, black in the winter sunshine. The tiger, checking himself in mid-leap just before he entered the shadow of the trees, caught fire in the air, became a tongue of flame lashing out at the dry black branches. . . .

But where the trees had stood a sudden cataract leaped from the hillside, an arch of silvery crashing water, thundering down upon the fire. But the fire was gone. . . .

For just a moment before the fisherman's staring eyes two hills rose—the green one he knew, and a new one, a bare, brown hillock ready to drink up the rushing waterfall. That passed so quickly it made Birt blink, and after blinking he blinked again, and moaned, for what he saw now was a great deal worse. Where the cataract had been there hovered a dragon. Black wings darkened all the hill, steel claws reached groping, and from the dark, scaly, gaping lips fire and steam shot out.

Beneath the monstrous creature stood Blackbeard, laughing.

"Take any shape you please, little Mr. Underhill!" he taunted. "I can match you. But the game grows tiresome. I want to look upon my treasure, upon Inalkil. Now, big dragon, little wizard, take your true shape. I command you by the power of your true name—Yevaud!"

Birt could not move at all, not even to blink. He cowered, staring whether he would or not. He saw the black dragon hang there in the air above Blackbeard. He saw the fire lick like many tongues from the scaly mouth, the steam jet from the red nostrils. He saw Blackbeard's face grow white, white as chalk, and the beard-fringed lips trembling.

"Your name is Yevaud!"

"Yes," said a great, husky, hissing voice. "My truename is Yevaud, and my true shape is this shape."

"But the dragon was killed—they found dragon-bones on Udrath Island—"

"That was another dragon," said the dragon, and then stooped like a hawk, talons outstretched. And Birt shut his eyes.

When he opened them the sky was clear, the hillside empty, except for a reddish-blackish trampled spot, and a few talon-marks in the grass.

Birt the fisherman got to his feet and ran. He ran across the common, scattering sheep to right and left, and straight down the village street to Palani's father's house. Palani was out in the garden weeding the nasturtiums. "Come with me!" Birt gasped. She stared. He grabbed her wrist and dragged her with him. She screeched a little, but did not resist. He ran with her straight to the pier, pushed her into his fishing-sloop the *Queenie,* untied the painter, took up the oars and set off rowing like a demon. The last that Sattins Island saw of him and Palani was the *Queenie*'s sail vanishing in the direction of the nearest island westward.

The villagers thought they would never stop talking about it, how Goody Guld's nephew Birt had lost his mind and sailed off with the schoolmistress on the very same day that the peddlar Blackbeard disappeared without a trace, leaving all his feathers and beads behind. But they did stop talking about it, three days later. They had other things to talk about, when Mr. Underhill finally came out of his cave.

Mr. Underhill had decided that since his truename was no longer a secret, he might as well drop his disguise. Walking was a lot harder than flying, and besides, it was a long, long time since he had had a real meal.

This fairy tale by CHARLES DICKENS *tells the story of a virtuous, sensible little princess who is given a magic fishbone by her fairy godmother. Although the little girl is a princess and her father is a king, this is really a satirical fairy tale about ordinary life in England. The pretended author is a little Victorian girl. Dickens' influence on the nineteenth century fairy tale was significant. In Dickens' day, the fairy tale was a popular literary form which, certain writers discovered, could be used for subversion of the reader's notions about society. Early in his career, Dickens was publicly opposed to this impure use of fairy tales, but here he uses the fairy tale as social allegory to take positions that his readers might have found unacceptable if stated directly using contemporary characters in familiar, realistic settings. Dickens was the most popular writer of the nineteenth century and one of the greatest of all prose fiction writers in English. This is one of his least-known tales.*

The Magic Fishbone
BY CHARLES DICKENS

ROMANCE. FROM THE PEN OF MISS ALICE RAINBIRD*

There was once a King, and he had a Queen, and he was the manliest of his sex, and she was the loveliest of hers. The King was, in his private profession, Under Government. The Queen's father had been a medical man out of town.

They had nineteen children, and were always having more. Seventeen of these children took care of the baby, and Alicia, the eldest, took care of them all. Their ages varied from seven years to seven months.

Let us now resume our story.

One day the King was going to the Office, when he stopped at the fishmonger's to buy a pound and a half of salmon not too near the tail, which the Queen (who was a careful housekeeper) had requested him to send home. Mr Pickles, the fishmonger, said, "Certainly, sir, is there any other article, good morning."

The King went on towards the Office in a melancholy mood, for Quarter Day was such a long way off, and several of the dear children were growing out of their clothes. He had not proceeded far, when Mr

---

* Aged seven

Pickles's errand-boy came running after him, and said, "Sir, you didn't notice the old lady in our shop."

"What old lady?" inquired the King. "I saw none."

Now, the King had not seen any old lady, because this old lady had been invisible to him, though visible to Mr Pickles's boy. Probably because he messed and splashed the water about to that degree, and flopped the pairs of soles down in that violent manner, that, if she had not been visible to him, he would have spoilt her clothes.

Just then the old lady came trotting up. She was dressed in shot-silk of the richest quality, smelling of dried lavender.

"King Watkins the First, I believe?" said the old lady.

"Watkins," replied the King, "is my name."

"Papa, if I am not mistaken, of the beautiful Princess Alicia?" said the old lady.

"And of eighteen other darlings," replied the King.

"Listen. You are going to the Office," said the old lady.

It instantly flashed upon the King that she must be a Fairy, or how could she know that?

"You are right," said the old lady, answering his thoughts, "I am the Good Fairy Grandmarina. Attend. When you return home to dinner, politely invite the Princess Alicia to have some of the salmon you bought just now."

"It may disagree with her," said the King.

The old lady became so very angry at this absurd idea, that the King was quite alarmed, and humbly begged her pardon.

"We hear a great deal too much about this thing disagreeing and that thing disagreeing," said the old lady, with the greatest contempt it was possible to express. "Don't be greedy. I think you want it all yourself."

The King hung his head under this reproof, and said he wouldn't talk about things disagreeing, any more.

"Be good then," said the Fairy Grandmarina, "and don't! When the beautiful Princess Alicia consents to partake of the salmon—as I think she will—you will find she will leave a fish-bone on her plate. Tell her to dry it, and to rub it, and to polish it till it shines like mother-of-pearl, and to take care of it as a present from me."

"Is that all?" asked the King.

"Don't be impatient, sir," returned the Fairy Grandmarina, scolding him severely. "Don't catch people short, before they have done speaking. Just the way with you grown-up persons. You are always doing it."

The King again hung his head, and said he wouldn't do so any more.

"Be good then," said the Fairy Grandmarina, "and don't! Tell the Princess Alicia, with my love, that the fish-bone is a magic present which can only be used once; but that it will bring her, that once, whatever she wishes for, PROVIDED SHE WISHES FOR IT AT THE RIGHT TIME. That is the message. Take care of it."

The King was beginning, "Might I ask the reason—?" when the Fairy became absolutely furious.

"*Will* you be good, sir?" she exclaimed, stamping her foot on the ground. "The reason for this, and the reason for that, indeed! You are always wanting the reason. No reason. There! Hoity toity me! I am sick of your grown-up reasons."

The King was extremely frightened by the old lady's flying into such a passion, and said he was very sorry to have offended her, and he wouldn't ask for reasons any more.

"Be good then," said the old lady, "and don't!"

With those words, Grandmarina vanished, and the King went on and on and on, till he came to the Office. There he wrote and wrote, till it was time to go home again. Then he politely invited the Princess Alicia, as the Fairy had directed him, to partake of the salmon. And when she had enjoyed it very much, he saw the fish-bone on her plate, as the Fairy had told him he would, and he delivered the Fairy's message, and the Princess Alicia took care to dry the bone, and to rub it, and to polish it till it shone like mother-of-pearl.

And so when the Queen was going to get up in the morning, she said, "O dear me, dear me, my head, my head!" And then she fainted away.

The Princess Alicia, who happened to be looking in at the chamber door, asking about breakfast, was very much alarmed when she saw her Royal Mamma in this state, and she rang the bell for Peggy,—which was the name of the Lord Chamberlain. But remembering where the smelling-bottle was, she climbed on a chair and got it, and after that she climbed on another chair by the bedside and held the smelling-bottle to the Queen's nose, and after that she jumped down and got some water, and after that she jupmed up again and wetted the Queen's forehead, and, in short, when the Lord Chamberlain came in, that dear old woman said to the little Princess, "What a Trot you are! I couldn't have done it better myself!"

But that was not the worst of the Queen's illness. O no! She was very ill indeed, for a long time. The Princess Alicia kept the seventeen young Princes and Princesses quiet, and dressed and undressed and danced the baby, and made the kettle boil, and heated the soup, and swept the hearth, and poured out the medicine, and nursed the Queen, and did all that ever she could, and was as busy busy busy, as busy could be. For there were not many servants at that Palace, for three reasons; because the King was short on money, because a rise in his office never seemed to come, and because quarter-day was so far off that it looked almost as far off and as little as one of the stars.

But on the morning when the Queen fainted away, where was the magic fish-bone? Why, there it was in the Princess Alicia's pocket. She had almost taken it out to bring the Queen to life again, when she put it back, and looked for the smelling bottle.

After the Queen had come out of her swoon that morning, and was dozing, the Princess Alicia hurried up-stairs to tell a most particular secret to a most particularly confidential friend of hers, who was a Duchess. People did suppose her to be a Doll, but she was really a Duchess, though nobody knew it except the Princess.

This most particular secret was the secret about the magic fish-bone, the history of which was well known to the Duchess, because the Princess told her everything. The Princess kneeled down by the bed on which the Duchess was lying, full dressed and wide-awake, and whispered the secret to her. The Duchess smiled and nodded. People might have supposed that she never smiled and nodded, but she often did, though nobody knew it except the Princess.

Then the Princess Alicia hurried down stairs again, to keep watch in the Queen's room. She often kept watch by herself in the Queen's room; but every evening, while the illness lasted, she sat there watching with the King. And every evening the King sat looking at her with a cross look, wondering why she never brought out the magic fish-bone. As often as she noticed this, she ran up stairs, whispered the secret to the Duchess over again, and said to the Duchess besides, "They think we children never have a reason or a meaning!" And the Duchess, though the most fashionable Duchess that ever was heard of, winked her eye.

"Alicia," said the King, one evening when she wished him Good Night.

"Yes, Papa."

"What is become of the magic fish-bone?"

"In my pocket, Papa."

"I thought you had lost it?"

"O no, Papa!"

"Or forgotten it?"

"No, indeed, Papa!"

And so another time the dreadful little snapping pug-dog next door made a rush at one of the young Princes as he stood on the steps coming home from school, and terrified him out of his wits, and he put his hand through a pane of glass, and bled bled bled. When the seventeen other young Princes and Princesses saw him bleed bleed bleed, they were terrified out of their wits too, and screamed themselves black in their seventeen faces all at once. But the Princess Alicia put her hands over all their seventeen mouths, one after another, and persuaded them to be quiet because of the sick Queen. And then she put the wounded Prince's hand in a basin of fresh cold water, while they stared with their twice seventeen are thirty-four put down four and carry three eyes, and then she looked in the hand for bits of glass, and there were fortunately no bits of glass there. And then she said to two chubby-legged Princes who were sturdy though small, "Bring me in the Royal rag-bag; I must snip and stitch and cut and contrive." So those two young Princes tugged at the Royal rag-bag and lugged it in, and the Princess Alicia sat down on the floor with a large pair of scissors and a needle and thread, and snipped and stitched and cut and contrived, and made a bandage and put it on, and it fitted beautifully, and so when it was all done she saw the King her Papa looking on by the door.

"Alicia."

"Yes, Papa."

"What have you been doing?"

"Snipping, stitching, cutting and contriving, Papa."

"Where is the magic fish-bone?"

"In my pocket, Papa."

"I thought you had lost it?"

"O no, Papa!"

"Or forgotten it?"

"No, indeed, Papa!"

After that, she ran up stairs to the Duchess and told her what had passed, and told her the secret over again, and the Duchess shook her flaxen curls and laughed with her rosy lips.

Well! and so another time the baby fell under the grate. The seventeen young Princes and Princesses were used to it, for they were almost always falling under the grate or down the stairs, but the baby was not used to it yet, and it gave him a swelled face and a black eye. The way the poor little darling came to tumble was, that he slid out of the Princess Alicia's lap just as she was sitting, in a great coarse apron that quite smothered her, in front of the kitchen fire, beginning to peel the turnips for the broth for dinner; and the way she came to be doing that was, that the King's cook had run away that morning with her own true love, who was a very tall but very tipsy soldier. Then, the seventeen young Princes and Princesses, who cried at everything that happened, cried and roared. But the Princess Alicia (who couldn't help crying a little herself) quietly called to them to be still, on account of not throwing back the Queen up stairs, who was fast getting well, and said, "Hold your tongues you wicked little monkeys, every one of you, while I examine baby!" Then she examined baby, and found that he hadn't broken anything, and she held cold iron to his poor dear eye, and smoothed his poor dear face, and he presently fell asleep in her arms. Then she said to the seventeen Princes and Princesses, "I am afraid to lay him down yet, lest he should wake and feel pain, be good and you shall all be cooks." They jumped for joy when they heard that, and began making themselves cooks' caps out of old newspapers. So to one she gave the salt-box, and to one she gave the barley, and to one she gave the herbs, and to one she gave the turnips, and to one she gave the carrots, and to one she gave the onions, and to one she gave the spice-box, till they were all cooks, and all running about at work, she sitting in the middle, smothered in the great coarse apron, nursing baby. By and by the broth was done, and the baby woke up, smiling like an angel, and was trusted to the sedatest Princess to hold, while the other Princes and Princesses were squeezed into a far-off corner to look at the Princess Alicia turning out the saucepan-full of broth, for fear (as they were always getting into trouble) they should get splashed and scalded. When the broth came tumbling out, steaming beautifully, and smelling like a nosegay good to eat, they clapped their hands. That made the baby clap his hands; and that, and his looking as if he had a comic toothache, made all the Princes and Princesses laugh. So the Princess Alicia said, "Laugh and be good, and after dinner we will make a nest on the floor in a corner, and he shall sit in his nest and see a dance of eighteen cooks." That delighted the young Princes and Princesses, and they ate up all the broth, and washed up all the plates and dishes, and cleared away, and pushed the table into a corner, and then they in their cooks' caps, and the Princess Alicia in the smothering coarse apron that belonged to the cook that had run away with her own true love that was the very tall but very tipsy soldier, danced a dance of eighteen cooks before the angelic baby, who forgot his swelled face and his black eye, and crowed with joy.

And so then, once more the Princess Alicia saw King Watkins the First, her father, standing in the doorway looking on; and he said: "What have you been doing Alicia?"

"Cooking and contriving, Papa."

"What else have you been doing, Alicia?"

"Keeping the children light-hearted, Papa."

"Where is the magic fish-bone, Alicia?"

"In my pocket, Papa."

"I thought you had lost it?"

"O no, Papa."

"Or forgotten it?"

"No, indeed, Papa."

The King then sighed so heavily, and seemed so low-spirited, and sat down so miserably, leaning his head upon his hand, and his elbow upon the kitchen table pushed away in the corner that the seventeen Princes and Princesses crept softly out of the kitchen, and left him alone with the Princess Alicia and the angelic baby.

"What is the matter, Papa?"

"I am dreadfully poor, my child."

"Have you no money at all, Papa?"

"None, my child."

"Is there no way left of getting any, Papa?"

"No way," said the King. "I have tried very hard, and I have tried all ways."

When she heard those last words, the Princess Alicia began to put her hand into the pocket where she kept the magic fish-bone.

"Papa," said she, "when we have tried very hard, and tried all ways, we must have done our very very best?"

"No doubt, Alicia."

"When we have done our very very best, Papa, and that is not enough, then I think the right time must have come for asking help of others." This was the very secret connected with the magic fish-bone, which she had found out for herself from the good fairy Grandmarina's words, and which she had so often whispered to her beautiful and fashionable friend the Duchess.

So she took out of her pocket the magic fish-bone that had been dried and rubbed and polished till it shone like mother-of-pearl, and she gave it one little kiss and wished it was quarter-day. And immediately it *was* quarter-day, and the King's quarter's salary came rattling down the chimney, and bounced into the middle of the floor.

But this was not half of what happened, no not a quarter, for immediately afterwards the good fairy Grandmarina came riding in, in a carriage and four (Peacocks), with Mr Pickles's boy up behind, dressed in silver and gold, with a cocked-hat, powdered hair, pink silk stockings, a jewelled cane, and a nosegay. Down jumped Mr Pickles's boy with his cocked-hat in his hand and wonderfully polite (being entirely changed by enchantment), and handed Grandmarina out, and there she stood, in her rich shot-silk smelling of dried lavender, fanning herself with a sparkling fan.

"Alicia, my dear," said this charming old Fairy, "how do you do, I hope I see you pretty well, give me a kiss."

The Princess Alicia embraced her, and then Grandmarina turned to the King, and said rather sharply: "Are you good?"

The King said he hoped so.

"I suppose you know the reason, *now*, why my god-Daughter here," kissing the Princess again, "did not apply to the fish-bone sooner?" said the Fairy.

The King made her a shy bow.

"Ah! But you didn't *then!*" said the Fairy.

The King made her a shyer bow.

"Any more reasons to ask for?" said the Fairy.

The King said no, and he was very sorry.

"Be good then," said the Fairy, "and live happy ever afterwards."

Then, Grandmarina waved her fan, and the Queen came in most splendidly dressed, and the seventeen young Princes and Princesses, no longer grown out of their clothes, came in, newly fitted out from top to toe, with tucks in everything to admit of its being let out. After that, the Fairy tapped the Princess Alicia with her fan, and the smothering coarse apron flew away, and she appeared exquisitely dressed, like a little Bride, with a wreath of orange-flowers, and a silver veil. After that, the kitchen dresser changed of itself into a wardrobe, made of beautiful woods and gold and looking-glass, which was full of dresses of all sorts, all for her and all exactly fitting her. After that, the angelic baby came in, running alone, with his face and eye not a bit the worse but much the better. Then, Grandmarina begged to be introduced to the Duchess, and when the Duchess was brought down many compliments passed between them.

A little whispering took place between the Fairy and the Duchess, and then the Fairy said out loud, "Yes, I thought she would have told you." Grandmarina then turned to the King and Queen, and said, "We are going in search of Prince Certainpersonio. The pleasure of your company is requested at church in half an hour precisely." So she and the Princess Alicia got into the carriage, and Mr Pickles's boy handed in the Duchess who sat by herself on the opposite seat, and then Mr Pickles's boy put up the steps and got up behind, and the Peacocks flew away with their tails spread.

Prince Certainpersonio was sitting by himself, eating barley-sugar and waiting to be ninety. When he saw the Peacocks followed by the carriage, coming in at the window, it immediately occurred to him that something uncommon was going to happen.

"Prince," said Grandmarina, "I bring you your Bride."

The moment the Fairy said those words, Prince Certainpersonio's face left off being sticky, and his jacket and corduroys changed to peach-bloom velvet, and his hair curled, and a cap and feather flew in like a bird and settled on his head. He got into the carriage by the Fairy's invitation, and there he renewed his acquaintance with the Duchess whom he had seen before.

In the church were the Prince's relations and friends, and the Princess Alicia's relations and friends, and the seventeen Prince and Princesses, and the baby, and a crowd of the neighbours. The marriage was beautiful beyond expression. The Duchess was bridesmaid, and beheld the ceremony from the pulpit where she was supported by the cushion of the desk.

Grandmarina gave a magnificent wedding feast afterwards, in which there was everything and more to eat, and everything and more to drink. The wedding cake was delicately ornamented with white satin ribbons, frosted silver and white lilies, and was forty-two yards round.

When Grandmarina had drunk her love to the young couple, and Prince Certainpersonio had made a speech, and everybody had cried Hip Hip Hip Hurrah! Grandmarina announced to the King and Queen that in future there would be eight quarter-days in every year, except in leap-year, when there would be ten. She then turned to Certainpersonio and Alicia, and said, "My dears, you will have thirty-five children, and they will all be good and beautiful. Seventeen of your children will be boys, and eighteen will be girls. The hair of the whole of your children will curl naturally. They will never have the measles, and will have recovered from the whooping-cough before being born."

On hearing such good news, everybody cried out, "Hip Hip Hip Hurrah!" again.

"It only remains," said Grandmarina in conclusion, "to make an end of the fish-bone."

So she took it from the hand of the Princess Alicia, and it instantly flew down the throat of the dreadful little snapping pug-dog next door and choked him, and he expired in convulsions.

In this story about faith, miracles, and alcoholism, a down-at-the-heels urban alcoholic is contrasted with a dying goddess, giving a modern, twilight-zone twist to the mythic story of the mortal who falls tragically in love with one of the immortals. MARGARET ST. CLAIR *flourished in the 1950s as a fantasy writer for the post-WWII, digest-size magazines, particularly* The Magazine of Fantasy & Science Fiction. *This story, however, is from* Beyond, *one of the short-lived but distinguished competitors of* F&SF *in the early 1950s.*

The Goddess on the Street Corner
BY MARGARET ST. CLAIR

She spoke to him on the street corner in the late afternoon, when Paul was only a little drunk. Afterwards, he wondered how he could have thought even for a moment that she was a human being. Womanhood was a mask that she wore insecurely. Behind it was a divinity that though old, worn, thin as a thread, was inescapably real. But in that first encounter he thought she was a woman, and he yielded to an imperative that rarely touched him. He took her with him past the liquor store, the grocery, the hock shop, and up to his room.

She stumbled a little as she went over the narrow threshold. Paul put out his hand to steady her, against her white arm. And then he knew.

It was as if he had touched something finer and more subtle than human flesh, something that thrilled with a cold, glowing, radiant life. No woman's arm could feel like that. He stared at her, his heart shaking with tenderness and reverential fear. His conviction was absolute. It was all he could do to keep from throwing himself at her feet.

There was silence. She smiled faintly. He did not know how to address her, by what name to call her. At last he said, "What has happened to you?"

"We get old. Even the gods get old," she answered gravely. She was very pale, and her voice was different from what it had been in the street. He saw under her clothing her silver body was old, old beyond imagining, but still ineffably beautiful. He didn't know what to do. She was so pale he feared she would faint. But do you ask a goddess to please sit down?

Mutely he drew the room's one chair from the wall for her. As she seated herself, he went to the cupboard and got out the sherry jug hesitantly. He put it back. He couldn't ask her to drink what he drank. At last he got brandy, from a pint he had bought last month when he was flush, and brought it to her in a glass.

She sipped at it. The blood—no, some diviner fluid—came back to her cheeks. He began to walk up and down the room, turning to look at her.

She was sitting back in the chair, her lips curved in that faint smile. He thought: "She's like a silver lamp, like having the evening star itself, in my room." Once she raised the glass to her lips and drank. The room seemed full of the reflections of her wrists and hands.

At last he said, "Where are you going to go? What's going to become of you?"

"I don't know."

Her words gave him courage. He said, in a rush, "Stay with me. Let me take care of you. You're—you make me feel that I belong to somebody. I never felt that before. Perhaps your power will come back. Why, you're immortal! You can't get old and—You'll be young again. Won't you please stay?"

She looked at him, and he thought there was gratitude in her bright brow. Slowly she inclined her head. For an instant he felt dizzy, sickened with incredulity as he realized that the foam-born daughter of Zeus had come to live with him.

Those were strange days. In the morning Paul would go to the liquor store and buy brandy for her, the best he could afford. It was the only human thing he had found that she could eat or drink. When he got back she would be sitting in the armchair, bathed and dressed, but quite exhausted. He would open the brandy. He never drank any of it himself; it was for her.

As the day wore on, her cheeks would be less white. He would sit on the floor beside her, quietly, in a voiceless communion. Now and again she would stretch out her divine hand and lay it on his human head. Then vast shining shapes would move through his mind. Once she told him a story, with long pauses between the words, about Achilles and the fighting around Troy. It was as if she unfolded some bright embroidered tapestry.

At night she slept in his bed and he on a blanket on the floor beside it. He would wake two or three times during the night to make sure that she was covered and sleeping quietly. In the darkness her body gave out a faint, pale, lovely silver light. He would kneel beside the bed watching, trembling with awe. Once he thought, "She owns me. Whether she wants to or not. I'm her dog."

He hoped she was getting better. He didn't know. He wanted it too much to trust his own hope.

On the sixth day his money ran out. The brandy he had been buying cost more than the sherry he was accustomed to drink, and his pension check would not come until the end of the month. He stood shivering in front of the liquor store, thinking of cheaper brandy and looking up absently at the sky. It was a dull slate blue; he thought it would snow before night. Then he turned and walked four blocks to the Blucher Laboratories and sold them a pint of his blood.

The nurse who took the blood was doubtful about him. She weighed him, and then said he was too thin. But Paul stood looking at her silently, and at last she pursed her lips and shrugged. He was permitted to lie down on the padded bench and have a vein in his upper arm opened. He went out with eight dollars in his hand.

He bought the bottle of brandy at the package goods store and started home with it. His footsteps were slow. He was feeling, not nauseated (the nurse had insisted on his swallowing coffee and a doughnut before she would dismiss him), but remote from himself and weak. His heart seemed to pound lightly and hollowly. The nurse had been right to be dubious over him.

It took him five minutes or so to get up the stairs. He had to stop often to rest. When he opened the door, she was sitting in the armchair. He looked at her with the objectivity induced by his feeling of exhaustion and remoteness. She was very pale. Paler, he thought, than she had been yesterday.

He opened the brandy and brought it to her in a glass. As she took it, she said, "You look tired, Paul. Do you have a girl somewhere? You were gone a long time."

For a moment he could only stare at her. A sudden bright indignation cut through the fog in his mind. Did she think, could she possibly think, that he, who sat by her feet in the day, who slept on the floor beside her in the night, could . . . could . . . ? Then the tenderness and benignity in her face reached him, and he saw the concern for him that had made her ask.

He looked away from her. "No, nothing like that. I'm . . . not so young any more," he answered, half in apology.

"Young!" For the first time he heard her laugh. The sound was like the sudden flash of sunlight on a wave. "Why, you're nothing but a boy. You don't know how young you are. Sit down by me on the floor, Paul."

As he obeyed, she put out one hand and tipped his face up to her. He shuddered all over at the touch. She studied him with her translucent golden eyes. Then she nodded and smiled.

"No, you're not handsome," she said, almost teasingly. "But . . . I cannot have lost all my power." For a moment her face changed. He saw that she was afraid. "I'll take care of you, oh, I know I can. Paul, the girls are going to be nice to you."

"That's good," he said awkwardly. In a flash of wry humor he thought, "She's optimistic because she has succeeded with even more unpromising human material than I am." Then the gentleness in her face shook him to the heart, and he repeated more warmly, "That's good."

She put her white hand over her eyes. "I never scorned human needs. Or human love."

On the next day she questioned him lightly, trying to hide her disappointment when he replied with negatives. The day after that she asked him more doubtfully; he saw that her self-confidence was going.

On the third day he excused himself at twilight and went out to walk in the street. Shivering, he paced up and down before the liquor store, the hock shop, the grocery (his overcoat had gone long ago), and invented the details of an amorous adventure. When his imagination was satisfied, he looked at the clock in the window of the second liquor store, and was dismayed to find that less than half an hour had passed. What he was going to say had happened couldn't have happened in under an hour; he had some forty minutes to kill. He walked back and forth, rehearsing his story and shivering. Then he ran up the stairs to her.

The light had not been turned on. Except for the pale, pale radiance from her body, the room was in darkness. He knelt by her feet, glad to be invisible, and told her his lies.

Once or twice she interrupted to put a question. He could feel that she was smiling. "So," she said, when he had come to the limits of his invention, "isn't it as I told you? Paul, didn't I tell you I'd take care of you?" There was a triumph in her voice.

"Yes. Thank you for it."

"And did you please *her?*" she asked after a moment, more gravely. "So that she gave you that final pleasure, of seeing a woman turned into more than a woman in your arms? I hope it was like that."

"It was like that."

The faint light of her body had grown stronger; he could perceive even in the dark that pleasure was making her smile. He was glad that he had lied to her. When he got to his feet and switched on the room's one weak bulb, he saw that her face was alive with her delight.

After that he told her many lies. He would walk up and down in the dusk, shivering uncontrollably as the year advanced and the winter grew more cold, and contrive stories of warm, perfumed rooms, wide couches, and girls with satin thighs. He got to know every watch and camera behind the metal lattice of the hock shop, every bottle in the window of the liquor stores. He thought none of the merchants in his street changed their displays often enough.

Once or twice he took twenty cents from the change in his pockets and went to the picture house on the corner, out of the cold, to sit through banging westerns and dramas of wealthy society, but usually he could not afford them, and after the third time he came the nurse at the Blucher Laboratories had refused to take any more blood from him, saying scoldingly, "What you need is less sherry to drink and more to eat. Why is it that you people don't ever want to eat?"—so he no longer had that source of revenue.

He bought freesias with two dollars of the money he got for the last pint of blood. He took the flowers in their green wrapper up the stairs to her, telling her he'd had a windfall, things were looking up for him. She received his story as yet another evidence of her success in taking care of him. The room was no more full of the delicate perfume of the flowers than it was of the silver reflections of her smiling lips and the movements of her hands.

He was always afraid that she would see past his lies to the cold, dirty reality, but somehow—whether because she had lost most of her power, or because it had not ever extended in that direction—she never did. She accepted his stories unquestioningly.

Yet, as the days passed and her body grew always lighter and more tenuous, it came to him that she was dying. His lies and his care could not help her. There were times when he thought she rallied, when he would permit himself to hope.

On Thursday he had no money left at all. He went to the laboratories. The nurse frowned at him through the window and shook her head menacingly. He went to the liquor store nearest the corner and stood about, fingering bottles, until the proprietor's back was turned. Then he put a pint of brandy in his pocket and walked out with it. She drank it slowly, growing a little less bloodless. Thursday was a good day.

Friday was bright and clear. Last night the moon had been full; it had snowed all night. The room had been full of the snow's cold radiance. He had wakened several times to look at her in the night. Now, in the hard light of morning, he could hardly see her. She was like a pale flame in the sun.

"How are you?" he asked anxiously as he prepared to leave her.

"Oh, I'm much better this morning, Paul. I almost think my power is coming back." She smiled at him. She seemed to believe it; he felt a tiny jet of hope as he went down the stair.

He had decided to try it again. He entered the liquor store and walked toward the back, where the brandy was. He waited carefully; then his hand went out. With shattering abruptness the proprietor spoke to him.

"Look here, Minton, you can't get away with this," he said sternly. "I saw you take that bottle yesterday, and I didn't say anything. You've been a good customer, and there are times when a man has to have a pint. But I'm not going to let you do it today too. A whole pint of brandy—what did you do with it?"

"I—" Paul's body had begun to shake.

"Well, I guess I know. You ought to've stuck to that sherry wine. Brandy costs too much. And there's no use your trying to lift a pint from Jake, at the other store. I told him about you."

Paul went out. The snow had been cleared from the sidewalks, but it still lay in the street. He bit his fingers desperately. Then he went to the laboratories and, despite the nurse's hostile frown, went in.

"Please," he said, "I've just got to—please—"

She looked at him for a long time, frowning and shaking her head. But at last she shrugged her shoulders, saying angrily, "Well, if you want to kill yourself!" and let him lie down on the bench. He thought she did not take quite the full pint.

He was slow getting back to his room. He had the brandy in his pocket, but he was dizzy, lightheaded, sick. The stairs had never seemed so long.

When he opened the door, she was standing beside the bed. He looked at her foolishly. "Did you see it?" she asked.

"See what?" he answered stupidly. Her voice, for all its excitement, had sounded remote and very weak.

"Why, what I made happen in the street. Didn't I tell you, Paul, that my power was coming back?" She smiled at him in triumph, but her body seemed to waver in the air.

"Oh. Yes, I—

"This morning I felt so much better. I thought I would try. And I succeeded. Surely you must have seen the masses of flowers near the window? Go over to the window and look out."

She was growing frightened. He obeyed her. He raised the sash and peered out dizzily.

For a moment he could see nothing. His eyes blurred; he had to blink them again and again. Then he made out, in the snow beneath the window, a tiny, tiny pale pink flower.

"Yes, you are right. Your power has come back to you. It is—a miracle. The whole street is full of flowers."

Her face grew devine with laughter. She held out her hands toward him, laughing, and he reached out for them. But the unearthly, beautiful body had grown as tenuous as smoke; he could not touch her. Still she smiled at him. For a moment a most wonderful perfume hovered in the air. There was a rainbow iridescence. Then she disappeared.

He stared stupidly at the spot where she had been. It was impossible; he would not believe it. But, as the moments passed and the room remained empty and silent, he realized that it had happened. He was alone now. She was gone; she had left him. Aphrodite was dead.

She had left him. He was all alone. And now—he tried to laugh as the irony came to him, but weeping choked him—and now, whose dog was he? The brandy was in his pocket, unopened. He would not have to sell any more blood for her. Who was going to take care of him?

The fantasy elements in this story about a witch who enchants a scarecrow, whom she names Feathertop, are the vehicles for wry social satire. Feathertop becomes virtually interchangeable with other young men, but Feathertop has an excuse for his shallowness: he has a pumpkin head. A prolific novelist, NATHANIEL HAWTHORNE (1804–1864) *also wrote a number of fantasy and supernatural stories, among them "Young Goodman Brown" and "Rappaccini's Daughter." "Feathertop" appears to be the one of his stories that influenced L. Frank Baum's Oz books.*

Feathertop:
A Moralized Legend
BY NATHANIEL HAWTHORNE

"Dickon," cried Mother Rigby, "a coal for my pipe!"

The pipe was in the old dame's mouth when she said these words. She had thrust it there after filling it with tobacco, but without stooping to light it at the hearth, where indeed there was no appearance of a fire having been kindled that morning. Forthwith, however, as soon as the order was given, there was an intense red glow out of the bowl of the pipe, and a whiff of smoke from Mother Rigby's lips. Whence the coal came, and how brought thither by an invisible hand, I have never been able to discover.

"Good!" quoth Mother Rigby, with a nod of her head. "Thank ye, Dickon! And now for making this scarecrow. Be within call, Dickon, in case I need you again."

The good woman had risen thus early (for as yet it was scarcely sunrise) in order to set about making a scarecrow, which she intended to put in the middle of her corn-patch. It was now the latter week of May, and the crows and blackbirds had already discovered the little, green, rolled-up leaf of the Indian corn just peeping out of the soil. She was determined, therefore, to contrive as lifelike a scarecrow as ever was seen, and to finish it immediately, from top to toe, so that it should begin its sentinel's duty that very morning. Now Mother Rigby (as everybody must have heard) was one of the most cunning and potent witches in New England, and might, with very little trouble, have made a scarecrow ugly enough to frighten the minister himself. But on this occasion, as she had awakened in an uncommonly pleasant humor, and was further dulcified by her pipe of tobacco, she resolved to produce something fine, beautiful, and splendid, rather than hideous and horrible.

"I don't want to set up a hobgoblin in my own corn-patch, and almost at my own doorstep," said Mother Rigby to herself, puffing out a whiff of smoke; "I could do it if I pleased, but I'm tired of doing marvellous things, and so I'll keep within the bounds of every-day business just for variety's sake. Besides, there is no use in scaring the little children for a mile roundabout, though 't is true I'm a witch."

It was settled, therefore, in her own mind, that the scarecrow should represent a fine gentleman of the period, so far as the materials at hand would allow. Perhaps it may be as well to enumerate the chief of the articles that went to the composition of this figure.

The most important item of all, probably, although it made so little show, was a certain broomstick, on which Mother Rigby had taken many an airy gallop at midnight, and which now served the scarecrow by way of a spinal column, or, as the unlearned phrase it, a backbone. One of its arms was a disabled flail which used to be wielded by Goodman Rigby, before his spouse worried him out of this troublesome world; the other, if I mistake not, was composed of the pudding stick and a broken rung of a chair, tied loosely together at the elbow. As for its legs, the right was a hoe handle, and the left an undistinguished and miscellaneous stick from the woodpile. Its lungs, stomach, and other affairs of that kind were nothing better than a meal bag stuffed with straw. Thus we have made out the skeleton and entire corporosity of the scarecrow, with the exception of its head; and this was admirably supplied by a somewhat withered and shrivelled pumpkin, in which Mother Rigby cut two holes for the eyes, and a slit for the mouth, leaving a bluish-colored knob in the middle to pass for a nose. It was really quite a respectable face.

"I've seen worse ones on human shoulders, at any rate," said Mother Rigby. "And many a fine gentleman has a pumpkin head, as well as my scarecrow."

But the clothes, in this case, were to be the making of the man. So the good old woman took down from a peg an ancient plum-colored coat of London make, and with relics of embroidery on its seams, cuffs, pocket-flaps, and button-holes, but lamentably worn and faded, patched at the elbows, tattered at the skirts, and threadbare all over. On the left breast was a round hole, whence either a star of nobility had been rent away, or else the hot heart of some former wearer had scorched it through and through. The neighbors said that this rich garment belonged to the Black Man's wardrobe, and that he kept it at Mother Rigby's cottage for the convenience of slipping it on whenever he wished to make a grand appearance at the governor's table. To match the coat there was a velvet waistcoat of very ample size, and formerly embroidered with foliage that had been as brightly golden as the maple leaves in October, but which had now quite vanished out of the substance of the velvet. Next came a pair of scarlet breeches, once worn by the French governor of Louisbourg, and the knees of which had touched the lower step of the throne of Louis le Grand. The Frenchman had given these smallclothes to an Indian powwow, who parted with them to the old witch for a gill of strong waters, at one of their dances in the forest. Furthermore, Mother Rigby produced a pair of silk stockings and put them on the figure's legs, where they showed as unsubstantial as a dream, with the wooden reality of the two sticks making itself miserably apparent through the holes. Lastly, she put her dead husband's wig on the bare scalp of the pumpkin, and surmounted the whole with a dusty three-cornered hat, in which was stuck the longest tail feather of a rooster.

Then the old dame stood the figure up in a corner of her cottage and chuckled to behold its yellow semblance of a visage, with its nobby little nose thrust into the air. It had a strangely self-satisfied aspect, and seemed to say, "Come look at me!"

"And you are well worth looking at, that's a fact!" quoth Mother Rigby, in admiration at her own handiwork. "I've made many a puppet since I've been a witch, but methinks this is the finest of them all. 'T is almost too good for a scarecrow. And, by the by, I'll just fill a fresh pipe of tobacco and then take him out to the corn-patch."

While filling her pipe the old woman continued to gaze with almost motherly affection at the figure in the corner. To say the truth, whether it were chance, or skill, or downright witchcraft, there was something wonderfully human in this ridiculous shape, bedizened with its tattered finery; and as for the countenance, it appeared to shrivel its yellow surface into a grin—a funny kind of expression betwixt scorn and merriment, as if it understood itself to be a jest at mankind. The more Mother Rigby looked the better she was pleased.

"Dickon," cried she sharply, "another coal for my pipe!"

Hardly had she spoken, than, just as before, there was a red-glowing coal on the top of the tobacco. She drew in a long whiff and puffed it forth again into the bar of morning sunshine which struggled through the one dusty pane of her cottage window. Mother Rigby always liked to flavor her pipe with a coal of fire from the particular chimney corner whence this had been brought. But where that chimney corner might be, or who brought the coal from it—further than that the invisible messenger seemed to respond to the name of Dickon—I cannot tell.

"That puppet yonder," thought Mother Rigby, still with her eyes fixed on the scarecrow, "is too good a piece of work to stand all summer in a corn-patch, frightening away the crows and blackbirds. He's capable of better things. Why, I've danced with a worse one, when partners happened to be scarce, at our witch meetings in the forest! What if I should let him take his chance among the other men of straw and empty fellows who go bustling about the world?"

The old witch took three or four more whiffs of her pipe and smiled.

"He'll meet plenty of his brethren at every street corner!" continued she. "Well; I didn't mean to dabble in witchcraft to-day, further than the lighting of my pipe, but a witch I am, and a witch I'm likely to be, and there's no use trying to shirk it. I'll make a man of my scarecrow, were it only for the joke's sake!"

While muttering these words, Mother Rigby took the pipe from her own mouth and thrust it into the crevice which represented the same feature in the pumpkin visage of the scarecrow.

"Puff, darling, puff!" said she. "Puff away, my fine fellow! your life depends on it!"

This was a strange exhortation, undoubtedly, to be addressed to a mere thing of sticks, straw, and old clothes, with nothing better than a shrivelled pumpkin for a head—as we know to have been the scarecrow's case. Nevertheless, as we must carefully hold in remembrance, Mother Rigby was a witch of singular power and dexterity; and, keeping this fact duly before our minds, we shall see nothing beyond credibility in the remarkable incidents of our story. Indeed, the great difficulty will be at once got over, if we can only bring ourselves to believe that, as soon as the old dame bade him puff, there came a whiff of smoke from the scarecrow's mouth. It was the very feeblest of whiffs, to be sure; but it was followed by another and another, each more decided than the preceding one.

"Puff away, my pet! puff away, my pretty one!" Mother Rigby

kept repeating, with her pleasantest smile. "It is the breath of life to ye; and that you may take my word for."

Beyond all question the pipe was bewitched. There must have been a spell either in the tobacco or in the fiercely-glowing coal that so mysteriously burned on top of it, or in the pungently-aromatic smoke which exhaled from the kindled weed. The figure, after a few doubtful attempts, at length blew forth a volley of smoke extending all the way from the obscure corner into the bar of sunshine. There it eddied and melted away among the motes of dust. It seemed a convulsive effort; for the two or three next whiffs were fainter, although the coal still glowed and threw a gleam over the scarecrow's visage. The old witch clapped her skinny hands together, and smiled encouragingly upon her handiwork. She saw that the charm worked well. The shrivelled, yellow face, which heretofore had been no face at all, had already a thin, fantastic haze, as it were of human likeness, shifting to and fro across it; sometimes vanishing entirely, but growing more perceptible than ever with the next whiff from the pipe. The whole figure, in like manner, assumed a show of life, such as we impart to ill-defined shapes among the clouds, and half deceive ourselves with the pastime of our own fancy.

If we must needs pry closely into the matter, it may be doubted whether there was any real change, after all, in the sordid, worn-out, worthless, and ill-jointed substance of the scarecrow; but merely a spectral illusion, and a cunning effect of light and shade so colored and contrived as to delude the eyes of most men. The miracles of witchcraft seem always to have had a very shallow subtlety; and, at least, if the above explanation does not hit the truth of the process, I can suggest no better.

"Well puffed, my pretty lad!" still cried old Mother Rigby. "Come, another good stout whiff, and let it be with might and main. Puff for thy life, I tell thee! Puff out of the very bottom of thy heart, if any heart thou hast, or any bottom to it! Well done, again! Thou didst suck in that mouthful as if for the pure love of it."

And then the witch beckoned to the scarecrow, throwing so much magnetic potency into her gesture that it seemed as if it must inevitably be obeyed, like the mystic call of the loadstone when it summons the iron.

"Why lurkest thou in the corner, lazy one?" said she. "Step forth! Thou hast the world before thee!"

Upon my word, if the legend were not one which I heard on my grandmother's knee, and which had established its place among things credible before my childish judgment could analyze its probability, I question whether I should have the face to tell it now.

In obedience to Mother Rigby's word, and extending its arm as if to reach her outstretched hand, the figure made a step forward—a kind of hitch and jerk, however, rather than a step—then tottered and almost lost its balance. What could the witch expect? It was nothing, after all, but a scarecrow stuck upon two sticks. But the strong-willed old beldam scowled, and beckoned, and flung the energy of her purpose so forcibly at this poor combination of rotten wood, and musty straw, and ragged garments, that it was compelled to show itself a man, in spite of the reality of things. So it stepped into the bar of sunshine. There it stood—poor devil of a contrivance that it was!—with only the thinnest vesture of human similitude about it, through which was evident the stiff, rickety, incongruous, faded, tattered, good-for-nothing patchwork of its substance, ready to sink in a heap upon the floor, as conscious of its own unworthiness to be erect. Shall I confess the truth? At its present point of vivification, the scarecrow reminds me of some of the lukewarm and abortive characters, composed of heterogeneous materials, used for the thousandth time, and never worth using, with which romance writers (and myself, no doubt, among the rest) have so over-peopled the world of fiction.

But the fierce old hag began to get angry and show a glimpse of her diabolic nature (like a snake's head, peeping with a hiss out of her bosom), at this pusillanimous behavior of the thing which she had taken the trouble to put together.

"Puff away, wretch!" cried she, wrathfully. "Puff, puff, puff, thou thing of straw and emptiness! thou rag or two! thou meal bag! thou pumpkin head! thou nothing! Where shall I find a name vile enough to call thee by? Puff, I say, and suck in thy fantastic life along with the smoke! else I snatch the pipe from thy mouth and hurl thee where that red coal came from."

Thus threatened, the unhappy scarecrow had nothing for it but to puff away for dear life. As need was, therefore, it applied itself lustily to the pipe, and sent forth such abundant volleys of tobacco smoke that the small cottage kitchen became all vaporous. The one sunbeam struggled mistily through, and could but imperfectly define the image of the cracked and dusty window pane on the opposite wall. Mother Rigby, meanwhile, with one brown arm akimbo and the other stretched towards the figure, loomed grimly amid the obscurity with such port and expression as when she was wont to heave a ponderous nightmare on her victims and stand at the bedside to enjoy their agony. In fear and trembling did this poor scarecrow puff. But its efforts it must be acknowledged, served an excellent purpose for, with each successive whiff, the figure lost more and more of its dizzy and perplexing tenuity and seemed to take denser substance. Its very garments, moreover, partook of the magical change, and shone with the gloss of novelty and glistened with the skilfully embroidered gold that had long ago been rent away. And, half revealed among the smoke, a yellow visage bent its lustreless eyes on Mother Rigby.

At last the old witch clinched her fist and shook it at the figure. Not that she was positively angry, but merely acting on the principle—perhaps untrue, or not the only truth, though as high a one as Mother Rigby could be expected to attain—that feeble and torpid natures, being incapable of better inspiration, must be stirred up by fear. But here was the crisis. Should she fail in what she now sought to effect, it was her ruthless purpose to scatter the miserable simulacre into its original elements.

"Thou hast a man's aspect," said she, sternly. "Have also the echo and mockery of a voice! I bid thee speak!"

The scarecrow gasped, struggled, and at length emitted a murmur, which was so incorporated with its smoky breath that you could scarcely tell whether it were indeed a voice or only a whiff of tobacco. Some narrators of this legend hold the opinion that Mother Rigby's conjurations and the fierceness of her will had compelled a familiar spirit into the figure, and that the voice was his.

"Mother," mumbled the poor stifled voice, "be not so awful with me! I would fain speak; but being without wits, what can I say?"

"Thou canst speak, darling, canst thou?" cried Mother Rigby, relaxing her grim countenance into a smile. "And what shalt thou say, quotha! Say, indeed! Art thou of the brotherhood of the empty skull, and demandest of me what thou shalt say? Thou shalt say a thousand things, and saying them a thousand times over, thou shalt still have said nothing! Be not afraid, I tell thee! When thou comest into the world (whither I purpose sending thee forthwith) thou shalt not lack the wherewithal to talk. Talk! Why, thou shalt babble like a millstream, if thou wilt. Thou hast brains enough for that, I trow!"

"At your service, mother," responded the figure.

"And that was well said, my pretty one," answered Mother Rigby. "Then thou speakest like thyself, and meant nothing. Thou shalt have a hundred such set phrases, and five hundred to the boot of them. And now, darling, I have taken so much pains with thee and thou art so beautiful, that, by my troth, I love thee better than any witch's puppet in the world; and I've made them of all sorts—clay, wax, straw, sticks, night fog, morning mist, sea foam, and chimney smoke. But thou art the very best. So give heed to what I say."

"Yes, kind mother," said the figure, "with all my heart!"

"With all thy heart!" cried the old witch, setting her hands to her sides and laughing loudly. "Thou hast such a pretty way of speaking. With all thy heart! And thou didst put thy hand to the left side of thy waistcoat as if thou really hadst one!"

So now, in high good humor with this fantastic contrivance of hers, Mother Rigby told the scarecrow that it must go and play its part in the great world, where not one man in a hundred, she affirmed, was gifted with more real substance than itself. And, that he might hold up his head with the best of them, she endowed him, on the spot, with an unreckonable amount of wealth. It consisted partly of a gold mine in Eldorado, and of ten thousand shares in a broken bubble, and of half a million acres of vineyard at the North Pole, and of a castle in the air, and a chateau in Spain, together with all the rents and income therefrom accruing. She further made over to him the cargo of a certain ship, laden with salt of Cadiz, which she herself, by her necromantic arts, had caused to founder, ten years before, in the deepest part of mid-ocean. If the salt were not dissolved, and could be brought to market, it would fetch a pretty penny among the fishermen. That he might not lack ready money, she gave him a copper farthing of Birmingham manufacture, being all the coin she had about her, and likewise a great deal of brass, which she applied to his forehead, thus making it yellower than ever.

"With that brass alone," quoth Mother Rigby, "thou canst pay thy way all over the earth. Kiss me, pretty darling! I have done my best for thee."

Furthermore, that the adventurer might lack no possible advantage towards a fair start in life, this excellent old dame gave him a token by which he was to introduce himself to a certain magistrate, member of the council, merchant, and elder of the church (the four capacities constituting but one man), who stood at the head of society in the neighboring metropolis. The token was neither more nor less than a single word, which Mother Rigby whispered to the scarecrow, and which the scarecrow was to whisper to the merchant.

"Gouty as the old fellow is, he'll run thy errands for thee, when once thou hast given him that word in his ear," said the old witch. "Mother Rigby knows the worshipful Justice Gookin, and the worshipful Justice knows Mother Rigby!"

Here the witch thrust her wrinkled face close to the puppet's, chuckling irrepressibly, and fidgeting all through her system, with delight at the idea which she meant to communicate.

"The worshipful Master Gookin," whispered she, "hath a comely maiden to his daughter. And hark ye, my pet! Thou hast a fair outside, and a pretty wit enough of thine own. Yea, a pretty wit enough! Thou wilt think better of it when thou hast seen more of other people's wits. Now, with thy outside and thy inside, thou art the very man to win a young girl's heart. Never doubt it! I tell thee it shall be so. Put but a bold face on the matter, sigh, smile, flourish thy hat, thrust forth thy leg like a dancing-master, put thy right hand to the left side of thy waistcoat, and pretty Polly Gookin is thine own!"

All this while the new creature had been sucking in and exhaling the vapory fragrance of his pipe, and seemed now to continue this occupation as much for the enjoyment it afforded as because it was an essential condition of his existence. It was wonderful to see how exceedingly like a human being it behaved. Its eyes (for it appeared to possess a pair) were bent on Mother Rigby, and at suitable junctures it nodded or shook its head. Neither did it lack words proper for the occasion: "Really! Indeed! Pray tell me! Is it possible! Upon my word! By no means! Oh! Ah! Hem!" and other such weighty utterances as imply attention, inquiry, acquiescence, or dissent on the part of the auditor. Even had you stood by and seen the scarecrow made, you could scarcely have resisted the conviction that it perfectly understood the cunning counsels which the old witch poured into its counterfeit of an ear. The more earnestly it applied its lips to the pipe, the more distinctly was its human likeness stamped among visible realities, the more sagacious grew its expression, the more lifelike its gestures and movements, and the more intelligibly audible its voice. Its garments, too, glistened so much the brighter with an illusory magnificence. The very pipe, in which burned the spell of all this wonderwork, ceased to appear as a smoke-blackened earthen stump, and became a meerschaum, with painted bowl and amber mouthpiece.

It might be apprehended, however, that as the life of the illusion seemed identical with the vapor of the pipe, it would terminate simultaneously with the reduction of the tobacco to ashes. But the beldam foresaw the difficulty.

"Hold thou the pipe, my precious one," said she, "while I fill it for thee again."

It was sorrowful to behold how the fine gentleman began to fade back into a scarecrow while Mother Rigby shook the ashes out of the pipe and proceeded to replenish it from her tobacco-box.

"Dickon," cried she, in her high, sharp tone, "another coal for this pipe!"

No sooner said than the intensely red speck of fire was glowing within the pipe-bowl; and the scarecrow, without waiting for the witch's bidding, applied the tube to his lips and drew in a few short, convulsive whiffs, which soon, however, became regular and equable.

"Now, mine own heart's darling," quoth Mother Rigby, "whatever may happen to thee, thou must stick to thy pipe. Thy life is in it; and that, at least, thou knowest well, if thou knowest nought besides. Stick to thy pipe, I say! Smoke, puff, blow thy cloud; and tell the people, if any question be made, that it is for thy health, and that so the physician orders thee to do. And, sweet one, when thou shalt find thy pipe getting low, go apart into some corner, and (first filling thyself with smoke) cry sharply, 'Dickon, a fresh pipe of tobacco!' and, 'Dickon, another coal for my pipe!' and have it into thy pretty mouth as speedily as may be. Else, instead of a gallant gentleman in a gold-laced coat, thou wilt be but a jumble of sticks and tattered clothes, and a bag of straw, and a withered pumpkin! Now depart, my treasure, and good luck go with thee!"

"Never fear, mother!" said the figure, in a stout voice, and sending forth a courageous whiff of smoke, "I will thrive, if an honest man and a gentleman may!"

"Oh, thou wilt be the death of me!" cried the old witch, convulsed with laughter. "That was well said. If an honest man and a gentleman may! Thou playest thy part to perfection. Get along with thee for a smart fellow; and I will wager on thy head, as a man of pith and substance, with a brain and what they call a heart, and all else that a man should have, against any other thing on two legs. I hold myself a better witch than yesterday, for thy sake. Did not I make thee? And I defy any witch in New England to make such another! Here; take my staff along with thee!"

The staff, though it was but a plain oaken stick, immediately took the aspect of a gold-headed cane.

"That gold head has as much sense in it as thine own," said Mother Rigby, "and it will guide thee straight to worshipful Master Gookin's door. Get thee gone, my pretty pet, my darling, my precious one, my treasure; and if any ask thy name, it is Feathertop. For thou hast a feather in thy hat, and I have thrust a handful of feathers into the hollow of thy head, and thy wig, too, is of the fashion they call Feathertop—so be Feathertop thy name!"

And, issuing from the cottage, Feathertop strode manfully towards town. Mother Rigby stood at the threshold, well pleased to see how the sunbeams glistened on him, as if all his magnificence were real, and how diligently and lovingly he smoked his pipe, and how handsomely he walked, in spite of a little stiffness of his legs. She watched him until out of sight, and threw a witch benediction after her darling, when a turn of the road snatched him from her view.

Betimes in the forenoon, when the principal street of the neighboring town was just at its acme of life and bustle, a stranger of very distinguished figure was seen on the sidewalk. His port as well as his garments betokened nothing short of nobility. He wore a richly-embroidered plum-colored coat, a waistcoat of costly velvet, magnificently adorned with golden foliage, a pair of splendid scarlet breeches, and the finest and glossiest of white silk stockings. His head was covered with a peruke, so daintily powdered and adjusted that it would have been sacrilege to disorder it with a hat; which, therefore (and it was a gold-laced hat, set off with a snowy feather), he carried beneath his arm. On the breast of his coat glistened a star. He managed his gold-headed cane with an airy grace, peculiar to the fine gentlemen of the period; and, to give the highest possible finish to his equipment, he had lace ruffles at his wrist, of a most ethereal delicacy, sufficiently avouching how idle and aristocratic must be the hands which they half concealed.

It was a remarkable point in the accoutrement of this brilliant personage that he held in his left hand a fantastic kind of a pipe, with an exquisitely painted bowl and an amber mouthpiece. This he applied to his lips as often as every five or six paces, and inhaled a deep whiff of smoke, which, after being retained a moment in his lungs, might be seen to eddy gracefully from his mouth and nostrils.

As may well be supposed, the street was all astir to find out the stranger's name.

"It is some great nobleman, beyond question," said one of the towns-people. "Do you see the star at his breast?"

"Nay; it is too bright to be seen," said another. "Yes; he must needs be a nobleman, as you say. But by what conveyance, think you, can his lordship have voyaged or travelled hither? There has been no vessel from the old country for a month past; and if he have arrived overland from the southward, pray where are his attendants and equipage?"

"He needs no equipage to set off his rank," remarked a third. "If he came among us in rags, nobility would shine through a hole in his elbow. I never saw such dignity of aspect. He has the old Norman blood in his veins, I warrant him."

"I rather take him to be a Dutchman, or one of your high Germans," said another citizen. "The men of those countries have always the pipe at their mouths."

"And so has a Turk," answered his companion. "But, in my judgment, this stranger hath been bred at the French court, and hath there learned politeness and grace of manner, which none understand so well as the nobility of France. That gait, now! A vulgar spectator might deem it stiff—he might call it a hitch and jerk—but, to my eye, it hath an unspeakable majesty, and must have been acquired by constant observation of the deportment of the Grand Monarque. The stranger's character and office are evident enough. He is a French ambassador, come to treat with our rulers about the cession of Canada."

"More probably a Spaniard," said another, "and hence his yellow complexion; or, most likely, he is from the Havana, or from some port on the Spanish main, and comes to make investigation about the piracies which our government is thought to connive at. Those settlers in Peru and Mexico have skins as yellow as the gold which they dig out of their mines."

"Yellow or not," cried a lady, "he is a beautiful man!—so tall, so slender! such a fine, noble face, with so well-shaped a nose, and all that delicacy of expression about the mouth! And, bless me, how bright his star is! It positively shoots out flames!"

"So do your eyes, fair lady," said the stranger, with a bow and a flourish of his pipe; for he was just passing at the instant. "Upon my honor, they have quite dazzled me."

"Was ever so original and exquisite a compliment?" murmured the lady, in an ecstasy of delight.

Amid the general admiration excited by the stranger's appearance, there were only two dissenting voices. One was that of an impertinent cur, which, after snuffing at the heels of the glistening figure, put its tail between its legs and skulked into its master's back yard, vociferating an execrable howl. The other dissentient was a young child, who squalled at the fullest stretch of his lungs, and babbled some unintelligible nonsense about a pumpkin.

Feathertop meanwhile pursued his way along the street. Except for the few complimentary words to the lady, and now and then a slight inclination of the head in requital of the profound reverences of the bystanders, he seemed wholly absorbed in his pipe. There needed no other proof of his rank and consequence than the perfect equanimity with which he comported himself, while the curiosity and admiration of the town swelled almost into clamor around him. With a crowd gathering behind his footsteps, he finally reached the mansion-house of the worshipful Justice Gookin, entered the gate, ascended the steps of the front door, and knocked. In the interim, before his summons was answered, the stranger was observed to shake the ashes out of his pipe.

"What did he say in that sharp voice?" inquired one of the spectators.

"Nay, I know not," answered his friend. "But the sun dazzles my eyes strangely. How dim and faded his lordship looks all of a sudden! Bless my wits, what is the matter with me?"

"The wonder is," said the other, "that his pipe, which was out only an instant ago, should be all alight again, and with the reddest coal I ever saw. There is something mysterious about this stranger. What a whiff of smoke was that! Dim and faded did you call him? Why, as he turns about the star on his breast is all ablaze."

"It is, indeed," said his companion; "and it will go near to dazzle pretty Polly Gookin, whom I see peeping at it out of the chamber window."

The door being now opened, Feathertop turned to the crowd, made a stately bend of his body like a great man acknowledging the reverence of the meaner sort, and vanished into the house. There was a mysterious kind of a smile, if it might not better be called a grin or grimace, upon his visage; but, of all the throng that beheld him, not an individual appears to have possessed insight enough to detect the illusive character of the stranger except a little child and a cur dog.

Our legend here loses somewhat of its continuity, and, passing over the preliminary explanation between Feathertop and the merchant, goes in quest of the pretty Polly Gookin. She was a damsel of a soft, round figure, with light hair and blue eyes, and a fair, rosy face, which seemed neither very shrewd nor very simple. This young lady had caught a glimpse of the glistening stranger while standing at the threshold, and had forthwith put on a laced cap, a string of beads, her finest kerchief, and her stiffest damask petticoat in preparation for the interview. Hurrying from her chamber to the parlor, she had ever since been viewing herself in the large looking-glass and practising pretty airs —now a smile, now a ceremonious dignity of aspect, and now a softer smile than the former, kissing her hand likewise, tossing her head, and managing her fan; while within the mirror an unsubstantial little maid repeated every gesture and did all the foolish things that Polly did, but without making her ashamed of them. In short, it was the fault of pretty Polly's ability rather than her will if she failed to be as complete an artifice as the illustrious Feathertop himself; and, when she thus tampered with her own simplicity, the witch's phantom might well hope to win her.

No sooner did Polly hear her father's gouty footsteps approaching the parlor door, accompanied with the stiff clatter of Feathertop's high-heeled shoes, than she seated herself bolt upright and innocently began warbling a song.

"Polly! daughter Polly!" cried the old merchant. "Come hither, child."

Master Gookin's aspect, as he opened the door, was doubtful and troubled.

"This gentleman," continued he, presenting the stranger, "is the Chevalier Feathertop—nay, I beg his pardon, my Lord Feathertop—who hath brought me a token of remembrance from an ancient friend of mine. Pay your duty to his lordship, child, and honor him as his quality deserves."

After these few words of introduction, the worshipful magistrate immediately quitted the room. But, even in that brief moment, had the fair Polly glanced aside at her father instead of devoting herself wholly to the brilliant guest, she might have taken warning of some mischief nigh at hand. The old man was nervous, fidgety, and very pale. Purposing a smile of courtesy, he had deformed his face with a sort of galvanic grin, which, when Feathertop's back was turned, he exchanged for a scowl, at the same time shaking his fist and stamping his gouty foot—an incivility which brought its retribution along with it. The truth appears to have been that Mother Rigby's word of introduction, whatever it might be, had operated far more on the rich merchant's fears than on his good will. Moreover, being a man of wonderfully acute observation, he had noticed that these painted figures on the bowl of Feathertop's pipe were in motion. Looking more closely, he became convinced that these figures were a party of little demons, each duly provided with horns and a tail, and dancing hand in hand, with gestures of diabolical merriment, round the circumference of the pipe bowl. As if to confirm his suspicions, while Master Gookin ushered his guest along a dusky passage from his private room to the parlor, the star on Feathertop's breast had scintillated actual flames, and threw a flickering gleam upon the wall, the ceiling, and the floor.

With such sinister prognostics manifesting themselves on all hands, it is not to be marvelled at that the merchant should have felt that he was committing his daughter to a very questionable acquaintance. He cursed, in his secret soul, the insinuating elegance of Feathertop's manners, as this brilliant personage bowed, smiled, put his hand on his heart, inhaled a long whiff from his pipe, and enriched the atmosphere with the smoky vapor of a fragrant and visible sigh. Gladly would poor Master Gookin have thrust his dangerous guest into the street, but there was a constraint and terror within him. This respectable old gentleman, we fear, at an earlier period of life, had given some pledge or other to the evil principle, and perhaps was now to redeem it by the sacrifice of his daughter.

It so happened that the parlor door was partly of glass, shaded by a silken curtain, the folds of which hung a little awry. So strong was the merchant's interest in witnessing what was to ensue between the fair Polly and the gallant Feathertop that, after quitting the room, he could by no means refrain from peeping through the crevice of the curtain.

But there was nothing very miraculous to be seen; nothing—except the trifles previously noticed—to confirm the idea of a supernatural peril environing the pretty Polly. The stranger it is true was evidently a thorough and practised man of the world, systematic and self-possessed, and therefore the sort of a person to whom a parent ought not to confide a simple, young girl without due watchfulness for the result. The worthy magistrate, who had been conversant with all degrees and qualities of mankind, could not but perceive every motion and gesture of the distinguished Feathertop came in its proper place; nothing had been left rude or native in him; a well-digested conventionalism had incorporated itself thoroughly with his substance and transformed him into a work of art. Perhaps it was this peculiarity that invested him with a species of ghastliness and awe. It is the effect of anything completely and consummately artificial, in human shape, that the person impresses us as an unreality and as having hardly pith enough to cast a shadow upon the floor. As regarded Feathertop, all this resulted in a wild, extravagant, and fantastical impression, as if his life and being were akin to the smoke that curled upward from his pipe.

But pretty Polly Gookin felt not thus. The pair were now promenading the room: Feathertop with his dainty stride and no less dainty grimace; the girl with a native maidenly grace, just touched, not spoiled, by a slightly affected manner, which seemed caught from the perfect artifice of her companion. The longer the interview continued, the more charmed was pretty Polly, until, within the first quarter of an hour (as the old magistrate noted by his watch), she was evidently beginning to be in love. Nor need it have been witchcraft that subdued her in such a hurry; the poor child's heart, it may be, was so very fervent that it melted her with its own warmth as reflected from the hollow semblance of a lover. No matter what Feathertop said, his words found depth and reverberation in her ear; no matter what he did, his action was heroic to her eye. And by this time it is to be supposed there was a blush on Polly's cheek, a tender smile about her mouth, and a liquid softness in her glance; while the star kept coruscating on Feathertop's breast, and the little demons careered with more frantic merriment than ever about the circumference of his pipe bowl. O pretty Polly Gookin, why should these imps rejoice so madly that a silly maiden's heart was about to be given to a shadow! Is it so unusual a misfortune, so rare a triumph?

By and by Feathertop paused, and throwing himself into an imposing attitude, seemed to summon the fair girl to survey his figure and resist him longer if she could. His star, his embroidery, his buckles glowed at that instant with unutterable splendor; the picturesque hues of his attire took a richer depth of coloring; there was a gleam and polish over his whole presence betokening the perfect witchery of well-ordered manners. The maiden raised her eyes and suffered them to linger upon her companion with a bashful and admiring gaze. Then, as if desirous of judging what value her own simple comeliness might have side by side with so much brilliancy, she cast a glance towards the full-length looking-glass in front of which they happened to be standing. It was one of the truest plates in the world and incapable of flattery. No sooner did the images therein reflected meet Polly's eye than she shrieked, shrank from the stranger's side, gazed at him for a moment in the wildest dismay, and sank insensible upon the floor. Feathertop likewise had looked towards the mirror, and there beheld, not the glittering mockery of his outside show, but a picture of the sordid patchwork of his real composition, stripped of all witchcraft.

The wretched simulacrum! We almost pity him. He threw up his arms with an expression of despair that went further than any of his previous manifestations towards vindicating his claims to be reckoned human; for, perchance the only time since this so often empty and deceptive life of mortals began its course, an illusion had seen and fully recognized itself.

Mother Rigby was seated by her kitchen hearth in the twilight of this eventful day, and had just shaken the ashes out of a new pipe, when she heard a hurried tramp along the road. Yet it did not seem so much the tramp of human footsteps as the clatter of sticks or the rattling of dry bones.

"Ha!" thought the old witch, "what step is that? Whose skeleton is out of its grave now, I wonder?"

A figure burst headlong into the cottage door. It was Feathertop! His pipe was still alight; the star still flamed upon his breast; the embroidery still glowed upon his garments; nor had he lost, in any degree or manner that could be estimated, the aspect that assimilated him with our mortal brotherhood. But yet, in some indescribable way (as is the case with all that has deluded us when once found out), the poor reality was felt beneath the cunning artifice.

"What has gone wrong?" demanded the witch. "Did yonder sniffling hypocrite thrust my darling from his door? The villain! I'll set twenty fiends to torment him till he offer thee his daughter on his bended knees!"

"No, mother," said Feathertop despondingly; "it was not that."

"Did the girl scorn my precious one?" asked Mother Rigby, her fierce eyes glowing like two coals of Tophet. "I'll cover her face with pimples! Her nose shall be as red as the coal in thy pipe! Her front teeth shall drop out! In a week hence she shall not be worth thy having!"

"Let her alone, mother," answered poor Feathertop; "the girl was half won; and methinks a kiss from her sweet lips might have made me altogether human. But," he added, after a brief pause and then a howl of self-contempt, "I've seen myself, mother! I've seen myself for the wretched, ragged, empty thing I am! I'll exist no longer!"

Snatching the pipe from his mouth, he flung it with all his might against the chimney, and at the same instant sank upon the floor, a medley of straw and tattered garments, with some sticks protruding from the heap, and a shrivelled pumpkin in the midst. The eyeholes were now lustreless; but the rudely-carved gap, that just before had been a mouth, still seemed to twist itself into a despairing grin, and was so far human.

"Poor fellow!" quoth Mother Rigby, with a rueful glance at the relics of her ill-fated contrivance. "My poor, dear, pretty Feathertop! There are thousands upon thousands of coxcombs and charlatans in the world, made up of just such a jumble of worn-out, forgotten, and good-for-nothing trash as he was! Yet they live in fair repute, and never see themselves for what they are. And why should my poor puppet be the only one to know himself and perish for it?"

While thus muttering, the witch had filled a fresh pipe of tobacco, and held the stem between her fingers, as doubtful whether to thrust it into her own mouth or Feathertop's.

"Poor Feathertop!" she continued. "I could easily give him another chance and send him forth again to-morrow. But no; his feelings are too tender, his sensibilities too deep. He seems to have too much heart to bustle for his own advantage in such an empty and heartless world. Well! well! I'll make a scarecrow of him after all. 'T is an innocent and useful vocation, and will suit my darling well; and, if each of his human brethren had as fit a one, 't would be the better for mankind; and as for this pipe of tobacco, I need it more than he."

So saying, Mother Rigby put the stem between her lips. "Dickon!" cried she, in her high, sharp tone, "another coal for my pipe!"

A magic ring that gives its wearer mathematical powers is the focus of this delightful mathematical fantasy, one of the few fantasies by WYMAN GUIN, *the most distinguished author of psychological science fiction of the 1950s. This story is a tonic and an antidote to the clichéd fantasy of wish-fulfillment and/or tragic punishment, addressing instead the problem of keeping hold of sanity in the face of the fantastic and the magical.*

The Root and the Ring
BY WYMAN GUIN

During the depression, I didn't have a job, but I married a lovely girl who did—and she held onto it.

One day, she declared to me, "I want to have a baby."

"Well," I said, "don't act as if I am an obstacle to that ambition."

"As a matter of fact, dear, you are."

Until she announced this blunt business, I had been sitting quietly, thinking, and bothering no one. Now I asserted testily, "You have no proof yet."

She came over and bent and kissed me, and the way she did this made it obvious that I was misunderstanding her. She then drew back and looked in my eyes, her pretty auburn head tilted a little to one side, her chin raised a degree.

Quite calmly, and with supreme logic, she observed, "If I am going to have a baby, you will have to have a job."

That is how I was launched on the road to success. I didn't dream in those days that I could owe as much money as I do now.

In fact, as the happy years rolled along, bringing two fine children and the carefully geared stages of success, I began to realize that I could probably be even more successful and accumulate more and more property and that certainly I would have bigger and bigger bills to worry about and more and more social obligations.

I got to thinking about that.

Presently I could see that being any more successful than I was right then, when we were so happy, wasn't very practical. Finally, it came to me that if I got to be as successful as some of the fellows around me, I wouldn't have the time and insight to sit down and realize I didn't want to be that successful.

"This is it," I said to myself at the office one day. "This is where I get off the train. I will have to find a way to stay moderately unsuccessful, the way I am now."

There seemed no better time than the present to go to work at it, so I scooped all the hot projects up off my desk and tossed them in a drawer to cool for a week or so. Then I sat there and thought about how I was going to tell my wife of the new plan.

I could see that wasn't going to be easy.

After a while, I was interrupted by my secretary coming in. She opened her mouth to speak and shut it. She stared at me, then at the clean desk-top. She started backing out of the office.

There was an unnatural rise in my voice as I asked her, "What is it?"

"It's all right. It can wait. I didn't realize you were busy thinking."

She closed the door with a lingering look of surprised respect.

What a hot new beginning I had made! A few more mistakes like that and I would be doomed to success. Just imagine, if the boss had come in and found me sitting there thinking . . .

Good Lord!—the words might have flashed through his mind—*this man has caliber. Just because he can't count beyond his fingers doesn't mean there isn't a place for him at the top.* That would be the one-way door. I would have to join the Riverdale Club and worry annually about the station wagon set voting me back in. I would have to develop ulcers and take them to Mayo's at the end of each fiscal year.

I would be like the man who bought a second-hand yacht because the price was so low—and then discovered it burned 900 gallons of fuel a day, needed a crew of four, including a captain, and that the boat made his clothes and house and car and wife look shabby—all of which explained why the previous owner had practically given it away. In a situation like that, you can take your beating and get out, or run yourself into bankruptcy trying to look and act and live as though you could afford a yacht.

Success is a lot harder to work your way out of; the gains and losses aren't so easy to see. When we were married, for instance, we lived in a furnished cottage and took buses. Then came raises. They meant, successively, better houses in better sections of town, taxis, then a car, then a car for each of us, period furniture, modern furniture, individually designed custom-built furniture, a record collection, a hi-fi sound system, TV screens at least as big as our neighbors', a liquor cabinet, then a small bar, finally a big one with something for every taste, a freezer, washing machine, a whole laundry room, a glassed-in stall shower, only one wasn't enough, which meant another bathroom, and so forth.

Here, let me make it even clearer. You know that the national budget is mostly indebtedness from past wars—I understand we're still paying off on 1812, and didn't somebody put in a claim for stuff appropriated in the Revolutionary War, except that the interest was disallowed? Well, I was still paying off on things from several raises ago, only the interest damned well was *not* disallowed. Any more raises and we'd be living in the most luxurious penury, complete with swimming pool, anybody could imagine!

So I hastily got out the hot projects and scattered them about my desk. I would just have to go on working hard at them, taking good care never to get anywhere with them. I settled down safely behind the paper barrier and began to think about how I would tell my wife.

I never got the chance. That night, while I was trying to get started, she gave me a wedding ring. I know that sounds strange, but it's like the problem of success—once you understand the facts, the whole thing becomes clear.

She gave me a wedding ring, even though we'd been married a long while and had two children, because, as I've mentioned, I didn't have a job when she and I were married. That is the concrete but not the symbolic reason why I had borrowed the money for the ring I gave her. I borrowed five dollars, the most money he has ever loaned in his life, from the fellow she was engaged to. Then I took this lovely girl who had said she would marry me, and we picked out a depression-style wedding ring for that price.

My wife's old boy-friend had money to start with. He is a perfect example of the strength of character that comes with an atmosphere of moderate *wealth.* Even while we were in college, he invested, little by little, in stuff that would make him really rich a few years later. After he was really rich, he put a fabulous engagement ring on this girl who just wasn't his type. She realized this and was unhappy about it.

So I borrowed five dollars from him to replace his ring and make her happy again.

My wife has never wanted any other ring. As a matter of principle, I didn't pay him back.

My wife always felt that I should have had a wedding ring, too. And the very day that I sat in my office, working out my plan to remain moderately unsuccessful, my wife was innocently arranging the time-payments on my wedding ring.

That evening, after our son and daughter had gone off to an early movie, we sat down to a quiet martini before dinner. I was bursting with my new plan, but I noticed that she kept looking at me sort of starry-eyed, and I saw the time wasn't ripe. She took my hands in hers and drew me down beside her on a couch.

"Darling, this is a little ceremony."

"Yes?" I asked uncomfortably, but with an appropriately eager smile.

She glanced obliquely at the coffee table, where there was a little box beside my martini. I picked it up, knowing it was a ring and that it meant a lot to her.

Practically all men wear rings—wedding rings, old school rings, lodge rings. Many buy and wear expensive rings of no special significance. I lost my high school class ring within a week of the time I got it, and I was surprised how strongly some of the fellows felt this to be a pretty shoddy piece of negligence. Even so, I have never cared much to wear a ring.

I decided, when I looked at this ring my wife was offering me, that it would be a small inconvenience if it made her a little happier. After she had slipped it on my finger, I kissed her gratefully. I admired its dull gold surfaces in silence for a while. Then I commented on how rich it looked. Finally I had a long sip from my nearly dry martini.

My wife rested her auburn head on my shoulder and held my hand and looked at the ring. "It would have been silly to get you a real wedding ring after fifteen years," she explained. "We will understand, just between us, that it's a wedding ring, won't we?"

"That's right. It's a real wedding ring to us."

"Did you notice that the raised work down the center is a line of symbols?"

"No, I didn't realize that." I lifted my hand and scrutinized the ring. I started to take it off for a better look and noticed the hasty, partial motion of her hand, as though she wished to prevent me. I pretended I had only meant to turn the ring on my finger to review the whole line of symbols. Then I saw the band had an odd half-twist.

"The words are ancient Arabic," she supplied. "It's a very old ring. Nobody knows how old. When the jeweler showed me this, I fell in love with it. You do like it, too, don't you?"

"Of course I do, darling. It's a very handsome thing."

"I thought you seemed a little hesitant about it."

I looked shocked. "Oh, no—*no*, I like it very much. And you're wonderful to want to give it to me."

"Aren't you curious about what the symbols mean, darling?"

"I was just going to ask. What do they mean?"

"You won't think it's a foolish notion?"

"Why should I think a thing like that? It isn't foolish, is it?"

"*I* don't think so."

"Well?"

"The jeweler wasn't sure, of course, but it says something about the person under the influence of this ring being favored above all men in the arts of numbers."

I glanced sharply at my wife's face. It looked completely innocent. Besides, she's not the practical-joker type, or any kind of joker, for that matter.

"Don't you think," I asked hesitantly, "that I'm a little inappropriate as the wearer? I can't even keep our checkbook balanced."

"Darling, the symbols are a beautiful design and we don't have to think about what they mean. I fell in love with the ring before I knew they meant anything. I wish now I hadn't told you."

"Forget it, dear," I said lightly. "I like it. I won't give the symbols another thought."

I have an old school friend in the anthropology department over at the university. The next day, I called on him, with the ring as heavy as a millstone on my finger.

I slipped it off and handed it to him. He poked it about in his palm for a while and then said, "Hmmmm!" Then, later, he said, "*Hmmmm!* It's a moebius curve, isn't it?"

I didn't say anything, figuring he was the guy with the answers. He got a reading glass out of his desk and studied the ring more closely.

Finally he asked, "Where did you get this?"

"One of the jewelers downtown picked it up in Europe for my wife."

"I've never heard of anything like it and I know the Gujarat goldwork of India pretty well."

"I thought it was supposed to be Arabic."

"Oh, there's some Arabic here. For that matter, there's some Latin, too. But the original inscription is in Gujarati. Near as I can make it out, it says, 'The ring of magic that brought our minds the zero.' That makes sense, naturally, because the zero makes its appearance in Gujarat inscriptions of the 6th century A.D."

"What does the Arabic say?"

"Can't read it. You've read the Latin, I suppose?"

"Flunked it."

"Well, your ring was blessed by Sylvester II."

"Who's he?"

He indicated an encyclopedia in the bookshelves. I found the name and read for a while.

"Well?"

"He was formerly known as Gerbert and he was the first man in Europe to use an abacus with ciphers. The story that he stole it from an Arab in Spain is discredited." I put the book back. "Maybe it was this ring he filched?"

My friend the anthropologist was certainly excited about it. The two of us pranced off to another room in the building, where a little bald-headed man studied the Arabic inscription under a glass.

He looked up and said, "Roughly, 'The magic ring of al-Khwarizmi, manipulator of emptiness.'"

I repeated, "Emptiness?"

"It's the Arabic word, *sifr*, from which our *cipher* is derived."

My friend the anthropologist said, "Al-Khwarizmi was the great Arabian mathematician who developed the decimal system. Do you realize this ring has followed the zero through three different cultures, from one revolution in mathematics to another?"

I asked the little bald-headed man, "Doesn't it say anything else in Arabic?"

He studied it again. "No, that's all the Arabic there is on it."

Somehow, I was doubly disturbed that the ring did not say what my wife had thought it said. *It actually said so much more.*

I took the ring from the little bald-headed man and slipped it back on my finger. I said, "I'll think about it," when my friend the anthropologist suggested I bring it back another time for him to study.

One week later, I lost the ring.

It happened that the director's monthly report for our company had been circulated the day before I lost the ring and, ever since glancing through those figures, my mind had been working out some remarkably simple changes in our operation that would result in a much better profit picture. The ease with which I grasped and replanned the financial structure of the company frightened me. I had no intention of drifting into more raises and more debts. Not when my plans called, instead, for loving my wife, raising my kids and building an amateur telescope in the backyard of the only house east of the Mississippi that I cared to own.

I knew the damned ring fitted my finger loosely. I had even mentioned this a couple of times to my wife. She assured me it was a good fit, but on Saturday, while I was building a retaining wall around the big apple tree on the steep slope of our back yard, I lost it. With my attention on the building of the retaining wall and my mind working miracles with the company figures, I didn't notice that the ring was gone until late in the afternoon. By then, I had already filled in the planting area behind the retaining wall and around the tree and planted ivy in the resulting bed.

I went into the house and explained carefully to my wife what had happened. For a moment, I thought she was going to cry.

I suggested the best thing would be to tear out the right side of the new retaining wall and start digging from there, because I was sure I had had the ring when I built up the left side.

My wife smiled, not too unkindly, and said, "No, darling. Let's forget it."

As the summer passed, she *did* seem to forget. But my guilt converted the ivy bed about the apple tree into a taboo place. When it came time to help the children pick the apples, I hated to walk under the tree. I watched the seared leaves tumble down the hill like arid supplicants and cling, trembling, in the ivy.

The frost came and then the snow and, as my love's token froze in ice, I feared she might one day see me out there, hacking at the iron earth with the pick-ax. If that day came, the terrible thing about it would be the ease with which I might find it. Some fugitive memory told me just where the ring lay—at the root of the apple tree.

The Christmas season came and we began to eat the apples we had picked.

Two nights before Christmas, we were down on the floor in front of the fireplace, the whole family, cutting stars and paper chains for the tree. My wife had sliced apples for us to eat while we worked. Outside, there was a raging blizzard and I had boomed up a birch fire on the grate. It occurred to me that we were a picture of the American family in a consumer-goods ad, it being impossible to tell, from all this happiness, how much we owed.

I suppose you could say that cutting the strips of paper for the tree reminded me of cutting a moebius curve, though I had never cut one before. I slit a strip of green paper about three feet long and two inches wide, and I said, "Hey, you guys, look at this trick."

I held the paper out in front of me. "You take one end in your left hand, with the thumb uppermost. The other end you take in your right hand, with the thumb down. Turn the fingers of the right hand down and in, like this, until they point to your body, and you've put a half-twist in the strip of paper. Now bring the left hand over without twisting and join the ends for gluing."

I proceeded to glue the ends.

My wife asked, "Do you have to interrupt us for that?"

"Now, now—this is a magic ring, because it has a half-twist in it. You see, you poke a scissor through the strip, like this, and start to slit it lengthwise and . . ."

Our daughter was ten and inclined to be a little impenetrable. But at this point, her face brightened and she said, "Oh, I see. That's clever. It has only one edge and one side."

I stared at her for a moment. "Yes. But you interrupted rather rudely."

"I'm sorry, Daddy."

"Now, you see, you keep cutting down the center of the strip . . ."

"Mother interrupted before," she insisted on reminding me.

"I forgive you both. You keep cutting down the center of the strip and—how many rings do you think you'll have when you're finished?"

"One," the boy stated. He was thirteen and inclined to make up his mind before he knew the facts.

"You're only guessing," I accused, approaching the end of the cut. "Look at the double ring hanging here below the scissors. Doesn't it seem to you I'll end up with two rings?"

"No. You'll end up with one."

I completed the cut. "Well, of course, you're right. It makes only one ring." I held up the ring. Everyone was looking at me.

My wife gave me a bitter-sweet smile.

My daughter returned without a word to the red-and-green paper chain she had been working on before I'd interrupted.

"That was a moebius curve," I explained. "It's a remarkable figure in geometry. Many illustrious mathematicians have been mystified by it."

"Anyone can see," my son said casually, "that it splits into one ring." His voice shifted to a shocking treble on the word "splits"—which was all that kept me from boxing his ears.

I got up and went into the kitchen and mixed myself a highball. Reluctantly, I went back to the living room and sat down with them again.

My wife glanced at my drink and then back to her work. "We'll need about ten feet more of that chain," she said to the girl.

The burning around my ears spread over my whole scalp. Such a smart damned family. Knew everything and didn't know anything. I would have just liked to stun them into a gibbering shock with the dynamic topology of space-time.

The wind slammed sleet into the storm-windows in great *whooshes* that were made up of a million icy clicks. My family planned the decoration of the tree while they worked.

Suddenly, I had hold of an enormous idea. It made the hair at the back of my neck stir. From burning with shame, I felt my face abruptly cool and go pale. There in my mind, as clearly and as illusively as the dancing flames on the grate, rose a nameless and intricate pattern.

I grabbed a piece of the green Christmas paper and a pencil and started drawing. If a plane were cut so—and so—the simple matter of a moebius curve would become . . .

Drawing rapidly, I felt my wife's eyes on me and the children looking up and becoming silent. By the time I had finished marking out the cuts and indicating the edges to be glued, my growing self-consciousness had obliterated the geometrical structure in my mind. The last lines I drew on the paper from my memory of what would *have* to be done. They no longer made sense to *me*.

Stubbornness buoyed me and I went to work with outward calm, cutting the paper and folding and gluing it the way I had marked. A hurried glance disclosed my son resting his chin in his hand and staring at me. My daughter's agate-green eyes and her round face were making an attempt to mimic one of her mother's moments of tolerant suspicion. I don't know what my wife's expression was like—I didn't dare look at her.

The wind outside was howling up a crescendo as I finished gluing the thing together and peered into its surfaces at a point that beckoned from infinity. If you pulled here with one hand, and here with the other, it began to fold in on itself with the complicated movements of an interdependent system. It was going to do something incredible if I stretched it any more.

It disappeared, completely and instantly, when I pulled.

My hands fell apart and there was nothing there. I was looking into three utterly astonished faces. The firelight danced like liquid gold on their wide eyes. Then there were squeals of laughter and the kids were saying, "Daddy, do it again!" "Do it again, Dad!"

My wife just sat there looking at me and a strange smile had come over her face. After a while, she got up from the floor and came over and knelt beside me. She kissed me first and then, close to my ear, she whispered, "Darling, I'm sorry we made you feel *that* badly. You didn't have to outdo yourself."

When she drew back, my daughter put her arms around me and hugged me tightly. "You're the most marvelous daddy in the world. Do it again, *please!*"

I looked into her proud face for a long moment. "I can't," I said slowly, and turned to my wife. "The directions were on the piece of paper."

"But, darling," my wife laughed, "surely you can remember how you did it."

I stared into the fire. "No, I haven't any idea."

My boy said, "Well, for the love of Mike!"

There was a long silence. Then my wife sighed. "That's a shame. It would have made a wonderful trick for parties. Come, children—let's get ready for bed."

I sat there for a while. Finally I got up and said, "Well, I'm pretty tired. I guess I'll go to bed, too."

They were discussing the time tomorrow that they would decorate the tree and they didn't hear me.

From where I lay in bed, a little later, I could occasionally see the limbs of the apple tree, ghostly in the sallow light from the street. The tree writhed violently in the storm like a live thing struggling up out of the frozen ivy. A wedding ring that was a moebius curve was buried there, a ring with a fantastic history that carried for me an irrational threat of unwanted eminence.

That structure I had built out of the Christmas paper . . . What unknown geometry had I tapped? It was an absurd notion that the ring had magic powers, let alone that it could contaminate the roots and fruit of the tree. Yet where else had that structure come from?

The threat from the ring had ballooned far beyond mere financial success. The first thing I knew, I would be writing world-shaking formulas like $E = mc^2$. Then some jockey would use my figures to power space flights. Then I would be directly responsible for the ugly interplanetary incidents that would follow, when tourists started throwing coke bottles and cigar butts in the canals of Mars. I would get the Nobel Peace Prize for making an interplanetary war possible.

Then an electrifying realization stiffened my back. Good Lord, the *whole family* was eating those apples!

Presently, my wife entered from her dressing room and got into her bed. I wanted very much to tell her about the threat to us all, but then, suddenly, the notion of a magic ring and contaminated apples seemed too absurd to talk about.

After a while in the dark, I said, "Darling, don't you think we're eating too many apples lately, just because we have so many of them? I don't think they're very good apples anyway."

"Oh, are you awake? I didn't come to kiss you because I thought you were asleep. They're perfectly good apples. We've eaten them for years."

"They keep me awake," I said honestly. "I thought the children were looking a little washed out."

"Darling, that's a silly notion. The children have a balanced diet. You won't mind if I *don't* come to kiss you, will you. I've got cream all over my face."

On New Year's Eve, she prepared an apple pie and it seemed ridiculous not to enjoy it.

When the next director's report came to my desk, I got to thinking again about how easily our corporate structure could be reorganized to provide a much more profitable operation. I was sitting at my desk, without one hot project before me, nothing but the report and a pad of paper where I had jotted down a few crucial calculations.

Then, of course, our president walked in.

Well, he had caught me redhanded in *thought*, so I would probably get a raise anyway. I sincerely liked the man and it seemed definitely unfair for me to sit there, a newly realized Einstein of the business world, and not tell him what I had learned. This was so big that I would be risking promotion to the board if I didn't play it down.

I explained it to him as off-handedly as I could and claimed I got a lot of the ideas from fellows around the office. I guess that was a mistake. The way he glanced at me, both of us knew nobody around that office had ideas like this. I tried to keep the development of the ideas from getting exciting, but I could hear the sparks crackling in his tycoonery.

When I walked into the living room that evening, my wife was reading the evening paper.

She looked up briefly. "Hello, darling. Did you have an interesting day?"

After losing the ring, I had never gotten around to telling her about my plan to stay unsuccessful. Till then, I had just quietly pursued the plan in my own way and today had been a necessary break in procedure, because I couldn't be dishonest with my boss. Now I found that, after twenty years of coming home to Mom and then fifteen years of coming home to my wife, it was impossible not to feel proud when I brought home the best report card, the biggest fish, an enemy's scalp or a raise.

"I had a wonderful day," I beamed.

"I did, too. Last week, I was listening to the women at the club talk about their husband's investments and I got to thinking I ought to know more about stocks. This morning, I took some books out of the library—" she indicated a formidable pile to the right of her chair— "and, dear, it's a fascinating subject. I think I'm going to be very good at it."

"Good at what?"

"Investing. I have a thousand dollars saved, you know."

"No, I didn't know."

"Oh, yes. I've always felt a wife should keep a nest egg. I feel now, since this is such an easy subject for me, that I ought to put some money to work for us."

"I thought we might have some martinis and celebrate a little."

"Not tonight, dear. You know how sleepy I get afterward and I want to get in some reading tonight." She indicated the formidable pile again.

"Oh."

"What was your news?"

"I got a raise of two thousand a year."

She lowered the paper to her lap. "Really, darling, I think that's wonderful. You've waited a long time for it, haven't you?"

"Well, not *that* long."

"I think it's wonderful, *however* long you've waited."

I stood there for a while, and then I said, "What are we having for dinner?"

"I fixed a cold buffet, because the children and I didn't care to eat right away. Each of us can eat when he wants to. You don't mind, do you?"

"No, that's all right. I think I'll eat now."

"Why don't you, dear? Dear?"

"Yes?"

"Aren't you going to kiss me?"

I kissed her and she went back to her stock quotations.

I had thought the boy might be interested in eating, which he usually was, but when I entered his room, I saw better. He had a bunch of "art-photo" and "girlie" magazines scattered across his desk. The blonde nude he had before him hit me right in the midriff, but he sat there, calm as a cucumber, measuring the distance from her navel to her chin with calipers.

He said, "Oh, hi, Dad."

I said, "Hello. How's the schoolwork going?"

"Oh, this isn't schoolwork."

I smiled. "I only said it for a joke."

There was a silence while he entered, on three different tabular sheets beside him, the delicate measurement he had just made.

"What on earth are you doing?" I asked at last.

He delayed answering while he spanned an even more intimate distance on the topology of the blonde. "Oh, just taking a healthy interest in girls, I guess you might say." His sparsely whiskered bass skidded with a shriek on the word "girls."

I looked around his desk at the busty, laughing array and felt the dull thud of middle age. "What has led you to believe," I asked carefully, "that such precise measurement of these undefended citadels will be necessary?"

"It isn't necessary to measure most of them. Most of them aren't any good."

I said to myself, "None of them are any good, my boy," and I grinned back knowingly at a sloe-eyed brunette. Aloud I asked, "What makes some of them good to measure?"

"Recognize any of the books in this picture?"

The page with the blonde on it was titled, *A Librarian's Day Off*. The blonde, wearing only a pair of horn-rimmed glasses, was cuddled up in a pile of books. She was good-naturedly sharing in the huge joke.

"Well, it's quite a library."

"That one there is in your library." He indicated an illustrated edition of Anatole France's *Thaïs*. "It measures nine and five-eighths inches from top to bottom and gives me a reference against which to convert the measurements of the girl."

"I see."

He indicated other pictures. "I found this beach ball at the sport-goods store and over here are standard boxing gloves. That cocktail glass looks a little oversized, doesn't it?"

I allowed as how it did.

"It isn't, though. It's just that she's a very small girl. I calculate she stands a little under four feet eleven inches."

This whole business was beginning to depress me and I was on the verge of protesting his mechanized approach, when he added an afterthought, "She's about six inches shorter than I am."

Here, at last, was a healthy sign. The boy did identify himself in a rôle, even if it was only one of comparative height. Well, a father ought to be more than a close friend. In a case like this, he ought to guide the child's interest toward more realistic goals.

I indicated a languidly sprawling creature and remarked with moderate enthusiasm, "This one's a lulu, isn't she?"

"What? Oh! Well, she's an ectomorphic mesomorph with a three in endomorphy."

Then I saw that he had pulled several texts from my library and among them were two of W. H. Sheldon's books on body types.

"You know," he explained, "that's her somatotype."

"You're sure it isn't her tomato-type?"

He tossed aside his calipers and assumed a man-to-man position in his chair. "You see, Dad, the female figure is much more interesting to me than the male, because it's a structural compromise between two functions. It's a second-rate muscular engine, because of its reproductive functions, but it's interesting how the compromise is worked out structurally in various female figures."

I looked at this boy of mine and I said to myself, "Here ends a proud line that sprang from the magnificent lust of a Viking who surprised a barbaric maid on Shannon's shore."

He didn't seem to worry about himself at all. "If I can find enough pictures containing a quantitative reference," he said, "I hope to establish a statistical ideal."

"And then you'll start looking for her?"

"Well, sure."

Not without some trepidation, I asked, "How are you going to be sure you've located a real-life ideal?"

He thought about that for a while. "I guess there'll be only one way to be sure."

I nodded. "Rope her, throw her to the floor and get out your calipers."

"I don't think it will come to that. Do *you?*"

I looked at my watch. "I thought you might like to eat with me. There's a cold buffet in the dining room."

He came back from his contemplation of the roping trick. "Oh, I couldn't leave this right now. I have three more pictures to measure and tabulate."

Some healthy interest in girls *he* had.

I went out into the dining room. The buffet was neatly laid out and the place was very quiet. I stood around a bit and looked at the food. Then I walked back to my daughter's room.

"Hi, Daddy."

"Hello," I said. "I thought you might like to eat now."

"Oh, do I *have* to, Daddy? I was just working on some figures."

"By God!" I thought. "This is too much!" Aloud I asked sternly, "What kind of figures?"

"Like this." She held up sheets of drawing paper from her desk. She had numerals drawn on them in all manner of styles and esoteric designs. "It's as much fun as arithmetic. Daddy, did you know that I'm getting one hundred in arithmetic every day now and Teacher says I'm a budding genius?"

"No, I didn't know that."

"But this is very interesting, too. Daddy, do you think the signs for the numbers mean anything else?"

"Not that I know of. Of course, the figure one and the word I are pretty much the same."

"Do you think the other signs were made up from the one and zero?"

"I don't think so."

"Well, you *can* make them up that way by using zeros and half-zeros, and then they look like this." She held up a sheet and then put it down and drew lines, relating the numerals in pairs. "See how they are married?"

1 2 3 4 5 6 7 8 9 0

"Well," I said, "that really *is* interesting."

"See, Daddy, if you lifted the two off the page and flipped it over, it would be a five. All you have to do is slide the six around on the page and it's a nine. Of course, the three is half of the eight, isn't it?"

"It is at that."

"The only one that disappoints me is the seven. It should be like the four, only it isn't. Not even a little."

I said contemplatively, "Since you're this deeply into the problem, I'll let you in on something. In Europe, people generally write the seven like this." I drew the figure on a piece of paper.

7

"Oh, Daddy! Is that really true?"

"I won't swear to the accuracy of my drawing," I hedged, "but they really do put a cross-bar on the seven."

"Look how it fits into the design!" she exclaimed, delighted.

"Very neatly," I confessed. "A tilted mirror-image of the four. I'll admit I never thought of tying the numbers together like this, but now that you've got it, what have you got?"

"Daddy, do you think the line of numbers connected this way is a message to us?"

"Absolutely. To me, it says quite clearly, 'Man does not live by figures alone.'" I heard my stomach growl and I asked again hesitantly, "Are you sure you wouldn't like to eat with me?"

"Oh, Daddy, I *couldn't!* This is too exciting."

Sometimes it seems to me that the quality of a lot of the prepared foods sold in this country rates a prison sentence. The manufacturers take all the nutrition out of wheat flour and it bakes up into a sandwich loaf that has a little texture only because it is pre-sliced and dried out. It's a laugh, what they call "cold-cuts"—sawdust pasted together with waste collagen. God knows what's in those sandwich spreads, but they can throw a man's digestion out of whack faster than a double dose of castor oil.

When I had finished my sandwich and a glass of warm milk, I went back to the buffet and looked around. There was half a cold apple pie there and when I went to pick it up, I dropped it on the floor. I was bending down to pick up the plate when I realized my wife was standing in the door.

She asked quietly, "Why did you do that?"

"Isn't the correct word 'how'?"

We looked at each other across the apple pie for a time and then my wife walked slowly past me to the window. I stood over the spilled pie, feeling foolish about not picking it up, but unable to take my eyes off my wife. She stood at the window and stared down across the snowy lawn at the apple tree.

Presently, she said without turning, "Perhaps there is a fate that follows the loss of a magic wedding ring. Do you believe this is happening to us?"

"It definitely is happening to all of us," I said bluntly. "I am not going to eat any more apples."

Her fine figure leaned back against the casing and her head relaxed toward the cold pane. Her bosom rose and fell tranquilly, without excitement. After a while, she declared, "I will continue to eat apples and prepare them for the children."

I went over to the window and took her hands in mine and turned her to me. I told her I wanted to avoid getting any more successful and why I felt that way.

"You don't really want more money," I concluded. "This foolishness about stocks just came about because of that wedding ring."

She chose to misinterpret what I had said. "There is nothing foolish about wedding rings," she said hotly, "except when people violate or lose them."

She drew away from me and stood very straight. "I'm going to make so much money, the Federal Reserve Bank will start sending us envoys."

When I got home the next evening, there was a robin's-egg-blue Cadillac parked in the drive. The gleaming hood was flanked by prodigious chrome trumpets. The upholstery was cream leather. About the only thing it lacked was a squirrel's plume on the buggy-whip aerial.

I went into the living room and there was my wife's old boy friend sitting in my favorite chair. I saw that he had lost quite a bit of hair, which probably explained the college-boy decorations on his Cadillac.

He stirred hugely in Scottish tweed and rose, extending a hand.

I said, "Well, the dim past returns in big live chunks, doesn't it?"

"It hasn't been as long ago as all that." He said this as if he would brook no further analysis on the point.

"It's been every bit as long ago as all that. Fifteen long years, to be exact."

His jaw jutted out against the fact.

I added, "That's the better part of a man's life."

My wife breezed in with a tray and a pitcher of martinis. "How nice to see you two getting reacquainted."

I lifted a glass off the tray as she went by me toward him. "We hardly recognized each other," I said wryly.

"Darling, we'll have to explain the occasion to you."

"Oh, I'm not going to insist on it."

"We've been together all day and we've formed a loose association."

I could only goggle silently at her.

"Business," he supplied. "Business association." He has always had a sense of humor like a stretch of Mohave Desert.

"He says I have a remarkable eye for figures."

"So does he," I insinuated.

My wife was disgusted. "Now you stop that. You are not going to spoil our chance to make millions."

He swallowed his anger and said, "Your wife has an almost magical grasp of the market. I have promised to pay her a thousand dollars a week as a consultant. This arrangement will give me the advantage of her insight and afford her money for her own investments."

"I don't like it," I stated. "It's out."

"But, darling, we can have all the things we want."

I looked at her for a long time. "What is it we want?"

"Well . . ."

"Do we want a yacht?"

"Of course not, dear."

"Do we need a third car?"

"Darling, please!"

"Do you want a mink coat?"

She declared levelly, "Yes, I do."

"Do you want some househelp?"

"Certainly."

"All right," I said. "You don't have to upset the national economy, after all. I'll get you the mink coat and a maid, and you call off this Hettie Green act."

My wife's old boy friend stuck his nose in solicitously. "I was thinking," he offered smoothly, "of putting you up for the Riverdale Club. And the children—they should be going to the proper schools. I can arrange to get them entered."

I thought about the Riverdale Club—and about the kids becoming nasty little prep-school snobs. I thought of the man who bought the second-hand yacht.

I walked over to him and smiled. "I owe you something."

He dodged back. Then he saw me pull the five dollars from my pocket and he recovered. "What's this for?"

"I borrowed it from you for my wedding ring."

He took it sullenly and stuffed it into his pocket.

"But I also owe you the interest," I added, and I cracked him a dilly under his second chin.

He collapsed all over the carpet and our wide-eyed kids seemed to appear from the woodwork.

The boy said, "Gee, Dad, you really lifted him up and laid him down!"

"Is he dead?" the girl asked, as if it were the second act in a TV show.

"My God, darling!" My wife said this as though she had found a dead horse in her living room. "What will we *do* with him?"

"Kids," I said softly, "you had better go on back to your rooms."

They went reluctantly. I took the flowers from a bowl on the mantle and dumped the bowl in his face. He began to splutter.

I left them alone to dissolve their "association." Out in the back hall, I put on a windbreaker and cap. I went down to the basement and carried the last bushel of apples out and dumped them in the garbage. I grinned down the lawn at the apple tree and went to the garage and got out the ax. I was sitting at the bench, honing it, when I heard the Cadillac start out of the drive.

Presently, my wife stepped through the door into the garage.

"Darling, you *wouldn't!*"

"Huh?" I asked vacantly, then saw her staring at the ax. "I love you. Besides, there are the children to think of—I can't manage them by myself."

"Silly, I didn't mean that. I mean I know what you're planning."

"In that case, I must say I *will.*"

"I won't let you. You have your choice of digging up that ring and wearing it the rest of your life, or living here with a family of apple eaters. Do you just resent wearing a ring because it makes you feel tied down?"

My wife can say the damnedest things. "Of course not."

"Don't you think that, whatever peculiarities there are about the ring I gave you, it was given in good faith?"

"Certainly I do."

"If it *is* a magic ring and fate has brought it down through history to you, don't you think you're trying to duck a pretty serious responsibility?"

I put down the ax and held up my hands. "All right, let's cut out the cross-examination."

She brought her beautiful body forward and stood over me. Her lovely head, which was still auburn, was tilted slightly to one side. Looking up into her exploring eyes, and thinking of what she had just said, I suddenly thought of Gerbert, who had quietly introduced the cipher into pre-Renaissance Europe. There *were* ways to use that ring.

Quite calmly and with supreme logic, she observed, "You know, you have assumed the responsibility of raising a couple of children. Don't you think you owe it to them to leave them the best possible world?"

I rose slowly and went over and collected the pick-ax and shovel. Then I grinned at her and went out of the garage and down the lawn toward the apple tree.

That is how I was relaunched on the road to success. I didn't dream then that you can be as quiet and unseen about it as I am now. I don't owe a cent—in fact, I own all sorts of businesses and property, through proxies, of course—yet I'll bet you've never heard of me. Maybe you've noticed I haven't told you my name or anybody else's in this account. That's one way it's done.

And I did rediscover the figure that vanished from my hands when I pulled. That was my first discovery.

There are lots more, but they won't be known for a long while.

Like the discovery of the zero, you see.

The "mathematics of magic" stories of L. SPRAGUE DE CAMP and FLETCHER PRATT were one of the most popular innovations of the famous magazine Unknown *in the early 1940s. Harold Shea, the protagonist of these fantasies, using symbolic logic, traveled to many familiar fantasy worlds, in each of which magic operated according to strict rules subject to mathematical analysis. The innovation of this series, mathematically rigorous rules, making magic subject to rational analysis, transformed magic into a kind of science. In each world, Shea used his knowledge of math to figure out the rules and survive the adventure. Even now, more than forty years later, one of the most universally held values in both the fantasy and science fiction fields is that world building, as the creation of such imaginary worlds is known, should be done carefully and according to rationalistic principles. "The Green Magician" (1953) is the last of the series, in which Shea inadvertently visits the world of Cúchulainn and other Celtic heroes from Irish mythology while trying to get home to Ohio.*

The Green Magician
BY L. SPRAGUE DE CAMP AND FLETCHER PRATT

In that suspended moment when the gray mists began to whirl around them, Harold Shea realized that although the pattern was perfectly clear, the details hadn't worked out right. It was all very well to realize that, as Doc Chalmers once said, "The world we live in is composed of impressions received through the senses, and if the senses can be attuned to receive a different series of impressions, we should infallibly find ourselves living in another of the infinite number of possible worlds." It was a scientific and personal triumph to have proved that, by the use of the sorites of symbolic logic, the gap to one of those possible worlds could be bridged.

The trouble was what happened after you got there. It amounted to living by one's wits. Once the jump across space-time had been made, and you were in the new environment, the conditions of the surroundings had to be accepted completely. It was no good trying to fire a revolver or scratch a match or light a flashlight in the world of Norse myth—these things did not form part of the surrounding mental pattern, and remained obstinately inert masses of useless material. On the other hand, magic . . .

The mist thickened and whirled, and Shea felt the pull of his wife Belphebe's hand, clutching his own desperately. The discovery that he could work simple magic in any continuum that permitted it was quite accidental, but fully as providential as the fact that Shea's skill in fencing and his spare, athletic figure gave him certain advantages in most of the continua he visited.

It was magic that had won him Belphebe, from the world of the *Faerie Queene*—and also magic that had landed them in their present difficulties. For you had to abide by the rules of magic as it was— wherever you landed—and Shea and Belphebe had landed in the Finnish Kalevala, to make the dismaying discovery that magical spells needed to be sung there; and Shea couldn't carry a tune across a room.

In one sense, to be sure, the expedition was a success. They had succeeded in rescuing Pete Brodsky, detective second class, from the limbo to which he had been transferred by stepping into the room when a sorites was going on. But there the success ended. Brodsky was completely unappreciative of the world of the Kalevala, and the inhabitants of that continuum were so unappreciative of their visitors that all three found themselves in a singularly dirty dungeon, facing the prospect of immediate decapitation.

It was then Shea took emergency action. There was no time to correlate the sorites with the descriptive properties of the various space-time continua. They had soared into this gray nothingness, with Shea operating generalized removal spells while Brodsky's impassioned rendition of *My Wild Irish Rose* provided the kind of motive power required by the laws of Kalevala magic. But it was taking an infernally long time.

Shea suddenly felt earth under his feet. Something hit him on the head and he realized that he was standing in a downpour. The rain was coming down vertically and with such intensity that he could not see more than a few yards in any direction. His first glance was toward Belphebe. She swung herself into his arms and they kissed damply.

"At least," she said, disengaging herself a little, "you are with me, my most dear lord, and so there's nought to fear."

They looked around, water running off their noses and chins. Shea's heavy woolen shirt was already so soaked that it stuck to his skin and Belphebe's neat hair was taking on a drowned rat appearance. She pointed and cried, "There's one!"

Shea peered toward a lumpish dark mass that had a shape vaguely resembling Pete Brodsky.

"Shea?" came a call and, without waiting for a reply, the lump started toward them. As it did so, the downpour lessened and the light brightened.

"Goddam it, Shea!" said Brodsky as he approached. "What kind of box is this? If I couldn't work my own racket better, I'd turn myself in for mopery. Where the hell are we?"

"Ohio, I hope," said Shea. "And look, Shamus, we're better off than we were, right? I'm sorry about this rain, but I didn't order it."

"All I got to say is, you better be right," said Brodsky gloomily. "You can get the book thrown at you for snatching an officer, and I ain't sure I can square the rap even now. Where's the other guy?"

Shea looked around for the fellow-scientist who had accompanied them into the world of the Kalevala. "Walter may be here, but it looks as though he didn't come through with us. And if you ask me, the question is not *where* we are, but *when* we are. It wouldn't do us much good to be back in Ohio in 700 A.D., which is about the time we left. If this rain would only let up . . ."

With surprising abruptness the rain did, backing away in a wall of small but intense downpours. Spots and bars of sky appeared among the clouds, wafted along by a brisk, steady current of air that penetrated Shea's wet shirt chillingly. The sun shot an occasional beam through the clouds to touch up the landscape.

Shea and his companions were standing in deep grass, overlooking an extent of rolling ground. This stretch in turn appeared to be the top of a plateau, falling away to the right. Mossy boulders shouldered up through the grass, which here and there gave way to patches of purple-flowered heather, while daisies nodded in the steady breeze. In the valley beyond the plateau, the lowland was covered with what appeared to be birch and oak. In the distance, as they turned to contemplate the scene, rose the crew-cropped heads of far blue mountains.

Brodsky was the first to speak. "If this is Ohio, I'm a purse snatcher," he said. "Listen, Shea, do I got to tell you again you ain't got much time? If those yaps from the D.A.'s office get started on this case, you might just as well hit yourself on the head and save them the trouble. So you better get me back home before people start asking questions."

Shea said rather desperately, "Pete, I'm doing all I can. I haven't the least idea where we are, or in what period, and until I do know, I don't dare try sending us anywhere else. We've already picked up a rather high charge of magical static coming here and any spell I use without knowing what kind of magic works around here is apt to make us simply disappear or end up in Hell—you know, real red hell with flames all around, like in a fundamentalist church sermon."

"Okay," said Brodsky. "You got the office. Me, I don't think you got more than a week, at the outside, to get us back where we belong."

Belphebe pointed. "Marry, are those not sheep?"

Shea shaded his eyes. "Right you are, darling," he said. The objects looked like a collection of white lice on green baize, but he trusted his wife's phenomenal eyesight.

"Sheep," said Brodsky. One could almost hear the gears grind in his brain as he looked around. "Sheep!" A beatific expression spread over his face. "Shea, you must of done it! Three, two and out, we're in Ireland—and if it is, you can hit me on the head if I *ever* want to go back."

Shea looked around. "It does rather look like it," he said. "But when—"

Something flew past with a rush of displaced air. It struck a nearby boulder with a terrific crash and burst into fragments that whizzed about like pieces of an artillery shell.

"*Duck!*" shouted Shea, throwing himself flat and dragging Belphebe down with him.

Brodsky went into a crouch, lips drawn tight over his teeth, looking around for the source of the missile. Nothing more happened. After a moment, Shea and Belphebe got up and went over to examine a twenty-pound hunk of sandy conglomerate.

Shea said, "Somebody is chucking hundred-pound boulders around. This may be Ireland, but I hope it isn't the time of Finn McCool or Strongbow."

"Jeez!" said Brodsky. "And me wit'out my heater. And you a shiv man with no shiv."

It occurred to Shea that at whatever period they had hit this place, he *was* in a singularly weaponless state. There was no sign of life except the distant, tiny sheep—not even a shepherd or a sheep-dog.

He sat down on a ledge of the boulder and considered. "Sweetheart," he said, addressing Belphebe, "it seems to me that whenever we are, the first thing we have to do is find people and get oriented. You're the guide. Which way?"

The girl shrugged. "My woodcraft is nought without trees," she said, "but if you put it so, I'd seek a valley, for people ever live by watercourses."

"Good idea," said Shea. "Let's go—"

Whizz!

Another boulder flew through the air, but not in their direction. It struck the turf a hundred yards away, bounced clumsily and rolled out of sight over the hill. Still, no one was visible.

Brodsky emitted a growl, but Belphebe laughed. "We are encouraged to begone," she said. "Come, my lord, let us do no less."

At that moment, another sound made itself audible. It was that of a team of horses and a vehicle with wheels in violent need of lubrication. With a drumming of hooves, a jingle of harness and a squealing of wheels, a chariot rattled up the slope and into view. It was drawn by two huge horses; one gray and one black. The chariot itself was built more on the lines of a sulky than those of the open-backed Graeco-Roman chariot, with a seat big enough for two or three persons across the back and the sides cut low in front to allow for entrance. The vehicle was ornamented with nail-heads and other trimmings in gold, and a pair of scythe-blades jutted ominously from the hubs.

The driver was a tall, thin, freckled man, with red hair trailing from under his golden fillet down over his shoulders. He wore a green kilt and, over that, a deer-skin cloak.

The chariot sped straight toward Shea and his companions, who dodged away from the scythes around the edge of the boulder. At the last instant, the charioteer reined to a walk and shouted, "Be off with you if you would keep the heads on your shoulders!"

"Why?" asked Shea.

"Because himself has a rage on. Tearing up trees and casting boulders he is, and a bad hour it will be for anyone who meets him this day."

"Who is himself?" said Shea.

Almost at the same time Brodsky said, "Who the hell are *you?*"

The charioteer pulled up with a look of astonishment on his face. "I am Laeg mac Riangabra," he said, "and who would himself be but Ulster's hound, the glory of Ireland, Cúchulainn the mighty? He is after killing his only son and has worked himself into a rage. *Ara!* It is ruining the countryside he is, and the sight of you Fomarians would make him the wilder."

The charioteer cracked his whip and the horses raced off over the curve of the hill, with flying clods dappling the sky. In the direction from which he had come, a good-sized sapling with dangling roots rose against the horizon and fell back.

"Come on!" said Shea, grabbing Belphebe's hand and starting down the slope after the chariot.

"*Hey!*" said Brodsky, tagging after them. "Come on back and pal up with this ghee. He's the number one hero of Ireland."

Another rock bounced on the sward and, from the distance, a kind of howling was audible.

"I've heard of him," said Shea "and if you want to, we can drop in on him later. But I think right now is a poor time for calls. He isn't in a pally mood."

Belphebe said, "You name him hero and yet you say he has slain his own son. How can this be?"

"It was a bum rap," Brodsky said. "This Cúchulainn got his girl friend Aoife pregnant way back when, and then gave her the air, see? So she's sore at him, see? So when the kid grows up, she sends him to Cúchulainn under a geas—"

"A moment," said Belphebe. "What would this geas be?"

"A taboo," said Shea.

Brodsky said, "It's a hell of a lot more than that. You got one of these geasas on you and you can't do the thing it's against, even if it was to save you from the hot seat. So like I was saying, this young ghee, his name is Conla, but he has this geas on him not to tell his name or that of his father to anyone. So when Aoife sends him to Cúchulainn, the big shot challenges the kid and then knocks him off. It ain't good."

"A tale to mourn, indeed," said Belphebe. "How are you so wise in these matters, Master Pete? Are you of this race?"

"I only wish I was," said Brodsky fervently. "It would of done me a lot of good on the force. But I ain't, see, so I doped it this way. I studied this Irish stuff till I knew more about it than anybody. And then I got innarested, see?"

They were well down the slope now, approaching the impassive sheep.

Belphebe said, "I trust we will come soon to where there are people. My bones protest I have not dined."

"Listen," said Brodsky, "this is Ireland, the best country in the world. If you want to feed your face, just knock off one of them sheep. It's on the house. They run the pitch that way."

"We have neither knife nor fire," said Belphebe.

"I think we can make out on the fire deal with the metal we have on us and a piece of flint," said Shea. "And if we have a sheep killed and a fire going, I'll bet it won't be long before somebody shows up with a knife to share our supper. Anyway, it's worth a try."

He walked over to a big tree and picked up a length of dead branch that lay near the base. By standing on it and heaving, he broke it somewhat raggedly in half, then handed one end to Brodsky. The resulting cudgels did not look especially efficient, but they could be made to do.

"Now," said Shea, "if we hide behind that boulder, Belphebe can circle around and drive the flock toward us."

"Would you be stealing our sheep now, darlings?" said a deep male voice.

Shea looked around. Out of nowhere, a group of men had appeared, standing on the slope above them. There were five of them, in kilts or trews, with mantles of deerskin or wolfhide fastened around their necks. One of them carried a brassbound club, one a clumsy-looking sword and the other three, spears.

Before Shea could say anything, the one with the club said, "The heads of the men will look fine in the hall, now. But I will have the woman first."

"Run!" cried Shea and took his own advice. The five ran after them.

Belphebe, being unencumbered, soon took the lead. Shea clung to his club, hating to have nothing to hit back with if he were run down. A glance backward showed that Brodsky had either dropped his or thrown it at the pursuers without effect.

"*Shea!*" yelled the detective. "Go on—they got me!"

They had not, as a matter of fact, but it was clear they soon would. Shea paused, turned, snatched up a stone about the size of a baseball and threw it past Brodsky's head at the pursuers. The spearman-target ducked, and they came on, spreading out in a crescent to surround their prey.

"I—can't—run no more," panted Brodsky. "Go on, kids."

"Like hell!" said Shea. "We can't go back without you. Let's both take the guy with the club."

Their stones arched through the air simultaneously. The clubman ducked, but not far enough. One missile caught his leather cap and sent him sprawling to the grass.

The others whooped and closed in with the evident intention of skewering and carving, when a terrific racket made everyone pause. Down the slope came the chariot that had passed Shea and his group before. The tall, red-haired charioteer was standing in the front yelling something like "Ulluullu" while, balancing in the back, was a small, rather dark man.

The chariot bounded and slewed toward them. Before Shea could take in the whole action one of the hub-head scythes caught a spearman, shearing on both legs neatly, just below the knee. The man fell, shrieking, and at the same instant, the small man drew back his arm and threw a javelin right through the body of another.

"It is himself!" cried one of them and the survivors turned to run.

The small, dark fellow spoke to the charioteer, who pulled up his horses. Cúchulainn leaped down from the vehicle, took a sling from his belt and whirled it around his head. The stone struck one of the men in the back of the neck and down he went. As the man fell, Cúchulainn wound up a second time. Shea thought this one would miss for sure, as the man was now a hundred yards away and going farther fast, but the missile hit him in the head and he pitched on his face.

"Get out the head-bag and fetch me the trophies, dear," said Cúchulainn.

II

Laeg rummaged in the rear of the chariot and produced a large bag and a heavy sword, with which he went calmly to work. Belphebe had turned back, as the rescuer came toward the three. He was not only an extremely handsome man—there was also a powerful play of musculature under his loose outer garment. The hero's face bore an expression of settled and brooding melancholy, and he was dressed in a long-sleeved white cloak, embroidered with gold thread, over a red tunic.

"Thanks a lot," said Shea. "You just saved our lives. How did you happen along?"

" 'Twas Laeg came to me with a tale of three strangers, who might be Fomorians by the look to them, and they were like to be set on by the Lagenians. Now I will be fighting any man in Ireland that gives me the time, but unless you are a hero, it is not good to fight at five to two, and it is time that these pigs of Lagenians learned their manners.

"So now it is time for you to be telling me who you are and where you come from and whither bound. If you are indeed Fomorians, the better for you—King Conchobar is friends with them this year."

Shea searched his mind for details of the culture-pattern of the men of Cúchulainn's Ireland. A slip at the beginning might result in their heads being added to the collection bumping each other in Laeg's bag like so many cantaloupes. Brodsky beat him to the punch.

"*Jeez!*" he said, in a tone which carried it own message. "Imagine holding heavy with a zinger like you! I'm Pete Brodsky. My friends here are Harold Shea and his wife Belphebe." He stuck out his hand.

"We do not come from Fomoria, but from America, an island beyond their land," added Shea.

Cúchulainn acknowledged the introduction with a stately nod of courtesy. His eyes swept over Brodsky, and he ignored the outstretched hand. He addressed Shea. "Why do you travel in company with such a mountain of ugliness, dear?"

Out of the corner of his eye, Shea could see the cop's wattles swell dangerously. He said hastily, "He may be no beauty, but he's useful. He's our slave and bodyguard, a good fighting man."

Brodsky had sense enough to keep quiet.

Cúchulainn accepted the explanation with the same sad courtesy and gestured toward the chariot. "You will be mounting up in the back of my car and I will drive you to my camp, where there will be an eating before you set out on your journey again."

He climbed to the front of the chariot himself, while the three wanderers clambered wordlessly to the back seat. Off they went. Shea found the ride a monstrously rough one, for the vehicle had no springs and the road was distinguished by its absence, but Cúchulainn lounged in the seat, apparently at ease.

Presently, there loomed ahead a small patch of woods at the bottom of the valley. Smoke rose from a fire. A score or more of men, rough and wild-looking, got to their feet and cheered as the chariot swept into the camp.

Cúchulainn sprang down lightly, acknowledged the greeting with a casual wave, then swung to Shea. "Mac Shea, I am thinking that you are of quality, and as you are not altogether the ugliest couple in the world, you will be eating with me." He waved an arm. "Bring the food, darlings."

Cúchulainn's henchmen busied themselves, with a vast amount of shouting, running about in patterns that would have made good cats' cradles. "Do you think they'll ever get around to feeding us?" said Belphebe in a low voice. But Cúchulainn merely looked on with a slight smile, seeming to regard the performance as somehow a compliment to himself.

After an interminable amount of coming and going, Cúchulainn, with a wave of his hand, indicated that the Sheas were to sit on the ground in front of him. The charioteer, Laeg, joined them on the ground, which was still decidedly damp after the rain.

A man brought a large wooden platter on which were heaped the champion's victuals, consisting of a huge cut of boiled pork, a mass of bread and a whole salmon.

Cúchulainn laid it on his knees and set to work on it with fingers and his dagger, saying with a ghost of a smile, "Now according to the custom of Ireland, mac Shea, you may challenge the champion for his portion. A man of your inches should be a blithe swordsman, and I have never fought with an American."

"Thanks," said Shea, "but I don't think I could eat that much and anyway, there's a—what do you call it?—a geas against my fighting anyone who had done something for me, so I couldn't after the way you saved us." He addressed himself to his slab of bread on which had been placed a pork chop and a piece of salmon, then glanced at Belphebe before he added, "Would it be too much trouble to ask for the loan of a pair of knives? We left in rather a hurry and without our tools."

A shadow flitted across the face of Cúchulainn. "It is not well for a man of his hands to be without his weapons," he said. "Are you sure, now, that they were not taken away from you?"

Belphebe said, "We came here on a magical spell and, as you doubtless know, there are some that cannot be spelled in the presence of cold iron."

"And what could be truer?" said Cúchulainn. He clapped his hands and called, "Bring two knives, darlings. The iron knives, not the bronze." He chewed, looking at Belphebe. "And where would you be journeying to, darlings?"

Shea said, "Back to America, I suppose. We sort of—dropped in to see the greatest hero in Ireland."

Cúchulainn appeared to take the compliment as a matter of course. "You come at a poor time. The expedition is over, and now I am going home to sit quietly with my wife Emer, so there will be no fighting."

Laeg looked up with his mouth full and said, "You will be quiet if the meddling Maev and Ailill will let you, Cucuc."

"When my time comes to be killed by the Connachta, then I will be killed by the men of Connacht," said Cúchulainn composedly. He was still looking at Belphebe.

Belphebe said, "Who stands at the head of the magical art here?"

Cúchulainn said, "None is greater, nor will be, than Ulster's Cathbadh, adviser to King Conchobar. And now you will rest and fit yourselves, and in the morning we will go to Muirthemne to see Emain Macha." He laid aside his empty platter and took another look at Belphebe.

"That's extremely kind of you," said Shea. It was so very kind that he felt a twinge of suspicion.

"It is not," said Cúchulainn. "For those with the gift of beauty, it is no more than their due that they should receive all courtesy."

He was still looking at Belphebe, who glanced up at the darkening sky. "My Lord," she said, "I am somewhat foredone. Would it not be well to seek our rest?"

Shea said, "It's an idea. Where do we sleep?"

Cúchulainn waved a hand toward the grove. "Where you will, darlings. No one will disturb you in the camp of Cúchulainn." He clapped his hands. "Gather moss for the bed of my friends."

When they were alone, Belphebe said in a low voice, "I like not the manner of his approach, though he has done us great good. Cannot you use your art to transport us back to Ohio?"

Shea said, "I'll take a chance on trying to work out the sorites in the morning. Remember, it won't do us any good to get back alone. We've got to take Pete with us or we'll be up on a charge of kidnapping or murdering him, and I don't want to go prowling through this place at night looking for him."

Early as they rose, the camp was already astir. While Shea and Belphebe wandered through the camp, looking for Brodsky, they noted it was strangely silent. Shea grabbed the arm of a bewhiskered desperado hurrying by to inquire the reason.

The man bent close and said in a fierce whisper: "Sure 'tis that himself is in his sad mood. If you would lose your head, it would be just as well to make a noise."

"There's Pete," said Belphebe.

The detective waved a hand and came toward them from under the trees. He had somehow acquired one of the deerskin cloaks, which was held under his chin with a brass brooch, and he looked unexpectedly cheerful.

"What's the office?" he asked in the same stage whisper the others were using.

"Come with us," said Shea. "We're going to try to get back to Ohio. Where'd you get the new clothes?"

"Aw, one of these muzzlers thought he could wrestle, so I slipped him a little jujitsu and won it. Listen, Shea, I ain't going back. This is the real McCoy."

"But we want to go back," said Belphebe, "and you told us just yesterday that if we showed up without you, our fate would be less than pleasant."

"Give it a rest. I'm on the legit here, and with that magical stuff of yours, you could be, too. At least, I want to stay for the big blow."

"Come this way," said Shea, moving away from the center of the camp to where there was less danger of their voices causing trouble. "What do you mean by the big blow?"

"From what I got," said Pete, "I figured out this Maev and Ailill are rustling out the mob and heeling them up to give Cúchulainn a bang on the head. They got all the cousins of people he's ever bumped off in on the caper, and that will make him go up against them all at once—and then, boom. I want to stay for the pay-off."

"Look here," said Shea, "you said only yesterday that we had to get you back within a week. Remember? It was something about your probably being seen going into our house and not coming out."

"Sure, sure. And if we go back, I'll alibi you. But what for? I'm teaching these guys to wrestle, and with your magic, maybe you could even take the geas off the big shot."

"Perhaps I could," said Shea. "It seems to amount to a kind of psychological compulsion by magical means. Between psychology and magic, I ought to make it. But I daren't take the chance with our hero making eyes at Belphebe."

They emerged from the clump of trees and were at the edge of the slope, with the early sun just touching the tops of the branches above them. Shea went on, "I'm sorry, Pete, but Belphebe and I don't want to spend the rest of our lives here. Now, you two hold hands. Give me your other hand, Belphebe."

Brodsky obeyed with a sullen expression. Shea closed his eyes and began, "If either A or (B or C) is true, and C or D is false . . ." motioning with his free hand up to the end of the sorites.

He opened his eyes again. They were still at the edge of a clump of trees, on a hill in Ireland, watching the smoke from the camp fire as it rose above the trees to catch the sunshine.

Belphebe said, "What appears to be amiss?"

"I don't *know*," said Shea desperately. "Wait a minute. Making this work depends on a radical alteration of sense impressions in accordance with the rules of symbolic logic and magic. Now we know that magic works here, so that can't be the trouble. But for symbolic logic to be effective, you have to submit to its effects—that is, be willing. Pete, you're the villain. You don't want to go back."

"Don't put the squeeze on me," said Brodsky. "I'll play ball."

"All right. Now remember, you're going back to Ohio and you

have a good job there and you like it. Besides, you were sent out to find us and you did. Okay?"

They joined hands again and Shea, constricting his brow with effort, ran through the sorites again. As he reached the end, time seemed to stand still for a second. Then—*crash!* A flash of vivid blue lightning struck the tree nearest them, splitting it from top to bottom.

Belphebe gave a little squeal, and a chorus of excited voices rose from the camp.

Shea gazed at the fragments of the splintered tree and said soberly, "I think that shot was meant for us, and that just about tears it, sweetheart. Pete, you get your wish. We're going to have to stay here, at least until I know more about the laws controlling magic in this continuum."

Two or three of Cúchulainn's men burst excitedly through the trees and came toward them, spears ready.

"Is it all right that you are?" one of them called.

"Just practicing a little magic," said Shea easily. "Come on, let's go back and join the others."

In the clearing, voices were no longer quenched. Cúchulainn stood watching the loading of the chariot, with a lofty and detached air. As the three travelers approached, he said, "Now it is to you I am grateful, mac Shea, with your magical spell for reminding me that things are better done at home than abroad. It is leaving at once we are."

"*Hey!*" said Brodsky. "I ain't had no breakfast."

The hero regarded him with distaste. "You will be telling me that I should postpone the journey for the condition of a slave's belly?" he said and, turning to Shea and Belphebe, added, "We can eat as we go."

The ride was smoother than the one of the previous day only because the horses went at a walk so as not to outdistance the column of retainers on foot. Conversation over the squeaking of the wheels began by being sparse and rather boring. But Cúchulainn apparently liked Belphebe's comments on the beauty of the landscape and began addressing her with an exclusiveness that Shea found disturbing.

The country around them got lower and flatter until, from the tops of the few rises, Shea glimpsed a sharp line of gray-blue across the horizon—the sea. Cultivation became more common, though there was still less of it than pasturage. Occasionally a lumpish-looking serf, clad in a length of ragged sacking-like cloth and a thick veneer of dirt, left off his labors to stare at the band and wave a languid greeting.

At last, over the manes of the horses, Shea saw that they were approaching a stockade of logs with a huge double gate.

Belphebe surveyed it critically and whispered behind her hand to Shea, "It could be taken with fire-arrows."

"I don't think they have many archers or very good ones," he whispered back. "Maybe you can show them something."

The gate was pushed open creakingly by more bearded warriors, who shouted, "Good day to you, Cucuc! Good luck to Ulster's hound!"

As the chariot rumbled through the opening, Shea glimpsed houses of various shapes and sizes, some of them evidently stables and barns. The biggest was the hall in the middle, its heavily thatched roof sloping down almost to the ground at the sides.

Laeg pulled up. Cúchulainn jumped down, waved his hand and cried, "Muirthemne welcomes you, Americans!" All the others applauded, as though he had said something particularly witty and brilliant.

He turned to speak to a fat man, rather better dressed than the rest, when another man came out of the main hall and walked rapidly toward them. The newcomer was thin, of medium height, with a long, white beard, slightly bent and carrying a stick on which he leaned now and again. A purple robe covered him impressively from neck to ankle.

"The best of the day to you, Cathbadh," said Cúchulainn. "This is surely a happy hour that brings you here, but where is my darling Emer?"

"Emer has gone to Emain Macha," said Cathbadh. "Conchobar summoned her—"

"*Ara!*" shouted Cúchulainn. "Is it a serf that I am, that the King can send for my wife every least last time he takes it into the head of him?"

"It is not that at all, at all," said Cathbadh. "He summons you, too, and for that he sent me instead of Levarcham, for he knows you might not heed her word if you took it into that willful head of yours to disobey, whereas it is myself can put a geas on you to go."

"And why does himself want us at Emain Macha?"

"Would I be knowing all the secrets in the heart of a King?"

Shea said, "Are you the court druid?"

Cathbadh became aware of him for the first time, and Cúchulainn made introductions. Shea explained, "It seems to me that the King might want you at the court for your own protection, so the druids can keep Maev's sorcerers from putting a spell on you. That's what she plans to do."

"How do you know of this?" asked Cathbadh with interest.

"Through Pete here. He sometimes knows about things that are going to happen before they actually take place. In our country we call it second sight."

Cúchulainn wrinked his nose and said, "That ugly slave?"

"Yeah, *me!*" said Brodsky, who had approached the group. "And you better watch your step, handsome, because somebody's going to hang you up to dry unless you do something about it."

"If it is destined, none can alter it," said Cúchulainn. "Fergus! Have the bathwater heated." He turned to Shea. "Once you are properly washed and garbed you will look well enough for the board in my beautiful house. I will lend you some proper garments, for I cannot bear the sight of those Fomorianlike rags."

III

Along the side of the main hall was an alcove made of screens of wattle, set at an angle which provided privacy for those within. In the alcove stood Cúchulainn's bathtub, a large and elaborate affair of bronze. A procession of the women of the manor was now coming from the well with jugs of water, which they emptied into the tub. Meanwhile, the men were poking up the fire at the end of the hall and adding stones of about five to ten pounds' weight.

Brodsky sidled up to Shea, as they stood in the half-light, orienting themselves. "Listen," he said, "I don't want to blow the whistle on a bum rap, but you better watch it. The racket they have here, this guy can make a pass at Belphebe in his own house, and it's legit."

"I was afraid of that," said Shea, unhappily.

"Give me time," Brodsky said. "I'll try to think of some way to rumble his line."

"*Make way!*" shouted a huge, whiskered retainer. The three dodged as the man ran past them, carrying a large stone, still smoking from the fire, in a pair of tongs. The man dashed into the alcove. There were a splash and a loud hiss. Another retainer followed with a second stone, while the first was on his return trip. In a few minutes, all the stones had been transferred to the bathtub. Shea looked around the screen and saw that the water was steaming gently.

Cúchulainn sauntered into the alcove and tested the water with an inquisitive finger. "That will do, dears," he said.

The retainers picked the stones out of the water with their tongs and piled them in the corner, then went around from behind the screen.

Cúchulainn reached up to pull off his tunic, then saw Shea. "I am going to undress for the bath," he said. "Surely, you would not be wanting to remain here, now."

Shea turned back into the main room just in time to see Brodsky smack one fist into the other palm. *"Got* it!" he said.

"Got what?" said Shea.

"How to needle this hot tomato." He looked around, then pulled Shea and Belphebe closer. "Listen, the big shot putting the scram on you now just reminded me. The minute he makes a serious pass at you, Belle, what you gotta do is go into a strip-tease. In public, where everybody can get a gander at it."

Belphebe gasped.

Shea said, "Are you out of your head? That sounds to me like trying to put a fire out with gasoline."

"I tell you, he can't take it!" Brodsky's voice was low but urgent. "They can't none of them. One time, when this guy was going to put the slug on everyone at the court, the King sent out a bunch of babes with bare topsides and they nearly had to pick him up in a basket."

"I like this not," said Belphebe, but Shea said, "A nudity taboo! That could be part of a culture pattern, all right. Do they all have it?"

"Yeah, and good," said Brodsky. "They even croak of it."

Cúchulainn stepped out of the aclove, buckling a belt around a fresh tunic, emerald-green with embroidery of golden thread. He scrubbed his long hair with a towel and ran a comb through it, while Laeg took his place behind the wattle screen.

Belphebe said, "Is there to be but one water for all?"

Cúchulainn said, "There is plenty of soapwort. Cleanliness befits beauty." He glanced at Brodsky. "The slave can bathe in the trough outside."

"Listen . . ." began Brodsky, but Shea put a hand on his arm and, to cover up, said, "Do your druids use spells of transportation—from one place to another?"

"There is little a good druid cannot do. But I would advise you not to use the spells of Cathbadh unless you are a hero as well as a maker of magic."

He turned to watch the preparations for dinner with somber satisfaction. Laeg presently appeared, his toilet made, and from another direction one of the women brought garments for Shea and Belphebe. Shea started to follow his wife, but remembered what Brodsky had said about the taboo and decided not to take a chance on shocking his hosts. She came out soon enough in a floor-length gown that clung to her all over, and he noted with displeasure that it was the same green and embroidery pattern as Cúchulainn's tunic.

His own costume, after he had dealt with water almost cold and a towel already damp, turned out to be a saffron tunic and tight knitted scarlet trews which he imagined as looking quite effective.

Belphebe was watching the women around the fire. Over in the shadows under the eaves sat Pete Brodsky, cleaning his fingernails with a bronze knife; a chunky, middle-aged man—a good hand in a fight, with his knowledge of jujitsu and his quick reflexes. Things would be a lot easier, though, if he hadn't fouled up the spell by wanting to stay where he was. Or had that been responsible?

Old Cathbadh came stumping up with his stick. "Mac Shea," he said, "the Little Hound is after telling me that you also are a druid who came here by magical arts from a distant place and can summon lightning from the skies."

"It's true enough," said Shea. "Doubtless you know those spells."

"Doubtless I do," said Cathbadh, looking sly. "We must hold converse on matters of our craft. We will be teaching each other some new spells, I am thinking."

Shea frowned. The only spell he was really interested in was one that would take Belphebe and himself—and Pete—back to Garaden, Ohio, and Cathbadh probably didn't know that one himself. He said, "I think we can be quite useful to each other. In America, where I come from, we have worked out some of the general principles of magic, so that it is only necessary to learn the procedures in various places."

Just then Cúchulainn came out of his private room and sat down without ceremony at the head of the table. The others gathered round.

Laeg took the place at one side of the hero and Cathbadh at the other. Shea and Belphebe were nodded to the next places, opposite each other.

Cúchulainn said to Cathbadh, "Will you make the sacrifice, dear?"

The druid stood up, spilled some wine on the floor and chanted to the gods, Bilé, Danu and Lér. Shea decided it was only imagination that he was hearing the sound of beating wings, and only the approach of the meal that gave him a powerful sense of internal comfort—but there was no doubt that Cathbadh knew his stuff.

Cathbadh knew it, too. "Was that not fine now?" he said, as he sat down next to Shea. "Can you show me anything in your outland magic ever so good?"

Shea thought it wouldn't do any harm to give the old codger a small piece of sympathetic magic. He said, "Move your wine cup over next to mine, and then watch it carefully."

There would have to be a spell to link the two if he were to make Cathbadh's wine disappear as he drank his own. The only one he could think of at the moment was the "Double, double" from *Macbeth,* so he murmured that under his breath, making the hand passes he had learned in Faerie.

Then he said, "Now watch," picked up his mug and set it to his lips.

Whoosh!

Out of Cathbadh's cup a geyser of wine leaped as though driven by a pressure hose, nearly reaching the ceiling before descending in a rain of glittering drops.

Cathbadh was a fast worker. He lifted his stick and struck the hurrying stream of liquid, crying something unintelligible in a high voice. Abruptly, the gusher was quenched and there was only the table, swimming with wine, and serf-women rushing to mop up the mess.

Cúchulainn said, "This is a very beautiful piece of magic, mac Shea, and it is a pleasure to have so notable a druid among us. But you would not be making fun of us, would you?" He looked dangerous.

"Not me," said Shea. "I only—"

Whatever he intended to say was cut off by a sudden burst of unearthly howling from outside. Shea glanced around rather wildly, feeling that things were getting out of hand, but Cúchulainn said, "You need not be minding that at all now. It will only be Uath, and because the moon has reached her term."

"I don't understand," said Shea.

"The women of Ulster were not good enough for Uath, so he must be going to Connacht and courting the daughter of Ollgaeth, the druid. This Ollgaeth is no very polite man. He said no Ultonian should have his daughter and, when Uath persisted, he put a geas on Uath that, when the moon fills, he must howl the night out, and a geas on his own daughter that she cannot abide the sound of howling. I am thinking that Ollgaeth's head is due for a place of honor."

Shea said, "But I still don't understand. If you can put a geas on someone, can't it be taken off again?"

Cúchulainn looked mournful, Cathbadh embarrassed and Laeg laughed. The charioteer said, "Now you will be making Cathbadh sad and our dear Cucuc is too polite to tell you—but the fact is no other than that Ollgaeth is so good a druid that no one can lift the spells he lays, nor lay one he cannot lift."

Outside, Uath's mournful howl rose again. Cúchulainn said to Belphebe, "Does he trouble you, dear? I can have him removed, or the upper part of him."

As the meal progressed, Shea noticed that Cúchulainn was putting away an astonishing quantity of the wine, talking almost exclusively with Belphebe, although the drink did not seem to have much effect on the hero. When the table was cleared Belphebe nodded significantly.

He got up and ran around the table to place a hand on her shoulder. Out of the corner of his eye, he saw Pete Brodsky getting up, too. Cúchulainn's face bore the faintest of smiles. "It is sorry to discommode you I am," he said, "but this is by the rules and not even a challenging matter. So now, Belphebe, darling, you will just come to my room."

He got up and started toward Belphebe, who got up, too, backing away. Shea racked his brain hopelessly for some kind of spell that might stop this business. Everyone else was standing up to watch the little drama.

Cúchulainn said, "Now you would not be getting in my way, would you, mac Shea, darling?" His voice was gentle, but there was something incredibly ferocious in the way he uttered the words.

Behind and to the left of Shea, Brodsky's voice rose, "Belle, you stiff, do like I told you!"

She turned back as Cúchulainn drew nearer and, with set face, crossed her arms and whipped the green gown off over her head. There she stood in her wispy bra and panties.

There was a simultaneous gasp and groan of horror from the audience.

"Go *on!*" yelled Brodsky in the background. "Give it the business!" He emphasized his meaning with a wolf-whistle.

Belphebe reached behind her to unhook her brassiere. Cúchulainn staggered as though he had been struck. He threw one arm across his eyes, reached the table and brought his face down on it, pounding the wood with the other fist.

"*Ara!*" he shouted. "Take her away! Is it killing me you will be and in my own hall, and me your host that has saved your life?"

"Will you let her alone?" asked Shea.

"I will that, for the night."

"Mac Shea, take his offer," advised Laeg from the head of the table. He looked rather greenish himself. "If his rage comes on him, none of us will be safe."

"Okay," said Shea and held Belphebe's dress for her.

Cúchulainn staggered to his feet. "It is not feeling well that I am, darlings," he said and, picking up the golden ewer of wine, made for his room.

IV

There was excited gabble among the retainers as Belphebe walked back to her place without looking to right or left, but they made room for Shea and Brodsky to join her.

The druid looked shrewdly at the closed door and said, "If the Little Hound drinks too much by himself he may be brooding on the wrong you are after doing him, and a sad day that would be. If he comes out with the hero-light playing round his head, run for your lives."

Belphebe said, "But where would we go?"

"Back to your own place. Where else?"

Shea frowned. "I'm not sure—" he began, when Brodsky cut in suddenly. "Say," he said, "your boss ain't really got no right to get bugged up. We had to play it that way."

Cathbadh swung to him. "And why, serf?"

"Don't call me serf. She's got a fierce geas on her. Any guy besides her husband that touches her gets a bellyache and dies of it. And Shea only stands for it because he's a magician. It's lucky we put the brakes on before he got her in that room, or he'd be ready for the lilies right now."

Cathbadh's eyebrows shot up like a seagull taking off. "Himself should know of this," he said. "There would be less bloodshed in Ireland if more people opened their mouths to explain things before they put their feet in them."

He got up, went to the bedroom door and knocked. There was a growl from within. Cathbadh entered and, a few minutes later, came out with Cúchulainn. The latter's step was visibly unsteady and his melancholy seemed to have deepened. He walked to the head of the table and sat down in the chair again.

"Sure, and this is the saddest tale in the world I'm hearing about your wife having such a bad geas on her. The evening is spoilt and all. I hope the black fit does not come on me now, for then it will be blood and death I'll need to restore me."

There were a couple of audible gasps and Laeg looked alarmed, but Cathbadh said hastily, "The evening is not so spoilt as you think, Cucuc. This mac Shea is evidently a very notable druid and spellmaker, but I think I am a better. Did you notice how quickly I put down his wine fountain? Would it not lift your heart now, to see the two of us engage in a contest of magic?"

Cúchulainn clapped his hands. "Never was truer word spoken."

Shea said, "I'm afraid I can't guarantee—but Belphebe plucked his sleeve and, with her head close to his, whispered, "Do it. There is a danger here."

"It isn't working right," Shea whispered back.

Outside rose the mournful sound of Uath's howling. "Can you not use your psychology on him out there?" the girl asked. "It will be magic to them."

"A real psychoanalysis would take days," said Shea. "Wait a minute, though—we seem to be in a world where the hysteric type is the norm. That means a high suggestibility. We might get something out of post-hypnotic suggestion."

Cúchulainn, from the head of the table, said, "It is not all night we have to wait." There was a note of menace in his voice.

Shea turned around and said aloud, "How would it be if I took the geas off that character out there? I understand that's something Cathbadh hasn't been able to do."

Cathbadh said, "If you can do this, it will be a thing worth seeing."

"All right," said Shea. "Bring him in."

"Laeg, dear, go get us Uath," said Cúchulainn. He took a drink, looked at Belphebe and his expression became morose again.

Shea said, "Let's see. I want a small bright object. May I borrow one of your rings, Cúchulainn? That one with the big stone would do nicely."

Cúchulainn slid the ring down the table as Laeg returned, firmly gripping the arm of a stocky young man, who seemed to be opposing some resistance to the process. Just as they got in the door, Uath flung back his head and emitted a bloodcurdling howl. Laeg dragged him forward.

Shea turned to the others. "If this magic is going to work, I'll need a little room. Don't come too near us while I'm spinning the spell, or you may be caught in it, too." He arranged a pair of seats well back from the table and attached a thread to the ring.

Laeg pushed Uath into one of the seats. "That's a bad geas you have there, Uath," said Shea, "and I want you to cooperate with me in getting rid of it. You'll do everything I tell you, won't you?"

The man nodded. Shea lifted the ring, said, "Watch this," and began twirling the thread back and forth between thumb and forefinger, so that the ring rotated first one way and then the other, sending out a flickering gleam of reflection from the rushlights. Meanwhile, Shea talked to Uath in a low voice, saying, "Sleep," now and then in the process. Behind him, he could hear an occasionally caught breath and could almost feel the atmosphere of suspense.

Uath went rigid.

Shea said in a low voice, "Can you hear me, Uath?"

"That I can."

"You will do what I say."

"That I will."

"When you wake up, you won't suffer from this howling geas any more."

"That I will not."

"To prove that you mean it, the first thing you do on waking will be to clap Laeg on the shoulder."

"That I will."

Shea repeated his directions several times, varying the words, and making Uath repeat them after him. At last he brought him out of the hypnotic trance with a snap of the fingers and a sharp, "Wake up!"

Uath stared about him with an air of bewilderment. Then he got up, walked over to the table and slapped Laeg on the shoulder. There was an appreciative murmur from the audience.

Shea said, "How do you feel, Uath?"

"It is just fine that I am feeling. I do not want to be howling at the moon at all now, and I'm thinking the geas is gone for good. I thank your honor." He came down the table, seized Shea's hand and kissed it, then joined the other retainers at the lower part of the table.

Cathbadh said, "That is a very good magic, indeed, and not the least of it was the small geas you put on him to lay his hand on Laeg's shoulder. And true it is that I have been unable to lift this spell. But as one man can run faster, so can another climb faster, and I will demonstrate by taking the geas off your wife, which you have evidently not been able to deal with."

"I'm not sure—" began Shea, doubtfully.

"Let not yourself be worried," said Cúchulainn. "It will not harm her at all and, in the future, she can be more courteous in the high houses she visits."

The druid rose and pointed a long, bony finger at Belphebe. He chanted some sort of rhythmic affair, which began in a gibberish of unknown language, but became more and more intelligible, ending with, ". . . and by oak, ash and yew, by the beauty of Aengus and the strength of Lér, and by authority as high druid of Ulster, let this geas be lifted from you, Belphebe! Let it pass! *Out* with it!"

He tossed up his arms and then sat down. "How do you feel, darling?"

"In good sooth, not much different than before," said Belphebe. "Should I?"

Cúchulainn said, "But how can we know that the spell has worked? *Aha!* I have it! Come with me." He rose, came around the table and, in response to Shea's exclamation of fury and Belphebe's of dismay, added, "Only as far as the door. Have I not given you my word?"

He bent over Belphebe, put one arm around her and reached for her hand, then reeled back, clutching his stomach with both hands and gasping for breath. Cathbadh and Laeg were on their feet. So was Shea.

Cúchulainn staggered against Laeg's arm, wiped a sleeve across his eyes and said, "Now the American is the winner, since your removal spell has failed, and it was like to be the death of me that the touch of her was. Do you be trying it yourself, Cathbadh, dear."

The druid reached out and laid a cautious finger on Belphebe's arm.

Nothing happened.

Laeg said, "Did not the serf say that a magician was proof against this geas?"

Cathbadh said, "You may have the right of it there, but I am thinking myself there is another reason. Cucuc wished to take her to his bed, while I was not thinking of that at all, at all."

Cúchulainn sat down again and addressed Shea. "A good thing it is, indeed, that I was protected from the work of this geas. Has it not proved obstinate even to the druids of your own country?"

"Very," said Shea. "I wish I could find someone who could deal with it." If possible, he had been more surprised than Cúchulainn by the latter's attack of cramps, but in the interval he had figured it out. Belphebe hadn't had any geas on her in the first place. Therefore, when Cathbadh tried to remove the spell, it took the opposite effect of laying on her a very good geas indeed. He felt rather grateful to Cathbadh.

Cathbadh said, "In America, there may be none to deal with such a matter, but in Ireland there is a man both bold and clever enough to lift the spell."

"Who's he?" asked Shea.

"That will be Ollgaeth of Cruachan, at the court of Ailill and Maev, who put the geas on Uath."

Brodsky from beside Shea spoke up. "He's the guy that's going to put one on Cúchulainn before the big mob takes him."

"*Wurra!*" said Cathbadh to Shea. "Your slave must have a second mind to go with his second sight. The last time he spoke, it would only be a spell that Ollgaeth would be putting on the Little Hound."

"Listen, punk," said Brodsky in a tone of exasperation, "get the stones out of your head. This is the pitch—this Maev and Ailill are mobbing up everybody that owes Cúchulainn here a score—and when they get them all together, they're going to put a geas on him that will make him fight them all at once, and it's too bad."

Cathbadh combed his beard with his fingers. "If this be true . . ." he began.

"It's the McCoy."

"I was going to say that, if it be true, it is high tidings from a low source. Nor do I see precisely how it may be dealt with."

Cúchulainn said with mournful and slightly alcoholic gravity, "I would fight them all without the geas, but if I am fated to fall, then that is an end of me."

Cathbadh turned to Shea. "You see the trouble we have with himself. Does your second sight reach farther, slave?"

Brodsky said, "Okay, lug, you asked for it. After Cúchulainn gets rubbed out, there'll be a war and practically everybody in the act gets knocked off, including you and Ailill and Maev. How do you like that?"

"As little as I like the look of your face," said Cathbadh. He addressed Shea. "Can this foretelling be trusted?"

"I've never known him to be wrong."

Cathbadh glanced from one to the other till one could almost hear his brains rumbling. Then he said, "I am thinking, mac Shea, that you will be having business at Ailill's court."

"What gives you such an idea?"

"You will be wanting to see Ollgaeth in this matter of your wife's geas, of course. A wife with a geas like that is like one with a bad eye—*and* you can never be happy until it is removed entirely. You will take your slave with you, and he will tell his tale and let Maev know that we know of her schemings, and they will be no more use than trying to feed a boar on bracelets."

Brodsky snapped his fingers and said, "Take him up," in a heavy whisper. But Shea said, "Look here, I'm not at all sure that I want to go to Ailill's court."

"I will even be going with you to see that you are properly received," said Cathbadh.

It struck Shea that this druid was extremely anxious to get him into a spot that might be dangerous. He said, "We can take a night to sleep on it and decide in the morning. Where do we sleep?"

"Finn will show you to a chamber," said Cúchulainn. "Myself and Cathbadh will be staying up the while." He smiled his charming and melancholy smile.

Finn guided the couple to a guest room at the back of the building, handed Shea a rushlight and closed the door, as Belphebe put up her arms to be kissed.

The next second, Shea was doubled up and knocked flat to the floor by a super-edition of the cramps that had seized Cúchulainn.

Belphebe bent over him. "Are you hurt, Harold?"

He pulled himself to a sitting posture with his back against the wall. "Not—seriously," he gasped. "It's that geas—it doesn't take time out for husbands."

The girl considered. "Could you not relieve me of it as you did the one who howled?"

Shea said, "I can try. But I can pretty well tell in advance that it won't work. Your personality is too tightly integrated—just the opposite of these hysterics around here."

"You might do it by magic."

Shea scrambled the rest of the way to his feet. "Not till I know more. Haven't you noticed I've been getting an overcharge—first that stroke of lightning and then the wine fountain? There's something in this continuum that seems to reverse my kind of magic."

She laughed a little. "If that's the law, why, there's an end. You have but to summon Pete and make a magic that would call for us to stay here, then—hey, presto!—we are returned."

"I don't dare take the chance, sweetheart. It might work and it might not—and even if it did, you'd be apt to wind up in Ohio with that geas still on you, and then we really would be in trouble."

There was a tap at the door. "Who is it?" called Belphebe.

"It's me—Pete."

As Shea opened, the detective slipped in and said, "Listen, I ain't got much time, but I gotta wise you up, see? Watch your step with this Cathbadh. The gang were telling me he's really bugged up at you for beating him on that geas deal. The only reason he doesn't send you to the cleaners right away is he's afraid of your kind of magic and wants to get wised up about it."

"Oh, Lord!" said Shea. "All the same, I don't see how we can avoid going with him to see Ollgaeth."

On top of that he had to sleep on the floor.

V

Harold Shea, Belphebe, Cathbadh and Pete Brodsky rode steadily across the central plain of Ireland. Their accouterments included serviceable broad-swords at the hips of Shea and Brodsky and a neat dagger at Belphebe's belt. Her request for a bow had brought forth only miserable sticks that pulled weakly and were quite useless beyond a range of fifty yards. These she had refused.

The first day, they followed the winding course of the Erne for some miles and splashed across it at a ford, then struck the boglands of western Cavan. Cathbadh appeared astonished at Brodsky's identifications of landmarks, but if he was really peeved at Shea, he did not show it, and his conversation even amused Belphebe.

By nightfall, they had covered at least half their journey. As they camped, with Belphebe busy at the fire, and the druid and Shea sitting against trees, Cathbadh said, "If it were me now, and I had the magic of the Americans, I would be doing a bit of it, and all this trouble of cooking would be saved."

Shea said, "But I like my wife's cooking."

"Not to be mentioning," said Cathbadh, as though he had not heard, "that a magician who calls lightning from the skies and comes here on a spell should be able to transport us to Cruachain without any trouble of riding at all, at all."

He was clearly fishing. Shea said, "That's an idea. I think maybe between the two of us we could work it. How about—"

Brodsky said suddenly, "Bag your head."

"—consulting with Allgaeth when we get there and seeing if we can't work out some good transportation magic," Shea finished smoothly.

Afterward, he got Brodsky aside and asked him, "Why the warning?"

"Listen," said Pete. "I'm a dick, see? I think I got this jerk's time. While we were riding back there, he wanted me to mob up with him and make prophecies. I'm telling you it ain't good. Nix him on everything."

"I see," said Shea. "Thanks—I'll try to be careful."

Morning showed mountains on their right, with a round peak in the midst of them. The journey went more slowly than on the previous day, principally because they had not yet developed riding callouses. They pulled up for the evening at the hut of a peasant rather more prosperous than the rest, and Brodsky more than paid for their food and lodging with tales out of Celtic myth.

The following day woke in rain and, though the peasant assured them Rath Cruachain was no more than a couple of hours' ride distant, the group became involved in fog and drizzle, so that it was not till afternoon that they skirted Loch Key and came to Magh Ai, the Plain of Livers.

There were about as many of the buildings as would constitute an incorporated village in their own universe, surrounded by the usual stockade and wide gate—unmistakably Cruachain of the Poets, the capital of Connacht.

At the gate of the stockade was a pair of hairy soldiers, but their spears were leaning against the posts and they were too engrossed in a game of knuckle-bones even to look up as the party rode through.

A number of people were moving about, most of whom paused to stare at Brodsky, who had flatly refused to discard the pants of his brown business suit and was evidently not dressed for the occasion.

The big house was built of heavy oak beams and had wooden shingles instead of the usual thatch. Shea stared with interest at windows with real glass in them, even though the panes were little diamond-shaped pieces half the size of a hand and far too irregular to see through.

There was a doorkeeper with a beard badly in need of trimming. Shea got off his horse and advanced to him, saying, "I am mac Shea, a traveler from beyond the island of the Fomorians, with my wife and bodyguard. May we have an audience with their majesties, and their great druid, Ollgaeth?"

The doorkeeper inspected the party with care and then grinned. "I am thinking," he said, "that your honor will please the Queen with your looks and your lady will please himself, so you had best go along in. But this ugly lump of a bodyguard will please neither, and as they are very sensitive, he had best stay with your mounts."

Shea glanced around in time to see Brodsky replace his expression of fury with the carefully cultivated blank look that policemen use under cross-examination, then helped Belphebe off her horse.

Inside, the main hall stretched away with the usual swords and spears in the usual places on the wall, and the usual rack of heads. In the middle, surrounded by retainers and soldiers, stood an oak dais, ornamented with strips of bronze and silver. It held two big carven armchairs, in which lounged, rather than sat, the famous sovereigns of Connacht.

Maev, who might have been in her early forties, was still strikingly beautiful, with a long, pale, unlined face, pale blue eyes and yellow hair hanging in long braids. For a blonde without the aid of cosmetics, she had remarkably red lips.

King Ailill was a less impressive figure than his consort. Some inches shorter, fat and paunchy, with small close-set eyes and a straggly pepper-and-salt beard, he seemed unable to keep his fingers still.

A young man in a blue kilt, wearing a silver-hilted shortsword over a tunic embroidered with gold thread, seemed to be acting as usher to make sure that nobody got to the royal couple out of turn. He spotted the newcomers at once and worked his way toward them.

"Will you be seeking an audience, or have you come merely to look at the greatest King in Ireland?" he asked. His eyes ran appreciatively over Belphebe's contours.

Shea identified himself, adding, "We have come to pay our respects to the King and Queen—ah . . ."

"Maine mac Aililla, Maine mo Epert," said the young man.

This would be one of the numerous sons of Ailill and Maev, who had all been given the same name. But he stood in their path without moving.

"Can we speak to them?" Shea said.

Maine mo Epert put back his head and looked down an aristocratic nose. "Since you are foreigners, you are evidently not knowing that it is the custom in Connacht to have a present for the man who brings you before the King. But I will be forgiving your ignorance." He smiled a charming smile.

Shea looked at Belphebe and she returned a glance of dismay.

Their total current possessions consisted of what they stood in. "But we have to see them," he said. "It may be important to them as well as to us."

Maine mo Epert smiled again.

Shea said, "How about a nice broadsword?" and pushed forward his hilt.

"I have a better one," said Maine mo Epert exasperatingly. "If it were a jewel now . . ."

Shea looked around. Cathbadh seemed to have disappeared. "Ollgaeth, the druid, is at the court, isn't he?"

"It is a rule that he will see none but those the Queen sends to him."

Shea felt like whipping out his sword and taking a crack at him. Suddenly, Belphebe from beside him said, "Jewels have we none, sirrah, but from your glances, there is something you would prize more. I am sure that, in accordance with your custom, my husband would be glad to loan me to you for the night."

Shea gasped, then remembered. That geas she had acquired could be handy as well as troublesome. But it had better not be removed till morning.

Maine mo Epert's smile turned into a grin that made Shea want more than ever to swat him, but the young man clapped his hands and began to push people aside.

Shea had just time to whisper, "Nice work, kid," when the usher pushed a couple of people from the end of a bench and sat them down in the front row, facing the royal pair. At the moment a couple of spearmen were holding a serf and giving evidence that he had stolen a pork chop.

Maev looked at Ailill, who said, "Ahem—since the lout was starving, perhaps we ought to exercise mercy and let him off with the loss of a hand."

"Do not be a fool," said Maev, "when it is not necessary at all. *What!* A man in Connacht, so famous for its heroes, is so weak-witted that he must starve? Hang him or burn him would be my decision if I were King."

"Very well, darling," said Ailill. "Let the man be hung."

Maine mo Epert said, "This is a pair from a distant island called America—the mac Shea and his wife, Belphebe. They wish to pay their respects."

"Let him speak," said Maev.

Shea wondered whether he ought to make an obeisance, but as no one else seemed to be doing it, he merely stepped forward and said, "Queen, you have become so famous that even in America we have heard of you, and we could not restrain the desire to see you. Also, I would like to see your famous druid, Ollgaeth, since my wife is suffering from a most unpleasant geas, and I am told he is an expert at removing them. Also, I have a message for you and the King, but that had better be given in private."

Maev rested her chin on her hand and surveyed him. "Handsome man," she said, "it is easy to see that you are not much used to deceiving people. Your embroidery is in the style of Ulster, and now you will be telling me at once what this message is and from whom it comes there."

"It doesn't come from there," said Shea. "It's true I have been in Ulster, at Cúchulainn's house of Muirthemne. And the message is that your plan against him will bring disaster."

King Ailill's fingers stopped their restless twitching and his mouth came open, while Maev's eyebrows formed a straight line. She said in a high voice, "And who told you of the plans of the King of Connacht?"

Look out, Shea thought. *This is thin ice.* Aloud he said, "Why, it's just that in my own country, I'm something of a magician, and I learned of it through spells."

The tension appeared to relax. "Magic," said Maev. "Handsome man, you have said a true word, that this message should be private. We will hear more of it later. You will be at our table tonight, and there you will meet Ollgaeth. For the now, our son, Maine Mingor, will show you to a place."

She waved her hand and Maine Mingor, a somewhat younger edition of Maine mo Epert, stepped out of the group and beckoned them to follow him. At the door, Belphebe giggled and said, "Handsome man."

Shea said, "Listen . . ."

"That I did," said Belphebe, "and heard her say that the message should be private. You're going to need a geas as much as I tonight."

The setting sun was shooting beams of gold and crimson through the low clouds. The horses had been tied to rings in the wall of the building, and Pete was waiting, with an expression of boredom. As Shea turned to follow Maine Mingor, he bumped into a tall, dark man, who was apparently waiting for just that purpose.

"Is it a friend of Cúchulainn of Muirthemne you are now?" asked this individual ominously.

"I've met him, but we're not intimates," said Shea. "Have you any special reason for asking?"

"I have that. He killed my father in his own house, he did. And I am thinking it is time he had one friend the less." His hand went to his hilt.

Maine Mingor said, "You will be leaving off with that, Lughaid. These people are messengers and under the protection of the Queen, my mother, so that if you touch them it will be both gods and men you must deal with."

"We will talk of this later," said Lughaid, and turned back to the palace.

Belphebe said, "I like that not."

Shea said, "Darling, I still know how to fence, and they don't."

VI

Dinner followed a pattern only slightly different from that at Muirthemne, with Maev and Ailill sitting on a dais facing each other across a small table. Shea and Belphebe were not given places as lofty as at Cúchulainn's board, but in partial compensation they had the two druids just opposite.

It became clear at once that Ollgaeth, a big stoutish man with a mass of white hair and beard, was one who asked a question only to trigger himself off on remarks of his own. He inquired about Shea's previous magical experience, and let him just barely touch on the illusions he had encountered in the Finnish Kalevala before taking off,

"Ah, now you would be thinking that was a great rare thing to see, would you not?" he said and gulped at barley beer. "Now let me tell you that of all the places in the world, Connacht produces the greatest illusions and the most beautiful. I remember, I do, the time when I was making a spell for Laerdach, for a better yield from his dun cow, and while I was in the middle of it, who should come by but his daughter, and she so beautiful that I stopped my chanting to look at her.

"Would you believe it now? The milk began to flow in a stream that would have drowned a man on horseback, and I had barely time to reverse the spell before it changed from illusion to reality and ravaged half a country."

Cathbadh nodded. Shea said, "Oh, I see. The chanting—"

Ollgaeth hurried on. "And there is a hill behind the rath of Maev this very moment. It looks no different from any other, but a hill of great magic, being one of the hills of the Sidhe and a gateway to their kingdom."

"Who—" began Shea, but the druid only raised his voice a little. "Mostly now, they would be keeping the gateways closed. But on a night like tonight, a good druid or even an ordinary one might open the gate."

"Why tonight?" asked Belphebe.

"What other night would it be but the Lúchnasaedh? Was it not for that you would be coming here? No, I forget. Forgive an old man." He smote his forehead to indicate the extent of his fault. "My dear friend, Cathbadh, would be just after telling me you came to discuss matters of high magic and a troublesome geas that lies on your lady. Wella, well ah. You have come to the right place."

Cathbadh said, "Still, he should not lose the sight of the hill of the Sidhe, for that will be a sight to take to his home in America with him."

"And it is myself will show it to him the night," said Ollgaeth. He turned to Cathbadh. "You will be coming with us, dear? And perhaps the mac Shea will be showing us some of his American magic when we come there, as I understand he is a rare good man with a spell."

Whatever reply Shea had in mind was cut off by King Ailill rapping on his table with the hilt of his knife and saying in his high voice, "We will now be hearing from Ferchertne, the bard, since this is the day of Lúgh, and a festival."

Serfs were whisking away the last of the food and benches were being moved to enlarge the space around Ferchertne, a youngish man with long hair and a lugubrious expression, who sat down on a stool with his harp, plucked a few melancholy twangs from the strings and in a bumpish baritone launched into the epic of the Fate of the Children of Tuirenn.

It wasn't very interesting and the voice was definitely bad. Shea glanced around and saw Brodsky fidgeting every time the harpist missed a quantity or struck a false note. Everyone else seemed to be affected almost to the point of tears, however, even Ollgaeth. Finally Ferchertne's voice went up in an atrocious discord and there was a violent snort from Pete.

The harp gave a twang and halted abruptly. Shea followed every eye in the room to the detective, who stared back belligerently.

"You would not be liking the music now, dear?" said Maev in a glacial voice.

"No, I wouldn't," said Brodsky. "If I couldn't do better than that with somebody holding my nose, I'd turn myself in."

"Better than that you shall do," said Maev. "Come forward, ugly man. Eiradh, you are to stand by this man with your sword, and if I signal you that he is less than the best, you are to bring me his head at once."

"Hey!" cried Shea, and Brodsky, "But I don't know the words."

Protest was useless. He was grabbed by half a dozen pairs of hands and pushed forward beside the bard's seat. Eiradh, a tall, bearded man, pulled out his sword and stood behind the pair, a smile of pleased anticipation on his face.

Brodsky looked around and then turned to the bard. "Give a guy a break, will you?" he said. "Go back over that last part till I catch the tune."

Ferchertne strummed obediently, while Brodsky leaned close, humming until he got the rather simple air that carried the words of the ballad. Then he straightened up, gesturing with one hand toward the harpist, who struck a chord and began to sing:

"Take these heads unto thy breast, O Brian . . ."

Pete Brodsky's voice soared over his, strong and confident, with no definite syllables, but carrying the tune for Ferchertne's words as the harp itself never had. Shea, watching Queen Maev, saw her stiffen, and then, as the melancholy ballad rolled on, two big tears came out on her cheek. Ailill was crying, too, and some of the audience were openly sobbing. It was like a collective soap-opera binge.

The epic came to an end at last, with Pete holding the high note after the harp had stopped. King Ailill lifted an arm and dried his streaming eyes on his sleeve, while Maev dried hers on her handkerchief. She said, "You have done more than you promised, American serf. I have not enjoyed the Fate of the Children more in my memory. Give him a new tunic and a gold ring." She stood up. "And now, handsome man, we will be hearing your message. You will attend me while the others dance."

As a pair of bagpipers stepped forward and gave a few preliminary howls on their instruments, Maev led the way through a door at the back, down the hall to a bedroom sumptuous by the standards that obtained here. There were rushlights against the wall and a soldier on guard at the door.

Maev said, *"Indech!* Poke up the fire, for it is cool the air is."

The soldier jabbed the fire with a poker, leaned his spear against the door and went out. Maev seemed in no hurry to come to business. She moved about the room restlessly.

"This," she said, "is the skull that belonged to Feradach mac Conchobra. I had him killed in payment for the taking of my dear Maine Morgor. See, I have had the eyeholes gilded."

Her dress, which had been a bright red in the stronger illumination of the hall, was a deep crimson here, and clung closely to a figure that, while full, was unquestionably well shaped.

"Would you be having a drop of Spanish wine now?" she said.

Shea felt a little trickle of perspiration gather on his chest and run down, and wished he were back with Ollgaeth. The druid was verbose and hopelessly vain, but he had furnished the tipoff on that chanting. It was some kind of quantity control for the spells that went with it. "Thanks," he said.

Maev poured wine into a golden cup for him, poured more for herself, and sat down on a stool. "Draw close beside me," she said, "for it is not right that we should be too much overheard. There. Now what is this of planning and disasters?"

Shea said, "In my own country I am something of a magician, or druid as you call it. Through this I have learned that you're going to get all Cúchulainn's enemies together, then put a geas on him to make him fight them all at once."

She looked at him through narrowed eyes. "You know too much, handsome man," she said, and there was a note of menace in her voice. "And the disasters?"

"Only that you had better not. The future of this is that you will succeed against Cúchulainn, but it will end up in a war in which you and your husband and most of your sons will be killed."

She sipped her wine, then stood up suddenly and began to pace the floor, moving like a crimson tide. Shea thought etiquette probably required him to get up, too, and he did so.

Not looking at him, Maev said, "And you have been at Muirthemne . . . and brought Cathbadh, the druid, with you here . . . and you know magical spells . . . *Ha!*"

She whirled with sudden pantherlike grace and faced Shea. "Tell me, handsome man, is it not true that you two came here to work on us with spells and magic and put a geas on us to defeat our purpose? Is it not true now that this tale of wars and disasters is something made up out of nothing?"

Shea said, "No, it isn't. I beat Cathbadh in a contest, and have reason to believe that he not only doesn't like me, but is cooking up something against me. And—"

She stamped. "Do not be lying to me. You have come here with your foreign magic to put a geas on Ollgaeth, and maybe on ourself, that we are to do your saying."

This was getting dangerous. Shea said, "Honest, I wouldn't put a geas on you. I don't know how."

"I do not care in the least at all," she said, "but you shall never make me do your bidding." She turned and stepped across the room, opened a big jewel case, from which she took a gold bracelet. "Come hither."

Shea stepped over to her. She rolled up his sleeves and snapped the bracelet on his arm, standing very close.

"Thanks," said Shea, "but I don't think I ought to accept—"

"And who are you to be saying what you will accept from Queen Maev? But touching the other, it is a thing decided, and I will go through with my project against Cúchulainn, no matter if it costs me my life and all. Come now."

She filled the wine cups again, took his hand, guided him to the stools and sat down close beside him. "Since life will be so brief, we may as well have what we can out of it," she said, drank off the cup and leaned back against Shea.

The thought leaped across his mind that, if he moved aside and let this imperious and rather beautiful woman slip to the floor, she would probably have his head taken off. He put an arm around her in self-defense. She caught the hand and guided it to her bosom, then reached for the other hand and led it to her belt. "The fastening is there," she said.

The door opened and Maine mo Epert came in, followed by Belphebe.

"Mother and Queen—" began the young man, and stopped.

To give Maev due credit she got to her feet with dignity and without apparent embarrassment. "Will you be forever behaving as though you were just hatched from the shell now?" she demanded.

"But I have a case against this woman. She made a promise to me, she did, and she has a geas on her that makes a man as ill as though bathed in venom."

"You will be having Ollgaeth take it off, then," said Maev.

" 'Tis the night of Lúgh. Ollgaeth is not to be found."

"Then you must even bed by yourself, then," said Maev. She looked from Shea to Belphebe and her expression was rather sour.

"I think we had better be going along, too, Harold," said Belphebe, sweetly.

VII

When they were outside Belphebe said, "Tell me not—I know. She looked so fine in that red robe that you wished to help her take it off."

Shea said, "Honest, Belphebe, I—"

"Oh, spare me your plaints. I'm not the first wife to have a husband made of glass, nor will I be the last. What is it that you have on your arm?"

"Listen, Belphebe, if you'll only let me tell you . . ."

A form stepped out of the shadows into moonlight, which revealed it as Ollgaeth. "The hour is met if you would see the hill of the Sidhe, mac Shea," he said.

She said, "Where's Cathbadh?"

"For bed, I think. He grew weary with his journey."

Shea turned to Belphebe. "Want to come along, kid?"

"Not I," she said and stifled an imaginary yawn. "I, too, am weary with the journey. Good night."

She took a couple of steps away. Shea stepped after her and bent his head close to hers. "Listen," he said, "you'd better come. Cathbadh was awfully anxious to have me go on this trip, and now he's cut himself out of the deal. I'm afraid he's cooking up something for you."

Belphebe shrugged off his hand. "I'm for bed," she said. "And with my geas to protect me."

He hated to leave her alone in her present mood, no matter how unjustified it was, but if he wanted to get any cooperation out of this vain druid, the man would have to be buttered up.

"All right," he said. "See you later, dear."

He turned to follow Ollgaeth through the dark streets. The guards at the gate were awake, a tribute to Maev's management, but they passed the druid and his companion readily enough.

Ollgaeth, stumbling along the track, said, "The Sidhe, now, they have the four great treasures of Ireland—Dagda's cauldron, that will never let a man go foodless, the stone of Fál, that strikes every man it is aimed at, Lugh's spear and Nuada's great manslaying sword, that is death to all before it, but protection to the bearer."

"Indeed," said Shea. "At the table you were saying—"

"Will you never let a man finish his tale?" said Ollgaeth. "The way of it is this—the Sidhe themselves may not use the treasures, for there is a geas on them that they can be handled only by a man of Milesian blood. Nor will they give them up, for fear the treasures may be used against them. And all who come into their land, they use hardly."

"I should think—" began Shea.

"I do call to mind there was a man named Goll tried it," said Ollgaeth. "But the Sidhe cut off both his ears and fed them to the pigs, and he was never the same man after. Ah, it's a queer race they are, and a good man one must be to sit at table with them."

The Hill of the Sidhe loomed in front of them.

"If you will look carefully, mac Shea," said Ollgaeth, "to the left of that little tree, you will see a darkish patch in the rocks. Let us move closer now." They climbed the base of the hill. "Now if you will be standing about here, watch the reflection of the moon on the spot there. Watch carefully."

Shea looked, moving his head from side to side—and made out a kind of reflection on the surface of the rock, not as definite and clear as it might be, more like that on a pond, wavering slightly with ripples. Clearly an area of high magical tension.

Ollgaeth said, "It is not to everyone I would be showing this or even telling it, but you will be going back to your America and it is as well for you to know that, because of the spells the Sidhe themselves place on these gates, they may be opened in this hour without the use of the ancient tongue. Watch now." He raised his arms and began to chant:

> *"The chiefs of the voyage over the sea*
> *By which the sons of Mil came . . ."*

It was not very long, ending:

> *"Who opens the gateway to Tír na n-Og?*
> *Who but I, Ollgaeth the druid?"*

He clapped his hands together sharply. The wavering reflection faded and Shea saw nothing but blackness, as if he were looking into a tunnel in the side of the hill.

"Approach, approach," said Ollgaeth. "It is not like that the Sidhe will be dangerous against a druid as powerful as myself."

Shea went nearer. Sure enough, he was looking down a tunnel that stretched some distance into blackness, with a faint light beyond. He put out his left hand—it went into the hole where solid rock had been without resistance, except for a slight tingly feeling.

As he turned the hand around, there was a low mumbling sound behind him and, at the same moment, something both clinging and resistant, like glue about to harden, gripped him from wrist to fingers. He half turned his head. Not three feet below on the slope in the moonlight stood Cathbadh, the druid, arms aloft and chanting in a low voice. Behind him was Ollgaeth.

"*You bastard!*" yelled Shea, but the chant went on and the tension was increasing. There wasn't going to be much time.

Suddenly, Shea remembered that cold iron was a prescriptive against most kinds of magic. He reached across his body, whipped out the broadsword and, with difficulty because he had to shorten his arm, made a slashing cut around the head, at the same time jerking mightily. It gave with a *plop*—and he went tumbling backward down the slope, cannoning into the chanting druid and sending the two of them sprawling in a tangle of legs and arms.

Shea rolled over once more, and jackknifed to his feet, his blade still pointed at Cathbadh, who climbed to his feet more slowly. He seemed to have something wrong with one arm.

Ollgaeth said, "Cathbadh, dear, I would be telling you now, that it's a bad day when you tamper with foreign druids, and now maybe you will be believing me. I remember—"

Shea said, "Shut up or it will be a worse night. I want to get to the bottom of this and find out some good reason why I shouldn't stick you both with this thing right now. You were in it together, weren't you?"

Ollgaeth said, "It was only to keep you there the while you told us some of the magic of the Americans. I have a geas on me that I cannot chant against anyone who has not harmed me or the Queen."

"Yet you didn't mind helping this lug trap a stranger who had done nothing to you. Stand still, you." He waved the point menacingly at Cathbadh, who showed signs of moving. "If you start another one of those chants, I'll let you have it."

"You need not be afraid at all, at all," said Ollgaeth. "Will you not be seeing he has hurt his arm and cannot lift it to raise a spell?"

"That's good," said Shea. "Now look here, Ollgaeth. You didn't actually throw any spells at me, so it won't hurt your geas, but you did get me out here where Cathbadh was going to lock me up, so you owe me something. Isn't that right?"

"It is not to be denied that the Queen might take such a view. But . . ."

Shea said, "All right, I'm ready to make a deal. Is this really the gate to the country of the Sidhe?"

"It is that."

"Then you're going to teach me how to use the spell on it. It might come in handy. And then we're going to tie dear Cathbadh up, where he won't make any more mischief for the night. And then we're going back to Cruachain, and you're going to take that geas off my wife. I'll call it square and say nothing to Maev, and even teach you some new magic in the morning. Agreed?"

He was thinking fast. If Ollgaeth showed good faith by taking off Belphebe's geas that night and teaching him to open the gate of the

Sidhe—and if it *was* a gate of the Sidhe—Pete could be collected in the morning and a swap be made for getting the three of them back to Ohio.

As for Cathbadh, a night under dew wouldn't hurt him, after what he tried to pull. And if Ollgaeth didn't work out right, it should be possible to retrieve Cathbadh in the morning and compel him by one process or another to take them to a druid who could both remove the geas and teach him enough to get back home.

Ollgaeth said, "I am thinking that this is as good a way to solve things as I have heard." He moved forward and, although the Ultonian druid looked malevolent even in the moonlight, began to tear strips from his outer robe to tie him up.

Ollgaeth, for a wonder, didn't say anything as they walked back, apparently sunk in deep purple thoughts. At the gate, the guard said to the druid, "It is herself wishes to see you and will be waiting wake," and Ollgaeth excused himself, saying he would be around later to deal with the geas if Shea were still awake. Shea said he would be, and tapped at the guest-house door.

"Who comes?" said Belphebe's voice.

"It's me—Harold."

The bolt clicked back, and the door opened to show her fully dressed, a line of worry in her forehead.

"My lord," she said, "I do pray your pardon for my angers. I see now 'twas no more your fault at Muirthemne. But we must be quick."

"What do you mean?"

She had their small items of gear all ready. "Pete was here but now. We are in deadly danger, among the Queen, Maine mo Epert and this Lughaid who accosted you. For your refusal to her, they have her permission to take our heads if they will."

Shea put his hand on his sword. "I'd like to see them try it."

"Foolish man! It is not the one or two, but a band—six, half a score. Come." She pulled him toward the door.

"But where's Pete?" he protested. "We can't go back without him. And I've made a deal with Ollgaeth."

"Nor can we go back at all if we do not live out the night," she said, leading him out into the dark, silent street. "Pete is doing what he may to gain us time. His singing's wholly caught them. All else yields before present necessity."

At the gate there was now only one guard, but he held his spear crosswise and said, "I cannot be letting you out the night. The Queen has sent word."

Belphebe gave a little cry. Shea half turned to see sparks of light dancing, back among the houses. Torches—and doubtless Ollgaeth the druid had been reached by Maev and would have some sort of geas to put on them if he came in sight. He swung around again, unsheathing his sword, and, without warning, drove a thrust at the guard's neck. The soldier jerked up his buckler just in time to catch Shea's point in the edge of the bronze decorations. Then he lowered his spear and drew it back for a jab.

Shea recovered, knocking the spear aside with his edge, but was unable to get around the shield for a return lunge. He thrust twice, feinting with the intention of driving home into an opening, but each time a slight movement of the buckler showed it would be futile. The soldier balanced, drew back for another thrust, then swore as Belphebe, who had slipped past him, caught the butt end of his weapon.

He shouted, *"Ho! An alarm!"*

They had to work fast. Shea aimed a cut at the man's head, but he ducked, simultaneously releasing the spear into Belphebe's hands, who went tumbling backward as the man did a quick sidestep and whipped out his sword.

Shea made a lightning estimate. The guard's face and neck were too small a target and too well protected by the shield, his torso doubly protected by shield and mail. Down.

He made a quick upward sweep that brought the buckler aloft, then drove the blade into the man's thigh, just above the knee and below the edge of the kilt. He felt the blade cleave meat—the man's leg buckled, spilling him to the ground in a clang of metal with a groaning shout.

Behind them in the rath, there were answering cries and the torchlight points turned. *"Come on!"* cried Belphebe, and began to run. She still clutched the big spear, but was so light on her feet it did not appear to matter. Shea, trying to keep up with his wife, heard more shouts behind them.

"The hill," he gasped and, as he ran, was suddenly glad the Irish of this period were not much good with bows.

He was getting short of breath, though Belphebe was running as lightly as ever. The hill loomed over them, dark now by reason of the movement of the moon. "This way," gasped Shea, and ran up the uneven slope. There was the black rock, still shining, queerly mirror-like. Shea lifted his arms over his head and began to chant, panting for breath:

"The chiefs of the voyage—over the sea—
By which—the sons of Mil came—"

Behind, one of the pursuers set up a view-halloo. Out of the corner of an eye, Shea saw Belphebe whirl and balance the spear as though for throwing, but he didn't have time to stop and tell her that such a weapon couldn't be used that way.

"Who but I, Harold mac Shea?" he finished, resoundingly. "Come on!"

He dragged Belphebe toward the dimly seen black opening, and through. When he entered the darkness he felt a tingling all over, as of a mild electric shock.

Then, abruptly, sunlight replaced moonlight. He and Belphebe were standing on the downward slope of another hill, like the one they had just entered. He had just time to take in the fact that the landscape was similar to the one they had quitted, before something crashed down on the back of his head and knocked him unconscious.

VIII

Briun mac Smetra, King of the Sidhe of Connacht, leaned forward in his carven chair and looked at the prisoners. Harold Shea looked back at him as calmly as he could, although his hands were bound behind his back and his head was splitting.

Briun was a tall, slender person with pale blond hair and blue eyes that seemed too big for his face. The others were a delicate-looking people, clad with Hellenic simplicity in wrap-around tunics.

"It will do you no good at all to be going on like this," said the King. "So now it is nothing at all you must lose but your heads for the Connachta you are."

"But we're not Connachta," said Shea. "As I told you . . ."

A husky man with black hair said, "They look like Gaels, they speak like Gaels and they are dressed like Gaels."

"And who should know better than Nera, the champion, who was a Gael himself before he became one of us?" said the King.

"Now look here, King," said Shea. "We can prove we're not Gaels by teaching you things no Gael ever knew."

"Can you now?" said Briun. "And what sort of things would those be?"

Shea said, "I think I can show your druids some new things about magic."

Beside him, Belphebe's clear voice seconded him. "I can show you how to make a bow that will shoot—two hundred yards."

Briun said, "Now it is to be seen that you are full of foolish lies. It is well known that we already have the best druids in the world, and no bow will shoot that far. This, now, is just an excuse to have us feed you for a time until it is proved you are lying, which is something we can see without any proof being needed. You are to lose your heads."

He made a gesture of dismissal and started to rise.

The black-thatched Nera said, "Let me—"

"Wait a minute!" cried Shea desperately. "This guy is a champion, isn't he? All right, how about it if I challenge him?"

The King sat down again and considered. "Since you are to lose your head anyway," he said, "we may as well have some enjoyment out of it. But you are without armor."

"Never use the stuff," said Shea. "Besides, if neither one of us has any, things will move faster." He heard Belphebe gasp beside him, but did not turn his head.

"Ha, ha!" said Nera. "Let him loose and I will be making him into pieces of fringe for your robe."

Somebody released Shea and he stretched his arms and flexed his muscles to restore circulation. He was pushed rather roughly toward the door, where the Tuatha Dé Danaan were forming a ring, and a sword was thrust into his hand. It was one of the usual Irish blades, almost pointless and suitable mainly for cutting.

"Hey!" he said. "I want my own sword, the one I had with me."

Briun stared at him a moment out of pale, suspicious eyes. "Bring the sword," he said and then called, *"Miach!"*

The broadsword that Shea had ground down to as fine a point as possible was produced and a tall old man stepped forward.

"You are to be telling me if there is a geas on this blade," said the King.

The druid took the blade and, holding it flat on both palms, ran his nose along it, sniffing. He looked up. "I do not find any smell of geas or magic about it," he said, then lifted his nose like a hound toward Shea. "But about his one there is certainly something that touches my profession."

"It will not save him," said Nera. "Come and be killed, Gael." He swung up his sword.

Shea just barely parried the downstroke. The man was strong as a horse and had a good deal of skill in the use of his clumsy weapon. For several panting minutes, the weapons clanged. Shea had to step back, and back again, and there were appreciative murmurs from the spectators.

Finally, Nera, showing a certain shortness of breath and visibly growing restive, shouted, "You juggling Greek!" He took a step backward and wound up for a two-handed overhead cut, intended to beat down his opponent's blade by sheer power. Instantly, Shea executed the maneuver known as an advance-thrust—dangerous against a fencer, but hardly a barbarian like this. He hopped forward, right foot first and shot his arm out straight. The point went right into Nera's chest.

Shea's intention was to jerk his blade loose with a twist to one side to avoid the downcoming slash. But the point stuck between his enemy's ribs and, in the instant it failed to yield, Nera's blade, weakened and wavering, came down on Shea's left shoulder. He felt the sting of steel and, in the same moment, the sword came loose as Nera folded up wordlessly.

"You're *hurt!*" cried Belphebe. "Let me loose!"

"Just a flesh wound," said Shea. "Do I win, King Briun?"

"Loose the woman," said the King, and tugged at his beard. "Indeed, and you do. A great liar you may be, but you are also a hero and champion, and it is our rule that you take Nera's place. You will be wanting his head for the pillars of the house you will have."

"Listen, King," said Shea. "I don't want to be a champion, and I'm not a liar. I can prove it. And I've got obligations. I really come from a land as far from the land of the Gaels as it is from Tír na n-Og, and if I don't get back there soon, I'm going to be in trouble."

"Miach!" called the King. "Is it the truth he is telling?"

The druid stepped forward, said, "Fetch me a bowl of water," and when it was brought, instructed Shea to dip a finger in it. Then he made a few finger-passes, murmuring to himself, and looked up.

"It's of the opinion I am," he said, "that this mac Shea has obligations elsewhere and, if he fails to fulfill them, a most unfavorable geas would come upon him."

"We may as well be comfortable over a mug of beer in deciding these questions," said the King.

Belphebe had been dabbing at Shea's shoulder. Now she caught his hand and they went in together. The big sword was awkward, and they had taken his scabbard as well, but he clung to it anyway.

When they were inside and King Briun had seated himself again, he said, "This is a hard case and requires thinking, but before we give judgment, we must know what there is to know. Now what is this of a new magic?"

"It's called sympathetic magic," said Shea. "I can show Miach how to do it, but I don't know the old tongue, so he'll have to help me. You see—I've been trying to get back to my own place, and I can't do it because of that."

He went on to explain about the court of Maev and Ailill, and the necessity of rescuing Pete and getting back with him. "Now," he said, "if someone will give me a little clay or wax, I'll show you how sympathetic magic is done."

Miach came forward and looked on with interest as someone brought a handful of damp clay to Shea, who placed it on a piece of wood and formed it into a rather crude and shapeless likeness of the seated King. "I'm going to do a spell to make him rise," said Shea, "and I'm afraid the effect will be too heavy if you don't chant. So when I start moving my hands, you sing."

"It shall be done," said Miach.

A verse or two of Shelley ought to make a good rising spell. Shea went over it in his head, then bent down and took hold of the piece of wood with one hand, while he murmured, "Arise, arise, arise," and with the other began to make the passes. He lifted the piece of wood. Miach's chant rose.

So did a shriek from the audience. Simultaneously, an intolerable weight developed on Shea's arm, a crack zigzagged across the floor and he half turned his head in time to see the royal palace and all its contents going up like an elevator, already past the lower branches of the trees, with one of the spectators clinging desperately to the doorsill by his fingertips.

Shea stopped his passes and hastily began repeating the poem backward, lowering his piece of wood. The palace came down with a jar that sent things tumbling from the walls and piled the court in a yelling heap. Miach looked dazed.

"I'm sorry," said Shea, "I . . ."

Patting his crown back into position, King Briun said sternly, "Is it ruining us you would be?"

Miach said, "O King, it is my opinion that this mac Shea has done no more than was asked, and that this is a very beautiful and powerful magic, and would be precious to the Sidhe."

"And you could remove the geas that lies on this woman and return the pair to their own place?"

Miach frowned. "The geas, yes—given only that it be removed in the place where it was laid. For the rest, I smell an inimical influence of a druid of the Gaels, and where he is present I cannot contend."

Shea said, "Look, you give it the old college try. I'll manage to keep Cathbadh off somehow. That's his name."

"Then hear our judgment." King Briun stretched forth a hand. "Now, mac Shea has killed our champion, and does not wish to take his place. There must be a balance against this, and we set it that it shall be this wonder-working bow of his wife's, which, if it is as good as his magic, will surely shoot holes through the sides of the mountains."

He paused and Shea nodded. The man could be quite reasonable after all.

"Secondly," Briun went on, "there is the matter of removing his wife's geas. Against this, we will place the teaching of this new magic to our druid. Now respecting the transfer of these two to their own country, it is our judgment that it should be paid for by having mac Shea undertake to remove us of the Sinech, since it is so troublesome a monster and he is so great a champion and magician."

"Just a minute," said Belphebe. "That doesn't help us find Pete or get him back and trouble will come on us if we don't. And we really ought to do something for Cúchulainn. Maev is going through with her plan against him."

"We would willingly help you in this matter, but you have no other prices to pay."

Miach said, "Yet there is a way to accomplish all they ask, save in the matter of the man Pete, in the finding of whom I have no power."

Briun said, "You will be telling us about it, then."

"Touching the Sinech," said Miach, "it is so great and dreadful a monster that even a champion like mac Shea will be hard put against it by his own strength alone. Therefore, let us loan him the treasure of Ireland, the invincible sword of Nuada, which is forbidden to us by its geas, but which he will be able to use without any trouble at all.

"Touching the geas, it will be needed that I accompany mac Shea's wife to the place where it was imposed, in order to lift it. Therefore, let the loan of the sword continue, and mac Shea can in turn loan it to this hero Cúchulainn, who will make a mighty slaughter of the Connachta we detest. Then, as I will be present, I can see that the blade is returned."

The King leaned his chin on one hand and frowned for a minute. Then he said, "It is our command that this be done as you advise."

IX

Miach was an apt pupil. At the third try, he succeeded in making a man he did not like break out in a series of beautiful yellow splotches. He was so delighted with the result that he promised Shea for the hunting of the Sinech not only the sword of Nuada but the enchanted shoes of Iubdan, that would enable him to walk on water.

He explained that the reason for the overcharge in Shea's magic was that the spells were in the wrong tongue, but as the magic wouldn't work at all without a spell of some kind and Shea didn't have time to learn another language, this was not much help.

About the Sinech itself, he was more encouraging. He did a series of divinations with bowls of water and blackthorn twigs. Though Shea did not know enough of the magic of this continuum to make out anything but a confused and cloudy movement below the clear surface of the bowl, Miach assured him that he had acquired a geas that would not allow his release until he had accomplished something that would alter the pattern of the continuum itself.

"Now tell me, mac Shea," he said, "was it not so in the other lands you visited? For I see by my divinations that you have visited many."

Shea, thinking of how he had helped break up the chapter of magicians in Faerie and rescued his wife from the Saracens of the *Orlando Furioso*, was forced to agree.

"It is just as I am telling you, for sure," said Miach. "And I am thinking that this geas has been with you since the day you left home without your ever knowing it. We all of us have them, we do, and a good man it is that does not have trouble with his geasas."

Belphebe looked up from the arrow she was shaping. Her bow was a success, but finding seasoned material from which to build shafts was a problem. "Still, master druid," she said, "it is no less than a problem to us that we may return to our own place late, and without our friend Pete. For this would place us deeply in trouble."

"Now I would not be worrying about that at all, at all," said Miach. "For the nature of a geas is that, once it is accomplished, it gives you no more trouble at all. And the time you are spending in the country of the Sidhe will be no more than a minute in the time of your own land, so that you need not be troubling till you are back among the Gaels."

"That's a break," said Shea. "Only I wish I could do something about Pete."

"Unless I can see him, my divination will not work on him at all," said Miach. "And now I am thinking it is time for you to try the shoes."

They went to one of the smaller lakes, not haunted by Sinechs, and Shea stepped out cautiously from the shore. The shoes sank in a little, forming a meniscus around them, but they seemed to give the lake-water beneath a jellylike consistency just strong enough to support him. A regular walking motion failed to yield good results. Shea found he had to skate along and he knew that, if he tripped over a wave, the result would be unfortunate, since the shoes would not keep the rest of him from breaking through the surface and, once submerged, would keep his head down.

Next morning, they went out in a procession to Loch Gara, the haunt of the monster, with King Briun, Belphebe and the assorted warriors of the Tuatha Dé Danaan. The latter had spears, but they did not look as though they would be much help. Two or three of them fell out and sat under the trees to compose poems and the rest were a dreamy-eyed lot.

Miach murmured a druid spell, unwrapped the sword of Nuada and handed it to Shea. It was better balanced than his own broadsword, coming down to a beautiful laurel-leaf point. As Shea swung it appreciatively, the blade began to ripple with light, as though there were some source of it within the steel itself.

He looked around. "Look, King," he said, "I'm going to try to do this right. If you'll cut down that small tree there, then hitch a rope to the top of that other tree beside it, then we'll bend down the second tree . . ."

Under his directions, the Tuatha did away with one tree and bent the other down by a rope running to the stump of the first. This rope continued on, Shea holding the rest of it in a coil.

"Ready?" he called.

"We are that," said King Briun, and Belphebe took up her shooting stance, with a row of arrows in the ground beside her.

Shea skated well out onto the lake, paying out the rope which dragged in the water behind him. The monster seemed in no hurry to put in an appearance.

"Hey!" called Shea. "Where are you, Sinech? Come on out, Loch Ness!"

As if in answer, the still surface of the lake broke like a shattered mirror some fifty yards away and, through the surface, there appeared something black and rubbery, which vanished and appeared again, much closer. The Sinech was moving toward him at a speed which did credit to its muscles.

Shea gripped the rope with both hands and shouted, *"Let her go!"*

The little figures on shore moved around, and there was a tremendous tug on the rope. The men had untied the tackle, so that the bent tree sprang upright. The pull on the rope sent Shea skidding shoreward as though he were water-skiing behind a motorboat. An arrow went past him and then another.

Shea began to slow down, then picked up again as a squad of King Briun's soldiers took hold of the rope and ran inland with it as fast as they could. His theory was that the Sinech would ground itself and, in that condition, could be dispatched by a combination of himself, the soldiers' spears and Belphebe's arrows.

But the soldiers on the rope did not yank hard enough to take up all the slack before Shea slowed down almost to a stop. Still twenty yards from shore, he could see the sandy bottom below him.

Behind him, he heard the water boiling and swishing under the urge of the Sinech's progress. Shea risked a glance over his shoulder to catch a glimpse of a creature somewhat like a mosasaur, with dozens of flippers along its sides in a long row. Just behind the pointed, lizardlike head that reared from the water a pair of arrows projected, and another had driven into its cheek-bone, evidently aimed for the eye.

The instant of looking back brought Shea's foot into contact with a boulder that lay with perhaps an inch projecting from the surface. Over it and down he went, head first into the water of the marge.

The Sinech's jaws snapped like a closing bank-vault door on empty air, while Shea's head drove down until his face ploughed into the sand of the bottom. His eyes open under the water, he could see nothing but clouds of sand stirred up by the monster's passage. The water swished around him as the Sinech came in contact with solid ground and threshed frantically in its efforts to make progress.

The shoes of Iubdan kept pulling Shea's feet up, but at last he bumped into the boulder he had stumbled over. His arms clawed its sides and his head came out of water with legs scrambling after.

The Sinech was still grounded, but not hopelessly so, and was making distinct progress toward Belphebe, who valiantly stood her ground, shooting arrow after arrow into the creature. The same glance told him that the spearmen of the Tuatha Dé Danaan had taken to their heels.

The monster, engrossed in Belphebe as its remaining opponent, threw back its head for a locomotive hiss, and Shea, skating toward it, saw her bend suddenly to seize up one of the abandoned spears in an attempt to distract it from him.

Tugging out the sword of Nuada, he aimed for the Sinech's neck, behind the head, where it lay half in and half out of water, the stiff mane standing up above Shea's head. As he drove toward the monster, the near eye spotted him and the head started to swivel back toward him.

In his rush, Shea drove the sword in up to the hilt, hoping for the big artery.

The Sinech writhed, throwing Shea back as it ejected the sword. There was a gush of blood, so dark it looked black. The creature threw back its head and emitted a kind of mournful, whistling roar of agony. Shea skated forward on his magical shoes for another thrust, almost stumbling over the neck. He reached down to grasp a bunch of mane in his left hand and climbed aboard, cutting and stabbing.

The Sinech threw back its head violently, to a height of thirty feet, it seemed. Shea's grip on the mane was broken, and he was thrown through the air. All he could think of was that he must hang onto the sword. He had hardly formulated this thought before he struck the water with a terrific splash.

When he got his head out against the resistance of the shoes at the other end of his anatomy, the Sinech was creaming the water with aimless writhings, its long head low on the bank, and its eyes already glassy.

The sword of Nuada had lived up to its reputation for giving mortal wounds all right. Shea had to develop a kind of dog paddle to carry him into shallow water past the throes of the subsiding monster.

Belphebe waded out to help him to his feet, regardless of the wet. She put both arms around him and gave him a quick, ardent kiss, which instantly doubled him over with cramps. Behind her the Sidhe were trickling out of the woods, headed by King Briun looking dignified, and Miach looking both amazed and pleased.

Shea said, "There's your job. Do you think that lets me out from under that geas you say I've got?"

Miach shook his head. "I am thinking it will not. A rare fine change you have made in the land of the Sidhe, but it is to the land of men you belong, and there you must do what is to be done. So we will just be going along to see if you can avert the fate that hangs over this Cúchulainn."

X

Shea and Belphebe were bouncing along in a chariot on the route from the section of Tír na n–Og corresponding to Connacht as the other world equivalent of Muirthemne to Ulster. They had agreed with Miach, who was coming in another chariot, that it would be better to go that way than re-enter as they had come and possibly have to fight their way through hostile Connacht, even though he was wearing the invincible sword of Nuada.

The country seemed very similar to that from which they had just come, though the buildings were generally poorer, and there were fewer of them. Indeed, none at all were in sight when they stopped at a furze-covered hill with a rocky outcrop near its base.

Miach signaled his charioteer to draw up and said, "Here stands another of the portals. You are to draw off a little while I cast my spell, as this is not one of the holy days and a magic of great power is required."

From the chariot, Shea could see him tossing his arms aloft, and caught an occasional word of the chant, which was in the old language. A blackness which seemed to suck up all the light of the day appeared around the outcrop, considerably larger than the tunnel Shea himself had opened. The charioteers got down to lead the horses, and they found themselves on the reverse slope, with Cúchulainn's stronghold of Muirthemne in the middle distance, smoke coming from its chimneys.

Shea said, "That's queer. I thought Cúchulainn was at Emain Macha with the King, but it looks as though he came back."

"By my thinking," said Belphebe, "he is most strangely set on having his own will and no other, so that not even the prophecy of death can drive him back."

Shea said, "I hope Cathbadh isn't with him. I'd hate to have to get into a hassel with him before that geas—" He was interrupted as a horseman suddenly burst from a clump of trees to the right, and went galloping across the rolling ground toward Cúchulainn's stronghold.

They went down a slope into a depression, where the fold of the ground and a screen of young trees on the opposite side hid the view of Muirthemne. As they climbed the slope, the charioteers reined in. At the same time, a line of men jumped out of cover, with spears and shields ready.

One of them advanced on the travelers. "Who might you be," he demanded truculently, "and for why are you here?"

Miach said, "I am a druid of the Sidhe and I am traveling with my friends to Muirthemne, to remove a geas that lies on one of them."

"You will not be doing that the day," said the man. "It is an order that no druids are to come nearer to Muirthemne than this line until himself has settled his differences with the Connachta."

"Woe's me!" said Miach, then turned toward Shea. "You will be seeing how your geas still rules. I am prevented from helping you at the one place where my help would be of avail."

"Be off with you now!" the man said and waved his spear.

Behind her hand, Belphebe said to Shea, "Is this not very unlike them?"

Shea said, "By George, you're right, sweetheart! That isn't Cúchulainn's psychology at all." He leaned toward the guard. "Hey, you, who gave the order and why?"

The man said, "I do not know by what right you are questioning me at all, but I will be telling you it was the Shamus."

An inspiration struck Shea. "You mean Pete, the American?"

"Who else?"

"We're the other Americans that were here before. Get him for us, will you? We can straighten this out. Tell him Shea is here."

The man looked at him suspiciously, then at Miach. He consulted with one of his companions, who stuck his spear in the ground, laid the shield beside it and trotted off toward Muirthemne.

Shea said, "How come Pete's giving orders around here?"

"Because it's the Shamus he is."

Shea said, "I recognize the title all right, but what I can't figure out is how Pete got away from Cruachain and got here to acquire it."

He was saved from further speculation by the creaking of a rapidly driven chariot, which drew up on the other side of the hedge. From it descended a Pete Brodsky strangely metamorphosed into something like the Connecticut Yankee at King Arthur's court. His disreputable trousers projected from beneath a brilliantly red tunic embroidered in gold, he had a kind of leather fillet around his head, a considerable growth of beard and, at his belt, swung not one, but two obviously homemade blackjacks.

"*Jeez!*" Brodsky said. "Am I glad to see *you!* It's all right, gang—let these guys through. They're part of my mob."

Shea made room for him to climb into their chariot and the spearmen fell back respectfully as Pete directed the driver through the winding gaps in the entanglement.

When they had cleared it, Shea said, "How did you get here, anyway?"

Pete said, "It was a pushover. They had me singing until I almost busted a gut. I tried to get this Ollgaeth to send me back to Ohio, but he nixed it and said I'd have to throw in with their mob when they came over here to rub out Cúchulainn. Well, hell, I know what's going to happen to the guys in that racket. They're going to end up with their heads looking for the rest of them.

"Anyway, I figured if you get anywhere after your fadeout, it will be here. So, one day when this Ollgaeth has me in the King's ice-house, showing me some of the flash, I figure it's a good chance to take along some presents. I let him have one on the conk, snatched everything I could carry and made a getaway."

"You mean you stole Ailill's crown jewels?" said Shea.

"Sure. I don't owe him nothing, do I? Well, when I get here with the ice, they roll out the carpet and send for this Cúchulainn. I give him a line about how this Maev mob is coming to hit him on the head, see? Only they're going to put a geas on all his gang so they'll go to sleep and can't do any fighting.

"That was different, see? They all want to get in on the cutting party, only they can't dope out what to do about it. I figure it's one of two things about these geasas. I been watching this Ollgaeth and the line I got is, if he can't get close enough, he can't make this geas business stick."

"That's good magicology," said Shea. "So that's why you have guards out."

"Yeah," said Pete. "Now the other line is this. I dope it that, if you got one of these magic spielers around, he'll sort of pull the stuff in from another one, so when this Cathbadh wants to get into the act I run him out, see?"

Shea heaved a sigh of relief. "That's good magicology, too, and I'm glad you did, because it's going to save us a lot of trouble. What I can't figure out is why you didn't get Cathbadh to send you home."

"*Home?*" said Pete. "What do you mean, home? When I come up with my line, they make me head Shamus of the force here; that's how I got to stash the combination around the place. Do you think I want to go back to Ohio and pound a beat?"

"Now, look here . . ." began Shea, but at that moment the gate of Muirthemne loomed over them, with Cúchulainn beside it, accompanied by a tall, beautiful woman who must be Emer.

The hero said, "It is glad to see you that I am, darlings. Your slave is less beautiful than ever, but you will be handselling him to me, for I think that with his help I may escape the doom that is predicted."

Shea climbed down and helped Belphebe out of the chariot. "Listen," he said. "Pete's already done all he can for you, and we don't dare go back to our own country without him."

Pete said, "Look, I'll write you a letter or something to put you in the clear. Leave a guy run his own racket, will you? This is my spot."

"Nothing doing," said Shea. "Any letter you write now would be in ancient Erse, and no more use than a third leg. Go ahead, Miach."

The druid lifted his arms, mumbled a phrase or two and lowered them again. "The geas is still upon you, mac Shea," he said. "And there is an odor of the magic of Cathbadh which I cannot overcome."

"Oh, I forgot," said Shea, and pulled the sword from his belt. "Here, Cúchulainn, this is the sword of Nuada which I borrowed from the Sidhe. You'll have to give it back to Miach here after you're through with the Connachta, but it will protect you better than Pete ever could. Does that make us square?"

"It does that," said Cúchulainn, holding the great sword up admiringly. Light rippled and flowed along the blade. "I will not be asking for your man now, at all."

"Now, Miach!" said Shea.

Miach raised his arms.

"Hey, I don't want—" began Pete as the chant rose.

Whoosh!

Shea, Belphebe and Brodsky arrived in the living room at Garaden, Ohio, with a rush of displaced air and almost in a heap. Behind them, the door of Shea's study stood open and, as the trio landed, a couple of heavy-set men with large feet turned startled faces. Their hands were full of Shea's papers.

Paying no attention to them, Shea gathered Belphebe in his arms and kissed her—experimentally at first and then ardently. The geas was gone, all right.

The heavy-set man gaped from them to Brodsky.

"By God," said one of them, "if it isn't Pete Brodsky, the synthetic harp, all dressed up in monkey suit! Wait till the boys at the precinct hear about this."

"And they're going to get an earful about the Auld Sod, the pack of head-hunters!" Brodsky retorted. "From now on, it's *Nazdrovie Pol-*

ska! That means 'Long live Poland!' " he explained politely to Belphebe, who was looking puzzled.

"Thank you," she managed to say before Shea pulled her back into his arms. "But you have shown that the geas has gone," she protested to Shea.

"That was the test," he said "Now comes the enjoyment!"

The fantasy stories of ROBERT A. HEINLEIN *are few, but influential. "Magic, Inc.," "They," and "The Unpleasant Profession of Jonathan Hoag," all from the magazine* Unknown *in the early 1940s, set standards for the use of magic in real world settings, treating magic as a super-science ("Magic, Inc.") or treating supernatural powers as the technology of godlike beings ("The Unpleasant Profession . . ."). "They" is an innovative psychological horror fantasy. "Our Fair City" is a later work (Weird Tales, 1949), but typical in tone and treatment of his earliest SF stories, such as "Let There Be Light." This story of a fantastic creature in an everyday setting is pulp fantasy at its most delightful, manipulating clichés and stereotypes for fantastic entertainment. Heinlein did not return to fantasy in a major way until the early 1960s, with his novel* Glory Road, *borrowed from Spenser's* The Fairie Queene, *an inimitable performance. But it is to Heinlein's early stories that other writers went for models in the 1940s and 1950s, when fantasy was a subsidiary endeavor to the science fiction field and Robert Heinlein was the dean of SF writers.*

Our Fair City
BY ROBERT A. HEINLEIN

Pete Perkins turned into the All-Nite Parking Lot and called out, "Hi, Pappy!"

The old parking lot attendant looked up and answered, "Be with you in a moment, Pete." He was tearing a Sunday comic sheet in narrow strips. A little whirlwind waltzed near him, picking up pieces of old newspaper and bits of dirt and flinging them in the faces of passing pedestrians. The old man held out to it a long streamer of the brightly colored funny-paper. "Here, Kitten," he coaxed. "Come, Kitten . . ."

The whirlwind hesitated, then drew itself up until it was quite tall, jumped two parked cars, and landed right near him.

It seemed to sniff at the offering.

"Take it, Kitten," the old man called softly and let the gay streamer slip from his fingers. The whirlwind whipped it up and wound it around its middle. He tore off another and yet another; the whirlwind wound them in a corkscrew through the loose mass of dirty paper and trash that constituted its visible body. Renewed by cold gusts that poured down the canyon of tall buildings, it swirled faster and ever taller, while it lifted the colored paper ribbons in a fantastic upswept hair-do. The old man turned, smiling. "Kitten does like new clothes."

"Take it easy, Pappy, or you'll have me believing in it."

"Eh? You don't have to believe in Kitten—you can *see* her."

"Yeah, sure—but you act as if she—I mean 'it'—could understand what you say."

"You still don't think so?" His voice was gently tolerant.

"Now, Pappy!"

"Hmm. . . . Lend me your hat." Pappy reached up and took it. "Here, Kitten," he called. "Come back, Kitten!" The whirlwind was playing around over their heads, several stories high. It dipped down.

"Hey! Where you going with that chapeau?" demanded Perkins.

"Just a moment . . . Here, Kitten!" The whirlwind sat down suddenly, spilling its load. The old man handed it the hat. The whirlwind snatched it and started it up a fast, long spiral.

"Hey!" yelped Perkins. "What do you think you're doing? That's not funny—that hat cost me six bucks only three years ago."

"Don't worry," the old man soothed. "Kitten will bring it back."

"She will, huh? More likely she'll dump it in the river."

"Oh, no! Kitten never drops anything she doesn't want to drop. Watch." The old man looked up to where the hat was dancing near the penthouse of the hotel across the street. "Kitten! Oh, Kitten! Bring it back."

The whirlwind hesitated, the hat fell a couple of stories. It swooped, caught it, and juggled it reluctantly. "Bring it *here,* Kitten."

The hat commenced a downward spiral, finishing in a long curving swoop. It hit Perkins full in the face. "She was trying to put it on your head," the attendant explained. "Usually she's more accurate."

"She is, eh?" Perkins picked up his hat and stood looking at the whirlwind, mouth open.

"Convinced?" asked the old man.

"Convinced? Oh, sho' sho.' " He looked back at his hat, then again at the whirlwind. "Pappy, this calls for a drink."

They went inside the lot's little shelter shack; Pappy found glasses; Perkins produced a pint, nearly full, and poured two generous slugs. He tossed his down, poured another, and sat down. "The first was in honor of Kitten," he announced. "This one is to fortify me for the Mayor's banquet."

Pappy cluck-clucked sympathetically. "You have to cover that?"

"Have to write a column about *something*, Pappy. 'Last night Hizzoner the Mayor, surrounded by a glittering galaxy of high-binders, grifters, sycophants, and ballot thieves, was the recipient of a testimonial dinner celebrating . . .' Got to write something, Pappy; the cash customers expect it. Why don't I brace up like a man and go on relief?"

"Today's column was good, Pete," the old man comforted him. He picked up a copy of the *Daily Forum;* Perkins took it from him and ran his eye down his own column.

" 'Our Fair City, by Peter Perkins,' " he read, and below that " 'What, No Horsecars? It is the tradition of our civic paradise that what was good enough for the founding fathers is good enough for us. We stumble over the very chuckhole in which great-uncle Tozier broke his leg in '09. It is good to know that the bath water, running out, is not gone forever, but will return through the kitchen faucet, thicker and disguised with chlorine, but the same. (Memo—Hizzoner uses bottled spring water. Must look into this.)

" 'But I must report a dismaying change. Someone has done away with the horsecars!

" 'You may not believe this. Our public conveyances run so seldom and slowly that you may not have noticed it; nevertheless I swear that I saw one wobbling down Grand Avenue with no horses of any sort. It seemed to be propelled by some newfangled electrical device.

" 'Even in the atomic age some changes are too much. I urge all citizens . . .' " Perkins gave a snort of disgust. "It's tackling a pillbox with a beanshooter, Pappy. This town is corrupt; it'll stay corrupt. Why should I beat out my brains on such piffle? Hand me the bottle."

"Don't be discouraged, Pete. The tyrant fears the laugh more than the assassin's bullet."

"Where'd you pick that up? Okay, so I'm not funny. I've tried laughing them out of office and it hasn't worked. My efforts are as pointless as the activities of your friend the whirling dervish."

The windows rattled under a gusty impact. "Don't talk that way about Kitten," the old man cautioned. "She's sensitive."

"I apologize." He stood up and bowed toward the door. "Kitten, I apologize. Your activities are *more* useful than mine." He turned to his host. "Let's go out and talk to her, Pappy. I'd rather do that than go to the Mayor's banquet, if I had my druthers."

They went outside, Perkins bearing with him the remains of the colored comic sheet. He began tearing off streamers. "Here, Kitty! Here, Kitty! Soup's on!"

The whirlwind bent down and accepted the strips as fast as he tore them. "She's still got the ones you gave her."

"Certainly," agreed Pappy. "Kitten is a pack rat. When she likes something she'll keep it indefinitely."

"Doesn't she ever get tired? There must be some calm days."

"It's never really calm here. It's the arrangement of the buildings and the way Third Street leads up from the river. But I think she hides her pet playthings on tops of buildings."

The newspaperman peered into the swirling trash. "I'll bet she's got newspapers from months back. Say, Pappy, I see a column in this, one about our trash collection service and how we don't clean our streets. I'll dig up some papers a couple of years old and claim that they have been blowing around town since publication."

"Why fake it?" answered Pappy, "Let's see what Kitten has." He whistled softly. "Come, baby—let Pappy see your playthings." The whirlwind bulged out; its contents moved less rapidly. The attendant plucked a piece of old newspaper from it in passing. "Here's one three months old."

"We'll have to do better than that."

"I'll try again." He reached out and snatched another. "Last June."

"That's better."

A car honked for service and the old man hurried away. When he returned Perkins was still watching the hovering column. "Any luck?" asked Pappy.

"She won't let me have them. Snatches them away."

"Naughty Kitten," the old man said. "Pete is a friend of ours. You be nice to him." The whirlwind fidgeted uncertainly.

"It's all right," said Perkins. "She didn't know. But look, Pappy—see that piece up there? A front page."

"You want it?"

"Yes. Look closely—the headline reads 'DEWEY' something. You don't suppose she's been hoarding it since the '44 campaign?"

"Could be. Kitten has been around here as long as I can remember. And she does hoard things. Wait a second." He called out softly. Shortly the paper was in his hands. "Now we'll see."

Perkins peered at it. "I'll be a short-term Senator! Can you top that, Pappy?"

The headline read: "Dewey Captures Manila"; the date was "1898."

Twenty minutes later they were still considering it over the last of Perkins' bottle. The newspaperman stared at the yellowed, filthy sheet. "Don't tell me this has been blowing around town for the last half century."

"Why not?"

"'Why not?' Well, I'll concede that the streets haven't been cleaned in that time, but this paper wouldn't last. Sun and rain and so forth."

"Kitten is very careful of her toys. She probably put it under cover during bad weather."

"For the love of Mike, Pappy, you don't really believe . . . But you do. Frankly, I don't care where she got it; the official theory is going to be that this particular piece of paper has been kicking around our dirty streets, unnoticed and uncollected, for the past fifty years. Boy, am I going to have fun!" He rolled the fragment carefully and started to put it in his pocket.

"Say, don't do that!" his host protested.

"Why not? I'm going to take it down and get a pic of it."

"You mustn't! It belongs to Kitten—I just borrowed it."

"Huh? Are you nuts?"

"She'll be upset if she doesn't get it back. Please, Pete—she'll let you look at it any time you want to."

The old man was so earnest that Perkins was stopped. "Suppose we never see it again? My story hangs on it."

"It's no good to *you*—*she* has to keep it, to make your story stand up. Don't worry—I'll tell her that she mustn't lose it under any circumstances."

"Well—okay." They stepped outside and Pappy talked earnestly to Kitten, then gave her the 1898 fragment. She promptly tucked it into the top of her column. Perkins said good-bye to Pappy, and started to leave the lot. He paused and turned around, looking a little befuddled. "Say, Pappy . . ."

"Yes, Pete?"

"You don't really think that whirlwind is alive, do you?"

"Why not?"

"Why not? Why not, the man says?"

"Well," said Pappy reasonably, "How do you know *you* are alive?"

"But . . . Why, because I—well, now, if you put it . . ." He stopped. "I don't know. You got me, pal."

Pappy smiled. "You see?"

"Uh, I guess so. G'night, Pappy. G'night, Kitten." He tipped his hat to the whirlwind. The column bowed.

The managing editor sent for Perkins. "Look, Pete," he said, chucking a sheaf of gray copy paper at him, "whimsy is all right, but I'd like to see some copy that wasn't dashed off in a gin mill."

Perkins looked over the pages shoved at him. "Our Fair City, by Peter Perkins. Whistle Up The Wind. Walking our streets always is a piquant, even adventurous, experience. We pick our way through the assorted trash, bits of old garbage, cigarette butts, and other less appetizing items that stud our sidewalks while our faces are assaulted by more bouyant souvenirs, the confetti of last Halloween, shreds of dead leaves, and other items too weather-beaten to be identified. However, I had always assumed that a constant turnover in the riches of our streets caused them to renew themselves at least every seven years . . ." The column then told of the whirlwind that contained the fifty-year-old newspaper and challenged any other city in the country to match it.

" 'Smatter with it?" demanded Perkins.

"Beating the drum about the filth in the streets is fine, Pete, but give it a factual approach."

Perkins leaned over the desk. "Boss, this *is* factual."

"Huh? Don't be silly, Pete."

"Silly, he says. Look . . ." Perkins gave him a circumstantial account of Kitten and the 1898 newspaper.

"Pete, you must have been drinking."

"Only Java and tomato juice, cross my heart and hope to die."

"How about yesterday? I'll bet the whirlwind came right up to the bar with you."

"I was cold, stone . . ." Perkins stopped himself and stood on his dignity. "That's my story. Print it, or fire me."

"Don't be like that, Pete. I don't want your job; I just want a column with some meat. Dig up some facts on man-hours and costs for street cleaning, compared with other cities."

"Who'd read that junk? Come down the street with me. I'll *show* you the facts. Wait a moment—I'll pick up a photographer."

A few minutes later Perkins was introducing the managing editor and Clarence V. Weems to Pappy. Clarence unlimbered his camera. "Take a pic of him?"

"Not yet, Clarence. Pappy, can you get Kitten to give us back the museum piece?"

"Why, sure." The old man looked up and whistled. "Oh, Kitten! Come to Pappy." Above their heads a tiny gust took shape, picked up bits of paper and stray leaves, and settled on the lot. Perkins peered into it.

"She hasn't got it," he said in aggrieved tones.

"She'll get it." Pappy stepped forward until the whirlwind enfolded him. They could see his lips move, but the words did not reach them.

"Now?" said Clarence.

"Not yet." The whirlwind bounded up and leapt over an adjoining building. The managing editor opened his mouth, closed it again.

Kitten was soon back. She dropped everything else and had just one piece of paper—*the* paper. "Now!" said Perkins. "Can you get a shot of that paper, Clarence—while it's in the air?"

"Natch," said Clarence, and raised his Speed Graphic. "Back a little, and hold it," he ordered, speaking to the whirlwind.

Kitten hesitated and seemed about to skitter away. "Bring it around slow and easy, Kitten," Pappy supplemented, "and turn it over —no, no! Not that way—the other edge up." The paper flattened out and sailed slowly past them, the headline showing.

"Did you get it?" Perkins demanded.

"Natch," said Clarence. "Is that all?" he asked the editor.

"Natc—I mean, that's all."

"Okay," said Clarence, picked up his case, and left.

The editor sighed. "Gentlemen," he said, "let's have a drink."

Four drinks later Perkins and his boss were still arguing. Pappy had left. "Be reasonable, Boss," Pete was saying, "you can't print an item about a live whirlwind. They'd laugh you out of town."

Managing editor Gaines straightened himself.

"It's the policy of the *Forum* to print all the news, and print it straight. This is news—we print it." He relaxed. "Hey! Waiter! More of the same—and not so much soda."

"But it's scientifically impossible."

"You saw it, didn't you?"

"Yes, but . . ."

Gaines stopped him. "We'll ask the Smithsonian Institution to investigate it."

"They'll laugh at you," Perkins insisted. "Ever hear of mass hypnotism?"

"Huh? No, that's no explanation—Clarence saw it, too."

"What does that prove?"

"Obvious—to be hypnotized you have to have a mind. *Ipso facto.*"

"You mean *Ipse dixit.*"

"Quit hiccuping. Perkins, you shouldn't drink in the daytime. Now start over and say it slowly."

"How do you know Clarence doesn't have a mind?"

"Prove it."

"Well, he's alive—he must have some sort of a mind, then."

"That's just what I was saying. The whirlwind is alive; therefore it has a mind. Perkins, if those longbeards from the Smithsonian are going to persist in their unscientific attitude, I for one will not stand for it. The *Forum* will not stand for it. You will not stand for it."

"Won't I?"

"Not for one minute. I want you to know the *Forum* is behind you, Pete. You go back to the parking lot and get an interview with that whirlwind."

"But I've got one. You wouldn't let me print it."

"Who wouldn't let you print it? I'll fire him! Come on, Pete. We're going to blow this town sky high. Stop the run. Hold the front page. Get busy!" He put on Pete's hat and strode rapidly into the men's room.

Pete settled himself at his desk with a container of coffee, a can of tomato juice, and the Midnight Final (late afternoon) edition. Under a four-column cut of Kitten's toy was his column, boxed and moved to the front page. Eighteen-point boldface ordered SEE EDITORIAL PAGE TWELVE. On page twelve another black line enjoined him to SEE OUR FAIR CITY PAGE ONE. He ignored this and read: MR. MAYOR—RESIGN! ! ! !

Pete read it and chuckled. "An ill wind—" "—symbolic of the spiritual filth lurking in the dark corners of the city hall." "—will grow to cyclonic proportions and sweep a corrupt and shameless administration from office." The editorial pointed out that the contract for street cleaning and trash removal was held by the Mayor's brother-in-law, and then suggested that the whirlwind could give better service cheaper.

The telephone jingled. He picked it up and said, "Okay—you started it."

"Pete—is that you?" Pappy's voice demanded. "They got me down at the station house."

"What for?"

"They claim Kitten is a public nuisance."

"I'll be right over." He stopped by the Art Department, snagged Clarence, and left. Pappy was seated in the station lieutenant's office, looking stubborn. Perkins shoved his way in. "What's he here for?" he demanded, jerking a thumb at Pappy.

The lieutenant looked sour. "What are you butting in for, Perkins? You're not his lawyer."

"Now?" said Clarence.

"Not yet, Clarence. For news, Dumbrosky—I work for a newspaper, remember? I repeat—what's he in for?"

"Obstructing an officer in the performance of his duty."

"That right, Pappy?"

The old man looked disgusted. "This character—" He indicated one of the policemen "—comes up to my lot and tries to snatch the Manila-Bay paper away from Kitten. I tell her to keep it up out of his way. Then he waves his stick at me and orders me to take it away from her. I tell him what he can do with his stick." He shrugged. "So here we are."

"I get it," Perkins told him, and turned to Dumbrosky. "You got a call from the city hall, didn't you? So you sent Dugan down to do the dirty work. What I don't get is why you sent Dugan. I hear he's so dumb you don't even let him collect the pay-off on his own beat."

"That's a lie!" put in Dugan. "I do so . . ."

"Shut up, Dugan!" his boss thundered. "Now, see here, Perkins—you clear out. There ain't no story here."

"No story?" Perkins said softly. "The police force tries to arrest a whirlwind and you say there's no story?"

"Now?" said Clarence.

"Nobody tried to arrest no whirlwind! Now scram."

"Then how come you're charging Pappy with obstructing an officer? What was Dugan doing—flying a kite?"

"He's not charged with obstructing an officer."

"He's not, eh? Just what have you booked him for?"

"He's not booked. We're holding him for questioning."

"So? not booked, no warrant, no crime alleged, just pick up a citizen and roust him around, Gestapo style." Perkins turned to Pappy. "You're not under arrest. My advice is to get up and walk out that door."

Pappy started to get up. "Hey!" Lieutenant Dumbrosky bounded out of his chair, grabbed Pappy by the shoulder and pushed him down. "I'm giving the orders around here. You stay . . ."

"Now!" yelled Perkins. Clarence's flash bulb froze them. Then Dumbrosky started up again.

"Who let him in here? Dugan—get that camera."

"Nyaannh!" said Clarence and held it away from the cop. They started doing a little Maypole dance, with Clarence as the Maypole.

"Hold it!" yelled Perkins. "Go ahead and grab the camera, Dugan —I'm just aching to write the story. 'Police Lieutenant Destroys Evidence of Police Brutality.' "

"What do you want I should do, Lieutenant?" pleaded Dugan.

Dumbrosky looked disgusted. "Siddown and close your face. Don't use that picture, Perkins—I'm warning you."

"Of what? Going to make me dance with Dugan? Come on, Pappy. Come on, Clarence." They left.

"Our Fair City" read the next day: "City Hall Starts Clean Up. While the city street cleaners were enjoying their usual siesta, Lieutenant Dumbrosky, acting on orders of Hizzoner's office, raided our Third Avenue whirlwind. It went sour, as Patrolman Dugan could not entice the whirlwind into the paddy wagon. Dauntless Dugan was undeterred; he took a citizen standing nearby, one James Metcalfe, parking-lot attendant, into custody as an accomplice of the whirlwind. An accomplice in what, Dugan didn't say—everybody knows that an accomplice is something pretty awful. Lieutenant Dumbrosky questioned the accomplice. See cut. Lieutenant Dumbrosky weighs 215 pounds, without his shoes. The accomplice weighs 119.

"Moral: Don't get underfoot when the police department is playing games with the wind.

"P.S. As we go to press, the whirlwind is still holding the 1898 museum piece. Stop by Third and Main and take a look. Better hurry— Dumbrosky is expected to make an arrest momentarily."

Pete's column continued needling the administration the following day: "Those Missing Files. It is annoying to know that any document needed by the Grand Jury is sure to be mislaid before it can be introduced in evidence. We suggest that Kitten, our Third Avenue Whirlwind, be hired by the city as file clerk extraordinary and entrusted with any item which is likely to be needed later. She could take the special civil exam used to reward the faithful—the one nobody ever flunks.

"Indeed, why limit Kitten to a lowly clerical job? She is persistent—and she hangs on to what she gets. No one will argue that she is less qualified than some city officials we have had.

"Let's run Kitten for Mayor! She's an ideal candidate—she has the common touch, she doesn't mind hurly-burly, she runs around in circles, she knows how to throw dirt, and the opposition can't pin anything on her.

"As to the sort of Mayor she would make, there is an old story—Aesop told it—about King Log and King Stork. We're fed up with King Stork; King Log would be welcome relief.

"Memo to Hizzoner—what *did* become of those Grand Avenue paving bids?

"P.S. Kitten still has the 1898 newspaper on exhibit. Stop by and see it before our police department figures out some way to intimidate a whirlwind."

Pete snagged Clarence and drifted down to the parking lot. The lot was fenced now; a man at a gate handed them two tickets but waved away their money. Inside he found a large circle chained off for Kitten and Pappy inside it. They pushed their way through the crowd to the old man. "Looks like you're coining money, Pappy."

"Should be, but I'm not. They tried to close me up this morning, Pete. Wanted me to pay the $50-a-day circus-and-carnival fee and post a bond besides. So I quit charging for the tickets—but I'm keeping track of them. I'll sue 'em, by gee."

"You won't collect, not in this town. Never mind, we'll make 'em squirm till they let up."

"That's not all. They tried to capture Kitten this morning."

"Huh? Who? How?"

"The cops. They showed up with one of those blower machines used to ventilate manholes, rigged to run backwards and take a suction. The idea was to suck Kitten down into it, or anyhow to grab what she was carrying."

Pete whistled. "You should have called me."

"Wasn't necessary. I warned Kitten and she stashed the Spanish-War paper someplace, then came back. She loved it. She went through that machine about six times, like a merry-go-round. She'd zip through and come out more full of pep than ever. Last time through she took Sergeant Yancel's cap with her and it clogged the machine and ruined his cap. They got disgusted and left."

Peter chortled. "You still should have called me. Clarence should have gotten a picture of that."

"Got it," said Clarence.

"Huh? I didn't know you were here this morning, Clarence."

"You didn't ast me."

Pete looked at him. "Clarence, darling—the idea of a news picture is to print it, not to hide it in the Art Department."

"On your desk," said Clarence.

"Oh. Well, let's move on to a less confusing subject. Pappy, I'd like to put up a big sign here."

"Why not! What do you want to say?"

"Kitten-for-Mayor—Whirlwind Campaign Headquarters. Stick a 24-sheet across the corner of the lot, where they can see it both ways. It fits in with—oh, oh! Company, girls!" He jerked his head toward the entrance.

Sergeant Yancel was back. "All right, all right!" he was saying. "Move on! Clear out of here." He and three cohorts were urging the spectators out of the lot. Pete went to him.

"What goes on, Yancel?"

Yancel looked around. "Oh, it's you, huh? Well, you, too—we got to clear this place out. Emergency."

Pete looked back over his shoulder. "Better get Kitten out of the way, Pappy!" he called out. *"Now,* Clarence."

"Got it," said Clarence.

"Okay," Pete answered. "Now, Yancel, you might tell me what it is we just took a picture of, so we can title it properly."

"Smart guy. You and your stooge had better scram if you don't want your heads blown off. We're setting up a bazooka."

"You're setting up a *what?"* Pete looked toward the squad car, unbelievingly. Sure enough, two of the cops were unloading a bazooka. "Keep shooting, kid," he said to Clarence.

"Natch," said Clarence.

"And quit popping your bubble gum. Now, look, Yancel—I'm just a newsboy. What in the world is the idea?"

"Stick around and find out, wise guy." Yancel turned away. "Okay there! Start doing it—commence firing!"

One of the cops looked up. "At what, Sergeant?"

"I thought you used to be a marine—at the whirlwind, of course."

Pappy leaned over Pete's shoulder. "What are they doing?"

"I'm beginning to get a glimmering. Pappy, keep Kitten out of range—I think they mean to put a rocket shell through her gizzard. It might bust up dynamic stability or something."

"Kitten's safe. I told her to hide. But this is crazy, Pete. They must be absolute, complete and teetotal nuts."

"Any law says a cop has to be sane to be on the force?"

"What whirlwind, Sergeant?" the bazooka man was asking. Yancel started to tell him, forcefully, then deflated when he realized that no whirlwind was available.

"You wait," he told him, and turned to Pappy. "You" he yelled. "You chased away that whirlwind. Get it back here."

Pete took out his notebook. "This is interesting, Yancel. Is it your professional opinion that a whirlwind can be ordered around like a trained dog? Is that the official position of the police department?"

"I . . . No comment! You button up, or I'll run you in."

"By all means. But you have that Buck-Rogers cannon pointed so that, after the shell passes through the whirlwind, if any, it should end up just about at the city hall. Is this a plot to assassinate Hizzoner?"

Yancel looked around suddenly, then let his gaze travel an imaginary trajectory.

"Hey, you lugs!" he shouted. "Point that thing the other way. You want to knock off the Mayor?"

"That's better," Peter told the Sergeant. "Now they have it trained on the First National Bank. I can't wait."

Yancel looked over the situation again. "Point it where it won't hurt nobody," he ordered. "Do I have to do all your thinking?"

"But, Sergeant . . ."

"Well?"

"You *point* it. We'll fire it."

Pete watched them. "Clarence," he sighed, "you stick around and get a pic of them loading it back into the car. That will be in about five minutes. Pappy and I will be in the Happy Hour Bar-Grill. Get a nice picture, with Yancel's features."

"Natch," said Clarence.

The next installment of "Our Fair City" featured three cuts and was headed "Police Declare War on Whirlwind." Pete took a copy and set out for the parking lot, intending to show it to Pappy.

Pappy wasn't there. Nor was Kitten. He looked around the neighborhood, poking his nose in lunchrooms and bars. No luck.

He headed back toward the *Forum* building, telling himself that Pappy might be shopping, or at a movie. He returned to his desk, made a couple of false starts on a column for the morrow, crumpled them up and went to the Art Department. "Hey! Clarence! Have you been down to the parking lot today?"

"Nah."

"Pappy's missing."

"So what?"

"Well, come along. We got to find him."

"Why?" But he came, lugging his camera.

The lot was still deserted, no Pappy, no Kitten—not even a stray breeze. Pete turned away. "Come on, Clarence—say, what are you shooting now?"

Clarence had his camera turned up toward the sky. "Not shooting," said Clarence. "Light is no good."

"What was it?"

"Whirlwind."

"Huh? Kitten?"

"Maybe."

"Here, Kitten—come Kitten." The whirlwind came back near him, spun faster, and picked up a piece of cardboard it had dropped. It whipped it around, then let him have it in the face.

"That's not funny, Kitten," Pete complained. "Where's Pappy?"

The whirlwind sidled back toward him. He saw it reach again for the cardboard. "No, you don't!" he yelped and reached for it, too.

The whirlwind beat him to it. It carried it up some hundred feet and sailed it back. The card caught him edgewise on the bridge of the nose. "Kitten!" Pete yelled. "Quit the horsing around."

It was a printed notice, about six by eight inches. Evidently it had been tacked up; there were small tears at all four corners. It read: "THE RITZ-CLASSIC" and under that, "Room 2013, Single Occupancy $6.00, Double Occupancy $8.00." There followed a printed list of the house rules.

Pete stared at it and frowned. Suddenly he chucked it back at the whirlwind. Kitten immediately tossed it back in his face.

"Come on, Clarence," he said briskly. "We're going to the Ritz-Classic—room 2013."

"Natch," said Clarence.

The Ritz-Classic was a colossal fleabag, favored by the bookie-and-madame set, three blocks away. Pete avoided the desk by using the basement entrance. The elevator boy looked at Clarence's camera and said, "No, you don't, Doc. No divorce cases in this hotel."

"Relax," Pete told him. "That's not a real camera. We peddle marijuana—that's the hay mow."

"Whyn't you say so? You hadn't ought to carry it in a camera. You make people nervous. What floor?"

"Twenty-one."

The elevator opertor took them up nonstop, ignoring other calls. "That'll be two bucks. Special service."

"What do you pay for the concession?" inquired Pete.

"You gotta nerve to beef—with your racket."

They went back down a floor by stair and looked up room 2013. Pete tried the knob cautiously; the door was locked. He knocked on it —no answer. He pressed an ear to it and thought he could hear movement inside. He stepped back, frowning.

Clarence said, "I just remember something," and trotted away. He returned quickly, with a red fire ax. "Now?" he asked Pete.

"A lovely thought, Clarence! Not yet." Pete pounded and yelled, "Pappy! Oh, Pappy!"

A large woman in a pink coolie coat opened the door behind them. "How do you expect a party to sleep?" she demanded.

Pete said, "Quiet, madame! We're on the air." He listened. This time there were sounds of struggling and then, "Pete! Pe——"

"*Now!*" said Pete. Clarence started swinging.

The lock gave up on the third swing. Pete poured in, with Clarence after him. He collided with someone coming out and sat down abruptly. When he got up he saw Pappy on a bed. The old man was busily trying to get rid of a towel tied around his mouth.

Pete snatched it away. "Get 'em!" yelled Pappy.

"Soon as I get you untied."

"I ain't tied. They took my pants. Boy, I thought you'd never come!"

"Took Kitten a while to make me understand."

"I got 'em," announced Clarence. "Both of 'em."

"Where?" demanded Pete.

"Here," said Clarence proudly, and patted his camera.

Pete restrained his answer and ran to the door. "They went thataway," said the large woman, pointing. He took out, skidded around the corner and saw an elevator door just closing.

Pete stopped, bewildered by the crowd just outside the hotel. He was looking uncertainly around when Pappy grabbed him. "There! That touring car!" The car Pappy pointed out was even then swinging out from the curb just beyond the rank of cabs in front of the hotel; with a deep growl it picked up speed, and headed away. Pete yanked open the door of the nearest cab.

"Follow that car!" he yelled. They all piled in.

"Why?" asked the hackie.

Clarence lifted the fire ax. "Now?" he asked.

The driver ducked. "Forget it," he said. "It was just a yak." He let in his clutch.

The hack driver's skill helped them in the downtown streets, but the driver of the touring car swung right on Third and headed for the river. They streamed across it, fifty yards apart, with traffic snarled behind them, and then were on the no-speed-limit freeway. The cabbie turned his head. "Is the camera truck keeping up?"

"What camera truck?"

"Ain't this a movie?"

"Good grief, no! That car is filled with kidnappers. Faster!"

"A snatch? I don't want no part of it." He braked suddenly.

Pete took the ax and prodded the driver. "You catch 'em!"

The hack speeded up again but the driver protested, "Not in this wreck. They got more power than me."

Pappy grabbed Pete's arm. "There's Kitten!"

"Where? Oh, never mind that now!"

"Slow down!" yelled Pappy. "Kitten, oh, Kitten—over here!"

The whirlwind swooped down and kept pace with them. Pappy called to it. "Here, baby! Go get that car! Up ahead—*get it!*"

Kitten seemed confused, uncertain. Pappy repeated it and she took off—like a whirlwind. She dipped and gathered a load of paper and trash as she flew.

They saw her dip and strike the car ahead, throwing paper in the face of the driver. The car wobbled. She struck again. The car veered, climbed the curb, ricocheted against the crash rail, and fetched up against a lamp post.

Five minutes later Pete, having left Kitten, Clarence, and the fire axe to hold the fort over two hoodlums suffering from abrasion, multiple contusions and shock, was feeding a dime into a pay phone at the nearest filling station. He dialed long distance. "Gimme the F.B.I.'s kidnap number," he demanded. "You know—the Washington, D.C., snatch number."

"My goodness," said the operator, "do you mind if I listen in?"

"Get me that number!"

"Right away!"

Presently a voice answered. "Federal Bureau of Investigation."

"Lemme talk to Hoover! Huh? Okay, okay—I'll talk to you. Listen this is a snatch case. I've got 'em on ice, for the moment, but unless you get one of your boys from your local office here pronto there won't be any snatch case—not if the city cops get here first. What?" Pete quieted down and explained who he was, where he was, and the more believable aspects of the events that had led up to the present situation. The government man cut in on him as he was urging speed and more speed and more speed and assured him that the local office was already being notified.

Pete got back to the wreck just as Lieutenant Dumbrosky climbed out of a squad car. Pete hurried up. "Don't do it, Dumbrosky," he yelled.

The big cop hesitated. "Don't do what?"

"Don't do anything. The F.B.I. are on their way now—and you're already implicated. Don't make it any worse."

Pete pointed to the two gunsels; Clarence was sitting on one and resting the spike of the ax against the back of the other. "These birds have already sung. This town is about to fall apart. If you hurry, you might be able to get a plane for Mexico."

Dumbrosky looked at him. "Wise guy," he said doubtfully.

"Ask them. They confessed."

One of the hoods raised his head. "We was threatened," he announced. "Take 'em in, lieutenant. They assaulted us."

"Go ahead," Pete said cheerfully. "Take us all in—together. Then you won't be able to lose that pair before the F.B.I. can question them. Maybe you can cop a plea."

"Now?" asked Clarence.

Dumbrosky swung around. "Put that ax down!"

"Do as he says, Clarence. Get your camera ready to get a picture as the G-men arrive."

"You didn't send for no G-men."

"Look behind you!"

A dark blue sedan slid quietly to a stop and four lean, brisk men got out. The first of them said, "Is there someone here named Peter Perkins?"

"Me," said Pete. "Do you mind if I kiss you?"

It was after dark but the parking lot was crowded and noisy. A stand for the new Mayor and distinguished visitors had been erected on one side, opposite it was a bandstand; across the front was a large illuminated sign: "HOME OF KITTEN—HONORARY CITIZEN OF OUR FAIR CITY."

In the fenced-off circle in the middle Kitten herself bounced and spun and swayed and danced. Pete stood on one side of the circle with Pappy opposite him; at four-foot intervals around it children were posted. "All set?" called out Pete.

"All set," answered Pappy. Together, Pete, Pappy and the kids started throwing serpentine into the ring. Kitten swooped, gathered the ribbons up and wrapped them around herself.

"Confetti!" yelled Pete. Each of the kids dumped a sackful toward the whirlwind—little of it reached the ground.

"Balloons!" yelled Pete. "Lights!" Each of the children started blowing up toy balloons; each had a dozen different colors. As fast as they were inflated they fed them to Kitten. Floodlights and searchlights came on; Kitten was transformed into a fountain of boiling, bubbling color, several stories high.

"Now?" said Clarence.

"Now!"

WONDERS

Stories filled with
events to astonish and delight

Much of the most biting and profound fantasy is written in reaction to other works. This story, in conscious imitation of Fritz Leiber's Fahfrd and Grey Mouser world (see p. 318), reacts against stories in which characters living in the distant past or in a world wildly different than our own think and act like twentieth-century Americans. JOANNA RUSS makes her point by posing the question: What if all those wild accounts of devils, angels, demons, and other creatures that we find in myths and legends are based upon realistic observation by people whose perceptual systems were different than ours are today? Her answer is disturbingly plausible. The best known of Joanna Russ' fantasies are among her "Alyx" stories, some of which are fantasy and some of which are science fiction. Others of her fantasy stories from the last twenty-five years, of ghosts and vampires and werewolves, are collected in her book, The Zanzibar Cat. *Here she manipulates setting and character in a wholly original manner, giving us a jolt of additional wonder at the end.*

The Man Who Could Not See Devils
BY JOANNA RUSS

My father, who saw devils at noonday, cursed me for a misbegotten abortion because I did not see them. But I saw nothing. Incubi, succubi, fiends, demons, werewolves, evil creatures of all sorts might do what they pleased for all of me; I could not eavesdrop on them and holy water turned to only water in my hands, though I have seen the victims carried in, bloodless, the next day, and indeed I carried one home myself, a boy with his throat cut from ear to ear, and that was the only time I got gratitude out of the pack of them. And for nothing.

My neighbors, I mean. "There! There! Don't you see?" they'd cry, the girls tumbling to get away from the hearth, the houselady fainting. "Don't you *see?*" But I saw nothing. Cats were possessed, strange shapes hovered in the air; in broad daylight one head turned, and then another, and then another, as I tried in vain, always in vain. "Don't you *see?*" Until I was twelve I lived terrified that I might bump into something some broad morning, out of sheer ignorance, and was never let abroad by myself. Then, when I was twelve and a half (if I had not been an only son, they might have let me alone, but I was too precious) a neighborhood conjuror tried to de-hex me of what he assured my parents was a particularly virulent curse—and failed—and I spent a night alone, by pure mistake, in a haunted ravine, trembling at every sound but emerging whole, and then repeating the experiment with a growing conviction that if I could not see the devils, perhaps it was because they could not see me.

When I told my father, he beat me.

"Those who cannot see devils, cannot see angels!" he roared.

I replied in a desperate fury that I should be glad enough to see some human beings, and when he reached for the poker I asked him, with mad inspiration, if he would like to spend the night in the ravine with me.

He turned pale. He said I was probably crazy and ought to be put to bed.

I said he would have to chain me up; but he could not do that every night; and as soon as I was free I would spend every night out in the woods and tell him about it in the daytime.

He said suicide was a sin.

I said I did not care.

"My poor boy," he said, trembling, "my poor boy, don't you see? Satan is deceiving you and giving you a false sense of security. Some day—"

"Show me Satan," I said.

"A ghost passed through this room three nights ago," he said, getting down on his knees, his beard wagging. "A ghost shaped like the body of a drowned girl, shining with a green light and we all saw it."

"I saw *you,*" I said. "And pretty fools you looked too, let me tell you, gaping at nothing."

"And it was wearing a white dress covered with seaweed," he went on in a singsong, "that shone in the darkness, and it passed through the candles and one by one they went out" (I had not seen that either) "and when it passed them they sprang up again and we saw each other's faces and we were all pale, all, all, except you" and to my amazement he burst into tears.

"I can't help that," I said, feeling uncomfortable.

"Didn't you see anything?" he said.

"Nothing."

"Anything?"

"Nothing."

I had never seen my father cry before, or since; in fact, this incident is my one even vaguely pleasant recollection of him, for the next day he was altogether himself. He thrashed me, thoroughly and formally, for no particular reason, and began that monotonous series of cursings that I have mentioned before. The story of the ghost (a distant cousin of my mother's) went the rounds of the village but with improvements—she had hovered over me, calling me by name; she had passed right through me; she had apostrophized me as one deaf and blind—

In three days no one would speak to me.

When I was sixteen, I ran away, got caught, and was brought back. They could beat me as much as they liked in the daytime, I said furiously, but they knew what would happen at night.

When I was seventeen, I ran away again, this time compounding the offense by stealing six silver pennies which is no more than the price of one-quarter of a not very good horse. I had the money wrested out of my hot hand (actually it was tied up in a tree and someone found it) and was set hoeing beans as a penance.

At nineteen I ransacked the house in a long, leisurely afternoon's search (by now they were terrified of me), locked one cousin securely in a closet (into which he had fled at the sight of me), pinned another to the wall with an old rapier I had found in the attic, stuffed the price of three farmhouse estates into the front of my shirt, and rode off humming to myself bitterly between my teeth. I had escaped for good—or so I thought.

It was the money, of course. It had to be the money. It was too much to lose, even with ten thousand imps clinging to each coin. I was thirty-five miles away, eating my soup like a peaceable citizen in a neighborhood inn, when I felt a hand descend on my shoulder and sprang to my feet to see—my uncle! the most tough-minded of the lot, who always said, "A good man need fear nothing," though in what his goodness consisted, his wife—God help her!—and his maidservants and his black-and-blue children did not seem quite able to tell. But here he was with twenty men with him, and a priest. It was the priest that made them so brave.

"Be careful," I said. "You don't know what may happen."

"My boy, my boy," he said, excessively kind, "we've had enough of this."

"Not half as much as you will have," I said while I tried to size them up and remembered bitterly that the money was still on me and so I was in a bad bargaining position—also there was no back door. "Not half as much," said I, "as—"

"You shall come home at once," said my uncle softly, "and we will find a way to cure you, my dear boy, oh we will."

"With my allies?" said I. He was moving closer.

"You have no allies, poor boy," said he, sweating visibly. "Poor boy; they are only the deceitful fancies of the—" But I, knowing them by now, made for the priest, and then there was a frightened row, with much cursing and screaming (though the money made them desperate) and in the end the poor holy man was sitting in a chair having his bleeding head bathed with vinegar and water, and there I was under a heap, or rather clump, of relatives. They found the money immediately and my father (who had hidden behind them in his fright) began sobbing and saying "Praise be to God" for his estate come back.

I told them fervently what would happen to them.

"Let him up, let him up," said my father, and they let me scramble to my feet, each retreating a little as the heat of the fight wore off.

"Give me a tenth and let me go," I said, out of breath.

"A tenth is for the church," said the priest, uncommonly keen all of a sudden, "and it would be blasphemous to do anything of the kind."

"I'll break your neck," I said intently, looking from one man to the other, "I'll break your spine, I'll make you die in slow torments, I'll—"

"Give it him, give it him," said my father, shaking all over, and he began to fumble among the money which my uncle immediately snatched away from him with the stern reminder that some people were too weak-minded for their own good.

"There is only one way to deal with this," said my uncle importantly, "and that is to take the boy home and exorcise him" (here his eyes gleamed) "and thrash him" (he tucked the money up neatly and buttoned it into the inside of his coat) "and make sure—sure" (said my uncle, hitting one fist into the other with slow relish) "make sure—sure, mind you—that this spell or devil or whatever it is, is driven out. Driven out!" added my uncle, loudly, to everyone's approbation. "Driven out! If we let him go, heaven only knows what may become of us. We may die in our sleep. Othor." Here he pushed a reluctant kinsman forward. "Tie him up." And, seeing that I was not to get away, not even penniless—I drove my head into the nearest stomach and called down such imprecations on them that they begged the innkeeper for a blanket to throw over me, the way you'd bag a cat, for my prophesying and cursing (as I could do nothing else) became every moment more frightful to their ears, seeing that I cursed them in curses they had never even heard before—as indeed they never had for I was making them all up.

"My God!" cried my uncle, "shut the boy up before it all comes true!" and as the innkeeper refused to interfere, someone went outside and got a horse blanket and it was with that abominable smell in my nose and throat that I stumbled blindly outside where I threw myself forward, I cared not where, and struck somebody's boots—or strongbox—or wall.

And that was the end of that, for the time.

I woke up sitting bolt upright on a stool set in the center of a room that looked vaguely familiar—it was my uncle's small estate—with a vague memory of riding dizzily in saying, "That's right, that's right, I'm only a servant"—and then a blur in one corner resolved itself into a small, redheaded cousin of mine, a brat so ugly and unpleasant that even his own mother disliked him, God help him.

"What?" I said stupidly. I saw the imp jump a little, and then settle back onto his feet. He was watching me suspiciously. He was hung all over with charms: bangles, crosses, hearts, lockets, medals, rings, bells, garlands, and staves, until he looked like a dirty, decorated Christmas tree; I suppose they had put him to guard because he was the most expendable member of the clan, for he was only thirteen and very scrawny.

"Well, they've got *you*," he said, with a certain satisfaction. "They're inside, deciding what to do with you." I shut my eyes for a few minutes, and when I opened them he was lounging against the wall, picking his teeth. He sprang to attention.

"What time is it?" I said, and he said, "Late," and then colored; I guessed that he was not supposed to talk to me. I had not thought I had slept when I shut my eyes and my head was still ringing; it occurred to me that I was perhaps still a little out of my mind, but that seemed quite all right at the time; I took out of my shirt one coin they had not found, a gold piece given me by my nurse when I was a child, and I held it up and turned it round so the candlelight made it twinkle. I could see my little cousin licking his lips in his corner.

"This could be yours," I said. He looked doubtful.

"Nyah," he said, and then he said, "Is it real?"

"It won't disappear," I said, "if that's what you mean. It's not bewitched."

"Don't believe it," he said, standing virtuously upright, on guard again.

"Then don't believe it," I said, and I tossed it on the floor in front of him. It rang on the stones and lay, winking.

After a short hesitation he picked it up. He whistled ecstatically.

"Say, you don't want this," he said.

"Yes I do; give it back," I said. He snorted.

"Nyah! Nyah! Feeble-mind!" he crowed. "Feeble-mind! Now I have it," and he tossed it up and caught it deftly backhand, as if to prove that it was real.

"You don't have it," I said.

He stuck out his tongue at me. I got off the stool and was at him in two strides; I covered his mouth and plucked the coin out of his hand; then I put it back, went back to my stool, and sat down. He stared at me dumbfounded.

"Do you really think," I said, "that they would let you keep it, if I told them about it?" (He thrust it into his coat.) "And do you think I wouldn't tell, if I felt like it?" (He threw it on the floor.) "No, no, keep it," I said carelessly. "Keep it. For a favor."

"Wouldn't do you a favor," he muttered, patting his magical garlands that encircled each wrist in the manner of a sacrificial lamb. "Wouldn't be right."

"Bah! nonsense," said I.

"*I'm* safe," he said, shaking his garlands, and tinkling all over. "Pooh," he added. He began to recite under his breath, imitating his father's nasal twang to perfection, a poor persecuted man whose crops always failed, whose babies always had the croup, whose attic leaked—

I took the boy by the arms and shook him till his teeth rattled.

"He—he—hel—" he said.

"Listen," I said, shaking him, "You numb-headed, misinformed baboon! You've known me all of your wretched life, you beast!" He began to cry. He stood there in the rags and tatters of his charms, bawling.

"Oh for God's sake," I said in despair, "shut up." And I sat back down on my stool and put my head between my knees.

He stopped crying. I said nothing. Then, after a considerable silence, he said: "You stole all that money?"

I nodded.

"Boy!" he said. There was a further silence.

"Hey, you wanna get out?" he said. I shook my head. "Sure you do. You wanna give me that gold money and get out?"

I shook my head again.

"Ah, come on," he said, "sure you do." And he sidled up to me and stood there in friendly fashion, his bells and jingles bumping lightly against me.

"Ah, come on," he said. I held up my hand with the coin in it. He took it and sprinted to the door, clanging; he flung open the door with spirit.

"I'm going to tell a story," he said. "I'm going to lie down and pretend to be dead."

"Bully for you," said I.

"I'll carry on," he said. "It'll be smashing. Shall I tell it to you?"

"No," I said, "and for God's sake, lower your voice."

"But it's so nice," he wheedled, "and it's—" So partly to shut him up and partly in a sudden liking for him (he was smiling a kind of gap-toothed, ecstatic smile and his orange freckles were aglow) I pulled off my ring—a cheap thing but my own—and gave it him.

"Hide it," I said, and slipped out into the courtyard.

Now I had a rough idea of where I was, but only a rough idea; so I went to the stables by taking what proved to be the longest way, hugging the walls and stumbling now and again against household remnants left out to freeze or dry, with a noise that I thought must waken the dead. I even saw the council through a window, and stood horribly bewitched for a moment, as if at my own funeral, until the sight gave me the shivers and I crept on. At the deserted stable I slashed the reins of all the horses, searched through saddlebags with my heart knocking at my teeth, found a small moneybag (my uncle's, one-quarter of a sheep this time) and mounted, snatching a torch from the wall, spurring toward the farm gate, dashing at the two guarding it, and firing the thatch above their heads.

What a blaze in an instant! What an uproar! Behind me in the court the freed beasts dashed effectively back and forth, barring everyone from the gate and then (in the most sensible manner possible) streaming behind me, leaving their owners horseless and homebound until someone should round them up the next morning. No one—not even my little cousin—would go out *that* night! The picture pleased me. As I rode through the windy black, I imagined uncles and cousins and grandfathers huddling uncomfortably in the dark of their charred and roofless rooms, seeing specters with every moan of the wind. It was damned cold. I was in my shirt. I stopped and searched the saddlebags again and heaven provided me with a jacket, knit by a suffering aunt. I became hysterical. The horse was stepping warily in the dark (we seemed to be traversing rocks) and we went around in circles until he simply stood still. I roared and rocked in the saddle. When I came to my senses, I headed south by the stars (who else but I even knew the stars? who else had spent nights in the open?) and saw the beautiful sun come up on my left, over gravelly hills, found a stream, washed and drank, and went on very much improved. But heaven proved to be remarkably improvident in the matter of food, and it was the next midday before I found a farm, stopped at it, and asked the hired girl—

She was off like a shot. I took advantage of my infamy and the sudden terror it produced to rifle the kitchen and change horses, leaving my uncle's to be de-hexed, de-bewitched, have chants chanted over it and expensive charms hung upon it and finally (I hoped) adopted and fed. Very likely my uncle would have to pay to have it back. I rode on in better spirits, but miserably fed, and finally, my infamy running out and reduced from a werewolf to a beggar, I sold the horse, proceeded on foot, sold my clothes and bought others cheaper and lighter and found—to my distress—that I had no money. None at all. In the north, where there was no food, I could have lived half a winter on that little bag. In the south, where the ricks ran over, I starved.

I do not like to remember what happened to me then. It was the only time in my life I saw things in simple truth. It seemed to me that the country was feeding off me, for as I got sicker I walked farther south and the spring came, and I fancied the wild mallows and the roses got their color from my blood; I was very sick. If I had not walked into houses at night and stolen, I think I would have died; for the people of the south do not disbelieve in demons, despite their cultivation; oh no. They would watch me, trembling behind the wall, as I stared at their pantry shelves, stared at the loaf in my hand, even forgetting why I had come. Sometimes I would put it down like a sleepwalker; once I lay on the grass by the open highway and wept for no reason, looking up at the stars. Someone saw me then, at dawn;

someone (once!) gave me good-day. It was as I walked up to the gates of my first city, low and gray in the wet dawn mist, that I knew I was going to die. As I went through the gates, they closed over me like the dull roar of water over one's head, and I lay down (as I thought) to quit this world.

But the world had other ideas.

I woke on a stone floor, with two faces bending over me, one thin, one fat; the fat man plump as a pig and oily, delighted, writhing, pious, all at once. I thought I had gone to heaven. Then he said, "My dear boy." He beamed. "My dear, poor boy, a treasure! A find! A find! What a find!"

"He needs some more," said the other face, laconically, and disappeared to fetch something. Somebody put a pillow under my head and I tried to sit up.

"No, no, no, no," said the fat face, serenely, twiddling a finger at me. "Lie down. That's good. Here" (to someone outside my field of vision), "here, help him up," and they propped me against a wall. "Dear boy" (someone drew a blanket over me), "dear foolish boy, you didn't even have the sense to beg," and began feeding me something I could not taste, smacking his lips as if I were a baby, and muttering to himself. I am seeing visions at last, I thought, and they are angels, and with this thought (which was rather distressing) I came bolt awake.

"Who the devil are you?" I croaked. Fat-face wreathed and writhed in delight and thin-face next to him put hands together and cast eyes piously upward. Then he scuttled out of my field of vision.

"Friends," said fat-face, beaming; "Orthgar, get me a napkin" (presumably to someone in the room, for I was lying on the floor of a kind of office, with ledgers open on a table and parchments and such gear all about the walls), and he began feeding me some more. Then he stopped and, ecstatically shutting his eyes, kissed me on the forehead.

"You," he said, "are going to make a lot of money."

"What?" said I. He patted my cheek, still beaming as if I were a prize pig.

"Later," he said. "Do you think you can sit up?" and I said possibly and they propped me in a chair where I could see (wonder of wonders!) a garden, and a gardener clipping fruit trees.

"My dear fellow," said fat-face, "you must tell me your name." And I did, and he said, "I am Rigg and this is Orthgar. Orthgar, get me a brandy." Orthgar disappeared. I stared up at my fat host in bewilderment (it grew no less in the next ten years!) and asked him—well, asked him—He put up one hand for silence.

"You mustn't talk," he said fondly, "you'll exhaust yourself. You sit there like a good little boy and *I*—" (he heaved himself ponderously off the table, where he had been perched like a great, fat finch) "and *I* will explain everything." He smiled. "I am a banker," he said, shutting his eyes and then, opening them, he added delicately, "but not a banker," and looked modestly at his hands, which were fastidiously picking up pages and turning them over.

"Well?" said I.

He looked beatific. "I," he said, squirming with modesty, "I—that is, we—all of us—we are Appropriators."

"What?" I said. He shrugged.

"Thieves," he said. "But that's a nasty name. Call me Rigg. Ah! the brandy," and he poured from his glass into another and gave the second to me.

"I am not a good thief at all," said I.

"You will be," he said. "You will be. Besides, my dear—" (and here he and Orthgar smirked at each other) "think of your great talent."

"Talent?" I said dully.

"Oh yes," he said, sliding off the seat and walking expansively around the room. "Orthgar found you at dawn in the city cemetery. Orthgar is protected by very strong charms. There you were, sleeping like a baby, obviously unharmed except for semistarvation, of course, perfectly oblivious to the danger you ran. That is, you didn't run. That's the point. It's a ghastly place; people go mad there, cut each other's throats, hang themselves on empty air, really dreadful."

"City ought to do something," interposed Orthgar.

"Certainly they ought," said my host emphatically. "But they won't. Who can? Only our friend here." He beamed. "And he won't, either. He'll be too busy. The present administration," said Rigg heatedly, "is rotten! Rotten! Luckily." He stopped. "Am I boring you?" he said.

"How can I be useful?" said I.

"'The clever fellow reaches conclusions more quickly than the stupid one,'" said Rigg, scratching behind his right ear and looking very piglike. "You ask good questions. Very. You see, when Orthgar brought you here—dear, brave fellow, Orthgar! I owe him a great deal

—when Orthgar brought you here, we gave you all sorts of tests to see if you were suited to the job. We spoke Awakening Spells over you. You snored. We conjured up your spirit. You snored. Finally I had Thring—Thring's a friend of ours, very useful fellow, Thring—go out and get a priest to exorcise you, cleanse you and anoint you. Nothing. Finally we put you to the ultimate test, pronounced a frightful malediction upon you, several frightful maledictions, in fact—"

"It was a strain to be in the room," said Orthgar.

"But nothing happened," said Rigg. "In fact, you opened your eyes and said something unprintable about your uncle."

"Yes," said I, thoughtfully.

"So then," continued Rigg excitedly, drinking his brandy and mine too, "so then we *knew!* My dear fellow, we *knew!* One man like you is worth a hundred of us! Do you know how many lockmakers there are in this city? Well, there are twice as many magicians. And there you have it." They clinked glasses. At this I laughed, and then I said that I wanted some brandy, too.

"You'll throw it up," said Rigg warningly, "it's too soon," but he gave me some anyway and keep it down I could not, and made a mess that the landlady had to clean up.

"Beggars," she said, and then she said, "You owe three weeks' rent."

"Madam," said my host with dignity, "I shall give you six. Do you see this paper?" and he showed her a page of a ledger.

"I can't read," said the landlady sullenly, going out the door with the slop basin. "But I can count," she said, putting her head in at the door, and then vanishing.

"I feel sick," I said, and Rigg took from a pocket a small green vial with a brass stopper.

"Here," he said, smiling shrewdly. "Oil of peppermint. Good for the stomach." He gave it to me. "Even yours," he said, with meaning. I drank some and closed my eyes. It burned and numbed my mouth and it made me feel a little better that there was medicine in the world for me, for me, yes, even me.

"Well?" he said.

"Well?"

"What share will you take?"

"One-quarter," I said.

"One-eighth," he said.

"One-quarter," I said. "You have to give me reasons for living."
He looked unhappy.
"One-sixth?" he said.
"Done."
"I told you," said Orthgar, and he cleared away the ledgers. "You'd best put them back on the shelves," he said. "They don't belong to us."
I laughed again.
"The unholy alliance," I said.
"Mm?" said Rigg, over his brandy.
"Nothing," I said.
"Well," said Rigg, "if you feel better, let's get you to bed. The proper soup and in three days you'll be on your feet."
"We'll have to travel," said Orthgar. "All six of us. His life won't be worth anything once they find out."
"Oh it'll take time," said Rigg serenely, his eyes sparkling. "It'll take time. They'll try spells first" (and he giggled) "and by then we'll be somewhere else." He looked out the window and sighed. "I hate the provinces," he said. He strolled over and helped Orthgar get me to bed. "Wait," he said, patting my cheek. "Drink soup. Think of wine, women, and song."
"I have never heard songs," I said, "and I hate women only a little less than men, I assure you." My foster father patted my cheek again.
"You'll like music," he said. "It shows in the shape of your ears." And waving gaily, he gathered up the brandy, bottle, glasses, tray and all, and strolled out. Orthgar stood at the door for a moment.
"He's not too bad," said Orthgar. "You can trust him." And then he too went out.

But I was not thinking of money. I was thinking rather of the oddness of the world and how strange it was that people bothered themselves with spells and counter-spells and did not investigate the really compelling questions, such as whether the sun's fire burned the same material as ordinary fires, for anyone can look into a wood fire, even a goldsmith's, but it is common knowledge that the sun dazzles the eyes for even a moment. And the moon must burn still another thing, for its fire in the daytime is pale white.

I remember my nurse, when I was little, asking me whether when the sun rose I did not see a great company of the heavenly host all crying Holy Holy Holy and I had said no, I saw only a round, red disk about the size of a penny coin. And then I wondered, drifting off to sleep to the sound of the gardener's shears, whether it might not be an advantage not to see demons and angels, and if it was, whether my children might not inherit the trait and pass it on to their children; and perhaps eventually (here the garden and its blossoming fruit trees wavered in the undulations of drowsiness) everyone would be like me, and if you asked people about the afreets, the succubi, the vampires, the angels and the fiends (very vaguely, far away, I could see the gardener cry out and back away from something, yet I knew I was safe; it might put its teeth into me and rage and roar and stamp—all silently—but I could sleep on), they would say *Those creatures? Oh, they're just legends; they don't exist.* . . .

From goats' eggs to three-legged Egyptian princes, the notions in these fanciful stories are so wildly imagined that during the author's lifetime they were published only in an edition of seven copies that never left the author's possession until after his death. HORACE WALPOLE, *the inventor of the Gothic novel, most likely intended these as children's stories, naming them "hieroglyphic," presumably because they are colorful word-pictures. They are years ahead of their time with their inspired fantastic notions, absurdity, and surrealism. This is the first time these stories have appeared in an anthology of fantasy.*

Hieroglyphic Tales
BY HORACE WALPOLE

A New Arabian Night's Entertainment

At the foot of the great mountain Hirgonqúu was anciently situated the kingdom of Larbidel. Geographers, who are not apt to make such just comparisons, said, it resembled a football just going to be kicked away; and so it happened; for the mountain kicked the kingdom into the ocean, and it has never been heard of since.

One day a young princess had climbed up to the top of the mountain to gather goat's eggs, the whites of which are excellent for taking off freckles. —Goat's eggs!—Yes—naturalists hold that all Beings are conceived in an egg. The goats of Hirgonqúu might be oviparous, and lay their eggs to be hatched by the sun. This is my supposition; no matter whether I believe it myself or not. I will write against and abuse any man that opposes my hypothesis. It would be fine indeed if learned men were obliged to believe what they assert.

The other side of the mountain was inhabited by a nation of whom the Larbidellians knew no more than the French nobility do of Great Britain, which they think is an island that some how or other may be approached by land. The princess had strayed into the confines of Cucurucu, when she suddenly found herself seized by the guards of the prince that reigned in that country. They told her in few words that she must be conveyed to the capital and married to the giant their lord and emperor. The giant, it seems, was fond of having a new wife every night, who was to tell him a story that would last till morning, and then have her head cut off—such odd ways have some folks of passing their wedding-nights! The princess modestly asked, why their master loved such long stories? The captain of the guard replied, his majesty did not sleep well—Well! said she, and if he does not!—not but I believe I can tell as long stories as any princess in Asia. Nay, I can repeat Leonidas by heart, and your emperor must be wakeful indeed if he can hold out against that.

By this time they were arrived at the palace. To the great surprise of the princess, the emperor, so far from being a giant, was but five feet one inch in height; but being two inches taller than any of his predecessors, the flattery of his courtiers had bestowed the name of *giant* on him; and he affected to look down upon any man above his own stature. The princess was immediately undressed and put to bed, his majesty being impatient to hear a new story.

Light of my eyes, said the emperor, what is your name? I call myself the princess Gronovia, replied she; but my real appellation is the frow Gronow. And what is the use of a name, said his majesty, but to be called by it? And why do you pretend to be a princess, if you are not? My turn is romantic, answered she, and I have ever had an ambition of being the heroine of a novel. Now there are but two conditions that entitle one to that rank; one must be a shepherdess or a princess. Well, content yourself, said the giant, you will die an empress, without being either the one or the other! But what sublime reason had you for lengthening your name so unaccountably? It is a custom in my family, said she: all my ancestors were learned men, who wrote about the Romans. It sounded more classic, and gave a higher opinion of their literature, to put a Latin termination to their names. All this is Japonese to me, said the emperor; but your ancestors seem to have been a parcel of mountebanks. Does one understand any thing the better for corrupting one's name? Oh, said the princess, but it showed taste too. There was a time when in Italy the learned carried this still farther; and a man with a large forehead, who was born on the fifth of January, called himself Quintus Januarius Fronto. More and more absurd, said the emperor. You seem to have a great deal of impertinent knowledge about a great many impertinent people; but proceed in your story: whence came you? Mynheer, said she, I was born in Holland—The deuce you was, said the emperor, and where is that? It was no where, replied the princess, spritelily, till my countrymen gained it from the sea—Indeed, moppet! said his majesty; and pray who were your countrymen, before you had any country? Your majesty asks a very shrewd question, said she, which I cannot resolve on a sudden; but I will step home to my library, and consult five or six thousand volumes of modern history, a hundred or two dictionaries, and an abridgment of geography in forty volumes in folio, and be back in an instant. Not so fast, my life, said the emperor, you must not rise till you go to execution; it is now one in the morning, and you have not begun your story.

My great grandfather, continued the princess, was a Dutch merchant, who passed many years in Japan—On what account? said the emperor. He went thither to abjure his religion, said she, that he might get money enough to return and defend it against Philip 2nd. You are a pleasant family, said the emperor; but though I love fables, I hate genealogies. I know in all families, by their own account, there never was any thing but good and great men from father to son; a sort of fiction that does not at all amuse me. In my dominions there is no nobility but flattery. Whoever flatters me best is created a great lord, and the titles I confer are synonimous to their merits. There is Kiss-my-breech-Can, my favourite; Adulation-Can, lord treasurer; Prerogative-Can, head of the law; and Blasphemy-Can, high-priest. Whoever speaks truth, corrupts his blood, and is ipso facto degraded. In Europe you allow a man to be noble because one of his ancestors was a flatterer. But every thing degenerates, the farther it is removed from its source. I will not hear a word of any of your race before your father: what was he?

It was in the height of the contests about the bull unigenitus—I tell you, interrupted the emperor, I will not be plagued with any more of those people with Latin names: they were a parcel of coxcombs, and seem to have infected you with their folly. I am sorry, replied Gronovia, that your sublime highness is so little acquainted with the state of Europe, as to take a papal ordinance for a person. Unigenitus is Latin for the Jesuits—And who the devil are the Jesuits? said the giant. You explain one nonsensical term by another, and wonder I am never the wiser. Sir, said the princess, if you will permit me to give you a short account of the troubles that have agitated Europe for these last two hundred years, on the doctrines of grace, free-will, predestination, reprobation, justification, &c. you will be more entertained, and will believe less, than if I told your majesty a long story of fairies and goblins. You are an eternal prater, said the emperor, and very self-sufficient; but talk your fill, and upon what subject you like, till tomorrow morning; but I swear by the soul of the holy Jirigi, who rode to heaven on the tail of a magpie, as soon as the clock strikes eight, you are a dead woman. Well, who was the Jesuit Unigenitus?

The novel doctrines that had sprung up in Germany, said Gronovia, made it necessary for the church to look about her. The disciples of Loyola—Of whom? said the emperor, yawning—Ignatius Loyola, the founder of the Jesuits, replied Gronovia, was—A writer of Roman history, I suppose, interrupted the emperor: what the devil were the Romans to you, that you trouble your head so much about them? The empire of Rome, and the church of Rome, are two distinct things, said the princess; and yet, as one may say, the one depends upon the other, as the new testament does on the old. One destroyed the other, and yet pretends a right to its inheritance. The temporalities of the church— What's o'clock, said the emperor to the chief eunuch? it cannot sure be far from eight—this woman has gossipped at least seven hours. Do you hear, my tomorrow-night's wife shall be dumb—cut her tongue out before you bring her to our bed. Madam, said the eunuch, his sublime highness, whose erudition passes the sands of the sea, is too well acquainted with all human sciences to require information. It is therefore that his exalted wisdom prefers accounts of what never happened, to any relation either in history or divinity—You lie, said the emperor; when I exclude truth, I certainly do not mean to forbid divinity—How many divinities have you in Europe, woman? The council of Trent, replied Gronovia, has decided—the emperor began to snore—I mean, continued Gronovia, that notwithstanding all father Paul has asserted, cardinal Palavicini affirms that in the three first sessions of that council —the emperor was now fast asleep, which the princess and the chief eunuch perceiving, clapped several pillows upon his face, and held them there till he expired. As soon as they were convinced he was dead, the princess, putting on every mark of despair and concern, issued to the divan, where she was immediately proclaimed empress. The emperor, it was given out, had died of an hermorrhoidal cholic, but to show her regard for his memory, her imperial majesty declared she would strictly adhere to the maxims by which he had governed. Accordingly she espoused a new husband every night, but dispensed with their telling her stories, and was graciously pleased also, upon their good behaviour, to remit the subsequent execution. She sent presents to all the learned men in Asia; and they in return did not fail to cry her up as a pattern of clemency, wisdom, and virtue: and though the panegyrics of the learned are generally as clumsy as they are fulsome, they ventured to assure her that their writings would be as durable as brass, and that the memory of her glorious reign would reach to the latest posterity.

The King and His Three Daughters

There was formerly a king, who had three daughters—that is, he would have had three, if he had had one more, but some how or other the eldest never was born. She was extremely handsome, had a great deal of wit, and spoke French in perfection, as all the authors of that age affirm, and yet none of them pretend that she ever existed. It is very certain that the two other princesses were far from beauties; the second had a strong Yorkshire dialect, and the youngest had bad teeth and but one leg, which occasioned her dancing very ill.

As it was not probable that his majesty would have any more children, being eighty-seven years, two months, and thirteen days old when his queen died, the states of the kingdom were very anxious to have the princesses married. But there was one great obstacle to this settlement, though so important to the peace of the kingdom. The king insisted that his eldest daughter should be married first, and as there was no such person, it was very difficult to fix upon a proper husband for her. The courtiers all approved his majesty's resolution; but as under the best princes there will always be a number of discontented, the nation was torn into different factions, the grumblers or patriots insisting that the second princess was the eldest, and ought to be declared heiress apparent to the crown. Many pamphlets were written pro and con, but the ministerial party pretended that the chancellor's argument was unanswerable, who affirmed, that the second princess could not be the eldest, as no princess-royal ever had a Yorkshire accent. A few persons who were attached to the youngest princess, took advantage of this plea for whispering that *her* royal highness's pretensions to the crown were the best of all; for as there was no eldest princess, and as the second must be the first, if there was no first, and as she could not be the second if she was the first, and as the chancellor had proved that she could not be the first, it followed plainly by every idea of law that she could be nobody at all; and then the consequence followed of course, that the youngest must be the eldest, if she had no elder sister.

It is inconceivable what animosities and mischiefs arose from these different titles; and each faction endeavoured to strengthen itself by foreign alliances. The court party having no real object for their attachment, were the most attached of all, and made up by warmth for the want of foundation in their principles. The clergy in general were devoted to this, which was styled *the first party*. The physicians embraced the second; and the lawyers declared for the third, or the faction of the youngest princess, because it seemed best calculated to admit of doubts and endless litigation.

While the nation was in this distracted situation, there arrived the prince of Quifferiquimini, who would have been the most accomplished hero of the age, if he had not been dead, and had spoken any language but the Egyptian, and had not had three legs. Notwithstanding these blemishes, the eyes of the whole nation were immediately turned upon him, and each party wished to see him married to the princess whose cause they espoused.

The old king received him with the most distinguished honours; the senate made the most fulsome addresses to him; the princesses were so taken with him, that they grew more bitter enemies than ever; and the court ladies and petit-maitres invented a thousand new fashions upon his account—every thing was to be á la Quifferiquimini. Both men and women of fashion left off rouge to look the more cadaverous; their cloaths were embroidered with hieroglyphics, and all the ugly characters they could gather from Egyptian antiquities, with which they were forced to be contented, it being impossible to learn a language that is lost; and all tables, chairs, stools, cabinets and couches, were made with only three legs; the last, however, soon went out of fashion, as being very inconvenient.

The prince, who, ever since his death, had had but a weakly constitution, was a little fatigued with this excess of attentions, and would often wish himself at home in his coffin. But his greatest difficulty of all was to get rid of the youngest princess, who kept hopping after him wherever he went, and was so full of admiration of his three legs, and so modest about having but one herself, and so inquisitive to know how his three legs were set on, that being the best natured man in the world, it went to his heart whenever in a fit of peevishness he happened to drop an impatient word, which never failed to throw her into an agony of tears, and then she looked so ugly that it was impossible for him to be tolerably civil to her. He was not much more inclined to the second princess—In truth, it was the eldest who made the conquest of his affections: and so violently did his passion increase one Tuesday morning, that breaking through all prudential considerations (for there were many reasons which ought to have determined his choice in favor of either of the other sisters) he hurried to the old king, acquainted him with his love, and demanded the eldest princess in marriage. Nothing could equal the joy of the good old monarch, who wished for nothing but to live to see the consummation of this match. Throwing his arms about the prince-skeleton's neck and watering his hollow cheeks with warm tears, he granted his request, and added, that he would immediately resign his crown to him and his favourite daughter.

I am forced for want of room to pass over many circumstances that would add greatly to the beauty of this history, and am sorry I must dash the reader's impatience by acquainting him, that notwithstanding the eagerness of the old king and youthful ardour of the prince, the nuptials were obliged to be postponed; the archbishop declaring that it was essentially necessary to have a dispensation from the pope, the parties being related within the forbidden degrees; a woman that never was, and a man that had been, being deemed first cousins in the eye of the canon law.

Hence arose a new difficulty. The religion of the Quifferiquiminians was totally opposite to that of the papists. The former believed in nothing but grace; and they had a high-priest of their own, who pretended that he was master of the whole fee-simple of grace, and by that possession could cause every thing to have been that never had been, and could prevent every thing that had been from ever having been. "We have nothing to do, said the prince to the king, but to send a solemn embassy to the high-priest of grace, with a present of a hundred thousand million of ingots, and he will cause your charming no-daughter to have been, and will prevent my having died, and then there will be no occasion for a dispensation from your old fool at Rome."—How! thou impious, atheistical bag of drybones, cried the old king; dost thou profane our holy religion? Thou shalt have no daughter of mine, thou three-legged skeleton—Go and be buried and be damned, as thou must be; for as thou art dead, thou art past repentance: I would sooner give my child to a baboon, who has one leg more than thou hast, than bestow her on such a reprobate corpse—You had better give your one-legged infanta to the baboon, said the prince, they are fitter for one another—As much a corpse as I am, I am perferable to nobody; and who the devil would have married your no-daughter, but a dead body! For my religion, I lived and died in it, and it is not in my power to change it now if I would—but for your part—a great shout interrupted this dialogue, and the captain of the guard rushing into the royal closet, acquainted his majesty, that the second princess, in revenge of the prince's neglect, had given her hand to a drysalter, who was a common-council-man, and that the city, in consideration of the match, had proclaimed them king and queen, allowing his majesty to retain the title for his life, which they had fixed for the term of six months; and ordering, in respect of his royal birth, that the prince should immediately lie in state and have a pompous funeral.

This revolution was so sudden and so universal, that all parties approved, or were forced to seem to approve it. The old king died the next day, as the courtiers said, for joy; the prince of Quifferiquimini was buried in spite of his appeal to the law of nations; and the youngest princess went distracted, and was shut up in a madhouse, calling out day and night for a husband with three legs.

The Dice-box: A Fairy Tale[1]

There was a merchant of Damascus named Aboulcasem, who had an only daughter called Pissimissi, which signifies *the waters of Jordan;* because a fairy foretold at her birth that she would be one of Solomon's concubines. Azaziel, the angel of death, having transported Aboulcasem to the regions of bliss, he had no fortune to bequeath to his beloved child but the shell of a pistachia-nut drawn by an elephant and

1) Translated from the French translation of the Countess Daunois, for the entertainment of Miss Caroline Campbell, eldest daughter of Lord William Campbell.

a ladybird. Pissimissi, who was but nine years old, and who had been kept in great confinement, was impatient to see the world; and no sooner was the breath out of her father's body than she got into the car, and whipping her elephant and ladybird, drove out of the yard as fast as possible, without knowing whither she was going. Her coursers never stopped till they came to the foot of a brazen tower, that had neither doors nor windows, in which lived an old enchantress, who had locked herself up there with seventeen thousand husbands. It had but one single vent for air, which was a small chimney grated over, through which it was scarce possible to put one's hand. Pissimissi, who was very impatient, ordered her coursers to fly with her up to the top of the chimney, which, as they were the most docile creatures in the world, they immediately did; but unluckily the fore paw of the elephant lighting on the top of the chimney, broke down the grate by its weight, but at the same time stopped up the passage so entirely, that all the enchantress's husbands were stifled for want of air. As it was a collection she had made with great care and cost, it is easy to imagine her vexation and rage. She raised a storm of thunder and lightning that lasted eight hundred and four years; and having conjured up an army of two thousand devils, she ordered them to slay the elephant alive, and dress it for her supper with anchovy sauce. Nothing could have saved the poor beast, if, struggling to get loose from the chimney, he had not happily broken wind, which it seems is a great preservative against devils. They all flew a thousand ways, and in their hurry carried away half the brazen tower, by which means the elephant, the car, the ladybird, and Pissimissi got loose; but in their fall tumbled through the roof of an apothecary's shop, and broke all his bottles of physic. The elephant, who was very dry with his fatigue, and who had not much taste, immediately sucked up all the medicines with his proboscis, which occasioned such a variety of effects in his bowels, that it was well he had such a strong constitution, or he must have died of it. His evacuations were so plentiful, that he not only drowned the tower of Babel, near which the apothecary's shop stood, but the current ran four score leagues till it came to the sea, and there poisoned so many whales and leviathans, that a pestilence ensued, and lasted three years, nine months and sixteen days. As the elephant was extremely weakened by what had happened, it was impossible for him to draw the car for eighteen months, which was a cruel delay to Pissimissi's impatience, who during all that time could not travel above a hundred miles a day, for as she carried the sick animal in her lap, the poor ladybird could not make longer stages with no assistance. Besides, Pissimissi bought every thing she saw wherever she came; and all was crowded into the car and stuffed into the seat. She had purchased ninety-two dolls, seventeen baby-houses, six cart-loads of sugar-plums, a thousand bales of gingerbread, eight dancing dogs, a bear and a monkey, four toy-shops with all their contents, and seven dozen of bibs and aprons of the newest fashion. They were jogging on with all this cargo over mount Caucasus, when an immense humming-bird, who had been struck with the beauty of the ladybird's wings, that I had forgot to say were of ruby spotted with black pearls, falling down at once upon her prey, swallowed ladybird, Pissimissi, the elephant, and all their commodities. It happened that the humming-bird belonged to Solomon; he let it out of its cage every morning after breakfast, and it constantly came home by the time the council broke up. Nothing could equal the surprise of his majesty and the courtiers, when the dear little creature arrived with the elephant's proboscis hanging out of its divine little bill. However, after the first astonishment was over, his majesty, who to be sure was wisdom itself, and who understood natural philosophy that it was a charm to hear him discourse of those matters, and who was actually making a collection of dried beasts and birds in twelve thousand volumes of the best fool's-cap paper, immediately perceived what had happened, and taking out of the side-pocket of his breeches a diamond toothpick-case of his own turning, with the toothpick made of the only unicorn's horn he ever saw, he stuck it into the elephant's snout, and began to draw it out: but all his philosophy was confounded, when jammed between the elephant's legs he perceived the head of a beautiful girl, and between her legs a baby-house, which with the wings extended thirty feet, out of the windows of which rained a torrent of sugar-plums, that had been placed there to make room. Then followed the bear, who had been pressed to the bales of gingerbread and was covered all over with it, and looked but uncouthly; and the monkey with a doll in every paw, and his pouches so crammed with sugar-plumbs that they hung on each side of him, and trailed on the ground behind like the duchess of ********'s beautiful breasts. Solomon, however, gave small attention to this procession, being caught with the charms of the lovely Pissimissi: he immediately began the song of songs extempore; and what he had seen—I mean, all that came out of the humming-bird's throat had made such a jumble in his ideas, that there was nothing so unlike to which he did not compare all Pissimissi's beauties. As he sung his canticles too to no tune, and god knows had but a bad voice, they were far from comforting Pissimissi: the elephant had torn her best bib and apron, and she cried and roared, and kept such a squalling, that though Solomon carried her in his arms, and showed her all the fine things in the temple, there was no pacifying her. The queen of Sheba, who was playing at backgammon with the high-priest, and who came every October to converse with Solomon, though she did not understand a word of Hebrew, hearing the noise, came running out of her dressing-room; and seeing the king with a squalling child in his arms, asked him peevishly, if it became his reputed wisdom to expose himself with his bastards to all the court? Solomon, instead of replying, kept singing, "We have a little sister, and she has no breasts;" which so provoked the Sheban princess, that happening to have one of the dice-boxes in her hand, she without any ceremony threw it at his head. The enchantress, whom I mentioned before, and who, though invisible, had followed Pissimissi, and drawn her into her train of misfortunes, turned the dice-box aside, and directed it to Pissimissi's nose, which being something flat, like madame de ********'s, it stuck there, and being of ivory, Solomon ever after compared his beloved's nose to the tower that leads to Damascus. The queen, though ashamed of her behaviour, was not in her heart sorry for the accident; but when she found that it only increased the monarch's passion, her contempt redoubled; and calling him a thousand old fools to herself, she ordered her postchaise and drove away in a fury, without leaving sixpence for the servants; and nobody knows what became of her or her kingdom, which has never been heard of since.

The Peach in Brandy:
A Milesian Tale[1]

Fitz Scanlan Mac Giolla l'ha druig, king[2] of Kilkenny, the thousand and fifty-seventh descendant in a direct line from Milesius king of Spain, had an only daughter called Great A, and by corruption Grata; who being arrived at years of discretion, and perfectly initiated by her royal parents in the arts of government, the fond monarch determined to resign his crown to her: having accordingly assembled the senate, he declared his resolution to them, and having delivered his sceptre into the princess's hand, he obliged her to ascend the throne; and to set the example, was the first to kiss her hand, and vow eternal obedience to her. The senators were ready to stifle the new queen with panegyrics and addresses; the people, though they adored the old king, were transported with having a new sovereign, and the university, according to custom immemorial, presented her majesty, three months after every body had forgotten the event, with testimonials of the excessive sorrow and excessive joy they felt on losing one monarch and getting another.

Her majesty was now in the fifth year of her age, and a prodigy of sense and goodness. In her first speech to the senate, which she lisped with inimitable grace, she assured them that her heart[3] was entirely Irish, and that she did not intend any longer to go in leading-strings, as a proof of which she immediately declared her nurse prime-minister. The senate applauded this sage choice with even greater encomiums than the last, and voted a free gift to the queen of a million of sugar-plums, and to the favourite of twenty thousand bottles of usquebaugh. Her majesty then jumping from her throne, declared it was her royal pleasure to play at blindman's-buff, but such a hub-bub arose from the senators pushing, and pressing, and squeezing, and punching one another, to endeavour to be the first blinded, that in the scuffle her maj-

---

1) This tale was written for Anne Liddel, countess of Ossary, wife of John Fitzpatrick, earl of Ossary. They had a daughter Anne, the subject of this story.
2) Read Lodge's Peerage of Ireland, in the family of Fitzpatrick.
3) Queen Anne in her first speech to the parliament said, her heart was entirely English.

esty was thrown down and got a bump on her forehead as big as a pigeon's egg, which set her a squalling, that you might have heard her to Tipperary. The old king flew into a rage, and snatching up the mace knocked out the chancellor's brains, who at that time happened not to have any; and the queen-mother, who sat in a tribune above to see the ceremony, fell into a fit and miscarried[4] of twins, who were killed by her majesty's fright; but the earl of Bullaboo, great butler of the crown, happening to stand next to the queen, catched up one of the dead children, and perceiving it was a boy, ran down to the king[5] and wished him joy of the birth of a son and heir. The king, who had now recovered his sweet temper, called him a fool and blunderer, upon which Mr. Phelim O' Torture, a zealous courtier, started up with great presence of mind and accused the earl of Bullaboo of high treason, for having asserted that his late majesty had had any other heir than their present most lawful and most religious sovereign queen Grata. An impeachment was voted by a large majority, though not without warm opposition, particularly from a celebrated Kilkennian orator, whose name is unfortunately not come down to us, it being erased out of the journals afterwards, as the Irish author whom I copy says, when he became first lord of the treasury, as he was during the whole reign of queen Grata's successor. The argument of this Mr. Killmorackill, says my author, whose name is lost, was, that her majesty the queen-mother having conceived a son before the king's resignation, that son was indubitably heir to the crown, and consequently the resignation void, is not signifying an iota whether the child was born alive or dead: it was alive, said he, when it was conceived—here he was called to order by Dr. O'Flaharty, the queen-mother's man-midwife and member for the borough of Corbelly, who entered into a learned dissertation on embrios; but he was interrupted by the young queen's crying for her supper, the previous question for which was carried without a negative; and then the house being resumed, the debate was cut short by the impatience of the majority to go and drink her majesty's health. This seeming violence gave occasion to a very long protest, drawn up by sir Archee Mac Sarcasm, in which he contrived to state the claim of the departed foetus so artfully, that it produced a civil war, and gave rise to those bloody ravages and massacres which so long laid waste the ancient kingdom of

4) Lady Ossary had miscarried just then of two sons.
5) The housekeeper, as soon as Lord Ossary came home, wished him joy of a son and heir, though both the children were born dead.

Kilkenny, and which were at last terminated by a lucky accident, well known, says my author, to every body, but which he thinks it his duty to relate for the sake of those who never may have heard it. These are his words:

It happened that the archbishop of Tuum (anciently called Meum by the Roman catholic clergy) the great wit of those times, was in the queen-mother's closet, who had the young queen in her lap.[6] His grace was suddenly seized with a violent fit of the cholic, which made him make such wry faces, that the queen-mother thought he was going to die, and ran out of the room to send for a physician, for she was a pattern of goodness, and void of pride. While she was stepped into the servant's hall to call somebody, according to the simplicity of those times, the archbishop's pains increased, when perceiving something on the mantle-piece, which he took for a peach in brandy, he gulped it all down at once without saying grace, God forgive him, and found great comfort from it. He had not done licking his lips before the queen-mother returned, when queen Grata cried out, "Mama, mama, the gentleman has eaten my little brother!" This fortunate event put an end to the contest, the male line entirely failing in the person of the devoured prince. The archbishop, however, who became pope by the name of Innocent the 3d. having afterwards a son by his sister, named the child Fitzpatrick, as having some of the royal blood in its veins; and from him are descended all the younger branches of the Fitzpatricks of our time. Now the rest of the acts of Grata and all that she did, are they not written in the book of the chronicles of the kings of Kilkenny?

---

6) Some commentators have ignorantly supposed that the Irish author is guilty of a great anachronism in this passage; for having said that the contested succession occasioned long wars, he yet speaks of queen Grata at the conclusion of them, as still sitting in her mother's lap as a child. Now I can confute them from their own state of the question. Like a child does not import that she actually was a child: she only sat like a child; and so she might though thirty years old. Civilians have declared at what period of his life a king may be of age before he is: but neither Grotius nor Puffendorffe, nor any of the tribe, have determined how long a king or queen may remain infants after they are past their infancy.

Mi Li:
A Chinese Fairy Tale

Mi Li, prince of China, was brought up by his godmother the fairy Hih, who was famous for telling fortunes with a tea-cup. From that unerring oracle she assured him, that he would be the most unhappy man alive unless he married a princess whose name was the same with her father's dominions. As in all probability there could not be above one person in the world to whom that accident had happened, the prince thought there would be nothing so easy as to learn who his destined bride was. He had been too well educated to put the question to his godmother, for he knew when she uttered an oracle, that it was with intention to perplex, not to inform; which has made people so fond of consulting all those who do not give an explicit answer, such as prophets, lawyers, and any body you meet on the road, who, if you ask the way, reply by desiring to know whence you came. Mi Li was no sooner returned to his palace than he sent for his governor, who was deaf and dumb, qualities for which the fairy had selected him, that he might not instil any bad principles into his pupil; however, in recompence, he could talk upon his fingers like an angel. Mi Li asked him directly who the princess was whose name was the same with her father's kingdom? This was a little exaggeration in the prince, but nobody ever repeats any thing just as they heard it: besides, it was excusable in the heir of a great monarchy, who of all things had not been taught to speak truth, and perhaps had never heard what it was. Still it was not the mistake of *kingdom* for *dominions* that puzzled the governor. It never helped him to understand any thing the better for its being rightly stated. However, as he had great presence of mind, which consisted in never giving a direct answer, and in looking as if he could, he replied, it was a question of too great importance to be resolved on a sudden. How came you to know that? said the prince—This youthful impetuosity told the governor that there was something more in the question than he had apprehended; and though he could be very solemn about nothing, he was ten times more so when there was something he did not comprehend. Yet that unknown something occasioning a conflict between his cunning and his ignorance, and the latter being the greater, always betrayed itself, for nothing looks so silly as a fool acting wisdom. The prince repeated his question; the governor demanded why he asked—the prince had not patience to spell the question over again on his fingers, but bawled it as loud as he could to no purpose. The courtiers ran in, and catching up the prince's words, and repeating them imperfectly, it soon flew all over Pekin, and thence into the provinces, and thence into Tartary, and thence to Muscovy, and so on, that the prince wanted to know who the princess was, whose name was the same as her father's. As the Chinese have not the blessing (for aught I know) of having family surnames as we have, and as what would be their christian-names, if they were so happy as to be christians, are quite different for men and women, the Chinese, who think that must be a rule all over the world because it is theirs, decided that there could not exist upon the square face of the earth a woman whose name was the same as her father's. They repeated this so often, and with so much deference and so much obstinacy, that the prince, totally forgetting the original oracle, believed that he wanted to know who the woman was who had the same name as her father. However, remembering there was something in the question that he had taken for royal, he always said *the king her father.* The prime minister consulted the red book or court-calendar, which was *his* oracle, and could find no such princess. All the ministers at foreign courts were instructed to inform themselves if there was any such lady; but as it took up a great deal of time to put these instructions into cypher, the prince's impatience could not wait for the couriers setting out, but he determined to go himself in search of the princess. The old king, who, *as is usual,* had left the whole management of affairs to his son the moment he was fourteen, was charmed with the prince's resolution of seeing the world, which he thought could be done in a few days, the facility of which makes so many monarchs never stir out of their own palaces till it is too late; and his majesty declared, that he should approve of his son's choice, be the lady who she would, provided she answered to the divine designation of having the same name as her father.

The prince rode post to Canton, intending to embark there on board an English man of war. With what infinite transport did he hear the evening before he was to embark, that a sailor knew the identic lady in question. The prince scalded his mouth with the tea he was drinking, broke the old china cup it was in, and which the queen his mother had given him at his departure from Pekin, and which had been given to her great great great great grandmother queen Fi by Confucius himself, and ran down to the vessel and asked for the man who knew his bride. It was honest Tom O'Bull, an Irish sailor, who by his interpreter Mr. James Hall, the supercargo, informed his highness that Mr. Bob Oliver of Sligo had a daughter christened of both his names, the fair miss Bob Oliver.[1] The prince by the plenitude of his power declared Tom a mandarin of the first class, and at Tom's desire promised to speak to his brother the king of Great Ireland, France and Britain, to have him made a peer in his own country, Tom saying he should be ashamed to appear there without being a lord as well as all his acquaintance.

The prince's passion, which was greatly inflamed by Tom's description of her highness Bob's charms, would not let him stay for a proper set of ladies from Pekin to carry to wait on his bride, so he took a dozen of the wives of the first merchants in Canton, and two dozen virgins as maids of honour, who however were disqualified for their employments before his highness got to St. Helena. Tom himself married one of them, but was so great a favourite with the prince, that she still was appointed maid of honour, and with Tom's consent was afterwards married to an English duke.

Nothing can paint the agonies of our royal lover when on his landing at Dublin he was informed that princess Bob had quitted Ireland, and was married to nobody knew whom. It was well for Tom that he was on Irish ground. He would have been chopped as small as rice, for it is death in China to mislead the heir of the crown through ignorance. To do it knowingly is no crime, any more than in other countries.

As a prince of China cannot marry a woman that has been married before, it was necessary for Mi Li to search the world for another lady equally qualified with miss Bob, whom he forgot the moment he was told he must marry somebody else, and fell equally in love with somebody else, though he knew not with whom. In this suspence he dreamt, *"that he would find his destined spouse, whose father had left the dominions which never had been his dominions, in a place where there was a bridge over no water, a tomb where nobody ever was buried nor ever would be buried, ruins that were more than they had ever been,*

---

1) There really was such a person.

a subterraneous passage in which there were dogs with eyes of rubies and emeralds, and a more beautiful menagerie of Chinese pheasants than any in his father's extensive gardens." This oracle seemed so impossible to be accomplished, that he believed it more than he had done the first, which showed his great piety. He determined to begin his second search, and being told by the lord lieutenant that there was in England a Mr. Banks,[2] who was going all over the world in search of he did not know what, his highness thought he could not have a better conductor, and sailed for England. There he learnt that the sage Banks was at Oxford, hunting in the Bodleian library for a MS. voyage of a man who had been in the moon, which Mr. Banks thought must have been in the western ocean, where the moon sets, and which planet if he could discover once more, he would take possession of in his majesty's name, upon condition that it should never be taxed, and so he lost again to this country like the rest of his majesty's dominions in that part of the world.

Mi Li took a hired post-chaise for Oxford, but as it was a little rotten it broke on the new road down to Henley. A beggar advised him to walk into general Conway's, who was the most courteous person alive, and would certainly lend him his own chaise. The prince travelled incog. He took the beggar's advice, but going up to the house was told the family were in the grounds, but he should be conducted to them. He was led through a venerable wood of beeches, to a menagerie[3] commanding a more glorious prospect than any in his father's dominions, and full of Chinese pheasants. The prince cried out in extasy, Oh! potent Hih! my dream begins to be accomplished. The gardiner, who knew no Chinese but the names of a few plants, was struck with the similitude of the sounds, but discreetly said not a word. Not finding his lady there, as he expected, he turned back, and plunging suddenly into the thickest gloom of the wood, he descended into a cavern totally dark, the intrepid prince following him boldly. After advancing a great way into this subterraneous vault, at last they perceived light, when on a sudden they were pursued by several small spaniels, and turning to look at them, the prince perceived their eyes[4] shone like emeralds and

---
2) The gentleman who discovered Otaheite, in company with Dr. Solander.
3) Lady Ailesbury's.
4) At Park-place there is such a passage cut through a chalk-hill: when dogs are in the middle, the light from the mouth makes their eyes appear in the manner here described.

rubies. Instead of being amazed, as Fo-Hi, the founder of his race, would have been, the prince renewed his exclamations, and cried, I advance! I advance! I shall find my bride! great Hih! thou art infallible! Emerging into light, the imperturbed[5] gardiner conducted his highness to a heap of artificial[6] ruins, beneath which they found a spacious gallery or arcade, where his highness was asked if he would not repose himself, but instead of answering he capered like one frantic, crying out, I advance! I advance! great Hih! I advance!—The gardiner was amazed, and doubted whether he was not conducting a madman, his master and lady, and hesitated whether he should proceed—but as he understood nothing the prince said, and perceiving he must be a foreigner, he concluded he was a Frenchman by his dancing. As the stranger too was so nimble and not at all tired with his walk, the sage gardiner proceeded down a sloping valley, between two mountains cloathed to their summits with cedars, firs, and pines, which he took care to tell the prince were all of his honour the general's own planting: but though the prince had learnt more English in three days in Ireland, than all the French in the world ever learnt in three years, he took no notice of the information, to the great offence of the gardiner, but kept running on, and increased his gambols and exclamations when he perceived the vale was terminated by a stupendous bridge, that seemed composed of the rocks which the giants threw at Jupiter's head, and had not a drop of water beneath it[7]— Where is my bride, my bride? cried Mi Li—I must be near her. The prince's shouts and cries drew a matron from a cottage that stood on a precipice near the bridge, and hung over the river—My lady is down at Ford-house, cried the good woman,[8] who was a little deaf, concluding they had called to her to know. The gardiner knew it was in vain to explain his distress to her, and thought that if the poor gentleman was really mad, his master the general would be the properest person to know how to manage him. Accordingly turning to the left, he led the prince along the banks of the river, which glittered through the opening fallows, while on the other hand a wilderness of shrubs climbed up the pendent cliffs of chalk, and

5) Copeland, the gardiner, a very grave person.
6) Consequently, they seem to have been larger.
7) The rustic bridge at Park-place was built by General Conway, to carry the road from Henley, and to leave the communication free between his grounds on each side of the road.
8) The old woman who kept the cottage built by General Conway to command a glorious prospect. Fordhouse is a farm house at the termination of the grounds.

contrasted with the verdant meads and fields of corn beyond the stream. The prince, insensible to such enchanting scenes, galloped wildly along, keeping the poor gardiner on a round trot, till they were stopped by a lonely tomb[9] surrounded by cypress, yews, and willows, that seemed the monument of some adventurous youth who had been lost in tempting the current, and might have suited the gallant and daring Leander. Here Mi Li first had presence of mind to recollect the little English he knew, and eagerly asked the gardiner whose tomb he beheld before him. It is nobody's—before he could proceed, the prince interrupted him, And will it never be any body's?—Oh! thought the gardiner, now there is no longer any doubt of his phrenzy—and perceiving his master and the family approaching towards them, he endeavoured to get the start, but the prince, much younger, and borne too on the wings of love, set out full speed the moment he saw the company, and particularly a young damsel with them. Running almost breathless up to lady Ailesbury, and seizing miss Campbell's hand—he cried, *Who she? who she?* Lady Ailesbury screamed, the young maiden squalled, the general, cool but offended, rushed between them, and if a prince could be collared, would have collared him—Mi Li kept fast hold with one arm, but pointing to his prize with the other, and with the most eager and supplicating looks entreating for an answer, continued to exclaim, *Who she? who she?* The general perceiving by his accent and manner that he was a foreigner, and rather tempted to laugh than be angry, replied with civil scorn, Why *she* is miss Caroline Campbell, daughter of lord William Campbell, his majesty's late governor of Carolina—Oh, Hih! I now recollect thy words! cried Mi Li—And so she became princess of China.

---

9) A fictitious tomb in a beautiful spot by the river, built for a point of view: it has a small pyramid on it.

A True Love Story

In the height of the animosities between the factions of the Guelfs and Ghibellines, a party of Venetians had made an inroad into the territories of the Viscontis, sovereigns of Milan, and had carried off the young Orondates, then at nurse. His family were at that time under a cloud, though they could boast of being descended from Canis Scaliger, lord of Verona. The captors sold the beautiful Orondates to a rich widow of the noble family of Grimaldi, who having no children, brought him up with as much tenderness as if he had been her son. Her fondness increased with the growth of his stature and charms, and the violence of his passions were augmented by the signora Grimaldi's indulgence. Is it necessary to say that love reigned predominantly in the soul of Orondates? Or that in a city like Venice a form like that of Orondates met with little resistance?

The Cyprian queen, not content with the numerous oblations of Orondates on her altars, was not satisfied while his heart remained unengaged. Across the canal, overagainst the palace of Grimaldi, stood a convent of Carmelite nuns, the abbess of which had a young African slave of the most exquisite beauty, called Azora, a year younger than Orondates. Jet and japan were tawny and without lustre, when compared to the hue of Azora. Africa never produced a female so perfect as Azora; as Europe could boast but of one Orondates.

The signora Grimaldi, though no bigot, was pretty regular at her devotions, but as lansquenet was more to her taste than praying, she hurried over her masses as fast as she could, to allot more of her precious time to cards. This made her prefer the church of the Carmelites, separated only by a small bridge, though the abbess was of a contrary faction. However, as both ladies were of equal quality, and had had no altercations that could countenance incivility, reciprocal curtsies always passed between them, the coldness of which each pretended to lay on their attention to their devotions, though the signora Grimaldi attended but little to the priest, and the abbess was chiefly employed in watching and criticising the inattention of the signora.

Not so Orondates and Azora. Both constantly accompanied their mistresses to mass, and the first moment they saw each other was decisive in both breasts. Venice ceased to have more than one fair in the eyes of Orondates, and Azora had not remarked till then that there could be more beautiful beings in the world than some of the Carmelite nuns.

The seclusion of the abbess, and the aversion between the two ladies, which was very cordial on the side of the holy one, cut off all hopes from the lovers. Azora grew grave and pensive and melancholy; Orondates surly and intractable. Even his attachment to his kind patroness relaxed. He attended her reluctantly but at the hours of prayer. Often did she find him on the steps of the church ere the doors were opened. The signora Grimaldi was not apt to make observations. She was content with indulging her own passions, seldom restrained those of others; and though good offices rarely presented themselves to her imagination, she was ready to exert them when applied to, and always talked charitably of the unhappy at her cards, if it was not a very unlucky deal.

Still it is probable that she never would have discovered the passion of Orondates, had not her woman, who was jealous of his favour, given her a hint; at the same time remarking, under affectation of good will, how well the circumstances of the lovers were suited, and that as her ladyship was in years, and would certainly not think of providing for a creature she had bought in the public market, it would be charitable to marry the fond couple, and settle them on her farm in the country.

Fortunately madame Grimaldi always was open to good impressions, and rarely to bad. Without perceiving the malice of her woman, she was struck with the idea of a marriage. She loved the cause, and always promoted it when it was honestly in her power. She seldom made difficulties, and never apprehended them. Without even examining Orondates on the state of his inclinations, without recollecting that madame Capello and she were of different parties, without taking any precautions to guard against a refusal, she instantly wrote to the abbess to propose a marriage between Orondates and Azora.

The latter was in madame Capello's chamber when the note arrived. All the fury that authority loves to console itself with for being under restraint, all the asperity of a bigot, all the acrimony of party, and all the fictitious rage that prudery adopts when the sensual enjoyments of others are concerned, burst out on the helpless Azora, who was unable to divine how she was concerned in the fatal letter. She was made to endure all the calumnies that the abbess would have been glad to have hurled at the head of madame Grimaldi, if her own character and the rank of that offender would have allowed it. Impotent menaces of revenge were repeated with emphasis, and as nobody in the convent dared to contradict her, she gratified her anger and love of prating with endless tautologies. In fine, Azora was strictly locked up and bread and water were ordered as sovereign cures for love. Twenty replies to madame Grimaldi were written and torn, as not sufficiently expressive of a resentment that was rather vociferous than eloquent, and her confessor was at last forced to write one, in which he prevailed to have some holy cant inserted, though forced to compound for a heap of irony that related to the antiquity of her family, and for many unintelligible allusions to vulgar stories which the Ghibelline party had treasured up against the Guelfs. The most lucid part of the epistle pronounced a sentence of eternal chastity on Azora, not without some sarcastic expressions against the promiscuous amours of Orondates, which ought in common decorum to have banished him long ago from the mansion of a widowed matron.

Just as this fulminatory mandate had been transcribed and signed by the lady abbess in full chapter, and had been consigned to the confessor to deliver, the portress of the convent came running out of breath, and announced to the venerable assembly, that Azora, terrified by the abbess's blows and threats, had fallen in labour and miscarried of four puppies: for be it known to all posterity, that Orondates was an Italian greyhound, and Azora a black spaniel.

The Bird's Nest

Guzalme, Queen of Serendip, was reposing in the Pavilion of Odours on a couch made of down from the wings of butterflies, when a voice that could be heard only in a dream, said Look! Look! She turned her head, without opening her eyes, and saw a few paces from the window a tree of transparent rosewood, that produced vast bunches of white china cups and saucers, which cast a perfume like the breath of the houries.

On one of the upper branches appeared a bird's nest, composed of shreds of mignionette, trolly, and Brussels lace. Impatient to see what the nest contained, she climbed up the tree, without stirring off her couch, when happening to touch a flageolet that lay under the nest, it immediately sung an Italian air beginning, Vita dell' alma mia.

The Queen could have listened forever to the silver notes, but a large bud on a neighbouring bough blowing at the same instant and disclosing itself into the shape of a heart-looking-glass, she was transported to see herself a thousand times handsomer than ever, though she was before more beautiful than Azrouz, Solomon's favourite mistress. Concluding this wonderful flower was a present from heaven, she thought it would be a wicked sin ever to cease looking in it, and accordingly adjusting herself into the most languishing posture she could contrive, she determined to remain in that position forever.

She had scarce taken this pious resolution, when she heard a violent chattering of teeth and strange inarticulate sounds. Casting down her eyes towards the ground, she beheld a vast vermilion baboon, at least ten feet high, who, for she had forgot that she stood on a very high branch, and that there was a good deal of wind, seemed to be eagerly gazing at her garters that were set with eyes of turtle doves, and made a kind of amorous twilight within the circle of her surrounding garments.

Never was a situation so critically sentimental as her Majesty's. If she climbed higher, as her first thought directed, she would but expose her person still farther. If she leaped down, the danger was yet greater.

What could she do? Nothing but what a woman always does in critical cases—that is, nothing.

She was sure she had had no ill intention—fortune was to blame, and could she govern fortune? Determining therefore not to be accessory to whatever might happen, she resolved to forget that the baboon was there; but as it is one's duty to contribute all in one's power to convince a lover that he has no hopes, and as nothing can put even a disagreeable lover out of one's head, except thinking on one's self, she set herself with increase of earnestness to look again in the marvellous glass, but she found it much more difficult to please herself with an attitude. She changed her posture so often, that the baboon, who was an excellent mimic, could not help imitating her, so that every bird in the forest laughed till it cried again.

She was going to be angry, but a watch made of a grain of millet which she wore in her ear, happening to strike six, instead of the baboon she beheld at the foot of the tree a venerable man, clothed with white robes made of seed pearl that fell down to his feet; and that were gathered round his waist by a girdle of emeralds set like fig leaves, but the clasp was quite worn out it had been unbuckled so often, for he bathed in the Euphrates seven times every day, and he was now five thousand nine hundred and thirteen years old.

Addressing himself to the Queen, he said, Bright star of the morning, dispel your fears; in me behold the Patriarch Abraham!

Lord bless me! said she, and how came you here?

When I was conveyed from this world, replied he, by Azuriel the Angel of Death, as he was carrying my soul to heaven, a voice from this forest, cried out, oh you old villain, was not it enough to leave me and my poor babe Ishmael to starve in this desert, but do you think you shall go to heaven too without me!

Azuriel, continued she, I insist upon your taking me along with that deceiver.

Dear Madam, said the Angel, that is impossible. Somehow or other Sarah has got thither before you, and there will be no living in peace if you should meet. All I can do for you is this. Abraham shall one day in every week wander about this desert with you for twelve hours—but as you will not be the better for his company since he will be nothing but soul, and as Sarah will still make a racket if she sees him with you in his human form, he shall take the shape of any animal he pleases—and this metamorphosis he must submit to, till a more beautiful woman than you, with the finest shape, the blackest eyes, and the reddest lips in the world, shall come a-bird's-nesting in this forest.

I have now, continued Abraham to the Queen, undergone this penance above five thousand years, without any hopes of being relieved from it till a quarter of an hour ago, when I saw you sleeping in the Pavilion of Odours. It was I who whispered to you to look at this tree, and the event has answered my expectation. I have seen a woman more beautiful than Hagar—nay, Madam, do not blush—and you will see the Bird of Solomon. Look! Look!

The Queen, hearing a chirping over her head, cast up her eyes, and within the nest on a white satin quilt fringed with diamonds and turquoises she saw a little purple fig made of a link amethyst. It had a bullfinch's head of ruby and jet, a bill of topaz, and a tail of peacock's feathers, flounced with rainbows.

This dear little creature, which was thirty times less than the smallest hummingbird, sat upon two ostrich's eggs of opal—which was not at all extraordinary, for everything that belonged to Solomon had the gift of dilating itself to any magnitude; and it was as easy for the sweet little creature to extend itself over two ostrich's eggs, as it is to make a million of people drunk with a single glass of champagne, which may be soon effected if you can but get them into a wilderness where there is not a drop of wine, for all the difficulty of commiting a miracle consists in the impossibility: any body might perform one if it were possible. On one of the eggs were strange characters; on the other, in Hebrew letters, were the words, Oroknoz Alapol.

For heaven's sake, cried Guzalme, tell me the meaning of those words: there must be some wonderful virtue in them.

They are the names of a great philosopher, said Abram, who is wiser than Solomon, and writes more nonsense. The characters you do not understand are in the language of a western island, and signify the same as Oroknoz Alapol, which being interpreted, is, *the leanest of true believers*. He will fall in love with you, and will write fairy tales for your entertainment—but give me your hand, and let me help you down.

Stay a minute, said she, I will only get a few seeds of this looking-glass flower; it is the whitest I ever saw. I will have them raised in my green-house, and furnish all my rooms with them.

Having said those words, she stretched out her arm to gather the flower, but her foot slipping, she fell down—and waked.

Postscript

The foregoing Tales are given for no more than they are worth: they are mere whimsical trifles, written chiefly for private entertainment, and for private amusement half a dozen copies only are printed. They deserve at most to be considered as an attempt to vary the stale and beaten class of stories and novels, which, though works of invention, are almost always devoid of imagination. It would scarcely be credited, were it not evident from the Bibliotheque des Romans, which contains the fictitious adventures that have been written in all ages and all countries, that there should have been so little fancy, so little variety, and so little novelty, in writings in which the imagination is fettered by no rules, and by no obligation of speaking truth. There is infinitely more invention in history, which has no merit if devoid of truth, than in romances and novels, which pretend to none.

"Bird of Prey" is a darkly amusing comment upon the realistic story of contemporary people and their problems: jealousy, adultery, sick pets, etc. JOHN COLLIER makes it impossible to determine whether their problems were supernaturally created or whether magical circumstances merely made things worse. Collier, a man with a limber imagination, was one of the finest fantasists of this century and a master of irony and horror. Many of his stories have been televised by such respected directors as Alfred Hitchcock and Rod Serling.

Bird of Prey
BY JOHN COLLIER

The house they call the Engineer's House is now deserted. The new man from Baton Rouge gave it up after living less than a month in it, and built himself a two-room shack with his own money, on the very farthest corner of the company's land.

The roof of the Engineer's House has caved in, and most of the windows are broken. Oddly enough, no birds nest in the shelter of the eaves, or take advantage of the forsaken rooms. An empty house is normally fine harborage for rats and mice and bats, but there is no squeak or rustle or scamper to disturb the quiet of this one. Only creatures utterly foreign, utterly remote from the most distant cousinhood to man, only the termite, the tarantula, and the scorpion indifferently make it their home.

All in a few years Edna Spalding's garden has been wiped out, as if it had never existed. The porch where she and Jack sat so happily in the evenings is rotten under its load of wind-blown twigs and sand. A young tree has already burst up the boards outside the living room window, so that they fan out like the stiff fingers of someone who is afraid. In this corner there still stands a strongly made parrot's perch, the wood of which has been left untouched even by the termite and the boring beetle.

The Spaldings had brought a parrot with them when first they came. It was a sort of extra wedding present, given them at the last moment by Edna's mother. It was something from home for Edna to take into the wilds.

The parrot was already old, and he was called Tom, and, like other parrots, he sat on his perch, and whistled and laughed and uttered his few remarks, which were often very appropriate. Edna and Jack were both very fond of him, and they were overwhelmingly fond of each other. They liked their house, and the country, and Jack's colleagues, and everything in life seemed to be delightful.

One night they had just fallen asleep when they were awakened by a tremendous squawking and fluttering outside on the porch. "Oh, Jack!" cried Edna. "Get up! Hurry! Run! It's one of those cats from the men's camp has got hold of poor Tom!"

Jack sprang out of bed, but caught his foot in the sheet, and landed on his elbow on the floor. Between rubbing his elbow and disentangling his foot, he wasted a good many seconds before he was up again. Then he dashed through the living room and out upon the porch.

All this time, which seemed an age, the squawking and fluttering increased, but as he flung open the door it ceased as suddenly as it had begun. The whole porch was bathed in the brightest moonlight, and at the farther end the perch was clearly visible, and on the floor beneath it was poor old Tom parrot, gasping amid a litter of his own feathers, and crying, "Oh! Oh! Oh!"

At any rate, he was alive. Jack looked right and left for traces of his assailant, and at once noticed the long heavy trailers of the trumpet vine were swinging violently, although there was not a breath of wind. He went to the rail and looked out and around, but there was no sign of a cat. Of course, it was not likely there would be. Jack was more interested in the fact that the swaying vines were spread over a length of several feet, which seemed a very great deal of disturbance for a fleeing cat to make. Finally, he looked up, and he thought he saw a bird —a big bird, an enormous bird—flying away. He just caught a glimpse of it as it crossed the brightness of the moon.

He turned back and picked up old Tom. The poor parrot's chain was broken, and his heart was pounding away like mad, and still, like a creature hurt and shocked beyond all endurance, he cried, "Oh! Oh! Oh!"

This was all the more odd, for it was seldom the old fellow came out with a new phrase, and Jack would have laughed heartily, except it sounded too pathetic. So he carefully examined the poor bird, and, finding no injury beyond the loss of a handful of feathers from his neck, he replaced him on the perch, and turned to reassure Edna, who now appeared in the doorway.

"Is he dead?" cried she.

"No," said Jack. "He's had a bit of shock, though. Something got hold of him."

"I'll bring him a piece of sugar," said Edna. "That's what he loves. That'll make him feel better."

She soon brought the sugar, which Tom took in his claw, but though usually he would nibble it up with the greatest avidity, this time he turned his lackluster eye only once upon it, and gave a short, bitter, despairing sort of laugh, and let it fall to the ground.

"Let him rest," said Jack. "He has had a bad tousling."

"It was a cat," said Edna. "It was one of those beastly cats the men have at the camp."

"Maybe," said Jack. "On the other hand—I don't know. I thought I saw an enormous bird flying away."

"It couldn't be an eagle," said Edna. "There are none ever seen here."

"I know," said Jack. "Besides, they don't fly at night. Nor do the buzzards. It might have been an owl, I suppose. But—"

"But what?" said Edna.

"But it looked very much larger than an owl," said Jack.

"It was your fancy," said Edna. "It was one of those beastly cats that did it."

This point was discussed very frequently during the next few days. Everybody was consulted, and everybody had an opinion. Jack might have been a little doubtful at first, for he had caught only the briefest glimpse as the creature crossed the moon, but opposition made him more certain, and the discussions sometimes got rather heated.

"Charlie says it was all your imagination," said Edna. "He says no owl would ever attack a parrot."

"How the devil does *he* know?" said Jack. "Besides, I said it was bigger than an owl."

"He says that shows you imagine things," said Edna.

"Perhaps he would like me to think I do," said Jack. "Perhaps you both would."

"Oh, Jack!" cried Edna. She was deeply hurt, and not without reason, for it showed that Jack was still thinking of a ridiculous mistake he had made, a real mistake, of the sort that young husbands sometimes do make, when they come suddenly into a room and people are startled without any reason for it. Charlie was young and free and easy and good-looking, and he would put his hand on your shoulder without even thinking about it, and nobody minded.

"I should not have said that," said Jack.

"No, indeed you shouldn't," said Edna, and she was right.

The parrot said nothing at all. All these days, he had been moping and ailing, and seemed to have forgotten even how to ask for sugar. He only groaned and moaned to himself, ruffled up his feathers, and every now and then shook his head in the most rueful, miserable way you can possibly imagine.

One day, however, when Jack came home from work, Edna put her finger to her lips and beckoned him to the window. "Watch Tom," she whispered.

Jack peered out. There was the old bird, lugubriously climbing down from his perch and picking some dead stalks from the vine, which he carried up till he gained a corner where the balustrade ran into the wall, and added his gatherings to others that were already there. He trod round and round, twisted his stalks in and out, and, always with the same doleful expression, paid great attention to the nice disposition of a feather or two, a piece of wool, a fragment of cellophane. There was no doubt about it.

"There's no doubt about it," said Jack.

"He's making a nest!" cried Edna.

"He!" cried Jack. *"He!* I like that. The old imposter! The old male impersonator! She's going to lay an egg. Thomasina—that's her name from now on."

Thomasina it was. Two or three days later the matter was settled beyond the shadow of a doubt. There, one morning, in the ramshackle nest, was an egg.

"I thought she was sick because of that shaking she got," said Jack. "She was broody, that's all."

"It's a monstrous egg," said Edna. "Poor birdie!"

"What do you expect, after God knows how many years?" said Jack, laughing. "Some birds lay eggs nearly as big as themselves—the kiwi or something. Still, I must admit it's a whopper."

"She doesn't look well," said Edna.

Indeed, the old parrot looked almost as sick as a parrot can be, which is several times sicker than any other living creature. Her eyes closed up, her head sank, and if a finger was put out to scratch her she turned her beak miserably away. However, she sat conscientiously on the prodigious egg she had laid, though every day she seemed a little feebler than before.

"Perhaps we ought to take the egg away," said Jack. "We could get it blown, and keep it as a memento."

"No," said Edna. "Let her have it. It's all she's had in all these years."

Here Edna made a mistake, and she realized it a few mornings later. "Jack," she called. "Do come. It's Tom—Thomasina, I mean. I'm afraid she's going to die."

"We ought to have taken the egg away," said Jack, coming out with his mouth full of breakfast. "She's exhausted herself. It's no good, anyway. It's bound to be sterile."

"Look at her!" cried Edna.

"She's done for," said Jack, and at that moment the poor old bird keeled over and gasped her last.

"The egg killed her," said Jack, picking it up. "I said it would. Do you want to keep it? Oh, good lord!" He put the egg down very quickly. "It's alive," he said.

"What?" said Edna. "What do you mean?"

"It gave me a turn," said Jack. "It's most extraordinary. It's against nature. There's a chick inside that egg, tapping."

"Let it out," said Edna. "Break the shell."

"I was right," said Jack. "It *was* a bird I saw. It must have been a stray parrot. Only it looked so big."

"I'm going to break the shell with a spoon," said Edna, running to fetch one.

"It'll be a lucky bird," said Jack when she returned. "Born with a silver spoon in its beak, so to speak. Be careful."

"I will," said Edna. "Oh, I do hope it lives!"

With that, she gingerly cracked the shell, the tapping increased, and soon they saw a well-developed beak tearing its way through. In another moment, the chick was born.

"Golly!" cried Jack. "What a monster!"

"It's because it's young," said Edna. "It'll grow lovely. Like its mother."

"Maybe," said Jack. "I must be off. Put it in the nest. Feed it pap. Keep it warm. Don't monkey with it too much. Goodbye, my love."

That morning Jack telephoned home two or three times to find out how the chick was, and if it ate. He rushed home at lunchtime. In the evening everyone came round to peep at the nestling and offer advice.

Charlie was there. "It ought to be fed every hour at least," said he. "That's how it is in nature."

"He's right," said Jack. "For the first month, at least, that's how it should be."

"It looks as if I'm going to be tied down a bit," said Edna ruefully.

"I'll look in when I pass and relieve your solitude," said Charlie.

"I'll manage to rush home now and then in the afternoons," said Jack, a little too thoughtfully.

Certainly, the hourly feeding seemed to agree with the chick, which grew at an almost alarming speed. It became covered with down, feathers sprouted; in a few months it was fully grown, and not in the least like its mother. For one thing, it was coal-black.

"It must be a hybrid," said Jack. "There *is* a black parrot; I've seen them in zoos. They didn't look much like this, though. I've half a mind to send a photograph of him somewhere."

"He looks so wicked," said Edna.

"He looks cunning," said Jack. "That bird knows everything, believe me. I bet he'll talk soon."

"It gave a sort of laugh," said Edna. "I forgot to tell you."

"When?" cried Jack. "A laugh?"

"Sort of," said Edna. "But it was horrible. It made Charlie nearly jump out of his skin."

"Charlie?" said Jack. "You didn't say he'd been here."

"Well, you know how often he drops in," said Edna.

"Do I?" said Jack. "I hope I do. God! What was that?"

"That's what I meant," said Edna. "A sort of laugh."

"What a horrible sound!" said Jack.

"Listen, Jack," said Edna. "I wish you wouldn't be silly about Charlie. You are, you know."

Jack looked at her. "I know I am," said he. "I know it when I look at you. And then I think I never will be again. But somehow it's got stuck in my mind, and the least little thing brings it on. Maybe I'm just a bit crazy, on that one subject."

"Well, he'll be transferred soon," said Edna. "And that'll be the end of it."

"Where did you hear that?" said Jack.

"He told me this afternoon," said Edna. "He was on his way back from getting the mail when he dropped in. That's why he told me first. Otherwise he'd have told you first. Only he hasn't seen you yet. Do you see?"

"Yes, I see," said Jack. "I wish I could be psychoanalyzed or something."

Soon Charlie made his farewells, and departed for his job on the company's other project. Edna was secretly glad to see him go. She wanted no problems, however groundless, to exist between herself and Jack. A few days later she felt sure that all the problems were solved forever.

"Jack," said she when he came home in the evening.

"Yes," said he.

"Something new," said she. "Don't play with that bird. Listen to me."

"Call him Polly," said Jack. They had named it Polly to be on the safe side. "You don't want to call him 'that bird.' The missus doesn't love you, Poll."

"Do you know, I don't!" said Edna, with quite startling vehemence. "I don't like him at all, Jack. Let's give him away."

"What? For heaven's sake!" cried Jack. "This rare, black, specially hatched Poll? This parrot of romantic origin? The cleverest Poll that ever—"

"That's it," said Edna. "He's too darned clever. Jack, I hate him. He's horrible."

"What? Has he said something you don't like?" said Jack, laughing. "I bet he will, when he talks. But what's the news, anyway?"

"Come inside," said Edna. "I'm not going to tell you with that creature listening." She led the way into the bedroom. "The news is," said she, "that I've got to be humored. And if I don't like anything, it's got to be given away. It's not going to be born with a beak because its mother was frightened by a hateful monstrosity of a parrot."

"What?" said Jack.

"That's what," said Edna, smiling and nodding.

"A brat?" cried Jack in delight. "A boy! Or a girl! It's bound to be one or the other. Listen, I was afraid to tell you how much I wanted one, Edna. Oh, boy! This is going to make everything very, very fine. Lie down. You're delicate. Put your feet up. I'm going to fix dinner. This is practice. Stay still. Oh, boy! Oh, boy! Or girl, as the case may be!"

He went out through the living room on his way to the kitchen. As he passed the window, he caught sight of the parrot on the dark porch outside, and he put his head through to speak to it.

"Have you heard the news?" said he. "Behold a father! You're going to be cut right out, my bird. You're going to be given away. Yes, sir, it's a baby."

The parrot gave a long low whistle. "You don't say so?" said he in a husky voice, a voice of apprehension, a quite astonishing imitation of Charlie's voice. "What about Jack?"

"What's that?" said Jack, startled.

"He'll think it's his," whispered the parrot in Edna's voice. "He's fool enough for anything. Phew-w-w! You don't say so? What about Jack? He'll think it's his, he's fool enough for anything."

Jack went out into the kitchen, and sat down with his head in his hands for several minutes.

"Hurry up!" cried Edna from the bedroom. "Hurry up—*Father!*"

"I'm coming," said Jack.

He went to his desk, and took out the revolver. Then he went into the bedroom.

At the sound of the cry and the shot, the parrot laughed. Then, lifting its claw, it took the chain in its beak, and bit through it as if it were paper.

Jack came out, holding the gun, his hand over his eyes. "Fool enough for anything!" said the parrot, and laughed.

Jack turned the gun on himself. As he did so, in the infinitesimal interval between the beginning and the end of the movement of his finger on the trigger, he saw the bird grow, spread its dark wings, and its eyes flamed, and it changed, and it launched itself toward him.

The gun went off. Jack dropped to the floor. The parrot, or whatever it was, sailing down, seized what came out of his ruined mouth, and wheeled back through the window, and was soon far away, visible for a moment only as it swept on broader wings past the new-risen moon.

"Detective of Dreams," written in GENE WOLFE's *pseudo-gothic mode, is reminiscent of Edgar Allan Poe's detective stories such as "Murders in the Rue Morgue." Rather than restoring the world of the story to rational order at the end, as Poe did at the end of "Rue Morgue," Wolfe has chosen to end his story with events every bit as peculiar as those that precede them. This is the kind of story Poe might write were he alive today. Gene Wolfe is the author of the four-volume* The Book of the New Sun, *a contemporary masterpiece of fantasy, and of many short stories of fantasy, as well as an impressive body of science fiction and other writings.*

The Detective of Dreams
BY GENE WOLFE

I was writing in my office in the rue Madeleine when Andrée, my secretary, announced the arrival of Herr D⎯⎯⎯. I rose, put away my correspondence, and offered him my hand. He was, I should say, just short of fifty, had the high, clear complexion characteristic of those who in youth (now unhappily past for both of us) have found more pleasure in the company of horses and dogs and the excitement of the chase than in the bottles and bordels of city life, and wore a beard and mustache of the style popularized by the late emperor. Accepting my invitation to a chair, he showed me his papers.

"You see," he said, "I am accustomed to acting as the representative of my government. In this matter I hold no such position, and it is possible that I feel a trifle lost."

"Many people who come here feel lost," I said. "But it is my boast that I find most of them again. Your problem, I take it, is purely a private matter?"

"Not at all. It is a public matter in the truest sense of the words."

"Yet none of the documents before me—admirably stamped, sealed, and beribboned though they are—indicates that you are other than a private gentleman traveling abroad. And you say you do not represent your government. What am I to think? What is this matter?"

"I act in the public interest," Herr D⎯⎯⎯ told me. "My fortune is not great, but I can assure you that in the event of your success you will be well recompensed; although you are to take it that I alone am your principal, yet there are substantial resources available to me."

"Perhaps it would be best if you described the problem to me?"

"You are not averse to travel?"

"No."

"Very well then," he said, and so saying launched into one of the most astonishing relations—no, *the* most astonishing relation—I have ever been privileged to hear. Even I, who had at first hand the account of the man who found Paulette Renan with the quince seed still lodged in her throat; who had received Captain Brotte's testimony concerning his finds amid the antarctic ice; who had heard the history of the woman called Joan O'Neil, who lived for two years behind a painting of herself in the Louvre, from her own lips—even I sat like a child while this man spoke.

When he fell silent, I said, "Herr D_____, after all you have told me, I would accept this mission though there were not a *sou* to be made from it. Perhaps once in a lifetime one comes across a case that must be pursued for its own sake; I think I have found mine."

He leaned forward and grasped my hand with a warmth of feeling that was, I believe, very foreign to his usual nature. "Find and destroy the Dream-Master," he said, "and you shall sit upon a chair of gold, if that is your wish, and eat from a table of gold as well. When will you come to our country?"

"Tomorrow morning," I said. "There are one or two arrangements I must make here before I go."

"I am returning tonight. You may call upon me at any time, and I will apprise you of new developments." He handed me a card. "I am always to be found at this address—if not I, then one who is to be trusted, acting in my behalf."

"I understand."

"This should be sufficient for your initial expenses. You may call on me should you require more." The cheque he gave me as he turned to leave represented a comfortable fortune.

I waited until he was nearly out the door before saying, "I thank you, Herr Baron." To his credit, he did not turn; but I had the satisfaction of seeing a flush red rising above the precise white line of his collar before the door closed.

Andrée entered as soon as he had left. "Who was that man? When you spoke to him—just as he was stepping out of your office—he looked as if you had struck him with a whip."

"He will recover," I told her. "He is the Baron H_____, of the secret police of K_____. D_____was his mother's name. He assumed that because his own desk is a few hundred kilometers from mine, and because he does not permit his likeness to appear in the daily papers, I would not know him; but it was necessary, both for the sake of his opinion of me and my own of myself, that he should discover that I am not so easily deceived. When he recovers from his initial irritation, he will retire tonight with greater confidence in the abilities I will devote to the mission he has entrusted to me."

"It is typical of you, monsieur," Andrée said kindly, "that you are concerned that your clients sleep well."

Her pretty cheek tempted me, and I pinched it. "I am concerned," I replied; "but the Baron will not sleep well."

My train roared out of Paris through meadows sweet with wild flowers, to penetrate mountain passes in which the danger of avalanches was only just past. The glitter of rushing water, sprung from on high, was everywhere; and when the express slowed to climb a grade, the song of water was everywhere, too, water running and shouting down the gray rocks of the Alps. I fell asleep that night with the descant of that icy purity sounding through the plainsong of the rails, and I woke in the station of L_____, the old capital of J_____, now a province of K_____.

I engaged a porter to convey my trunk to the hotel where I had made reservations by telegraph the day before, and amused myself for a few hours by strolling about the city. Here I found the Middle Ages might almost be said to have remained rather than lingered. The city wall was complete on three sides, with its merloned towers in repair; and the cobbled streets surely dated from a period when wheeled traffic of any kind was scarce. As for the buildings—Puss in Boots and his friends must have loved them dearly: there were bulging walls and little panes of bull's-eye glass, and overhanging upper floors one above another until the structures seemed unbalanced as tops. Upon one grey old pile with narrow windows and massive doors, I found a plaque informing me that though it had been first built as a church, it had been successively a prison, a custom house, a private home, and a school. I investigated further, and discovered it was now an arcade, having been divided, I should think at about the time of the first Louis, into a multitude of dank little stalls. Since it was, as it happened, one of the addresses mentioned by Baron H_____, I went in.

Gas flared everywhere, yet the interior could not have been said to be well lit—each jet was sullen and secretive, as if the proprietor in whose cubicle it was located wished it to light none but his own wares. These cubicles were in no order; nor could I find any directory or guide to lead me to the one I sought. A few customers, who seemed to have visited the place for years, so that they understood where everything was, drifted from one display to the next. When they arrived at each, the proprietor came out, silent (so it seemed to me) as a specter, ready to answer questions or accept a payment; but I never heard a question asked, or saw any money tendered—the customer would finger the edge of a kitchen knife, or hold a garment up to her own shoulders, or turn the pages of some moldering book; and then put the thing down again, and go away.

At last, when I had tired to peeping into alcoves lined with booths still gloomier than the ones on the main concourse outside, I stopped at a leather merchant's and asked the man to direct me to Fräulein A_____.

"I do not know her," he said.

"I am told on good authority that her business is conducted in this building, and that she buys and sells antiques."

"We have several antique dealers here. Herr M_____–"

"I am searching for a young woman. Has your Herr M_____ a niece or a cousin?"

"—handles chairs and chests, largely. Herr O_____, near the guildhall—"

"It is within this building."

"—stocks pictures, mostly. A few mirrors. What is it you wish to buy?"

At this point we were interrupted, mercifully, by a woman from the next booth. "He wants Fräulein A_____. Out of here, and to your left; past the wigmaker's, then right to the stationer's, then left again. She sells old lace."

I found the place at last, and sitting at the very back of her booth Fräulein A_____ herself, a pretty, slender, timid-looking young woman. Her merchandise was spread on two tables; I pretended to examine it and found that it was not old lace she sold but old clothing, much of it trimmed with lace. After a few moments she rose and came out to talk to me, saying, "If you could tell me what you require? . . ." She was taller than I had anticipated, and her flaxen hair would have been very attractive if it were ever released from the tight braids coiled round her head.

"I am only looking. Many of these are beautiful—are they expensive?"

"Not for what you get. The one you are holding is only fifty marks."

"That seems like a great deal."

"They are the fine dresses of long ago—for visiting, or going to the ball. The dresses of wealthy women of aristocratic taste. All are like new; I will not handle anything else. Look at the seams in that one you hold, the tiny stitches all done by hand. Those were the work of dressmakers who created only four or five in a year, and worked twelve and fourteen hours a day, sewing at the first light, and continuing under the lamp, past midnight."

I said, "I see that you have been crying, Fräulein. Their lives were indeed miserable, though no doubt there are people today who suffer equally."

"No doubt there are," the young woman said. "I, however, am not one of them." And she turned away so that I should not see her tears.

"I was informed otherwise."

She whirled about to face me. "You know him? Oh, tell him I am not a wealthy woman, but I will pay whatever I can. Do you really know him?"

"No." I shook my head. "I was informed by your own police."

She stared at me. "But you are an outlander. So is he, I think."

"Ah, we progress. Is there another chair in the rear of your booth? Your police are not above going outside your own country for help, you see, and we should have a little talk."

"They are not our police," the young woman said bitterly, "but I will talk to you. The truth is that I would sooner talk to you, though you are French. You will not tell them that?"

I assured her that I would not; we borrowed a chair from the flower stall across the corridor, and she poured forth her story.

"My father died when I was very small. My mother opened this booth to earn our living—old dresses that had belonged to her own mother were the core of her original stock. She died two years ago, and since that time I have taken charge of our business and used it to support myself. Most of my sales are to collectors and theatrical companies. I do not make a great deal of money, but I do not require a great deal, and I have managed to save some. I live alone at Number 877 _____strasse; it is an old house divided into six apartments, and mine is the gable apartment."

"You are young and charming," I said, "and you tell me you have a little money saved. I am surprised you are not married."

"Many others have said the same thing."

"And what did you tell them, Fräulein?"

"To take care of their own affairs. They have called me a manhater —Frau G_____, who had the confections in the next corridor but two, called me that because I would not receive her son. The truth is that I do not care for people of either sex, young or old. If I want to live by myself and keep my own things to myself, is not it my right to do so?"

"I am sure it is; but undoubtedly it has occurred to you that this person you fear so much may be a rejected suitor who is taking his revenge on you."

"But how could he enter and control my dreams?"

"I do not know, Fräulein. It is you who say that he does these things."

"I should remember him, I think, if he had ever called on me. As it is, I am quite certain I have seen him somewhere, but I cannot recall where. Still . . ."

"Perhaps you had better describe your dream to me. You have the same one again and again, as I understand it?"

"Yes. It is like this. I am walking down a dark road. I am both frightened and pleasurably excited, if you know what I mean. Sometimes I walk for a long time, sometimes for what seems to be only a few moments. I think there is moonlight, and once or twice I have noticed stars. Anyway, there is a high, dark hedge, or perhaps a wall, on my right. There are fields to the left, I believe. Eventually I reach a gate of iron bars, standing open—it's not a large gate for wagons or carriages, but a small one, so narrow I can hardly get through. Have you read the writings of Dr. Freud of Vienna? One of the women here mentioned once that he had written concerning dreams, and so I got them from the library, and if I were a man I am sure he would say that entering that gate meant sexual commerce. Do you think I might have unnatural leanings?" Her voice had dropped to a whisper.

"Have you ever felt such desires?"

"Oh, no. Quite the reverse."

"Then I doubt it very much," I said. "Go on with your dream. How do you feel as you pass through the gate?"

"As I did when walking down the road, but more so—more frightened, and yet happy and excited. Triumphant, in a way."

"Go on."

"I am in the garden now. There are fountains playing, and nightingales singing in the willows. The air smells of lilies, and a cherry tree in blossom looks like a giantess in her bridal gown. I walk on a straight, smooth path; I think it must be paved with marble chips, because it is white in the moonlight. Ahead of me is the *Schloss*—a great building. There is music coming from inside."

"What sort of music?"

"Magnificent—joyous, if you know what I am trying to say, but not the tinklings of a theater orchestra. A great symphony. I have never been to the opera at Bayreuth; but I think it must be like that—yet a happy, quick tune."

She paused, and for an instant her smile recovered the remembered music. "There are pillars, and a grand entrance, with broad steps. I run up—I am so happy to be there—and throw open the door. It is brightly lit inside; a wave of golden light, almost like a wave from the ocean, strikes me. The room is a great hall, with a high ceiling. A long table is set in the middle and there are hundreds of people seated at it, but one place, the one nearest me, is empty. I cross to it and sit down; there are beautiful golden loaves on the table, and bowls of honey with roses floating at their centers, and crystal carafes of wine, and many other good things I cannot remember when I awake. Everyone is eating and drinking and talking, and I begin to eat too."

I said, "It is only a dream, Fräulein. There is no reason to weep."

"I dream this each night—I have dreamed so every night for months."

"Go on."

"Then he comes. I am sure he is the one who is causing me to dream like this because I can see his face clearly, and remember it when the dream is over. Sometimes it is very vivid for an hour or more after I wake—so vivid that I have only to close my eyes to see it before me."

"I will ask you to describe him in detail later. For the present, continue with your dream."

"He is tall, and robed like a king, and there is a strange crown on his head. He stands beside me, and though he says nothing, I know that the etiquette of the place demands that I rise and face him. I do this. Sometimes I am sucking my fingers as I get up from his table."

"He owns the dream palace, then."

"Yes, I am sure of that. It is his castle, his home; he is my host. I stand and face him, and I am conscious of wanting very much to please him, but not knowing what it is I should do."

"That must be painful."

"It is. But as I stand there, I become aware of how I am clothed, and—"

"How are you clothed?"

"As you see me now. In a plain, dark dress—the dress I wear here at the arcade. But the others—all up and down the hall, all up and down the table—are wearing the dresses I sell here. These dresses." She held one up for me to see, a beautiful creation of many layers of lace, with buttons of polished jet. "I know then that I cannot remain; but the king signals to the others, and they seize me and push me toward the door."

"You are humiliated then?"

"Yes, but the worst thing is that I am aware that he knows that I could never drive myself to leave, and he wishes to spare me the struggle. But outside—some terrible beast has entered the garden. I smell it —like the hyena cage at the *Tiergarten*—as the door opens. And then I wake up."

"It is a harrowing dream."

"You have seen the dresses I sell. Would you credit it that for weeks I slept in one, and then another, and then another of them?"

"You reaped no benefit from that?"

"No. In the dream I was clad as now. For a time I wore the dresses always—even here to the stall, and when I bought food at the market. But it did no good."

"Have you tried sleeping somewhere else?"

"With my cousin who lives on the other side of the city. That made no difference. I am certain that this man I see is a real man. He is in my dream, and the cause of it; but he is not sleeping."

"Yet you have never seen him when you are awake?"

She paused, and I saw her bite at her full lower lip. "I am certain I have."

"Ah!"

"But I cannot remember when. Yet I am sure I have seen him—that I have passed him in the street."

"Think! Does his face associate itself in your mind with some particular section of the city?"

She shook her head.

When I left her at last, it was with a description of the Dream-Master less precise than I had hoped, though still detailed. It tallied in almost all respects with the one given me by Baron H_____; but that proved nothing, since the baron's description might have been based largely on Fräulein A_____'s.

The bank of Herr R_____ was a private one, as all the greatest banks in Europe are. It was located in what had once been the town house of some noble family (their arms, overgrown now with ivy, were still visible above the door) and bore no identification other than a small brass plate engraved with the names of Herr R_____ and his partners. Within, the atmosphere was more dignified—even if, perhaps, less tasteful—than it could possibly have been in the noble family's time. Dark pictures in gilded frames lined the walls, and the clerks sat at inlaid tables upon chairs upholstered in tapestry. When I asked for Herr R_____, I was told that it would be impossible to see him that afternoon; I sent in a note with a sidelong allusion to "unquiet dreams," and within five minutes I was ushered into a luxurious office that must once have been the bedroom of the head of the household.

Herr R_____ was a large man—tall, and heavier (I thought) than his physician was likely to have approved. He appeared to be about fifty; there was strength in his wide, fleshy face; his high forehead and capacious cranium suggested intellect; and his small, dark eyes, forever flickering as they took in the appearance of my person, the expression of my face, and the position of my hands and feet, ingenuity.

No pretense was apt to be of service with such a man, and I told him flatly that I had come as the emissary of Baron H_____, that I knew what troubled him, and that if he would cooperate with me I would help him if I could.

"I know you, monsieur," he said, "by reputation. A business with which I am associated employed you three years ago in the matter of a certain mummy." He named the firm. "I should have thought of you myself."

"I did not know that you were connected with them."

"I am not, when you leave this room. I do not know what reward Baron H_____ has offered you should you apprehend the man who is oppressing me, but I will give you, in addition to that, a sum equal to that you were paid for the mummy. You should be able to retire to the south then, should you choose, with the rent of a dozen villas."

"I do not choose," I told him, "and I could have retired long before. But what you just said interests me. You are certain that your persecutor is a living man?"

"I know men." Herr R_____ leaned back in his chair and stared at the painted ceiling. "As a boy I sold stuffed cabbage-leaf rolls in the street—did you know that? My mother cooked them over wood she collected herself where buildings were being demolished, and I sold them from a little cart for her. I lived to see her with half a score of footmen and the finest house in Lindau. I never went to school; I learned to add and subtract in the streets—when I must multiply and divide I have my clerk do it. But I learned men. Do you think that now, after forty years of practice, I could be deceived by a phantom? No, he is a man—let me confess it, a stronger man than I—a man of flesh and blood and brain, a man I have seen somewhere, sometime, here in this city—and more than once."

"Describe him."

"As tall as I. Younger—perhaps thirty or thirty-five. A brown, forked beard, so long." (He held his hand about fifteen centimeters beneath his chin.) "Brown hair. His hair is not yet grey, but I think it may be thinning a little at the temples."

"Don't you remember?"

"In my dream he wears a garland of roses—I cannot be sure."

"Is there anything else? Any scars or identifying marks?"

Herr R_____ nodded. "He has hurt his hand. In my dream, when he holds out his hand for the money, I see blood in it—it is his own, you understand, as though a recent injury had reopened and was beginning to bleed again. His hands are long and slender—like a pianist's."

"Perhaps you had better tell me your dream."

"Of course." He paused, and his face clouded, as though to recount the dream were to return to it. "I am in a great house. I am a person of importance there, almost as though I were the owner; yet I am not the owner—"

"Wait," I interrupted. "Does this house have a banquet hall? Has it a pillared portico, and is it set in a garden?"

For a moment Herr R———'s eyes widened. "Have you also had such dreams?"

"No," I said. "It is only that I think I have heard of this house before. Please continue."

"There are many servants—some work in the fields beyond the garden. I give instructions to them—the details differ each night, you understand. Sometimes I am concerned with the kitchen, sometimes with the livestock, sometimes with the draining of a field. We grow wheat, principally, it seems; but there is a vineyard too, and a kitchen garden. And of course the house itself must be cleaned and swept and kept in repair. There is no wife; the owner's mother lives with us, I think, but she does not much concern herself with the housekeeping— that is up to me. To tell the truth, I have never actually seen her, though I have the feeling that she is there."

"Does this house resemble the one you bought for your own mother in Lindau?"

"Only as one large house must resemble another."

"I see. Proceed."

"For a long time each night I continue like that, giving orders, and sometimes going over the accounts. Then a servant, usually it is a maid, arrives to tell me that the owner wishes to speak to me. I stand before a mirror—I can see myself there as plainly as I see you now—and arrange my clothing. The maid brings rose-scented water and a cloth, and I wipe my face; then I go in to him.

"He is always in one of the upper rooms, seated at a table with his own account book spread before him. There is an open window behind him, and through it I can see the top of a cherry tree in bloom. For a long time—oh, I suppose ten minutes—I stand before him while he turns over the pages of his ledger."

"You appear somewhat at a loss, Herr R———not a common condition for you, I believe. What happens then?"

"He says, 'You owe . . .'" Herr R——— paused. "That is the problem, monsieur, I can never recall the amount. But it is a large sum. He says, 'And I must require that you make payment at once.'

"I do not have the amount, and I tell him so. He says, 'Then you must leave my employment.' I fall to my knees at this and beg that he will retain me, pointing out that if he dismisses me I will have lost my source of income, and will never be able to make payment. I do not enjoy telling you this, but I weep. Sometimes I beat the floor with my fists."

"Continue. Is the Dream-Master moved by your pleading?"

"No. He again demands that I pay the entire sum. Several times I have told him that I am a wealthy man in this world, and that if only he would permit me to make payment in its currency, I would do so immediately."

"That is interesting—most of us lack your presence of mind in our nightmares. What does he say then?"

"Usually he tells me not to be a fool. But once he said, 'That is a dream—you must know it by now. You cannot expect to pay a real debt with the currency of sleep.' He holds out his hand for the money as he speaks to me. It is then that I see the blood in his palm."

"You are afraid of him?"

"Oh, very much so. I understand that he has the most complete power over me. I weep, and at last I throw myself at his feet—with my head under the table, if you can credit it, crying like an infant."

"Then he stands and pulls me erect, and says, 'You would never be able to pay all you owe, and you are a false and dishonest servant. But your debt is forgiven, forever.' And as I watch, he tears a leaf from his account book and hands it to me."

"Your dream has a happy conclusion, then."

"No. It is not yet over. I thrust the paper into the front of my shirt and go out, wiping my face on my sleeve. I am conscious that if any of the other servants should see me, they will know at once what has happened. I hurry to reach my own counting room; there is a brazier there, and I wish to burn the page from the owner's book."

"I see."

"But just outside the door of my own room, I meet another servant—an upper-servant like myself, I think, since he is well dressed. As it happens, this man owes me a considerable sum of money, and to conceal from him what I have just endured, I demand that he pay at once." Herr R―――― rose from his chair and began to pace the room, looking sometimes at the painted scenes on the walls, sometimes at the Turkish carpet at his feet. "I have had reason to demand money like that often, you understand. Here in this room.

"The man falls to his knees, weeping and begging for additional time; but I reach down, like this, and seize him by the throat."

"And then?"

"And then the door of my counting room opens. But it is not my counting room with my desk and the charcoal brazier, but the owner's own room. He is standing in the doorway, and behind him I can see the open window, and the blossoms of the cherry tree."

"What does he say to you?"

"Nothing. He says nothing to me. I release the other man's throat, and he slinks away."

"You awaken then?"

"How can I explain it? Yes, I wake up. But first we stand there; and while we do I am conscious of . . . certain sounds."

"If it is too painful for you, you need not say more."

Herr R⎯⎯⎯ drew a silk handkerchief from his pocket and wiped his face. "How can I explain?" he said again. "When I hear those sounds, I am aware that the owner possesses certain other servants, who have never been under my direction. It is as though I have always known this, but had no reason to think of it before."

"I understand."

"They are quartered in another part of the house—in the vaults beneath the wine cellar, I think sometimes. I have never seen them, but I know—then—that they are hideous, vile and cruel; I know too that he thinks me but little better than they, and that as he permits me to serve him, so he allows them to serve him also. I stand—we stand—and listen to them coming through the house. At last a door at the end of the hall begins to swing open. There is a hand like the paw of some filthy reptile on the latch."

"Is that the end of the dream?"

"Yes." Herr R⎯⎯⎯ threw himself into his chair again, mopping his face.

"You have this experience each night?"

"It differs," he said slowly, "in some details."

"You have told me that the orders you give the under-servants vary."

"There is another difference. When the dreams began, I woke when the hinges of the door at the passage-end craaked. Each night now the dream endures a moment longer. Perhaps a tenth of a second. Now I see the arm of the creature who opens that door, nearly to the elbow."

I took the address of his home, which he was glad enough to give me, and leaving the bank made my way to my hotel.

When I had eaten my roll and drunk my coffee the next morning, I went to the place indicated by the card given me by Baron H_____, and in a few minutes was sitting with him in a room as bare as those tents from which armies in the field are cast into battle. "You are ready to begin the case this morning?" he asked.

"On the contrary. I have already begun; indeed, I am about to enter a new phase of my investigation. You would not have come to me if your Dream-Master were not torturing someone other than the people whose names you gave me. I wish to know the identity of that person, and to interrogate him."

"I told you that there were many other reports. I—"

"Provided me with a list. They are all of the petite bourgeoisie, when they are not persons still less important. I believed at first that it might be because of the urgings of Herr R_____ that you engaged me; but when I had time to reflect on what I know of your methods, I realized that you would have demanded that he provide my fee had that been the case. So you are sheltering someone of greater importance, and I wish to speak to him."

"The Countess—" Baron H_____ began.

"Ah!"

"The Countess herself has expressed some desire that you should be presented to her. The Count opposes it."

"We are speaking, I take it, of the governor of this province?"

The Baron nodded. "Of Count von V_____. He is responsible, you understand, only to the Queen Regent herself."

"Very well. I wish to hear the Countess, and she wishes to talk with me. I assure you, Baron, that we will meet; the only question is whether it will be under your auspices."

The Countess, to whom I was introduced that afternoon, was a woman in her early twenties, deep-breasted and somber-haired, with skin like milk, and great dark eyes welling with fear and (I thought) pity, set in a perfect oval face.

"I am glad you have come, monsieur. For seven weeks now our good Baron H_____ has sought this man for me, but he has not found him."

"If I had known my presence here would please you, Countess, I would have come long ago, whatever the obstacles. You then, like the others, are certain it is a real man we seek?"

"I seldom go out, monsieur. My husband feels we are in constant danger of assassination."

"I believe he is correct."

"But on state occasions we sometimes ride in a glass coach to the *Rathaus*. There are uhlans all around us to protect us then. I am certain that—before the dreams began—I saw the face of this man in the crowd."

"Very well. Now tell me your dream."

"I am here, at home—"

"In this palace, where we sit now?"

She nodded.

"That is a new feature, then. Continue, please."

"There is to be an execution. In the garden." A fleeting smile crossed the Countess's lovely face. "I need not tell you that that is not where the executions are held; but it does not seem strange to me when I dream.

"I have been away, I think, and have only just heard of what is to take place. I rush into the garden. The man Baron H_____ calls the Dream-Master is there, tied to the trunk of the big cherry tree; a squad of soldiers faces him, holding their rifles; their officer stands beside them with his saber drawn, and my husband is watching from a pace or two away. I call out for them to stop, and my husband turns to look at me. I say: 'You must not do it, Karl. You must not kill this man.' But I see by his expression that he believes that I am only a foolish, tenderhearted child. Karl is . . . several years older than I."

"I am aware of it."

"The Dream-Master turns his head to look at me. People tell me that my eyes are large—do you think them large, monsieur?"

"Very large, and very beautiful."

"In my dream, quite suddenly, his eyes seem far, far larger than mine, and far more beautiful; and in them I see reflected the figure of my husband. Please listen carefully now, because what I am going to say is very important, though it makes very little sense, I am afraid."

"Anything may happen in a dream, Countess."

"When I see my husband reflected in this man's eyes, I know—I cannot say how—that it is this reflection, and not the man who stands near me, who is the real Karl. The man I have thought real is only a reflection of that reflection. Do you follow what I say?"

I nodded. "I believe so."

"I plead again: 'Do not kill him. Nothing good can come of it. . . .' My husband nods to the officer, the soldiers raise their rifles, and . . . and . . .'"

"You wake. Would you like my handkerchief, Countess? It is of coarse weave; but it is clean, and much larger than your own."

"Karl is right—I am only a foolish little girl. No, monsieur, I do not wake—not yet. The soldiers fire. The Dream-Master falls forward, though his bonds hold him to the tree. And Karl flies to bloody rags beside me."

On my way back to my hotel, I purchased a map of the city; and when I reached my room I laid it flat on the table there. There could be no question of the route of the Countess's glass coach—straight down the Hauptstrasse, the only street in the city wide enough to take a carriage surrounded by cavalrymen. The most probable route by which Herr R⎯⎯ might go from his house to his bank coincided with the Hauptstrasse for several blocks. The path Fräulein A⎯⎯ would travel from her flat to the arcade crossed the Hauptstrasse at a point contained by that interval. I needed to know no more.

Very early the next morning I took up my post at the intersection. If my man were still alive after the fusillade Count von V⎯⎯ fired at him each night, it seemed certain that he would appear at this spot within a few days, and I am hardened to waiting. I smoked cigarettes while I watched the citizens of L⎯⎯ walk up and down before me. When an hour had passed, I bought a newspaper from a vendor, and stole a few glances at its pages when foot traffic was light.

Gradually I became aware that I was watched—we boast of reason, but there are senses over which reason holds no authority. I did not know where my watcher was, yet I felt his gaze on me, whichever way I turned. So, I thought, you know me, my friend. Will I too dream now? What has attracted your attention to a mere foreigner, a stranger, waiting for who-knows-what at this corner? Have you been talking to Fraulein A⎯⎯? Or to someone who has spoken with her?

Without appearing to do so, I looked up and down both streets in search of another lounger like myself. There was no one—not a drowsing grandfather, not a woman or a child, not even a dog. Certainly no tall man with a forked beard and piercing eyes. The windows then—I studied them all, looking for some movement in a dark room behind a seemingly innocent opening. Nothing.

Only the buildings behind me remained. I crossed to the opposite side of the Hauptstrasse and looked once more. Then I laughed.

They must have thought me mad, all those dour burghers, for I fairly doubled over, spitting my cigarette to the sidewalk and clasping my hands to my waist for fear my belt would burst. The presumption, the impudence, the brazen insolence of the fellow! The stupidity, the wonderful stupidity of myself, who had not recognized his old stories! For the remainder of my life now, I could accept any case with pleasure, pursue the most inept criminal with zest, knowing that there was always a chance he might outwit such an idiot as I.

For the Dream-Master had set up His own picture, and full-length and in the most gorgeous colors, in His window. Choking and spluttering I saluted it, and then, still filled with laughter, I crossed the street once more and went inside, where I knew I would find Him. A man awaited me there—not the one I sought, but one who understood Whom it was I had come for, and knew as well as I that His capture was beyond any thief-taker's power. I knelt, and there, though not to the satisfaction I suppose of Baron H_____, Fräulein A_____, Herr R_____, and the Count and Countess von V_____, I destroyed the Dream-Master as He has been sacrificed so often, devouring His white, wheaten flesh that we might all possess life without end.

Dear people, dream on.

FRANK R. STOCKTON was one of the most popular writers of the late nineteenth century in the United States. He wrote stories of all sorts, the most famous of all being "The Lady or the Tiger." His fantasy fiction stories were among the first published for adults in the United States, especially the stories contained in The Bee-man of Orn and Other Fanciful Tales *(1887). Stockton published fiction in* St. Nicholas, *the most famous of children's magazines, absorbing the children's fantasy tradition of his day and transmuting it in "The Bee-man of Orn," a bizarre and wonder-filled fantasy quest, and other stories.*

The Bee-man of Orn
BY FRANK R. STOCKTON

In the ancient country of Orn, there lived an old man who was called the Bee-man, because his whole time was spent in the company of bees. He lived in a small hut, which was nothing more than an immense beehive, for these little creatures had built their honey-combs in every corner of the one room it contained, on the shelves, under the little table, all about the rough bench on which the old man sat, and even about the head-board and along the sides of his low bed. All day the air of the room was thick with buzzing insects, but this did not interfere in any way with the old Bee-man, who walked in among them, ate his meals, and went to sleep, without the slightest fear of being stung. He had lived with the bees so long, they had become so accustomed to him, and his skin was so tough and hard, that the bees no more thought of stinging him than they would of stinging a tree or a stone. A swarm of bees had made their hive in a pocket of his old leathern doublet; and when he put on this coat to take one of his long walks in the forest in search of wild bees' nests, he was very glad to have this hive with him, for, if he did not find any wild honey, he would put his hand in his pocket and take out a piece of a comb for a luncheon. The bees in his pocket worked very industriously, and he was always certain of having something to eat with him wherever he went. He lived principally upon honey; and when he needed bread or meat, he carried some fine combs to a village not far away and bartered them for other food. He was ugly, untidy, shrivelled, and brown. He was poor, and the bees seemed to be his only friends. But, for all that, he was happy and contented; he had all the honey he wanted, and his bees, whom he considered the best company in the world, were as friendly and sociable as they could be, and seemed to increase in number every day.

One day, there stopped at the hut of the Bee-man a Junior Sorcerer. This young person, who was a student of magic, necromancy, and the kindred arts, was much interested in the Bee-man, whom he had frequently noticed in his wanderings, and he considered him an admirable subject for study. He had got a great deal of useful practice by endeavoring to find out, by the various rules and laws of sorcery, exactly why the old Bee-man did not happen to be something that he was not, and why he was what he happened to be. He had studied a long time at this matter, and had found out something.

"Do you know," he said, when the Bee-man came out of his hut, "that you have been transformed?"

"What do you mean by that?" said the other, much surprised.

"You have surely heard of animals and human beings who have been magically transformed into different kinds of creatures?"

"Yes, I have heard of these things," said the Bee-man; "but what have I been transformed from?"

"That is more than I know," said the Junior Sorcerer. "But one thing is certain—you ought to be changed back. If you will find out what you have been transformed from, I will see that you are made all right again. Nothing would please me better than to attend to such a case."

And, having a great many things to study and investigate, the Junior Sorcerer went his way.

This information greatly disturbed the mind of the Bee-man. If he had been changed from something else, he ought to be that other thing, whatever it was. He ran after the young man, and overtook him.

"If you know, kind sir," he said, "that I have been transformed, you surely are able to tell me what it is that I was."

"No," said the Junior Sorcerer, "my studies have not proceeded far enough for that. When I become a senior I can tell you all about it. But, in the meantime, it will be well for you to try to discover for yourself your original form, and when you have done that, I will get some of the learned masters of my art to restore you to it. It will be easy enough to do that, but you could not expect them to take the time and trouble to find out what it was."

And, with these words, he hurried away, and was soon lost to view.

Greatly disquieted, the Bee-man retraced his steps, and went to his hut. Never before had he heard any thing which had so troubled him.

"I wonder what I was transformed from?" he thought, seating himself on his rough bench. "Could it have been a giant, or a powerful prince, or some gorgeous being whom the magicians or the fairies wished to punish? It may be that I was a dog or a horse, or perhaps a fiery dragon or a horrid snake. I hope it was not one of these. But, whatever it was, every one has certainly a right to his original form, and I am resolved to find out mine. I will start early to-morrow morning, and I am sorry now that I have not more pockets to my old doublet, so that I might carry more bees and more honey for my journey."

He spent the rest of the day in making a hive of twigs and straw, and, having transferred to this a number of honey-combs and a colony of bees which had just swarmed, he rose before sunrise the next day, and having put on his leathern doublet, and having bound his new hive to his back, he set forth on his quest; the bees who were to accompany him buzzing around him like a cloud.

As the Bee-man passed through the little village the people greatly wondered at his queer appearance, with the hive upon his back. "The Bee-man is going on a long expedition this time," they said; but no one imagined the strange business on which he was bent. About noon he sat down under a tree, near a beautiful meadow covered with blossoms, and ate a little honey. Then he untied his hive and stretched himself out on the grass to rest. As he gazed upon his bees hovering about him, some going out to the blossoms in the sunshine, and some returning laden with the sweet pollen, he said to himself, "They know just what they have to do, and they do it; but alas for me! I know not what I may have to do. And yet, whatever it may be, I am determined to do it. In some way or other I will find out what was my original form, and then I will have myself changed back to it."

And now the thought came to him that perhaps his original form might have been something very disagreeable, or even horrid.

"But it does not matter," he said sturdily. "Whatever I was that shall I be again. It is not right for any one to retain a form which does not properly belong to him. I have no doubt I shall discover my original form in the same way that I find the trees in which the wild bees hive. When I first catch sight of a bee-tree I am drawn towards it, I know not how. Something says to me: 'That is what you are looking for.' In the same way I believe that I shall find my original form. When I see it, I shall be drawn towards it. Something will say to me: 'That is it.' "

When the Bee-man was rested he started off again, and in about an hour he entered a fair domain. Around him were beautiful lawns, grand trees, and lovely gardens; while at a little distance stood the stately palace of the Lord of the Domain. Richly dressed people were walking about or sitting in the shade of the trees and arbors; splendidly caparisoned horses were waiting for their riders; and everywhere were seen signs of opulence and gayety.

"I think," said the Bee-man to himself, "that I should like to stop here for a time. If it should happen that I was originally like any of these happy creatures it would please me much."

He untied his hive, and hid it behind some bushes, and taking off his old doublet, laid that beside it. It would not do to have his bees flying about him if he wished to go among the inhabitants of this fair domain.

For two days the Bee-man wandered about the palace and its grounds, avoiding notice as much as possible, but looking at every thing. He saw handsome men and lovely ladies; the finest horses, dogs, and cattle that were ever known; beautiful birds in cages, and fishes in crystal globes, and it seemed to him that the best of all living things were here collected.

At the close of the second day, the Bee-man said to himself: "There is one being here toward whom I feel very much drawn, and that is the Lord of the Domain. I cannot feel certain that I was once like him, but it would be a very fine thing if it were so; and it seems impossible for me to be drawn toward any other being in the domain when I look upon him, so handsome, rich, and powerful. But I must observe him more closely, and feel more sure of the matter, before applying to the sorcerers to change me back into a lord of a fair domain."

The next morning, the Bee-man saw the Lord of the Domain walking in his gardens. He slipped along the shady paths, and followed him so as to observe him closely, and find out if he were really drawn toward this noble and handsome being. The Lord of the Domain walked on for some time, not noticing that the Bee-man was behind him. But suddenly turning, he saw the little old man.

"What are you doing here, you vile beggar?" he cried; and he gave him a kick that sent him into some bushes that grew by the side of the path.

The Bee-man scrambled to his feet, and ran as fast as he could to the place where he had hidden his hive and his old doublet.

"If I am certain of any thing," he thought, "it is that I was never a person who would kick a poor old man. I will leave this place. I was transformed from nothing that I see here."

He now travelled for a day or two longer, and then he came to a great black mountain, near the bottom of which was an opening like the mouth of a cave.

This mountain he had heard was filled with caverns and underground passages, which were the abodes of dragons, evil spirits, horrid creatures of all kinds.

"Ah me!" said the Bee-man with a sigh, "I suppose I ought to visit this place. If I am going to do this thing properly, I should look on all sides of the subject, and I may have been one of those horrid creatures myself."

Thereupon he went to the mountain, and as he approached the opening of the passage which led into its inmost recesses he saw, sitting upon the ground, and leaning his back against a tree, a Languid Youth.

"Good-day," said this individual when he saw the Bee-man. "Are you going inside?"

"Yes," said the Bee-man, "that is what I intend to do."

"Then," said the Languid Youth, slowly rising to his feet, "I think I will go with you. I was told that if I went in there I should get my energies toned up, and they need it very much; but I did not feel equal to entering by myself, and I thought I would wait until some one came along. I am very glad to see you, and we will go in together."

So the two went into the cave, and they had proceeded but a short distance when they met a very little creature, whom it was easy to recognize as a Very Imp. He was about two feet high, and resembled in color a freshly polished pair of boots. He was extremely lively and active, and came bounding toward them.

"What did you two people come here for?" he asked.

"I came," said the Languid Youth, "to have my energies toned up."

"You have come to the right place," said the Very Imp. "We will tone you up. And what does that old Bee-man want?"

"He has been transformed from something, and wants to find out what it is. He thinks he may have been one of the things in here."

"I should not wonder if that were so," said the Very Imp, rolling his head on one side, and eying the Bee-man with a critical gaze.

"All right," said the Very Imp; "he can go around, and pick out his previous existence. We have here all sorts of vile creepers, crawlers, hissers, and snorters. I suppose he thinks any thing will be better than a Bee-man."

"It is not because I want to be better than I am," said the Bee-man, "that I started out on this search. I have simply an honest desire to become what I originally was."

"Oh! that is it, is it?" said the other. "There is an idiotic moon-calf here with a clam head, which must be just like what you used to be."

"Nonesense," said the Bee-man. "You have not the least idea what an honest purpose is. I shall go about, and see for myself."

"Go ahead," said the Very Imp, "and I will attend to this fellow who wants to be toned up." So saying he joined the Languid Youth.

"Look here," said that individual, regarding him with interest, "do you black and shine yourself every morning?"

"No," said the other, "it is water-proof varnish. You want to be invigorated, don't you? Well, I will tell you a splendid way to begin. You see that Bee-man has put down his hive and his coat with the bees in it. Just wait till he gets out of sight, and then catch a lot of those bees, and squeeze them flat. If you spread them on a sticky rag, and make a plaster, and put it on the small of your back, it will invigorate you like every thing, especially if some of the bees are not quite dead."

"Yes," said the Languid Youth, looking at him with his mild eyes, "but if I had energy enough to catch a bee I would be satisfied. Suppose you catch a lot for me."

"The subject is changed," said the Very Imp. "We are now about to visit the spacious chamber of the King of the Snap-dragons."

"That is a flower," said the Languid Youth.

"You will find him a gay old blossom," said the other. "When he has chased you round his room, and; has blown sparks at you, and has snorted and howled, and cracked his tail, and snapped his jaws like a pair of anvils, your energies will be toned up higher than ever before in your life."

"No doubt of it," said the Languid Youth; "but I think I will begin with something a little milder."

"Well then," said other, "there is a flat-tailed Demon of the Gorge in here. He is generally asleep, and, if you say so, you can slip into the farthest corner of his cave, and I'll solder his tail to the opposite wall. Then he will rage and roar, but he can't get at you, for he doesn't reach all the way across his cave; I have measured him. It will tone you up wonderfully to sit there and watch him."

"Very likely," said the Languid Youth; "but I would rather stay outside and let you go up in the corner. The performance in that way will be more interesting to me."

"You are dreadfully hard to please," said the Very Imp. "I have offered them to you loose, and I have offered them fastened to a wall, and now the best thing I can do is to give you a chance at one of them that can't move at all. It is the Ghastly Griffin and is enchanted. He can't stir so much as the tip of his whiskers for a thousand years. You can go to his cave and examine him just as if he were stuffed, and then you can sit on his back and think how it would be if you should live to be a thousand years old, and he should wake up while you are sitting there. It would be easy to imagine a lot of horrible things he would do to you when you look at his open mouth with its awful fangs, his dreadful claws, and his horrible wings all covered with spikes."

"I think that might suit me," said the Languid Youth. "I would much rather imagine the exercises of these monsters than to see them really going on."

"Come on, then," said the Very Imp, and he led the way to the cave of the Ghastly Griffin.

The Bee-man went by himself through a great part of the mountain, and looked into many of its gloomy caves and recesses, recoiling in horror from most of the dreadful monsters who met his eyes. While he was wandering about, an awful roar was heard resounding through the passages of the mountain, and soon there came flapping along an enormous dragon, with body black as night, and wings and tail of fiery red. In his great fore-claws he bore a little baby.

"Horrible!" exclaimed the Bee-man. "He is taking that little creature to his cave to devour it."

He saw the dragon enter a cave not far away, and following looked in. The dragon was crouched upon the ground with the little baby lying before him. It did not seem to be hurt, but was frightened and crying. The monster was looking upon it with delight, as if he intended to make a dainty meal of it as soon as his appetite should be a little stronger.

"It is too bad!" thought the Bee-man. "Somebody ought to do something." And turning around, he ran away as fast as he could.

He ran through various passages until he came to the spot where he had left his bee-hive. Picking it up, he hurried back, carrying the hive in his two hands before him. When he reached the cave of the dragon, he looked in and saw the monster still crouched over the weeping child. Without a moment's hesitation, the Bee-man rushed into the cave and threw his hive straight into the face of the dragon. The bees, enraged by the shock, rushed out in an angry crowd and immediately fell upon the head, mouth, eyes, and nose of the dragon. The great monster, astounded by this sudden attack, and driven almost wild by the numberless stings of the bees, sprang back to the farthest portion of his cave, still followed by his relentless enemies, at whom he flapped wildly with his great wings and struck with his paws. While the dragon was thus engaged with the bees, the Bee-man rushed forward, and, seizing the child, he hurried away. He did not stop to pick up his doublet, but kept on until he reached the entrance of the caves. There he saw the Very Imp hopping along on one leg, and rubbing his back and shoulders with his hands, and stopped to inquire what was the matter, and what had become of the Languid Youth.

"He is no kind of a fellow," said the Very Imp. "He disappointed me dreadfully. I took him up to the Ghastly Griffin, and told him the thing was enchanted, and that he might sit on its back and think about what it could do if it was awake; and when he came near it the wretched creature opened its eyes, and raised its head, and then you ought to have seen how mad that simpleton was. He made a dash at me and seized me by the ears; he kicked and beat me till I can scarcely move."

"His energies must have been toned up a good deal," said the Bee-man.

"Toned up! I should say so!" cried the other. "I raised a howl, and a Scissor-jawed Clipper came out of his hole, and got after him; but that lazy fool ran so fast that he could not be caught."

The Bee-man now ran on and soon overtook the Languid Youth.

"You need not be in a hurry now," said the latter, "for the rules of this institution don't allow the creatures inside to come out of this opening, or to hang around it. If they did, they would frighten away visitors. They go in and out of holes in the upper part of the mountain."

The two proceeded on their way.

"What are you going to do with that baby?" said the Languid Youth.

"I shall carry it along with me," said the Bee-man, "as I go on with my search, and perhaps I may find its mother. If I do not, I shall give it to somebody in that little village yonder. Any thing would be better than leaving it to be devoured by that horrid dragon."

"Let me carry it. I feel quite strong enough now to carry a baby."

"Thank you," said the Bee-man, "but I can take it myself. I like to carry something, and I have now neither my hive nor my doublet."

"It is very well that you had to leave them behind," said the Youth, "for the bees would have stung the baby."

"My bees never sting babies," said the other.

"They probably never had a chance," remarked his companion.

They soon entered the village, and after walking a short distance the youth exclaimed: "Do you see that woman over there sitting at the door of her house? She has beautiful hair and she is tearing it all to pieces. She should not be allowed to do that."

"No," said the Bee-man. "Her friends should tie her hands."

"Perhaps she is the mother of this child," said the Youth, "and if you give it to her she will no longer think of tearing her hair."

"But," said the Bee-man, "you don't really think this is her child?"

"Suppose you go over and see," said the other.

The Bee-man hesitated a moment, and then he walked toward the woman. Hearing him coming, she raised her head, and when she saw the child she rushed towards it, snatched it into her arms, and screaming with joy she covered it with kisses. Then with happy tears she begged to know the story of the rescue of her child, whom she never expected to see again; and she loaded the Bee-man with thanks and blessings. The friends and neighbors gathered around and there was great rejoicing. The mother urged the Bee-man and the Youth to stay with her, and rest and refresh themselves, which they were glad to do as they were tired and hungry.

They remained at the cottage all night, and in the afternoon of the next day the Bee-man said to the Youth: "It may seem an odd thing to you, but never in all my life have I felt myself drawn towards any living being as I am drawn towards this baby. Therefore I believe that I have been transformed from a baby."

"Good!" cried the Youth. "It is my opinion that you have hit the truth. And now would you like to be changed back to your original form?"

"Indeed I would!" said the Bee-man, "I have the strongest yearning to be what I originally was."

The Youth, who had now lost every trace of languid feeling, took a great interest in the matter, and early the next morning started off to inform the Junior Sorcerer that the Bee-man had discovered what he had been transformed from, and desired to be changed back to it.

The Junior Sorcerer and his learned Masters were filled with enthusiasm when they heard this report, and they at once set out for the mother's cottage. And there by magic arts the Bee-man was changed back into a baby. The mother was so grateful for what the Bee-man had done for her that she agreed to take charge of this baby, and to bring it up as her own.

"It will be a grand thing for him," said the Junior Sorcerer, "and I am glad that I studied his case. He will now have a fresh start in life, and will have a chance to become something better than a miserable old man living in a wretched hut with no friends or companions but buzzing bees."

The Junior Sorcerer and his Masters then returned to their homes, happy in the success of their great performance; and the Youth went back to his home anxious to begin a life of activity and energy.

Years and years afterward, when the Junior Sorcerer had become a Senior and was very old indeed, he passed through the country of Orn, and noticed a small hut about which swarms of bees were flying. He approached it, and looking in at the door he saw an old man in a leathern doublet, sitting at a table, eating honey. By his magic art he knew this was the baby which had been transformed from the Bee-man.

"Upon my word!" exclaimed the Sorcerer, "He has grown into the same thing again!"

"The Red Hawk" is a saga-like tale of a woman given control of the weather while one of the gods takes a rest. ELIZABETH A. LYNN won the World Fantasy Award for both short fiction and the novel in the 1970s, but has published only rarely since. *"The Red Hawk"* has heretofore appeared only in a limited edition, which garnered a World Fantasy Award nomination. This tale is a particularly fine example of the fantasy world that does not owe a great deal to any historical or mythic convention but is clearly and carefully planned as original.

The Red Hawk
BY ELIZABETH A. LYNN

This story comes from the youth of the world, from a time when even the gods were young. At that time the land of Ryoka lay much as it lies now, bordered to the east by the ocean and to the west by desert, to the south by the Crystal Lake, and to the north by mountains.

The mountains were taller then. The tallest of them were known as the Gray Peaks. Goats and foxes and red hawks lived upon them, and on clear days they seemed to float above the clouds, a place of wonder and mystery to those who lived below in the green valleys of the Ippan massif.

One day Tukalina the Black Goddess, shaper of the world, decided to leave Ryoka for a time and visit with Sedi, goddess of the moon, whose home is beneath the sea. She gazed at the earth, examining the greater patterns and the lesser, and it seemed to her that all was in order. . . . Yet the sister of order is mischief, and of all the creatures of the earth the winds are the most capricious, for they are formed of the very fabric of chaos. So Tukalina went to her son Vaikkenen. Vaikkenen was very dear to her, for he was still young and had come to his full strength, and he was very beautiful, with a ruddy face, and golden hair and beard.

Tukalina found him by a riverbank, sporting with a pride of hunting cats, and she said to him, *Dear son. I have decided to visit thy sister. I will be gone a little time. While I am gone, wilt thou cease thy play and take upon thyself the governance of the winds? For of all created beings, they are most treacherous.*

Vaikkenen lifted his shinning face to his mother's gaze and said, *I do not wish to halt my play. Do not ask it of me!* He stroked with his bare foot the flank of the tiger lolling at his side.

I will not, Tukalina said indulgently. *But while I am absent from the earth, be prudent, son of mine. In all thy amusements, do nothing to awaken thy grandmother!*

Vaikkenen swore that he would not. For when the Old One, the Mother, lies sleeping in Her cave which is the Void, it is not wise to awaken Her.

Tukalina bid a loving farewell to her son. She did not entirely trust his promise. But she knew that at the moment he so swore, he had meant each word that he said. For such is the nature of Vaikkenen, that he means whatever he says, though what he says may change from one moment to the next.

Tukalina then considered to whom she might entrust the governance of the winds. There were wise folk aplenty in Ryoka. But Tukalina did not want to entrust such power to a witch or wizard. She wanted someone who did not crave power, or fame, or fortune, someone who craved only knowledge, but cared little for magic; someone who was, in addition, solitary, a patient hermit.

And Tukalina remembered the astronomer of Ippa.

Tekkelé of Ippa had been born and bred in Nakasé County, on the great green floodplains where there are no mountains. But at the age when other girls are taking lovers, Tekkelé apprenticed herself to a stargazer, and by the time she was thirty her reputation had spread far beyond the borders of Nakasé and even into eastern Ryoka, to the seaport of Skyeggo, where the seabirds cry. Great honor might have been hers as navigator to one of the sealords, but Tekkelé had rejected such offers and chosen to travel to Ippa, to the Gray Peaks, to live in a cave on a bleak and stony hillside and watch the infinite patterns of the stars.

The mountain dwellers respected her and sometimes brought her news and food, but no one went to visit her save an old woman named Oshka, who once or twice a year appeared at the cave mouth, and she came to talk about the stars. Oshka was an avatar of Tukalina, who found Tekkelé's obsession with the stars rather restful. But this Tekkelé did not know.

So the ebony-skinned goddess wrapped about her the Cloak of Storms and spread her wings to the sky. She found the astronomer awake, as was her habit, observing the dawn. Tukalina stood within the cave and the stars glittered in her hair.

Tekkelé dropped to her knees in the dust.

"Get up, astronomer," Tukalina said. "Don't be afraid. You know me, although you do not know it." Tekkelé rose. Her knees hurt, and her heart was pounding. "I am not displeased with you. Diligently have you studied the movements of the stars, and there is much truth in what you know of wind and cloud and sky. But you will soon know much more, for into your hands, for a little time, I intend to entrust the winds' governance."

As the goddess spoke, the air in the cave began to whirl and coalesce. Out of that vortex five beings emerged to stand before the dumbfounded astronomer. The first was a golden-skinned child who smelled of ripe wheat ears, the second a red-maned mare, the third a leafclad dancing boy with the green eyes of a demon, and the fourth an ebony-skinned warrior with indigo eyes and hair. And the fifth was like a white winged man, but he had no hands or feet, only talons. They grinned at the astronomer and did not speak. "The yellow one is the east wind, and the red the south," the goddess said, "the green one is the west wind. The blue one is the north."

"And the other?" Tekkelé said.

"That is the wind of the upper sky, who never touches earth."

"I see," said Tekkelé dryly, though in all her years of study she had never heard of the wind of the upper sky. She gazed at the elementals, trying not to show her terror of them.

Tukalina approved of her courage. She will do, she thought. "Come here," she said. Tekkelé went across the cavern to where the goddess stood, and upon her narrow shoulders Tukalina laid the Cloak of Storms.

Then, to Tekkelé's further astonishment, the goddess changed into the frail and wrinkled old woman with whom she had spoken only half a year before. "You see, we have met," said the goddess gently.

But Tekkelé clasped her hands together and shivered where she stood. It did not help that she recognized Oshka. Did I patronize her? she wondered. She might have; she was more used to the company of hawks and goats than she was to goddesses. "Dread goddess," she began, and stopped. She had forgotten how to use her tongue. "I am honored by your trust in me. Nevertheless, I beg you, choose another for this task. I am a stupid mortal woman, who—"

"Mortal," Tukalina said, "but not stupid."

"I would not know what to say to them."

The goddess-crone smiled. "I will tell you," she said. "Follow me." Tekkelé followed her to the bare rock plateau outside the cave. It was protected on the north and was the astronomer's frequent stargazing platform. Drawing Tekkelé to her, Tukalina touched her tongue to Tekkelé's eyelids, nose, and mouth. "Now, look!" she said, and released her.

Tekkelé gasped. The rocks enclosing the plateau seemed to melt. She stood upon the very crown of a high peak, and below her, visible in all its length and breadth, stretched the land of Ryoka. She saw into every corner of it, from the shores of the ocean where the ships of the sealords prowled, to the meanest hill farm in the Ippan range, to the orchards of the Talvelai clan in Issho, to the caravans of the nomads camped by the shores of the Crystal Lake. *I had not known there were so many people on the earth,* she thought. And then she saw—no, felt —no, *knew*—another thing. She *knew* where on that earth the rain had to fall, the sun to shine. She knew how the cloud packs gathered. She knew where the lightning was born. She knew it with the certainty that accompanied no other piece of knowledge in her soul, except that knowledge every woman has of her own body which is given to her by the Mother.

And despite her confusion, her heart rejoiced. *Perhaps,* she thought, *perhaps I may even see the patterns of the stars with this sight.*

"You shall come here in the morning," Tukalina said, "before dawn. You shall look out on the earth. You shall put around you the Cloak of Storms, and when you have seen, as you are seeing now, the patterns of wind and light and weather, the winds will feel your power, and they will come. Hold in your soul that pattern you discern, and the winds will perceive it too. Then say to them, 'Go about thy daily business, O winds!' They will obey."

Tekkelé stared uneasily at the dancing wind wraiths. "They will?"

"I have so charged them," Tukalina said.

Tekkelé did not doubt the Black Goddess's power. Clenching her fingers on the Cloak, she said, "Go about thy daily business, O winds!"

The winds bowed, and sped into the sunrise.

"It is as I thought," said Tukalina. "Your strength will master them." She lifted her arms. Before Tekkelé could say another word, the old woman had vanished. A giant raven stood in her place. The red hawks screamed homage as the raven circled the rocks. Then, swifter than a new-shot arrow, it rose above the mountains and headed east.

Tekkelé the astronomer sighed. I wish I had had some time to think about it, she thought. But one did not dispute a goddess. I thought I was a stargazer. Now I am a hero. . . . She looked at her hands. They were not heroic; they were not even comely; they were rough and scarred, ink-stained now, the knuckles swollen, and they pained her in the winter. Walking to her sleeping place, she stretched her fingers toward the fire.

Aloud she said, "I have not changed. I am what I have always been."

She slipped the Cloak of Storms from her shoulders, marveling at its lack of weight. Folding it in a square, she laid it in the wooden chest that sat by her bed. Then, yawning, she went to roll her charts and store her tools away, for now that day had come, she would sleep.

One month passed.

Two months passed, then half a year. For the folk of Ryoka it seemed a year like any other: sun and moon followed their accustomed paths. Spring yielded to summer, to autumn, to winter; children were born; the old died, and their souls fell through the cracks in the earth to the void, where they waited to be reborn at the will of the Mother. Only the wise, who study the gods, knew that something had changed, and only the greatest of those knew what it was.

But for Tekkelé the astronomer, everything had changed. It had happened slowly, but it had happened; she was no longer solitary. Faces surrounded her. She saw them when she rose from sleep in the afternoons. She read them in her books and in her star-charts: the faces of women whose children starved when the harvest failed, the faces of men whose entire crop had been flattened by a hailstorm. They came between her and the stars. Fiercely she told them: "I did not do it!" The faces did not care. "I only see the patterns, I do not make them." In her mind they cursed her. In the silences of night, pacing the caverns, she cried to the rocks, "I cannot bear this grief, I am too weak!" Yet she bore it, and she endured the presence of the winds each morning. They did not speak to her: she did not know if they could speak, but sometimes they laughed.

She guessed that they were laughing at her guilt, and hated them for it. She wished she were not human, as they were not. She wished she could not feel.

Sometimes she wished that she were dead.

The months wore on. Each day Tekkelé prayed that Tukalina would soon appear and take her torment from her. But Tukalina did not come. It seemed to Tekkelé that the goddess had chosen not to honor her for her strength and diligence, but to punish her. She grew bitter. She began to hate herself, and all Ryoka, including the gods, and even the stars in their serene, indifferent glory.

The Cloak of Storms seemed to grow heavier each time she put it on.

Meanwhile, Vaikkenen played in the western hills. Though a year had passed for the folk of Ryoka, for Vaikkenen his mother had been absent from the earth a week: time moves differently for mortals than for elementals. He had barely noted her departure anyway; he was occupied with whatever young gods do when no one is watching them. But though he was young, his power was growing, and its aura clung to him as heat to flame. So the winds in their journeys sought him out, hoping to amuse him by what they told him. In this they were being true to their natures—for they could see that Vaikkenen the god had a much greater capacity for mischief than they did.

From the winds Vaikkenen learned that a mortal woman had been entrusted with the governance of the winds, that she lived in the north, and that her name was Tekkelé. At first he paid scant attention to what the winds said of her, but after a while their descriptions piqued his interest. It intrigued him that she lived alone, that she watched the stars, and that his mother had chosen her to govern the winds. Seeing his curiosity aroused, the cunning winds spoke often of Tekkelé, until Vaikkenen began to think that he would go and look upon this astronomer. It rather annoyed him that his mother had put the winds into her care. *He* was destined for such power. It should not have been given to a mortal. So Vaikkenen reasoned, choosing to forget that when Tukalina offered him governance of the winds, he had preferred to play.

Therefore Vaikkenen took the shape of a red hawk, and flew to the Ippan range. In the lower mountains below the Gray Peaks he again changed shape. "I am a wizard from the desert," he told the mountainfolk, casually dropping a ruby from his mouth. "My name is Tiera. I seek Tekkelé the stargazer. What do you know of her?"

They would have told him anything. "She is old," said one hunter, "aged beyond her years."

"She speaks with no one. She refuses visitors."

"She even refuses food! I left half a goat, fresh-killed, near her cave last week; when I passed by two days later, it was still there."

"You know," said a woman thoughtfully, "she was not like this before."

"When did she change?" Vaikkenen asked.

The mountainfolk conferred. "She has been like this for months," they said.

Donning the red hawk shape, Vaikkenen flew to Tekkelé's cave. It was sunset. Stars were blooming in the east. Perching on a crag, he preened his feathers and waited for the astronomer to emerge from her sleeping place.

He waited. The sky darkened. At last she appeared, a thin and colorless woman, moving slowly, clad in tattered furs. Vaikkenen was unimpressed. She was scrawny, he thought, her face care-lined, her mouth too severe. But then he noticed the thick length of hair falling down her back, and the uncommon grace of her carriage, and the tremendous intelligence in her eyes. She was not ugly, he decided; indeed, a discerning viewer might say that she was beautiful. The mountainfolk had exaggerated their few glimpses of her into untruths.

Then Vaikkenen was aroused, and the feathers of the hawk glittered like flame. Sharp-eyed Tekkelé saw the glow out of the corner of her eye. First she thought it a trick of the light, and then she thought it was the south wind come to tease her, and, angered, she called, "Come out!" Vaikkenen abandoned the hawk shape and resumed the form of the youthful wizard that he had worn that day. But it was not the same shape, not quite. That shape had been simple and as diffident as a god pretending to be a wizard can be. This shape was not diffident. It was young, and beautiful, and filled with promise.

And Tekkelé said, "Who are you, stranger?" She was not happy to see him. The sight of any human face was a reproach to her; she wanted nothing to do with humankind.

Vaikkenen said, "I am Tiera, a wizard from the western hills. But I was told that an ugly crone lived amid these rocks. I find a beautiful woman. I must go to punish the fools who told me lies." He transformed himself into the hawk shape, and spread his wings as if to fly away.

"Wait!" Tekkelé cried, for she did not want him to go. Like most mortals that Vaikkenen encounters, she thought him the most beautiful of men, with his honey-red skin and his wheat-gold hair, and his jet black eyes. . . . But Tekkelé, like the mountain dwellers, had been deceived by her own pain: she thought herself ugly. She said with grim regret, "Do not hurt the folk who spoke to you. They told the truth."

Vaikkenen became Tiera once more. "They lied," he insisted. "Look at yourself." A mirror appeared between his two spread hands.

And, as Tekkelé gazed into it, he took away the pain that ruled her face and the coarse poverty of her garments, and clothed her in warmth and comfort. Tekkelé gasped at the feel of silk on her skin. She stared at her clothes: they were her own to look at, but they felt like—like—

"Stop!" she said.

"As you wish," said Vaikkenen. He returned to her the poverty of her tunic, her old leather boots, her grime-encrusted furs. But he did not give her back her pain. Instead, taking her hand, he led her out of the chill waste of twilight to her sleeping cave. There he took her in his arms and said, "I love you." And, because at that moment he believed what he said, Tekkelé believed him too, and loved him, and put her arms about him in turn, and brought him in delight to her bed.

Just before dawn she rose. The cave smelled of sex and sweat and roses, at least she thought it was roses; it had been months since she had smelled a rose. Pressed against the wall on her narrow cot, Tiera the wizard slept, arms and legs sprawling. Next to him lay the depression where she had lain through the night. As she watched, he muttered something and reached to it, to her. Kneeling to remove the Cloak of Storms from her chest, Tekkelé damned herself for seven kinds of a fool. He was a stranger. He was beautiful, while she was, if not ugly, then certainly plain. He was, she guessed, twenty, or a little older, and she was forty-two, and a recluse, and her bones hurt. . . . He opened his eyes and looked at her. "Are you going away?" he said, plaintive as a child, and her heart melted all over again.

"Sleep," she said to him, rising with the Cloak of Storms in her palm. "I will return soon."

She closed the chest lid and walked from her sleeping cave to the vale of stone, where she would meet the winds. Standing in its center, she put over her shoulders the Cloak of Storms. Grimly she endured the knowledge of future famines, droughts, and human agony that came to her; courageously she invited the presence of the winds. They came and danced about her, and it seemed to her that they laughed at her more than ever that morning, especially the red south wind. Shaking with pain, she returned to the cave to find Tiera the wizard sitting against the wall, waiting for her.

"Come," he said, "let me smooth the lines from your face."

Tekkelé caught his hands as he reached for her. "Wait," she said. "You are—this has been lovely. But I know you cannot mean to stay here—" He stopped the rest of the sentence with a kiss.

"I will do anything you bid me do," he said when their lips parted, "except leave your side."

Because he meant it, she believed him.

So Vaikkenen stayed in the cave of Tekkelé the astronomer. He praised her beauty until she began to believe that she was indeed beautiful; he marveled at her knowledge of the stars until she began to think that maybe there was value to the work she had months ago ceased doing. She taught him to read star-charts, and he sat with her uncomplaining through the coldest nights, his body heat keeping her warm. When she needed to be alone, he went walking in the mountains until she desired him back. In exchange for her teaching him the patterns of the stars, he taught her a shape-changing spell, a simple one. At first she was afraid to use it, but one day he coaxed her into taking hawk shape. . . . Tekkelé was entranced. Never had she known such freedom. In hawk shape she could escape the earth and all its pain. "They are cleaner than humankind," she exclaimed to Tiera. She watched them as she watched the stars, and discovered that they, too, followed patterns: that the female hawks tended to be larger than the males, for instance, and that they mated for life. As hawk—as in her lover's arms—she could escape the faces whose torment wrung her soul.

Eight months to the day that Tiera the wizard had come to her, Tekkelé was delivered of girl twins. She named the first of them Laikkimi, which means "hawk." The second she named Shiro, which means "ruby."

The children grew quickly. By the time they were three years old —three years in which Tekkelé, who had never intended to have children and had thought that she did not like children, observed them with the hunger she once reserved for the stars—they had the semblance and poise and intelligence of children who are eight years old. Tekkelé thought them wonderful. It amazed her that they were so distinct: she had expected that two beings who looked alike would behave alike, yet they were different. Laikkimi was gentle and generous and laughed a great deal, and Shiro was fierce. "Thous should have had they sister's name," Tekkelé told her, "for thou are as swift in anger and in defense as a young hawk." Yet the twins were alike, too, and in the manner of all children, they grew restless. To assuage their restlessness, and because she did not want her daughters to grow used to solitude, Tekkelé began to change her reclusive habits.

The first time she entered the village of the mountainfolk—the same Vaikkenen had spoken with, four years back—they did not recognize her.

"I am the stargazer," she told them. She pushed Shiro and Laikkimi in front of her. "These are my daughters."

They were wary. "Who was their father?" a woman asked.

"Tiera the wizard."

"The one who drips rubies when he talks?"

Tekkelé laughed. Tiera had showed her that trick. "The same. Look, his daughter does it too. Shiro, my heart, do as thy father taught thee. Let a red jewel slip from thy tongue."

"He did not teach me," Shiro said. "I did it by myself." But thus coaxed, she spat a ruby into her mother's palm. "I thought," Tekkelé said, "since we are neighbors, that I might bring my children here sometimes. It grows lonely in the cave."

"Of course," said the villagers, wondering if Shiro could be induced to do her trick again, "anytime."

One more year passed. Laikkimi and Shiro grew like weeds in a marsh. One night, as Tekkelé sat gazing at star-patterns, at that configuration of stars which astronomers before her had named the Lizard, she realized that something about it was different. In the cluster of stars —four large ones, two small ones—which made up the Lizard's left front claw, there were two new stars.

She hurried to her charts. Perhaps she was mistaken. But the stars were not in her star-charts. She hunted through her books, squinting at the light, wondering if her charts were wrong. Her charts were not wrong. She raced out again, ignoring Tiera's muttered protest at the rush of cold that swept the cavern. The new stars were still there. She went back to her chart room, and, hands shaking, mixed up ink and found a sharp-nibbed pen. Then she marked the new stars on the chart and wrote in the margin: "Observed, this 17th day of the month of the

Goat, in the Year of the Fish, two stars, white, separated two degrees from one another and one degree southwest of their nearest neighbor in the cluster which is the left front talon of the constellation Lizard, the 4th hour after midnight, by Tekkelé of Ippa."

She signed her name. Then she entered their sleeping room and shook wakeful her daughters. "Come. I want you to see something."

"I don't want to," Shiro said.

Laikkimi whined, "It's too cold."

But Tekkelé was not cold; she did not think she would ever be cold again. Patiently she pushed them outside and told them where to look, insisted that they find the Lizard's claw, remember the Lizard? They did. See that little red star, and then the other red star close by, and next to it the two white stars?

They saw them. So?

"So," said Tekkelé, "those two stars were not there last night. Or the night before. Or ever before."

Laikkimi was polite. "That's interesting, Mama." Shiro grumbled, and went back to bed. Tekkelé stared at the night sky, smiling. She decided she had never been so happy. She wondered if she should wake Tiera and show him the new stars, and decided it would wait until the next night. Even the mocking wind wraiths held little terror for her now. Too excited to sleep, she paced the caverns composing a message to Jouvi of Nakasé, her old teacher.

But Vaikkenen was bored. Tekkelé and her stars had ceased to interest him. He was still fond of her, but he was a young god, and his attention span was short. He had forgotten what he had come north to do. It had involved the wind wraiths; probably it had not been important. The weeks, in his perception, that he had been Tiera the wizard had been amusing. Tekkelé, he knew, would miss him. He would miss her, for a while.

He did not think he would miss the children; he preferred tiger cubs.

So the next day, when Tekkelé and the children traveled down the mountain trails to the nearest large village, hoping to find someone to carry a message south, Vaikkenen departed. He left no farewell, for the gods are not accustomed to explaining themselves. He had come as the red hawk; he would leave as the red hawk, wild and free, needing nothing.

At the last moment, knowing that Tekkelé would thank him for rendering her unable to do a task she hated, he removed the Cloak of Storms from the chest by the bed they had shared and took it with him.

The journey down the mountain was arduous but uneventful. Tekkelé was still euphoric. Laikkimi and Shiro were excited; they had never been farther from home than the mountaindwellers' huts, and now they were going to a big village, almost a town! Tekkelé beguiled them with descriptions of the bazaar and the treasures it held—"ribbons, and iron pots, brass rings, bells, lace and cloth." Their eyes grew wide to think of it.

It took several hours to reach the village. It was indeed more than a cluster of huts. It had four streets. A wooden statute of Tukalina greeted travelers as they came through the gate. Tekkelé bowed to it, thinking as she did that it did not much resemble that austere goddess. For one thing, it had no nose.

"I hear music, Mama," said Laikkimi.

"So do I," Tekkelé answered. "Go see where it is. Mind your manners! I shall be here." She pointed to the headman's house. While the children scampered toward the bazaar, Tekkelé knocked, and was admitted. The headman's name was Arpa, the mountainfolk had told her, and he was slow. It was generally believed that his wife, Shouk, was the true administrator of the village.

The house was small but clean; it smelled of goat's milk and tallow. Arpa was a chubby, slow-speaking man with fat little hands like a baby's. Shouk was thin and quick, with yellow teeth. When Tekkelé introduced herself, she was asked to sit, and Shouk brought tea. She had heard of this woman, whose daughters dripped rubies from their tongues, and whose husband was a wizard.

Tekkelé came right to the point. "I need someone to take a message to Nakasé."

Arpa blinked. Tekkelé thought idly that he looked like a toad. "I will pay five rubies," she said.

The headman frowned. People were not usually so direct with him; it confused him. He glanced at his wife.

"Uma could go," she said. "He has been to Nakasé twice. He knows the roads." The two women gazed at one another and acknowledged that kinship between them which all women are given and which comes to them from the Mother.

"I should like to meet this Uma," Tekkelé said. Uma was sent for. He was a broad-featured man of about Tekkelé's age.

"What shall I say, and to whom?" he asked.

"You shall seek out Jouvi the astronomer, and you shall say to him, the Lizard's left foot has grown new toes. If he is dead, may the Mother show him mercy, give that message to whoever inherited his charts. Be sure to say the message comes from Tekkelé of Ippa."

Uma repeated the message. He wondered if the astronomer was mad, with this talk of lizards and toes, but there was a woman in Nakasé he liked better than his wife, who was older than he, and nagged. "And my pay?"

"When will you leave?"

"If I am paid today, I will leave tomorrow."

"Your pay is two rubies," Tekkelé said. She spilled five rubies from the pouch around her neck—she had coaxed them from Shiro that morning—and laid them in Arpa's palm. He held one to the light, rolled it between his fingers, and passed it and a second to Uma.

Shouk said. "He is an honorable man."

"Thank you," Tekkelé said. Suddenly there was a patter of hands against the door, and Shiro and Laikkimi burst into the headman's hut.

"Mama, look what a man gave me!" cried Shiro, waving a blue scarf. Laikkimi rang a brightly polished bell.

"These are my daughters," Tekkelé said, catching each by an ear. "Stand quietly, imps!" Arpa's dull eyes grew moist; he was sentimental about children, especially girls. "Compose thyselves; we must go."

But the twins set up a wail. "Please, Mama, I want to stay," Laikkimi implored.

Imperious Shiro hit her mother on the leg. "I want to ride the goat!"

Shouk lifted the lid from the pot on the hearth. The meat smell made Tekkelé's knees buckle. She had not eaten since sunset of the night before. Prompted by his wife's gaze, Arpa cleared his throat and muttered something about the midday meal.

I do need food, Tekkelé thought. Not to stay would be impolite. . . . "Thank you," she said. Shrieking with pleasure, the girls raced from the hut.

The meat was goat's meat, and it was very good. Tekkelé ate meat and rice, and drank tea, as did Shouk. Arpa drank some milky beverage which, Shouk said, was fermented goat's milk. Tekkelé tried some. It made her loquacious. While Arpa went for a walk, she told Shouk about the new stars and about her golden lover who had come to her in the shape of a hawk. Shouk shared with her the gossip about Uma's wife, who got drunk and threw pots.

The day waned. At last Tekkelé rose to leave. She walked, with Shouk, to the bazaar to find the children. The weather had turned chill; the merchants were shuttering their shops. Gray clouds coursed southward across the sky.

"The lowlands will have rain tonight," said Shouk.

As she spoke, a gust of wind nearly blew them off their feet. An awning tore loose from the front of a nearby shop. Swearing, a man seized it and began to roll it up. "Stargazer," the village woman said, "you should not climb the mountain in such ugly weather. Stay the night. Sleep in our hut."

Tekkelé was touched. But in seventeen years she had not spent a night away from her cave. "I cannot," she said.

"Then let your children stay," Shouk said. "They have not the strength to battle this wind."

Tekkelé frowned. The weather *was* foul. It would do no harm for Laikkimi and Shiro to sleep in the village for one night.

She called them. "How would you like to sleep here tonight?"

They were overjoyed. "But where will you be, Mama?" Laikkimi asked.

"I will go home to Papa. He will be lonely if I do not. But we shall come get you tomorrow. Do not be a trouble to these kind folk!"

"Oh, no," said Shiro. Tekkelé kissed them, wondering if she were doing right. I should not have had that taste of goat's milk, she thought.

Arpa and Shouk escorted her to the foot of the trail. "Take care," Arpa said. " 'Ware winds."

"I do not fear the winds," answered Tekkelé.

The fermented goat's milk was warm within her as she fought her way up the trail. The winds swirled, plucking at her clothes as if they sought to jar her from her perch. The rocks tore her hands. She bound them and went on. Once she glimpsed a flock of mountain goats, and marveled at their uncanny balance, and once she saw—or thought she saw, in the growing darkness—a huge sapphire-eyed black bear that she knew to be an avatar of the north wind.

Tired beyond thought, she stumbled through the cave into calm. "Tiera," she called, "I am here."

But Tiera was not. He was not in the sleeping room, nor in the chart room, nor in that open space from which she ordered the winds, nor in the storage cave. Panicked, Tekkelé screamed his name to the night, but only the winds answered. Heedless of her own peril, she looked for him, sure that he had fallen while gathering herbs and lying on the stones, broken, lost. . . . She did not find him. At last, too worn to weep, she returned to her bed.

In the morning she opened her chest and discovered that the Cloak of Storms was missing.

Shiro and Laikkimi woke with the sun. They had been put to bed in a hayloft, which they found exciting. Both had acquired fleas. They ate the morning meal with the headman and his wife, and even picky Laikkimi ate everything that was set before her. After all, their mother had told them not to be a trouble. They then went to play in the bazaar, where they fought with the village children and tormented the merchants.

As the day wore on, Shouk grew concerned. Tekkelé had said she and her man would return for the twins, and Tekkelé, she felt sure, was not the sort of woman to betray a promise. Fearing that the astronomer had injured herself climbing to her cave, Shouk spoke with her husband. "Someone should go and see."

He disagreed. "What can harm a wizard?"

But Shouk had her way, and two men were sent on the journey to the astronomer's cave. They went up swiftly.

They came more swiftly down, and their yellow faces were gray as ash. "What did you see?" Shouk said.

"Ruin," they said, shuddering. "Ruin and devastation. No one was there. Everything was burnt. We found neither man nor woman, just a red hawk which sat on a smoking pile and screamed at us."

"Were there charts?" Shouk asked, although she was not sure what a chart was. "Clothing, foodstuffs—"

"Nothing!" said the younger of the two, and the whites of his eyes showed. "Some angry god has been there. We did not dare stay—" A wild shriek interrupted him. A great red hawk soared above their heads. Shouk recalled that Tekkelé had told her that Tiera had first come to her in the shape of a red hawk. It is the wizard, she thought. And she wondered what dreadful fate had befallen Tekkelé of Ippa.

"The poor babes," she said. "To lose at one time both mother and father. We must care for them." For she thought, practically, one of them spits rubies, and who knows what the other can do? Her own children were grown. "The poor lost babes," she said. Arpa agreed. He was sentimental about children, especially girl children.

So Shouk called Shiro and Laikkimi to her and told them what the men had seen. "Your mother and father are gone, but you shall live with us." She expected them to be afraid, and to weep, and then, in the manner of the young, to forget. But Shiro and Laikkimi were the daughters of Tekkelé and Vaikkenen, and they were not like other children.

Stony-faced, they stared at Shouk. "I do not believe you," Shiro said.

"Our mother would not leave her cave," said Laikkimi.

"Our father is a wizard. No one harms a wizard."

"We will see," they declared in unison. To Shouk's astonishment, they marched from the hut and began to ascend the trail to the peak.

"Huh," grunted one old woman who claimed wisdom. "They are not children at all, but demons." Intrigued whispers echoed around the village. If we harbor them, some folk said, perhaps we, too, will offend the gods. The men who had been to the cave described what they had seen there, with elaborations.

And when Laikkimi and Shiro returned, faces chalk-white, they were met by a host of frightened, angry people throwing stones and yelling curses.

"Go away!" the villagers shouted, except for Arpa, who disliked noise, and Shouk, who stayed within her house and fumed at her neighbors' stupidity. "You are not wanted!"

"We will go," said Shiro fiercely, "but you will be sorry!" With that childish, ominous threat the twins turned and ran from the village. Sick at heart, and not a little frightened by what had happened to their home, they struggled south. Suddenly a hawk's raucous call shrilled above them. They glanced up. A great red hawk was circling over them, calling. It was a familiar sound.

"Perhaps Father sent it," Laikkimi said hopefully. She had frequently heard from her mother how her father had come to the cave in the guise of a hawk.

"I think it means for us to follow it," Shiro said. So follow they did, to a half-fallen lean-to at the edge of a stream. "We can sleep here," said Shiro. The hawk, screaming agreement, plunged to perch on the roof-beam. Shiro prodded the still standing planks. "This wood is good, not rotten." They pushed inside. "Look, here is a blanket, and a cooking pot, and a ring of stones for a hearth. You shall have to make a fire, Laiki." For that was one of Laikkimi's gifts, that she could make fire flow from her fingers.

They gathered wood, and Laikkimi made a fire in the hearth. Shiro made a broom out of a pine branch, and swept the lean-to clean. She found a rope, and two fishhooks, and a knife, and, elated, took them outside, where she quickly caught first one fish, then another. She hit them with a stone to kill them. Cleaning them was messy, but she managed it, and, leaving what she did not want for the hawk, brought the flesh to the fire and laid it on the stones. Afterward the girls lay in the dark hut with their arms about each other, and did what they had refused to do in front of the villagers—they wept.

"I hate those people," Shiro said. "They threw rocks at us. I would like to hurt them. We could burn their huts."

But Laikkimi disagreed. "That woman was kind to us, and she did not throw stones. I don't want to burn her hut."

They did not burn the village. But they did not return to it for fear of being met with stones. They made their home in the lean-to, and survived by trapping small animals and fishing in the stream, and, occasionally, stealing from the village. After a few weeks the villagers decided that they had been hasty—as Shouk pointed out, throwing stones at ten-year-old girls won no favor of the gods—and sent to see if the twins would return. But Laikkimi and Shiro wanted nothing to do with humankind. "Be off," Shiro cried, "or we shall kill you and skin you and wrap your hides about our feet!" Such was the power of Vaikkenen's daughters that the villagers believed them, and ran, while overhead, in a voice filled with menace, the red hawk wheeled, screaming.

And in the fertile meadows of Ryoka, Vaikkenen played. He thought not at all of Tekkelé the astronomer or of his two abandoned daughters: he was having too much fun seducing the maidens of the rich, scattering the cattle of the poor, and riding wild horses until they foundered from exhaustion. Possessing the Cloak of Storms gave him mastery over the winds, but such is his nature that, having attained what he wanted, he no longer wanted it. At first he did what Tekkelé had done: each morning before sunrise he would call the winds and order them to be about their business. But though a god, Vaikkenen does not share his mother's knowledge, and so he could not see what they had to do. Without knowledge, the power to command means very little. Therefore, it began to bore him. The task was the same each time; there was no challenge in it, no spice or excitement. So he ceased to do it—it was a task fit only for mortals, he told himself—and ordered the capricious winds one morning to "Do what thou wilt!"

They were happy to obey him. Directionless, they scattered, driving all before them across the world. A month passed. Two months; then half a year. Across the face of Ryoka, lamentation and misery started to rise. Rain no longer fell when it should or where it should. Crops withered in the soil. Snow did not fall in winter, and the rivers no longer rose in spring to flood the land. Grain did not sprout. Patterns that had held for generations failed. There was no food, no water save salt water, which humanfolk cannot drink. Balance and order shattered, and rich and poor alike died.

In terror people knelt in prayer, mouths against the earth, begging mercy from the Mother. All over Ryoka women and men spoke. And in Her sleep, the Old One heard. She did not wake, but, troubled in dream, She shifted uneasily on Her bed.

The stricken earth groaned. Fissures gaped. Springs dried. Fires spouted from the stone. Humankind trembled, and in her cave beneath the sea, Sedi lifted her head and exclaimed, *Grandmother is restless! What can be wrong?*

Tukalina, who had felt it, too, said grimly, *I do not know, and I should. This has been a pleasant visit, daughter.* Rising up through the sea, the goddess cloaked herself in cloud and rode the back of a waterspout to the nearest point of land. It turned out to be Skyeggo harbor, the great trading port of the east. She looked for the sails of the trading ships and did not see them. She went to the docks. The ships lay broken on the sand, and about them lay corpses. In the city streets she found more dead. The city seemed a charnel house. She sniffed the air, the moist air that flows from the sea and drives pestilence before it. It was bitter, hot, and dry.

The winds are loose, ungoverned, the goddess thought. *I smell chaos.* And spreading her dark wings over the wretched city, Tukalina flew north to the Gray Peaks.

There she found ruin, and the memory of pain. The pain shouted at her from the walls as she stood in Tekkelé's empty chambers. There was no sign of the astronomer's presence—the malicious winds had long since scattered the scraps of her charts—but as Tukalina walked through the caverns a glint of red caught her eye. She bent and picked it up. It was a ruby.

The Black Goddess stalked to the stone plateau from which Tekkelé had called the winds, and spread her arms to the sky. She did not have the Cloak of Storms, but then, she did not need it. Filled with righteous anger, she summoned the errant winds. She waited. And waited, and still they did not come; they were far from the sound of even a goddess's voice, playing on the edge of the world. At last they heard the puissant call, and came and bowed before her, trembling. Only the icy wind of the sky did not quake, for he knew that, rage as she might, even Tukalina could not unmake them.

But she could, she pointed out to them in asperity, return them to the Void, that great vast darkness beneath the earth, and summon other spirits to take their places in the unbounded sky. "Others can assume the duties you have so shamefully neglected. Look at what you have done! Ryoka lies in torment, and who will its poor people blame? Me! You owe me an accounting. Tell me what happened to Tekkelé of Ippa."

So the winds that had refused to speak to Tekkelé spoke to their mistress of Tekkelé's anguish at her task, of Vaikkenen's curiosity, of his coming to the Gray Peaks, and of what had occurred in the five years he remained there.

When they finished, the goddess said, "Well do I know, O winds, that my son would not have come to this place if he had not been told of it, and who should tell him of it but you? I do not hold you guiltless in these matters. You"—she pointed to the golden-skinned child and the red-maned mare—"shall go and find for me the Cloak of Storms which my son has no doubt dropped or thrown aside or hidden in some place he has since forgotten, and bring it to me." The east and south winds bowed and danced into the sky. "You"—pointing to the leafclad boy and the ebony-skinned warrior—"shall find Tekkelé of Ippa. "They also bowed and disappeared. "And you," she said to the white wind of the sky, "shall find my son."

"I go," he said, and went.

The yellow east wind found the Cloak of Storms wrapped around a thorn bush in a swamp. Plucking it from that fetid place, he called the south wind to him. Together they returned to Tukalina and laid the Cloak at her feet. The white wind of the sky returned and said, "I have seen your son. He lies in a bower domed with flowers that he has built in the southern plains."

"I see," Tukalina said. How like my son, she mused. The land starves around him, and he builds a house of flowers in which to hide. O Vaikkenen! Saddened, she awaited the return of the west and north winds. At last they came. "Well," demanded the goddess, "where is Tekkelé?"

"O Tukalina," they answered, "we cannot find her."

The Black Goddess drew herself to her full height and spread her wings. They blotted out the sun. "O winds," she said, "now hope within they malignant hearts that Tekkelé is not dead. For if she has gone before her time to the Void, I promise you shall return there as well to serve her shade. Begone from my sight!"

The chastened winds departed to take up the tasks they had ignored for so long. Tukalina, her rage subsiding, held the Cloak of Storms to the light. It was tattered from its sojourn in the thorn bush. She healed its rents with a touch and let it fall around her shoulders. O Vaikkenen, she thought, would that I could as easily heal the ills that you unthinking heaped upon Ryoka!

Then, setting aside her divinity, Tukalina assumed the guise of the old woman Oshka. She did not expect to find Tekkelé: but somewhere on the mountainside were Laikkimi and Shiro, Tekkelé's children, and even immortals hate to incur debts. Tukalina could not help but feel she owed them something.

Life had not been easy for Laikkimi and Shiro since their parents had vanished from the cave and they had been driven from the village. Life had grown hard in the mountains. Winter lasted overlong that year, and the spring foliage took a long time to rise: when it did, the buds were shriveled and stunted. The leaf-eating animals of the slopes moved south; the predators, bereft of food, began to attack the mountaindwellers. First they killed the cattle, then the human beings. The villagers left their homes, those that could. Those that could not, died.

Laikkimi and Shiro survived by watching the goats and eating what they did, and by stealing from the villagers as they succumbed to starvation. They stole bows and arrows and guessed how to use them;

they stole pots and pans and metal things that they could not make for themselves. The red hawk nested in an ancient spruce tree near the shack. She had stayed with them, and on days when they could not find food she hunted for them, bringing them rabbits and forest birds and even an occasional chicken. She screamed to warn them when the hunting cats of the mountains came too close, and once had flown at a panther which, drawn by the scent of the two girls, had approached the hut at dusk. Sometimes she would disappear for days on end, only to reappear battered and tired, with a few feathers missing.

Laikkimi first saw the old woman while gathering the soft inner bark of the sweet birch, which is good to eat. Ceasing to strip the bark, she watched the stranger climb slowly and steadily along the trail. Then, gathering up what she had foraged, Laikkimi went to find Shiro.

Shiro heard the news with surprise and unease. "Who can it be? Is it one of the village folk? I thought they were dead."

"No," Laikkimi said. "I do not know her. She is old; her hair is gray and her skin dry and wrinkled."

Shiro fingered her bow and arrows. "If she is an enemy," she declared, "I will kill her."

Laikkimi said, "I do not think she is an enemy."

"You are sure you do not know her?"

"I'm sure," Laikkimi said.

And when Tukalina arrived at the shack beside the stream, she found Shiro standing in the doorway, bow strung, aiming an arrow at her breast. She knew that she had found those she sought.

"Peace to you," she said gravely. "Do not shoot; I mean no harm."

"Who are you?" Shiro said.

"My name is Oshka."

"What do you want?"

"I am looking for someone who used to live north of here."

Laikkimi emerged from the shack. "Who?"

"Tekkelé the astronomer."

Laikkimi gasped. "You know her?" Shiro said.

"I did know her. She lived in a cave on the peak."

"She is not there," Shiro said. "Go back to where you came from and tell them that she is gone."

"Is she dead?" Tukalina asked.

"No!" the children cried in unison.

"I will tell them," said Tukalina. She gazed at the two, marveling at their size and strength. Human children do not grow so fast, she thought. Do they know what they are? They were lean as dogs. "May I offer you food? I have some."

Laikkimi licked her lips. Shiro's arrow tip sagged. "What sort of food?" she asked. Her sister shot her a reproachful glance. What did it matter what sort of food it was? They would eat it.

"This," said the disguised goddess, and she caused four small but perfect peaches to appear in her hands. They were yellow and pink and soft with down. A sweet fragrance drifted across the clearing to the famished children.

Shiro moaned, and dropped the bow. The girls ran like goats to Tukalina's side. Two of the peaches vanished so swiftly that it seemed as if they had been swallowed whole. The girls reached for the next two —and hesitated.

Laikkimi said, "One of these is yours, Old One."

"I have had mine," said Tukalina. Their generosity despite their hunger pleased her greatly. "Take them."

Suddenly a hawk's scream ripped the air. It was the red hawk, returning from the hunt. She dived, still shrieking, coming to protect the children who were dear to her as her life. Tukalina recognized the human soul under the bristling feathers, and even her immortal heart was wrung.

"Tekkelé!" she said, and gestured with one hand, casting off her own disguise as she did so. So named in mid-strike, Tekkelé the red hawk faltered. Her feathers dropped away; she landed on the earth a human woman wearing tattered clothes.

"Mother!" cried the girls, and ran to touch her.

She backed from them, shivering, and her eyes were vague and wild.

"Wait," said the goddess. The children stared, awestruck, at the majestic winged woman whose skin was black as night. "In a moment she will know you. Watch her eyes." And as the children waited, hearts pounding, the wild eyes changed and became those of Tekkelé, their mother whom they had lost.

They went to her, and held her, weeping.

"Mother," said Shiro, torn between delight and tears, "how is it you are so little?" For the twins were taller than their mother. Tekkelé's hair, once black, was gray, and she was spare and lean as the hawk whose shape she had stolen.

She gazed at Tukalina with a hawk's steady stare.

"Tekkelé of Ippa," said the goddess, "can you speak?" For mortals who have worn animal shape sometimes lose their power to make human sounds.

"I speak," said Tekkelé. The words emerged in a hoarse croak, but they were human.

"Can you listen?"

"I listen."

"Then know," said the Black Goddess, "that the being you knew as Tiera the wizard is in truth Vaikkenen, my son. Deeply has he wronged you, and all Ryoka, by his theft of the Cloak of Storms. For this, and for his having disturbed his grandmother, he shall be punished. Is there aught he might do for you to make amends for the harm he has already done?"

Tekkelé cocked her head to one side. With the passion that she once had reserved for the stars, she hated Tiera the wizard. Long distances had she flown in her hawk shape, hoping to find him. Her fingers curled like talons.

"I want to eat his eyes," she said.

"That you may not do," said the Black Goddess.

Tekkelé's fingers uncurled; the wildness left her face, and weariness replaced it. "Then I want nothing," she said. Her human intelligence was coming back to her. She had had enough, she thought, of gods and goddesses and of the gifts of gods and goddesses. . . .

"Do you wish to remain here?" Tukalina said. "I can return you to Nakasé."

But the twins objected to this. "She shall stay with us!" exclaimed Shiro. The twins watched their mother anxiously. Much had happened that they did not understand: the hawk that had guarded them for half a year had turned out to be their mother; their father, it seemed, was a god, and their mother hated him although once she had loved him. . . .

"I will stay," Tekkelé said. "It is as good as any other place." She gazed indifferently at the shack, the stubby blue trees, the stream, the mountains, and then at her daughters. "Perhaps it is better than some others."

She needs rest, the goddess thought. The frailty of mortals constantly surprised her. She spread her wings until their tips brushed the sky. "I will see that you are not disturbed," the Black Goddess promised.

Her shadow fell over the valley. The winds regarded it, and understood that neither storm nor heat nor flood was to touch it. The spirits of earth likewise saw it. Small animals sensed it and began to move toward the hut, hoping that there they would be safe from predators. Tukalina folded her wings. Then, wrapping the Cloak of Storms about her, she sped south.

She found Vaikkenen asleep beneath his bower, and woke him by removing it. The sun fell upon his upturned face. Vaikkenen opened his eyes to find his mother looming over him. He recognized immediately that she was displeased. Sighing to himself, for he hated scenes, he rose from his couch, graceful as a gazelle, and knelt at her feet, smiling sweetly.

O my mother, welcome back to Ryoka, he said. *I trust my sister is well. How may I serve thee?*

Get up, said Tukalina tartly. *You have already served me, and all Ryoka, ill.*

Rising, Vaikkenen assumed a penitent mien. *What have I done?*

You seduced my servant Tekkelé and then left her and her daughters, your daughters, unprotected. You stole the Cloak of Storms, which I entrusted to Tekkelé, and then threw it away, creating great misery across this land. Have you not felt it? And most important, you disturbed your grandmother, when I expressly warned you not to do so! What have you to say?

Vaikkenen squirmed. How degrading, he thought, for a god to have to defend himself. *It is all the fault of the winds. They told me about Tekkelé of Ippa. They practically dared me to steal the Cloak! I did not mean to do it,* he began.

His mother interrupted him. *That is no excuse. You did it. And there are no amends you can make to the souls whom your thoughtless behavior sent to the Void before their time. For this, and for your temerity in daring to disturb your grandmother, you shall leave Ryoka.*

Where shall I go? Vaikkenen asked, for he could see that Tukalina was truly angry, and that only obedience would mollify her.

You shall go to the Void, Tukalina said. Vaikkenen paled. The Void is where the souls of the dead go to await rebirth, and immortals, who can neither die nor be reborn, hate it. *You shall go to Cendrai the Gatekeeper, and you shall offer her your services, and do what she tells you.*

For how long? Vaikkenen asked grimly.

Until the souls who entered the Void after your theft of the Cloak of Storms are judged and reborn.

This was not, as immortals count time, very long, and Vaikkenen knew it. Yet any time was too long to spend in the Void. He wondered if there was some way to avoid his mother's judgment.

There is not, said Tukalina, knowing her son's thought. She pointed at the ground and spoke. The ground shuddered. A dark tunnel, like an open mouth, appeared in the fabric of the earth.

Vaikkenen went. The souls that filled the caverns of the Void were astonished to see the bright god coming toward them. He halted at the Gate, where the throng was thickest. Cendrai the Gatekeeper greeted him roughly. "What are you doing here, Trickster? This is no place for an immortal. Be off!"

Vaikkenen said, "Oh Cendrai, I would obey you if I could. But I have been sent to offer you my services until all the souls who entered here after I stole the Cloak of Storms from Tekkelé of Ippa have been judged and reborn." He put on his most winning expression. Whatever task she finds me, he thought, may not be too bad.

Cendrai clapped her hands in delight. "Good!" she cried. "I need a rest. I have not left this Gate for centuries. You will take my place, and I will return to the sunlight. Come, immortal!" With a grin she stepped aside.

So Vaikkenen the Trickster became the warden of the dead. It is a wearisome task, for the dead are eager to leave the Void and must be watched, lest they sneak through the Gate and return to the world before their proper time. Vaikkenen despised the task. He spent a great deal of time planning the trick which he intended to play on the winds to repay them for their part in his theft, and when that grew dull, he designed another trick which he hoped to play on Cendrai. He half-expected her to take advantage of him and not return—it was the sort of thing he himself might do—but when the last soul who had entered the Void since his theft of the Cloak of Storms from Tekkelé was judged and reborn, Cendrai reappeared.

"Come back anytime!" she yelled as Vaikkenen with a shout of joy left the Gate and sped toward the sunlight.

Vaikkenen did eventually repay the winds for their part in the theft, and the trick he played on Cendrai is one of the Six Great Tricks, and is much sung of across Ryoka. Tukalina the raven-winged was later to say that her son learned nothing from his sojourn in the Void, except caution. Tekkelé the astronomer lived long in Ravenswood, as the valley came to be called. Eventually Shiro and Laikkimi left the valley, and went to have their own adventures, as befitted the daughters of a god. The hawks returned to the mountaintop, and the people to their villages; beavers dammed the stream, and it turned into a lake filled with fish.

At last Tekkelé grew bored with solitude. To amuse herself, she would leave her hut and wander to the nearest town, where she would sit in the sunlight and tell stories to the children. "Once upon a time," she would say, "there was a woman who lived on a mountain, maybe this mountain, and her name was Tekkelé, and she watched the stars. . . ." And she told them about Tekkelé the stargazer, who loved a wizard with golden hair. To the older ones she spoke of the stars, showing them the patterns, and of the life of the red hawks that nested in the mountains. Twice a year Shiro and Laikkimi returned, as dutiful daughters should, to visit their mother. They had grown to be beautiful and loving women and had remained true to their natures: Shiro was wild and fierce, and had gone to the castles of the folk of the Crystal Lake and become a warrior, and Laikkimi had gone east to the city of Skyeggo and there met a man who loved her, and by him bore two children, a girl whom she named Tekkelé, and a boy named Ruha, after his father's father. Both her children had golden hair.

It is not clear when Tekkelé of Ippa first became known as a sibyl. But as time went on, men and women would come to the village by the lake, approach her, and beg her to instruct them if such and such an act would be pleasing to the gods. At first Tekkelé thought this funny. "You are fools," she said, "to think that the gods care for your petty problems!" But whatever she said, people would repeat it, and take it to heart. They left the village telling each other how wise she was.

That spring Shiro and Laikkimi returned, as they did every spring, to visit their mother. They rode into Ravenswood on two tall horses. But when they entered Tekkelé's hut, which stood where the old lean-to had stood, they found it empty, and the hearthstone, when they touched it, was cold. They sought out the headman of the village. "We are looking for Tekkelé of Ippa," they said.

The headman answered, "She is gone."

"Gone where?" said Shiro, ever fierce. The headman spread his hands and shrugged. "Do you mean that she's dead?"

"Oh, no," the headman said. "Not that. She was very wise. Now the gods have taken her."

"I doubt it," said Laikkimi dryly. Neither of the twins, being part-devine themselves, had much use for the gods. They searched through Ravenswood for traces of their mother but found nothing, and no one who could tell them anything, except one girl who admitted that the day before Tekkelé's disappearance she had heard the old woman standing beside the lake, whispering to herself.

"What was she saying?" Laikkimi asked.

"I did not understand it—she spoke of faces, many faces," answered the child.

Shiro and Laikkimi turned this over in their minds, but could make no sense of it. Puzzled and sad, they decided that Tekkelé—who was very old by now—had lost her footing and fallen into the lake. Lovingly they spoke the death ritual for her, that her soul might not fly continually through the vast caverns of the Void.

At the last moment, as the twins made ready to leave the peaceful valley, Shiro said, "Wait."

"What is it?" Laikkimi said.

Shiro pointed toward the mountaintop. "What if—?" Laikkimi nodded. It had been many years since they had left the cave in which Tekkelé had borne them; they did not miss it. But perhaps, they thought, Tekkelé the stargazer had chosen to return there, to die amid the rocks, listening to the wild music of the winds and the hawks' shrill cries.

They started up the mountain trail. But they had not gone very far before they heard above them the rustle of wings. A red hawk—female, by the size of it, and gaunt with age—soared toward them from the ever-present bank of cloud that surrounded, and still surrounds, the Gray Peaks. The sun glinted on its wings. Silently it circled once, twice, three times over their heads.

Laikkimi lifted her arms to the bird. "Mother!"

The red hawk screamed—in assent, confusion, challenge? Its yellow eyes gleamed. Then, veering, it flew north. Laikkimi and Shiro waited on the trail, hoping that it would return. But it did not. At last they retraced their steps to the hut where they had left their horses grazing, and, mounting, turned their faces away from Ravenswood.

But as they rode, Tekkelé's daughters smiled, for they believed they knew what had become of their mother. And no one has seen or heard of anybody who has seen Tekkelé of Ippa since that time.

Although the traditions of fantasy and the American tall tale are related, it is a rare story that comfortably fits our notions of both. This fanciful story about a visit from a sad-eyed door-to-door salesman is first and foremost a tall tale, with a canny believe-it-or-not narrator. But the salesman and his sad plight evoke the optimistic wonderment of fantastic possibility and the mourning for a lost, half-forgotten past which is characteristic of the fantasy story. MARK TWAIN's *major contribution to fantasy is his satire on Arthurian fantasy,* A Connecticut Yankee in King Arthur's Court *(1889). "The Canvasser's Tale" is one of only two short fantasy stories (the other being "The Facts Concerning the Recent Carnival of Crime in Connecticut") that Twain wrote. It has not previously been reprinted in a fantasy anthology.*

The Canvasser's Tale
BY MARK TWAIN

Poor, sad-eyed stranger! There was that about his humble mien, his tired look, his decayed-gentility clothes, that almost reached the mustard-seed of charity that still remained, remote and lonely, in the empty vastness of my heart, notwithstanding I observed a portfolio under his arm, and said to myself, Behold, Providence hath delivered his servant into the hands of another canvasser.

Well, these people always get one interested. Before I well knew how it came about, this one was telling me his history, and I was all attention and sympathy. He told it something like this:—

My parents died, alas, when I was a little, sinless child. My uncle Ithuriel took me to his heart and reared me as his own. He was my only relative in the wide world; but he was good and rich and generous. He reared me in the lap of luxury. I knew no want that money could satisfy.

In the fulness of time I was graduated, and went with two of my servants—my chamberlain and my valet—to travel in foreign countries. During four years I flitted upon careless wing amid the beauteous gardens of the distant strand, if you will permit this form of speech in one whose tongue was ever attuned to poesy; and indeed I so speak with confidence, as one unto his kind, for I perceive by your eyes that you too, sir, are gifted with the divine inflation. In those far lands I revelled in the ambrosial food that fructifies the soul, the mind, the heart. But of all things, that which most appealed to my inborn aesthetic taste was the prevailing custom there, among the rich, of making collections of elegant and costly rarities, dainty *objets de vertu,* and in an evil hour I tried to uplift my uncle Ithuriel to a plane of sympathy with this exquisite employment.

I wrote and told him of one gentleman's vast collection of shells; another's noble collection of meerschaum pipes; another's elevating and refining collection of undecipherable autographs; another's priceless collection of old china; another's enchanting collection of postage stamps—and so forth and so on. Soon my letters yielded fruit. My uncle began to look about for something to make a collection of. You may know, perhaps, how fleetly a taste like this dilates. His soon became a raging fever, though I knew it not. He began to neglect his great pork business; presently he wholly retired and turned an elegant leisure into a rabid search for curious things. His wealth was vast, and he spared it not. First he tried cow-bells. He made a collection which filled five large *salons,* and comprehended all the different sorts of cow-bells that ever had been contrived, save one. That one—an antique, and the only specimen extant—was possessed by another collector. My uncle offered enormous sums for it, but the gentleman would not sell. Doubtless you know what necessarily resulted. A true collector attaches no value to a collection that is not complete. His great heart breaks, he sells his hoard, he turns his mind to some field that seems unoccupied.

Thus did my uncle. He next tried brickbats. After piling up a vast and intensely interesting collection, the former difficulty supervened; his great heart broke again; he sold out his soul's idol to the retired brewer who possessed the missing brick. Then he tried flint hatchets and other implements of Primeval Man, but by and by discovered that the factory where they were made was supplying other collectors as well as himself. He tried Aztec inscriptions and stuffed whales—another failure, after incredible labor and expense. When his collection seemed at last perfect, a stuffed whale arrived from Greenland and an Aztec inscription from the Cundurango regions of Central America that made all former specimens insignificant. My uncle hastened to secure these noble gems. He got the stuffed whale, but another collector got the inscription. A real Cundurango, as possibly you know, is a possession of such supreme value that, when once a collector gets it, he will rather part with his family than with it. So my uncle sold out, and saw his darlings go forth, never more to return; and his coal-black hair turned white as snow in a single night.

Now he waited, and thought. He knew another disappointment might kill him. He was resolved that he would choose things next time that no other man was collecting. He carefully made up his mind, and once more entered the field—this time to make a collection of echoes.

"Of what?" said I.

Echoes, sir. His first purchase was an echo in Georgia that repeated four times; his next was a six-repeater in Maryland; his next was a thirteen-repeater in Maine; his next was a nine-repeater in Kansas; his next was a twelve-repeater in Tennessee, which he got cheap, so to speak, because it was out of repair, a portion of the crag which reflected it having tumbled down. He believed he could repair it at a cost of a few thousand dollars, and, by increasing the elevation with masonry, treble the repeating capacity; but the architect who undertook the job had never built an echo before, and so he utterly spoiled this one. Before he meddled with it, it used to talk back like a mother-in-law, but now it was only fit for the deaf and dumb asylum. Well, next he bought a lot of cheap little double-barrelled echoes, scattered around over various States and Territories; he got them at twenty per cent off by taking the lot. Next he bought a perfect Gatling gun of an echo in Oregon, and it cost a fortune, I can tell you. You may know, sir, that in the echo market the scale of prices is cumulative, like the carat-scale in diamonds; in fact, the same phraseology is used. A single-carat echo is worth but ten dollars over and above the value of the land it is on; a two-carat or double-barrelled echo is worth thirty dollars; a five-carat is worth nine hundred and fifty; a ten-carat is worth thirteen thousand. My uncle's Oregon echo, which he called the Great Pitt Echo, was a twenty-two carat gem, and cost two hundred and sixteen thousand dollars—they threw the land in, for it was four hundred miles from a settlement.

Well, in the mean time my path was a path of roses. I was the accepted suitor of the only and lovely daughter of an English earl, and was beloved to distraction. In that dear presence I swam in seas of bliss. The family were content, for it was known that I was sole heir to an uncle held to be worth five millions of dollars. However, none of us knew that my uncle had become a collector, at least in anything more than a small way, for aesthetic amusement.

Now gathered the clouds above my unconscious head. That divine echo, since known throughout the world as the Great Koh-i-noor, or Mountain of Repetitions, was discovered. It was a sixty-five-carat gem. You could utter a word and it would talk back at you for fifteen minutes, when the day was otherwise quiet. But behold, another fact came to light at the same time: another echo-collector was in the field. The two rushed to make the peerless purchase. The property consisted of a couple of small hills with a shallow swale between, out yonder among the back settlements of New York State. Both men arrived on the ground at the same time, and neither knew the other was there. The echo was not all owned by one man; a person by the name of Williamson Bolivar Jarvis owned the east hill, and a person by the name of Harbison J. Bledso owned the west hill; the swale between was the dividing line. So while my uncle was buying Jarvis's hill for three million two hundred and eighty-five thousand dollars, the other party was buying Bledso's hill for a shade over three million.

Now, do you perceive the natural result? Why, the noblest collection of echoes on earth was forever and ever incomplete, since it possessed but the one half of the king echo of the universe. Neither man was content with this divided ownership, yet neither would sell to the other. There were jawings, bickerings, heart-burnings. And at last, that other collector, with a malignity which only a collector can ever feel toward a man and a brother, proceeded to cut down his hill!

You see, as long as he could not have the echo, he was resolved that nobody should have it. He would remove his hill, and then there would be nothing to reflect my uncle's echo. My uncle remonstrated with him, but the man said, "I own one end of this echo; I choose to kill my end; you must take care of your own end yourself."

Well, my uncle got an injunction put on him. The other man appealed and fought it in a higher court. They carried it on up, clear to the Supreme Court of the United States. It made no end of trouble there. Two of the judges believed that an echo was personal property, because it was impalpable to sight and touch, and yet was purchasable, salable, and consequently taxable; two others believed that an echo was real estate, because it was manifestly attached to the land, and was not removable from place to place; other of the judges contended that an echo was not property at all.

It was finally decided that the echo was property; that the hills were property; that the two men were separate and independent owners of the two hills, but tenants in common in the echo; therefore defendant was at full liberty to cut down his hill, since it belonged solely to him, but must give bonds in three million dollars as indemnity for damages which might result to my uncle's half of the echo. This decision also debarred my uncle from using defendant's hill to reflect his part of the echo, without defendant's consent; he must use only his own hill; if his part of the echo would not go, under these circumstances, it was sad, of course, but the court could find no remedy. The court also debarred defendant from using my uncle's hill to reflect *his* end of the echo, without consent. You see the grand result! Neither man would give consent, and so that astonishing and most noble echo had to cease from its great powers; and since that day that magnificent property is tied up and unsalable.

A week before my wedding day, while I was still swimming in bliss and the nobility were gathering from far and near to honor our espousals, came news of my uncle's death, and also a copy of his will, making me his sole heir. He was gone; alas, my dear benefactor was no more. The thought surcharges my heart even at this remote day. I handed the will to the earl; I could not read it for the blinding tears. The earl read it; then he sternly said, "Sir, do you call this wealth?—but doubtless you do in your inflated country. Sir, you are left sole heir to a vast collection of echoes—if a thing can be called a collection that is scattered far and wide over the huge length and breadth of the American continent; sir, this is not all; you are head and ears in debt; there is not an echo in the lot but has a mortgage on it; sir, I am not a hard man, but I must look to my child's interest; if you had but one echo which you could honestly call your own, if you had but one echo which was free from incumbrance, so that you could retire to it with my child, and by humble, painstaking industry, cultivate and improve it, and thus wrest from it a maintenance, I would not say you nay; but I cannot marry my child to a beggar. Leave his side, my darling; go, sir; take your mortgage-ridden echoes and quit my sight forever."

My noble Celestine clung to me in tears, with loving arms, and swore she would willingly, nay, gladly marry me, though I had not an echo in the world. But it could not be. We were torn asunder, she to pine and die within the twelvemonth, I to toil life's long journey sad and lone, praying daily, hourly, for that release which shall join us together again in that dear realm where the wicked cease from troubling and the weary are at rest. Now, sir, if you will be so kind as to look at these maps and plans in my portfolio, I am sure I can sell you an echo for less money than any man in the trade. Now this one, which cost my uncle ten dollars, thirty years ago, and is one of the sweetest things in Texas, I will let you have for—

"Let me interrupt you," I said. "My friend, I have not had a moment's respite from canvassers this day. I have bought a sewing-machine which I did not want; I have bought a map which is mistaken in all its details; I have bought a clock which will not go; I have bought a moth poison which the moths prefer to any other beverage; I have bought no end of useless inventions, and now I have had enough of this foolishness. I would not have one of your echoes if you were even to give it to me. I would not let it stay on the place. I always hate a man that tries to sell me echoes. You see this gun? Now take your collection and move on; let us not have bloodshed."

But he only smiled a sad, sweet smile, and got out some more diagrams. You know the result perfectly well, because you know that when you have once opened the door to a canvasser, the trouble is done and you have got to suffer defeat.

I compromised with this man at the end of an intolerable hour. I bought two double-barrelled echoes in good condition, and he threw in another, which he said was not salable because it only spoke German. He said, "She was a perfect polyglot once, but somehow her palate got down."

CREATURES

Stories of strange and unusual
beasts and entities

One of the great contemporary unicorn stories, "The Silken-swift . . ." is a revisionist retelling of the traditional legend, reinterpreting it to reflect modern ideas about virtue while retaining the legend's eternal essence, that unicorns are associated with pure womanhood. THEODORE STURGEON, *whose career in fantasy produced one of the major and influential bodies of short fiction of the twentieth century, was nowhere more central to the development of adult fantasy than in this classic, which sparked such other works as Peter Beagle's* The Last Unicorn *and Harlan Ellison's "On the Downhill Side."*

The Silken-swift . . .
BY THEODORE STURGEON

There's a village by the Bogs, and in the village is a Great House. In the Great House lived a squire who had land and treasures and, for a daughter, Rita.

In the village lived Del, whose voice was a thunder in the inn when he drank there; whose corded, cabled body was golden-skinned, and whose hair flung challenges back to the sun.

Deep in the Bogs, which were brackish, there was a pool of purest water, shaded by willows and wide-wondering aspen, cupped by banks of a moss most marvellously blue. Here grew mandrake, and there were strange pipings in mid-summer. No one ever heard them but a quiet girl whose beauty was so very contained that none of it showed. Her name was Barbara.

There was a green evening, breathless with growth, when Del took his usual way down the lane beside the manor and saw a white shadow adrift inside the tall iron pickets. He stopped, and the shadow approached, and became Rita. "Slip around to the gate," she said, "and I'll open it for you."

She wore a gown like a cloud and a silver circlet round her head. Night was caught in her hair, moonlight in her face, and in her great eyes, secrets swam.

Del said, "I have no business with the squire."

"He's gone," she said. "I've sent the servants away. Come to the gate."

"I need no gate." He leaped and caught the top bar of the fence, and in a continuous fluid motion went high and across and down beside her. She looked at his arms, one, the other; then up at his hair. She pressed her small hands tight together and made a little laugh, and then she was gone through the tailored trees, lightly, swiftly, not looking back. He followed, one step for three of hers, keeping pace with a new pounding in the sides of his neck. They crossed a flower bed and a wide marble terrace. There was an open door, and when he passed through it he stopped, for she was nowhere in sight. Then the door clicked shut behind him and he whirled. She was there, her back to the panel, laughing up at him in the dimness. He thought she would come to him then, but instead she twisted by, close, her eyes on his. She smelt of violets and sandalwood. He followed her into a great hall, quite dark but full of the subdued lights of polished wood, cloisonné, tooled leather and gold-threaded tapestry. She flung open another door, and they were in a small room with a carpet made of rosy silences, and a candle-lit table. Two places were set, each with five different crystal glasses and old silver as prodigally used as the iron pickets outside. Six teakwood steps rose to a great oval window. "The moon," she said, "will rise for us there."

She motioned him to a chair and crossed to a sideboard, where there was a rack of decanters—ruby wine and white; one with a strange brown bead; pink, and amber. She took down the first and poured. Then she lifted the silver domes from the salvers on the table, and a magic of fragrance filled the air. There were smoking sweets and savories, rare seafood and slivers of fowl, and morsels of strange meat wrapped in flower petals, spitted with foreign fruits and tiny soft seashells. All about were spices, each like a separate voice in the distant murmur of a crowd: saffron and sesame, cumin and marjoram and mace.

And all the while Del watched her in wonder, seeing how the candles left the moonlight in her face, and how completely she trusted her hands, which did such deftness without supervision—so composed she was, for all the silent secret laughter that tugged at her lips, for all the bright dark mysteries that swirled and swam within her.

They ate, and the oval window yellowed and darkened while the candlelight grew bright. She poured another wine, and another, and with the courses of the meal they were as May to the crocus and as frost to the apple.

Del knew it was alchemy and he yielded to it without question. That which was purposely over-sweet would be piquantly cut; this induced thirst would, with exquisite timing, be quenched. He knew she was watching him; he knew she was aware of the heat in his cheeks and the tingle at his fingertips. His wonder grew, but he was not afraid.

In all this time she spoke hardly a word; but at last the feast was over and they rose. She touched a silken rope on the wall, and panelling slid aside. The table rolled silently into some ingenious recess and the panel returned. She waved him to an L-shaped couch in one corner, and as he sat close to her, she turned and took down the lute which hung on the wall behind her. He had his moment of confusion; his arms were ready for her, but not for the instrument as well. Her eyes sparkled, but her composure was unshaken.

Now she spoke, while her fingers strolled and danced on the lute, and her words marched and wandered in and about the music. She had a thousand voices, so that he wondered which of them was truly hers. Sometimes she sang; sometimes it was a wordless crooning. She seemed at times remote from him, puzzled at the turn the music was taking, and at other times she seemed to hear the pulsing roar in his eardrums, and she played laughing syncopations to it. She sang words which he almost understood:

> *Bee to blossom, honey dew,*
> *Claw to mouse, and rain to tree,*
> *Moon to midnight, I to you;*
> *Sun to starlight, you to me . . .*

and she sang something wordless:

> *Ake ya rundefle, rundefle fye,*
> *Orel ya rundefle kown,*
> *En yea, en yea, ya bunderbee bye*
> *En sor, en see, en sown.*

which he also almost understood.

In still another voice she told him the story of a great hairy spider and a little pink girl who found it between the leaves of a half-open book; and at first he was all fright and pity for the girl, but then she went on to tell of what the spider suffered, with his home disrupted by this yawping giant, and so vividly did she tell of it that at the end he was laughing at himself and all but crying for the poor spider.

So the hours slipped by, and suddenly, between songs, she was in his arms; and in the instant she had twisted up and away from him, leaving him gasping. She said, in still a new voice, sober and low, "No, Del. We must wait for the moon."

His thighs ached and he realized that he had half-risen, arms out, hands clutching and feeling the extraordinary fabric of her gown though it was gone from them; and he sank back to the couch with an odd, faint sound that was wrong for the room. He flexed his fingers and, reluctantly, the sensation of white gossamer left them. At last he looked across at her and she laughed and leapt high lightly, and it was as if she stopped in midair to stretch for a moment before she alighted beside him, bent and kissed his mouth, and leapt away.

The roaring in his ears was greater, and at this it seemed to acquire a tangible weight. His head bowed; he tucked his knuckles into the upper curve of his eye sockets and rested his elbows on his knees. He could hear the sweet sussurrus of Rita's gown as she moved about the room; he could sense the violets and sandalwood. She was dancing, immersed in the joy of movement and of his nearness. She made her own music, humming, sometimes whispering to the melodies in her mind.

And at length he became aware that she had stopped; he could hear nothing, though he knew she was still near. Heavily he raised his head. She was in the center of the room, balanced like a huge white moth, her eyes quite dark now with their secrets quiet. She was staring at the window, poised, waiting.

He followed her gaze. The big oval was black no longer, but dusted over with silver light. Del rose slowly. The dust was a mist, a loom, and then, at one edge, there was a shard of the moon itself creeping and growing.

Because Del stopped breathing, he could hear her breathe; it was rapid and so deep it faintly strummed her versatile vocal cords.

"Rita . . ."

Without answering she ran to the sideboard and filled two small glasses. She gave him one, then, "Wait," she breathed, "oh, wait!"

Spellbound, he waited while the white stain crept across the window. He understood suddenly that he must be still until the great oval was completely filled with direct moonlight, and this helped him, because it set a foreseeable limit to his waiting; and it hurt him, because nothing in life, he thought, had ever moved so slowly. He had a moment of rebellion, in which he damned himself for falling in with her complex pacing; but with it he realized that now the darker silver was wasting away, now it was a finger's breadth, and now a thread, and now, and *now*—.

She made a brittle feline cry and sprang up the dark steps to the window. So bright was the light that her body was a jet cameo against it. So delicately wrought was her gown that he could see the epaulettes of silver light the moon gave her. She was so beautiful his eyes stung.

"Drink," she whispered. "Drink with me, darling, darling . . ."

For an instant he did not understand her at all, and only gradually did he become aware of the little glass he held. He raised it toward her and drank. And of all the twists and titillations of taste he had had this night, this was the most startling; for it had no taste at all, almost no substance, and a temperature almost exactly that of blood. He looked stupidly down at the glass and back up at the girl. He thought that she had turned about and was watching him, though he could not be sure, since her silhouette was the same.

And then he had his second of unbearable shock, for the light went out.

The moon was gone, the window, the room, Rita was gone.

For a stunned instant he stood tautly, stretching his eyes wide. He made a sound that was not a word. He dropped the glass and pressed his palms to his eyes, feeling them blink, feeling the stiff silk of his lashes against them. Then he snatched the hands away, and it was still dark, and more than dark; this was not a blackness. This was like trying to see with an elbow or with a tongue; it was not black, it was *Nothingness.*

He fell to his knees.

Rita laughed.

An odd, alert part of his mind seized on the laugh and understood it, and horror and fury spread through his whole being; for this was the laugh which had been tugging at her lips all evening, and it was a hard, cruel, self-assured laugh. And at the same time, because of the anger or in spite of it, desire exploded whitely within him. He moved toward the sound, groping, mouthing. There was a quick, faint series of rustling sounds from the steps, and then a light, strong web fell around him. He struck out at it, and recognized it for the unforgettable thing it was— her robe. He caught at it, ripped it, stamped upon it. He heard her bare feet run lightly down and past him, and lunged, and caught nothing. He stood, gasping painfully.

She laughed again.

"I'm blind," he said hoarsely. "Rita, I'm blind!"

"I know," she said coolly, close beside him. And again she laughed.

"What have you done to me?"

"I've watched you be a dirty animal of a man," she said.

He grunted and lunged again. His knees struck something—a chair, a cabinet—and he fell heavily. He thought he touched her foot.

"Here, lover, here!" she taunted.

He fumbled about for the thing which had tripped him, found it, used it to help him upright again. He peered uselessly about.

"Here, lover!"

He leaped, and crashed into the door jamb: cheekbone, collarbone, hip-bone, ankle were one straight blaze of pain. He clung to the polished wood.

After a time he said, in agony, "Why?"

"No man has ever touched me and none ever will," she sang. Her breath was on his cheek. He reached and touched nothing, and then he heard her leap from her perch on a statue's pedestal by the door, where she had stood high and leaned over to speak.

No pain, no blindness, not even the understanding that it was her witch's brew working in him could quell the wild desire he felt at her nearness. Nothing could tame the fury that shook him as she laughed. He staggered after her, bellowing.

She danced around him, laughing. Once she pushed him into a clattering rack of fire-irons. Once she caught his elbow from behind and spun him. And once, incredibly, she sprang past him and, in midair, kissed him again on the mouth.

He descended into Hell, surrounded by the small, sure patter of bare feet and sweet cool laughter. He rushed and crashed, he crouched and bled and whimpered like a hound. His roaring and blundering took an echo, and that must have been the great hall. Then there were walls that seemed more than unyielding; they struck back. And there were panels to lean against, gasping, which became opening doors as he leaned. And always the black nothingness, the writhing temptation of the pat-pat of firm flesh on smooth stones, and the ravening fury.

It was cooler, and there was no echo. He became aware of the whisper of the wind through trees. The balcony, he thought; and then, right in his ear, so that he felt her warm breath, "Come, lover . . ." and he sprang. He sprang and missed, and instead of sprawling on the terrace, there was nothing, and nothing, and nothing, and then, when he least expected it, a shower of cruel thumps as he rolled down the marble steps.

He must have had a shred of consciousness left, for he was vaguely aware of the approach of her bare feet, and of the small, cautious hand that touched his shoulder and moved to his mouth, and then his chest. Then it was withdrawn, and either she laughed or the sound was still in his mind.

Deep in the Bogs, which were brackish, there was a pool of purest water, shaded by willows and wide-wondering aspens, cupped by banks of a moss most marvellously blue. Here grew mandrake, and there were strange pipings in mid-summer. No one ever heard them but a quiet girl whose beauty was so very contained that none of it showed. Her name was Barbara.

No one noticed Barbara, no one lived with her, no one cared. And Barbara's life was very full, for she was born to receive. Others are born wishing to receive, so they wear bright masks and make attractive sounds like cicadas and operettas, so others will be forced, one way or another, to give to them. But Barbara's receptors were wide open, and always had been, so that she needed no substitute for sunlight through a tulip petal, or the sound of morning-glories climbing, or the tangy sweet smell of formic acid which is the only death cry possible to an ant, or any other of the thousand things overlooked by folk who can only wish to receive. Barbara had a garden and an orchard, and took things in to market when she cared to, and the rest of the time she spent in taking what was given. Weeds grew in her garden, but since they were welcomed, they grew only where they could keep the watermelons from being sunburned. The rabbits were welcome, so they kept to the two rows of carrots, the one of lettuce, and the one of tomato vines which were planted for them, and they left the rest alone. Goldenrod shot up beside the bean hills to lend a hand upward, and the birds ate only the figs and peaches from the waviest top branches, and in return patrolled the lower ones for caterpillars and egg-laying flies. And if a fruit stayed green for two weeks longer until Barbara had time to go to market, or if a mole could channel moisture to the roots of the corn, why it was the least they could do.

For a brace of years Barbara had wandered more and more, impelled by a thing she could not name—if indeed she was aware of it at all. She knew only that over-the-rise was a strange and friendly place, and that it was a fine thing on arriving there to find another rise to go over. It may very well be that she now needed someone to love, for loving is a most receiving thing, as anyone can attest who has been loved without returning it. It is the one who is loved who must give and give. And she found her love, not in her wandering, but at the market. The shape of her love, his colors and sounds, were so much with her that when she saw him first it was without surprise; and thereafter, for a very long while, it was quite enough that he lived. He gave to her by being alive, by setting the air athrum with his mighty voice, by his stride, which was, for a man afoot, the exact analog of what the horseman calls a "perfect seat."

After seeing him, of course, she received twice and twice again as much as ever before. A tree was straight and tall for the magnificent sake of being straight and tall, but wasn't straightness a part of him, and being tall? The oriole gave more now than song, and the hawk more than walking the wind, for had they not hearts like his, warm blood and his same striving to keep it so for tomorrow? And more and more, over-the-rise was the place for her, for only there could there be more and still more things like him.

But when she found the pure pool in the brackish Bogs, there was no more over-the-rise for her. It was a place without hardness or hate, where the aspens trembled only for wonder, and where all contentment was rewarded. Every single rabbit there was *the* champion nose-twinkler, and every waterbird could stand on one leg the longest, and proud of it. Shelf-fungi hung to the willow-trunks, making that certain, single purple of which the sunset is incapable, and a tanager and a cardinal gravely granted one another his definition of "red."

Here Barbara brought a heart light with happiness, large with love, and set it down on the blue moss. And since the loving heart can receive more than anything else, so it is most needed, and Barbara took the best bird songs, and the richest colors, and the deepest peace, and all the other things which are most worth giving. The chipmunks brought her nuts when she was hungry and the prettiest stones when she was not. A green snake explained to her, in pantomime, how a river of jewels may flow uphill, and three mad otters described how a bundle of joy may slip and slide down and down and be all the more joyful for it. And there was the magic moment when a midge hovered, and then a honeybee, and then a bumblebee, and at last a hummingbird; and there they hung, playing a chord in A sharp minor.

Then one day the pool fell silent, and Barbara learned why the water was pure.

The aspens stopped trembling.

The rabbits all came out of the thicket and clustered on the blue bank, backs straight, ears up, and all their noses as still as coral.

The waterbirds stepped backwards, like courtiers, and stopped on the brink with their heads turned sidewise, one eye closed, the better to see with the other.

The chipmunks respectfully emptied their cheek pouches, scrubbed their paws together and tucked them out of sight; then stood still as tent pegs.

The pressure of growth around the pool ceased: the very grass waited.

The last sound of all to be heard—and by then it was very quiet—was the soft *whick!* of an owl's eyelids as it awoke to watch.

He came like a cloud, the earth cupping itself to take each of his golden hooves. He stopped on the bank and lowered his head, and for a brief moment his eyes met Barbara's, and she looked into a second universe of wisdom and compassion. Then there was the arch of the magnificent neck, the blinding flash of his golden horn.

And he drank, and he was gone. Everyone knows the water is pure, where the unicorn drinks.

How long had he been there? How long gone? Did time wait too, like the grass?

"And couldn't he stay?" she wept. "Couldn't he stay?"

To have seen the unicorn is a sad thing; one might never see him more. But then—to have seen the unicorn!

She began to make a song.

It was late when Barbara came in from the Bogs, so late the mood was bleached with cold and fleeing to the horizon. She struck the high-road just below the Great House and turned to pass it and go out to her garden house.

Near the locked main gate an animal was barking. A sick animal, a big animal. . . .

Barbara could see in the dark better than most, and soon saw the creature clinging to the gate, climbing, uttering that coughing moan as it went. At the top it slipped, fell outward, dangled; then there was a ripping sound, and it fell heavily to the ground and lay still and quiet.

She ran to it, and it began to make the sound again. It was a man, and he was weeping.

It was her love, her love, who was tall and straight and so very alive—her love, battered and bleeding, puffy, broken, his clothes torn, crying.

Now of all times was the time for a lover to receive, to take from the loved one his pain, his trouble, his fear. "Oh, hush, hush," she whispered, her hands touching his bruised face like swift feathers. "It's all over now. It's all over."

She turned him over on his back and knelt to bring him up sitting. She lifted one of his thick arms around her shoulder. He was very heavy, but she was very strong. When he was upright, gasping weakly, she looked up and down the road in the waning moonlight. Nothing, no one. The Great House was dark. Across the road, though, was a meadow with high hedgerows which might break the wind a little.

"Come, my love, my dear love," she whispered. He trembled violently.

All but carrying him, she got him across the road, over the shallow ditch, and through a gap in the hedge. She almost fell with him there. She gritted her teeth and set him down gently. She let him lean against the hedge, and then ran and swept up great armfuls of sweet broom. She made a tight springy bundle of it and set it on the ground beside him, and put a corner of her cloak over it, and gently lowered his head until it was pillowed. She folded the rest of the cloak about him. He was very cold.

There was no water near, and she dared not leave him. With her kerchief she cleaned some of the blood from his face. He was still very cold. He said, "You devil. You rotten little devil."

"Shh." She crept in beside him and cradled his head. "You'll be warm in a minute."

"Stand still," he growled. "Keep running away."

"I won't run away," she whispered. "Oh, my darling, you've been hurt, so hurt. I won't leave you. I promise I won't leave you."

He lay very still. He made the growling sound again.

"I'll tell you a lovely thing," she said softly. "Listen to me, think about the lovely thing," she crooned.

"There's a place in the bog, a pool of pure water, where the trees live beautifully, willow and aspen and birch, where everything is peaceful, my darling, and the flowers grow without tearing their petals. The moss is blue and the water is like diamonds."

"You tell me stories in a thousand voices," he muttered.

"Shh. Listen, my darling. This isn't a story, it's a real place. Four miles north and a little west, and you can see the trees from the ridge with the two dwarf oaks. And I know why the water is pure!" she cried gladly. "I know why!"

He said nothing. He took a deep breath and it hurt him, for he shuddered painfully.

"The unicorn drinks there," she whispered. "I saw him!"

Still he said nothing. She said, "I made a song about it. Listen, this is the song I made:"

> *And He—suddenly gleamed! My dazzled eyes*
> *Coming from outer sunshine to this green*
> *And secret gloaming, met without surprise*
> *The vision. Only after, when the sheen*
> *And splendor of his going fled away,*
> *I knew amazement, wonder and despair,*
> *That he should come—and pass—and would not stay,*
> *The Silken-swift—the gloriously Fair!*
> *That he should come—and pass—and would not stay,*
> *So that, forever after, I must go,*
> *Take the long road that mounts against the day,*
> *Travelling in the hope that I shall know*
> *Again that lifted moment, high and sweet,*
> *Somewhere—on purple moor or windy hill—*
> *Remembering still his wild and delicate feet,*
> *The magic and the dream—remembering still!*

His breathing was more regular. She said, "I truly *saw* him!"

"I'm blind," he said. "Blind, I'm blind."

"Oh, my dear . . ."

He fumbled for her hand, found it. For a long moment he held it. Then, slowly, he brought up his other hand and with them both he felt her hand, turned it about, squeezed it. Suddenly he grunted, half sitting. "You're here!"

"Of course, darling. Of course I'm here."

"Why?" he shouted. "Why? *Why?* Why all of this? Why blind me?" He sat up, mouthing, and put his great hand on her throat. "Why do all that if . . ." The words ran together into an animal noise. Wine and witchery, anger and agony boiled in his veins.

Once she cried out.

Once she sobbed.

"Now," he said, "you'll catch no unicorns. Get away from me." He cuffed her.

"You're mad. You're sick," she cried.

"Get away," he said ominously.

Terrified, she rose. He took the cloak and hurled it after her. It almost toppled her as she ran away, crying silently.

After a long time, from behind the hedge, the sick, coughing sobs began again.

Three weeks later Rita was in the market when a hard hand took her upper arm and pressed her into the angle of a cottage wall. She did not start. She flashed her eyes upward and recognized him, and then said composedly, "Don't touch me."

"I need you to tell me something," he said. "And tell me you *will!*" His voice was as hard as his hand.

"I'll tell you anything you like," she said. "But don't touch me."

He hesitated, then released her. She turned to him casually. "What is it?" Her gaze darted across his face and its almost-healed scars. The small smile tugged at one corner of her mouth.

His eyes were slits. "I have to know this: why did you make up all that . . . prettiness, that food, that poison . . . just for me? You could have had me for less."

She smiled. "Just for you? It was your turn, that's all."

He was genuinely surprised. "It's happened before?"

She nodded. "Whenever it's the full of the moon—and the squire's away."

"You're lying!"

"You forget yourself!" she said sharply. Then, smiling, "It is the truth, though."

"I'd 've heard talk—"

"Would you now? And tell me—how many of your friends know about your humiliating adventure?"

He hung his head.

She nodded. "You see? They go away until they're healed, and they come back and say nothing. And they always will."

"You're a devil . . . why do you do it? Why?"

"I told you," she said openly. "I'm a woman and I act like a woman in my own way. No man will ever touch me, though. I am virgin and shall remain so."

"You're *what?*" he roared.

She held up a restraining, ladylike glove. "Please," she said, pained.

"Listen," he said, quietly now, but with such intensity that for once she stepped back a pace. He closed his eyes, thinking hard. "You told me—the pool, the pool of the unicorn, and a song, wait. 'The Silken-swift, the gloriously Fair . . .' Remember? And then I—I saw to it that *you'd* never catch a unicorn!"

She shook her head, complete candor in her face. "I like that, 'the Silken-swift.' Pretty. But believe me—no! That isn't mine."

He put his face close to hers, and though it was barely a whisper, it came out like bullets. "Liar! Liar! I couldn't forget. I was sick, I was hurt, I was poisoned, but I know what I did!" He turned on his heel and strode away.

She put the thumb of her glove against her upper teeth for a second, then ran after him. "Del!"

He stopped but, rudely, would not turn. She rounded him, faced him. "I'll not have you believing that of me—it's the one thing I have left," she said tremulously.

He made no attempt to conceal his surprise. She controlled her expression with a visible effort, and said, "Please. Tell me a little more —just about the pool, the song, whatever it was."

"You don't remember?"

"I don't *know!*" she flashed. She was deeply agitated.

He said with mock patience, "You told me of a unicorn pool out on the Bogs. You said you had seen *him* drink there. You made a song about it. And then I—"

"Where? Where was this?"

"You forget so soon?"

"Where? Where did it happen?"

"In the meadow, across the road from your gate, where you followed me," he said. "Where my sight came back to me, when the sun came up."

She looked at him blankly, and slowly her face changed. First the imprisoned smile struggling to be free, and then—she was herself again, and she laughed. She laughed a great ringing peal of the laughter that had plagued him so, and she did not stop until he put one hand behind his back, then the other, and she saw his shoulders swell with the effort to keep from striking her dead.

"You animal!" she said, goodhumoredly. "Do you know what you've done? Oh, you . . . you *animal!*" She glanced around to see that there were no ears to hear her. "I left you at the foot of the terrace steps," she told him. Her eyes sparkled. "Inside the gates, you understand? And you . . ."

"Don't laugh," he said quietly.

She did not laugh. "That was someone else out there. Who, I can't imagine. But it wasn't I."

He paled. "You followed me out."

"On my soul I did not," she said soberly. Then she quelled another laugh.

"That can't be," he said. "I couldn't have . . ."

"But you were blind, blind and crazy, Del-my-lover!"

"Squire's daughter, take care," he hissed. Then he pulled his big hand through his hair. "It can't be. It's three weeks; I'd have been accused . . ."

"There are those who wouldn't," she smiled. "Or—perhaps she will, in time."

"There has never been a woman so foul," he said evenly, looking her straight in the eye. "You're lying—you know you're lying."

"What must I do to prove it—aside from that which I'll have no man do?"

His lip curled. "Catch the unicorn," he said.

"If I did, you'd believe I was virgin?"

"I must," he admitted. He turned away, then said, over his shoulder, "But—*you?*"

She watched him thoughtfully until he left the marketplace. Her eyes sparkled; then she walked briskly to the goldsmith's, where she ordered a bridle of woven gold.

If the unicorn pool lay in the Bogs nearby, Rita reasoned, someone who was familiar with that brakish wasteland must know of it. And when she made a list in her mind of those few who travelled the Bogs, she knew whom to ask. With that, the other deduction came readily. Her laughter drew stares as she moved through the marketplace.

By the vegetable stall she stopped. The girl looked up patiently.

Rita stood swinging one expensive glove against the other wrist, half-smiling. "So you're the one." She studied the plain, inward-turning, peaceful face until Barbara had to turn her eyes away. Rita said, without further preamble, "I want you to show me the unicorn pool in two weeks."

Barbara looked up again, and now it was Rita who dropped her eyes. Rita said, "I can have someone else find it, of course. If you'd rather not." She spoke very clearly, and people turned to listen. They looked from Barbara to Rita and back again, and they waited.

"I don't mind," said Barbara faintly. As soon as Rita had left, smiling, she packed up her things and went silently back to her house.

The goldsmith, of course, made no secret of such an extraordinary commission; and that, plus the gossips who had overheard Rita talking to Barbara, made the expedition into a cavalcade. The whole village turned out to see; the boys kept firmly in check so that Rita might lead the way; the young bloods ranged behind her (some a little less carefree than they might be) and others snickering behind their hands. Behind them the girls, one or two a little pale, others eager as cats to see the squire's daughter fail, and perhaps even . . . but then, only she had the golden bridle.

She carried it casually, but casualness could not hide it, for it was not wrapped, and it swung and blazed in the sun. She wore a flowing white robe, trimmed a little short so that she might negotiate the rough bogland; she had on a golden girdle and little gold sandals, and a gold chain bound her head and hair like a coronet.

Barbara walked quietly a little behind Rita, closed in with her own thoughts. Not once did she look at Del, who strode somberly by himself.

Rita halted a moment and let Barbara catch up, then walked beside her. "Tell me," she said quietly, "why did you come? It needn't have been you."

"I'm his friend," Barbara said. She quickly touched the bridle with her finger. "The unicorn."

"Oh," said Rita. "The unicorn." She looked archly at the other girl. "You wouldn't betray all your friends, would you?"

Barbara looked at her thoughtfully, without anger. "If—when you catch the unicorn," she said carefully, "what will you do with him?"

"What an amazing question! I shall keep him, of course!"

"I thought I might persuade you to let him go."

Rita smiled, and hung the bridle on her other arm. "You could never do that."

"I know," said Barbara. "But I thought I might, so that's why I came." And before Rita could answer, she dropped behind again.

The last ridge, the one which overlooked the unicorn pool, saw a series of gasps as the ranks of villagers topped it, one after the other, and saw what lay below; and it was indeed beautiful.

Surprisingly, it was Del who took it upon himself to call out, in his great voice, "Everyone wait here!" And everyone did; the top of the ridge filled slowly, from one side to the other, with craning, murmuring people. And then Del bounded after Rita and Barbara.

Barbara said, "I'll stop here."

"Wait," said Rita, imperiously. Of Del she demanded, "What are you coming for?"

"To see fair play," he growled. "The little I know of witchcraft makes me like none of it."

"Very well," she said calmly. Then she smiled her very own smile. "Since you insist, I'd rather enjoy Barbara's company too."

Barbara hesitated. "Come, he won't hurt you, girl," said Rita. "He doesn't know you exist."

"Oh," said Barbara, wonderingly.

Del said gruffly, "I do so. She has the vegetable stall."

Rita smiled at Barbara, the secrets bright in her eyes. Barbara said nothing, but came with them.

"You should go back, you know," Rita said silkily to Del, when she could. "Haven't you been humiliated enough yet?"

He did not answer.

She said, "Stubborn animal! Do you think I'd have come this far if I weren't sure?"

"Yes," said Del, "I think perhaps you would."

They reached the blue moss. Rita shuffled it about with her feet and then sank gracefully down to it. Barbara stood alone in the shadows of the willow grove. Del thumped gently at an aspen with his fist. Rita, smiling, arranged the bridle to cast, and laid it across her lap.

The rabbits stayed hid. There was an uneasiness about the grove.

Barbara sank to her knees, and put out her hand. A chipmunk ran to nestle in it.

This time there was a difference. This time it was not the slow silencing of living things that warned of his approach, but a sudden babble from the people on the ridge.

Rita gathered her legs under her like a sprinter, and held the bridle poised. Her eyes were round and bright, and the tip of her tongue showed between her white teeth. Barbara was a statue. Del put his back against his tree, and became as still as Barbara.

Then from the ridge came a single, simultaneous intake of breath, and silence. One knew without looking that some stared speechless, that some buried their faces or threw an arm over their eyes.

He came.

He came slowly this time, his golden hooves choosing his paces like so many embroidery needles. He held his splendid head high. He regarded the three on the bank gravely, and then turned to look at the ridge for a moment. At last he turned, and came round the pond by the willow grove. Just on the blue moss, he stopped to look down into the pond. It seemed that he drew one deep clear breath. He bent his head then, and drank, and lifted his head to shake away the shining drops.

He turned toward the three spellbound humans and looked at them each in turn. And it was not Rita he went to, at last, nor Barbara. He came to Del, and he drank of Del's eyes with his own just as he had partaken of the pool—deeply and at leisure. The beauty and wisdom were there, and the compassion, and what looked like a bright white point of anger. Del knew that the creature had read everything then, and that he knew all three of them in ways unknown to human beings.

There was a majestic sadness in the way he turned then, and dropped his shining head, and stepped daintily to Rita. She sighed, and rose up a little, lifting the bridle. The unicorn lowered his horn to receive it—

—and tossed his head, tore the bridle out of her grasp, sent the golden thing high in the air. It turned there in the sun, and fell into the pond.

And the instant it touched the water, the pond was a bog and the birds rose mourning from the trees. The unicorn looked up at them, and shook himself. Then he trotted to Barbara and knelt, and put his smooth, stainless head in her lap.

Barbara's hands stayed on the ground by her sides. Her gaze roved over the warm white beauty, up to the tip of the golden horn and back.

The scream was frightening. Rita's hands were up like claws, and she had bitten her tongue; there was blood on her mouth. She screamed again. She threw herself off the now withered moss toward the unicorn and Barbara. "She can't be!" Rita shrieked. She collided with Del's broad right hand. "It's wrong, I tell you, she, you, I. . . ."

"I'm satisfied," said Del, low in his throat. "Keep away, squire's daughter."

She recoiled from him, made as if to try to circle him. He stepped forward. She ground her chin into one shoulder, then the other, in a gesture of sheer frustration, turned suddenly and ran toward the ridge. "It's mine, it's mine," she screamed. "I tell you it can't be hers, don't you understand? I never once, I never did, but she, but she—"

She slowed and stopped, then, and fell silent at the sound that rose from the ridge. It began like the first patter of rain on oak leaves, and it gathered voice until it was a rumble and then a roar. She stood looking up, her face working, the sound washing over her. She shrank from it.

It was laughter.

She turned once, a pleading just beginning to form on her face. Del regarded her stonily. She faced the ridge then, and squared her shoulders, and walked up the hill, to go into the laughter, to go through it, to have it follow her all the way home and all the days of her life.

Del turned to Barbara just as she bent over the beautiful head. She said, "Silken-swift . . . go free."

The unicorn raised its head and looked up at Del. Del's mouth opened. He took a clumsy step forward, stopped again. *"You!"*

Barbara's face was wet. "You weren't to know," she choked. "You weren't ever to know . . . I was so glad you were blind, because I thought you'd never know."

He fell on his knees beside her. And when he did, the unicorn touched her face with his satin nose, and all the girl's pent-up beauty flooded outward. The unicorn rose from his kneeling, and whickered softly. Del looked at her, and only the unicorn was more beautiful. He put out his hand to the shining neck, and for a moment felt the incredible silk of the mane flowing across his fingers. The unicorn reared then, and wheeled, and in a great leap was across the bog, and in two more was on the crest of the farther ridge. He paused there briefly, with the sun on him, and then was gone.

Barbara said, "For us, he lost his pool, his beautiful pool."

And Del said, "He will get another. He must." With difficulty he added, "He couldn't be . . . punished . . . for being so gloriously Fair."

A Victorian tale of good and evil, "The New Mother" is the story of two children who, if they yield to temptation, will get into trouble from which their loving mother cannot rescue them. Although the overt morality proselytized by the story is pure Victorian drawing room, LUCY CLIFFORD'S imagination seems a much stranger place. This fantastic tale, originally published in a children's magazine, was reprinted in Clifford's best fantasy collection, Anyhow Stories *(1882). Clifford is one of the nineteenth-century writers currently being rediscovered in the contemporary search for the roots of fantasy.*

The New Mother
BY LUCY CLIFFORD

The children were always called Blue-Eyes and the Turkey. The elder one was like her dear father who was far away at sea; for the father had the bluest of blue eyes, and so gradually his little girl came to be called after them. The younger one had once, while she was still almost a baby, cried bitterly because a turkey that lived near the cottage suddenly vanished in the middle of the winter; and to console her she had been called by its name.

Now the mother and Blue-Eyes and the Turkey and the baby all lived in a lonely cottage on the edge of the forest. It was a long way to the village, nearly a mile and a half, and the mother had to work hard and had not time to go often herself to see if there was a letter at the post-office from the dear father, and so very often in the afternoon she used to send the two children. They were very proud of being able to go alone. When they came back tired with the long walk, there would be the mother waiting and watching for them, and the tea would be ready, and the baby crowing with delight; and if by any chance there was a letter from the sea, then they were happy indeed. The cottage room was so cosy: the walls were as white as snow inside as well as out. The baby's high chair stood in one corner, and in another there was a cupboard, in which the mother kept all manner of surprises.

"Dear children," the mother said one afternoon late in the autumn, "it is very chilly for you to go to the village, but you must walk quickly, and who knows but what you may bring back a letter saying that dear father is already on his way to England. Don't be long," the mother said, as she always did before they started. "Go the nearest way and don't look at any strangers you meet, and be sure you do not talk with them."

"No, mother," they answered; and then she kissed them and called them dear good children, and they joyfully started on their way.

The village was gayer than usual, for there had been a fair the day before. "Oh, I *do* wish we had been here yesterday," Blue-Eyes said as they went on to the grocer's, which was also the post-office. The postmistress was very busy and just said "No letter for you to-day." Then Blue-Eyes and the Turkey turned away to go home. They had left the village and walked some way, and then they noticed, resting against a pile of stones by the wayside, a strange wild-looking girl, who seemed very unhappy. So they thought they would ask her if they could do anything to help her, for they were kind children and sorry indeed for any one in distress.

The girl seemed to be about fifteen years old. She was dressed in very ragged clothes. Round her shoulders there was an old brown shawl. She wore no bonnet. Her hair was coal-black and hung down uncombed and unfastened. She had something hidden under her shawl; on seeing them coming towards her, she carefully put it under her and sat upon it. She sat watching the children approach, and did not move or stir till they were within a yard of her; then she wiped her eyes just as if she had been crying bitterly, and looked up.

The children stood still in front of her for a moment, staring at her. "Are you crying?" they asked shyly.

To their surprise she said in a most cheerful voice, "Oh dear, no! quite the contrary. Are you?"

"Perhaps you have lost yourself?" they said gently.

But the girl answered promptly, "Certainly not. Why, you have just found me. Besides," she added, "I live in the village."

The children were surprised at this, for they had never seen her before, and yet they thought they knew all the village folk by sight.

Then the Turkey, who had an inquiring mind, put a question. "What are you sitting on?" she asked.

"On a peardrum," the girl answered.

"What is a peardrum?" they asked.

"I am surprised at your not knowing," the girl answered. "Most people in good society have one." And then she pulled it out and showed it to them. It was a curious instrument, a good deal like a guitar in shape; it had three strings, but only two pegs by which to tune them. But the strange thing about the peardrum was not the music it made, but a little square box attached to one side.

"Where did you get it?" the children asked.

"I bought it," the girl answered.

"Didn't it cost a great deal of money?" they asked.

"Yes," answered the girl slowly, nodding her head, "it cost a great deal of money. I am very rich," she added.

"You don't look rich," they said, in as polite a voice as possible.

"Perhaps not," the girl answered cheerfully.

At this, the children gathered courage, and ventured to remark, "You look rather shabby."

"Indeed?" said the girl in a voice of one who had heard a pleasant but surprising statement. "A little shabbiness is very respectable," she added in a satisfied voice. "I must really tell them this," she continued. And the children wondered what she meant. She opened the little box by the side of the peardrum, and said, just as if she were speaking to some one who could hear her. "They say I look rather shabby; it is quite lucky isn't it?"

"Why, you are not speaking to any one!" they said, more surprised than ever.

"Oh dear, yes! I am speaking to them both."

"Both?" they said, wondering.

"Yes. I have here a little man dressed as a peasant, and a little woman to match. I put them on the lid of the box, and when I play they dance most beautifully."

"Oh! let us see; do let us see!" the children cried.

Then the village girl looked at them doubtfully. "Let you see!" she said slowly. "Well, I am not sure that I can. Tell me, are you good?"

"Yes, yes," they answered eagerly, "we are very good!"

"Then it's quite impossible," she answered, and resolutely closed the lid of the box.

They stared at her in astonishment. "But we are good," they cried, thinking she must have misunderstood them. "We are very good. Then can't you let us see the little man and woman?"

"Oh dear, no!" the girl answered. "I only show them to naughty children. And the worse the children the better do the man and woman dance."

She put the peardrum carefully under her ragged cloak, and prepared to go on her way. "I really could not have believed that you were good," she said reproachfully, as if they had accused themselves of some great crime. "Well, good day."

"Oh, but we will be naughty," they said in despair.

"I am afraid you couldn't," she answered, shaking her head. "It requires a great deal of skill to be naughty well."

And swiftly she walked away, while the children felt their eyes fill with tears, and their hearts ache with disappointment.

"If we had only been naughty," they said, "we should have seen them dance."

"Suppose," said the Turkey, "we try to be naughty to-day; perhaps she would let us see them to-morrow."

"But, oh!" said Blue-Eyes, "I don't know how to be naughty; no one ever taught me."

The Turkey thought for a few minutes in silence. "I think I can be naughty if I try," she said. "I'll try to-night."

"Oh, don't be naughty without me!" she cried. "It would be so unkind of you. You know I want to see the little man and woman just as much as you do. You are very, very unkind."

And so, quarrelling and crying, they reached their home.

Now, when their mother saw them, she was greatly astonished, and, fearing they were hurt, ran to meet them.

"Oh, my children, oh, my dear, dear children," she said; "what is the matter?"

But they did not dare tell their mother about the village girl and the little man and woman, so they answered, "Nothing is the matter," and cried all the more.

"Poor children!" the mother said to herself, "They are tired, and perhaps they are hungry; after tea they will be better." And she went back to the cottage, and made the fire blaze; and she put the kettle on to boil, and set the tea-things on the table. Then she went to the little cupboard and took out some bread and cut it on the table, and said in a loving voice, "Dear little children, come and have your tea, and see, there is the baby waking from her sleep; she will crow at us while we eat."

But the children made no answer to the dear mother; they only stood still by the window and said nothing.

"Come, children," the mother said again. "Come, Blue-Eyes, and come, my Turkey; here is nice sweet bread for tea." Then suddenly she looked up and saw that the Turkey's eyes were full of tears.

"Turkey!" she exclaimed, "my dear little Turkey! what is the matter? Come to mother, my sweet." And putting the baby down, she held out her arms, and the Turkey ran swiftly into them.

"Oh, mother," she sobbed, "Oh, dear mother! I do so want to be naughty. I do so want to be very, very naughty."

And then Blue-Eyes left her chair also, and rubbing her face against her mother's shoulder, cried sadly. "And so do I, mother. Oh, I'd give anything to be very, very naughty."

"But, my dear children," said the mother, in astonishment, "Why do you want to be naughty?"

"Because we do; oh, what shall we do?" they cried together.

"I should be very angry if you were naughty. But you could not be, for you love me," the mother answered.

"Why couldn't we?" they asked.

Then the mother thought a while before she answered; and she seemed to be speaking rather to herself than to them.

"Because if one loves well," she said gently, "one's love is stronger than all bad feelings in one, and conquers them."

"We don't know what you mean," they cried; "and we do love you; but we want to be naughty."

"Then I should know you did not love me," the mother said.

"If we were very, very, very naughty, and wouldn't be good, what then?"

"Then," said the mother sadly—and while she spoke her eyes filled with tears, and a sob almost choked her—"then," she said, "I should have to go away and leave you, and to send home a new mother, with glass eyes and wooden tail."

II

"Good-day," said the village girl, when she saw Blue-Eyes and the Turkey approach. She was again sitting by the heap of stones, and under her shawl the peardrum was hidden.

"Are the little man and woman there?" the children asked.

"Yes, thank you for inquiring after them," the girl answered; "they are both here and quite well. The little woman has heard a secret—she tells it while she dances."

"Oh do let us see," they entreated.

"Quite impossible, I assure you," the girl answered promptly. "You see, you are good."

"Oh!" said Blue-Eyes, sadly; "but mother says if we are naughty she will go away and send home a new mother, with glass eyes and a wooden tail."

"Indeed," said the girl, still speaking in the same unconcerned voice, "that is what they all say. They all threaten that kind of thing. Of course really there are no mothers with glass eyes and wooden tails; they would be much too expensive to make." And the common sense of this remark the children saw at once.

"We think you might let us see the little man and woman dance."

"The kind of thing you would think," remarked the village girl.

"But will you if we are naughty?" they asked in despair.

"I fear you could not be naughty—that is, really—even if you tried," she said scornfully.

"But if we are very naughty to-night, will you let us see them to-morrow?"

"Questions asked to-day are always best answered to-morrow," the girl said, and turned round as if to walk on. "Good day," she said blithely; "I must really go and play a little to myself."

For a few minutes the children stood looking after her, then they broke down and cried. The Turkey was the first to wipe away her tears. "Let us go home and be very naughty," she said; "then perhaps she will let us see them to-morrow."

And that afternoon the dear mother was sorely distressed, for, instead of sitting at their tea as usual with smiling happy faces, they broke their mugs and threw their bread and butter on the floor, and when the mother told them to do one thing they carefully did another, and only stamped their feet with rage when she told them to go upstairs until they were good.

"Do you remember what I told you I should do if you were very very naughty?" she asked sadly.

"Yes, we know, but it isn't true," they cried. "There is no mother with a wooden tail and glass eyes, and if there were we should just stick pins into her and send her away; but there is none."

Then the mother became really angry, and sent them off to bed, but instead of crying and being sorry at her anger, they laughed for joy, and sat up and sang merry songs at the top of their voices.

The next morning quite early, without asking leave from the

mother, the children got up and ran off as fast as they could to look for the village girl. She was sitting as usual by the heap of stones with the peardrum under her shawl.

"Now please show us the little man and woman," they cried, "and let us hear the peardrum. We were very naughty last night." But the girl kept the peardrum carefully hidden.

"So you say," she answered. "You were not half naughty enough. As I remarked before, it requires a great deal of skill to be naughty well."

"But we broke our mugs, we threw our bread and butter on the floor, we did everything we could to be tiresome."

"Mere trifles," answered the village girl scornfully. "Did you throw cold water on the fire, did you break the clock, did you pull all the tins down from the walls, and throw them on the floor?"

"No," exclaimed the children, aghast, "we did not do that."

"I thought not," the girl answered. "So many people mistake a little noise and foolishness for real naughtiness." And before they could say another word she had vanished.

"We'll be much worse," the children cried, in despair. "We'll go and do all the things she says"; and then they went home and did all these things. And when the mother saw all that they had done she did not scold them as she had the day before, but she just broke down and cried, and said sadly—

"Unless you are good to-morrow, my poor Blue-Eyes and Turkey, I shall indeed have to go away and come back no more, and the new mother I told you of will come to you."

They did not believe her; yet their hearts ached when they saw how unhappy she looked, and they thought within themselves that when they once had seen the little man and woman dance, they would be good to the dear mother for ever afterwards.

The next morning, before the birds were stirring, the children crept out of the cottage and ran across the fields. They found the village girl sitting by the heap of stones, just as if it were her natural home.

"We have been very naughty," they cried. "We have done all the things you told us; now will you show us the little man and woman?" The girl looked at them curiously. "You really seem quite excited," she said in her usual voice. "You should be calm."

"We have done all the things you told us," the children cried again, "and we do so long to hear the secret. We have been so very naughty, and mother says she will go away to-day and send home a new mother if we are not good."

"Indeed," said the girl. "Well, let me see. When did your mother say she would go?"

"But if she goes, what shall we do?" they cried in despair. "We don't want her to go; we love her very much."

"You had better go back and be good, you are really not clever enough to be anything else; and the little woman's secret is very important; she never tells it for make-believe naughtiness."

"But we did all the things you told us," the children cried.

"You didn't throw the looking-glass out of the window, or stand the baby on its head."

"No, we didn't do that," the children gasped.

"I thought not," the girl said triumphantly. "Well, good-day. I shall not be here to-morrow."

"Oh, but don't go away," they cried. "Do let us see them just once."

"Well, I shall go past your cottage at eleven o'clock this morning," the girl said. "Perhaps I shall play the peardrum as I go by."

"And will you show us the man and woman?" they asked.

"Quite impossible, unless you have really deserved it; make-believe naughtiness is only spoilt goodness. Now if you break the looking-glass and do the things that are desired . . ."

"Oh, we will," they cried. "We will be very naughty till we hear you coming."

Then again the children went home, and were naughty, oh, so very very naughty that the dear mother's heart ached and her eyes filled with tears, and at last she went upstairs and slowly put on her best gown and her new sun-bonnet, and she dressed the baby all in its Sunday clothes, and then she came down and stood before Blue-Eyes and the Turkey, and just as she did so the Turkey threw the looking-glass out of the window, and it fell with a loud crash upon the ground.

"Good-bye, my children," the mother said sadly, kissing them. "The new mother will be home presently. Oh, my poor children!" and then weeping bitterly, the mother took the baby in her arms and turned to leave the house.

"But mother, we will be good at half-past eleven, come back at half-past eleven," they cried, "and we'll both be good; we must be naughty till eleven o'clock." But the mother only picked up the little bundle in which she had tied up her cotton apron, and went slowly out at the door. Just by the corner of the fields she stopped and turned, and waved her handkerchief, all wet with tears, to the children at the window; she made the baby kiss its hand; and in a moment mother and baby had vanished from their sight.

Then the children felt their hearts ache with sorrow, and they cried bitterly, and yet they could not believe that she had gone. And the broken clock struck eleven, and suddenly there was a sound, a quick, clanging, jangling sound, with a strange discordant note at intervals. They rushed to the open window, and there they saw the village girl dancing along and playing as she did so.

"We have done all you told us," the children called. "Come and see; and now show us the little man and woman."

The girl did not cease her playing or her dancing, but she called out in a voice that was half speaking half singing. "You did it all badly. You threw the water on the wrong side of the fire, the tin things were not quite in the middle of the room, the clock was not broken enough, you did not stand the baby on its head."

She was already passing the cottage. She did not stop singing, and all she said sounded like part of a terrible song. "I am going to my own land," the girl sang, "to the land where I was born."

"But our mother is gone," the children cried; "our dear mother will she ever come back?"

"No," sang the girl, "she'll never come back. She took a boat upon the river; she is sailing to the sea; she will meet your father once again, and they will go sailing on."

Then the girl, her voice getting fainter and fainter in the distance, called out once more to them. "Your new mother is coming. She is already on her way; but she only walks slowly, for her tail is rather long, and her spectacles are left behind; but she is coming, she is coming—coming—coming."

The last word died away; it was the last one they ever heard the village girl utter. On she went, dancing on.

Then the children turned, and looked at each other and at the little cottage home, that only a week before had been so bright and happy, so cosy and spotless. The fire was out, the clock all broken and spoilt. And there was the baby's high chair, with no baby to sit in it; there was the cupboard on the wall, and never a sweet loaf on its shelf; and there were the broken mugs, and the bits of bread tossed about, and the greasy boards which the mother had knelt down to scrub until they were as white as snow. In the midst of all stood the children, looking at the wreck they had made, their eyes blinded with tears, and their poor little hands clasped in misery.

"I don't know what we shall do if the new mother comes," cried Blue-Eyes. "I shall never, never like any other mother."

The Turkey stopped crying for a minute, to think what should be done. "We will bolt the door and shut the window; and we won't take any notice when she knocks."

All through the afternoon they sat watching and listening for fear of the new mother; but they saw and heard nothing of her, and gradually they became less and less afraid lest she should come. They fetched a pail of water and washed the floor; they found some rags, and rubbed the tins; they picked up the broken mugs and made the room as neat as they could. There was no sweet loaf to put on the table, but perhaps the mother would bring something from the village, they thought. At last all was ready, and Blue-Eyes and the Turkey washed their faces and their hands, and then sat and waited, for of course they did not believe what the village girl had said about their mother sailing away.

Suddenly, while they were sitting by the fire, they heard a sound as of something heavy being dragged along the ground outside, and then there was a loud and terrible knocking at the door. The children felt their hearts stand still. They knew it could not be their own mother, for she would have turned the handle and tried to come in without any knocking at all.

Again there came a loud and terrible knocking.

"She'll break the door down if she knocks so hard," cried Blue-Eyes.

"Go and put your back to it," whispered the Turkey, "and I'll peep out of the window and try to see if it is really the new mother."

So in fear and trembling Blue-Eyes put her back against the door, and the Turkey went to the window. She could just see a black satin poke bonnet with a frill round the edge, and a long bony arm carrying a black leather bag. From beneath the bonnet there flashed a strange bright light, and Turkey's heart sank and her cheeks turned pale, for she knew it was the flashing of two glass eyes. She crept up to Blue-Eyes. "It is—it is—it is!" she whispered, her voice shaking with fear, "it is the new mother!"

Together they stood with the two little backs against the door.

There was a long pause. They thought perhaps the new mother had made up her mind that there was no one at home to let her in, and would go away, but presently the two children heard through the thin wooden door the new mother move a little, and then say to herself— "I must break the door open with my tail."

For one terrible moment all was still, but in it the children could almost hear her lift up her tail, and then, with a fearful blow, the little painted door was cracked and splintered. With a shriek the children darted from the spot and fled through the cottage, and out at the back door into the forest beyond. All night long they stayed in the darkness and the cold, and all the next day and the next, and all through the cold, dreary days and the long dark nights that followed.

They are there still, my children. All through the long weeks and months have they been there, with only green rushes for their pillows and only the brown dead leaves to cover them, feeding on the wild strawberries in the summer, or on the nuts when they hang green; on the blackberries when they are no longer sour in the autumn, and in the winter on the little red berries that ripen in the snow. They wander about among the tall dark firs or beneath the great trees beyond. Sometimes they stay to rest beside the little pool near the copse, and they long and long, with a longing that is greater than words can say, to see their own dear mother again, just once again, to tell her that they'll be good for evermore—just once again.

And still the new mother stays in the little cottage, but the windows are closed and the doors are shut, and no one knows what the inside looks like. Now and then, when the darkness has fallen and the night is still, hand in hand Blue-Eyes and the Turkey creep up near the home in which they once were so happy, and with beating hearts they watch and listen; sometimes a blinding flash comes through the window, and they know it is the light from the new mother's glass eyes, or they hear a strange muffled noise, and they know it is the sound of her wooden tail as she drags it along the floor.

This story by one of the founders of contemporary fantasy, ANTHONY BOUCHER, *derives its psychological force, as does Philip K. Dick's "The King of the Elves" (p. 375), from the tension between what is real and what is not. Adult fantasy fiction in English would not be as advanced or sophisticated as it is today were it not for the career of Boucher, the founding (in 1949) co-editor of* The Magazine of Fantasy & Science Fiction. *His erudition and good taste drew many of the best writers of the post-WWII period to his magazine, from Shirley Jackson and Charles G. Finney to Richard Matheson, Theodore Sturgeon, Poul Anderson, and a host of others.*

Mr. Lupescu
BY ANTHONY BOUCHER

The teacups rattled, and flames flickered over the logs.

"Alan, I *do* wish you could do something about Bobby."

"Isn't that rather Robert's place?"

"Oh you know *Robert*. He's so busy doing good in nice abstract ways with committees in them."

"And headlines."

"He can't be bothered with things like Mr. Lupescu. After all, Bobby's only his *son.*"

"And yours, Marjorie."

"And mine. But things like this take a *man,* Alan."

The room was warm and peaceful; Alan stretched his long legs by the fire and felt domestic. Marjorie was soothing even when she fretted. The firelight did things to her hair and the curve of her blouse.

A small whirlwind entered at high velocity and stopped only when Marjorie said, "Bob-*by!* Say hello nicely to Uncle Alan."

Bobby said hello and stood tentatively on one foot.

"Alan . . ." Marjorie prompted.

Alan sat up straight and tried to look paternal. "Well, Bobby," he said. "And where are you off to in such a hurry?"

"See Mr. Lupescu 'f course. He usually comes afternoons."

"Your mother's been telling me about Mr. Lupescu. He must be quite a person."

"Oh gee I'll say he is, Uncle Alan. He's got a great big red nose and red gloves and red eyes—not like when you've been crying but really red like yours're brown—and little red wings that twitch only he can't fly with them cause they're ruddermentary he says. And he talks like—oh gee I can't do it, but he's swell, he is."

"Lupescu's a funny name for a fairy godfather, isn't it, Bobby?"

"Why? Mr. Lupescu always says why do all the fairies have to be Irish because it takes all kinds, doesn't it?"

"*Alan!*" Marjorie said. "I don't see that you're doing a *bit* of good. You talk to him seriously like that and you simply make him think it *is* serious. And you *do* know better, don't you, Bobby? You're just joking with us."

"Joking? About *Mr. Lupescu?*"

"Marjorie, you don't— Listen, Bobby. Your mother didn't mean to insult you or Mr. Lupescu. She just doesn't believe in what she's never seen, and you can't blame her. Now, supposing you took her and me out in the garden and we could all see Mr. Lupescu. Wouldn't that be fun?"

"Uh-uh." Bobby shook his head gravely. "Not for Mr. Lupescu. He doesn't like people. Only little boys. And he says if I ever bring people to see him, then he'll let Gorgo get me. G'bye now." And the whirlwind departed.

Marjorie sighed. "At least thank heavens for Gorgo. I never can get a very clear picture out of Bobby, but he says Mr. Lupescu tells the most *terrible* things about him. And if there's any trouble about vegetables or brushing teeth, all I have to say is *Gorgo* and hey presto!"

Alan rose. "I don't think you need worry, Marjorie. Mr. Lupescu seems to do more good than harm, and an active imagination is no curse to a child."

"You haven't *lived* with Mr. Lupescu."

"To live in a house like this, I'd chance it," Alan laughed. "But please forgive me now—back to the cottage and the typewriter . . . Seriously, why don't you ask Robert to talk with him?"

Marjorie spread her hands helplessly.

"I know. I'm always the one to assume responsibilities. And yet you married Robert."

Marjorie laughed. "I don't know. Somehow there's something *about* Robert . . ." Her vague gesture happened to include the original Dégas over the fireplace, the sterling tea service, and even the liveried footman who came in at that moment to clear away.

Mr. Lupescu was pretty wonderful that afternoon, all right. He had a little kind of an itch like in his wings and they kept twitching all the time. Stardust, he said. It tickles. Got it up in the Milky Way. Friend of mine has a wagon route up there.

Mr. Lupescu had lots of friends, and they all did something you wouldn't ever think of, not in a squillion years. That's why he didn't like people, because people don't do things you can tell stories about. They just work or keep house or are mothers or something.

But one of Mr. Lupescu's friends, now, was captain of a ship, only it went in time, and Mr. Lupescu took trips with him and came back and told you all about what was happening this very minute five hundred years ago. And another of the friends was a radio engineer, only he could tune in on all the kingdoms of faery and Mr. Lupescu would squidgle up his red nose and twist it like a dial and make noises like all the kingdoms of faery coming in on the set. And then there was Gorgo, only he wasn't a friend—not exactly; not even to Mr. Lupescu.

They'd been playing for a couple of weeks—only it must've been really hours, cause Mamselle hadn't yelled about supper yet, but Mr. Lupescu says Time is funny—when Mr. Lupescu screwed up his red eyes and said, "Bobby, let's go in the house."

"But there's people in the house, and you don't—"

"I know I don't like people. That's why we're going in the house. Come on, Bobby, or I'll—"

So what could you do when you didn't even want to hear him say Gorgo's name?

He went into Father's study through the French window, and it was a strict rule that nobody *ever* went into Father's study, but rules weren't for Mr. Lupescu.

Father was on the telephone telling somebody he'd try to be at a luncheon but there was a committee meeting that same morning but he'd see. While he was talking, Mr. Lupescu went over to a table and opened a drawer and took something out.

When Father hung up, he saw Bobby first and started to be very mad. He said, "Young man, you've been trouble enough to your Mother and me with all your stories about your red-winged Mr. Lupescu, and now if you're to start bursting in—"

You have to be polite and introduce people. "Father, this is Mr. Lupescu. And see, he does too have red wings."

Mr. Lupescu held out the gun he'd taken from the drawer and

shot Father once right through the forehead. It made a little clean hole in front and a big messy hole in back. Father fell down and was dead.

"Now, Bobby," Mr. Lupescu said, "a lot of people are going to come here and ask you a lot of questions. And if you don't tell the truth about exactly what happened, I'll send Gorgo to fetch you."

Then Mr. Lupescu was gone through the French window.

"It's a curious case, Lieutenant," the medical examiner said. "It's fortunate I've dabbled a bit in psychiatry; I can at least give you a lead until you get the experts in. The child's statement that his fairy godfather shot his father is obviously a simple flight mechanism, susceptible of two interpretations. A, the father shot himself; the child was so horrified by the sight that he refused to accept it and invented this explanation. B, the child shot the father, let us say by accident, and shifted the blame to his imaginary scapegoat. B has, of course, its more sinister implications: if the child had resented his father and created an ideal substitute, he might make the substitute destroy the reality. . . . But there's the solution to your eyewitness testimony; which alternative is true, Lieutenant, I leave up to your researches into motive and the evidence of ballistics and fingerprints. The angle of the wound jibes with either."

The man with the red nose and eyes and gloves and wings walked down the back lane to the cottage. As soon as he got inside, he took off his coat and removed the wings and the mechanism of strings and rubber that made them twitch. He laid them on top of the ready pile of kindling and lit the fire. When it was well started, he added the gloves. Then he took off the nose, kneaded the putty until the red of its outside vanished into the neutral brown of the mass, jammed it into a crack in the wall, and smoothed it over. Then he took the red-irised contact lenses out of his brown eyes and went into the kitchen, found a hammer, pounded them to powder, and washed the powder down the sink.

Alan started to pour himself a drink and found, to his pleased surprise, that he didn't especially need one. But he did feel tired. He could lie down and recapitulate it all, from the invention of Mr. Lupescu (and Gorgo and the man with the Milky Way route) to today's success and on into the future when Marjorie—pliant, trusting Marjorie—would be more desirable than ever as Robert's widow and heir. And Bobby would need a *man* to look after him.

Alan went into the bedroom. Several years passed by in the few seconds it took him to recognize what was waiting on the bed, but then, Time is funny.

Alan said nothing.

"Mr. Lupescu, I presume?" said Gorgo.

In this wonderfully inventive story, a famous conductor who has a tail steals the affections of the elusive woman whom a young man loves. STEPHEN VINCENT BENÉT's use of folk tale and fantasy for clever social satire links him to John Collier (see "Bird of Prey," p. 189) and Saki (see "Tobermory," p. 368), each using fantasy as a device to transform what would otherwise be a conventional mainstream fiction. Benét won the Pulitzer Prize for his poetry in 1929. His adult fantasy, The Devil and Daniel Webster *(1937), as well as his use of fantasy in his poetry, make him one of the significant fantasists of the first half of this century in the United States.*

The King of the Cats
BY STEPHEN VINCENT BENÉT

"But, my *dear*," said Mrs. Culverin, with a tiny gasp, "you can't actually mean—a *tail!*"

Mrs. Dingle nodded impressively. "Exactly. I've seen him. Twice, Paris, of course, and then, a command appearance at Rome—we were in the Royal box. He conducted—my dear, you've never heard such effects from an orchestra—and, my dear," she hesitated slightly, "he conducted *with it.*"

"How perfectly, fascinatingly too horrid for words!" said Mrs. Culverin in a dazed but greedy voice. "We *must* have him to dinner as soon as he comes over—he is coming over, isn't he?"

"The twelfth," said Mrs. Dingle with a gleam in her eyes. "The New Symphony people have asked him to be guest-conductor for three special concerts—I do hope you can dine with *us* some night while he's here—he'll be very busy, of course—but he's promised to give us what time he can spare——"

"Oh, thank you, dear," said Mrs. Culverin, abstractedly, her last raid upon Mrs. Dingle's pet British novelist still fresh in her mind. "You're always so delightfully hospitable—but you mustn't wear yourself out—the rest of us must do *our* part—I know Harry and myself would be only too glad to——"

"That's very sweet of you, darling." Mrs. Dingle also remembered the larceny of the British novelist. "But we're just going to give Monsieur Tibault—sweet name, isn't it! They say he's descended from the Tybalt in 'Romeo and Juliet' and that's why he doesn't like Shakespeare—we're just going to give Monsieur Tibault the simplest sort of time—a little reception after his first concert, perhaps. He hates," she looked around the table, "large, mixed parties. And then, of course, his —er—little idiosyncrasy——" she coughed delicately. "It makes him feel a trifle shy with strangers."

"But I don't understand yet, Aunt Emily," said Tommy Brooks, Mrs. Dingle's nephew. "Do you really mean this Tibault bozo has a tail? Like a monkey and everything?"

"Tommy dear," said Mrs. Culverin, crushingly, "in the first place Monsieur Tibault is not a bozo—he is a very distinguished musician—the finest conductor in Europe. And in the second place——"

"He has," Mrs. Dingle was firm. "He has a tail. He conducts with it."

"Oh, but honestly!" said Tommy, his ears pinkening, "I mean—of course, if you say so, Aunt Emily, I'm sure he has—but still, it sounds pretty steep, if you know what I mean! How about it, Professor Tatto?"

Professor Tatto cleared his throat. "Tck," he said, putting his fingertips together cautiously, "I shall be very anxious to see this Monsieur Tibault. For myself, I have never observed a genuine specimen of *homo caudatus,* so I should be inclined to doubt, and yet . . . In the Middle Ages, for instance, the belief in men—er—tailed or with caudal appendages of some sort, was both widespread and, as far as we can gather, well-founded. As late as the Eighteenth Century, a Dutch sea-captain with some character for veracity, recounts the discovery of a pair of such creatures in the island of Formosa. They were in a low state of civilization, I believe, but the appendages in question were quite distinct. And in 1860, Dr. Grimbrook, the English surgeon, claims to have treated no less than three African natives with short but evident tails—though his testimony rests upon his unsupported word. After all, the thing is not impossible, though doubtless unusual. Web feet—rudimentary gills—these occur with some frequency. The appendix we have with us always. The chain of our descent from the ape-like form is by no means complete. For that matter," he beamed around the table, "what can we call the last few vertebrae of the normal spine but the beginnings of a concealed and rudimentary tail? Oh, yes—yes—it's possible—quite—that in an extraordinary case—a reversion to type—a survival—though, of course——"

"I told you so," said Mrs. Dingle triumphantly. *"Isn't* it fascinating? Isn't it, Princess?"

The Princess Vivrakanarda's eyes, blue as a field of larkspur, fathomless as the center of heaven, rested lightly for a moment on Mrs. Dingle's excited countenance.

"Ve-ry fascinating," she said, in a voice like stroked, golden velvet. "I should like—I should like ve-ry much to meet this Monsieur Tibault."

"Well, *I* hope he breaks his neck!" said Tommy Brooks, under his breath—but nobody ever paid much attention to Tommy.

Nevertheless, as the time for Mr. Tibault's arrival in these States drew nearer and nearer, people in general began to wonder whether the Princess had spoken quite truthfully—for there was no doubt of the fact that, up till then, she had been the unique sensation of the season—and you know what social lions and lionesses are.

It was, if you remember, a Siamese season, and genuine Siamese were at quite as much of a premium as Russian accents had been in the quaint old days when the Chauve-Souris was a novelty. The Siamese Art Theater, imported at terrific expense, was playing to packed houses at the Century Theater. "Gushuptzgu," an epic novel of Siamese farm life, in nineteen closely-printed volumes, had just been awarded the Nobel prize. Prominent pet-and-newt dealers reported no cessation in the appalling demand for Siamese cats. And upon the crest of this wave of interest in things Siamese, the Princess Vivrakanarda poised with the elegant nonchalance of a Hawaiian water-baby upon his surf-board. She was indispensable. She was incomparable. She was everywhere.

Youthful, enormously wealthy, allied on one hand to the Royal Family of Siam and on the other to the Cabots (and yet with the first eighteen of her twenty-one years shrouded from speculation in a golden zone of mystery), the mingling of races in her had produced an exotic beauty as distinguished as it was strange. She moved with a feline, effortless grace, and her skin was as if it had been gently powdered with tiny grains of the purest gold—yet the blueness of her eyes, set just a trifle slantingly, was as pure and startling as the sea on the rocks of Maine. Her brown hair fell to her knees—she had been offered extraordinary sums by the Master Barbers' Protective Association to have it shingled. Straight as a waterfall tumbling over brown rocks, it had a vague perfume of sandalwood and suave spices and held tints of rust and the sun. She did not talk very much—but then she did not have to —her voice had an odd, small, melodious huskiness that haunted the mind. She lived alone and was reputed to be very lazy—at least it was known that she slept during most of the day—but at night she bloomed like a moonflower and a depth came into her eyes.

It was no wonder that Tommy Brooks fell in love with her. The wonder was that she let him. There was nothing exotic or distinguished about Tommy—he was just one of those pleasant, normal young men who seem created to carry on the bond business by reading the newspapers in the University Club during most of the day, and can always be relied upon at night to fill an unexpected hole in a dinner-party. It is true that the Princess could hardly be said to do more than tolerate any of her suitors—no one had ever seen those aloofly arrogant eyes enliven at the entrance of any male. But she seemed to be able to tolerate Tommy a little more than the rest—and that young man's infatuated day-dreams were beginning to be beset by smart solitaires and imaginary apartments on Park Avenue, when the famous M. Tibault conducted his first concert at Carnegie Hall.

Tommy Brooks sat beside the Princess. The eyes he turned upon her were eyes of longing and love, but her face was as impassive as a Benda mask, and the only remark she made during the preliminary bustlings was that there seemed to be a number of people in the audience. But Tommy was relieved, if anything, to find her even a little more aloof than usual, for, ever since Mrs. Culverin's dinner-party, a vague disquiet as to the possible impression which this Tibault creature might make upon her, had been growing in his mind. It shows his devotion that he was present at all. To a man whose simple Princetonian nature found in "Just a Little Love, a Little Kiss," the quintessence of musical art, the average symphony was a positive torture, and he looked forward to the evening's program itself with a grim, brave smile.

"Ssh!" said Mrs. Dingle, breathlessly. "He's coming!" It seemed to the startled Tommy as if he were suddenly back in the trenches under a heavy barrage, as M. Tibault made his entrance to a perfect bombardment of applause.

Then the enthusiastic noise was sliced off in the middle and a gasp took its place—a vast, windy sigh, as if every person in that multitude had suddenly said "Ah." For the papers had not lied about him. The tail was there.

They called him theatric—but how well he understood the uses of theatricalism! Dressed in unrelieved black from head to foot (the black dress-shirt had been a special token of Mussolini's esteem), he did not walk on, he strolled, leisurely, easily, aloofly, the famous tail curled nonchalantly about one wrist—a suave, black panther lounging through a summer garden with that little mysterious weave of the head that panthers have when they pad behind bars—the glittering darkness of his eyes unmoved by any surprise or elation. He nodded, twice, in regal acknowledgment, as the clapping reached an apogee of frenzy. To Tommy there was something dreadfully reminiscent of the Princess in the way he nodded. Then he turned to his orchestra.

A second and louder gasp went up from the audience at this point, for, as he turned, the tip of that incredible tail twined with dainty carelessness into some hidden pocket and produced a black baton. But Tommy did not even notice. He was looking at the Princess instead.

She had not even bothered to clap, at first, but now—— He had never seen her moved like this, never. She was not applauding, her hands were clenched in her lap, but her whole body was rigid, rigid as a steel bar, and the blue flowers of her eyes were bent upon the figure of M. Tibault in a terrible concentration. The pose of her entire figure was so still and intense that for an instant Tommy had the lunatic idea that any moment she might leap from her seat beside him as lightly as a moth, and land, with no sound, at M. Tibault's side to—yes—to rub her proud head against his coat in worship. Even Mrs. Dingle would notice in a moment.

"Princess—" he said, in a horrified whisper, "Princess—"

Slowly the tenseness of her body relaxed, her eyes veiled again, she grew calm.

"Yes, Tommy?" she said, in her usual voice, but there was still something about her . . .

"Nothing, only—oh, hang—he's starting!" said Tommy, as M. Tibault, his hands loosely clasped before him, turned and *faced* the audience. His eyes dropped, his tail switched once impressively, then gave three little preliminary taps with his baton on the floor.

Seldom has Gluck's overture to "Iphigenie in Aulis" received such an ovation. But it was not until the Eighth Symphony that the hysteria of the audience reached its climax. Never before had the New Symphony been played so superbly—and certainly never before had it been led with such genius. Three prominent conductors in the audience were sobbing with the despairing admiration of envious children toward the close, and one at least was heard to offer wildly ten thousand dollars to a well-known facial surgeon there present for a shred of evidence that tails of some variety could by any stretch of science be grafted upon a normally decaudate form. There was no doubt about it—no mortal hand and arm, be they ever so dexterous, could combine the delicate élan and powerful grace displayed in every gesture of M. Tibault's tail.

A sable staff, it dominated the brasses like a flicker of black lightning; an ebon, elusive whip, it drew the last exquisite breath of melody from the woodwinds and ruled the stormy strings like a magician's rod. M. Tibault bowed and bowed again—roar after roar of frenzied admiration shook the hall to its foundations—and when he finally staggered, exhausted, from the platform, the president of the Wednesday Sonata Club was only restrained by force from flinging her ninety-thousand-dollar string of pearls after him in an excess of esthetic appreciation. New York had come and seen—and New York was conquered. Mrs. Dingle was immediately besieged by reporters, and Tommy Brooks looked forward to the "little party" at which he was to meet the new hero of the hour with feelings only a little less lugubrious than those that would have come to him just before taking his seat in the electric chair.

The meeting between his Princess and M. Tibault was worse and better than he expected. Better because, after all, they did not say much to each other—and worse because it seemed to him, somehow, that some curious kinship of mind between them made words unnecessary. They were certainly the most distinguished-looking couple in the room, as he bent over her hand. "So darlingly foreign, both of them, and yet so different," babbled Mrs. Dingle—but Tommy couldn't agree.

They were different, yes—the dark, lithe stranger with that bizarre appendage tucked carelessly in his pocket, and the blue-eyed, brown-haired girl. But that difference only accentuated what they had in common—something in the way they moved, in the suavity of their gestures, in the set of their eyes. Something deeper, even, than race. He tried to puzzle it out—then, looking around at the others, he had a flash of revelation. It was as if that couple were foreign, indeed—not only to New York but to all common humanity. As if they were polite guests from a different star.

Tommy did not have a very happy evening, on the whole. But his mind worked slowly, and it was not until much later that the mad suspicion came upon him in full force.

Perhaps he is not to be blamed for his lack of immediate comprehension. The next few weeks were weeks of bewildered misery for him. It was not that the Princess's attitude toward him had changed—she was just as tolerant of him as before, but M. Tibault was always there. He had a faculty of appearing as out of thin air—he walked, for all his height, as lightly as a butterfly—and Tommy grew to hate that faintest shuffle on the carpet that announced his presence as he had never hated the pound of the guns.

And then, hang it all, the man was so smooth, so infernally, unrufflably smooth! He was never out of temper, never embarrassed. He treated Tommy with the extreme of urbanity, and yet his eyes mocked, deep-down, and Tommy could do nothing. And, gradually, the Princess became more and more drawn to this stranger, in a soundless communion that found little need for speech—and that, too, Tommy saw and hated, and that, too, he could not mend.

He began to be haunted not only by M. Tibault in the flesh but by M. Tibault in the spirit. He slept badly, and when he slept, he dreamed —of M. Tibault, a man no longer, but a shadow, a specter, the limber ghost of an animal whose words came purringly between sharp little pointed teeth. There was certainly something odd about the whole shape of the fellow—his fluid ease, the mold of his head, even the cut of his fingernails—but just what it was escaped Tommy's intensest cogitation. And when he did put his finger on it at length, at first he refused to believe.

A pair of petty incidents decided him, finally, against all reason. He had gone to Mrs. Dingle's, one winter afternoon, hoping to find the Princess. She was out with his aunt, but was expected back for tea, and he wandered idly into the library to wait. He was just about to switch on the lights, for the library was always dark even in summer, when he heard a sound of light breathing that seemed to come from the leather couch in the corner. He approached it cautiously and dimly made out the form of M. Tibault, curled up on the couch, peacefully asleep.

The sight annoyed Tommy so that he swore under his breath and was back near the door on his way out, when the feeling we all know and hate, the feeling that eyes we cannot see are watching us, arrested him. He turned back—M. Tibault had not moved a muscle of his body to all appearance—but his eyes were open now. And those eyes were black and human no longer. They were green—Tommy could have sworn it—and he could have sworn that they had no bottom and gleamed like little emeralds in the dark. It only lasted a moment, for Tommy pressed the light-button automatically—and there was M. Tibault, his normal self, yawning a little but urbanely apologetic, but it gave Tommy time to think. Nor did what happened a trifle later increase his peace of mind.

They had lit a fire and were talking in front of it—by now, Tommy hated M. Tibault so thoroughly that he felt that odd yearning for his company that often occurs in such cases. M. Tibault was telling some anecdote and Tommy was hating him worse than ever for basking with such obvious enjoyment in the heat of the flames and the ripple of his own voice.

Then they heard the street-door open, and M. Tibault jumped up—and jumping, caught one sock on a sharp corner of the brass fire-rail and tore it open in a jagged flap. Tommy looked down mechanically at the tear—a second's glance, but enough—for M. Tibault, for the first time in Tommy's experience, lost his temper completely. He swore violently in some spitting, foreign tongue—his face distorted suddenly—he clapped his hand over his sock. Then, glaring furiously at Tommy, he fairly sprang from the room, and Tommy could hear him scaling the stairs in long, agile bounds.

Tommy sank into a chair, careless for once of the fact that he heard the Princess's light laugh in the hall. He didn't want to see the Princess. He didn't want to see anybody. There had been something revealed when M. Tibault had torn that hole in his sock—and it was not the skin of a man. Tommy had caught a glimpse of—black plush. Black velvet. And then had come M. Tibault's sudden explosion of fury. Good *Lord*—did the man wear black velvet stockings under his ordinary socks? Or could he—could he—but here Tommy held his fevered head in his hands.

He went to Professor Tatto that evening with a series of hypothetical questions, but as he did not dare confide his real suspicions to the Professor, the hypothetical answers he received served only to confuse him the more. Then he thought of Billy Strang. Billy was a good sort, and his mind had a turn for the bizarre. Billy might be able to help.

He couldn't get hold of Billy for three days and lived through the interval in a fever of impatience. But finally they had dinner together at Billy's apartment, where his queer books were, and Tommy was able to blurt out the whole disordered jumble of his suspicions.

Billy listened without interrupting until Tommy was quite through. Then he pulled at his pipe. "But, my dear *man*——" he said, protestingly.

"Oh, I know—I know——" said Tommy, and waved his hands, "I know I'm crazy—you needn't tell me that—but I tell you, the man's a cat all the same—no, I don't see how he could be, but he is—why, hang it, in the first place, everybody knows he's got a *tail!*"

"Even so," said Billy, puffing. "Oh, my dear Tommy, I don't doubt you saw, or think you saw, everything you say. But, even so——" He shook his head.

"But what about those other birds, werwolves and things?" said Tommy.

Billy looked dubious. "We-ll," he admitted, "you've got me there, of course. At least—a tailed man *is* possible. And the yarns about werwolves go back far enough, so that—well, *I* wouldn't say there aren't or haven't been werwolves—but then I'm willing to believe more things than most people. But a wer-cat—or a man that's a cat and a cat that's a man—honestly, Tommy——"

"If I don't get some real advice I'll go clean off my hinge. For Heaven's sake, tell me something to *do!*"

"Lemme think," said Billy. "First, you're pizen-sure this man is——"

"A cat. Yeah," and Tommy nodded violently.

"Check. And second—if it doesn't hurt your feelings, Tommy—you're afraid this girl you're in love with has—er—at least a streak of—felinity—in her—and so she's drawn to him?"

"Oh, Lord, Billy, if I only knew!"

"Well—er—suppose she really is, too, you know—would you still be keen on her?"

"I'd marry her if she turned into a dragon every Wednesday!" said Tommy, fervently.

Billy smiled. "H'm," he said, "then the obvious thing to do is to get rid of this M. Tibault. Lemme think."

He thought about two pipes full, while Tommy sat on pins and needles. Then, finally, he burst out laughing.

"What's so darn funny?" said Tommy, aggrievedly.

"Nothing, Tommy, only I've just thought of a stunt—something so blooming crazy—but if he is—h'm—what you think he is—it *might* work———" And, going to the bookcase, he took down a book.

"If you think you're going to quiet my nerves by reading me a bedtime story———"

"Shut up, Tommy, and listen to this—if you really want to get rid of your feline friend."

"What is it?"

"Book of Agnes Repplier's. About cats. Listen.

" 'There is also a Scandinavian version of the ever famous story which Sir Walter Scott told to Washington Irving, which Monk Lewis told to Shelley and which, in one form or another, we find embodied in the folklore of every land'—now, Tommy, pay attention—'the story of the traveler who saw within a ruined abbey, a procession of cats, lowering into a grave a little coffin with a crown upon it. Filled with horror, he hastened from the spot; but when he had reached his destination, he could not forbear relating to a friend the wonder he had seen. Scarcely had the tale been told when his friend's cat, who lay curled up tranquilly by the fire, sprang to its feet, cried out, "Then I am the King of the Cats!" and disappeared in a flash up the chimney.'

"Well?" said Billy, shutting the book.

"By gum!" said Tommy, staring. "By gum! Do you think there's a chance?"

"*I* think we're both in the booby-hatch. But if you want to try it———"

"Try it! I'll spring it on him the next time I see him. But—listen—I can't make it a ruined abbey———"

"Oh, use your imagination! Make it Central Park—anywhere. Tell it as if it happened to you—seeing the funeral procession and all that. You can lead into it somehow—let's see—some general line—oh, yes—'Strange, isn't it, how fact so often copies fiction. Why, only yesterday———' See?"

"Strange, isn't it, how fact so often copies fiction," repeated Tommy dutifully, "Why, only yesterday———"

"I happened to be strolling through Central Park when I saw something very odd."

"I happened to be strolling through—here, gimme that book!" said Tommy, "I want to learn the rest of it by heart!"

Mrs. Dingle's farewell dinner to the famous Monsieur Tibault, on the occasion of his departure for his Western tour, was looked forward to with the greatest expectations. Not only would everybody be there, including the Princess Vivrakanarda, but Mrs. Dingle, a hinter if there ever was one, had let it be known that at this dinner an announcement of very unusual interest to Society might be made. So every one, for once, was almost on time, except for Tommy. He was at least fifteen minutes early, for he wanted to have speech with his aunt alone. Unfortunately, however, he had hardly taken off his overcoat when she was whispering some news in his ear so rapidly that he found it difficult to understand a word of it.

"And you mustn't breathe it to a soul!" she ended, beaming. "That is, not before the announcement—I think we'll have *that* with the salad —people never pay very much attention to salad——"

"Breathe what, Aunt Emily?" said Tommy, confused.

"The Princess, darling—the dear Princess and Monsieur Tibault —they just got engaged this afternoon, dear things! Isn't it *fascinating?*"

"Yeah," said Tommy, and started to walk blindly through the nearest door. His aunt restrained him.

"Not there, dear—not in the library. You can congratulate them later. They're just having a sweet little moment alone there now——" And she turned away to harry the butler, leaving Tommy stunned.

But his chin came up after a moment. He wasn't beaten yet.

"Strange, isn't it, how often fact copies fiction?" he repeated to himself in dull mnemonics, and, as he did so, he shook his fist at the library door.

Mrs. Dingle was wrong, as usual. The Princess and M. Tibault were not in the library—they were in the conservatory, as Tommy discovered when he wandered aimlessly past the glass doors.

He didn't mean to look, and after a second he turned away. But that second was enough.

Tibault was seated in a chair and she was crouched on a stool at his side, while his hand, softly, smoothly, stroked her brown hair. Black cat and Siamese kitten. Her face was hidden from Tommy, but he could see Tibault's face. And he could hear.

They were not talking, but there was a sound between them. A warm and contented sound like the murmur of giant bees in a hollow tree—a golden, musical rumble, deep-throated, that came from Tibault's lips and was answered by hers—a golden purr.

Tommy found himself back in the drawing-room, shaking hands with Mrs. Culverin, who said, frankly, that she had seldom seen him look so pale.

The first two courses of the dinner passed Tommy like dreams, but Mrs. Dingle's cellar was notable, and by the middle of the meat course, he began to come to himself. He had only one resolve now.

For the next few moments he tried desperately to break into the conversation, but Mrs. Dingle was talking, and even Gabriel will have a time interrupting Mrs. Dingle. At last, though, she paused for breath and Tommy saw his chance.

"Speaking of that," said Tommy, piercingly, without knowing in the least what he was referring to, "Speaking of that——"

"As I was saying," said Professor Tatto. But Tommy would not yield. The plates were being taken away. It was time for salad.

"Speaking of that," he said again, so loudly and strangely that Mrs. Culverin jumped and an awkward hush fell over the table. "Strange, isn't it, how often fact copies fiction?" There, he was started. His voice rose even higher. "Why, only to-day I was strolling through——" and, word for word, he repeated his lesson. He could see Tibault's eyes glowing at him, as he described the funeral. He could see the Princess, tense.

He could not have said what he had expected might happen when he came to the end. But it was not bored silence, everywhere, to be followed by Mrs. Dingle's acrid, "Well, Tommy, is that *quite* all?"

He slumped back in his chair, sick at heart. He was a fool and his last resource had failed. Dimly he heard his aunt's voice, saying, "Well, then——" and realized that she was about to make the fatal announcement.

But just then Monsieur Tibault spoke.

"One moment, Mrs. Dingle," he said, with extreme politeness, and she was silent. He turned to Tommy.

"You are—positive, I suppose, of what you saw this afternoon, Brooks?" he said, in tones of light mockery.

"Absolutely," said Tommy sullenly. "Do you think I'd——"

"Oh, no, no, no," Monsieur Tibault waved the implication aside, "but—such an interesting story—one likes to be sure of the details—and, of course, you *are* sure—*quite* sure—that the kind of crown you describe was on the coffin?"

"Of course," said Tommy, wondering, "but——"

"Then I'm the King of the Cats!" cried Monsieur Tibault in a voice of thunder, and, even as he cried it, the house-lights blinked—there was the soft thud of an explosion that seemed muffled in cotton-wool from the minstrel gallery—and the scene was lit for a second by an obliterating and painful burst of light that vanished in an instant and was succeeded by heavy, blinding clouds of white, pungent smoke.

"Oh, those *horrid* photographers," came Mrs. Dingle's voice in a melodious wail. "I *told* them not to take the flashlight picture till dinner was over, and now they've taken it *just* as I was nibbling lettuce!"

Some one tittered a little nervously. Some one coughed. Then, gradually the veils of smoke dislimned and the green-and-black spots in front of Tommy's eyes died away.

They were blinking at each other like people who have just come out of a cave into brilliant sun. Even yet their eyes stung with the fierceness of that abrupt illumination and Tommy found it hard to make out the faces across the table from him.

Mrs. Dingle took command of the half-blinded company with her accustomed poise. She rose, glass in hand. "And now, dear friends," she said in a clear voice, "I'm sure all of us are very happy to——" Then she stopped, open-mouthed, an expression of incredulous horror on her features. The lifted glass began to spill its contents on the table-cloth in a little stream of amber. As she spoke, she had turned directly to Monsieur Tibault's place at the table—and Monsieur Tibault was no longer there.

Some say there was a bursting flash of fire that disappeared up the chimney—some say it was a giant cat that leaped through the window at a bound, without breaking the glass. Professor Tatto puts it down to a mysterious chemical disturbance operating only over M. Tibault's chair. The butler, who is pious, believes the devil in person flew away with him, and Mrs. Dingle hesitates between witchcraft and a malicious ectoplasm dematerializing on the wrong cosmic plane. But be that as it may, one thing is certain—in the instant of fictive darkness which followed the glare of the flashlight, Monsieur Tibault, the great conductor, disappeared forever from mortal sight, tail and all.

Mrs. Culverin swears he was an international burglar and that she was just about to unmask him, when he slipped away under cover of the flashlight smoke, but no one else who sat at that historic dinner-table believes her. No, there are no sound explanations, but Tommy thinks he knows, and he will never be able to pass a cat again without wondering.

Mrs. Tommy is quite of her husband's mind regarding cats—she was Gretchen Woolwine, of Chicago *(you* know the Woolwines!)—for Tommy told her his whole story, and while she doesn't believe a great deal of it, there is no doubt in her heart that one person concerned in the affair was a *perfect* cat. Doubtless it would have been more romantic to relate how Tommy's daring finally won him his Princess—but, unfortunately, it would not be veracious. For the Princess Vivrakanarda, also, is with us no longer. Her nerves, shattered by the spectacular dénouement of Mrs. Dingle's dinner, required a sea-voyage, and from that voyage she has never returned to America.

Of course, there are the usual stories—one hears of her, a nun in a Siamese convent, or a masked dancer at Le Jardin de ma Sœur—one hears that she has been murdered in Patagonia or married in Trebizond —but, as far as can be ascertained, not one of these gaudy fables has the slightest basis in fact. I believe that Tommy, in his heart of hearts, is quite convinced that the sea-voyage was only a pretext, and that by some unheard-of means, she has managed to rejoin the formidable Monsieur Tibault, wherever in the world of the visible or the invisible he may be—in fact, that in some ruined city or subterranean palace they reign together now, King and Queen of all the mysterious Kingdom of Cats. But that, of course, is quite impossible.

An uplifting tale of wondrous possibilities, "Uncle Einar" is just one of several stories RAY BRADBURY wrote about a very strange family, creatures all, who nevertheless are just plain folks. Other stories in the cycle include "Homecoming" (1946), "The Traveller" (1946), and "The April Witch" (1952). Under the influence of science fiction/fantasy writers Theodore Sturgeon and Henry Kuttner, the young Ray Bradbury began to develop his own brand of sentimental irony in the 1940s in such stories as these, using all the clichés of fantasy for children and translating them into mature and provocative structures for the adult audience. Witches, werewolves, vampires, and all the paraphernalia of evil become human, sympathetic, and morally transformed. There is a gentle but persistent feeling that Bradbury was in fact playing with the surreal in constructing his absurd but believable images.

Uncle Einar
BY RAY BRADBURY

"It will take only a minute," said Uncle Einar's sweet wife.

"I refuse," he said. "And that takes but a *second.*"

"I've worked all morning," she said, holding to her slender back, "and you won't help? It's drumming for a rain."

"Let it rain," he cried, morosely. "I'll not be pierced by lightning just to air your clothes."

"But you're so quick at it."

"Again, I refuse." His vast tarpaulin wings hummed nervously behind his indignant back.

She gave him a slender rope on which were tied four dozen fresh-washed clothes. He turned it in his fingers with distaste. "So it's come to this," he muttered, bitterly. "To this, to this, to this." He almost wept angry and acid tears.

"Don't cry; you'll wet them down again," she said. "Jump up, now, run them about."

"Run them about." His voice was hollow, deep, and terribly wounded. "I say: let it thunder, let it pour!"

"If it was a nice, sunny day I wouldn't ask," she said, reasonably. "All my washing gone for nothing if you don't. They'll hang about the house——"

That *did* it. Above all, he hated clothes flagged and festooned so a man had to creep under on the way across a room. He jumped up. His vast green wings boomed. "Only so far as the pasture fence!"

Whirl: up he jumped, his wings chewed and loved the cool air. Before you'd say Uncle Einar Has Green Wings he sailed low across his farmland, trailing the clothes in a vast fluttering loop through the pounding concussion and back-wash of his wings!

"Catch!"

Back from the trip, he sailed the clothes, dry as popcorn, down on a series of clean blankets she'd spread for their landing.

"Thank you!" she cried.

"Gahh!" he shouted, and flew off under the apple tree to brood.

Uncle Einar's beautiful silk-like wings hung like sea-green sails behind him, and whirred and whispered from his shoulders when he sneezed or turned swiftly. He was one of the few in the Family whose talent was visible. All his dark cousins and nephews and brothers hid in small towns across the world, did unseen mental things or things with witch-fingers and white teeth, or blew down the sky like fire-leaves, or loped in forests like moon-silvered wolves. They lived comparatively safe from normal humans. Not so a man with great green wings.

Not that he hated his wings. Far from it! In his youth he'd always flown nights, because nights were rare times for winged men! Daylight held dangers, always had, always would; but nights, ah, nights, he had sailed over islands of cloud and seas of summer sky. With no danger to himself. It had been a rich, full soaring, an exhilaration.

But now he could not fly at night.

On his way home to some high mountain pass in Europe after a Homecoming among Family members in Mellin Town, Illinois (some years ago) he had drunk too much rich crimson wine. "I'll be all right," he had told himself, vaguely, as he beat his long way under the morning stars, over the moon-dreaming country hills beyond Mellin Town. And then—crack out of the sky——

A high-tension tower.

Like a netted duck! A great sizzle! His face blown black by a blue sparkler of wire, he fended off the electricity with a terrific back-jumping percussion of his wings, and fell.

His hitting the moonlit meadow under the tower made a noise like a large telephone book dropped from the sky.

Early the next morning, his dew-sodden wings shaking violently, he stood up. It was still dark. There was a faint bandage of dawn stretched across the east. Soon the bandage would stain and all flight would be restricted. There was nothing to do but take refuge in the forest and wait out the day in the deepest thicket until another night gave his wings a hidden motion in the sky.

In this fashion he met his wife.

During the day, which was warm for November first in Illinois country, pretty young Brunilla Wexley was out to udder a lost cow, for she carried a silver pail in one hand as she sidled through thickets and pleaded cleverly to the unseen cow to please return home or burst her gut with unplucked milk. The fact that the cow would have most certainly come home when her teats really needed pulling did not concern Brunilla Wexley. It was a sweet excuse for forest-journeying, thistle-blowing, and flower chewing; all of which Brunilla was doing as she stumbled upon Uncle Einar.

Asleep near a bush, he seemed a man under a green shelter.

"Oh," said Brunilla, with a fever. "A man. In a camp-tent."

Uncle Einar awoke. The camp-tent spread like a large green fan behind him.

"Oh," said Brunilla, the cow-searcher. "A man with wings."

That was how she took it. She was startled, yes, but she had never been hurt in her life, so she wasn't afraid of anyone, and it was a fancy thing to see a winged man and she was proud to meet him. She began to talk. In an hour they were old friends, and in two hours she'd quite forgotten his wings were there. And he somehow confessed how he happened to be in this wood.

"Yes, I noticed you looked banged around," she said. "That right wing looks very bad. You'd best let me take you home and fix it. You won't be able to fly all the way to Europe on it, anyway. And who wants to live in Europe these days?"

He thanked her, but he didn't quite see how he could accept.

"But I live alone," she said. "For, as you see, I'm quite ugly."

He insisted she was not.

"How kind of you," she said. "But I am, there's no fooling myself. My folks are dead, I've a farm, a big one, all to myself, quite far from Mellin Town, and I'm in need of talking company."

But wasn't she afraid of him? he asked.

"Proud and jealous would be more near it," she said. *"May I?"*

And she stroked his large green membraned veils with careful envy. He shuddered at the touch and put his tongue between his teeth.

So there was nothing for it but that he come to her house for medicaments and ointments, and my! what a burn across his face, beneath his eyes! "Lucky you weren't blinded," she said. "How'd it happen?"

"Well . . ." he said, and they were at her farm, hardly noticing they'd walked a mile, looking at each other.

A day passed, and another, and he thanked her at her door and said he must be going, he much appreciated the ointment, the care, the lodging. It was twilight and between now, six o'clock, and five the next morning, he must cross an ocean and a continent. "Thank you; goodby," he said, and started to fly off in the dusk and crashed right into a maple tree.

"Oh!" she screamed, and ran to his unconscious body.

When he waked the next hour he knew he'd fly no more in the dark again ever; his delicate night-perception was gone. The winged telepathy that had warned him where towers, trees, houses and hills stood across his path, the fine clear vision and sensibility that guided him through mazes of forest, cliff, and cloud, all were burnt forever by that strike across his face, that blue electric fry and sizzle.

"How?" he moaned softly. "How can I go to Europe? If I flew by day, I'd be seen and—miserable joke—maybe shot down! Or kept for a zoo perhaps, what a life *that'd* be! Brunilla, tell me, what shall I do?"

"Oh," she whispered, looking at her hands. "We'll think of something. . . ."

They were married.

The Family came for the wedding. In a great autumnal avalanche of maple, sycamore, oak, elm leaf they hissed and rustled, fell in a shower of horse-chestnut, thumped like winter apples on the earth, with an over-all scent of farewell-summer on the wind they made in their rushing. The ceremony? The ceremony was brief as a black candle lit, blown out, and smoke left still on the air. Its briefness, darkness, upside-down and backward quality escaped Brunilla, who only listened to the great tide of Uncle Einar's wings faintly murmuring above them as they finished out the rite. And as for Uncle Einar, the wound across his nose was almost healed and, holding Brunilla's arm, he felt Europe grow faint and melt away in the distance.

He didn't have to see very well to fly straight up, or come straight down. It was only natural that on this night of their wedding he take Brunilla in his arms and fly right up into the sky.

A farmer, five miles over, glanced at a low cloud at midnight, saw faint glows and crackles.

"Heat lightning," he observed, and went to bed.

They didn't come down till morning, with the dew.

The marriage took. She had only to look at him, and it lifted her to think she was the only woman in the world married to a winged man. "Who else could say it?" she asked her mirror. And the answer was: "No one!"

He, on the other hand, found great beauty behind her face, great kindness and understanding. He made some changes in his diet to fit her thinking, and was careful with his wings about the house; knocked porcelains and broken lamps were nerve-scrapers, he stayed away from them. He changed his sleeping habits, since he couldn't fly nights now anyhow. And she in turn fixed chairs so they were comfortable for his wings, put extra padding here or took it out there, and the things she said were the things he loved her for. "We're in our cocoons, all of us. See how ugly I am?" she said. "But one day I'll break out, spread wings as fine and handsome as you."

"You broke out long ago," he said.

She thought it over. "Yes," she had to admit. "I know just which day it was, too. In the woods when I looked for a cow and found a tent!" They laughed, and with him holding her she felt so beautiful she knew their marriage had slipped her from her ugliness, like a bright sword from its case.

They had children. At first there was fear, all on his part, that they'd be winged.

"Nonsense, I'd love it!" she said, "Keep them out from under foot."

"Then," he exclaimed, "they'd be in your *hair!*"

"Ow!" she cried.

Four children were born, three boys and a girl, who, for their energy, seemed to have wings. They popped up like toadstools in a few years, and on hot summer days asked their father to sit under the apple tree and fan them with his cooling wings and tell them wild starlit tales of island clouds and ocean skies and textures of mist and wind and how a star tastes melting in your mouth, and how to drink cold mountain air, and how it feels to be a pebble dropped from Mt. Everest, turning to a green bloom, flowering your wings just before you strike bottom!

This was his marriage.

And today, six years later, here sat Uncle Einar, here he was, festering under the apple tree, grown impatient and unkind; not because this was his desire, but because after the long wait, he was still unable to fly the wild night sky; his extra sense had never returned. Here he sat despondently, nothing more than a summer sun-parasol, green and discarded, abandoned for the season by the reckless vacationers who once sought the refuge of its translucent shadow. Was he to sit here forever, afraid to fly by day because someone might see him? Was his only flight to be as a drier of clothes for his wife, or a fanner of children on hot August noons? His one occupation had *always* been flying Family errands, quicker than storms. A boomerang, he'd whickled over hills and valleys and like a thistle, landed. He had always had money; the Family had good use for their winged man! But now? Bitterness! His wings jittered and whisked the air and made a captive thunder.

"Papa," said little Meg.

The children stood looking at his thought-dark face.

"Papa," said Ronald. "Make more thunder!"

"It's a cold March day, there'll soon be rain and plenty of thunder," said Uncle Einar.

"Will you come watch us?" asked Michael.

"Run on, run on! Let papa brood!"

He was shut of love, the children of love, and the love of children. He thought only of heavens, skies, horizons, infinities, by night or day, lit by star, moon, or sun, cloudy or clear, but always it was skies and heavens and horizons that ran ahead of you forever when you soared. Yet here he was, sculling the pasture, kept low for fear of being seen.

Misery in a deep well!

"Papa, come watch us; it's March!" cried Meg. "And we're going to the Hill with all the kids from town!"

Uncle Einar grunted. "What hill is that?"

"The Kite Hill, of course!" they all sang together.

Now he looked at them.

Each held a large paper kite, their faces sweating with anticipation and an animal glowing. In their small fingers were balls of white twine.

From the kites, colored red and blue and yellow and green, hung caudal appendages of cotton and silk strips.

"We'll fly our kites!" said Ronald. "Won't you come?"

"No," he said, sadly. "I mustn't be seen by anyone or there'd be trouble."

"You could hide and watch from the woods." said Meg. "We made the kites ourselves. Just because we know how."

"How do you know how?"

"You're our father!" was the instant cry. "That's why!"

He looked at his children for a long while. He sighed. "A kite festival, is it?"

"Yes, sir!"

"I'm going to win," said Meg.

"No, *I'm!*" Michael contradicted.

"Me, *me!*" piped Stephen.

"God up the chimney!" roared Uncle Einar, leaping high with a deafening kettledrum of wings. "Children! Children, I love you dearly!"

"Father, what's wrong?" said Michael, backing off.

"Nothing, nothing, nothing!" chanted Einar. He flexed his wings to their greatest propulsion and plundering. Whoom! they slammed like cymbals. The children fell flat in the backwash! "I have it, I *have* it! I'm free again! Fire in the flue! Feather on the wind! Brunilla!" Einar called to the house. His wife appeared. "I'm free!" he called, flushed and tall, on his toes. "Listen, Brunilla, I don't need the night any more! I can fly by day! I don't need the night! I'll fly *every* day and *any* day of the year from now on!—but, God, I waste time, talking. Look!"

And as the worried members of his family watched, he seized the cotton tail from one of the little kites, tied it to his belt behind, grabbed the twine ball, held one end in his teeth, gave the other end to his children, and up, up into the air he flew, away into the March wind!

And across the meadows and over the farms his children ran, letting out string to the daylit sky, bubbling and stumbling, and Brunilla stood back in the farmyard and waved and laughed to see what was happening; and her children marched to the far Kite Hill and stood, the four of them, holding the ball of twine in their eager, proud fingers, each tugging and directing and pulling. And the children from Mellin Town came running with *their* small kites to let up on the wind, and they saw the great green kite leap and hover in the sky and exclaimed:

"Oh, oh, what a kite! What a kite! Oh, I wish I'd a kite like that! Where, where did you *get* it!"

"Our father made it!" cried Meg and Michael and Stephen and Ronald, and gave an exultant pull on the twine and the humming, thundering kite in the sky dipped and soared and made a great and magical exclamation mark across a cloud!

FRITZ LEIBER is one of the great contemporary writers of fantasy fiction. Early in his career, in the late 1930s and early 1940s, he was devoted to Lovecraftian supernatural horror literature but, at the same time, developed his enduring Sword & Sorcery series featuring the lovable and roguish duo, Fafhrd and the Grey Mouser, in the invented world of Newhon (a rich transformation of prehistoric Europe), out of fondness for the adventures of Robert E. Howard's Conan the Barbarian. He went on to become one of the most distinguished and innovative science fiction writers of the past four decades, but never lost his enthusiasm for fantasy in all its forms. The following story is somewhat reminiscent of the early horror fantasies of Ray Bradbury dealing with children, but has Leiber's characteristic grace, elegance, and ironic humor.

Space-Time for Springers
BY FRITZ LEIBER

Gummitch was a superkitten, as he knew very well, with an I.Q. of about 160. Of course, he didn't talk. But everybody knows that I.Q. tests based on language ability are very one-sided. Besides, he would talk as soon as they started setting a place for him at table and pouring him coffee. Ashurbanipal and Cleopatra ate horsemeat from pans on the floor and they didn't talk. Baby dined in his crib on milk from a bottle and he didn't talk. Sissy sat at table but they didn't pour her coffee and she didn't talk—not one word. Father and Mother (whom Gummitch had nicknamed Old Horsemeat and Kitty-Come-Here) sat at table and poured each other coffee and they *did* talk. Q.E.D.

Meanwhile, he would get by very well on thought projection and intuitive understanding of all human speech—not even to mention cat patois, which almost any civilized animal could play by ear. The dramatic monologues and Socratic dialogues, the quiz and panel-show appearances, the felidological expedition to darkest Africa (where he would uncover the real truth behind lions and tigers), the exploration of the outer planets—all these could wait. The same went for the books for which he was ceaselessly accumulating material: *The Encyclopedia of Odors, Anthropofeline Psychology, Invisible Signs and Secret Wonders, Space-Time for Springers, Slit Eyes Look at Life,* et cetera. For the present it was enough to live existence to the hilt and soak up knowledge, missing no experience proper to his age level—to rush about with tail aflame.

So to all outward appearances Gummitch was just a vividly normal kitten, as shown by the succession of nicknames he bore along the magic path that led from blue-eyed infancy toward puberty: Little One, Squawker, Portly, Bumble (for purring not clumsiness), Old Starved-to-Death, Fierso, Loverboy (affection not sex), Spook and Catnik. Of these only the last perhaps requires further explanation: the Russians had just sent Muttnik up after Sputnik, so that when one evening Gummitch streaked three times across the firmament of the living room floor in the same direction, past the fixed stars of the humans and the comparatively slow-moving heavenly bodies of the two older cats, and Kitty-Come-Here quoted the line from Keats:

Then felt I like some watcher of the skies
When a new planet swims into his ken;

it was inevitable that Old Horsemeat would say, "Ah—Catnik!"

The new name lasted all of three days, to be replaced by Gummitch, which showed signs of becoming permanent.

The little cat was on the verge of truly growing up, at least so Gummitch overheard Old Horsemeat comment to Kitty-Come-Here. A few short weeks, Old Horsemeat said, and Gummitch's fiery flesh would harden, his slim neck thicken, the electricity vanish from everything but his fur, and all his delightful kittenish qualities rapidly give way to the earth-bound singlemindedness of a tom. They'd be lucky, Old Horsemeat concluded, if he didn't turn completely surly like Ashurbanipal.

Gummitch listened to these predictions with gay unconcern and with secret amusement from his vantage point of superior knowledge, in the same spirit that he accepted so many phases of his outwardly conventional existence: the murderous sidelong looks he got from Ashurbanipal and Cleopatra as he devoured his own horsemeat from his little tin pan, because they sometimes were given canned catfood but he never; the stark idiocy of Baby, who didn't know the difference between a live cat and a stuffed teddy bear and who tried to cover up his ignorance by making goo-goo noises and poking indiscriminately at all eyes; the far more serious—because cleverly hidden—

maliciousness of Sissy, who had to be watched out for warily—especially when you were alone—and whose retarded—even warped—development, Gummitch knew, was Old Horsemeat and Kitty-Come-Here's deepest, most secret, worry (more of Sissy and her evil ways soon); the limited intellect of Kitty-Come-Here, who despite the amounts of coffee she drank was quite as featherbrained as kittens are supposed to be and who firmly believed, for example, that kittens operated in the same space-time as other beings—that to get from *here* to *there* they had to cross the space *between*—and similar fallacies; the mental stodginess of even Old Horsemeat, who although he understood quite a bit of the secret doctrine and talked intelligently to Gummitch when they were alone, nevertheless suffered from the limitations of his status—a rather nice old god but a maddeningly slow-witted one.

But Gummitch could easily forgive all this massed inadequacy and downright brutishness in his felino-human household, because he was aware that he alone knew the real truth about himself and about other kittens and babies as well, the truth which was hidden from weaker minds, the truth that was as intrinsically incredible as the germ theory of disease or the origin of the whole great universe in the explosion of a single atom.

As a baby kitten Gummitch had believed that Old Horsemeat's two hands were hairless kittens permanently attached to the ends of Old Horsemeat's arms but having an independent life of their own. How he had hated and loved those two five-legged sallow monsters, his first playmates, comforters and battle-opponents!

Well, even that fantastic discarded notion was but a trifling fancy compared to the real truth about himself!

The forehead of Zeus split open to give birth to Minerva. Gummitch had been born from the waist-fold of a dirty old terrycloth bathrobe, Old Horsemeat's basic garment. The kitten was intuitively certain of it and had proved it to himself as well as any Descartes or Aristotle. In a kitten-size tuck of that ancient bathrobe the atoms of his body had gathered and quickened into life. His earliest memories were of snoozing wrapped in terrycloth, warmed by Old Horsemeat's heat. Old Horsemeat and Kitty-Come-Here were his true parents. The other theory of his origin, the one he heard Old Horsemeat and Kitty-Come-Here recount from time to time—that he had been the only surviving kitten of a litter abandoned next door, that he had had the shakes from vitamin deficiency and lost the tip of his tail and the hair on his paws and had to be nursed back to life and health with warm yellowish milk-and-vitamins fed from an eyedropper—that other theory was just one of those rationalizations with which mysterious nature cloaks the birth of heroes, perhaps wisely veiling the truth from minds unable to bear it, a rationalization as false as Kitty-Come-Here and Old Horsemeat's touching belief that Sissy and Baby were their children rather than the cubs of Ashurbanipal and Cleopatra.

The day that Gummitch had discovered by pure intuition the secret of his birth he had been filled with a wild instant excitement. He had only kept it from tearing him to pieces by rushing out to the kitchen and striking and devouring a fried scallop, torturing it fiendishly first for twenty minutes.

And the secret of his birth was only the beginning. His intellectual faculties aroused, Gummitch had two days later intuited a further and greater secret: since he was the child of humans he would, upon reaching this maturation date of which Old Horsemeat had spoken, turn not into a sullen tom but into a godlike human youth with reddish golden hair the color of his present fur. He would be poured coffee; and he would instantly be able to talk, probably in all languages. While Sissy (how clear it was now!) would at approximately the same time shrink and fur out into a sharp-clawed and vicious she-cat dark as her hair, sex and self-love her only concerns, fit harem-mate for Cleopatra, concubine to Ashurbanipal.

Exactly the same was true, Gummitch realized at once, for all kittens and babies, all humans and cats, wherever they might dwell. Metamorphosis was as much a part of the fabric of their lives as it was of the insects'. It was also the basic fact underlying all legends of werewolves, vampires and witches' familiars.

If you just rid your mind of preconceived notions, Gummitch told himself, it was all very logical. Babies were stupid, fumbling, vindictive creatures without reason or speech. What more natural than that they should grow up into mute sullen selfish beasts bent only on rapine and reproduction? While kittens were quick, sensitive, subtle, supremely alive. What other destiny were they possibly fitted for except to become the deft, word-speaking, book-writing, music-making, meat-getting-and-dispensing masters of the world? To dwell on the physical differences, to point out that kittens and men, babies and cats, are rather unlike in appearance and size, would be to miss the forest for the trees

—very much as if an entomologist should proclaim metamorphosis a myth because his microscope failed to discover the wings of a butterfly in a caterpillar's slime or a golden beetle in a grub.

Nevertheless it was such a mind-staggering truth, Gummitch realized at the same time, that it was easy to understand why humans, cats, babies and perhaps most kittens were quite unaware of it. How safely explain to a butterfly that he was once a hairy crawler, or to a dull larva that he will one day be a walking jewel? No, in such situations the delicate minds of man- and feline-kind are guarded by a merciful mass amnesia, such as Velikovsky has explained prevents us from recalling that in historical times the Earth was catastrophically bumped by the planet Venus operating in the manner of a comet before settling down (with a cosmic sigh of relief, surely!) into its present orbit.

This conclusion was confirmed when Gummitch in the first fever of illumination tried to communicate his great insight to others. He told it in cat patois, as well as that limited jargon permitted, to Ashurbanipal and Cleopatra and even, on the off chance, to Sissy and Baby. They showed no interest whatever, except that Sissy took advantage of his unguarded preoccupation to stab him with a fork.

Later, alone with Old Horsemeat, he projected the great new thoughts, staring with solemn yellow eyes at the old god, but the latter grew markedly nervous and even showed signs of real fear, so Gummitch desisted. ("You'd have sworn he was trying to put across something as deep as the Einstein theory or the doctrine of original sin," Old Horsemeat later told Kitty-Come-Here.)

But Gummitch was a man now in all but form, the kitten reminded himself after these failures, and it was part of his destiny to shoulder secrets alone when necessary. He wondered if the general amnesia would affect him when he metamorphosed. There was no sure answer to this question, but he hoped not—and sometimes felt that there was reason for his hopes. Perhaps he would be the first true kitten-man, speaking from a wisdom that had no locked doors in it.

Once he was tempted to speed up the process by the use of drugs. Left alone in the kitchen, he sprang onto the table and started to lap up the black puddle in the bottom of Old Horsemeat's coffee cup. It tasted foul and poisonous and he withdrew with a little snarl, frightened as well as revolted. The dark beverage would not work its tongue-loosening magic, he realized, except at the proper time and with the proper ceremonies. Incantations might be necessary as well. Certainly unlawful tasting was highly dangerous.

The futility of expecting coffee to work any wonders by itself was further demonstrated to Gummitch when Kitty-Come-Here, wordlessly badgered by Sissy, gave a few spoonfuls to the little girl, liberally lacing it first with milk and sugar. Of course Gummitch knew by now that Sissy was destined shortly to turn into a cat and that no amount of coffee would ever make her talk, but it was nevertheless instructive to see how she spat out the first mouthful, drooling a lot of saliva after it, and dashed the cup and its contents at the chest of Kitty-Come-Here.

Gummitch continued to feel a great deal of sympathy for his parents in their worries about Sissy and he longed for the day when he would metamorphose and be able as an acknowledged man-child truly to console them. It was heart-breaking to see how they each tried to coax the little girl to talk, always attempting it while the other was absent, how they seized on each accidentally wordlike note in the few sounds she uttered and repeated it back to her hopefully, how they were more and more possessed by fears not so much of her retarded (they thought) development as of her increasingly obvious maliciousness, which was directed chiefly at Baby . . . though the two cats and Gummitch bore their share. Once she had caught Baby alone in his crib and used the sharp corner of a block to dot Baby's large-domed, lightly downed head with triangular red marks. Kitty-Come-Here had discovered her doing it, but the woman's first action had been to rub Baby's head to obliterate the marks so that Old Horsemeat wouldn't see them. That was the night Kitty-Come-Here hid the abnormal psychology books.

Gummitch understood very well that Kitty-Come-Here and Old Horsemeat, honestly believing themselves to be Sissy's parents, felt just as deeply about her as if they actually were and he did what little he could under the present circumstances to help them. He had recently come to feel a quite independent affection for Baby—the miserable little proto-cat was so completely stupid and defenseless—and so he unofficially constituted himself the creature's guardian, taking his naps behind the door of the nursery and dashing about noisily whenever Sissy showed up. In any case he realized that as a potentially adult member of a felino-human household he had his natural responsibilities.

Accepting responsibilities was as much a part of a kitten's life,

Gummitch told himself, as shouldering unsharable intuitions and secrets, the number of which continued to grow from day to day.

There was, for instance, the Affair of the Squirrel Mirror.

Gummitch had early solved the mystery of ordinary mirrors and of the creatures that appeared in them. A little observation and sniffing and one attempt to get behind the heavy wall-job in the living room had convinced him that mirror beings were insubstantial or at least hermetically sealed into their other world, probably creatures of pure spirit, harmless imitative ghosts—including the silent Gummitch Double who touched paws with him so softly yet so coldly.

Just the same, Gummitch had let his imagination play with what would happen if one day, while looking into the mirror world, he should let loose his grip on his spirit and let it slip into the Gummitch Double while the other's spirit slipped into his body—if, in short, he should change places with the scentless ghost kitten. Being doomed to a life consisting wholly of imitation and completely lacking in opportunities to show initiative—except for the behind-the-scenes judgment and speed needed in rushing from one mirror to another to keep up with the real Gummitch—would be sickeningly dull, Gummitch decided, and he resolved to keep a tight hold on his spirit at all times in the vicinity of mirrors.

But that isn't telling about the Squirrel Mirror. One morning Gummitch was peering out the front bedroom window that overlooked the roof of the porch. Gummitch had already classified windows as semi-mirrors having two kinds of space on the other side: the mirror world and that harsh region filled with mysterious and dangerously organized-sounding noises called the outer world, into which grownup humans reluctantly ventured at intervals, donning special garments for the purpose and shouting loud farewells that were meant to be reassuring but achieved just the opposite effect. The coexistence of two kinds of space presented no paradox to the kitten who carried in his mind the 27-chapter outline of *Space-Time for Springers*—indeed, it constituted one of the minor themes of the book.

This morning the bedroom was dark and the outer world was dull and sunless, so the mirror world was unusually difficult to see. Gummitch was just lifting his face toward it, nose twitching, his front paws on the sill, when what should rear up on the other side, exactly in the space that the Gummitch Double normally occupied, but a dirty brown, narrow-visaged image with savagely low forehead, dark evil wall-eyes, and a huge jaw filled with shovel-like teeth.

Gummitch was enormously startled and hideously frightened. He felt his grip on his spirit go limp, and without volition he teleported himself three yards to the rear, making use of that faculty for cutting corners in space-time, traveling by space-warp in fact, which was one of his powers that Kitty-Come-Here refused to believe in and that even Old Horsemeat accepted only on faith.

Then, not losing a moment, he picked himself up by his furry seat, swung himself around, dashed downstairs at top speed, sprang to the top of the sofa, and stared for several seconds at the Gummitch Double in the wall-mirror—not relaxing a muscle strand until he was completely convinced that he was still himself and had not been transformed into the nasty brown apparition that had confronted him in the bedroom window.

"Now what do you suppose brought that on?" Old Horsemeat asked Kitty-Come-Here.

Later Gummitch learned that what he had seen had been a squirrel, a savage, nut-hunting being belonging wholly to the outer world (except for forays into attics) and not at all to the mirror one. Nevertheless he kept a vivid memory of his profound momentary conviction that the squirrel had taken the Gummitch Double's place and been about to take his own. He shuddered to think what would have happened if the squirrel had been actively interested in trading spirits with him. Apparently mirrors and mirror-situations, just as he had always feared, were highly conducive to spirit transfers. He filed the information away in the memory cabinet reserved for dangerous, exciting and possibly useful information, such as plans for climbing straight up glass (diamond-tipped claws!) and flying higher than the trees.

These days his thought cabinets were beginning to feel filled to bursting and he could hardly wait for the moment when the true rich taste of coffee, lawfully drunk, would permit him to speak.

He pictured the scene in detail: the family gathered in conclave at the kitchen table, Ashurbanipal and Cleopatra respectfully watching from floor level, himself sitting erect on chair with paws (or would they be hands?) lightly touching his cup of thin china, while Old Horsemeat poured the thin black steaming stream. He knew the Great Transformation must be close at hand.

At the same time he knew that the other critical situation in the household was worsening swiftly. Sissy, he realized now, was far older than Baby and should long ago have undergone her own somewhat less glamorous though equally necessary transformation (the first tin of raw horsemeat could hardly be as exciting as the first cup of coffee). Her time was long overdue. Gummitch found increasing horror in this mute vampirish being inhabiting the body of a rapidly growing girl, though inwardly equipped to be nothing but a most bloodthirsty she-cat. How dreadful to think of Old Horsemeat and Kitty-Come-Here having to care all their lives for such a monster! Gummitch told himself that if any opportunity for alleviating his parents' misery should ever present itself to him, he would not hesitate for an instant.

Then one night, when the sense of Change was so burstingly strong in him that he knew tomorrow must be the Day, but when the house was also exceptionally unquiet with boards creaking and snapping, taps adrip, and curtains mysteriously rustling at closed windows (so that it was clear that the many spirit worlds including the mirror one must be pressing very close), the opportunity came to Gummitch.

Kitty-Come-Here and Old Horsemeat had fallen into especially sound, drugged sleeps, the former with a bad cold, the latter with one unhappy highball too many (Gummitch knew he had been brooding about Sissy). Baby slept too, though with uneasy whimperings and joggings—moonlight shone full on his crib past a window shade which had whirringly rolled itself up without human or feline agency. Gummitch kept vigil under the crib, with eyes closed but with widely excited mind pressing outward to every boundary of the house and even stretching here and there into the outer world. On this night of all nights sleep was unthinkable.

Then suddenly he became aware of footsteps, footsteps so soft they must, he thought, be Cleopatra's.

No, softer than that, so soft they might be those of the Gummitch Double escaped from the mirror world at last and padding up toward him through the darkened halls. A ribbon of fur rose along his spine.

Then into the nursery Sissy came prowling. She looked slim as an Egyptian princess in her long, thin, yellow nightgown and as sure of herself, but the cat was very strong in her tonight, from the flat intent eyes to the dainty canine teeth slightly bared—one look at her now would have sent Kitty-Come-Here running for the telephone number she kept hidden, the telephone number of the special doctor—and

Gummitch realized he was witnessing a monstrous suspension of natural law in that this being should be able to exist for a moment without growing fur and changing round pupils for slit eyes.

He retreated to the darkest corner of the room, suppressing a snarl.

Sissy approached the crib and leaned over Baby in the moonlight, keeping her shadow off him. For a while she gloated. Then she began softly to scratch his cheek with a long hatpin she carried, keeping away from his eye, but just barely. Baby awoke and saw her and Baby didn't cry. Sissy continued to scratch, always a little more deeply. The moonlight glittered on the jeweled end of the pin.

Gummitch knew he faced a horror that could not be countered by running about or even spitting and screeching. Only magic could fight so obviously supernatural a manifestation. And this was also no time to think of consequences, no matter how clearly and bitterly etched they might appear to a mind intensely awake.

He sprang up onto the other side of the crib, not uttering a sound, and fixed his golden eyes on Sissy's in the moonlight. Then he moved forward straight at her evil face, stepping slowly, not swiftly, using his extraordinary knowledge of the properties of space *to walk straight through her hand and arm as they flailed the hatpin at him.* When his nose-tip finally paused a fraction of an inch from hers, his eyes had not blinked once, and she could not look away. Then he unhesitatingly flung his spirit into her like a fistful of flaming arrows and he worked the Mirror Magic.

Sissy's moonlit face, feline and terrified, was in a sense the last thing that Gummitch, the real Gummitch-kitten, ever saw in this world. For the next instant he felt himself enfolded by the foul, black blinding cloud of Sissy's spirit, which his own had displaced. At the same time he heard the little girl scream, very loudly but even more distinctly, *"Mommy!"*

That cry might have brought Kitty-Come-Here out of her grave, let alone from sleep merely deep or drugged. Within seconds she was in the nursery, closely followed by Old Horsemeat, and she had caught up Sissy in her arms and the little girl was articulating the wonderful word again and again, and miraculously following it with the command—there could be no doubt, Old Horsemeat heard it too—"Hold me tight!"

Then Baby finally dared to cry. The scratches on his cheek came to attention and Gummitch, as he had known must happen, was banished to the basement amid cries of horror and loathing, chiefly from Kitty-Come-Here.

The little cat did not mind. No basement would be one-tenth as dark as Sissy's spirit that now enshrouded him for always, hiding all the file drawers and the labels on all the folders, blotting out forever even the imagining of the scene of first coffee-drinking and first speech.

In a last intuition, before the animal blackness closed in utterly, Gummitch realized that the spirit, alas, is not the same thing as the consciousness and that one may lose—sacrifice—the first and still be burdened with the second.

Old Horsemeat had seen the hatpin (and hit it quickly from Kitty-Come-Here) and so he knew that the situation was not what it seemed and that Gummitch was at the very least being made into a sort of scapegoat. He was quite apologetic when he brought the tin pans of food to the basement during the period of the little cat's exile. It was a comfort to Gummitch, albeit a small one. Gummitch told himself, in his new black halting manner of thinking, that after all a cat's best friend is his man.

From that night Sissy never turned back in her development. Within two months she had made three years' progress in speaking. She became an outstandingly bright, light-footed, high-spirited little girl. Although she never told anyone this, the moonlit nursery and Gummitch's magnified face were her first memories. Everything before that was inky blackness. She was always very nice to Gummitch in a careful sort of way. She could never stand to play the game "Owl Eyes."

After a few weeks Kitty-Come-Here forgot her fears and Gummitch once again had the run of the house. But by then the transformation Old Horsemeat had always warned about had fully taken place. Gummitch was a kitten no longer but an almost burly tom. In him it took the psychological form not of sullenness or surliness but an extreme dignity. He seemed at times rather like an old pirate brooding on treasures he would never live to dig up, shores of adventure he would never reach. And sometimes when you looked into his yellow eyes you felt that he had in him all the materials for the book *Slit Eyes Look at*

Life— three or four volumes at least—although he would never write it. And that was natural when you come to think of it, for as Gummitch knew very well, bitterly well indeed, his fate was to be the only kitten in the world that did not grow up to be a man.

This unusual story is about a traveler in Turkey who is looking for a good time and has a strange adventure with a young woman. The author, AVRAM DAVIDSON, is one of the contemporary masters of adult fantasy. His novel, The Phoenix and the Mirror, *is a classic, and his volumes of short stories are filled with gems. Davidson has been awarded the Life Achievement Award by the World Fantasy Convention and won World Fantasy Awards for specific works twice. His fantasy fiction is polished and elegant, witty and compressed. This story is from his early collection,* Or All the Seas with Oysters *(1962).*

Great Is Diana
BY AVRAM DAVIDSON

"Whenever the sexes separate, at a party like this, I mean, after dinner," Jim Lucas said, "I keep feeling we ought to have walnuts and port and say *'Gempmun, the Queen!'* like in the old English novels."

"Naa, you don't want any *port,*" Don Slezak, who was the host, said, opening the little bar. "What you want—"

Fred Bishop, who had taken a cigar out of his pocket, put it back. "Speaking of the old English," he began. But Don didn't want to speak of the old English.

"I want you to try this," he said. "It's something I invented myself. Doesn't even have a name yet." He produced a bottle and a jug and ice and glasses. Jim looked interested; Fred, resigned. "It's really a very simple little drink," Don observed, pouring. "You take white rum —any good white rum—and cider. But it's got to be *real* cider. None of this pasteurized apple juice that they allow them to sell nowadays as cider. So much of this . . . so much of that. Drink up."

They drank. "Not bad at all. In fact," Fred smacked his lips, "very good. Strange, how fashions in drink change. Rum was it until gin came in; then whisky. Now, in the seventeen hundreds . . ."

Don got up and noisily prepared three more rum-and-ciders. "Ah," he said, quaffing, "it goes down like mother's milk, doesn't it." Jim put his glass down empty with a clatter. Don promptly made more.

"Mother's milk," Jim said. He was reflective. "Talk about fashions in *drink* . . . dextrose, maltose, corn syrup, and what the hell else they put into the babies nowadays. How come the women aren't born flat-chested, explain me *that,* Mr. Bishop?"

Fred smiled blandly. "Proves there's nothing *to* this evolution nonsense, doesn't it. Particularly after that sordid Pilt-down business . . ."

Don Slezak poured himself another. "Got to go a little bit easy on the cider," he said. "Rum, you can get rum anywhere, but real cider . . . That's a *revolting* idea!" he exclaimed, struck by a delayed thought. "Flat-chested. Ugh."

Jim said, defensively, that it would serve the women right. "Dextrose, maltose, corn syrup. No wonder the kids nowadays are going to Hell in a hotrod. They're rotten with chemicals before they can even *walk!*"

"The poor kids." Don choked down a sob. Jim waved his glass.

"Another thing. Besides that, Nature *meant* women to nurse their babies. Nature meant them to have *twins*. 'Sobvious. Or else they'd just have *one*. In the middle. Like a cyclops or something. And how many women do *you* know or do I know, who have twins? Precious damn few, let *me* tell you . . . Oh, Margaret Sanger has a lot to answer for," he said, darkly.

Don smirked. "Spotted the flaw in *that* argument right away. According to *you,* cows should have quadruplets." He began to laugh, then to cough. Jim's face fell. Fred Bishop at once put his cigar back again.

"Curious you should bring that up. The late Alexander Graham Bell passed the latter years of his life developing a breed of sheep which would produce quadruplets. In order for the ewes to be able to nourish these multiple births they had to possess four functioning teats instead of the usual two."

Don squirmed. "I wish you'd pronounce that word as it's spelled," he said. "It sounds so *vulgar* when you rhyme it with *'pits.'* "

Jim crunched a piece of ice, nodded his head slowly. Then he spat out the pieces. "Just occurred to me: Doesn't something like that sometimes occur in women? *'Polymam-'* something? Once knew a woman who was a custom brassiere-maker, and she claimed that—"

A dreamy look had come into Don's eyes. "Suppose a fellow was one of these whatdayacallits? a breast-fetishist." He got the latter word out with some difficulty. "Why, he'd go *crazy—*"

"Why don't you mix up another round, Don?" Fred suggested, craftily. "Jim could help you. And I will tell you about the interesting career of Mr. Henry Taylor, who was, in a way, an example of what

Aldous Huxley calls the glorious eccentrics who enliven every age by their presence."

Mr. Henry Taylor [Fred continued] was an Englishman, which is a thing glorious enough in itself. He was not, even by our foolish modern standards, too much of an eccentric; which is an argument in favor of free will over heredity. His grandfather, Mr. Fulke Taylor, in unsolicited response to the controversies between the Houses of Hanover and Stuart, had managed to plague both—and the Houses of Parliament as well—with genealogical pamphlets he had written in favor of the claims (which existed only in his own mind) of a distant, distaff branch of the Tudors. He also willed a sum of money to be used in translating the works of Dryden into the Cornish language. The task was duly carried out by a prolific and penniless clergyman named Pendragon, or Pendennis, or Pen-something; it did much to prevent the extinction of the latter's family, but had, alas, no such effect upon the Cornish language.

Trevelyan Taylor, Henry's father, was much taken up—you will recall this was in the seventeen hundreds—with what he called *"These new and wonderful Discoveries"*: meaning the efforts of Robert Bakewell and the brothers Bates in the recently developed science of selective breeding. *"Previously,"* wrote Trevelyan Taylor, *"Animal Husbandry was left entirely to the animals themselves. We shall alter that."*

Others might inbreed, crossbreed, linebreed, and outbreed in the interest of larger udders or leaner bacon; old Trevelyan spent thirty devoted years in the exclusive purpose of developing a strain of white sheep with black tails. There has seldom been a longer experiment in the realm of pure science, but after the old man's death the whole flock (known locally as Taylor's Tails) was sold to an unimaginative and pre-Mendelian drover named Huggins, thus becoming history. And mutton.

The flock, if it produced no profit, at least paid for itself, and its owner had spent little on other things. Henry Taylor, who had enjoyed a comfortable allowance, now found himself with an even more comfortable income. He turned ancestral home and estate over to his younger brother, Laurence (later, first Baron Osterwold), and set forth on his travels. London saw him no more—*"London, where I have passed so much of my youth,"* as he wrote in a letter to his brother, *"in profligate Courses as a Rake and a Deist."* These two terms are, of course, not necessarily synonymous.

Henry Taylor crossed over to the continent with his carriage, his horses, his valet, clothes, commode, dressing case, and toilet articles. No one had yet begun to vulcanize or galvanize or do whatever it is to rubber which is done, but he had a portable, collapsible sailcloth bath —all quite in the Grand Tradition of the English Milord. Throughout all the years that he continued his letters—throughout, at least, all of the European and part of the Asiatic term of his travels—he insisted that his tour was for educational purposes.

"*I devote myself,*" he wrote, "*to the study of those Institutions of which I count myself best qualified to judge. I leave to others the Governance and Politick of Nations, and their Laws and Moral Philosophies. My Inquiries—empirick, all—are directed towards their Food, their Drink, their Tobacco, and their Women.* Especially *their Women! Glorious Creatures, all, of whatsoever Nation. I love them all and I love every Part of them, Tresses, Eyes, Cheeks, Lips, Necks, Napes, Arms, Bosoms . . .*

"*Why do Women cloack their lovely Bosoms, Brother?*" he demands to know. "*Why conceal their Primest Parts? So much better to reveal them pridefully, as do the Females in the Isles of Spice. . . . I desire you'll send* [he adds] *by next vessel to stop at Leghorn, 6 lbs. fine Rappee Snuff and 4 cases Holland Gin.*"

Taylor passed leisurely through France, the Low Countries, various German States, Denmark, Poland, Austria, Venice, Lombardy, Modena, Tuscany, the Papal Dominions, the Kingdom of Naples and the two Sicilies, and—crossing the Adriatic—entered the Turkish hegemonies in Europe by way of Albania . . . the tobacco was much better than in Italy, but he complained against the eternal sherbets of the Turks, who were, he said, in the manner of not offering strong waters to their guests, "*no better than the Methodies or other dehydrated Sectarians.*" He was not overpleased with the Greek practice of putting resin in their wine, and noted that "*they eat much Mutton and little Beef and drink a poor sort of Spirits called Rockee.*" He liked their curdled milk, however, and—of course—their women.

"*The Men here wear Skirts,*" Henry Taylor says, "*and the Women wear Pantalones . . . I have made diligent Inquiry and learned that this unnatural Reversal doth not obtain in* all *Matters domestick, however.*" He cites details to support this last statement.

There is a picture of him done at this time by an itinerant Italian painter of miniatures. It shows a well-made man in his thirties, dressed in the English styles of the year of Taylor's departure, with a line of whisker curling down his jaw; clean-shaven chin and upper-lip, and a rather full mouth. He began to learn Turkish and the Romaic, or vernacular Greek, to sit cross-legged and to suck at a hookah, to like the tiny cups of black and syrupy coffee, and—eventually—to dispense with an interpreter. He spoke face to face with the pasha of each district he passed. He rather liked the Turks.

"There is among them none of this Hypocritical Nonsense, as with us, of having One Wife, to whom we are eternally yoked unless we care to display our Horns and our Money to the House of Lords." He reports a conversation he had with *"a Black Eunuch in Adrianople. I asked him quite Boldly if he were not sensible of his Great Loss, and he pointed to an Ass which was grazing nearby and said with a Laugh—"* But I really cannot repeat what he said.

Taylor said he *"admired his Wit, but was not happy at the aptness of his Analogy."*

From the Balkans he went on to Asia Minor, where he made a closer acquaintance of the famous Circassian women—the raising and the sale of whom was seemingly the chief business of their native hills. He pauses in his flow of metaphors to ask a question. *"If I compare the Breasts of the Turkish Women to full Moons, with what shall I compare those glorious Features possessed by the Circassians? I would liken them to the warm Sun, were the Sun Twins."*

"Polymastia!" Jim exclaimed. He smiled happily. Fred blinked. Don said, "Huh?"

"Not *'polymam-'* something, but polymastia: 'Having many breasts.' Just now remembered. Came across it once, in a dictionary."

"Just like that, huh?" Don asked. "Were you considering becoming a latter-day A. G. Bell with the human race instead of sheep?"

"Go on, Fred," Jim said, hastily. "I didn't mean to interrupt."

Taylor's next letter [Fred continued, after a very slight pause] was dated more than a year later, from Jerusalem. He had conceived a desire to visit the more remote regions of Western Asia Minor, eventually heading for the coast, whence he hoped to visit certain of the Grecian islands. As large areas were impassable to his carriage, he was obliged to hire mules. He gives a description, as usual, of the nature of the country and people, but without his usual lively humor. Suddenly, without any connecting phrases, the letter plunges into an incident which had occurred that day in Jerusalem.

"I visited a synagogue of the Polish Jews here, having some business of minor Importance with one of their Melamedins, or Ushers. It is a small room, below Street-level, furnished as well as their Poverty permits of. There was an Inscription of some sort at the Lectern, but they had been burning Candles by it for so long that it was obscured by Soot and Smoke.

"Only the single word Hamatho *was visible, and I confess to you, Dear Brother, that when I saw this word, which means, His Wrath, a Shudder seized me, and I groaned aloud. Alas! How much have I done to merit His Wrath. . . ."*

And then, without further explanation, he reverts to his ramble in Asia Minor. His party had come over the Duzbel Pass to a miserable Turkish village east of Mt. Koressos, *"a wretched marshy neighborhood where I was loth to stop, fearing the Ague. But some of the Mules required to be shod, and we were preceded at the forge by some Turkishes officers, Yezz Bashy or Bimm Bashi, or like preposterous Rank and Title. So there was no help for it. It promised to take Hours, and I went a-walking."* Henry Taylor soon left the village behind and found himself in wild country. He had no fears for his safety, or of being lost, he explained, because he had pistols and a small horn always about him. By and by he entered a sort of small valley down which a stream rushed, and there, drinking at a pool, he saw a woman.

"She was dark, with black Eyes and Hair, buxom and exceedingly comely. I thought of the Line in the Canticle: I am black but beautiful. Alas! That I did not call to mind those other lines, also of Solomon, about the Strange Woman. And yet it was, I suppose, just as well, for 'Out of the Strong came forth Sweet.' "

On seeing her, he freely confesses, he had no hopes other than for an anormous adventure, and was encouraged by her lack of shyness. He spoke to her in Turkish, but she shook her head. She understood Greek, however, though her accent was strange to him, and she said that her name was Diana. She offered him a drink from her cup, he accepted, and they fell into conversation. *"Although she gave no Details about her Home, and I pressed her for none, I understood that she was without present Family and was in what we should call Reduced Circumstances. For she spoke of Times past, when she had many Maid Servants and much Wealth, and the tears stood in her Eyes. I took her hand and she offered no objections."*

The next lines are written in ink of a different color, as if he had put off writing until another time. Then, *"In short, Brother, I pursued the Way usual to me in those Days, and although she gave me her Lips, I was not content to stop, but was emboldened to thrust my Hand into her Bodice . . . and thus perceived in very short order that she was not a Human Female but an Unnatural Monstrosity. I firmly believe, and was encouraged in Belief by a worthy Divine of the Eastern Church to whom I revealed the Matter, that this Creature who called herself Diana had no Natural Existence, but was a Dœmon, called forth, I first thought, by the Devil himself. . . .*

"I am now convinced that she was a very Type of Lust, sent to test or prove me. That is, to horrify me in that same Sin in which I had so long wallowed, and to turn those Features, in which I had intended to take illicit Delight, into a Terror and Revulsion. I ran, I am not ashamed to own it, until I fell bleeding and exhausted at the Forge, and was taken by a Fever of which I am long recovering. . . .

According to the standards of his time there was only one thing for him to do under the circumstances, and he did it. He got religion. There had lately been established in Jerusalem an office of the British and Overseas Society for the Circulation of Uncorrupted Anglican Versions of the Scriptures; Henry Taylor became a colporteur, or agent, of this Society, and was sent among the native Christians of Mesopotamia, Kurdistan, and Persia.

He never knew, because he died before it became known, that the Turkish village where he had his shocking experience was near the site of the ancient city of Ephesus. Its famous Temple of Diana was one of the Seven Wonders of the World and was served by hundreds of priestesses and visited by pilgrims in throngs. But that was before the Apostle Paul came that way and *"Many of those which used curious arts brought their books together and burned them before all men."* But not every one in Ephesus was so quickly convinced.

A certain *"Demetrius, a silversmith, which made silver shrines for Diana . . . called together the workmen of like occupation, and said . . . that not alone in Ephesus, but almost throughout all Asia, this Paul hath persuaded and turned away much people, saying that they be no gods, which are made with hands: So that not only this our craft is in danger . . . but also that the temple of the great goddess Diana should be despised, and her magnificence be destroyed, whom all Asia and the world worshippeth. And when they heard these sayings, they were full of wrath, and cried out saying, Great is Diana of the Ephesians. And the whole city was filled with confusion. . . ."*

"I am also filled with confusion," Don said. "First we hear about this Limey, Taylor: he tries to grab a feel and gets the screaming meemies. All of a sudden—a Bible class."

Jim clicked his tongue. "That *word*—it's slipped my mind again Poly—? Ploy—?"

"Patience," Fred pleaded. "Why aren't you more patient?"

The confusion in Ephesus [Fred said] was finally ended by a city official who *"appeased"* the mob by asking, *"What man is there that knoweth not now that the City of the Ephesians is a worshipper of the great goddess Diana, and of the image which fell down from Jupiter? . . . Ye ought to be quiet, and to do nothing rashly."*

Long after Henry Taylor's time, the archeologists uncovered the temple site. Among the many images they found was one which may perhaps be that same one *"which fell down from Jupiter."* It is carven from black meteoric stone, and was obviously intended for reverence in fertility rituals, for the goddess is naked to the waist, and has, not two breasts, but a multitude, a profusion of them, clustering over the front of the upper torso. . . .

"Well, you're not going to make too much out of this story, are you?" Jim asked. "Obviously this condition was hereditary in that district, and your pal, H. Taylor, just happened to meet up with a woman who had it, as well as the name Diana."

"It is certainly a curious coincidence, if nothing more," said Fred.

Don wanted to know what finally became of Henry Taylor. "He convert any of the natives?"

"No. They converted him. He became a priest."

"You mean, *he gave up women?*"

"Oh, no: Celibacy is not incumbent upon priests of the Eastern Church. He married."

"But not one of those babes from the Greater Ephesus area, I'll bet," Don said.

Jim observed, musingly, "It's too bad old Alexander Graham Bell didn't know about this. He needn't have bothered with sheep. Of course, it *takes* longer with people—"

Fred pointed out that Dr. Bell had been an old man at the time.

"He could have set up a foundation. I would have been *glad* to carry on the great work. It wouldn't frighten *me,* like it did Taylor. . . . Say, you wouldn't know, approximately, how *many* this Diana had—?"

"It must sure have taken a lot out of Taylor, all right," Don said. "I bet he was never much good at anything afterwards."

Fred took one last swallow of his last drink. The jug and bottle, he observed, were empty. "Oh, I don't know about that," he said. "In the last letter he wrote to his brother before the latter's death, he says: *'My dear Wife has observed my sixty-fifth Birthday by presenting me with my Fifth Son and ninth Child. . . . I preach Sunday next on the Verse, "His Leaf Also Shall not Wither" (Psalms).'"*

Here are giants, dwarves, and adventures! This rare story from the time of P. T. Barnum chronicles the adventures of a boy who discovers, on a tropical island, the last two surviving members of a race of benevolent giants. CHRISTOPHER PEARSE CRANCH, *an important American poet and literary figure in the nineteenth century, wrote two books of uniquely American fantasy, departing significantly from the British fairy tale conventions (in the British stories, the land of the fairies is usually a park or garden nearby, inhabited by small creatures) by mixing in the element of realistic adventure. The books were not particularly successful in Cranch's day and have languished, nearly forgotten, in rare book libraries. This is the first time in a century that "The Last of the Huggermuggers" has been reprinted.*

The Last of the Huggermuggers:
A GIANT STORY
BY CHRISTOPHER PEARSE CRANCH

CHAPTER 1
HOW LITTLE JACKET WOULD GO TO SEA

I dare say there are not many of my young readers who have heard about Jacky Cable, the sailor-boy, and of his wonderful adventures on Huggermugger's Island. Jacky was a smart Yankee lad, and was always remarkable for his dislike of staying at home, and a love of lounging upon the wharves, where the sailors used to tell him stories about sea-life. Jacky was always a little fellow. The country people, who did not much like the sea, or encourage Jacky's fondness for it, used to say, that he took so much salt air and tar smoke into his lungs that it stopped his growth. The boys used to call him Little Jacket. Jacky, however, though small in size, was big in wit, being an uncommonly smart lad, though he did play truant sometimes, and seldom knew well his school-lessons. But some boys learn faster out of school than in school, and this was the case with Little Jacket. Before he was ten years old, he knew every rope in a ship, and could manage a sailboat or a row-boat with equal ease. In fine, salt water seemed to be his element; and he was never so happy or so wide awake as when he was lounging with the sailors in the docks. The neighbors thought he was a sort of good-for-nothing, idle boy, and his parents often grieved that he was not fonder of home and of school. But Little Jacket was not a bad boy, and was really learning a good deal in his way, though he did not learn it all out of books.

Well, it went on so, and Little Jacket grew fonder and fonder of the sea, and pined more and more to enlist as a sailor, and go off to the strange countries in one of the splendid big ships. He did not say much about it to his parents, but they saw what his longing was, and after thinking and talking the matter over together, they concluded that it was about as well to let the boy have his way.

So when Little Jacket was about fifteen years old, one bright summer's day, he kissed his father and mother, and brothers and sisters, and went off as a sailor in a ship bound to the East Indies.

CHAPTER 2

HIS GOOD AND HIS BAD LUCK AT SEA

It was a long voyage, and there was plenty of hard work for Little Jacket, but he found several good fellows among the sailors, and was so quick, so bright, so ready to turn his hand to every thing, and withal of so kind and social a disposition, that he soon became a favorite with the Captain and mates, as with all the sailors. They had fine weather, only too fine, the Captain said, for it was summer time, and the sea was often as smooth as glass. There were lazy times then for the sailors, when there was little work to do, and many a story was told among them as they lay in the warm moonlight nights on the forecastle. But now and then there came a blow of wind, and all hands had to be stirring—running up the shrouds, taking in sails, pulling at ropes, plying the pump; and there was many a hearty laugh among them at the ducking some poor fellow would get, as now and then a wave broke over the deck.

Things went on, however, pretty smoothly with Little Jacket, on the whole, for some time. They doubled the Cape of Good Hope, and were making their way as fast as they could to the coast of Java, when the sky suddenly darkened, and there came on a terrible storm. They took in all the sails they could, after having several carried away by the wind. The vessel scudded, at last, almost under bare poles. The storm was so violent as to render her almost unmanageable, and they were carried a long way out of their course. Everybody had tremendous work to perform, and Little Jacket began to wish he were safe on dry land again. Day after day the poor vessel drifted and rolled. The sky was so dark, that the Captain could not take an observation to tell in what part of the ocean they were. At last, they saw that they were driving towards some enormous cliffs that loomed up in the darkness. Every one lost hope of the ship being saved. Still they neared the cliffs, and now they saw the white breakers ahead, close under them. The Captain got the boats out, to be in readiness for the worst. But the sea was too rough to use them. At last, with a mighty crash, the great ship struck upon the black rocks. All was confusion and wild rushing of the salt waves over them, and poor Jacky found himself in the foaming surge. Struggling to reach the shore, a great wave did what he could not have done himself. He was thrown dripping wet, and bruised, upon the rocks. When he came to himself, he discovered that several of his companions had also reached the shore, but nothing more was seen of the ship. She had gone down in the fearful tempest, and carried I know not how many poor fellows down with her.

CHAPTER 3

HOW HE FARED ON SHORE

All this was bad enough, as Little Jacket thought. But he was very thankful that he was alive and on shore, and able to use his limbs, and that he found some companions still left. He was not long either in using his wits, and in making the best use of the chances still left him. He found himself upon a rocky promontory. But on climbing a little higher up, he could see that there was beyond it, and joining on to it, a beautiful smooth beach. The rocks were enormous, and he and his comrades had hard work to clamber over them. It took them a good while to do so, exhausted as they were by fatigue, and dripping with wet. At length they reached the beach, the sands of which were of very large grain, and so loose that they had to wade nearly knee deep through them. The country back of the shore seemed very rocky and rough, and here and there were trees of an enormous magnitude. Every thing seemed on a gigantic scale, even to the weeds and grasses that grew on the edge of the beach, where it sloped up to join the main land. And they could see, by mounting on a stone, the same great gloomy cliffs which they saw before the ship struck, but some miles inland. But what most attracted their attention, was the enormous and beautiful great sea-shells, which lay far up on the shore. They were not only of the most lovely colors, but quite various in form, and so large that a man might creep into them. Little Jacket was not long in discovering the advantage of this fact, for they might be obliged, when night came on, to retire into these shells, as they saw no house anywhere within sight. Now, Little Jacket had read *Robinson Crusoe,* and *Gulliver's Travels,* and had half believed the wonderful stories of Brobdignag; but he never thought that he should ever be actually wrecked on a giant's island. There now seemed to be a probability that it might be so, after all. What meant these enormous weeds, and trees, and rocks, and grains of sand, and these huge shells? What meant these great cliffs in the distance? He began to feel a little afraid. But he thought about Gulliver, and how well he fared after all, and, on the whole, looked forward rather with pleasure at the prospect of some strange adventure. Now and then he thought he could make out something like huge footprints on the shore—but this might be fancy. At any rate, if they could only find some food to live upon, they might get on tolerably well for a time. And perhaps this was only a fancy about giants, and they might yet find civilized beings like themselves living here.

Now Little Jacket began to be very hungry, and so did his companions—there were six of them—and they all determined to look about as far inland as they dared to go, for some kind of fruit or vegetable which might satisfy their appetites. They were not long in discovering a kind of beach-plum, about as big as watermelons, which grew on a bush so tall, that they had to reach the fruit at arm's length, and on tiptoe. The stalks were covered with very sharp thorns, about a foot long. Some of these thorns they cut off (they had their knives in their pockets still), for Little Jacket thought they might be of service to them in defending themselves against any wild animal which might prowl around at night. It chanced that Little Jacket found good use for his in the end, as we shall see. When they had gathered enough of these great plums, they sat down and dined upon them. They found them a rather coarse, but not unpalatable fruit. As they were still very wet, they took off their clothes, and dried them in the sun; for the storm had ceased, and the sun now came out very warm. The great waves, however, still dashed up on the beach. When their clothes were dry, they put them on, and feeling a good deal refreshed, spent the rest of the day in looking about to see what was to be done for the future. As night came on, they felt a good deal dispirited; but Little Jacket encouraged his companions, by telling stories of sailors who had been saved, or had been taken under the protection of the kings of the country, and had married the king's daughters, and all that. So they found a group of the great shells near each other, seven of them, lying high and dry out of the reach of the dashing waves, and, after bidding each other good night, they crept in. Little Jacket found his dry and clean, and having curled himself up, in spite of his anxiety about the future, was soon fast asleep.

CHAPTER 4

HOW HUGGERMUGGER CAME ALONG

Now it happened that Little Jacket was not altogether wrong in his fancies about giants, for there *was* a giant living in this island where the poor sailors were wrecked. His name was Huggermugger, and he and his giantess wife lived at the foot of the great cliffs they had seen in the distance. Huggermugger was something of a farmer, something of a hunter, and something of a fisherman. Now, it being a warm, clear, moonlight night, and Huggermugger being disposed to roam about, thought he would take a walk down to the beach to see if the late storm had washed up any clams or oysters, or other shell-fish, of which he was very fond. Having gathered a good basket full, he was about returning, when his eye fell upon the group of great shells in which Little Jacket and his friends were reposing, all sound asleep.

"Now," thought Huggermugger, "my wife has often asked me to fetch home one of these big shells. She thinks it would look pretty on her mantel-piece, with sunflowers sticking in it. Now I may as well gratify her, though I can't exactly see the use of a shell without a fish in it. Mrs. Huggermugger must see something in these shells that I don't."

So he didn't stop to choose, but picked up the first one that came to his hand, and put it in his basket. It was the very one in which Little Jacket was asleep. The little sailor slept too soundly to know that he was travelling, free of expense, across the country at a railroad speed, in a carriage made of a giant's fish-basket. Huggermugger reached his house, mounted his huge stairs, set down his basket, and placed the big shell on the mantel-piece.

"Wife," says he, "here's one of those good-for-nothing big shells you have often asked me to bring home."

"Oh, what a beauty," says she, as she stuck a sunflower in it, and stood gazing at it in mute admiration. But, Huggermugger being hungry, would not allow her to stand idle.

"Come," says he, "let's have some of these beautiful clams cooked for supper—they are worth all your fine shells with nothing in them."

So they sat down, and cooked and ate their supper, and then went to bed.

Little Jacket, all this time, heard nothing of their great rumbling voices, being in as sound a sleep as he ever enjoyed in his life. He awoke early in the morning, and crept out of his shell—but he could hardly believe his eyes, and thought himself still dreaming, when he found himself and his shell on a very high, broad shelf, in a room bigger than any church he ever saw. He fairly shook and trembled in his shoes, when the truth came upon him that he had been trapped by a giant, and was here a prisoner in his castle. He had time enough, however, to become cool and collected, for there was not a sound to be heard, except now and then something resembling a thunderlike snoring, as from some distant room. "Aha," thought Little Jacket to himself, "it is yet very early, and the giant is asleep, and there may be time yet to get myself out of his clutches."

He was a brave little fellow, as well as a true Yankee in his smartness and ingenuity. So he took a careful observation of the room, and its contents. The first thing to be done was to let himself down from the mantel-piece. This was not an easy matter, as it was very high. If he jumped, he would certainly break his legs. He was not long in discovering one of Huggermugger's fishing-lines tied up and lying not far from him. This he unrolled, and having fastened one end of it to a nail which he managed just to reach, he let the other end drop (it was as large as a small rope) and easily let himself down to the floor. He then made for the door, but that was fastened. Jacky, however, was determined to see what could be done, so he pulled out his jackknife, and commenced cutting into the corner of the door at the bottom, where it was a good deal worn, as if it had been gnawed by the rats. He thought that by cutting a little now and then, and hiding himself when the giant should make his appearance, in time he might make an opening large enough for him to squeeze himself through. Now Huggermugger was by this time awake, and heard the noise which Jacky made with his knife.

"Wife," says he, waking her up—she was dreaming about her beautiful shell—"wife, there are those eternal rats again, gnawing, gnawing at that door; we must set the trap for them to-night."

Little Jacket heard the giant's great voice, and was very much astonished that he spoke English. He thought that giants spoke nothing but "chow-chow-whangalorum-hallaballoo with a-ruffle-bull-bagger!" This made him hope that Huggermugger would not eat him. So he grew very hopeful, and determined to persevere. He kept at his work, but as softly as he could. But Huggermugger heard the noise again, or fancied he heard it, and this time came to see if he could not kill the rat that gnawed so steadily and so fearlessly. Little Jacket heard him coming, and rushed to hide himself. The nearest place of retreat was one of the giant's great boots, which lay on the floor, opening like a cave before him. Into this he rushed. He had hardly got into it before Huggermugger entered.

CHAPTER 5

WHAT HAPPENED TO LITTLE JACKET IN THE GIANT'S BOOT

Huggermugger made a great noise in entering, and ran up immediately to the door at which Little Jacket had been cutting, and threshed about him with a great stick, right and left. He then went about the room, grumbling and swearing, and poking into all the corners and holes in search of the rat; for he saw that the hole under the door had been enlarged, and he was sure that the rats had done it. So he went peeping and poking about, making Little Jacket not a little troubled, for he expected every moment that he would pick up the boot in which he was concealed, and shake him out of his hiding-place. Singularly enough, however, the giant never thought of looking into his own boots, and very soon he went back to his chamber to dress himself.

Little Jacket now ventured to peep out of the boot, and stood considering what was next to be done. He hardly dared to go again to the door, for Huggermugger was now dressed, and his wife too, for he heard their voices in the next room, where they seemed to be preparing their breakfast. Little Jacket now was puzzling his wits to think what he should do, if the giant should take a fancy to put his boots on before he could discover another hiding-place. He noticed, however, that there were other boots and shoes near by, and so there was a chance that Huggermugger might choose to put on some other pair. If this should be the case, he might lie concealed where he was during the day, and at night work away again at the hole in the door, which he hoped to enlarge enough soon, to enable him to escape. He had not much time, however, for thought; for the giant and his wife soon came in. By peeping out a little, he could just see their great feet shuffling over the wide floor.

"And now, wife," says Huggermugger, "bring me my boots." He was a lazy giant, and his wife spoiled him, by waiting on him too much.

"Which boots, my dear," says she.

"Why, the long ones," says he; "I am going a hunting to-day, and shall have to cross the marshes."

Little Jacket hoped the long boots were not those in one of which he was concealed, but unfortunately they were the very ones. So he felt a great hand clutch up the boots, and him with them, and put them down in another place. Huggermugger then took up one of the boots and drew it on, with a great grunt. He now proceeded to take up the other. Little Jacket's first impulse was to run out and throw himself on the giant's mercy, but he feared lest he should be taken for a rat. Besides he now thought of a way to defend himself, at least for a while. So he drew from his belt one of the long thorns he had cut from the bush by the seaside, and held it ready to thrust it into his adversary's foot, if he could. But he forgot that though it was as a sword in *his* hand, it was but a thorn to a giant. Huggermugger had drawn the boot nearly on, and Little Jacket's daylight was all gone, and the giant's great toes were pressing down on him, when he gave them as fierce a thrust as he could with his thorn.

"Ugh!" roared out the giant, in a voice like fifty mad bulls; "wife, wife, I say!"

"What's the matter, dear?" says wife.

"Here's one of your confounded needles in my boot. I wish to gracious you'd be more careful how you leave them about!"

"A needle in your boot?" said the giantess, "how can that be? I haven't been near your boots with my needles."

"Well, you feel there yourself, careless woman, and you'll see."

Whereupon the giantess took the boot, and put her great hand down into the toe of it, when Little Jacket gave another thrust with his weapon.

"O-o-o-o!!" screams the wife. "There's something here, for it ran into my finger; we must try to get it out." She then put her hand in again, but very cautiously, and Little Jacket gave it another stab, which made her cry out more loudly than before. Then Huggermugger put his hand in, and again he roared out as he felt the sharp prick of the thorn.

"It's no use," says he, flinging down the boot in a passion, almost breaking Little Jacket's bones, as it fell. "Wife, take that boot to the cobbler, and tell him to take that sharp thing out, whatever it is, and send it back to me in an hour, for I must go a hunting today."

So off the obedient wife trotted to the shoemaker's, with the boot under her arm. Little Jacket was curious to see whether the shoemaker was a giant too. So when the boot was left in his workshop, he contrived to peep out a little, and saw, instead of another Huggermugger, only a crooked little dwarf, not more than two or three times bigger than himself. He went by the name of Kobboltozo.

"Tell your husband," says he, "that I will look into his boot presently—I am busy just at this moment—and will bring it myself to his house."

Little Jacket was quite relieved to feel that he was safe out of the giant's house, and that the giantess had gone. "Now," thought he, "I think I know what to do."

After a while, Kobboltozo took up the boot and put his hand down into it slowly and cautiously. But Little Jacket resolved to keep quiet this time. The dwarf felt around so carefully, for fear of having his finger pricked, and his hand was so small in comparison with that of the giant's, that Little Jacket had time to dodge around his fingers and down into the toe of the boot, so that Kobboltozo could feel nothing there. He concluded, therefore, that whatever it was that hurt the giant and his wife, whether needle, or pin, or tack, or thorn, it must have dropped out on the way to his shop. So he laid the boot down, and went for his coat and hat. Little Jacket knew that now was his only chance of escape—he dreaded being carried back to Huggermugger—so he resolved to make a bold move. No sooner was the dwarf's back turned, as he went to reach down his coat, than Little Jacket rushed out of the boot, made a spring from the table on which it lay, reached the floor, and made his way as fast as he could to a great pile of old boots and shoes that lay in a corner of the room, where he was soon hidden safe from any present chance of detection.

CHAPTER 6

HOW LITTLE JACKET ESCAPED FROM KOBBOLTOZO'S SHOP

Great was Huggermugger's astonishment, and his wife's, when they found that the shoemaker told them the truth, and that there was nothing in the boot which could in any way interfere with the entrance of Mr. Huggermugger's toes. For a whole month and a day, it puzzled him to know what it could have been that pricked him so sharply.

Leaving the giant and his wife to their wonderment, let us return to Little Jacket. As soon as he found the dwarf was gone, and that all was quiet, he came out from under the pile of old shoes, and looked around to see how he should get out. The door was shut, and locked on the outside, for Kobboltozo had no wife to look after the shop while he was out. The window was shut too, the only window in the shop. This window, however, not being fastened on the outside, the little sailor thought he might be able to open it by perseverance. It was very high, so he pushed along a chair towards a table, on which he succeeded in mounting, and from the table, with a stick which he found in the room, he could turn the bolt which fastened the window inside. This, to his great joy, he succeeded in doing, and in pulling open the casement. He could now, with ease, step upon the window sill. The thing was now to let himself down on the other side. By good luck, he discovered a large piece of leather on the table. This he took and cut into strips, and tying them together, fastened one end to a nail inside, and boldly swung himself down in sailor fashion, as he had done at the giant's, and reached the ground. Then looking around, and seeing nobody near, he ran off as fast as his legs could carry him. But alas! he knew not where he was. If he could but find a road which would lead him back to the seaside where his companions were, how happy would he have been! He saw nothing around him but huge rocks and trees, with here and there an enormous fence or stone wall. Under these fences, and through the openings in the stone walls he crept, but could find no road. He wandered on for some time, clambering over great rocks and wading through long grasses, and began to be very tired and very hungry; for he had not eaten any thing since the evening before, when he feasted on the huge beach plums. He soon found himself in a sort of blackberry pasture, where the berries were as big as apples; and having eaten some of these, he sat down to consider what was to be done. He felt that he was all alone in a great wilderness, and out of which he feared he never could free himself. Poor Jacky felt lonely and sad enough, and almost wished he had discovered himself to the dwarf, for whatever could have happened to him, it could not have been worse than to be left to perish in a wilderness alone.

CHAPTER 7

HOW HE MADE USE OF HUGGERMUGGER IN TRAVELLING

While Little Jacket sat pondering over his situation, he heard voices not far off, as of two persons talking. But they were great voices, as of trumpets and drums. He looked over the top of the rock against which he was seated, and saw for the first time the entire forms of Huggermugger and his wife, looming up like two great light-houses. He knew it must be they, for he recognized their voices. They were standing on the other side of a huge stone wall. It was the giant's garden.

"Wife," said Huggermugger, "I think now I've got my long boots on again, and my toe feels so much better, I shall go through the marsh yonder and kill a few frogs for your dinner; after that, perhaps I may go down again to the seashore, and get some more of those delicious clams I found last night."

"Well, husband," says the wife, "you may go if you choose for your clams, but be sure you get me some frogs, for you know how fond I am of them."

So Huggermugger took his basket and his big stick, and strode off to the marsh. "Now," thought the little sailor, "is my time. I must watch which way he goes, and if I can manage not to be seen, and can only keep up with him—for he goes at a tremendous pace—we shall see!"

So the giant went to the marsh, in the middle of which was a pond, while Little Jacket followed him as near as he dared to go. Pretty soon, he saw the huge fellow laying about him with his big stick, and making a great splashing in the water. It was evident he was killing Mrs. Huggermugger's frogs, a few of which he put in his basket, and then strode away in another direction. Little Jacket now made the best use of his little legs that ever he made in his life. If he could only keep the giant in sight! He was much encouraged by perceiving that Huggermugger, who, as I said before, was a lazy giant, walked at a leisurely pace, and occasionally stopped to pick the berries that grew everywhere in the fields. Little Jacket could see his large figure towering up some miles ahead. Another fortunate circumstance, too, was, that the giant was smoking his pipe as he went, and even when Little Jacket almost lost sight of him, he could guess where he was from the clouds of smoke floating in the air, like the vapor from a high-pressure Mississippi steamboat. So the little sailor toiled along, scrambling over rocks, and through high weeds and grass and bushes, till they came to a road. Then Jacky's spirits began to rise, and he kept along as cautiously, yet as fast as he could, stopping only when the giant stopped. At last, after miles and miles of walking, he caught a glimpse of the sea through the huge trees that skirted the road. How his heart bounded! "I shall at least see my messmates again," he said, "and if we are destined to remain long in this island, we will at least help each other, and bear our hard lot together."

It was not long before he saw the beach, and the huge Huggermugger groping in the wet sand for his shellfish. "If I can but reach my companions without being seen, tell them my strange adventures, and all hide ourselves till the giant is out of reach, I shall be only too happy." Very soon he saw the group of beautiful great shells, just as they were when he left them, except that *his* shell, of course, was not there, as it graced Mrs. Huggermugger's domestic fireside. When he came near enough, he called some of his comrades by name, not too loud, for fear of being heard by the shellfish-loving giant. They knew his voice, and one after another looked out of his shell. They had already seen the giant, as they were out looking for their lost companion, and had fled to hide themselves in their shells.

"For heaven's sake," cried the little sailor, "Tom, Charley, all of you! don't stay here; the giant will come and carry you all off to his house under the cliffs; his wife has a particular liking for those beautiful houses of yours. I have just escaped, almost by miracle. Come, come with me—here—under the rocks—in this cave—quick, before he sees us!"

So Little Jacket hurried his friends into a hole in the rocks, where the giant would never think of prying. Huggermugger did not see them. They were safe. As soon as he had filled his basket, he went off, and left nothing but his footprints and the smoke of his pipe behind him.

After all, I don't think the giant would have hurt them, had he seen them. For he would have known the difference between a sailor and a shell-fish at once, and was no doubt too good-natured to injure them, if they made it clear to his mind that they were not by any means fish; but, on the contrary, might disagree dreadfully with his digestion, should he attempt to swallow them.

CHAPTER 8

HOW LITTLE JACKET AND HIS FRIENDS LEFT THE GIANT'S ISLAND

Very soon the sailors found a nice, large, dry cave in the rocks. There they brought dry sea-weed and made it into beds, and lived on the fish and fruits, which they had not much difficulty in obtaining. They even dragged their beautiful shells into the cave, and made little closets and cupboards of them. Their cups and plates were made of smaller bivalve shells. Their drink was clear spring-water, which they discovered near by, mixed with the juice of fruits.

They lived in this way for several weeks, always hoping some good luck would happen. At last, one day, they saw a ship a few miles from the shore. They all ran to the top of a rock, and shouted and waved their hats. Soon, to their indescribable joy, they saw a boat approaching the shore. They did not wait for it to reach the land, but being all good swimmers, with one accord plunged into the sea and swam to the boat. The sailors in the boat proved to be all Americans, and the ship was the *Nancy Johnson,* from Portsmouth, N. H., bound to the East Indies, but being out of water had made for land to obtain a supply.

The poor fellows were glad enough to get on board ship again. As they sailed off, they fancied they saw in the twilight, the huge forms of the great Mr. and Mrs. Huggermugger on the rocks, gazing after them with open eyes and mouths. They pointed them out to the people of the ship, as Little Jacket related his wonderful adventures; but the sailors only laughed at them, and saw nothing but huge rocks and trees; and they whispered among themselves, that the poor fellows had lived too long on tough clams and sour berries, and cold water, and that a little jolly life on board ship would soon cure their disordered imaginations.

CHAPTER 9

MR. NABBUM

Little Jacket and his friends were treated very kindly by the Captain and crew of the *Nancy Johnson,* and as a few more sailors were wanted on board, their services were gladly accepted. They all arrived safely at Java, where the ship took in a cargo of coffee. Little Jacket often related his adventures in the giant's island, but the sailors, though many of them were inclined to believe in marvellous stories, evidently did not give much credit to Jacky's strange tale, but thought he must have dreamed it all.

There was, however, one man who came frequently on board the ship while at Java, who seemed not altogether incredulous. He was a tall, powerful Yankee, who went by the name of Zebedee Nabbum. He had been employed as an agent of Barnum, to sail to the Indies and other countries in search of elephants, rhinoceroses, lions, tigers, baboons, and any wild animals he might chance to ensnare. He had been fitted out with a large ship and crew, and all the men and implements necessary for this exciting and dangerous task, and had been successful in entrapping two young elephants, a giraffe, a lion, sixteen monkeys, and a great number of parrots. He was now at Java superintending the manufacture of a very powerful net of grass-ropes, an invention of his own, with which he hoped to catch a good many more wild animals, and return to America, and make his fortune by exhibiting them for Mr. Barnum.

Now Zebedee Nabbum listened with profound attention to Little Jacket's story, and pondered and pondered over it.

"And after all," he said to himself, "why shouldn't it be true? Don't we read in Scripter that there war giants once? Then why hadn't there ought to be some on 'em left—in some of them remote islands whar nobody never was? Grimminy! If it should be true—if we should find Jacky's island—if we should see the big critter alive, or his wife—if we could slip a noose under his legs and throw him down—or carry along the great net and trap him while he war down on the beach arter his clams, and manage to tie him and carry him off in my ship! He'd kick, I know. He'd a kind o' roar and struggle, and maybe swamp the biggest raft we could make to fetch him. But couldn't we starve him into submission? Or, if we gave him plenty of clams, couldn't we keep him quiet? Or couldn't we give the critter *Rum?*—I guess he don't know nothin' of ardent sperets—and obfusticate his wits—and get him reglar boozy—couldn't we do any thing we chose to, then? An't it worth tryin', any how? If we *could* catch him, and get him to Ameriky alive, or only his skeleton, my fortune's made, I cal'late. I kind o' can't think that young fellow's been a gullin' me. He talks as though he'd seen the awful big critters with his own eyes. So do the other six fellows—they couldn't all of 'em have been dreamin'."

So Zebedee had a conversation one day with the Captain of the *Nancy Johnson,* and found out from him that he had taken the latitude and longitude of the coast where they took away the shipwrecked sailors. The Captain also described to Zebedee the appearance of the coast; and, in short, Zebedee contrived to get all the information about the place the Captain could give him, without letting it appear that he had any other motive in asking questions than mere curiosity.

CHAPTER 10

ZEBEDEE AND JACKY PUT THEIR HEADS TOGETHER

Zebedee now communicated to Little Jacket his plans about sailing for the giant's coast, and entrapping Huggermugger and carrying him to America. Little Jacket was rather astonished at the bold scheme of the Yankee, and tried to dissuade him from attempting it. But Zebedee had got his head so full of the notion now, that he was determined to carry out his project, if he could. He even tried to persuade Little

Jacket to go with him, and his six companions, and finally succeeded. The six other sailors, however, swore that nothing would tempt them to expose themselves again on shore to the danger of being taken by the giant. Little Jacket agreed to land with Zebedee and share all danger with him, on condition that Zebedee would give him half the profits Barnum should allow them from the exhibition of the giant in America. But Little Jacket made Zebedee promise that he would be guided by his advice, in their endeavors to ensnare the giant. Indeed, a new idea had entered Jacky's head as to the best way of getting Huggermugger into their power, and that was to try persuasion rather than stratagem or force. I will tell you the reasons he had for so thinking.

1. The Huggermuggers were not Ogres or Cannibals. They lived on fish, frogs, fruit, vegetables, grains, &c.

2. The Huggermuggers wore clothes, lived in houses, and were surrounded with various indications of civilization. They were not savages.

3. The Huggermuggers spoke English, with a strange accent, to be sure. They seemed sometimes to prefer it to their own language. They must, then, have been on friendly terms with English or Americans, at some period of their lives.

4. The Huggermuggers were not wicked and blood-thirsty. How different from the monsters one reads about in children's books! On the contrary, though they had little quarrels together now and then, they did not bite nor scratch, but seemed to live together as peaceably and lovingly, on the whole, as most married couples. And the only time he had a full view of their faces, Little Jacket saw in them an expression which was really good and benevolent.

All these facts came much more forcibly to Jacky's mind, now that the first terror was over, and calm, sober reason had taken the place of vague fear.

He, therefore, told Mr. Nabbum, at length, his reasons for proposing, and even urging, that unless Huggermugger should exhibit a very different side to his character from that which he had seen, nothing like force or stratagem should be resorted to.

"For," said Little Jacket, "even if you succeeded, Mr. Nabbum, in throwing your net over his head, or your noose round his leg, as you would round an elephant's, you should consider how powerful and intelligent, and, if incensed, how furious an adversary you have to deal with. None but a man out of his wits would think of carrying him off to your ship by main force. And as to your idea of making him drunk, and taking him abroad in that condition, there is no knowing whether drink would not render him quite furious, and ten times more unmanageable than ever. No, take my word for it, Mr. Nabbum, that I know Huggermugger too well to attempt any of your tricks with him. You cannot catch him as you would an elephant or a hippopotamus. Be guided by me, and see if my plan don't succeed better than yours."

"Well," answered Zebedee, "I guess, arter all, Jacky, you may be right. You've seen the big varmint, and feel a kind o' acquainted with him, so you see I won't insist on my plan, if you've any better. Now, what I want to know is, what's your idee of comin' it over the critter?"

"You leave that to me," said Little Jacket; "if talking and making friends with him can do any thing, I think I can do it. We may coax him away; tell him stories about our country, and what fun he'd have among the people so much smaller than himself, and how they'd all look up to him as the greatest man they ever had, which will be true, you know; and that perhaps the Americans will make him General Huggermugger, or His Excellency President Huggermugger; and you add a word about our nice oysters, and clam-chowders.

"I think there'd be room for him in your big ship. It's warm weather, and he could lie on deck, you know; and we could cover him up at night with matting and old sails; and he'd be so tickled at the idea of going to sea, and seeing strange countries, and we'd show him such whales and porpoises, and tell him such good stories, that I think he'd keep pretty quiet till we reached America. To be sure, it's a long voyage, and we'd have to lay in an awful sight of provisions, for he's a great feeder; but we can touch at different ports as we go along, and replenish our stock.

"One difficulty will be, how to persuade him to leave his wife—for there wouldn't be room for two of them. We must think the matter over, and it will be time enough to decide what to do when we get there. Even if we find it impossible to get him to go with us, we'll get somebody to write his history, and an account of our adventures, and make a book that will sell."

CHAPTER 11

THEY SAIL FOR HUGGERMUGGER'S ISLAND

So Little Jacket sailed with Mr. Zebedee Nabbum, in search of the giant's island. They took along a good crew, several bold elephant-hunters, an author to write their adventures, an artist to sketch the Huggermuggers, Little Jacket's six comrades, grappling-irons, nets, ropes, harpoons, cutlasses, pistols, guns, the two young elephants, the lion, the giraffe, the monkeys, and the parrots.

They had some difficulty in rowing the island, but by taking repeated observations, they at last discovered land that they thought must be it. They came near, and were satisfied that they were not deceived. There were the huge black cliffs—there were the rocky promontory—the beach. It was growing dusk, however, and they determined to cast anchor, and wait till morning before they sent ashore a boat.

Was it fancy or not, that Little Jacket thought he could see in the gathering darkness, a dim, towering shape, moving along like a pillar of cloud, now and then stooping to pick up something on the shore—till it stopped, and seemed looking in the direction of the ship, and then suddenly darted off towards the cliffs, and disappeared in the dark woods.

CHAPTER 12

THE HUGGERMUGGERS IN A NEW LIGHT

I think the giant must have seen the ship, and ran home at full speed to tell his wife about it. For in the morning early, as Little Jacket and Nabbum and several others of the boldest of the crew had just landed their boat, and were walking on the beach, whom should they see but Huggermugger and his wife hastening towards them with rapid strides. Their first impulse was to rush and hide themselves, but the Huggermuggers came too fast towards them to allow them to do so. There was nothing else to do but face the danger, if danger there was. What was their surprise to find that the giant and giantess wore the most beaming smiles on their broad faces. They stooped down and patted their heads with their huge hands, and called them, in broken English, "pretty little dolls and dears, and where did they come from, and how long it was since they had seen any little men like them—and wouldn't they go home and see them in their big house under the cliffs?" Mrs. Huggermugger, especially, was charmed with them, and would have taken them home in her arms—"she had no children of her own, and they should live with her and be her little babies." The sailors did not exactly like the idea of being treated like babies, but they were so astonished and delighted to find the giants in such good humor, that they were ready to submit to all the good woman's caresses.

Little Jacket then told them where they came from, and related his whole story of having been shipwrecked there, and all his other adventures. As he told them how Huggermugger had carried home the big shell with him in it, sound asleep; how he had let himself down from the mantel-piece, and had tried to escape by cutting at the door; and how, when he heard Huggermugger coming, he had rushed into the boot, and how he had pricked the giant's toe when he attempted to draw his boot on, and how the boot and he were taken to the cobbler's —then Huggermugger and his wife could contain themselves no longer, but burst into such peals of laughter, that the people in the ship, who were watching their movements on shore through their spy-glasses, and expected every moment to see their companions all eaten alive or carried off to be killed, knew not what to make of it. Huggermugger and his wife laughed till the tears ran down their faces, and made such a noise in their merriment, that the sailors wished they were further off. They, however, were in as great glee as the giant and giantess, and began to entertain such a good opinion of them, that they were ready to assent to any thing the Huggermuggers proposed. In fact, except in matter of size, they could see very little difference between the giants and themselves. All Zebedee Nabbum's warlike and elephant-trapping schemes melted away entirely, and he even began to have a sort of conscientious scruple against enticing away the big fellow who proved to be such a jolly good-humored giant. He was prepared for resistance. He would have even liked the fun of throwing a noose over his head, and pulling him down and harpooning him, but this good-humored, merry laughter, this motherly caressing, was too much for Zebedee. He was overcome. Even Little Jacket was astonished. The once dreaded giant was in all respects like them—only O, so much bigger!

So, after a good deal of friendly talk, Huggermugger invited the whole boat's crew to go home with him to dinner, and even to spend some days with him, if they would. Little Jacket liked the proposal, but Zebedee said they must first send back a message to the ship, to say where they were going. Huggermugger sent his card by the boat, to the rest of the ship's company—it was a huge piece of pasteboard, as big as a dining-table—saying, that he and Mrs. H. would be happy, some other day, to see all who would do him the honor of a visit. He would come himself and fetch them in his fish-basket, as the road was rough, and difficult for such little folks to travel.

CHAPTER 13

HUGGERMUGGER HALL

The next morning Huggermugger appeared on the beach with his big basket, and took away about half a dozen of the sailors, Zebedee and Little Jacket went with them. It was a curious journey, jogging along in his basket, and hanging at such a height from the ground. Zebedee could not help thinking what a capital thing it would be in America to have a few big men like him to lift heavy stones for building, or to carry the mail bags from city to city, at a railroad speed. But, as to travelling in his fish-basket, he certainly preferred our old-fashioned railroad cars.

They were all entertained very hospitably at Huggermugger Hall. They had a good dinner of fish, frogs, fruit, and vegetables, and drank a kind of beer, made of berries, out of Mrs. Huggermugger's thimble, much to the amusement of all. Mrs. Huggermugger showed them her beautiful shell, and made Little Jacket tell how he had crept out of it, and let himself down by the fishing-line. And Huggermugger made him act over again the scene of hiding in the boot. At which all laughed again. The little people declined their hosts' pressing invitation to stay all night, so Huggermugger took them all back to their boat. They had enough to tell on board ship about their visit. The next day, and the day after, others of the crew were entertained in the same way at Huggermugger Hall, till all had satisfied their curiosity. The giant and his wife being alone in the island, they felt that it was pleasant to have their solitude broken by the arrival of the little men. There were several dwarfs living here and there in the island, who worked for the giants, of whom Kobboltozo was one; but there were no other giants. The Huggermuggers were the last of their race. Their history, however, was a secret they kept to themselves. Whether they or their ancestors came from Brobdignag, or whether they were descended from Gog and Magog, or Goliath of Gath, they never would declare.

Mr. Scrawler, the author, who accompanied the ship, was very curious to know something of their history and origin. He ascertained that they learned English of a party of adventurers who once landed on their shore, many years before, and that the Huggermugger race had long inhabited the island. But he could learn nothing of their origin. They looked very serious whenever this subject was mentioned. There was evidently a mystery about them, which they had particular reasons never to unfold. On all other subjects they were free and communicative. On this, they kept the strictest and most guarded silence.

CHAPTER 14

KOBBOLTOZO ASTONISHES MR. SCRAWLER

Now it chanced that some of the dwarfs I have spoken of, were not on the best of terms with the Huggermuggers. Kobboltozo was one of these. And the only reason why he disliked them, as far as could be discovered, was, that they were giants, and he (though a good deal larger than an ordinary sized man) was but a dwarf. He could never be as big as they were. He was like the frog that envied the ox, and his envy and hatred sometimes swelled him almost to bursting. All the favors that the Huggermuggers heaped upon him, had no effect in softening him. He would have been glad at almost any misfortune that could happen to them.

Now Kobboltozo was at the giant's house one day when Mr. Scrawler was asking questions of Huggermugger about his origin, and observed his disappointment at not being furnished with all the information he was so eager to obtain; for Mr. Scrawler calculated to make a book about the Huggermuggers and all their ancestors, which would sell. So while Mr. Scrawler was taking a stroll in the garden, Kobboltozo came up to him and told him he had something important to communicate to him. They then retired behind some shrubbery, where

Kobboltozo, taking a seat under the shade of a cabbage, and requesting Mr. Scrawler to do the same, looked around cautiously, and spoke as follows:—

"I perceive that you are very eager to know something about the Huggermuggers' origin and history. I think that I am almost the only one in this island, besides them, who can gratify your curiosity in this matter. But you must solemnly promise to tell no one, least of all the giants, in what way you came to know what I am going to tell you, unless it be after you have left the island, for I dread Huggermugger's vengeance if he knows the story came from me."

"I promise," said Scrawler.

"Know then," said Kobboltozo, "that the ancestors of the Huggermuggers—the Huggers on the male side, and the Muggers on the female—were men and women not much above the ordinary size—smaller than me, the poor dwarf. Hundreds of years ago they came to this island, directed hither by an old woman, a sort of witch, who told them that if they and their children, and their children's children, ate constantly of a particular kind of shell-fish, which was found in great abundance here, they would continue to increase in size, with each successive generation, until they became proportioned to all other growth in the island—till they became giants—such giants as the Huggermuggers. But that the last survivors of the race would meet with some great misfortune, if this secret should ever be told to more than one person out of the Huggermugger family. I have reasons for believing that Huggermugger and his wife are the last of their race; for all their ancestors and relations are dead, and they have no children, and are likely to have none. *Now there are two persons who have been told the secret. It was told to me, and I tell it to you!*"

As Kobboltozo ended, his face wore an almost fiendish expression of savage triumph, as if he had now settled the giants' fate forever.

"But," said Scrawler, "how came *you* into possession of this tremendous secret; and, if true, why do you wish any harm to happen to the good Huggermuggers?"

"I hate them!" said the dwarf. "They are rich—I am poor. They are big and well-formed—I am little and crooked. Why should not my race grow to be as shapely and as large as they; for *my* ancestors were as good as theirs, and I have heard that they possessed the island before the Huggermuggers came into it? No! I am weary of the Huggermuggers. I have more right to the island than they. But they have grown by enchantment, while my race only grew to a certain size, and then we stopped and grew crooked. But the Huggermuggers, if there should be any more of them, will grow till they are like the trees of the forest.

"Then as to the way I discovered their mystery. I was taking home a pair of shoes for the giantess, and was just about to knock at the door, when I heard the giant and his wife talking. I crept softly up and listened. They have great voices—not difficult to hear *them*. They were talking about a secret door in the wall, and of something precious which was locked up within a little closet. As soon as their voices ceased, I knocked, and was let in. I assumed an appearance as if I had heard nothing, and they did not suspect me. I went and told Hammawhaxo, the carpenter—a friend of mine, and a dwarf like me. I knew he didn't like Huggermugger much. Hammawhaxo was employed at the time to repair the bottom of a door in the giant's house, where the rats had been gnawing. So he went one morning before the giants were up, and tapped all around the wainscoting of the walls with his hammer, till he found a hollow place, and a sliding panel, and inside the wall he discovered an old manuscript in the ancient Hugger language, in which was written the secret I have told you. And now we will see if the old fortune-teller's prophecy is to come true or not."

CHAPTER 15

MRS. HUGGERMUGGER GROWS THIN AND FADES AWAY

Scrawler, though delighted to get hold of such a story to put into his book, could not help feeling a superstitious fear that the prediction might be verified, and some misfortune befall the good Huggermuggers. It could not come from him or any of his friends, he was sure; for Zebedee Nabbum's first idea of entrapping the giant was long since abandoned. If he was ever to be taken away from the island, it could only be by the force of persuasion, and he was sure that Huggermugger would not voluntarily leave his wife.

Scrawler only hinted then to Huggermugger, that he feared Kobboltozo was his enemy. But Huggermugger laughed, and said he knew the dwarf was crabbed and spiteful, but that he did not fear him. Huggermugger was not suspicious by nature, and it never came into his thoughts that Kobboltozo, or any other dwarf could have the least idea of his great secret.

Little Jacket came now frequently to the giant's house, where he became a great favorite. He had observed, for some days, that Mrs. Huggermugger's spirits were not so buoyant as usual. She seldom laughed—she sometimes sat alone and sighed, and even wept. She ate very little of shell-fish—even her favorite frog had lost its relish. She was growing thin—the once large, plump woman. Her husband, who really loved her, though his manner towards her was sometimes rough, was much concerned. He could not enjoy his lonely supper—he scarcely cared for his pipe. To divert his mind, he would sometimes linger on the shore, talking to the little men, as he called them. He would strip off his long boots and his clothes, and wade out into the sea to get a nearer view of the ship. He could get near enough to talk to them on board. "How should you like to go with us," said the little men, one day, "and sail away to see new countries? We could show you a great deal that you haven't seen. If you went to America with us, you would be the greatest man there."

Huggermugger laughed, but not one of his hearty laughs—his mind was ill at ease about his wife. But the idea was a new one, of going away from giant-land to a country of pygmies. Could he ever go? Not certainly without his wife—and she would never leave the island. Why should he wish to go away? "To be sure," he said, "it is rather lonely here—all our kindred dead—nobody to be seen but little ugly dwarfs. And I really like these little sailors, and shall be sorry to part with them. No, here I shall remain, wife and I, and here we shall end our days. We are the last of the giants—let us not desert our native soil."

Mrs. Huggermugger grew worse and worse. It seemed to be a rapid consumption. No cause could be discovered for her sickness. A dwarf doctor was called in, but he shook his head—he feared he could do nothing. Little Jacket came with the ship's doctor, and brought some medicines. She took them, but they had no effect. She could not now rise from her bed. Her husband sat by her side all the time. The good-hearted sailors did all they could for her, which was not much. Even Zebedee Nabbum's feelings were touched. He told her Yankee stories, and tales of wild beasts—of elephants, not bigger than one of her pigs—of lions and bears as small as lapdogs—of birds not larger than one of their flies. All did what they could to lessen her sufferings.

"To think," said Zebedee, "aint it curious—who'd a thought that great powerful critter could ever get sick and waste away like this!"

CHAPTER 16

THE SORROWS OF HUGGERMUGGER

At last, one morning while the sailors were lounging about on the beach, they saw the great Huggermugger coming along, his head bent low, and the great tears streaming down his face. They all ran up to him. He sat, or rather threw himself down on the ground. "My dear little friends," said he, "it's all over. I never shall see my poor wife again—never again—never again—I am the last of the Huggermuggers. She is gone. And as for me—I care not now whither I go. I can never stay here—not here—it will be too lonely. Let me go and bury my poor wife, and then farewell to giant-land! I will go with you, if you will take me!"

They were all much grieved. They took Huggermugger's great hands, as he sat there, like a great wrecked and stranded ship, swayed to and fro by the waves and surges of his grief, and their tears mingled with his. He took them in his arms, the great Huggermugger, and kissed them. "You are the only friends left me now," he said, "take me with you from this lonely place. She who was so dear to me is gone to the great Unknown, as on a boundless ocean; and this great sea which lies before us is to me like it. Whether I live or die, it is all one—take me with you. I am helpless now as a child!"

CHAPTER 17

HUGGERMUGGER LEAVES HIS ISLAND

Zebedee Nabbum could not help thinking how easily he had obtained possession of his giant. There was now nothing to do but to make room for him in the ship, and lay in a stock of those articles of food which the giant was accustomed to eat, sufficient for a long voyage.

Huggermugger laid his wife in a grave by the sea-shore, and covered it over with the beautiful large shells which she so loved. He then went home, opened the secret door in the wall, took out the ancient manuscript, tied a heavy stone to it, and sunk it in a deep well under the rocks, into which he also threw the key of his house, after having taken every thing he needed for his voyage, and locked the doors.

The ship was now all ready to sail. The sailors had made a large raft, on which the giant sat and paddled himself to the ship, and climbed on board. The ship was large enough to allow him to stand, when the sea was still, and even walk about a little; but Huggermugger preferred the reclining posture, for he was weary and needed repose.

During the first week or two of the voyage, his spirits seemed to revive. The open sea, without any horizon, the sails spreading calmly above him, the invigorating salt breeze, the little sailors clambering up the shrouds and on the yards, all served to divert his mind from his great grief. The sailors came around him and told him stories, and described the country to which they were bound; and sometimes Mr. Nabbum brought out his elephants, which Huggermugger patted and fondled like dogs. But poor Huggermugger was often sea-sick, and could not sit up. The sailors made him as comfortable as they could. By night they covered him up and kept him warm, and by day they stretched an awning above him to protect him from the sun. He was so accustomed to the open air, that he was never too cold nor too warm. But poor Huggermugger, after a few weeks more, began to show the symptoms of a more serious illness than sea-sickness. A nameless melancholy took possession of him. He refused to eat—he spoke little, and only lay and gazed up at the white sails and the blue sky. By degrees, he began to waste away, very much as his wife did. Little Jacket felt a real sorrow and sympathy, and so did they all. Zebedee Nabbum, however, it must be confessed, "though he felt a kind o' sorry for the poor critter," thought more of the loss it would be to him, as a money speculation, to have him die before they reached America. "It would be too bad," he said, "after all the trouble and expense I've had, and when the critter was so willin', too, to come aboard, to go and have him die. We must feed him well, and try hard to save him; for we can't afford to lose him. Why, he'd be worth at least 50,000 dollars—yes, 100,000 dollars, in the United States." So Zebedee would bring him dishes of his favorite clams, nicely cooked and seasoned, but the giant only sighed and shook his head. "No," he said, "my little friends, I feel that I shall never see your country. Your coming to my island has been in some way fatal for me. My secret must have been told. The prophecy, ages ago, has come true!"

CHAPTER 18

THE LAST OF HUGGERMUGGER

Mr. Scrawler now thought it was time for him to speak. He had only refrained from communicating to Huggermugger what the dwarf had told him, from the fear of making the poor giant more unhappy and ill than ever. But he saw that he could be silent no longer, for there seemed to be a suspicion in Huggermugger's mind, that it might be these very people, in whose ship he had consented to go, who had found out and revealed his secret.

Mr. Scrawler then related to the giant what the dwarf had told him in the garden, about the concealed MS., and the prophecy it contained.

Huggermugger sunk his head in his hands, and said: "Ah, the dwarf—the dwarf! Fool that I was; I might have known it. His race always hated mine. Ah, wretch! that I had punished thee as thou deservest!

"But, after all, what matters it?" he added, "I am the last of my race. What matters it, if I die a little sooner than I thought? I have little wish to live, for I should have been very lonely in my island. Better is it that I go to other lands—better, perhaps, that I die ere reaching land.

"Friends, I feel that I shall never see your country—and why should I wish it? How could such a huge being as I live among you? For a little while I should be amused with you, and you astonished at me. I might find friends here and there, like you; but your people could never understand my nature, nor I theirs. I should be carried about as a spectacle; I should not belong to myself, but to those who exhibited me. There could be little sympathy between your people and mine. I might, too, be feared, be hated. Your climate, your food, your houses, your laws, your customs—every thing would be unlike what mine has been. I am too old, too weary of life, to begin it again in a new world."

So, my young readers, not to weary you with any more accounts of Huggermugger's sickness, I must end the matter, and tell you plainly that he died long before they reached America, much to Mr. Nabbum's vexation. Little Jacket and his friends grieved very much, but they could not help it, and thought that, on the whole, it was best it should be so. Zebedee Nabbum wished they could, at least, preserve the giant's body, and exhibit it in New York. But it was impossible. All they could take home with them was his huge skeleton; and even this, by some mischance, was said to be incomplete.

Some time after the giant's death, Mr. Scrawler, one day when the ship was becalmed, and the sailors wished to be amused, fell into a poetic frenzy, and produced the following song, which all hands sung, (rather slowly) when Mr. Nabbum was not present, to the tune of Yankee Doodle:—

>   *Yankee Nabbum went to sea*
>   *A huntin' after lions;*
>   *He came upon an island where*
>   *There was a pair of giants.*
>   *He brought his nets and big harpoon,*
>   *And thought he'd try to catch 'em,*
>   *But Nabbum found out very soon*
>   *There was no need to fetch 'em.*
>
>   *Yankee Nabbum went ashore,*
>   *With Jacky and some others,*
>   *But Huggermugger treated them*
>   *Just like his little brothers.*
>   *He took 'em up and put 'em in*
>   *His thunderin' big fish basket;*
>   *He took 'em home and gave 'em all*
>   *They wanted, ere they asked it.*
>
>   *The giants were as sweet to them*
>   *As two great lumps of sugar—*
>   *A very Queen of Candy was*
>   *Good Mrs. Huggermugger.*
>   *But, ah! the good fat woman died,*
>   *The giant too departed,*
>   *And came himself on Nabbum's ship,*
>   *Quite sad and broken hearted.*

> *He came aboard and sailed with us,*
> *A sadder man and wiser—*
> *But pretty soon, just like his wife,*
> *He sickened and did die, Sir.*
> *But Nabbum kept his mighty bones—*
> *How they will stare to see 'em,*
> *When Nabbum has them all set up*
> *In Barnum's great Museum!*

Nothing is clearly known, strange to say, as to what became of this skeleton. In the Museum, at Philadelphia, there are some great bones, which are usually supposed to be those of the Great Mastodon. It is the opinion, however, of others, that they are none other than those of the great Huggermugger—all that remains of the last of the giants.

Note.—I was told, several years since, that Mr. Scrawler's narrative of his adventures in Huggermugger's island, was nearly completed, and that he was only waiting for a publisher. As, however, nothing has as yet been heard of his long expected book, I have taken the liberty to print what I have written, from the story, as I heard it from Little Jacket himself, who is now grown to be a man. I have been told that Little Jacket, who is now called Mr. John Cable, has left the sea, and is now somewhere out in the Western States, settled down as a farmer, and has grown so large and fat, that he fears he must have eaten some of those strange shell-fish, by which the Huggermugger race grew to be so great. Other accounts, however, say that he is as fond of the sea as ever, and has got to be the captain of a great ship; and that he and Mr. Nabbum are still voyaging round the world, in hopes of finding other Huggermuggers.

In this amusing tale, the mere power of speech is not all that is necessary for pleasant conversation, even with a cat. H. H. Munro, who wrote under the name SAKI, *was an important writer of the contemporary short story and among those British writers who died in World War I. Saki was a humorist and ironist whose wit drew him to the fantastic and the absurd. He does not so much write fantasy as use it for special effect.*

Tobermory
BY SAKI

It was a chill, rain-washed afternoon of a late August day, that indefinite season when partridges are still in security or cold storage, and there is nothing to hunt—unless one is bounded on the north by the Bristol Channel, in which case one may lawfully gallop after fat red stags. Lady Blemley's house-party was not bounded on the north by the Bristol Channel, hence there was a full gathering of her guests round the tea-table on this particular afternoon. And, in spite of the blankness of the season and the triteness of the occasion, there was no trace in the company of that fatigued restlessness which means a dread of the pianola and a subdued hankering for auction bridge. The undisguised open-mouthed attention of the entire party was fixed on the homely negative personality of Mr Cornelius Appin. Of all her guests, he was the one who had come to Lady Blemley with the vaguest reputation. Someone had said he was "clever," and he had got his invitation in the moderate expectation, on the part of his hostess, that some portion at least of his cleverness would be contributed to the general entertainment. Until tea-time that day she had been unable to discover in what direction, if any, his cleverness lay. He was neither a wit nor a croquet champion, a hypnotic force nor a begetter of amateur theatricals. Neither did his exterior suggest the sort of man in whom women are willing to pardon a generous measure of mental deficiency. He had subsided into mere Mr Appin, and the Cornelius seemed a piece of transparent baptismal bluff. And now he was claiming to have launched on the world a discovery beside which the invention of gunpowder, of the printing press, and of steam locomotion were inconsiderable trifles. Science had made bewildering strides in many directions during recent decades, but this thing seemed to belong to the domain of the miracle rather than to scientific achievement.

"And do you really ask us to believe," Sir Wilfred was saying, "that you have discovered a means for instructing animals in the art of human speech and that dear old Tobermory has proved your first successful pupil?"

"It is a problem at which I have worked for the last seventeen years," said Mr Appin, "but only during the last eight or nine months have I been rewarded with glimmerings of success. Of course I have experimented with thousands of animals, but latterly only with cats, those wonderful creatures which have assimilated themselves so marvellously with our civilization while retaining all their highly developed feral instincts. Here and there among cats one comes across an outstanding superior intellect, just as one does among the ruck of human beings, and when I made the acquaintance of Tobermory a week ago I saw at once that I was in contact with a 'Beyond-cat' of extraordinary intelligence. I had gone far along the road to success in recent experiments; with Tobermory, as you call him, I have reached the goal."

Mr Appin concluded his remarkable statement in a voice which he strove to divest of a triumphant infection. No one said "Rats," though Clovis's lips moved in a monosyllabic contortion which probably invoked those rodents of disbelief.

"And do you mean to say," asked Miss Resker, after a slight pause, "that you have taught Tobermory to say and understand easy sentences of one syllable?"

"My dear Miss Resker," said the wonder-worker patiently, "one teaches little children and savages and backward adults in that piecemeal fashion; when one has solved the problem of making a beginning with an animal of highly developed intelligence one has no need for those halting methods. Tobermory can speak our language with perfect correctness."

This time Clovis very distinctly said, "Beyond-rats!" Sir Wilfred was more polite, but equally sceptical.

"Hadn't we better have the cat in and judge for ourselves?" suggested Lady Blemley.

Sir Wilfred went in search of the animal, and the company settled themselves down to the languid expectation of witnessing some more or less adroit drawing-room ventriloquism.

In a minute Sir Wilfred was back in the room, his face white beneath its tan and eyes dilated with excitement.

"By gad, it's true!"

His agitation was unmistakably genuine, and his hearers started forward in a thrill of awakened interest.

Collapsing into an armchair he continued breathlessly: "I found him dozing in the smoking-room, and called out to him to come for his tea. He blinked at me in his usual way, and I said, 'Come on, Toby; don't keep us waiting'; and, by Gad! he drawled out in a most horribly natural voice that he'd come when he dashed well pleased! I nearly jumped out of my skin!"

Appin had preached to absolutely incredulous hearers; Sir Wilfred's statement carried instant conviction. A Babel-like chorus of startled exclamation arose, amid which the scientist sat mutely enjoying the first fruit of his stupendous discovery.

In the midst of the clamour Tobermory entered the room and made his way with velvet tread and studied unconcern across to the group seated round the tea-table.

A sudden hush of awkwardness and constraint fell upon the company. Somehow there seemed an element of embarrassment in addressing on equal terms a domestic cat of acknowledged mental ability.

"Will you have some milk, Tobermory?" asked Lady Blemley in a rather strained voice.

"I don't mind if I do," was the response, couched in a tone of even indifference. A shiver of surpressed excitement went through the listeners, and Lady Blemley might be excused for pouring out the saucerful of milk rather unsteadily.

"I'm afraid I've spilt a good deal of it," she said apologetically.

"After all, it's not my Axminster," was Tobermory's rejoinder.

Another silence fell on the group, and then Miss Resker, in her best district-visitor manner, asked if the human language had been difficult to learn. Tobermory looked squarely at her for a moment and then fixed his gaze serenely on the middle distance. It was obvious that boring questions lay outside his scheme of life.

"What do you think of human intelligence?" asked Mavis Pellington lamely.

"Of whose intelligence in particular?" asked Tobermory coldly.

"Oh, well, mine for instance," said Mavis, with a feeble laugh.

"You put me in an embarrassing position," said Tobermory, whose tone and attitude certainly did not suggest a shred of embarrassment. "When your inclusion in this house-party was suggested Sir Wilfred protested that you were the most brainless woman of his acquaintance, and that there was a broad distinction between hospitality and the care of the feeble-minded. Lady Blemley replied that your lack of brain-power was the precise quality which had earned you your invitation, as you were the only person she could think of who might be idiotic enough to buy their old car. You know, the one they call 'The Envy of Sisyphus,' because it goes quite nicely uphill if you push it."

Lady Blemley's protestations would have had greater effect if she had not casually suggested to Mavis only that morning that the car in question would be just the thing for her down at her Devonshire home.

Major Barfield plunged in heavily to effect a diversion.

"How about your carryings-on with the tortoiseshell puss up at the stables, eh?"

The moment he had said it everyone realized the blunder.

"One does not usually discuss these matters in public," said Tobermory frigidly. "From a slight observation of your ways since you've been in this house I should imagine you'd find it inconvenient if I were to shift the conversation on to your own little affairs."

The panic which ensued was not confined to the major.

"Would you like to go and see if cook has got your dinner ready?" suggested Lady Blemley hurriedly, affecting to ignore the fact that it wanted at least two hours to Tobermory's dinner-time.

"Thanks," said Tobermory, "not quite so soon after my tea. I don't want to die of indigestion."

"Cats have nine lives, you know," said Sir Wilfred heartily.

"Possibly," answered Tobermory; "but only one liver."

"Adelaide!" said Mrs Cornett, "do you mean to encourage that cat to go out and gossip about us in the servants' hall?"

The panic had indeed become general. A narrow ornamental balustrade ran in front of most of the bedroom windows at the Towers, and it was recalled with dismay that this had formed a favorite promenade for Tobermory at all hours, whence he could watch the pigeons—and heaven knew what else besides. If he intended to become reminiscent in his present outspoken strain the effect would be something more than disconcerting. Mrs Cornett, who spent much time at her toilet table, and whose complexion was reputed to be of a nomadic though punctual disposition, looked as ill at ease as the Major. Miss Scrawen, who wrote fiercely sensuous poetry and led a blameless life, merely displayed irritation; if you are methodical and virtuous in private you don't necessarily want everyone to know it. Bertie van Tahn, who was so depraved at seventeen that he had long ago given up trying to be any worse, turned a dull shade of gardenia white, but he did not commit the error of dashing out of the room like Odo Finsberry, a young gentleman who was understood to be reading for the Church and who was possibly disturbed at the thought of scandals he might hear concerning other people. Clovis had the presence of mind to maintain a composed exterior; privately he was calculating how long it would take to procure a box of fancy mice through the agency of the *Exchange and Mart* as a species of hush-money.

Even in a delicate situation like the present, Agnes Resker could not endure to remain too long in the background.

"Why did I ever come down here?" she asked dramatically.

Tobermory immediately accepted the opening.

"Judging by what you said to Mrs Cornett on the croquet-lawn yesterday, you were out for food. You described the Blemleys as the dullest people to stay with that you knew, but said they were clever enough to employ a first-rate cook; otherwise they'd find it difficult to get anyone to come down a second time."

"There's not a word of truth in it! I appeal to Mrs Cornett—" exclaimed the discomfited Agnes.

"Mrs Cornett repeated your remark afterwards to Bertie van Tahn," continued Tobermory, and said, "That woman is a regular Hunger Marcher; she'd go anywhere for four square meals a day, and Bertie van Tahn said—"

At this point the chronicle mercifully ceased. Tobermory had caught a glimpse of the big yellow Tom from the Rectory working his way through the shrubbery towards the stable wing. In a flash he had vanished through the open French window.

With the disappearance of his too brilliant pupil Cornelius Appin found himself beset by a hurricane of bitter upbraiding, anxious enquiry, and frightened entreaty. The responsibility for the situation lay with him, and he must prevent matters from becoming worse. Could Tobermory impart his dangerous gift to other cats? was the first question he had to answer. It was possible, he replied, that he might have initiated his intimate friend the stable puss into his new accomplishment, but it was unlikely that his teaching could have taken a wider range as yet.

"Then," said Mrs Cornett, "Tobermory may be a valuable cat and a great pet; but I'm sure you'll agree, Adelaide, that both he and the stable cat must be done away with without delay."

"You don't suppose I've enjoyed the last quarter of an hour, do you?" said Lady Blemley bitterly. "My husband and I are very fond of Tobermory—at least, we were before this horrible accomplishment was infused into him; but now, of course, the only thing is to have him destroyed as soon as possible."

"We can put some strychnine in the scraps he always gets at dinner-time," said Sir Wilfred, "and I will go and drown the stable cat myself. The coachman will be very sore at losing his pet, but I'll say a very catching form of mange has broken out in both cats and we're afraid of it spreading to the kennels."

"But my great discovery!" expostulated Mr Appin; "after all my years of research and experiment—"

"You can go and experiment on the short-horns at the farm, who are under proper control," said Mrs Cornett, "or the elephants at the Zoological Gardens. They're said to be highly intelligent, and they have this recommendation, that they don't come creeping about our bedrooms and under chairs, and so forth."

An archangel ecstatically proclaiming the Millenium, and then finding that it clashed unpardonably with Henley and would have to be indefinitely postponed, could hardly have felt more crestfallen than Cornelius Appin at the reception of his wonderful achievement. Public opinion, however, was against him—in fact, had the general voice been consulted on the matter it is probable that a strong minority would have been in favour of including him in the strychnine diet.

Defective train arrangements and a nervous desire to see matters brought to a finish prevented an immediate dispersal of the party, but dinner that evening was not a social success. Sir Wilfred had had rather a trying time with the stable cat and subsequently with the coachman. Agnes Resker ostentatiously limited her repast to a morsel of dry toast, which she bit as though it were a personal enemy; whilst Mavis Pellington maintained a vindictive silence throughout the meal. Lady Blemley kept up a flow of what she hoped was conversation, but her attention was fixed on the doorway. A plateful of carefully dosed fish scraps was in readiness on the sideboard, but sweets and savoury and dessert went their way, and no Tobermory appeared either in the dining-room or kitchen.

The sepulchral dinner was cheerful compared to the subsequent vigil in the smoking-room. Eating and drinking had at least supplied a distraction and cloak to the prevailing embarrassment. Bridge was out of the question in the general tension of nerves and tempers, and after Odo Finsberry had given a lugubrious rendering of "Melisande in the Wood" to a frigid audience, music was tacitly avoided. At eleven the servants went to bed, announcing that the small window in the pantry had been left open as usual for Tobermory's private use. The guests read steadily through the current batch of magazines, and fell back gradually on the "Badminton Library" and bound volumes of *Punch*. Lady Blemley made periodic visits to the pantry, returning each time with an expression of listless depression which forestalled questioning.

At two o'clock Clovis broke the dominating silence.

"He won't turn up tonight. He's probably in the local newspaper office at the present moment, dictating the first instalment of his reminiscences. Lady What's-her-name's book won't be in it. It will be the event of the day."

Having made this contribution to the general cheerfulness, Clovis went to bed. At long intervals the various members of the house-party followed his example.

The servants taking round the early tea made a uniform announcement to a uniform question. Tobermory had not returned.

Breakfast was, if anything, a more unpleasant function than dinner had been, but before its conclusion the situation was relieved. Tobermory's corpse was brought in from the shrubbery, where a gardener had just discovered it. From the bites on his throat and the yellow fur which coated his claws it was evident that he had fallen in unequal combat with the big Tom from the Rectory.

By midday most of the guests had quitted the Towers, and after lunch Lady Blemley had sufficiently recovered her spirits to write an extremely nasty letter to the Rectory about the loss of her valuable pet.

Tobermory had been Appin's one successful pupil, and he was destined to have no successor. A few weeks later an elephant in the Dresden Zoological Garden, which had shown no previous signs of irritability, broke loose and killed an Englishman who had apparently been teasing it. The victim's name was variously reported in the papers as Oppin and Eppelin, but his front name was faithfully rendered Cornelius.

"If he was trying German irregular verbs on the poor beast," said Clovis, "he deserved all he got."

Suddenly one rainy night the landscape around the town of Derryville is transformed into a fantasy world. This story is about the seductiveness of fantasy worlds, about small, bedraggled elves and big, ugly trolls. PHILIP K. DICK, *one of the great science fiction writers of the century, often turned his hand to fantasy in short fiction during the first few years of his career in the 1950s, when he was a student of Anthony Boucher, one of the founders of contemporary fantasy.*

The King of the Elves
BY PHILIP K. DICK

It was raining and getting dark. Sheets of water blew along the row of pumps at the edge of the filling station; the trees across the highway bent against the wind.

Shadrach Jones stood just inside the doorway of the little building, leaning against an oil drum. The door was open and gusts of rain blew in onto the wood floor. It was late; the sun had set, and the air was turning cold. Shadrach reached into his coat and brought out a cigar. He bit the end off it and lit it carefully, turning away from the door. In the gloom, the cigar burst into life, warm and glowing. Shadrach took a deep draw. He buttoned his coat around him and stepped out onto the pavement.

"Darn," he said. "What a night!" Rain buffeted him, wind blew at him. He looked up and down the highway, squinting. There were no cars in sight. He shook his head, locked up the gasoline pumps.

He went back into the building and pulled the door shut behind him. He opened the cash register and counted the money he'd taken in during the day. It was not much.

Not much, but enough for one old man. Enough to buy him tobacco and firewood and magazines, so that he could be comfortable as he waited for the occasional cars to come by. Not very many cars came along the highway any more. The highway had begun to fall into disrepair; there were many cracks in its dry, rough surface, and most cars preferred to take the big state highway that ran beyond the hills. There was nothing in Derryville to attract them, to make them turn toward it. Derryville was a small town, too small to bring in any of the major industries, too small to be very important to anyone. Sometimes hours went by without—

Shadrach tensed. His fingers closed over the money. From outside came a sound, the melodic ring of the signal wire stretched along the pavement.

Dinggg!

Shadrach dropped the money into the till and pushed the drawer closed. He stood up slowly and walked toward the door, listening. At the door, he snapped off the light and waited in the darkness, staring out.

He could see no car there. The rain was pouring down, swirling with the wind; clouds of mist moved along the road. And something was standing beside the pumps.

He opened the door and stepped out. At first, his eyes could make nothing out. Then the old man swallowed uneasily.

Two tiny figures stood in the rain, holding a kind of platform between them. Once, they might have been gaily dressed in bright garments, but now their clothes hung limp and sodden, dripping in the rain. They glanced half-heartedly at Shadrach. Water streaked their tiny faces, great drops of water. Their robes blew about them with the wind, lashing and swirling.

On the platform, something stirred. A small head turned wearily, peering at Shadrach. In the dim light, a rain-streaked helmet glinted dully.

"Who are you?" Shadrach said.

The figure on the platform raised itself up. "I'm the King of the Elves and I'm wet."

Shadrach stared in astonishment.

"That's right," one of the bearers said. "We're all wet."

A small group of elves came straggling up, gathering around their king. They huddled together forlornly, silently.

"The King of the Elves," Shadrach repeated. "Well, I'll be darned."

Could it be true? They were very small, all right, and their dripping clothes were strange and oddly colored.

But *Elves?*

"I'll be darned. Well, whatever you are, you shouldn't be out on a night like this."

"Of course not," the king murmured. "No fault of our own. No fault . . ." His voice trailed off into a choking cough. The Elf soldiers peered anxiously at the platform.

"Maybe you better bring him inside," Shadrach said. "My place is up the road. He shouldn't be out in the rain."

"Do you think we like being out on a night like this?" one of the bearers muttered. "Which way is it? Direct us."

Shadrach pointed up the road. "Over there. Just follow me. I'll get a fire going."

He went down the road, feeling his way onto the first of the flat stone steps that he and Phineas Judd had laid during the summer. At the top of the steps, he looked back. The platform was coming slowly along, swaying a little from side to side. Behind it, the Elf soldiers picked their way, a tiny column of silent dripping creatures, unhappy and cold.

"I'll get the fire started," Shadrach said. He hurried them into the house.

Wearily, the Elf King lay back against the pillow. After sipping hot chocolate, he had relaxed and his heavy breathing sounded suspiciously like a snore.

Shadrach shifted in discomfort.

"I'm sorry," the Elf King said suddenly, opening his eyes. He rubbed his forehead. "I must have drifted off. Where was I?"

"You should retire, Your Majesty," one of the soldiers said sleepily. "It is late and these are hard times."

"True," the Elf King said, nodding. "Very true." He looked up at the towering figure of Shadrach, standing before the fireplace, a glass of beer in his hand. "Mortal, we thank you for your hospitality. Normally, we do not impose on human beings."

"It's those Trolls," another of the soldiers said, curled up on a cushion of the couch.

"Right," another soldier agreed. He sat up, groping for his sword. "Those reeking Trolls, digging and croaking—"

"You see," the Elf King went on, "as our party was crossing from the Great Low Steps toward the Castle, where it lies in the hollow of the Towering Mountains—"

"You mean Sugar Ridge," Shadrach supplied helpfully.

"The Towering Mountains. Slowly we made our way. A rain storm came up. We became confused. All at once a group of Trolls appeared, crashing through the underbrush. We left the woods and sought safety on the Endless Path—"

"The highway. Route Twenty."

"So that is why we're here." The Elf King paused a moment. "Harder and harder it rained. The wind blew around us, cold and bitter. For an endless time we toiled along. We had no idea where we were going or what would become of us."

The Elf King looked up at Shadrach. "We knew only this: Behind us, the Trolls were coming, creeping through the woods, marching through the rain, crushing everything before them."

He put his hand to his mouth and coughed, bending forward. All the Elves waited anxiously until he was done. He straightened up.

"It was kind of you to allow us to come inside. We will not trouble you for long. It is not the custom of the Elves—"

Again he coughed, covering his face with his hand. The Elves drew toward him apprehensively. At last the king stirred. He sighed.

"What's the matter?" Shadrach asked. He went over and took the cup of chocolate from the fragile hand. The Elf King lay back, his eyes shut.

"He has to rest," one of the soldiers said. "Where's your room? The sleeping room."

"Upstairs," Shadrach said. "I'll show you where."

Late that night, Shadrach sat by himself in the dark, deserted living room, deep in meditation. The Elves were asleep above him, upstairs in the bedroom, the Elf King in the bed, the others curled up together on the rug.

The house was silent. Outside, the rain poured down endlessly, blowing against the house. Shadrach could hear the tree branches slapping in the wind. He clasped and unclasped his hands. What a strange business it was—all these Elves, with their old, sick king, their piping voices. How anxious and peevish they were!

But pathetic, too; so small and wet, with water dripping down from them, and all their gay robes limp and soggy.

The Trolls—what were they like? Unpleasant and not very clean. Something about digging, breaking and pushing through the woods . . .

Suddenly, Shadrach laughed in embarrassment. What was the

matter with him, believing all this? He put his cigar out angrily, his ears red. What was going on? What kind of joke was this?

Elves? Shadrach grunted in indignation, Elves in Derryville? In the middle of Colorado? Maybe there were Elves in Europe. Maybe in Ireland. He had heard of that. But here? Upstairs in his own house, sleeping in his own bed?

"I've heard just about enough of this," he said. "I'm not an idiot, you know."

He turned toward the stairs, feeling for the banister in the gloom. He began to climb.

Above him, a light went on abruptly. A door opened.

Two Elves came slowly out onto the landing. They looked down at him. Shadrach halted halfway up the stairs. Something on their faces made him stop.

"What's the matter?" he asked hesitantly.

They did not answer. The house was turning cold, cold and dark, with the chill of the rain outside and the chill of the unknown inside.

"What is it?" he said again. "What's the matter?"

"The king is dead," one of the Elves said. "He died a few moments ago."

Shadrach stared up, wide-eyed. "He did? But—"

"He was very old and very tired." The Elves turned away, going back into the room, slowly and quietly shutting the door.

Shadrach stood, his fingers on the banister, hard, lean fingers, strong and thin.

He nodded his head blankly.

"I see," he said to the closed door. "He's dead."

The Elf soldiers stood around him in a solemn circle. The living room was bright with sunlight, the cold white glare of early morning.

"But wait," Shadrach said. He plucked at his necktie. "I have to get to the filling station. Can't you talk to me when I come home?"

The faces of the Elf soldiers were serious and concerned.

"Listen," one of them said. "Please hear us out. It is very important to us."

Shadrach looked past them. Through the window he saw the highway, steaming in the heat of day, and down a little way was the gas station, glittering brightly. And even as he watched, a car came up to it and honked thinly, impatiently. When nobody came out of the station, the car drove off again down the road.

"We beg you," a soldier said.

Shadrach looked down at the ring around him, the anxious faces, scored with concern and trouble. Strangely, he had always thought of Elves as carefree beings, flitting without worry or sense—

"Go ahead," he said. "I'm listening." He went over to the big chair and sat down. The Elves came up around him. They conversed among themselves for a moment, whispering, murmuring distantly. Then they turned toward Shadrach.

The old man waited, his arms folded.

"We cannot be without a king," one of the soldiers said. "We could not survive. Not these days."

"The Trolls," another added. "They multiply very fast. They are terrible beasts. They're heavy and ponderous, crude, bad-smelling—"

"The odor of them is awful. They come up from the dark wet places, under the earth, where the blind, groping plants feed in silence, far below the surface, far from the sun."

"Well, you ought to elect a king, then," Shadrack suggested. "I don't see any problem there."

"We do not elect the King of the Elves," a soldier said. "The old king must name his successor."

"Oh," Shadrach replied. "Well, there's nothing wrong with that method."

"As our old king lay dying, a few distant words came forth from his lips," a soldier said. "We bent closer, frightened and unhappy, listening."

"Important, all right," agreed Shadrach. "Not something you'd want to miss."

"He spoke the name of him who will lead us."

"Good. You caught it, then. Well, where's the difficulty?"

"The name he spoke was—was your name."

Shadrach stared. *"Mine?"*

"The dying king said: 'Make him, the towering mortal, your king. Many things will come if he leads the Elves into battle against the Trolls. I see the rising once again of the Elf Empire, as it was in the old days, as it was before—' "

"Me!" Shadrach leaped up. "Me? King of the Elves?"

Shadrach walked about the room, his hands in his pockets. "Me,

Shadrach Jones, King of the Elves," He grinned a little. "I sure never thought of it before."

He went to the mirror over the fireplace and studied himself. He saw his thin, graying hair, his bright eyes, dark skin, his big Adam's apple.

"King of the Elves," he said. "King of the Elves. Wait till Phineas Judd hears about this. Wait till I tell him!"

Phineas Judd would certainly be surprised!

Above the filling station, the sun shown, high in the clear blue sky.

Phineas Judd sat playing with the accelerator of his old Ford truck. The motor raced and slowed. Phineas reached over and turned the ignition key off, then rolled the window all the way down.

"What did you say?" he asked. He took off his glasses and began to polish them, steel rims between slender, deft fingers that were patient from years of practice. He restored his glasses to his nose and smoothed what remained of his hair into place.

"What was it, Shadrach?" he said. "Let's hear that again."

"I'm King of the Elves," Shadrach repeated. He changed position, bringing his other foot up on the runningboard. "Who would have thought it? Me, Shadrach Jones, King of the Elves."

Phineas gazed at him. "How long have you been—King of the Elves, Shadrach?"

"Since the night before last."

"I see. The night before last." Phineas nodded. "I see. And what, may I ask, occurred the night before last?"

"The Elves came to my house. When the old Elf king died, he told them that—"

A truck came rumbling up and the driver leaped out. "Water!" he said. "Where the hell is the hose?"

Shadrach turned reluctantly. "I'll get it." He turned back to Phineas. "Maybe I can talk to you tonight when you come back from town. I want to tell you the rest. It's very interesting."

"Sure," Phineas said, starting up his little truck. "Sure, Shadrach. I'm very interested to hear."

He drove off down the road.

Later in the day, Dan Green ran his flivver up to the filling station.

"Hey, Shadrach," he called. "Come over here! I want to ask you something."

Shadrach came out of the little house, holding a waste-rag in his hand.

"What is it?"

"Come here." Dan leaned out the window, a wide grin on his face, splitting his face from ear to ear. "Let me ask you something, will you?"

"Sure."

"Is it true? Are you really the King of the Elves?"

Shadrach flushed a little. "I guess I am," he admitted, looking away. "That's what I am, all right."

Dan's grin faded. "Hey, you trying to kid me? What's the gag?"

Shadrach became angry. "What do you mean? Sure, I'm the King of the Elves. And anyone who says I'm not—"

"All right, Shadrach," Dan said, starting up the flivver quickly. "Don't get mad. I was just wondering."

Shadrach looked very strange.

"All right," Dan said. "You don't hear me arguing, do you?"

By the end of the day, everyone around knew about Shadrach and how he had suddenly become King of the Elves. Pop Richey, who ran the Lucky Store in Derryville, claimed Shadrach was doing it to drum up trade for the filling station.

"He's a smart old fellow," Pop said. "Not very many cars go along there any more. He knows what he's doing."

"I don't know," Dan Green disagreed. "You should hear him. I think he really believes it."

"King of the Elves?" They all began to laugh. "Wonder what he'll say next."

Phineas Judd pondered. "I've known Shadrach for years. I can't figure it out." He frowned, his face wrinkled and disapproving. "I don't like it."

Dan looked at him. "Then you think he believes it?"

"Sure," Phineas said. "Maybe I'm wrong, but I really think he does."

"But how could he believe it?" Pop asked. "Shadrach is no fool. He's been in business for a long time. He must be getting something out of it, the way I see it. But what, if it isn't to build up the filling station?"

"Why, don't you know what he's getting?" Dan said, grinning. His gold tooth shone.

"What?" Pop demanded.

"He's got a whole kingdom to himself, that's what—to do with like he wants. How would you like that, Pop? Wouldn't you like to be King of the Elves and not have to run this old store any more?"

"There isn't anything wrong with my store," Pop said. "I ain't ashamed to run it. Better than being a clothing salesman."

Dan flushed. "Nothing wrong with that, either." He looked at Phineas. "Isn't that right? Nothing wrong with selling clothes, is there, Phineas?"

Phineas was staring down at the floor. He glanced up. "What? What was that?"

"What you thinking about?" Pop wanted to know. "You look worried."

"I'm worried about Shadrach," Phineas said. "He's getting old. Sitting out there by himself all the time, in the cold weather, with the rain water running over the floor—it blows something awful in the winter, along the highway—"

"Then you *do* think he believes it?" Dan persisted. "You *don't* think he's getting something out of it?"

Phineas shook his head absently and did not answer.

The laughter died down. They all looked at one another.

That night, as Shadrach was locking up the filling station, a small figure came toward him from the darkness.

"Hey!" Shadrach called out. "Who are you?"

An Elf soldier came into the light, blinking. He was dressed in a little gray robe, buckled at the waist with a band of silver. On his feet were little leather boots. He carried a short sword at his side.

"I have a serious message for you," the Elf said. "Now, where did I put it?"

He searched his robe while Shadrach waited. The Elf brought out a tiny scroll and unfastened it, breaking the wax expertly. He handed it to Shadrach.

"What's it say?" Shadrach asked. He bent over, his eyes close to the vellum. "I don't have my glasses with me. Can't quite make out these little letters."

"The Trolls are moving. They've heard that the old king is dead, and they're rising, in all the hills and valleys around. They will try to break the Elf Kingdom into fragments, scatter the Elves—"

"I see," Shadrach said. "Before your new king can really get started."

"That's right." The Elf soldier nodded. "This is a crucial moment for the Elves. For centuries, our existence has been precarious. There are so many Trolls, and Elves are very frail and often take sick—"

"Well, what should I do? Are there any suggestions?"

"You're supposed to meet with us under the Great Oak tonight. We'll take you into the Elf Kingdom, and you and your staff will plan and map the defense of the Kingdom."

"What?" Shadrach looked uncomfortable. "But I haven't eaten dinner. And my gas station—tomorrow is Saturday, and a lot of cars—"

"But you are King of the Elves," the soldier said.

Shadrach put his hand to his chin and rubbed it slowly.

"That's right," he replied. "I am, ain't I?"

The Elf soldier bowed.

"I wish I'd known this sort of thing was going to happen," Shadrach said. "I didn't suppose being King of the Elves—"

He broke off, hoping for an interruption. The Elf soldier watched him calmly, without expression.

"Maybe you ought to have someone else as your king," Shadrach decided. "I don't know very much about war and things like that, fighting and all that sort of business." He paused, shrugged his shoulders. "It's nothing I've ever mixed in. They don't have wars here in Colorado. I mean they don't have wars between human beings."

Still the Elf soldier remained silent.

"Why was I picked?" Shadrach went on helplessly, twisting his hands. "I don't know anything about it. What made him go and pick me? Why didn't he pick somebody else?"

"He trusted you," the Elf said. "You brought him inside your house, out of the rain. He knew that you expected nothing for it, that there was nothing you wanted. He had known few who gave and asked nothing back."

"Oh." Shadrach thought it over. At last he looked up. "But what about my gas station? And my house? And what will they say, Dan Green and Pop down at the store—"

The Elf soldier moved away, out of the light. "I have to go. It's getting late, and at night the Trolls come out. I don't want to be too far away from the others."

"Sure," Shadrach said.

"The Trolls are afraid of nothing, now that the old king is dead. They forage everywhere. No one is safe."

"Where did you say the meeting is to be? And what time?"

"At the Great Oak. When the moon sets tonight, just as it leaves the sky."

"I'll be there, I guess," Shadrach said. "I suppose you're right. The King of the Elves can't afford to let his kingdom down when it needs him most."

He looked around, but the Elf soldier was already gone.

Shadrach walked up the highway, his mind full of doubts and wonderings. When he came to the first of the flat stone steps, he stopped.

"And the old oak tree is on Phineas's farm! What'll Phineas say?"

But he was the Elf King and the Trolls were moving in the hills. Shadrach stood listening to the rustle of the wind as it moved through the trees beyond the highway, and along the far slopes and hills.

Trolls? Were there really Trolls there, rising up, bold and confident in the darkness of the night, afraid of nothing, afraid of no one?

And this business of being Elf King . . .

Shadrach went on up the steps, his lips pressed tight. When he reached the top of the stone steps, the last rays of sunlight had already faded. It was night.

Phineas Judd stared out the window. He swore and shook his head. Then he went quickly to the door and ran out onto the porch. In the cold moonlight a dim figure was walking slowly across the lower field, coming toward the house along the cow trail.

"Shadrach!" Phineas cried. "What's wrong? What are you doing out this time of night?"

Shadrach stopped and put his fists stubbornly on his hips.

"You go back home," Phineas said. "What's got into you?"

"I'm sorry, Phineas," Shadrach answered. "I'm sorry I have to go over your land. But I have to meet somebody at the old oak tree."

"At this time of night?"

Shadrach bowed his head.

"What's the matter with you, Shadrach? Who in the world you going to meet in the middle of the night on my farm?"

"I have to meet with the Elves. We're going to plan out the war with the Trolls."

"Well, I'll be damned," Phineas Judd said. He went back inside the house and slammed the door. For a long time he stood thinking. Then he went back out on the porch again. "What did you say you were doing? You don't have to tell me, of course, but I just—"

"I have to meet the Elves at the old oak tree. We must have a general council of war against the Trolls."

"Yes, indeed. The Trolls. Have to watch for the Trolls all the time."

"Trolls are everywhere," Shadrach stated, nodding his head. "I never realized it before. You can't forget them or ignore them. They never forget you. They're always planning, watching you—"

Phineas gaped at him, speechless.

"Oh, by the way," Shadrach said. "I may be gone for some time. It depends on how long this business is going to take. I haven't had much experience in fighting Trolls, so I'm not sure. But I wonder if you'd mind looking after the gas station for me, about twice a day, maybe once in the morning and once at night, to make sure no one's broken in or anything like that."

"You're going away?" Phineas came quickly down the stairs. "What's all this about Trolls? Why are you going?"

Shadrach patiently repeated what he had said.

"But what for?"

"Because I'm the Elf King. I have to lead them."

There was silence. "I see," Phineas said, at last. "That's right, you *did* mention it before, didn't you? But, Shadrach, why don't you come inside for a while and you can tell me about the Trolls and drink some coffee and—"

"Coffee?" Shadrach looked up at the pale moon above him, the moon and the bleak sky. The world was still and dead and the night was very cold and the moon would not be setting for some time.

Shadrach shivered.

"It's a cold night," Phineas urged. "Too cold to be out. Come on in—"

"I guess I have a little time," Shadrach admitted. "A cup of coffee wouldn't do any harm. But I can't stay very long . . ."

Shadrach stretched his legs out and sighed. "This coffee sure tastes good, Phineas."

Phineas sipped a little and put his cup down. The living room was quite and warm. It was a very neat little living room with solemn pictures on the walls, gray uninteresting pictures that minded their own business. In the corner was a small reed organ with sheet music carefully arranged on top of it.

Shadrach noticed the organ and smiled. "You still play, Phineas?"

"Not much any more. The bellows don't work right. One of them won't come back up."

"I suppose I could fix it sometime. If I'm around, I mean."

"That would be fine," Phineas said. "I was thinking of asking you."

"Remember how you used to play 'Vilia' and Dan Green came up with that lady who worked for Pop during the summer? The one who wanted to open a pottery shop?"

"I sure do," Phineas said.

Presently, Shadrach set down his coffee cup and shifted in his chair.

"You want more coffee?" Phineas asked quickly. He stood up. "A little more?"

"Maybe a little. But I have to be going pretty soon."

"It's a bad night to be outside."

Shadrach looked through the window. It was darker; the moon had almost gone down. The fields were stark. Shadrach shivered. "I wouldn't disagree with you," he said.

Phineas turned eagerly. "Look, Shadrach. You go on home where it's warm. You can come out and fight Trolls some other night. There'll always be Trolls. You said so yourself. Plenty of time to do that later, when the weather's better. When it's not so cold."

Shadrach rubbed his forehead wearily. "You know, it all seems like some sort of a crazy dream. When did I start talking about Elves and Trolls? When did it all begin?" His voice trailed off. "Thank you for the coffee." He got slowly to his feet. "It warmed me up a lot. And I appreciated the talk. Like old times, you and me sitting here the way we used to."

"Are you going?" Phineas hesitated. *"Home?"*

"I think I better. It's late."

Phineas got quickly to his feet. He led Shadrach to the door, one arm around his shoulder.

"All right, Shadrach, you go on home. Take a good hot bath before you go to bed. It'll fix you up. And maybe just a little snort of brandy to warm the blood."

Phineas opened the front door and they went slowly down the porch steps, onto the cold, dark ground.

"Yes, I guess I'll be going," Shadrach said. "Good night—"

"You go on home." Phineas patted him on the arm. "You run along home and take a good hot bath. And then go straight to bed."

"That's a good idea. Thank you, Phineas. I appreciate your kindness." Shadrach looked down at Phineas's hand on his arm. He had not been that close to Phineas for years.

Shadrach contemplated the hand. He wrinkled his brow, puzzled.

Phineas's hand was huge and rough and his arms were short. His fingers were blunt, his nails broken and cracked. Almost black, or so it seemed in the moonlight.

Shadrach looked up at Phineas. "Strange," he murmured.

"What's strange, Shadrach?"

In the moonlight, Phineas's face seemed oddly heavy and brutal. Shadrach had never noticed before how the jaw bulged, what a great protruding jaw it was. The skin was yellow and coarse, like parchment. Behind the glasses, the eyes were like two stones, cold and lifeless. The ears were immense, the hair stringy and matted.

Odd that he had never noticed before. But he had never seen Phineas in the moonlight.

Shadrach stepped away, studying his old friend. From a few feet off, Phineas Judd seemed unusually short and squat. His legs were slightly bowed. His feet were enormous. And there was something else—

"What is it?" Phineas demanded, beginning to grow suspicious. "Is there something wrong?"

Something was completely wrong. And he had never noticed it, not in all the years they had been friends. All around Phineas Judd was an odor, a faint, pungent stench of rot, of decaying flesh, damp and moldy.

Shadrach glanced slowly about him. "Something wrong?" he echoed. "No, I wouldn't say that."

By the side of the house was an old rain barrel, half fallen apart. Shadrach walked over to it.

"No, Phineas. I wouldn't exactly say there's something wrong."

"What are you doing?"

"Me?" Shadrach took hold of one of the barrel staves and pulled it loose. He walked back to Phineas, carrying the barrel stave carefully. "I'm King of the Elves. Who—or what—are you?"

Phineas roared and attacked with his great murderous shovel hands.

Shadrach smashed him over the head with the barrel stave. Phineas bellowed with rage and pain.

At the shattering sound, there was a clatter and from underneath the house came a furious horde of bounding, leaping creatures, dark bent-over things, their bodies heavy and squat, their feet and heads immense. Shadrach took one look at the flood of dark creatures pouring out from Phineas's basement. He knew what they were.

"Help!" Shadrach shouted. "Trolls! Help!"

The Trolls were all around him, grabbing hold of him, tugging at him, climbing up him, pummeling his face and body.

Shadrach fell to with the barrel stave, swung again and again, kicking Trolls with his feet, whacking them with the barrel stave. There seemed to be hundreds of them. More and more poured out from under Phineas's house, a surging black tide of pot-shaped creatures, their great eyes and teeth gleaming in the moonlight.

"Help!" Shadrach cried again, more feebly now. He was getting winded. His heart labored painfully. A Troll bit his wrist, clinging to his arm. Shadrach flung it away, pulling loose from the horde clutching his trouser legs, the barrel stave rising and falling.

One of the Trolls caught hold of the stave. A whole group of them helped, wrenching furiously, trying to pull it away. Shadrach hung on desperately. Trolls were all over him, on his shoulders, clinging to his coat, riding his arms, his legs, pulling his hair—

He heard a high-pitched clarion call from a long way off, the sound of some distant golden trumpet, echoing in the hills.

The Trolls suddenly stopped attacking. One of them dropped off Shadrach's neck. Another let go of his arm.

The call came again, this time more loudly.

"Elves!" a Troll rasped. He turned and moved toward the sound, grinding his teeth and spitting with fury.

"Elves!"

The Trolls swarmed forward, a growing wave of gnashing teeth and nails, pushing furiously toward the Elf columns. The Elves broke formation and joined battle, shouting with wild joy in their shrill, piping voices. The tide of Trolls rushed against them, Troll against Elf, shovel nails against golden sword, biting jaw against dagger.

"Kill the Elves!"

"Death to the Trolls!"

"Onward!"

"Forward!"

Shadrach fought desperately with the Trolls that were still clinging to him. He was exhausted, panting and gasping for breath. Blindly, he whacked on and on, kicking and jumping, throwing Trolls away from him, through the air and across the ground.

How long the battle raged, Shadrach never knew. He was lost in a sea of dark bodies, round and evil-smelling, clinging to him, tearing, biting, fastened to his nose and hair and fingers. He fought silently, grimly.

All around him, the Elf legions clashed with the Troll horde, little groups of struggling warriors on all sides.

Suddenly Shadrach stopped fighting. He raised his head, looking uncertainly around him. Nothing moved. Everything was silent. The fighting had ceased.

A few Trolls still clung to his arms and legs. Shadrach whacked one with the barrel stave. It howled and dropped to the ground. He staggered back, struggling with the last troll, who hung tenaciously to his arm.

"Now you!" Shadrach gasped. He pried the Troll loose and flung it into the air. The Troll fell to the ground and scuttled off into the night.

There was nothing more. No Troll moved anywhere. All was silent across the bleak moon-swept fields.

Shadrach sank down on a stone. His chest rose and fell painfully. Red specks swam before his eyes. Weakly, he got out his pocket handkerchief and wiped his neck and face. He closed his eyes, shaking his head from side to side.

When he opened his eyes again, the Elves were coming toward

him, gathering their legion together again. The Elves were disheveled and bruised. Their golden armor was gashed and torn. Their helmets were bent or missing. Most of their scarlet plumes were gone. Those that still remained were drooping and broken.

But the battle was over. The war was won. The Troll hordes had been put to flight.

Shadrach got slowly to his feet. The Elf warriors stood around him in a circle, gazing up at him with silent respect. One of them helped steady him as he put his handkerchief away in his pocket.

"Thank you," Shadrach murmured. "Thank you very much."

"The Trolls have been defeated," an Elf stated, still awed by what had happened.

Shadrach gazed around at the Elves. There were many of them, more than he had ever seen before. All the Elves had turned out for the battle. They were grim-faced, stern with the seriousness of the moment, weary from the terrible struggle.

"Yes, they're gone, all right," Shadrach said. He was beginning to get his breath. "That was a close call. I'm glad you fellows came when you did. I was just about finished, fighting them all by myself."

"All alone, the King of the Elves held off the entire Troll army," an Elf announced shrilly.

"Eh?" Shadrach said, taken aback. Then he smiled. "That's true, I *did* fight them alone for a while. I *did* hold off the Trolls all by myself. The whole darn Troll army."

"There is more," an Elf said.

Shadrach blinked. "More?"

"Look over here, O King, mightiest of all the Elves. This way. To the right."

The Elves led Shadrach over.

"What is it?" Shadrach murmured, seeing nothing at first. He gazed down, trying to pierce the darkness. "Could we have a torch over here?"

Some Elves brought little pine torches.

There, on the frozen ground, lay Phineas Judd, on his back. His eyes were blank and staring, his mouth half open. He did not move. His body was cold and stiff.

"He is dead," an Elf said solemnly.

Shadrach gulped in sudden alarm. Cold sweat stood out abruptly on his forehead. "My gosh! My old friend! What have I done?"

"You have slain the Great Troll."

Shadrach paused.

"I *what?*"

"You have slain the Great Troll, leader of all the Trolls."

"This has never happened before," another Elf exclaimed excitedly. "The Great Troll has lived for centuries. Nobody imagined he could die. This is our most historic moment."

All the Elves gazed down at the silent form with awe, awe mixed with more than a little fear.

"Oh, go on!" Shadrach said. "That's just Phineas Judd."

But as he spoke, a chill moved up his spine. He remembered what he had seen a little while before, as he stood close by Phineas, as the dying moonlight crossed his old friend's face.

"Look." One of the Elves bent over and unfastened Phineas's blue-serge vest. He pushed the coat and vest aside. "See?"

Shadrach bent down to look.

He gasped.

Underneath Phineas Judd's blue-serge vest was a suit of mail, an encrusted mesh of ancient, rusting iron, fastened tightly around the squat body. On the mail stood an engraved insignia, dark and time-worn, embedded with dirt and rust. A moldering half-obliterated emblem. The emblem of a crossed owl leg and toadstool.

The emblem of the Great Troll.

"Golly," Shadrach said. "And *I* killed him."

For a long time he gazed silently down. Then, slowly, realization began to grow in him. He straightened up, a smile forming on his face.

"What is it, O King?" an Elf piped.

"I just thought of something," Shadrach said. "I just realized that—that since the Great Troll is dead and the Troll army has been put to flight—"

He broke off. All the Elves were waiting.

"I thought maybe I—that is, maybe if you don't need me any more—"

The Elves listened respectfully. "What is it, Mighty King? Go on."

"I thought maybe now I could go back to the filling station and not be king any more." Shadrach glanced hopefully around at them. "Do you think so? With the war over and all. With him dead. What do you say?"

For a time, the Elves were silent. They gazed unhappily down at the ground. None of them said anything. At last they began moving away, collecting their banners and pennants.

"Yes, you may go back," an Elf said quietly. "The war is over. The Trolls have been defeated. You may return to your filling station, if that is what you want."

A flood of relief swept over Shadrach. He straightened up, grinning from ear to ear. "Thanks! That's fine. That's really fine. That's the best news I've heard in my life."

He moved away from the Elves, rubbing his hands together and blowing on them.

"Thanks an awful lot." He grinned around at the silent Elves. "Well, I guess I'll be running along, then. It's late. Late and cold. It's been a hard night. I'll—I'll see you around."

The Elves nodded silently.

"Fine. Well, good night." Shadrach turned and started along the path. He stopped for a moment, waving back at the Elves. "It was quite a battle, wasn't it? We really licked them." He hurried on along the path. Once again he stopped, looking back and waving. "Sure glad I could help out. Well, good night!"

One or two of the Elves waved, but none of them said anything.

Shadrach Jones walked slowly toward his place. He could see it from the rise, the highway that few cars traveled, the filling station falling to ruin, the house that might not last as long as himself, and not enough money coming in to repair them or buy a better location.

He turned around and went back.

The Elves were still gathered there in the silence of the night. They had not moved away.

"I was hoping you hadn't gone," Shadrach said, relieved.

"And we were hoping you would not leave," said a soldier.

Shadrach kicked a stone. It bounced through the tight silence and stopped. The Elves were still watching him.

"Leave?" Shadrach asked. "And me King of the Elves?"

"Then you will remain our king?" an Elf cried.

"It's a hard thing for a man of my age to change. To stop selling gasoline and suddenly be a king. It scared me for a while. But it doesn't any more."

"You will? You *will?*"

"Sure," said Shadrach Jones.

The little circle of Elf torches closed in joyously. In their light, he saw a platform like the one that had carried the old King of the Elves. But this one was much larger, big enough to hold a man, and dozens of the soldiers waited with proud shoulders under the shafts.

A soldier gave him a happy bow. "For you, Sire."

Shadrach climbed aboard. It was less comfortable than walking, but he knew this was how they wanted to take him to the Kingdom of the Elves.

WORLDS

Stories of other places,
where wonders abide

WORLDS

L. FRANK BAUM's Wonderful Wizard of Oz *(1900), perhaps the greatest of all American fairy tales, is so synonymous with Baum's name that the rest of his writings have been forgotten to a large extent. This is a shame, since certain of his other fantasy novels, such as* The Sea Fairies, *are substantially better than some of the lesser Oz books. It is not generally known that Baum set out intentionally to create specifically American fairy tales, in the belief that America should have its own new stories, in its own environment, generated by its own culture and not merely pale imitations of the British genre that seemed to dominate. Baum was most probably unfamiliar with the Huggermugger books of Christopher Pearse Cranch (see p. 339), which must surely rank with Baum's efforts as American originals. Nevertheless, Baum set about writing a rich body of works, both long and short, and in the end succeeded in being the first to promote the idea of American fantasy successfully as a new kind of children's literature. The four short tales included here, from his book* American Fairy Tales, *are examples of the force and breadth of Baum's powers of invention.*

4 American Fairy Tales
BY L. FRANK BAUM

The Glass Dog

An accomplished wizard once lived on the top floor of a tenement house and passed his time in thoughtful study and studious thought. What he didn't know about wizardry was hardly worth knowing, for he possessed all the books and recipes of all the wizards who had lived before him; and moreover, he had invented several wizardments himself.

This admirable person would have been completely happy but for the numerous interruptions to his studies caused by folk who came to consult him about their troubles (in which he was not interested), and by the loud knocks of the iceman, the milkman, the baker's boy, the laundryman and the peanut woman. He never dealt with any of these people; but they rapped at his door every day to see him about this or that or to try to sell him their wares. Just when he was most deeply interested in his books or engaged in watching the bubbling of a cauldron there would come a knock at his door. And after sending the intruder away he always found he had lost his train of thought or ruined his compound.

At length these interruptions aroused his anger, and he decided he must have a dog to keep people away from his door. He didn't know where to find a dog, but in the next room lived a poor glass-blower with whom he had a slight acquaintance; so he went into the man's apartment and asked:

"Where can I find a dog?"

"What sort of a dog?" inquired the glass-blower.

"A good dog. One that will bark at people and drive them away. One that will be no trouble to keep and won't expect to be fed. One that has no fleas and is neat in his habits. One that will obey me when I speak to him. In short, a good dog," said the wizard.

"Such a dog is hard to find," returned the glass-blower, who was busy making a blue glass flower pot with a pink glass rosebush in it, having green glass leaves and yellow glass roses.

The wizard watched him thoughtfully.

"Why cannot you blow me a dog out of glass?" he asked, presently.

"I can," declared the glass-blower; "but it would not bark at people, you know."

"Oh, I'll fix that easily enough," replied the other. "If I could not make a glass dog bark I would be a mighty poor wizard."

"Very well; if you can use a glass dog I'll be pleased to blow one for you. Only, you must pay for my work."

"Certainly," agreed the wizard. "But I have none of that horrid stuff you call money. You must take some of my wares in exchange."

The glass-blower considered the matter for a moment.

"Could you give me something to cure my rheumatism?" he asked.

"Oh, yes; easily."

"Then it's a bargain. I'll start the dog at once. What color of glass shall I use?"

"Pink is a pretty color," said the wizard, "and it's unusual for a dog, isn't it?"

"Very," answered the glass-blower; "but it shall be pink."

So the wizard went back to his studies and the glass-blower began to make the dog.

Next morning he entered the wizard's room with the glass dog under his arm and set it carefully upon the table. It was a beautiful pink in color, with a fine coat of spun glass, and about its neck was twisted a blue glass ribbon. Its eyes were specks of black glass and sparkled intelligently, as do many of the glass eyes worn by men.

The wizard expressed himself pleased with the glass-blower's skill and at once handed him a small vial.

"This will cure your rheumatism," he said.

"But the vial is empty!" protested the glass-blower.

"Oh, no; there is one drop of liquid in it," was the wizard's reply.

"Will one drop cure my rheumatism?" inquired the glass-blower, in wonder.

"Most certainly. That is a marvelous remedy. The one drop contained in the vial will cure instantly any kind of disease ever known to humanity. Therefore it is especially good for rheumatism. But guard it well, for it is the only drop of its kind in the world, and I've forgotten the recipe."

"Thank you," said the glass-blower, and went back to his room.

Then the wizard cast a wizzy spell and mumbled several very learned words in the wizardese language over the glass dog. Whereupon the little animal first wagged its tail from side to side, then winked his left eye knowingly, and at last began barking in a most frightful manner—that is, when you stop to consider the noise came from a pink glass dog. There is something almost astonishing in the magic arts of wizards; unless, of course, you know how to do the things yourself, when you are not expected to be surprised at them.

The wizard was as delighted as a school teacher at the success of his spell, although he was not astonished. Immediately he placed the dog outside his door, where it would bark at anyone who dared knock and so disturb the studies of its master.

The glass-blower, on returning to his room, decided not to use the one drop of wizard cure-all just then.

"My rheumatism is better to-day," he reflected, "and I will be wise to save the medicine for a time when I am very ill, when it will be of more service to me."

So he placed the vial in his cupboard and went to work blowing more roses out of glass. Presently he happened to think the medicine might not keep, so he started to ask the wizard about it. But when he reached the door the glass dog barked so fiercely that he dared not knock, and returned in great haste to his own room. Indeed, the poor man was quite upset at so unfriendly a reception from the dog he had himself so carefully and skillfully made.

The next morning, as he read his newspaper, he noticed an article stating that the beautiful Miss Mydas, the richest young lady in town, was very ill, and the doctors had given up hope of her recovery.

The glass-blower, although miserably poor, hard-working and homely of feature, was a man of ideas. He suddenly recollected his precious medicine, and determined to use it to better advantage than relieving his own ills. He dressed himself in his best clothes, brushed his hair and combed his whiskers, washed his hands and tied his necktie, blackened his shoes and sponged his vest, and then put the vial of magic cure-all in his pocket. Next he locked the door, went downstairs and walked through the streets to the grand mansion where the wealthy Miss Mydas resided.

The butler opened the door and said:

"No soaps, no chromos, no vegetables, no hair oil, no books, no baking powder. My young lady is dying and we're well supplied for the funeral."

The glass-blower was grieved at being taken for a peddler.

"My friend," he began, proudly; but the butler interrupted him saying:

"No tombstones, either; there's a family graveyard and the monument's built."

"The graveyard won't be needed if you will permit me to speak," said the glass-blower.

"No doctors, sir; they've given up my young lady, and she's given up the doctors," continued the butler, calmly.

"I'm no doctor," returned the glass-blower.

"Nor are the others. But what is your errand?"

"I called to cure your young lady by means of a magical compound."

"Step in, please, and take a seat in the hall. I'll speak to the housekeeper," said the butler, more politely.

So he spoke to the housekeeper and the housekeeper mentioned the matter to the steward and the steward consulted the chef and the chef kissed the lady's maid and sent her to see the stranger. Thus, are the very wealthy hedged around with ceremony, even when dying.

When the lady's maid heard from the glass-blower that he had a medicine which would cure her mistress, she said:

"I'm glad you came."

"But," said he, "if I restore your mistress to health she must marry me."

"I'll make inquiries and see if she's willing," answered the maid, and went at once to consult Miss Mydas.

The young lady did not hesitate an instant.

"I'd marry any old thing rather than die!" she cried. "Bring him here at once!"

So the glass-blower came, poured the magic drop into a little water, gave it to the patient, and the next minute Miss Mydas was as well as she had ever been in her life.

"Dear me!" she exclaimed; "I've an engagement at the Fritters' reception to-night. Bring my pearl-colored silk, Marie, and I will begin my toilet at once. And don't forget to cancel the order for the funeral flowers and your mourning gown."

"But, Miss Mydas," remonstrated the glass-blower, who stood by, "you promised to marry me if I cured you."

"I know," said the young lady, "but we must have time to make proper announcement in the society papers and have the wedding cards engraved. Call to-morrow and we'll talk it over."

The glass-blower had not impressed her favorably as a husband, and she was glad to find an excuse for getting rid of him for a time. And she did not want to miss the Fritters' reception.

Yet the man went home filled with joy; for he thought his stratagem had succeeded and he was about to marry a rich wife who would keep him in luxury forever afterward.

The first thing he did on reaching his room was to smash his glass-blowing tools and throw them out of the window.

He then sat down to figure out ways of spending his wife's money.

The following day he called upon Miss Mydas, who was reading a novel and eating chocolate creams as happily as if she had never been ill in her life.

"Where did you get the magic compound that cured me?" she asked.

"From a learned wizard," said he; and then, thinking it would interest her, he told how he had made the glass dog for the wizard, and how it barked and kept everybody from bothering him.

"How delightful!" she said. "I've always wanted a glass dog that could bark."

"But there's only one in the world," he answered, "and it belongs to the wizard."

"You must buy it for me," said the lady.

"The wizard cares nothing for money," replied the glass-blower.

"Then you must steal it for me," she retorted. "I can never live happily another day unless I have a glass dog that can bark."

The glass-blower was much distressed at his, but said he would see what he could do. For a man should always try to please his wife, and Miss Mydas had promised to marry him within a week.

On his way way home he purchased a heavy sack, and when he passed the wizard's door and the pink glass dog ran out to bark at him he threw the sack over the dog, tied the opening with a piece of twine, and carried him away to his own room.

The next day he sent the sack by a messenger boy to Miss Mydas, with his compliments, and later in the afternoon he called upon her in person, feeling quite sure he would be received with gratitude for stealing the dog she so greatly desired.

But when he came to the door and the butler opened it, what was his amazement to see the glass dog rush out and begin barking at him furiously.

"Call off your dog," he shouted, in terror.

"I can't sir," answered the butler. "My young lady has ordered the glass dog to bark whenever you call here. You'd better look out, sir," he added, "for if it bites you, you may have glassophobia!"

This so frightened the poor glass-blower that he went away hurriedly. But he stopped at a drug store and put his last dime in the telephone box so he could talk to Miss Mydas without being bitten by the dog.

"Give me Pelf 6742!" he called.

"Hello! What is it?" said a voice.

"I want to speak with Miss Mydas," said the glass-blower.

Presently a sweet voice said: "This is Miss Mydas. What is it?"

"Why have you treated me so cruelly and set the glass dog on me?" asked the poor fellow.

"Well, to tell the truth," said the lady, "I don't like your looks.

Your cheeks are pale and baggy, your hair is coarse and long, your eyes are small and red, your hands are big and rough, and you are bow-legged."

"But I can't help my looks!" pleaded the glass-blower; "and you really promised to marry me."

"If you were better looking I'd keep my promise," she returned. "But under the circumstances you are no fit mate for me, and unless you keep away from my mansion I shall set my glass dog on you!" Then she dropped the 'phone and would have nothing more to say.

The miserable glass-blower went home with a heart bursting with disappointment and began tying a rope to the bedpost by which to hang himself.

Some one knocked at the door, and, upon opening it, he saw the wizard.

"I've lost my dog," he announced.

"Have you, indeed?" replied the glass-blower tying a knot in the rope.

"Yes; some one has stolen him."

"That's too bad," declared the glass-blower, indifferently.

"You must make me another," said the wizard.

"But I cannot; I've thrown away my tools."

"Then what shall I do?" asked the wizard.

"I do not know, unless you offer a reward for the dog."

"But I have no money," said the wizard.

"Offer some of your compounds, then," suggested the glass-blower, who was making a noose in the rope for his head to go through.

"The only thing I can spare," replied the wizard, thoughtfully, "is a Beauty Powder."

"What!" cried the glass-blower, throwing down the rope, "have you really such a thing?"

"Yes, indeed. Whoever takes the powder will become the most beautiful person in the world."

"If you will offer that as a reward," said the glass-blower, eagerly, "I'll try to find the dog for you, for above everything else I long to be beautiful."

"But I warn you the beauty will only be skin deep," said the wizard.

"That's all right," replied the happy glass-blower; "when I lose my skin I shan't care to remain beautiful."

"Then tell me where to find my dog and you shall have the powder," promised the wizard.

So the glass-blower went out and pretended to search, and by-and-by he returned and said:

"I've discovered the dog. You will find him in the mansion of Miss Mydas."

The wizard went at once to see if this were true, and, sure enough, the glass dog ran out and began barking at him. Then the wizard spread out his hands and chanted a magic spell which sent the dog fast asleep, when he picked him up and carried him to his own room on the top floor of the tenement house.

Afterward he carried the Beauty Powder to the glass-blower as a reward, and the fellow immediately swallowed it and became the most beautiful man in the world.

The next time he called upon Miss Mydas there was no dog to bark at him, and when the young lady saw him she fell in love with his beauty at once.

"If only you were a count or a prince," she sighed, "I'd willingly marry you."

"But I am a prince," he answered; "the Prince of Dogblowers."

"Ah!" said she; "then if you are willing to accept an allowance of four dollars a week I'll order the wedding cards engraved."

The man hesitated, but when he thought of the rope hanging from his bedpost he consented to the terms.

So they were married, and the bride was very jealous of her husband's beauty and led him a dog's life. So he managed to get into debt and made her miserable in turn.

As for the glass dog, the wizard set him barking again by means of his wizardness and put him outside his door. I suppose he is there yet, and am rather sorry, for I should like to consult the wizard about the moral to this story.

The Queen of Quok

A king once died, as kings are apt to do, being as liable to shortness of breath as other mortals.

It was high time this king abandoned his earth life, for he had lived in a sadly extravagant manner, and his subjects could spare him without the slightest inconvenience.

His father had left him a full treasury, both money and jewels being in abundance. But the foolish king just deceased had squandered every penny in riotous living. He had then taxed his subjects until most of them became paupers, and this money vanished in more riotous living. Next he sold all the grand old furniture in the palace; all the silver and gold plate and bric-a-brac; all the rich carpets and furnishings and even his own kingly wardrobe, reserving only a soiled and moth-eaten ermine robe to fold over his threadbare raiment. And he spent the money in further riotous living.

Don't ask me to explain what riotous living is. I only know, from hearsay, that it is an excellent way to get rid of money. And so this spendthrift king found it.

He now picked all the magnificent jewels from his kingly crown and from the round ball on the top of his scepter, and sold them and spent the money. Riotous living, of course. But at last he was at the end of his resources. He couldn't sell the crown itself, because no one but the king had the right to wear it. Neither could he sell the royal palace, because only the king had the right to live there.

So, finally, he found himself reduced to a bare palace, containing only a big mahogany bedstead that he slept in, a small stool on which he sat to pull off his shoes and the moth-eaten ermine robe.

In this strait he was reduced to the necessity of borrowing an occasional dime from his chief counselor, with which to buy a ham sandwich. And the chief counselor hadn't many dimes. One who counseled his king so foolishly was likely to ruin his own prospects as well.

So the king, having nothing more to live for, died suddenly and left a ten-year-old son to inherit the dismantled kingdom, the moth-eaten robe and the jewel-stripped crown.

No one envied the child, who had scarcely been thought of until he became king himself. Then he was recognized as a personage of some importance, and the politicians and hangers-on, headed by the chief counselor of the kingdom, held a meeting to determine what could be done for him.

These folk had helped the old king to live riotously while his money lasted, and now they were poor and too proud to work. So they tried to think of a plan that would bring more money into the little king's treasury, where it would be handy for them to help themselves.

After the meeting was over the chief counselor came to the young king, who was playing peg-top in the courtyard, and said:

"Your majesty, we have thought of a way to restore your kingdom to its former power and magnificence."

"All right," replied his majesty, carelessly. "How will you do it?"

"By marrying you to a lady of great wealth," replied the counselor.

"Marrying me!" cried the king. "Why, I am only ten years old!"

"I know; it is to be regretted. But your majesty will grow older, and the affairs of the kingdom demand that you marry a wife."

"Can't I marry a mother, instead?" asked the poor little king, who had lost his mother when a baby.

"Certainly not," declared the counselor. "To marry a mother would be illegal; to marry a wife is right and proper."

"Can't you marry her yourself?" inquired his majesty, aiming his peg-top at the chief counselor's toe, and laughing to see how he jumped to escape it.

"Let me explain," said the other. "You haven't a penny in the world, but you have a kingdom. There are many rich women who would be glad to give their wealth in exchange for a queen's coronet—even if the king is but a child. So we have decided to advertise that the one who bids the highest shall become the queen of Quok."

"If I must marry at all," said the king, after a moment's thought, "I prefer to marry Nyana, the armorer's daughter."

"She is too poor," replied the counselor.

"Her teeth are pearls, her eyes are amethysts, and her hair is gold," declared the little king.

"True, your majesty. But consider that your wife's wealth must be used. How would Nyana look after you have pulled her teeth of pearls, plucked out her amethyst eyes and shaved her golden head?"

The boy shuddered.

"Have your own way," he said, despairingly. "Only let the lady be as dainty as possible and a good playfellow."

"We shall do our best," returned the chief counselor, and went away to advertise throughout the neighboring kingdoms for a wife for the boy king of Quok.

There were so many applicants for the privilege of marrying the little king that it was decided to put him up at auction, in order that the largest possible sum of money should be brought into the kingdom. So, on the day appointed, the ladies gathered at the palace from all the surrounding kingdoms—from Bilkon, Mulgravia, Junkum and even as far away as the republic of Macvelt.

The chief counselor came to the palace early in the morning and had the king's face washed and his hair combed; and then he padded the inside of the crown with old newspapers to make it small enough to fit his majesty's head. It was a sorry looking crown, having many big and little holes in it where the jewels had once been; and it had been neglected and knocked around until it was quite battered and tarnished. Yet, as the counselor said, it was the king's crown, and it was quite proper he should wear it on the solemn occasion of his auction.

Like all boys, be they kings or paupers, his majesty had torn and soiled his one suit of clothes, so that they were hardly presentable; and there was no money to buy new ones. Therefore the counselor wound the old ermine robe around the king and sat him upon the stool in the middle of the otherwise empty audience chamber.

And around him stood all the courtiers and politicians and hangers-on of the kingdom, consisting of such people as were too proud or lazy to work for a living. There was a great number of them, you may be sure, and they made an imposing appearance.

Then the doors of the audience chamber were thrown open, and the wealthy ladies who aspired to being queen of Quok came trooping in. The king looked them over with much anxiety, and decided they were each and all old enough to be his grandmother, and ugly enough to scare away the crows from the royal cornfields. After which he lost interest in them.

But the rich ladies never looked at the poor little king squatting upon his stool. They gathered at once about the chief counselor, who acted as auctioneer.

"How much am I offered for the coronet of the queen of Quok?" asked the counselor, in a loud voice.

"Where is the coronet?" inquired a fussy old lady who had just buried her ninth husband and was worth several millions.

"There isn't any coronet at present," explained the chief counselor, "but whoever bids highest will have the right to wear one, and she can then buy it."

"Oh," said the fussy old lady, "I see." Then she added: "I'll bid fourteen dollars."

"Fourteen thousand dollars!" cried a sour-looking woman who was thin and tall and had wrinkles all over her skin—"like a frosted apple," the king thought.

The bidding now became fast and furious, and the poverty-stricken courtiers brightened up as the sum began to mount into the millions.

"He'll bring us a very pretty fortune, after all," whispered one to his comrade, "and then we shall have the pleasure of helping him spend it."

The king began to be anxious. All the women who looked at all kindhearted or pleasant had stopped bidding for lack of money, and the slender old dame with the wrinkles seemed determined to get the coronet at any price, and with it the boy husband. This ancient creature finally became so excited that her wig got crosswise of her head and her false teeth kept slipping out, which horrified the little king greatly; but she would not give up.

At last the chief counselor ended the auction by crying out:

"Sold to Mary Ann Brodjinsky de la Porkus for three million, nine hundred thousand, six hundred and twenty-four dollars and sixteen cents!" And the sour-looking old woman paid the money in cash and on the spot, which proves this is a fairy story.

The king was so disturbed at the thought that he must must marry this hideous creature that he began to wail and weep; whereupon the woman boxed his ears soundly. But the counselor reproved her for punishing her future husband in public, saying:

"You are not married yet. Wait until to-morrow, after the wedding takes place. Then you can abuse him as much as you wish. But at present we prefer to have people think this is a love match."

The poor king slept but little that night, so filled was he with terror of his future wife. Nor could he get the idea out of his head that he preferred to marry the armorer's daughter, who was about his own age. He tossed and tumbled around upon his hard bed until the moonlight came in at the window and lay like a great white sheet upon the bare floor. Finally, in turning over for the hundredth time, his hand struck against a secret spring in the headboard of the big mahogany bedstead, and at once, with a sharp click, a panel flew open.

The noise caused the king to look up, and, seeing the open panel, he stood upon tiptoe, and, reaching within, drew out a folded paper. It had several leaves fastened together like a book, and upon the first page was written:

> *"When the king is in trouble*
> *This leaf he must double*
> *And set it on fire*
> *To obtain his desire."*

This was not very good poetry, but when the king had spelled it out in the moonlight he was filled with joy.

"There's no doubt about my being in trouble," he exclaimed; "so I'll burn it at once, and see what happens."

He tore off the leaf and put the rest of the book in its secret hiding place. Then, folding the paper double, he placed it on the top of his stool, lighted a match and set fire to it.

It made a horrid smudge for so small a paper, and the king sat on the edge of the bed and watched it eagerly.

When the smoke cleared away he was surprised to see, sitting upon the stool, a round little man, who, with folded arms and crossed legs, sat calmly facing the king and smoking a black briarwood pipe.

"Well, here I am," said he.

"So I see," replied the little king. "But how did you get here?"

"Didn't you burn the paper?" demanded the round man, by way of answer.

"Yes, I did," acknowledged the king.

"Then you are in trouble, and I've come to help you out of it. I'm the Slave of the Royal Bedstead."

"Oh!" said the king. "I didn't know there was one."

"Neither did your father, or he would not have been so foolish as to sell everything he had for money. By the way, it's lucky for you he did not sell this bedstead. Now, then, what do you want?"

"I'm not sure what I want," replied the king; "But I know what I don't want, and that is the old woman who is going to marry me."

"That's easy enough," said the Slave of the Royal Bedstead. "All you need do is to return her the money she paid the chief counselor and declare the match off. Don't be afraid. You are the king, and your word is law."

"To be sure," said his majesty. "But I am in great need of money. How am I going to live if the chief counselor returns to Mary Ann Brodjinsky her millions?"

"Phoo! That's easy enough," again answered the man, and, putting his hand in his pocket, he drew out and tossed to the king an old-fashioned leather purse. "Keep that with you," said he, "and you will always be rich, for you can take out of the purse as many twenty-five-cent silver pieces as you wish, one at a time. No matter how often you take one out, another will instantly appear in its place within the purse."

"Thank you," said the king, gratefully. "You have rendered me a rare favor; for now I shall have money for all my needs and will not be obliged to marry anyone. Thank you a thousand times!"

"Don't mention it," answered the other, puffing his pipe slowly and watching the smoke curl into the moonlight. "Such things are easy to me. Is that all you want?"

"All I can think of just now," returned the king.

"Then, please close that secret panel in the bedstead," said the man; "the other leaves of the book may be of use to you some time."

The boy stood upon the bed as before and, reaching up, closed the opening so that no one else could discover it. Then he turned to face his visitor, but the Slave of the Royal Bedstead had disappeared.

"I expected that," said his majesty; "yet I am sorry he did not wait to say good-by."

With a lightened heart and a sense of great relief the boy king placed the leathern purse underneath his pillow, and climbing into bed again slept soundly until morning.

When the sun rose his majesty rose also, refreshed and comforted, and the first thing he did was to send for the chief counselor.

That mighty personage arrived looking glum and unhappy, but the boy was too full of his own good fortune to notice it. Said he:

"I have decided not to marry anyone, for I have just come into a fortune of my own. Therefore I command you to return to that old woman the money she has paid you for the right to wear the coronet of the queen of Quok. And make public declaration that the wedding will not take place."

Hearing this the counselor began to tremble, for he saw the young king had decided to reign in earnest; and he looked so guilty that his majesty inquired:

"Well! what is the matter now?"

"Sire," replied the wretch, in a shaking voice, "I cannot return the woman her money, for I have lost it!"

"Lost it!" cried the king, in mingled astonishment and anger.

"Even so, your majesty. On my way home from the auction last night I stopped at the drug store to get some potash lozenges for my throat, which was dry and hoarse with so much loud talking; and your majesty will admit it was through my efforts the woman was induced to pay so great a price. Well, going into the drug store I carelessly left the package of money lying on the seat of my carriage, and when I came out again it was gone. Nor was the thief anywhere to be seen."

"Did you call the police?" asked the king.

"Yes, I called; but they were all on the next block, and although they have promised to search for the robber I have little hope they will ever find him."

The king sighed.

"What shall we do now?" he asked.

"I fear you must marry Mary Ann Brodjinsky," answered the chief counselor; "unless, indeed, you order the executioner to cut her head off."

"That would be wrong," declared the king. "The woman must not be harmed. And it is just that we return her money, for I will not marry her under any circumstances."

"Is that private fortune you mentioned large enough to repay her?" asked the counselor.

"Why, yes," said the king, thoughtfully, "but it will take some time to do it, and that shall be your task. Call the woman here."

The counselor went in search of Mary Ann, who, when she heard she was not to become a queen, but would receive her money back, flew into a violent passion and boxed the chief counselor's ears so viciously that they stung for nearly an hour. But she followed him into the king's audience chamber, where she demanded her money in a loud voice, claiming as well the interest due upon it over night.

"The counselor has lost your money," said the boy king, "but he shall pay you every penny out of my own private purse. I fear, however, you will be obliged to take it in small change."

"That will not matter," she said, scowling upon the counselor as if she longed to reach his ears again; "I don't care how small the change is so long as I get every penny that belongs to me, and the interest. Where is it?"

"Here," answered the king, handing the counselor the leathern purse. "It is all in silver quarters, and they must be taken from the purse one at a time; but there will be plenty to pay your demands, and to spare."

So, there being no chairs, the counselor sat down upon the floor in one corner and began counting out silver twenty-five-cent pieces from the purse, one by one. And the old woman sat upon the floor opposite him and took each piece of money from his hand.

It was a large sum: three million nine hundred thousand six hundred and twenty-four dollars and sixteen cents. And it takes four times as many twenty-five-cent pieces as it would dollars to make up the amount.

The king left them sitting there and went to school, and often thereafter he came to the counselor and interrupted him long enough to get from the purse what money he needed to reign in a proper and dignified manner. This somewhat delayed the counting, but as it was a long job, anyway, that did not matter much.

The king grew to manhood and married the pretty daughter of the armorer, and they now have two lovely children of their own. Once in awhile they go into the big audience chamber of the palace and let the little ones watch the aged, hoary-headed counselor count out silver twenty-five-cent pieces to a withered old woman, who watches his every movement to see that he does not cheat her.

It is a big sum, three million nine hundred thousand six hundred and twenty-four dollars and sixteen cents in twenty-five-cent pieces.

But this is how the counselor was punished for being so careless with the woman's money. And this is how Mary Ann Brodjinsky de la Porkus was also punished for wishing to marry a ten-year-old king in order that she might wear the coronet of the queen of Quok.

The Magic Bonbons

There lived in Boston a wise and ancient chemist by the name of Dr. Daws, who dabbled somewhat in magic. There also lived in Boston a young lady by the name of Claribel Sudds, who was possessed of much money, little wit and an intense desire to go upon the stage.

So Claribel went to Dr. Daws and said:

"I can neither sing nor dance; I cannot recite verse nor play upon the piano; I am no acrobat nor leaper nor high kicker; yet I wish to go upon the stage. What shall I do?"

"Are you willing to pay for such accomplishments?" asked the wise chemist.

"Certainly," answered Claribel, jingling her purse.

"Then come to me to-morrow at two o'clock," said he.

All that night he practiced what is known as chemical sorcery; so that when Claribel Sudds came next day at two o'clock he showed her a small box filled with compounds that closely resembled French bonbons.

"This is a progressive age," said the old man, "and I flatter myself your Uncle Daws keeps right along with the procession. Now, one of your old-fashioned sorcerers would have made you some nasty, bitter pills to swallow; but I have consulted your taste and convenience. Here are some magic bonbons. If you eat this one with the lavender color you can dance thereafter as lightly and gracefully as if you had been trained a lifetime. After you consume the pink confection you will sing like a nightingale. Eating the white one will enable you to become the finest elocutionist in the land. The chocolate piece will charm you into playing the piano better than Rubenstein, while after eating the lemon-yellow bonbon you can easily kick six feet above your head."

"How delightful!" exclaimed Claribel, who was truly enraptured. "You are certainly a most clever sorcerer as well as a considerate compounder," and she held out her hand for the box.

"Ahem!" said the wise one; "A check, please."

"Oh, yes; to be sure! How stupid of me to forget it," she returned.

He considerately retained the box in his own hand while she signed a check for a large amount of money, after which he allowed her to hold the box herself.

"Are you sure you have made them strong enough?" she inquired, anxiously; "it usually takes a great deal to affect me."

"My only fear," replied Dr. Daws, "is that I have made them too strong. For this is the first time I have ever been called upon to prepare these wonderful confections."

"Don't worry," said Claribel; "the stronger they act the better I shall act myself."

She went away, after saying this, but stopping in at a dry goods store to shop, she forgot the precious box in her new interest and left it lying on the ribbon counter.

Then little Bessie Bostwick came to the counter to buy a hair ribbon and laid her parcels beside the box. When she went away she gathered up the box with her other bundles and trotted off home with it.

Bessie never knew, until after she had hung her coat in the hall closet and counted up her parcels, that she had one too many. Then she opened it and exclaimed:

"Why, it's a box of candy! Someone must have mislaid it. But it is too small a matter to worry about; there are only a few pieces." So she dumped the contents of the box into a bonbon dish that stood upon the hall table and picking out the chocolate piece—she was fond of chocolates—ate it daintily while she examined her purchases.

These were not many, for Bessie was only twelve years old and was not yet trusted by her parents to expend much money at the stores. But while she tried on the hair ribbon she suddenly felt a great desire to play upon the piano, and the desire at last became so overpowering that she went into the parlor and opened the instrument.

The little girl had, with infinite pains, contrived to learn two "pieces" which she usually executed with a jerky movement of her right hand and a left hand that forgot to keep up and so made dreadful discords. But under the influence of the chocolate bonbon she sat down and ran her fingers lightly over the keys producing such exquisite harmony that she was filled with amazement at her own performance.

That was the prelude, however. The next moment she dashed into Beethoven's seventh sonata and played it magnificently.

Her mother, hearing the unusual burst of melody, came downstairs to see what musical guests had arrived; but when she discovered it was her own little daughter who was playing so divinely she had an attack of palpitation of the heart (to which she was subject) and sat down upon a sofa until it should pass away.

Meanwhile Bessie played one piece after another with untiring energy. She loved music, and now found that all she needed do was to sit at the piano and listen and watch her hands twinkle over the keyboard.

Twilight deepened in the room and Bessie's father came home and hung up his hat and overcoat and placed his umbrella in the rack. Then he peeped into the parlor to see who was playing.

"Great Caesar!" he exclaimed. But the mother came to him softly with her finger on her lips and whispered: "Don't interrupt her, John. Our child seems to be in a trance. Did you ever hear such superb music?"

"Why, she's an infant prodigy!" gasped the astounded father. "Beats Blind Tom all hollow! It's—it's wonderful!"

As they stood listening the senator arrived, having been invited to dine with them that evening. And before he had taken off his coat the Yale professor—a man of deep learning and scholarly attainments—joined the party.

Bessie played on; and the four elders stood in a huddled but silent and amazed group, listening to the music and waiting for the sound of the dinner gong.

Mr. Bostwick, who was hungry, picked up the bonbon dish that lay on the table beside him and ate the pink confection. The professor was watching him, so Mr. Bostwick courteously held the dish toward him. The professor ate the lemon-yellow piece and the senator reached out his hand and took the lavender piece. He did not eat it, however, for, chancing to remember that it might spoil his dinner, he put it in his vest pocket. Mrs. Bostwick, still intently listening to her precocious daughter, without thinking what she did, took the remaining piece, which was the white one, and slowly devoured it.

The dish was now empty, and Claribel Sudds' precious bonbons had passed from her possession forever!

Suddenly Mr. Bostwick, who was a big man, began to sing in a shrill, tremolo soprano voice. It was not the same song Bessie was playing, and the discord was so shocking that the professor smiled, the senator put his hands to his ears and Mrs. Bostwick cried in a horrified voice:

"William!"

Her husband continued to sing as if endeavoring to emulate the famous Christine Nilsson, and paid no attention whatever to his wife or his guests.

Fortunately the dinner gong now sounded, and Mrs. Bostwick dragged Bessie from the piano and ushered her guests into the dining-room. Mr. Bostwick followed, singing "The Last Rose of Summer" as if it had been an encore demanded by a thousand delighted hearers.

The poor woman was in despair at witnessing her husband's undignified actions and wondered what she might do to control him. The professor seemed more grave than usual; the senator's face wore an offended expression, and Bessie kept moving her fingers as if she still wanted to play the piano.

Mrs. Bostwick managed to get them all seated, although her husband had broken into another aria; and then the maid brought in the soup.

When she carried a plate to the professor, he cried, in an excited voice:

"Hold it higher! Higher—I say!" And springing up he gave it a sudden kick that sent it nearly to the ceiling, from whence the dish descended to scatter soup over Bessie and the maid and to smash in pieces upon the crown of the professor's bald head.

At this atrocious act the senator rose from his seat with an exclamation of horror and glanced at his hostess.

For some time Mrs. Bostwick had been staring straight ahead, with a dazed expression; but now, catching the senator's eye, she bowed gracefully and began reciting "The Charge of the Light Brigade" in forceful tones.

The senator shuddered. Such disgraceful rioting he had never seen nor heard before in a decent private family. He felt that his reputation was at stake, and, being the only sane person, apparently, in the room, there was no one to whom he might appeal.

The maid had run away to cry hysterically in the kitchen; Mr. Bostwick was singing "O Promise Me;" the professor was trying to kick the globes off the chandelier; Mrs. Bostwick had switched her recitation to "The Boy Stood on the Burning Deck," and Bessie had stolen into the parlor and was pounding out the overture from the "Flying Dutchman."

The senator was not at all sure he would not go crazy himself, presently; so he slipped away from the turmoil, and, catching up his hat and coat in the hall, hurried from the house.

That night he sat up late writing a political speech he was to deliver the next afternoon at Faneuil Hall, but his experiences at the Bostwicks' had so unnerved him that he could scarcely collect his thoughts, and often he would pause and shake his head pityingly as he remembered the strange things he had seen in that usually respectable home.

The next day he met Mr. Bostwick on the street, but passed him by with a stony glare of oblivion. He felt he really could not afford to know this gentleman in the future. Mr. Bostwick was naturally indignant at the direct snub; yet in his mind lingered a faint memory of some quite unusual occurrences at his dinner party the evening before, and he hardly knew whether he dared resent the senator's treatment or not.

The political meeting was the feature of the day, for the senator's eloquence was well known in Boston. So the big hall was crowded with people, and in one of the front rows sat the Bostwick family, with the learned Yale professor beside them. They all looked tired and pale, as if they had passed a rather dissipated evening, and the senator was rendered so nervous by seeing them that he refused to look in their direction a second time.

While the mayor was introducing him the great man sat fidgeting in his chair; and, happening to put his thumb and finger into his vest pocket, he found the lavender-colored bonbon he had placed there the evening before.

"This may clear my throat," thought the senator, and slipped the bonbon into his mouth.

A few minutes afterwards he arose before the vast audience, which greeted him with enthusuastic plaudits.

"My friends," began the senator, in a grave voice, "this is a most impressive and important occasion."

Then he paused, balanced himself upon his left foot, and kicked his right leg into the air in the way favored by ballet-dancers!

There was a hum of amazement and horror from the spectators, but the senator appeared not to notice it. He whirled around upon the tips of his toes, kicked right and left in a graceful manner, and startled a baldheaded man in the front row by casting a languishing glance in his direction.

Suddenly Claribel Sudds, who happened to be present, uttered a scream and sprang to her feet. Pointing an accusing finger at the dancing senator, she cried in a loud voice:

"That's the man who stole my bonbons! Seize him! Arrest him! Don't let him escape!"

But the ushers rushed her out of the hall, thinking she had gone suddenly insane; and the senator's friends seized him firmly and carried him out the stage entrance to the street, where they put him into an open carriage and instructed the driver to take him home.

The effect of the magic bonbon was still powerful enough to control the poor senator, who stood upon the rear seat of the carriage and danced energetically all the way home, to the delight of the crowd of small boys who followed the carriage and the grief of the sober-minded citizens, who shook their heads sadly and whispered that "another good man had gone wrong."

It took the senator several months to recover from the shame and humiliation of this escapade; and, curiously enough, he never had the slightest idea what had induced him to act in so extraordinary a manner. Perhaps it was fortunate the last bonbon had now been eaten, for they might easily have caused considerably more trouble than they did.

Of course Claribel went again to the wise chemist and signed a check for another box of magic bonbons; but she must have taken better care of these, for she is now a famous vaudeville actress.

This story should teach us the folly of condemning others for actions that we do not understand, for we never know what may happen to ourselves. It may also serve as a hint to be careful about leaving parcels in public places, and, incidentally, to let other people's packages severely alone.

The Dummy That Lived

In all Fairyland there is no more mischievous a person than Tanko-Mankie the Yellow Ryl. He flew through the city one afternoon—quite invisible to mortal eyes, but seeing everything himself—and noticed a figure of a wax lady standing behind the big plate glass window of Mr. Floman's department store.

The wax lady was beautifully dressed, and extended in her stiff left hand was a card bearing the words:

"RARE BARGAIN!
This Stylish Costume
(Imported from Paris)
Former Price, $20,
REDUCED TO ONLY $19.98."

This impressive announcement had drawn before the window a crowd of women shoppers, who stood looking at the wax lady with critical eyes.

Tanko-Mankie laughed to himself the low, gurgling little laugh that always means mischief. Then he flew close to the wax figure and breathed twice upon its forehead.

From that instant the dummy began to live, but so dazed and astonished was she at the unexpected sensation that she continued to stand stupidly staring at the women outside and holding out the placard as before.

The ryl laughed again and flew away. Anyone but Tanko-Mankie would have remained to help the wax lady out of the troubles that were sure to overtake her; but this naughty elf thought it rare fun to turn the inexperienced lady loose in a cold and heartless world and leave her to shift for herself.

Fortunately it was almost six o'clock when the dummy first realized that she was alive, and before she had collected her new thoughts and decided what to do a man came around and drew down all the window shades, shutting off the view from the curious shoppers.

Then the clerks and cashiers and floorwalkers and cash girls went home and the store was closed for the night, although the sweepers and scrubbers remained to clean the floors for the following day.

The window inhabited by the wax lady was boxed in, like a little room, one small door being left at the side for the window-trimmer to creep in and out of. So the scrubbers never noticed that the dummy, when left to herself, dropped the placard to the floor and sat down upon a pile of silks to wonder who she was, where she was, and how she happened to be alive.

For you must consider, dear reader, that in spite of her size and her rich costume, in spite of her pink cheeks and fluffy yellow hair, this lady was very young—no older, in reality, than a baby born but half an hour. All she knew of the world was contained in the glimpse she had secured of the busy street facing her window; all she knew of people lay in the actions of the group of women which had stood before her on the other side of the window pane and criticised the fit of her dress or remarked upon its stylish appearance.

So she had little enough to think about, and her thoughts moved somewhat slowly; yet one thing she really decided upon, and that was not to remain in the window and be insolently stared at by a lot of women who were not nearly so handsome or well dressed as herself.

By the time she reached this important conclusion, it was after midnight; but dim lights were burning in the big, deserted store, so she crept through the door of her window and walked down the long aisles, pausing now and then to look with much curiosity at the wealth of finery confronting her on every side.

When she came to the glass cases filled with trimmed hats she remembered having seen upon the heads of the women in the street similar creations. So she selected one that suited her fancy and placed it carefully upon her yellow locks. I won't attempt to explain what instinct it was that made her glance into a near-by mirror to see if the hat was straight, but this she certainly did. It didn't correspond with her dress very well, but the poor thing was too young to have much taste in matching colors.

When she reached the glove counter she remembered that gloves were also worn by the women she had seen. She took a pair from the case and tried to fit them upon her stiff, wax-coated fingers; but the gloves were too small and ripped in the seams. Then she tried another pair, and several others, as well; but hours passed before she finally succeeded in getting her hands covered with a pair of pea-green kids.

Next she selected a parasol from a large and varied assortment in the rear of the store. Not that she had any idea what it was used for; but other ladies carried such things, so she also would have one.

When she again examined herself critically in the mirror she decided her outfit was now complete, and to her inexperienced eyes there was no perceptible difference between her and the women who had stood outside the window. Whereupon she tried to leave the store, but found every door fast locked.

The wax lady was in no hurry. She inherited patience from her previous existence. Just to be alive and to wear beautiful clothes was sufficient enjoyment for her at present. So she sat down upon a stool and waited quietly until daylight.

When the janitor unlocked the door in the morning the wax lady swept past him and walked with stiff but stately strides down the street. The poor fellow was so completely whuckered at seeing the well-known wax lady leave her window and march away from the store that he fell over in a heap and only saved himself from fainting by striking his funny bone against the doorstep. When he recovered his wits she had turned the corner and disappeared.

The wax lady's immature mind had reasoned that, since she had come to life, her evident duty was to mix with the world and do whatever other folks did. She could not realize how different she was from people of flesh and blood; nor did she know she was the first dummy that had ever lived, or that she owed her unique experience to Tanko-Mankie's love of mischief. So ignorance gave her a confidence in herself that she was not justly entitled to.

It was yet early in the day, and the few people she met were hurrying along the streets. Many of them turned in to restaurants and eating houses, and following their example the wax lady also entered one and sat upon a stool before a lunch counter.

"Coffee 'n' rolls!" said a shop girl on the next stool.

"Coffee 'n' rolls!" repeated the dummy, and soon the waiter placed them before her. Of course she had no appetite, as her constitution, being mostly wood, did not require food; but she watched the shop girl, and saw her put the coffee to her mouth and drink it. Therefore the wax lady did the same, and the next instant was surprised to feel the hot liquid trickling out between her wooden ribs. The coffee also blistered her wax lips, and so disagreeable was the experience that she arose and left the restaurant, paying no attention to the demands of the waiter for "20 cents, mum." Not that she intended to defraud him, but the poor creature had no idea what he meant by "20 cents, mum."

As she came out she met the window-trimmer at Floman's store. The man was rather near-sighted, but seeing something familiar in the lady's features he politely raised his hat. The wax lady also raised her hat, thinking it the proper thing to do, and the man hurried away with a horrified face.

Then a woman touched her arm and said:

"Beg pardon, Ma'am; but there's a price-mark hanging on your dress behind."

"Yes, I know," replied the wax lady, stiffly; "it was originally $20, but it's been reduced to $19.98."

The woman looked surprised at such indifference and walked on. Some carriages were standing at the edge of the sidewalk, and seeing the dummy hesitate a driver approached her and touched his cap.

"Cab, ma'am?" he asked.

"No," said she, misunderstanding him; "I'm wax."

"Oh!" he exclaimed, and looked after her wonderingly.

"Here's yer mornin' paper!" yelled a newsboy.

"Mine, did you say?" she asked.

"Sure! Chronicle, 'Quirer, R'public 'n' 'Spatch! Wot'll ye 'ave?"

"What are they for?" inquired the wax lady, simply.

"W'y, ter read, o'course. All the news, you know."

She shook her head and glanced at a paper.

"It looks all speckled and mixed up," she said. "I'm afraid I can't read."

"Ever ben to school?" asked the boy, becoming interested.

"No; what's school?" she inquired.

The boy gave her an indignant look.

"Say!" he cried, "ye'r just a dummy, that's wot ye are!" and ran away to seek a more promising customer.

"I wonder what he means," thought the poor lady. "Am I really different in some way from all the others? I look like them, certainly; and I try to act like them; yet that boy called me a dummy and seemed to think I acted queerly."

This idea worried her a little, but she walked on to the corner, where she noticed a street car stop to let some people on. The wax lady, still determined to do as others did, also boarded the car and sat down quietly in a corner.

After riding a few blocks the conductor approached her and said: "Fare, please!"

"What's that?" she inquired, innocently.

"Your fare!" said the man, impatiently.

She stared at him stupidly, trying to think what he meant.

"Come, come!" growled the conductor, and he grabbed her rudely by the arm and lifted her to her feet. But when his hand came in contact with the hard wood of which her arm was made the fellow was filled with surprise. He stooped down and peered into her face, and, seeing it was wax instead of flesh, he gave a yell of fear and jumped from the car, running as if he had seen a ghost.

At this the other passengers also yelled and sprang from the car, fearing a collision; and the motorman, knowing something was wrong, followed suit. The wax lady, seeing the others run, jumped from the car last of all, and stepped in front of another car coming at full speed from the opposite direction.

She heard cries of fear and of warning on all sides, but before she understood her danger she was knocked down and dragged for half a block.

When the car was brought to a stop a policeman reached down and pulled her from under the wheels. Her dress was badly torn and soiled, her left ear was entirely gone, and the left side of her head was caved in; but she quickly scrambled to her feet and asked for her hat. This a gentleman had already picked up, and when the policeman handed it to her and noticed the great hole in her head and the hollow place it disclosed, the poor fellow trembled so frightfully that his knees actually knocked together.

"Why—why, ma'am, you're—killed!" he gasped.

"What does it mean to be killed?" asked the wax lady.

The policeman shuddered and wiped the perspiration from his forehead.

"You're it!" he answered, with a groan.

The crowd that had collected were looking upon the lady wonderingly, and a middle-aged gentleman now exclaimed:

"Why she's wax!"

"Wax!" echoed the policeman.

"Certainly. She's one of those dummies they put in the windows," declared the middle-aged man.

The crowd pressed nearer and several shouted: "You're right!" "That's what she is!" "She's a dummy!"

"Are you?" inquired the policeman, sternly.

The wax lady did not reply. She began to fear she was getting into trouble, and the staring crowd seemed to embarrass her.

Suddenly a bootblack attempted to solve the problem by saying: "You guys is all wrong! Can a dummy talk? Can a dummy walk? Can a dummy live?"

"Hush!" murmured the policeman. "Look here!" and he pointed to the hole in the lady's head. The newsboy looked, turned pale and whistled to keep himself from shivering.

A second policeman now arrived, and after a brief conference it was decided to take the strange creature to headquarters. So they called a hurry-up wagon, and the damaged wax lady was helped inside and driven to the police station. There the policemen locked her in a cell and hastened to tell Inspector Mugg their wonderful story.

Inspector Mugg had just eaten a poor breakfast, and was not in a pleasant mood; so he roared and stormed at the unlucky policemen, saying they were themselves dummies to bring such a fairy tale to a man of sense. He also hinted that they had been guilty of intemperance.

The policemen tried to explain, but Inspector Mugg would not listen; and while they were still disputing in rushed Mr. Floman, the owner of the department store.

"I want a dozen detectives, at once, inspector!" he cried.

"What for?" demanded Mugg.

"One of the wax ladies has escaped from my store and eloped with a $19.98 costume, a $4.23 hat, a $2.19 parasol and a 76-cent pair of gloves, and I want her arrested!"

While he paused for breath the inspector glared at him in amazement.

"Is everybody going crazy at the same time?" he inquired, sarcastically. "How could a wax dummy run away?"

"I don't know; but she did. When my janitor opened the door this morning he saw her run out."

"Why didn't he stop her?" asked Mugg.

"He was too frightened. But she's stolen my property, your honor, and I want her arrested!" declared the storekeeper.

The inspector thought for a moment.

"You wouldn't be able to prosecute her," he said, "for there is no law against dummies stealing."

Mr. Floman sighed bitterly.

"Am I to lose that $19.98 costume and the $4.23 hat and—"

"By no means," interrupted Inspector Mugg. "The police of this city are ever prompt to act in defense of our worthy citizens. We have already arrested the wax lady, and she is locked up in cell No. 16. You may go there and recover your property, if you wish, but before you prosecute her for stealing you'd better hunt up a law that applies to dummies."

"All I want," said Mr. Floman, "is that $19.98 costume and—"

"Come along!" interrupted the policeman. "I'll take you to the cell."

But when they entered No. 16 they found only a lifeless dummy lying prone upon the floor. Its wax was cracked and blistered, its head was badly damaged, and the bargain costume was dusty, soiled and much bedraggled. For the mischief loving Tanko-Mankie had flown by and breathed once more upon the poor wax lady, and in that instant her brief life ended.

"It's just as I thought," said Inspector Mugg, leaning back in his chair contentedly. "I knew all the time the thing was a fake. It seems sometimes as though the whole world would go crazy if there wasn't some level-headed man around to bring 'em to their senses. Dummies are wood and wax, an' that's all there is of 'em."

"That may be the rule," whispered the policeman to himself, "but this one were a dummy as lived!"

In SAMUEL R. DELANY's reinterpretation of the sword and sorcery story, the castles, dragons, and dungeons are different, not in name or form, but in meaning. They are peripheral and atmospheric, not central images. One of the foremost SF writers, Delany has produced his major work in the last decade in adult fantasy, in a series of stories and novels set in the imaginary world of Nevèrÿon. Vivid and realistic in detail, yet strange, distant, and barbaric in setting, Nevèrÿon is populated with complex and psychologically rounded characters not often found in fantasy fiction, and is a world constantly analyzed from new vantage points in each of the stories in the series. The selection here is from Delany's first volume, Tales of Nevèrÿon. *The series now includes three more volumes,* Nevèrÿona, Flight from Nevèrÿon, *and* The Bridge of Lost Desire.

The Tale of Dragons and Dreamers
BY SAMUEL R. DELANY

But there is a negative work to be carried out first: we must rid ourselves of a whole mass of notions, each of which, in its own way, diversifies the theme of continuity. They may not have a very rigorous conceptual structure, but they have a very precise function. Take the notion of tradition: it is intended to give a special temporal status to a group of phenomena that are both successive and identical (or at least similar); it makes it possible to rethink the dispersion of history in the form of the same; it allows a reduction of the difference proper to every beginning, in order to pursue without discontinuity the endless search for origin . . .
—Michel Foucault
The Archeology of Knowledge

1

Wide wings dragged on stone, scales a polychrome glister with seven greens. The bony gum yawned above the iron rail. The left eye, fist-sized and packed with stained foils, did not blink its transverse lid. A stench of halides; a bilious hiss.

"But why have you penned it up in here?"

"Do you think the creature unhappy, my Vizerine? Ill-fed, perhaps? Poorly exercised—less well cared for than it would be at Ellamon?"

"How could anyone know?" But Myrgot's chin was down, her lower lip out, and her thin hands joined tightly before the lap of her shift.

"I know *you,* my dear. You hold it against me that I should want some of the 'fable' that has accrued to these beasts to redound on me. But you know; I went to great expense (and I don't just mean the bribes, the gifts, the money) to bring it here . . . Do you know what a dragon is? For me? Let me tell you, dear Myrgot: it is an expression of some natural sensibility that cannot be explained by pragmatics, that cannot survive unless someone is hugely generous before it. These beasts are a sport. If Olin—yes, Mad Olin, and it may have been the highest manifestation of her madness—had not decided, on a tour through the mountain holds, the creatures were beautiful, we wouldn't have them today. You know the story? She came upon a bunch of brigands slaughtering a nest of them and sent her troops to slaughter the brigands. Everyone in the mountains had seen the wings, but no one was sure the creatures could actually fly till two years after Olin put them under her protection, and the grooms devised their special training programs that allowed the beasts to soar. And their flights, though lovely, are short and rare. The creatures are not survival oriented—unless you want to see them as part of a survival relationship with the vicious little harridans who are condemned to be their riders: another of your crazed great aunt's more inane institutions. Look at that skylight. The moon outside illumines it now. But the expense I have gone to in order to arrive at those precise green panes! Full sunlight causes the creature's eyes to inflame, putting it in great discomfort. They can only fly a few hundred yards or so, perhaps a mile with the most propitious drafts, and unless they land on the most propitious ledge, they cannot take off again. Since they cannot elevate from flat land, once set down in an ordinary forest, say, they are doomed. In the wild, many live their entire lives without flying, which, given how easily their wing membranes tear through or become injured, is understandable. They are egg-laying creatures who know nothing of physical intimacy. Indeed, they are much more tractable when kept from their fellows. This one is bigger, stronger, and generally healthier than any you'll find in the Falthas—in or out of the Ellamon corals. Listen to her trumpet her joy over her present state!"

Obligingly, the lizard turned on her splay claws, dragging the chain from her iron collar, threw back her bony head beneath the tower's many lamps, and hissed—not a trumpet, the Vizerine reflected, whatever young Strethi might think. "My dear, why don't you just turn it loose?"

"Why don't *you* just have me turn loose the poor wretch chained in the dungeon?" At the Vizerine's bitter glance, the Suzeraine chuckled. "No, dear Myrgot. True, I could haul on those chains there, which would pull back the wood and copper partitions you see on the other side of the pen. My beast could then waddle to the ledge and soar out from our tower here, onto the night. (Note the scenes of hunting I have had the finest craftsmen beat into the metal work. Myself, I think they're stunning.) But such a creature as this in a landscape like the one about here could take only a single flight—for, really, without a rider they're simply too stupid to turn around and come back to where they took off. And I am not a twelve year old girl; what's more, I couldn't bear to have one about the castle who could ride the creature aloft when I am too old and too heavy." (The dragon was still hissing.) "No, I could only conceive of turning it loose if my whole world were destroyed and—indeed—my next act would be to cast myself down from that same ledge to the stones!"

"My Suzeraine, I much preferred you as a wild-haired, horse-proud seventeen-year-old. You were beautiful and heartless . . . in some ways rather a bore. But you have grown up into another over-refined soul of the sort our aristocracy is so good at producing and which produces so little itself save ways to spend unconscionable amounts on castles, clothes, and complex towers to keep comfortable impossible beasts. You remind me of a cousin of mine—the Baron Inige? Yet what I loved about you, when you were a wholly ungracious provincial heir whom I had just brought to court, was simply that *that* was what I could never imagine you."

"Oh, I remember what you loved about me! And I remember your cousin too—though it's been years since I've seen him. Among those pompous and self-important dukes and earls, though I doubt he liked me any better than the rest did, I recall a few times when he went out of his way to be kind . . . I'm sure I didn't deserve it. How is Curly?"

"Killed himself three years ago." The Vizerine shook her head. "*His* passion, you may recall, was flowers—which I'm afraid totally took over in the last years. As I understand the story—for I wasn't there when it happened—he'd been putting together another collection of particularly rare weeds. One he was after apparently turned out to be the wrong color, or couldn't be found, or didn't exist. The next day his servants discovered him in the arboretum, his mouth crammed with the white blossoms of some deadly mountain flower." Myrgot shuddered. "Which I've always suspected is where such passions as his—and yours—are too likely to lead, given the flow of our lives, the tenor of our times."

The Suzeraine laughed, adjusting the collar of his rich robe with his forefinger. (The Vizerine noted that the blue eyes were much paler in the prematurely lined face than she remembered; and the boyish nailbiting had passed on, in the man, to such grotesque extents that each of his bony fingers now ended in a perfect pitted wound.) Two slaves at the door, their own collars covered with heavily jeweled neckpieces, stepped forward to help him, as they had long since been instructed, when the Suzeraine's hand fell again into the robe's folds, the adjustment completed. The slaves stepped back. The Suzeraine, oblivious, and the Vizerine, feigning obliviousness and wondering if the Suzeraine's obliviousness were feigned or real, strolled through the low stone arch between them to the uneven steps circling down the tower.

"Well," said the blond lord, stepping back to let his lover of twenty years ago precede, "now we return to the less pleasant aspect of your stay here. You know, I sometimes find myself dreading any visit from the aristocracy. Just last week two common women stopped at my castle—one was a redhaired island woman, the other a small creature in a mask who hailed from the Western Crevasse. They were traveling together, seeking adventure and fortune. The Western Woman had once for a time worked in the Falthas, training the winged beasts and the little girls who ride them. The conversation was choice! The island woman could tell incredible tales, and was even using skins and inks to mark down her adventures. And the masked one's observations were very sharp. It was a fine evening we passed. I fed them and housed them. They entertained me munificently. I gave them useful gifts, saw them depart, and would be delighted to see either return. Now, were the stars in a different configuration, I'm sure that the poor wretch that we've got strapped in the dungeon and his little friend who escaped might have come wandering by in the same wise. But no, we have to bind one to the plank in the cellar and stake a guard out for the other

... You really wish me to keep up the pretence to that poor mule that it is Krodar, rather than you, who directs his interrogation?"

"You object?" Myrgot's hand, out to touch the damp stones at the stair's turning, came back to brush at the black braids that looped her forehead. "Once or twice I have seen you enjoy such an inquisition session with an avidity that verged on the unsettling."

"Inquisition? But this is merely questioning. The pain—at your own orders, my dear—is being kept to a minimum." (Strethi's laugh echoed down over Myrgot's shoulder, recalling for her the enthusiasm of the boy she could no longer find when she gazed full at the man.) "I have neither objection nor approbation, my Vizerine. We have him; we do with him as we will . . . Now, I can't help seeing how you gaze about at my walls, Myrgot! I must tell you, ten years ago when I had this castle built over the ruins of my parents' farm, I really thought the simple fact that all my halls had rooves would bring the aristocracy of Nevèrÿon flocking to my court. Do you know, you are my only regular visitor—at least the only one who comes out of anything other than formal necessity. And I do believe you would come to see me even if I lived in the same draughty farmhouse I did when you first met me. Amazing what we'll do out of friendship . . . The other one, Myrgot; I wonder what happened to our prisoner's little friend. They both fought like devils. Too bad the boy got away."

"We have the one I want," Myrgot said.

"At any rate, you have your reasons—your passion, for politics and intrigue. That's what comes of living most of your life in Kolhari. Here in Avila, it's—well, it's not that different for me. You have your criticism of my passions—and I have mine of yours. Certainly I should like to be much more straightforward with the dog: make my demand and chop his head off if he didn't meet it. This endless play is not really my style. Yet I am perfectly happy to assist you in your desires. And however disparaging you are of my little pet, whose welfare is my life, I am sure there will come a time when one or another of your messengers will arrive at my walls bearing some ornate lizard harness of exquisite workmanship you have either discovered in some old storeroom or—who knows—have had specially commissioned for me by the latest and finest artist. When it happens, I shall be immensely pleased."

And as the steps took them around and down the damp tower, the Suzeraine of Strethi slipped up beside the Vizerine to take her aging arm.

2

And again Small Sarg ran.

He struck back low twigs, side-stepped a wet branch clawed with moonlight, and leaped a boggy puddle. With one hand he shoved away a curtain of leaves, splattering himself face to foot with night-dew, to reveal the moonlight castle. (How many other castles had he so revealed . . .) Branches chattered to behind him.

Panting, he ducked behind a boulder. His muddy hand pawed beneath the curls like scrap brass at his neck. The hinged iron was there; and locked tight—a droplet trickled under the metal. He swatted at his hip to find his sword: the hilt was still tacky under his palm where he had not had time to clean it. The gaze with which he took in the pile of stone was not a halt in his headlong dash so much as a continuation of it, the energy propelling arms and legs momentarily diverted into eyes, ears, and all inside and behind them; then it was back in his feet; his feet pounded the shaley slope so that each footfall, even on his calloused soles, was a constellation of small pains; it was back in his arms; his arms pumped by his flanks so that his fists, brushing his sides as he jogged, heated his knuckles by friction.

A balustrade rose, blotting stars.

There would be the unlocked door (as he ran, he clawed over memories of the seven castles he had already run up to; seven side doors, all unlocked . . .); and the young barbarian, muddy to the knees and elbows, his hair at head and chest and groin matted with leaf-bits and worse, naked save the sword thonged about his hips and the slave collar locked about his neck, dashed across moonlit stubble and gravel into a tower's shadow, toward the door . . . and slowed, pulling in cool breaths of autumn air that grew hot inside him and ran from his nostrils; more air ran in.

"Halt!" from the brand that flared high in the doorframe.

Sarg, in one of those swipes at his hip, had moved the scabbard around behind his buttock; it was possible, if the guard had not really been looking at Sarg's dash through the moonlight, for the boy to have seemed simply a naked slave. Sarg's hand was ready to grab at the hilt.

"Who's there?"

Small Sarg raised his chin, so that the iron would show. "I've come back," and thought of seven castles. "I got lost from the others, this morning. When they were out."

"Come now, say your name and rank."

"It's only Small Sarg, master—one of the slaves in the Suzeraine's labor pen. I was lost this morning—"

"Likely story!"

"—and I've just found my way back." With his chin high, Sarg walked slowly and thought: I am running, I am running . . .

"See here, boy—" The brand came forward, fifteen feet, ten, five, three . . .

I am running. And Small Sarg, looking like a filthy field slave with some thong at his waist, jerked his sword up from the scabbard (which bounced on his buttock) and with a grunt sank it into the abdomen of the guard a-glow beneath the high-held flare. The guard's mouth opened. The flare fell, rolled in the mud so that it burned now only on one side. Small Sarg leaned on the hilt, twisting—somewhere inside the guard the blade sheered upward, parting diaphragm, belly, lungs. The guard closed his eyes, drooled blood, and toppled. Small Sarg almost fell on him—till the blade sucked free. And Sarg was running again, blade out for the second guard (in four castles before there had been a second guard), who was, it seemed as Sarg swung around the stone newel and into the stairwell where his own breath was a roaring echo, not there.

He hurried up and turned into a side corridor that would take him down to the labor pen. (Seven castles, now. Were all of them designed by one architect?) He ran through the low hall, guided by that glowing spot in his mind where memory was flush with desire; around a little curve, down the steps—

"What the—?"

—and jabbed his sword into the shoulder of the guard who'd started forward (already hearing the murmur behind the wooden slats), yanking it free of flesh, the motion carrying it up and across the throat of the second guard (here there was always a second guard) who had turned, surprised; the second guard released his sword (it had only been half drawn), which fell back into its scabbard. Small Sarg hacked at the first again (who was screaming): the man fell, and Small Sarg leaped over him, while the man gurgled and flopped. But Sarg was pulling at the boards, cutting at the rope. Behind the boards and under the screams, like murmuring flies, hands and faces rustled about one another. (Seven times now they had seemed like murmuring flies.) And rope was always harder hacking than flesh. The wood, in at least two other castles, had simply splintered under his hands (under his hands, wood splintered) so that, later, he had wondered if the slaughter and the terror was really necessary.

Rope fell away.

Sarg yanked again.

The splintered gate scraped out on stone.

"You're free!" Sarg hissed into the mumbling; mumblings silenced at the word. "Go on, get out of here now!" (How many faces above their collars were clearly barbarian like his own? Memory of other labor pens, rather than what shifted and murmured before him, told him most were.) He turned and leaped bodies, took stairs at double step —while memory told him that only a handful would flee at once; another handful would take three, four, or five minutes to talk themselves into fleeing; and another would simply sit, terrified in the foul straw, and would be sitting there when the siege was over.

He dashed up stairs in the dark. (Dark stairs fell down beneath dashing feet . . .) He flung himself against the wooden door with the strip of light beneath and above it. (In two other castles the door had been locked); it fell open. (In one castle the kitchen midden had been deserted, the fire dead.) He staggered in, blinking in firelight.

The big man in the stained apron stood up from over the cauldron, turned, frowning. Two women carrying pots stopped and stared. In the bunk beds along the midden's far wall, a red-headed kitchen boy raised himself up on one arm, blinking. Small Sarg tried to see only the collars around each neck. But what he saw as well (he had seen it before . . .) was that even here, in a lord's kitchen, where slavery was already involved with the acquisition of the most rudimentary crafts and skills, most of the faces were darker, the hair was coarser, and only the shorter of the women was clearly a barbarian like himself.

"You are free . . . !" Small Sarg said, drawing himself up, dirty, blood splattered. He took a gulping breath. "The guards are gone below. The labor pens have already been turned loose. You are free . . . !"

The big cook said: "What . . . ?" and a smile, with worry flickering through, slowly overtook his face. (This one's mother, thought Small Sarg, was a barbarian: he had no doubt been gotten on her by some free northern dog.) "What are you talking about, boy? Better put that shoat-sticker down or you'll get yourself in trouble."

Small Sarg stepped forward, hands out from his sides. He glanced left at his sword. Blood trailed a line of drops on the stone below it.

Another slave with a big pot of peeled turnips in his hands strode into the room through the far archway, started for the fire rumbling behind the pot hooks, grilling spits, and chained pulleys. He glanced at Sarg, looked about at the others, stopped.

"Put it down now," the big cook repeated, coaxingly. (The slave who'd just come in, wet from perspiration, with a puzzled look started to put his turnip pot down on the stones—then gulped and hefted it back against his chest.) "Come on—"

"What do you think, I'm some berserk madman, a slave gone off my head with the pressure of the iron at my neck?" With his free hand, he thumbed toward his collar. "I've fought my way in here, freed the laborers below you; you have only to go now yourselves. You're free, do you understand?"

"Now wait, boy," said the cook, his smile wary. "Freedom is not so simple a thing as that. Even if you're telling the truth, just what do you propose we're free to do? Where do you expect us to go? If we leave here, what do you expect will happen to us? We'll be taken by slavers before dawn tomorrow, more than likely. Do you want us to get lost in the swamps to the south? Or would you rather we starve to death in the mountains to the north? Put down your sword—just for a minute—and be reasonable."

The barbarian woman said, with her eyes wide and no barbarian accent at all: "Are you well, boy? Are you hungry? We can give you food: you can lie down and sleep a while if you—"

"I don't want sleep. I don't want food. I want you to understand that you're free and I want you to move. Fools, fools, don't you know that to stay slaves is to stay fools?"

"Now that sword, boy—" The big slave moved.

Small Sarg raised his blade.

The big slave stopped. "Look, youth. Use your head. We can't just—"

Footsteps; armor rattled in another room—clearly guards' sounds. (How many times now—four out of the seven?—had he heard those sounds?) What happened (again) was:

"Here, boy—!" from the woman who had till now not spoken. She shifted her bowl under one arm and pointed toward the bunks.

Small Sarg sprinted toward them, sprang—into the one below the kitchen boy's. As he sprang, his sword point caught the wooden support beam, jarred his arm full hard; the sword fell clanking to the stone floor. As Sarg turned to see it, the kitchen boy in the bunk above flung down a blanket. Sarg collapsed in the straw, kicked rough cloth (it was stiff at one end as though something had spilled on it and dried) down over his leg, and pulled it up over his head at the same time. Just before the blanket edge cut away the firelit chamber, Sarg saw the big slave pull off his stained apron (underneath the man was naked as Sarg) to fling it across the floor to where it settled, like a stained sail, over Sarg's fallen weapon. (And the other slave had somehow managed to set his turnip pot down directly over those blood drops.) Under the blanket dark, he heard the guard rush in.

"All right, you! A hoard of bandits—probably escaped slaves—have stormed the lower floors. They've already taken the labor pen—turned loose every cursed dog in them." (Small Sarg shivered and grinned: how many times now, three, or seven, or seventeen, had he watched slaves suddenly think with one mind, move together like the leaves on a branch before a single breeze!) More footsteps. Beneath the blanket, Small Sarg envisioned a second guard running in to collide with the first, shouting (over the first's shoulder?): "Any of you kitchen scum caught aiding and abetting these invading lizards will be hung up by the heels and whipped till the flesh falls from your backs—and you know we mean it. There must be fifty of them or more to have gotten in like that! And don't think they won't slaughter *you* as soon as they would *us!*"

The pair of footsteps retreated; there was silence for a drawn breath.

Then bare feet were rushing quickly toward his bunk.

Small Sarg pushed back the blanket. The big slave was just snatching up his apron. The woman picked up the sword and thrust it at Sarg.

"All right," said the big slave, "we're running."

"Take your sword," the woman said. "And good luck to you, boy."

They ran—the redheaded kitchen boy dropped down before Small Sarg's bunk and took off around the kitchen table after them. Sarg vaulted now, and landed (running), his feet continuing the dash that had brought him into the castle. The slaves crowded out the wooden door through which Small Sarg had entered. Small Sarg ran out through the arch by which the guards had most probably left.

Three guards stood in the anteroom, conferring. One looked around and said, "Hey, what are—"

A second one who turned and just happened to be a little nearer took Small Sarg's sword in his belly; it tore loose out his side, so that the guard, surprised, fell in the pile of his splatting innards. Sarg struck another's bare thigh—cutting deep—and then the arm of still another (his blade grated bone). The other ran, trailing a bass howl: "They've come! They're coming in here, now! Help! They're breaking in—" breaking to tenor in some other corridor.

Small Sarg ran, and a woman, starting into the hallway from the right, saw him and darted back. But there was a stairwell to his left; he ran up it. He ran, up the cleanly hewn stone, thinking of a tower with spiral steps, that went on and on and on, opening on some high, moon-lit parapet. After one turn, the stairs stopped. Light glimmered from dozens of lamps, some on ornate stands, some hanging from intricate chains.

A thick, patterned carpet cushioned the one muddy foot he had put across the sill. Sarg crouched, his sword out from his hip, and brought his other foot away from the cool stone behind.

The man at the great table looked up, frowned—a slave, but his collar was covered by a wide neckpiece of heavy white cloth sewn about with chunks of tourmaline and jade. He was very thin, very lined, and bald. (In how many castles had Sarg seen slaves who wore their collars covered so? Six, now? All seven?) "What are you doing here, boy . . . ?" The slave pushed his chair back, the metal balls on the forelegs furrowing the rug.

Small Sarg said: "You're free."

Another slave in a similar collar-cover turned on the ladder where she was replacing piles of parchment on a high shelf stuffed with manuscripts. She took a step down the ladder, halted. Another youth (same covered collar), with double pointers against a great globe in the corner, looked perfectly terrified—and was probably the younger brother of the kitchen boy, from his bright hair. (See only the collars, Small Sarg thought. But with the jeweled and damasked neckpieces, it was hard, very hard.) The bald slave at the table, with the look of a tired man, said: "You don't belong here, you know. And you are in great danger." The slave, a wrinkled forty, had the fallen pectorals of the quickly aging.

"You're free!" Small Sarg croaked.

"And you are a very naïve and presumptuous little barbarian. How many times have I had this conversation—four? Five? At least six? You are here to free us of the iron collars." The man dug a forefinger beneath the silk and stones to drag up, on his bony neck, the iron band beneath. "Just so you'll see it's there. Did you know that *our* collars are much heavier than yours?" He released the iron; the same brown forefinger hooked up the jeweled neckpiece—almost a bib—which sagged and wrinkled up, once pulled from its carefully arranged position. "These add far more weight to the neck than the circle of iron they cover." (Small Sarg thought: Though I stand here, still as stone, I am running, running . . .) "We make this castle function, boy—at a level of efficiency that, believe me, is felt in the labor pens as much as in the audience chambers where our lord and owner entertains fellow nobles. You think you are rampaging through the castle, effecting your own eleemosynary manumissions. What you are doing is killing free men and making the lives of slaves more miserable than, of necessity, they already are. If slavery is a disease and a rash on the flesh of Nevèrÿon—" (I am running, like an eagle caught up in the wind, like a snake sliding down a gravel slope . . .) "—your own actions turn an ugly eruption into a fatal infection. You free the labor pens into a world where, at least in the cities and the larger towns, a wage-earning populace, many of them, is worse off than here. And an urban merchant class can only absorb a fraction of the skills of the middle level slaves you turn loose from the middens and smithies. The Child Empress herself has many times declared that she is opposed to the institution of bondage, and the natural drift of our nation is away from slave labor anyway—so that all your efforts do is cause restrictions to become tighter in those areas where the institution would naturally die out of its own accord in a decade or so. Have you considered: your efforts may even be prolonging the institution you would abolish." (Running, Small Sarg thought, rushing, fleeing, dashing . . .) "But the simple truth is that the particular skills *we*—the ones who must cover our collars in jewels—master to run such a complex house as an aristocrat's castle are just not needed by the growing urban class. Come around here, boy, and look for yourself." The bald slave pushed his chair back even further and gestured for Small Sarg to approach. "Yes. Come, see."

Small Sarg stepped, slowly and carefully, across the carpet. (I am running, he thought; flesh tingled at the backs of his knees, the small of his back. Every muscle, in its attenuated motion, was geared to some coherent end that, in the pursuit of it, had become almost invisible within its own glare and nimbus.) Sarg walked around the table's edge.

From a series of holes in the downward lip hung a number of heavy cords, each with a metal loop at the end. (Small Sarg thought: In one castle they had simple handles of wood tied to them; in another the handles were cast from bright metal set with red and green gems, more ornate than the jeweled collars of the slaves who worked them.) "From this room," explained the slave, "we can control the entire castle—really, it represents far more control, even, than that of the Suzeraine who owns all you see, including us. If I pulled this cord here, a bell would ring in the linen room and summon the slave working there; if I pulled it twice, that slave would come with linen for his lordship's chamber, which we would then inspect before sending it on to be spread. Three rings, and the slave would come bearing the sheets and hangings for the guests' chambers. Four rings, and we would receive the sheets for our own use—and they are every bit as elegant, believe me, as the ones for his lordship. One tug on this cord here and wine and food would be brought for his lordship . . . at least if the kitchen staff is still functioning. Three rings, and a feast can be brought for us, here in these very rooms, that would rival any indulged by his Lordship. A bright lad like you, I'm sure, could learn the strings to pull very easily. Here, watch out for your blade and come stand beside me. That's right. Now give that cord there a quick, firm tug and just see what happens. No, don't be afraid. Just reach out and pull it. Once, mind you—not twice or three times. That means something else entirely. Go ahead . . ."

Sarg moved his hand out slowly, looking at his muddy, bloody fingers. (Small Sarg thought: Though it may be a different cord in each castle, it is *always* a single tug! My hand, with each airy inch, feels like it is running, running to hook the ring . . .)

". . . with only a little training," went on the bald slave, smiling, "a smart and ambitious boy like you could easily become one of us. From here, you would wield more power within these walls than the Suzeraine himself. And such power as that is not to be—"

Then Small Sarg whirled (no, he had never released his sword) to shove his steel into the loose belly. The man half-stood, with open mouth, then fell back, gargling. Blood spurted, hit the table, ran down the cords. "You fool . . . !" the bald man managed, trying now to grasp one handle.

Small Sarg, with his dirty hand, knocked the bald man's clean one away. The chair overturned and the bald man curled and uncurled on the darkening carpet. There was blood on his collar piece now.

"You think I am such a fool that I don't know you can call guards in here as easily as food-bearers and house-cleaners?" Small Sarg looked at the woman on the ladder, the boy at the globe. "I do not like to kill slaves. But I do not like people who plot to kill me—especially such a foolish plot. Now: are the rest of you such fools that you cannot understand what it means when I say, 'You're free'?"

Parchments slipped from the shelf, unrolling on the floor, as the woman scurried down the ladder. The boy fled across the room, leaving a slowly turning globe. Then both were into the arched stairwell from which Small Sarg had come. Sarg hopped over the fallen slave and ran into the doorway through which (in two other castles) guards, at the (single) tug of a cord, had come swarming: a short hall, more steps, another chamber. Long and short swords hung on the wooden wall. Leather shields with colored fringes leaned against the stone one. A helmet lay on the floor in the corner near a stack of grieves. But there were no guards. (Till now, in the second castle only, there had been no guards.) I am free, thought Small Sarg, once again I am free, running, running through stone arches, down tapestried stairs, across dripping halls, up narrow corridors, a-dash through time and possibility. (Somewhere in the castle people were screaming.) Now I am free to free my master!

Somewhere, doors clashed. Other doors, nearer, clashed. Then the chamber doors swung back in firelight. The Suzeraine strode through, tugging them to behind him. "Very well—" (Clash!—"we can get on with our little session." He reached up to adjust his collar and two slaves in jeweled collar pieces by the door (they were oiled, pale, strong men with little wires sewn around the backs of their ears; besides the collar pieces they wore only leather clouts) stepped forward to take his cloak. "Has he been given any food or drink?"

The torturer snored on the bench, knees wide, one hand hanging, calloused knuckles the color of stone, one on his knee, the fingers smeared red here and there dried to brown; his head lolled on the wall.

"I asked: Has he had anything to—Bah!" This to the slave folding his cloak by the door: "That man is fine for stripping the flesh from the backs of your disobedient brothers. But for anything more subtle . . . well, we'll let him sleep." The Suzeraine, who now wore only a leather kilt and very thick-soled sandals (the floor of this chamber sometimes became very messy), walked to the slant board from which hung chains and ropes and against which leaned pokers and pincers. On a table beside the plank were several basins—in one lay a rag which had already turned the water pink. Within the furnace, which took up most of one wall (a ragged canvas curtain hung beside it) a log broke; on the opposite wall the shadow of the grate momentarily darkened and flickered. "How are you feeling?" the Suzeraine asked perfunctorily. "A little better? That's good. Perhaps you enjoy the return of even that bit of good feeling enough to answer my questions accurately and properly. I can't really impress upon you enough how concerned my master is for the answers. He is a very hard taskman, you know—that is, if you know him at all. Krodar wants—but then, we need not sully such an august name with the fetid vapors of this place. The stink of the iron that binds you to that board—I remember a poor, guilty soul lying on the plank as you lie now, demanding of me: 'Don't you even wash the bits of flesh from the last victim off the chains and manacles before you bind up the new one?' " The Suzeraine chuckled. " 'Why should I?' was my answer. True, it makes the place reek. But that stench is a very good reminder—don't you feel it?—of the mortality that is, after all, our only real playing piece in this game of time and pain." The Suzeraine looked up from the bloody basin: a heavy arm, a blocky bicep, corded with high veins, banned at the joint with thin ligament; a jaw in which a muscle quivered under a snarl of patchy beard, here gray, there black, at another place ripped from reddened skin, at still another cut by an old scar; a massive thigh down which sweat trickled, upsetting a dozen other droplets caught in that thigh's coarse hairs, till here a link, there a cord, and elsewhere a rope, dammed it. Sweat crawled under, or overflowed, the dams. "Tell me, Gorgik, have you ever been employed by a certain southern lord, a Lord Aldamir, whose hold is in the Garth Peninsula, only a stone's throw from the Vygernangx Monastery, to act as a messenger between his Lordship and certain weavers, jewelers, potters, and iron mongers in port Kolhari?"

"I have . . . have never . . ." The chest tried to rise under a metal band that would have cramped the breath of a smaller man than Gorgik. ". . . never set foot within the precinct of Garth. Never, I tell you . . . I have told you. . . ."

"And yet—" The Suzeraine, pulling the wet rag from its bowl where it dripped a cherry smeer on the table, turned to the furnace. He wound the rag about one hand, picked up one of the irons sticking from the furnace rack, and drew it out to examine its tip: an ashen rose. "—for reasons you still have not explained to my satisfaction, you wear, on a chain around your neck—" The rose, already dimmer, lowered over Gorgik's chest; the chest hair had been singed in places, adding to the room's stink. "—that." The rose clicked the metal disk that lay on Gorgik's sternum. "These navigational scales, the map etched there, the grid of stars that turns over it and the designs etched around it all speak of its origin in—"

The chest suddenly heaved; Gorgik gave up some sound that tore in the cartilages of his throat.

"Is that getting warm?" The Suzeraine lifted the poker tip. An off-center scorch-mark marred the astrolabe's verdigris. "I was saying: the workmanship is clearly from the south. If you haven't spent time there, why else would you be wearing it?" Then the Suzeraine pressed the poker tip to Gorgik's thigh; Gorgik screamed. The Suzeraine, after a second or two, removed the poker from the blistering mark (amidst the cluster of marks, bubbled, yellow, some crusted over by now). "Let me repeat something to you, Gorgik, about the rules of the game we're playing: the game of time and pain. I said this to you before we began. I say it to you again, but the context of several hour's experience may reweight its meaning for you—and before I repeat it, let me tell you that I shall, as I told you before, eventually repeat it yet again: When the pains are small, in this game, then we make the time very, very long. Little pains, spaced out over the seconds, the minutes—no more than a minute between each—for days on end. Days and days. You have no idea how much I enjoy the prospect. The timing, the ingenuity, the silent comparisons between your responses and the responses of the many, many others I have had the pleasure to work with—that is all my satisfaction. Remember this: on the simplest and most basic level, the infliction of these little torments gives me far more pleasure than would your revealing the information that is their occasion. So if you want to get back at me, to thwart me in some way, to cut short my real pleasure in all of this, perhaps you had best—"

"I told you! I've answered your questions! I've answered them and answered them truthfully! I have never set foot in the Garth! The astrolabe was a gift to me when I was practically a child. I cannot even recall the circumstances under which I received it. Some noble man or woman presented it to me on a whim at some castle or other that I stayed at." (The Suzeraine replaced the poker on the furnace rack and turned to a case, hanging on the stone wall, of small polished knives.) "I am a man who has stayed in many castles, many hovels; I have slept under bridges in the cities, in fine inns and old alleys. I have rested for the night in fields and forests. And I do not mark my history the way you do, cataloguing the gifts and graces I have been lucky enough to—" Gorgik drew a sharp breath.

"The flesh between the fingers—terribly sensitive." The Suzeraine lifted the tiny knife, where a blood drop crawled along the cutting edge. "As is the skin between the toes, on even the most calloused feet. I've known men—not to mention women—who remained staunch under hot pokers and burning pincers who, as soon as I started to make the fewest, smallest cuts in the flesh between the fingers and toes (really, no more than a dozen or so) became astonishingly cooperative. I'm quite serious." He put down the blade on the table edge, picked up the towel from the basin and squeezed; reddened water rilled between his fingers into the bowl. The Suzeraine swabbed at the narrow tongue of blood that moved down the plank below Gorgik's massive (twitching a little now) hand. "The thing wrong with having you slanted like this, head up and feet down, is that even the most conscientious of us finds himself concentrating more on your face, chest, and stomach than, say, on your feet, ankles, and knees. Some exquisite feelings may be produced in the knee: a tiny nail, a small mallet . . . First I shall make a few more cuts. Then I shall wake our friend snoring against the wall. (You scream and he still sleeps! Isn't it amazing? But then, he's had so much of this!) We shall reverse the direction of the slant—head down, feet up —so that we can spread our efforts out more evenly over the arena of your flesh." In another basin, of yellow liquid, another cloth was submerged. The Suzeraine pulled the cloth out and spread it, dripping. "A little vinegar . . ."

Gorgik's head twisted in the clamp across his forehead that had already rubbed to blood at both temples as the Suzeraine laid the cloth across his face.

"A little salt. (Myself, I've always felt that four or five small pains, each of which alone would be no more than a nuisance, when applied all together can be far more effective than a single great one.)" The Suzeraine took up the sponge from the coarse crystals heaped in a third basin (crystals clung, glittering, to the brain-shape) and pressed it against Gorgik's scorched and fresh-blistered thigh. "Now the knife again . . ."

Somewhere, doors clashed.

Gorgik coughed hoarsely and repeatedly under the cloth. Frayed threads dribbled vinegar down his chest. The cough broke into another scream, as another bloody tongue licked over the first.

Other doors, nearer, clashed.

One of the slaves with the wire sewn in his ears turned to look over his shoulder.

The Suzeraine paused in sponging off the knife.

On his bench, without ceasing his snore, the torturer knuckled clumsily at his nose.

The chamber door swung back, grating. Small Sarg ran in, leaped on the wooden top of a cage bolted to the wall (that could only have held a human being squeezed in a very unnatural position), and shouted: "All who are slaves here are now free!"

The Suzeraine turned around with an odd expression. He said: "Oh, not again! Really, this is the *last* time!" He stepped from the table, his shadow momentarily falling across the vinegar rag twisting on Gorgik's face. He moved the canvas hanging aside (furnace light lit faint stairs rising), stepped behind it; the ragged canvas swung to—there was a small, final clash of bolt and hasp.

Small Sarg was about to leap after him, but the torturer suddenly opened his bloodshot eyes, the forehead below his bald skull wrinkled; he lumbered up, roaring.

"Are you free or slave?" Small Sarg shrieked, sword out.

The torturer wore a wide leather neck collar, set about with studs of rough metal, a sign (Small Sarg thought; and he had thought it before) that, if any sign could or should indicate a state somewhere between slavery and freedom, would be it. "Tell me," Small Sarg shrieked again, as the man, eyes bright with apprehension, body sluggish with sleep, lurched forward, "are you slave or free?" (In three castles the studded leather had hidden the bare neck of a free man; in two, the iron collar.) When the torturer seized the edge of the plank where Gorgik was bound—only to steady himself, and yet . . .—Sarg leaped, bringing his sword down. Studded leather cuffing the torturer's forearm deflected the blade; but the same sleepy lurch threw the hulking barbarian (for despite his shaved head, the torturer's heavy features and gold skin spoke as pure a southern origin as Sarg's own) to the right; the blade, aimed only to wound a shoulder, plunged into flesh at the bronze haired solar plexus.

The man's fleshy arms locked around the boy's hard shoulders, joining them in an embrace lubricated with blood. The torturer's face, an inch before Sarg's, seemed to explode in rage, pain, and astonishment. Then the head fell back, eyes opened, mouth gaping. (The torturer's teeth and breath were bad, very bad: this was the first time Small Sarg had ever actually killed a torturer.) The grip relaxed around Sarg's back; the man fell; Sarg staggered, his sword still gripped in one hand, wiping at the blood that spurted high as his chin with the other. "You're free . . . !" Sarg called over his shoulder; the sword came loose from the corpse.

The door slaves, however, were gone. (In two castles, they had gone seeking their own escape; in one, they had come back with guards . . .) Small Sarg turned toward the slanted plank, pulled the rag away from Gorgik's rough beard, flung it to the floor. "Master . . . !"

"So, you are . . . here—again—to . . . free me!"

"I have followed your orders, Master; I have freed every slave I encountered on my way . . ." Suddenly Small Sarg turned back to the corpse. On the torturer's hand-wide belt, among the gnarled studs, was a hook and from the hook hung a clutch of small instruments. Small Sarg searched for the key among them, came up with it. It was simply a metal bar with a handle on one end and a flat side at the other. Sarg ducked behind the board and began twisting the key in locks. On the upper side of the plank, chains fell away and clamps bounced loose. Planks squeaked beneath flexing muscles.

Sarg came up as the last leg clamp swung away from Gorgik's ankle (leaving it red indentations) and the man's great foot hit the floor. Gorgik stood, kneading one shoulder; he pushed again and again at his flank with the heel of one hand. A grin broke his beard. "It's good to see you, boy. For a while I didn't know if I would or not. The talk was all of small pains and long times."

"What did they want from you—this time?" Sarg took the key and reached around behind his own neck, fitted the key in the lock, turned it (for these were barbaric times; the mountain man, named Belham, who had invented the lock and key, had only made one, and no one had yet thought to vary them: different keys for different locks was a refinement not to come for a thousand years), unhinged his collar, and stood, holding it in his soiled hands.

"This time it was some nonsense about working as a messenger in the south—your part of the country." Gorgik took the collar, raised it to his own neck, closed it with a clink. "When you're under the hands of a torturer, with all the names and days and questions, you lose your grip on your own memory. Everything he says sounds vaguely familiar, as if something like it might have once occurred. And even the things you once were sure of lose their patina of reality." A bit of Gorgik's hair had caught in the lock. With a finger, he yanked it loose—at a lull in the furnace's crackling, you could hear hair tear. "Why should I ever go to the Garth? I've avoided it so long I can no longer remember my reasons." Gorgik lifted the bronze disk from his chest and frowned at it. "Because of this, he assumed I must have been there. Some noble gave this to me, how many years ago now? I don't even recall if it was a man or a woman, or what the occasion was." He snorted and let the disk fall. "For a moment I thought they'd melt it into my chest with their cursed pokers." Gorgik looked around, stepped across gory stone. "Well, little master, you've proved yourself once more; and yet once more I suppose it's time to go." He picked up a broad sword leaning against the wall among a pile of weapons, frowned at the edge, scraped at it with the blunt of his thumb. "This will do."

Sarg, stepping over the torturer's body, suddenly bent, hooked a finger under the studded collar, and pulled it down. "Just checking on this one, hey, Gorgik?" The neck, beneath the leather, was iron bound.

"Checking what, little master?" Gorgik looked up from his blade.

"Nothing. Come on, Gorgik."

The big man's step held the ghost of a limp; Small Sarg noted it and beat the worry from his mind. The walk would grow steadier and steadier. (It had before.) "Now we must fight our way out of here and flee this crumbling pile."

"I'm ready for it, little master."

"Gorgik?"

"Yes, master?"

"The one who got away . . . ?"

"The one who was torturing me with his stupid questions?" Gorgik stepped to the furnace's edge, pulled aside the hanging. The door behind it, when he jiggled its rope handle, was immobile and looked to be of plank too thick to batter in. He let the curtain fall again. And the other doors, anyway, stood open.

"Who was he, Gorgik?"

The bearded man made a snorting sound. "We have our campaign, master—to free slaves and end the institution's inequities. The lords of Nevèrÿon have their campaign, their intrigues, their schemes and whims. What you and I know, or should know by now, is how little our and their campaigns actually touch . . . though in place after place they come close enough so that no man or woman can slip between without encounter, if not injury."

"I do not understand . . . ?"

Gorgik laughed, loud as the fire. "That's because I am the slave that I am and you are the master you are." And he was beside Sarg and past him; Small Sarg, behind him, ran.

3

The women shrieked—most of them. Gorgik, below swinging lamps, turned with raised sword to see one of the silent ones crouching against the wall beside a stool—an old woman, most certainly used to the jeweled collar cover, though hers had come off somewhere. There was only iron at her neck now. Her hair was in thin black braids, clearly dyed, and looping her brown forehead. Her eyes caught Gorgik's and perched on his gaze like some terrified creature's, guarding infinite secrets. For a moment he felt an urge, though it did not quite rise clear enough to take words, to question them. Then, in the confusion, a lamp chain broke; burning oil spilled. Guards and slaves and servants ran through a growing welter of flame. The woman was gone. And Gorgik turned, flailing, taking with him only her image. Somehow the castle had (again) been unable to conceive of its own fall at the hands of a naked man—or boy—and had, between chaos and rumor, collapsed into mayhem before the ten, the fifty, the hundred-fifty brigands who had stormed her. Slaves with weapons, guards with pot-tops and farm implements, paid servants carrying mysterious packages either for safety or looting, dashed there and here, all seeming as likely to be taken for foe as friend. Gorgik shouldered against one door; it splintered, swung out, and he was through—smoke trickled after him. He ducked across littered stone, following his shadow flickering with back light, darted through another door that was open

Silver splattered his eyes. He was outside; moonlight splintered through the low leaves of the catalpa above him. He turned, both to see where he'd been and if he were followed, when a figure already clear in the moon, hissed, "Gorgik!" above the screaming inside.

"Hey, little master!" Gorgik laughed and jogged across the rock.

Small Sarg seized Gorgik's arm. "Come on, Gorgik! Let's get out of here. We've done what we can, haven't we?"

Gorgik nodded and, together, they turned to plunge into the swampy forests of Strethi.

Making their way beneath branches and over mud, with silver spills shafting the mists, Small Sarg and Gorgik came, in the humid autumn night, to a stream, a clearing, a scarp—where two women sat at the white ashes of a recent fire, talking softly. And because these were primitive times when certain conversational formalities had not yet grown up to contour discourse among strangers, certain subjects that more civilized times might have banished from the evening were here brought quickly to the fore.

"I see a bruised and tired slave of middle age," said the woman who wore a mask and who had given her name as Raven. With ankles crossed before the moonlit ash, she sat with her arms folded on her raised knees. "From that, one assumes that the youngster is the owner."

"But the boy," added the redhead kneeling beside her, who had given her name as Norema, "is a barbarian, and in this time and place it is the southern barbarians who, when they come this far north, usually end up slaves. The older, for all his bruises, has the bearing of a Kolhari man, whom you'd expect to be the owner."

Gorgik, sitting with one arm over one knee, said: "We are both free men. For the boy the collar is symbolic—of our mutual affection, our mutual protection. For myself, it is sexual—a necessary part in the pattern that allows both action and orgasm to manifest themselves within the single circle of desire. For neither of us is its meaning social, save that it shocks, offends, or deceives."

Small Sarg, also crosslegged but with his shoulders hunched, his elbows pressed to his sides, and his fists on the ground, added, "My master and I are free."

The masked Raven gave a shrill bark that it took seconds to recognize as laughter: "You both claim to be free, yet one of you bears the title 'master' and wears a slave collar at the same time? Surely you are two jesters, for I have seen nothing like this in the length and breadth of this strange and terrible land."

"We are lovers," said Gorgik, "and for one of us the symbolic distinction between slave and master is necessary to desire's consummation."

"We are avengers who fight the institution of slavery wherever we find it," said Small Sarg, "in whatever way we can, and for both of us it is symbolic of our time in servitude and our bond to all men and women still so bound."

"If we have not pledged ourselves to death before capture, it is only because we both know that a living slave can rebel and a dead slave cannot," said Gorgik.

"We have sieged more than seven castles now, releasing the workers locked in the laboring pens, the kitchen and house slaves, and the administrative slaves alike. As well, we have set upon those men who roam through the land capturing and selling men and women as if they were property. Between castles and countless brigands, we have freed many who had only to find a key for their collars. And in these strange and barbaric times, any key will do."

The redheaded Norema said: "You love as master and slave and you fight the institution of slavery? The contradiction seems as sad to me as it seemed amusing to my friend."

"As one word uttered in three different situations may mean three entirely different things, so the collar worn in three different situations may mean three different things. They are not the same: sex, affection, and society," said Gorgik. "Sex and society relate like an object and its image in a reflecting glass. One reverses the other—are you familiar with the phenomenon, for these *are* primitive times, and mirrors are rare—"

"I am familiar with it," said Norema and gave him a long, considered look.

Raven said: "We are two women who have befriended each other in this strange and terrible land, and we have no love for slavers. We've killed three now in the two years we've traveled together—slavers who've thought to take us as property. It is easy, really, here where the men expect the women to scream and kick and bite and slap, but not to plan and place blades in their gut."

Norema said: "Once we passed a gang of slavers with a herd of ten women in collars and chains, camped for the night. We descended on them—from their shouts they seemed to think they'd been set on by a hundred fighting men."

Sarg and Gorgik laughed; Norema and Raven laughed—all recognizing a phenomenon.

"You know," mused Norema, when the laughter was done, "the only thing that allows you and ourselves to pursue our liberations with any success is that the official policy of Nevèrÿon goes against slavery under the edict of the Child Empress."

"Whose reign," said Gorgik, absently, "is just and generous."

"Whose reign," grunted the masked woman, "is a sun-dried dragon turd."

"Whose reign—" Gorgik smiled—"is currently insufferable, if not insecure."

Norema said: "To mouth those conservative formulas and actively oppose slavery seems to me the same sort of contradiction as the one you first presented us with." She took a reflective breath. "A day ago we stopped near here at the castle of the Suzeraine of Strethi. He was amused by us and entertained us most pleasantly. But we could not help notice that his whole castle was run by slaves, men and women. But we smiled, and ate slave-prepared food—and were entertaining back."

Gorgik said: "It was the Suzeraine's castle that we last sieged."

Small Sarg said: "And the kitchen slaves, who probably prepared your meal, are now free."

The two women, masked and unmasked, smiled at each other, smiles within which were inscribed both satisfaction and embarrassment.

"How do you accomplish these sieges?" Raven asked.

"One of the other of us, in the guise of a free man without collar, approaches a castle where we have heard there are many slaves and delivers an ultimatum." Gorgik grinned. "Free your slaves or . . ."

"Or what?" asked Raven.

"To find an answer to that question, they usually cast the one of us who came into the torture chamber. At which point the other of us, decked in the collar—it practically guarantees one entrance if one knows which doors to come in by—lays siege to the hold."

"Only," Small Sarg said, "this time it didn't work like that. We were together, planning our initial strategy, when suddenly the Suzeraine's guards attacked us. They seemed to know who Gorgik was. They called him by name and almost captured us both."

"Did they, now?" asked Norema.

"They seemed already to have their questions for me. At first I thought they knew what we had been doing. But these are strange and barbaric times; and information travels slowly here."

"What did they question you about?" Raven wanted to know.

"Strange and barbaric things," said Gorgik. "Whether I had worked as a messenger for some southern lord, carrying tales of children's bouncing balls and other trivial imports. Many of their questions centered about . . ." He looked down, fingering the metal disk hanging against his chest. As he gazed, you could see, from his tensing cheek muscle, a thought assail him.

Small Sarg watched Gorgik. "What is it . . . ?"

Slowly Gorgik's brutish features formed a frown. "When we were fighting our way out of the castle, there was a woman . . . a slave. I'm sure she was a slave. She wore the collar . . . But she reminded me of another woman, a noble woman, a woman I knew a long time ago . . ." Suddenly he smiled. "Though she too wore the collar from time to time, much for the same reasons as I."

The matted haired barbarian, the western woman in her mask, the island woman with her cropped hair sat about the silvered ash and watched the big man turn the disk. "When I was in the torture chamber, my thoughts were fixed on my own campaign for liberation and not on what to me seemed the idiotic fixations of my oppressor. Thus all their questions and comments are obscure to me now. By the same token, the man I am today obscures my memories of the youthful slave released from the bondage of the mines by this noble woman's whim. Yet, prompted by that face this evening, vague memories of then and now emerge and confuse themselves without clarifying. They turn about this instrument, for measuring time and space . . . they have to do with the name Krodar . . ."

The redhead said: "I have heard that name, Krodar . . ."

Within the frayed eyeholes, the night-blue eyes narrowed; Raven glanced at her companion.

Gorgik said: "There was something about a monastery in the south, called something like the Vygernangx . . ."

The masked woman said: "Yes, I know of the Vygernangx . . ."

The redhead glanced back at her friend with a look set between complete blankness and deep knowingness.

Gorgik said: "And there was something about the balls, the toys we played with as children . . . or perhaps the rhyme we played to . . . ?"

Small Sarg said: "When I was a child in the jungles of the south, we would harvest the little modules of sap that seeped from the scars in certain broadleafed palms and save them up for the traders who would come every spring for them . . ."

Both women looked at each other now, then at the men, and remained silent.

"It is as though—" Gorgik held up the verdigrised disk with its barbarous chasings—"all these things would come together in a logical pattern, immensely complex and greatly beautiful, tying together slave and empress, commoner and lord—even gods and demons—to show how all are related in a negotiable pattern, like some sailor's knot, not yet pulled taut, but laid out on the dock in loose loops, so that simply to see it in such form were to comprehend it even when yanked tight. And yet . . ." He turned the astrolabe over. ". . . they will *not* clear in my mind to any such pattern!"

Raven said: "The lords of this strange and terrible land indeed live lives within such complex and murderous knots. We have all seen them whether one has sieged a castle or been seduced by the hospitality of one; we have all had a finger through at least a loop in such a knot. You've talked of mirrors, pretty man, and of their strange reversal effect. I've wondered if our ignorance isn't simply a reversed image of their knowledge."

"And I've wondered—" Gorgik said, "slave, free-commoner, lord —if each isn't somehow a reflection of the other; or a reflection of a reflection."

"They are not," said Norema with intense conviction. "*That* is the most horrendous notion I've ever heard." But her beating lids, her astonished expression as she looked about in the moonlight, might have suggested to a sophisticated enough observer a conversation somewhere in her past of which this was the reflection.

Gorgik observed her, and waited.

After a while Norema picked up a stick, poked in the ashes with it: a single coal turned up ruby in the silver scatter and blinked.

After a moments, Norema said: "Those balls . . . that the children play with in summer on the streets of Kolhari . . . Myself, I've always wondered where they came from—I mean I know about the orchards in the south. But I mean *how* do they get to the city every year."

"You don't know that?" Raven turned, quite astonished, to her redheaded companion. "You mean to tell me, island woman, that you and I have traveled together for over a year and a half, seeking fortune and adventure, and you have never asked me this nor have I ever told you?"

Norema shook her head.

Again Raven loosed her barking laughter. "Really, what is most strange and terrible about this strange and terrible land is how two women can be blood friends, chattering away for days at each other, saving one another's lives half a dozen times running and yet somehow never really talk! Let me tell you: the Western Crevasse, from which I hail, has, running along its bottom, a river that leads to the Eastern Ocean. My people live the whole length of the river, and those living at the estuary are fine, seafaring women. It is our boats, crewed by these sailing women of the Western Crevasse, who each year have sailed to the south in our red ships and brought back these toys to Kolhari, as indeed they also trade them up and down the river." A small laugh now, a sort of stifled snorting. "I was twenty and had already left my home before I came to one of your ports and the idea struck me that a man could actually *do* the work required on a boat."

"Aye," said Gorgik, "I saw those boats in my youth—but we were always scared to talk with anyone working on them. The captain was always a man; and we assumed, I suppose, that he must be a very evil person to have so many women within his power. Some proud, swaggering fellow—as frequently a foreigner as one of your own men—"

"Yes," said Norema. "I remember such a boat. The crew was all women and the captain was a great, black-skinned fellow who terrified everyone in my island village—"

"The captain a man?" The masked woman frowned beneath her mask's ragged hem. "I know there are boats from your Ulvayn islands on which men and women work together. But a man for a captain on a boat of my people . . . ? It is so unlikely that I am quite prepared to dismiss it as an outright imposs—" She stopped; then she barked, "Of course. The man on the boat! Oh, yes, my silly heathen woman, of course there is a man on the boat. There's always a man on the boat. But he's certainly *not* the Captain. Believe me, my friend, even though I have seen men fulfil it, Captain is a woman's job: and in our land it is usually the eldest sailor on the boat who takes the job done by your captain."

"If it wasn't the captain, then," asked Norema, "who was he?"

"How can I explain it to you . . . ?" Raven said. "There is always a man in a group of laboring women in my country. But he is more like a talisman, or a good-luck piece the women take with them, than a working sailor—much less an officer. He is a figure of prestige, yes, which explains his fancy dress; but he is not a figure of power. Indeed, do you know the wooden women who are so frequently carved on the prow of your man-sailored ships? Well he fulfils a part among our sailors much as that wooden woman does among yours. I suppose to you it seems strange. But in our land, a single woman lives with a harem of men; and in our land, any group of women at work always keeps a single man. Perhaps it is simply another of your reflections? But you, in your strange and terrible land, can see nothing *but* men at the heads of things. The captain indeed! A pampered pet who does his exercises every morning on the deck, who preens and is praised and shown off at every port—that is what men are for. And, believe me, they love it, no matter what they say. But a man . . . a *man* with power and authority and the right to make decisions? You must excuse me, for though I have been in your strange and terrible land for years and know such things exist here, I still cannot think of such things among my own people without laughing." And here she gave her awkward laugh, while with her palm she beat her bony knee. "Seriously," she said when her laugh was done, "such a pattern for work seems so natural to me that I cannot really believe you've never encountered anything like it before—" she was talking to Norema now—"even here."

Norema smiled, a little strangely. "Yes, I . . . I have heard of something like it before."

Gorgik again examined the redhead's face, as if he might discern, inscribed by eye-curve and cheek-bone and forehead-line and lip-shape what among her memories reflected this discussion.

Something covered the moon.

First masked Raven, then the other three, looked up. Wide wings labored off the light.

"What is such a mountain beast doing in such a flat and swampy land?" asked Small Sarg.

"It must be the Suzeraine's pet," Norema said. "But why should he have let it go?"

"So," said Raven, "once again tonight we are presented with a mysterious sign and no way to know whether it completes a pattern or destroys one." The laugh this time was something that only went on behind her closed lips. "They cannot fly very far. There is no ledge for her to perch on. And once she lands, in this swampy morass, she won't be able to regain flight. Her wings will tear in the brambles and she will never fly again."

But almost as if presenting the image of some ironic answer, the wings flapped against a sudden, high, unfelt breeze, and the beast, here shorn of all fables, rose and rose—for a while—under the night.

The first novel set in fairyland in the English language is Phantasmion *by* SARA COLERIDGE, *and as such, its historical importance cannot be underestimated.* Phantasmion *was written by the daughter of the poet Samuel Taylor Coleridge, whose contributions to the fantastic in poetry are second only to Poe. It was popular enough to be reprinted in the latter part of the nineteenth century but has not been republished since.*

from *Phantasmion*
BY SARA COLERIDGE

CHAPTER I

THE FAIRY POTENTILLA APPEARS TO THE YOUNG PRINCE PHANTASMION

A young boy hid himself from his nurse in sport, and strayed all alone in the garden of his father, a rich and mighty prince; he followed the bees from flower to flower, and wandered further than he had ever gone before, till he came to the hollow tree where they hived, and watched them entering their storehouse laden with the treasures they had collected; he lay upon the turf, laughing and talking to himself, and, after a while, he plucked a long stiff blade of grass, and was about to thrust it in at the entrance of the hive, when a voice just audible above the murmur of the bees, cried "Phantasmion!" Now the child thought that his nurse was calling him in strange tones, and he started, saying, "Ah! Leeliba!" and looked round; but casting up his eyes he saw that there stood before him an ancient woman, slenderer in figure than his nurse, yet more firm and upright, and with a countenance which made him afraid. "What dost thou here, Phantasmion?" said the stranger to the little boy, and he made no answer: then she looked sweetly upon the child, for he was most beautiful and she said to him, "Whom dost thou take me for?" and he replied, "At first I took thee for my nurse, but now I see plainly that thou art not like her." "And how am I different from thy nurse?" said the strange woman. The boy was about to answer, but he stopped short and blushed; then after a pause he said, "One thing that thou hast wings upon thy shoulders, and she has none." "Phantasmion!" she replied, "I am not like thy nurse: I can do that which is beyond her skill, great as thou thinkest it." At this the boy laughed, and said with a lively countenance, pointing to the hollow tree, "Could'st thou make the bees that have gone in there fly out of their hive all in one swarm?" The fairy stayed not to answer, but touched the decayed trunk with her wand, and the bees poured out of their receptacle by thousands and thousands, and hung in a huge cluster from the branch of a sycamore; and as the child looked upon the swarm, it seemed to be composed of living diamonds, and glanced so brilliantly in the sunshine that it dazzled the sight. And the beautiful boy laughed aloud, and leaped into the air, and clapped his hands for joy. Then the fairy placed her wand within his little palm, saying, "Strike the tree, and say, 'Go in!' and they shall all enter the hive again." The cheeks of the young boy blushed brighter than ever, and his eyes sparkled, as he struck the hollow trunk with all his might, and cried, "Go in! Go in!" No sooner had he done this than the whole multitude quitted the branch of the sycamore, and disappeared within the body of the tree.

Then the ancient woman said to the little prince, "Wilt thou give me that pomegranate?" and she pointed to the only ripe one which grew on a tree hard by. One member of the trunk of this pomegranate tree leaned forward, and invited the adventurous child to mount; he quickly crept along it, and having plucked the fruit which the fairy had pointed out, he turned round and tried to descend: but finding that he should slip if he attempted to return by the way he came, having measured the height from the ground with his eye, he boldly sprang at once from the bough to the turf below, and presented his prize to the stranger. With that she took it from his hand, and, looking kindly upon him, she said, "My little Phantasmion, thou needest no fairy now to work wonders for thee, being yet so young that all thou beholdest is new and marvellous in thine eyes. But the day must come when this happiness will fade away; when the stream, less clear than at its outset, will no longer return such bright reflections; then, if thou wilt repair to this pomegranate tree, and call upon the name of Potentilla, I will appear before thee, and exert all my power to renew the delights and wonders of thy childhood."

After speaking these words, Potentilla vanished; the child opened his eyes wide, and, now feeling afraid to be alone, he ran homeward as fast as possible, and in a little time heard the voice of his mother calling to him in quick tones; for she had outrun his nurse, who was also hastening in search of him. The child bounded up to her, and with breathless eagerness sought to describe the strange things which he had seen. "All the bees came out in a cluster," cried he, "and they were dressed in diamonds! thousands and millions of them hung together upon a branch! and I my own self made every one of the bees go back again into their hive, with the shining stick which the old woman lent me." "What old woman?" replied Queen Zalia to her little son; "was it one of the gardeners' wives?" "O no!" said he; "an old woman with wings on her shoulders, and she flew up and vanished away, like the bubbles which I blow through my pipe." "Thou hast been dreaming, my sweet boy," said his mother; "thou hast fallen asleep in the sunshine, and hast dreamt all this." "No, no! my mother," the child replied; "indeed, indeed it was quite unlike those dreams which I have at night. I wish the bees could speak that they might tell thee all about it, for they saw the winged woman as well as I."

CHAPTER II

POTENTILLA FULFILS HER PROMISE TO PHANTASMION

Soon afterwards Phantasmion's fair mother, Zalia, fell sick and died. Her young son was kept from the chamber of death, and, roaming about the palace in search of her, he found a little child sitting on the floor of a lonely chamber, afraid to stir because he was by himself. "The people are all gone away," cried Phantasmion; "Come, I will take thee abroad to see the pretty flowers, now the sun shines so bright." The child was glad to have fresh air and company, and, holding fast by the older boy's hand, he sped along with short quick steps further than his tiny feet had ever carried him before, lisping about the bees and hornets, which, in his ignorance he would fain have caught, as they buzzed past him, and laughing merrily when his frolicsome guide led him right through a bed of feathered columbines, for the sake of seeing the urchin's rosy cheek brushed by soft blossoms and powdered with flower dust. At last they entered the queen's pleasure ground, where only one gardener remained, and he was sitting on the path, gathering berries in a basket. "Where is my mother?" cried the prince, leaping suddenly behind him; "hast thou hidden her away, old man?" "Thy mother is dead!" answered he, looking up in the boy's face; and it was the glance of his eye, more than the words he spoke, which made Phantasmion shudder. The menial smoothed his brow, and with humble courtesy offered a branch of crimson fruit to the young prince, who flung it on the ground, crying in a haughty tone, "How darest thou say that my mother is dead?" "Go to her chamber, and see;" replied the man sternly. "And how can I see her if she is dead?" rejoined the boy, with a tremulous laugh; "can I see the cloud of yesterday in yon clear sky? like clouds the dead vanish away, and we see them no more." Just then he spied the young child lying down, with the fruit-branch dropping out of his fingers, and his face buried in a flowery tuft. "What! hiding among the heartsease?" cried he; "ah! let me hide too." Then, putting his face close to that of his charge, "How cold the little cheek is!" he cried; "come, raise it up to the warm sun." Hearing these words the gardener turned the child's face upwards, and behold he was dead; his lips smeared with berry juice, and his pale swollen cheeks covered with purple spots! Then he held out the body to the startled boy, and showing the slack limbs and glazed eye, while his own shot fire like that of a panther:—"So look the dead," cried he, "ere they vanish away: just so Queen Zalia is looking!" Phantasmion shrieked, and hastening home, he met his mother's funeral procession going forth from the palace. The body was wrapped in a shroud, and black plumes nodded over the face; but he saw the dead hands, and the limbs stretched upon the bier. From that time forth he never spoke of Queen Zalia, but he often beheld her in dreams, and often he dreamed of the old man who told him she was dead, and who disappeared, on the same day, from the royal household.

Phantasmion grieved but little when his father died a year afterwards; for he scarcely knew King Dorimant's face, that warlike prince having been wholly engaged, since the birth of his child, in a fruitless search after mines of iron. It was commonly believed that ill success in this matter hastened his end; but the people about the palace well knew that he died of eating poisoned honey.

Thus Phantasmion was yet too young, when he inherited the throne of Palmland, to be a king in reality; and those who governed the land sought to keep him a child as long as possible. They prevented him from learning how to reign, but could not succeed in making him content with mere pomp and luxury; for his pleasures were so closely set that they hindered one another's growth, and, by the time that he attained to his full stature, nothing gratified him, except the society of a noble youth who came to visit his court from a foreign country, and who interested his mind by curious histories and glowing descriptions. Dariel of Tigridia was well skilled in the management of fruit trees and flowers; he had brought seeds of many fine sorts from distant lands, and at the desire of Phantasmion, he sowed them in the royal garden. One morning he came to the prince, saying, "The rare plant has put forth leaves; come and look at it!" "Earlier even than we expected!" cried the prince, rising joyfully from his seat. "I will not only see, but taste and try." The two youths took their way through a flowery labyrinth, talking much of the wondrous plant and the virtues of its leaves; but just as they were drawing nigh to the nook where it grew, several scorpions fastened all at once on Dariel's sandaled foot, and stung it with such violence, that, quitting his comrade's arm, he sprang into the air, and then fell prostrate under the towering lilies. Phantasmion carried him to the palace, and placed him tenderly on a couch. After a time, seeing that he continued in a languishing state, he made an infusion of the leaves which his friend had so highly extolled, and silently gave it to Dariel instead of the drink which the physician had ordered; but, just as he expected to see the poor youth revived by this kind act, his head sank on the pillow, a blue tinge stole over his cheek, and, when the prince had gazed upon his altered face for a few minutes, he plainly saw that it told no longer of sickness, but of death. Not, however, till decay had wrought a still more ghastly change in Dariel's comely countenance, Phantasmion quitted the side of his couch; then, overpowered with sorrow, he roamed abroad, and sought the forest of lilies which his comrade's hand had reared: the sun was bright, the air fresh, but all that flowery multitude was drooping and ready to perish; cankerworms had gnawed their roots, and the wondrous plant itself had been attacked by such numbers of insects that scarce a trace of it remained.

This circumstances deepened the melancholy which had seized on the spirit of Phantasmion. He began to think that all persons and things connected with himself were doomed to misfortune; and when this channel of thought was once opened, a hundred rills poured into it at once, and filled it to the brim.

He reflected on the early deaths of his father and mother, as he had never reflected on them before: the black plumes and solemn tapers of the chamber where King Dorimant lay in state rose up before him, while Zalia stretched on her bier, and the strange man holding out his little comrade's body, visited him again as in the dreams of his childhood. These and other remembrances, grouped together under one aspect of gloom, all wore the same visionary twilight hue, and inspired the same sadness. He turned away from cheerful faces, and was constantly expecting to see the ghost of Dariel, a shadowy image of his swollen corpse.

Phantasmion had spent many days in this state of dejection, when he wandered forth after a sleepless night, one clear morning, and, refreshed by the breath of early dawn, began to slumber under the boughs of a pomegranate tree. No sooner had he closed his eyes than the fairy, whom he had formerly seen on that very spot, seemed to stand there again. In his dream she touched him with her wand, and forthwith leafy branches, like those which drooped over him, sprouted from his shoulders; imperceptibly those branches changed into green wings and up he soared, feeling as if his whole body were inflated with air. As he floated along in the sky a group of angel faces shone before him: he surveyed them, and all were lovely, but one was far lovelier than the rest, and, while he gazed upon that countenance, it grew more and more exquisite, the others becoming indistinct and fading gradually away. Suddenly, like a balloon exhausted of air, down he dropped to the earth, and was snatched away from the vision. "Potentilla!" he cried aloud; starting up in the intensity of feeling, and stretching out both his hands, "Potentilla! help! help!" No sooner had he uttered that long forgotten name, than he opened his eyes, and saw the little old fairy smiling in his face. "Phantasmion," she said, "what shall I do for thee? I am queen of the insect realm, and powers like those which insects have, are mine to bestow." "Give me wings!" he cried; for still he had a vague hope that he might once more behold that heavenly face if he could but soar aloft.

Potentilla waved her wand, and soon the air was filled with butterflies, those angel insects pouring from every region of the heavens. Here came a long train arrayed in scarlet, waving up and down altogether like a flag of triumph; there floated a band clad in deep azure, and flanked on either side by troops in golden panoply. Some were like flights of green leaves, others twinkled in robes of softest blue besprent with silver, like young princesses at a festival; and, in front of the whole multitude, a gorgeous crowd, adorned with peacock eyes flew round and round in a thousand starry wheels, while here and there one butterfly would flit aloof for a few moments, then sink into the circle and revolve indistinguishably with the rest: now the entire wheel flew off into splinters, now reconstructed itself at once, as if but a single life informed its several parts.

Again Potentilla waved her wand, and the bloomy throng descended on trees and shrubs, attiring every bough in fresh blossoms, which quivered without a breeze. Phantasmion saw that he was to choose from this profusion of specimens the wings that pleased him best, and he fixed on a set like those which he wore in his dream. The moment that Potentilla touched him with her wand a sensation of lightness ran throughout his body, and instantly afterwards he perceived that wings played on his shoulders, wings of golden green adorned with black embroidery: beneath an emerald coronet his radiant locks clustered in large soft rings, and wreathed themselves around his snowy forehead: robes of white silk floated over his buoyant limbs, and his full eyes, lately closed in languor, beamed with joyful expectation, while more than child-like bloom rose mantling to his cheek. Potentilla had seen an eagle teaching her young ones to fly, gradually widening her airy circles, and mounting in a spiral line that swelled as it rose, while the sun burnished her golden plumes; just so she flew before the winged youth, who timidly followed where she led the way, trembling in his first career when he saw the earth beneath him. But, gaining confidence, all at once he shot away from his guide, like a spark from a sky-rocket; he soared and gyred and darted on high, describing as many different figures as a skater on the ice, while from the groves and flowery meads below this choral strain resounded:—

> *See the bright stranger!*
> *On wings of enchantment,*
> *See how he soars!*
> *Eagles! that high on the crest of the mountain,*
> *Beyond where the cataracts gush from their fountain,*
> *Look out o'er the sea and her glistering shores,*
> *Cast your sun-gazing eyes on his pinions of light!*
> *Behold how he glitters*
> *Transcendently bright!*
>
> *Whither, ah whither,*
> *To what lofty region*
> *His course will he bend?*

See him! O, see him! the clouds overtaking,
As though the green earth he were blythely forsaking;
Ah now, in swift circles behold him descend!
Now again like a meteor he shoots through the sky,
Or a star glancing upward,
To sparkle on high!

CHAPTER III

PHANTASMION SEES AND HEARS STRANGE THINGS BY THE SEA SHORE

Phantasmion left the shadows of earth behind him, while he soared so high that green fields, and blue waters, gardens, and groves, all melted into one, and even that heavenly sight which had first made him pray for wings was itself forgotten in the pleasure of flying. He thought it a delightful novelty to rush down upon the heron like the trained hawk, or aim a javelin at some bird of prey as she stooped upon her quarry; to whirl upward with the glede, drop down like a shot side by side with the jer-falcon, disperse the swallows in the midst of their aerial dances, or sweep the cope of heaven in pursuit of the swift: then hovering aloft in perfect stillness, with green pinions and floating robes, he attracted crowds of gazers, who marvelled how a bird of paradise could look so large at such a wondrous height. One fine clear day he flew southward to the ocean, and pursued a sea eagle to the highest ether. At first setting off he was rudely brushed by vultures, hurrying down to feast upon a carcase which lay rocking on the waves: he thrust among them with his drawn sword, and pushed onward, leaving a cloud of his delicate plumelets fluttering in the air. Having arrived at last where the atmosphere was too thin for anything but a bird to breathe, he hastily began to descend; but, faint and weary, scarce saw his way before him, and dropped full on the back of the eagle's mate, jerking out of her clutches a load of fish just caught for her young. Enraged at this loss, she pursued Phantasmion, and with her strong beak shattered one of his pinions ere he had time to gain a cliff towards which he was steering; so that, being no longer able to direct his course aright, he fell with violence, and lay stunned upon the rugged shore. While he leaned upon his arm, just recovering from the shock, and surveyed the ocean with dazzled eyes, he perceived a strange woman's form rising out of the waves, and gliding towards the beach: a wreath of living moving flowers, like sea-anemones, clung round her head, from which the slimy locks of whitish blue hung down till they met the waters; her skin was thick and glistering; there was a glaze upon it which made Phantasmion shiver; and, trailing her sinuous body beside the place where the youth lay, she cast a glance towards him, with her moony eyes of yellow green, at which his blood ran cold: but on she went, and turned round a crag which jutted into the sea beyond the fallen prince. Still scarce recovered, Phantasmion arose and leaned against the lower end of this rock, which, like a buttress, projected from the main body of the cliff; the shattered pinion drooped to the ground, while the wings on the left side were half-expanded, and lay languidly against the white stone, like a green branch amid unseasonable snow. And now other sounds caught his ear, beside the roar and hiss of advancing and retiring waves. He stood on tiptoe, and looking down into a recess on the other side of the rock, beheld the shape that had lately passed him, reclining on the shore, and staring up in the face of a lofty dame, who talked aloud with passionate tones and gestures. She whose voice Phantasmion heard stood with her back towards him; he saw not her face, but he observed that she wore purple robes and a jewelled crown. "Ah me!" she cried, "the beautiful Iarine! Glandreth has called her 'the beautiful Iarine:' teach me how to countervail the charms of this fair girl, and to secure the heart of Glandreth." To this the fishy woman made no reply, save a murmuring sound of laughter; whereat the crowned lady exclaimed, in a shrill voice, "Remember thy vow to the king, my father, when he caught thee in his toils upon the shore." Then the woman-fish replied, "Have I not redeemed that vow? Did I not lend thee spells to bewitch the heart of Albinian? and is it not through me that thou art Queen of this Land of Rocks? Without guerdon I will serve thee no longer." The crowned lady put her hands before her face, and groaned deeply. At length she made answer, "Be satisfied, Seshelma! the babe shall be thine. Help me to remove Iarine from the sight of Glandreth; help me to destroy the hostile house of Magnart, and thou shalt have thy desire." Then the crowned woman sat down below the rock, and listened to the words of her whom she called Seshelma, and the two seemed to be contriving some plot. Phantasmion could not understand all that was said, for Seshelma discoursed in a low gurgling murmur; but he heard her speak of poisonous fish, and of a charmed vessel, and of a damsel named Iarine. In the end she drew from an oyster-shell a glittering net, and offered it to her companion, who took it from her flabby hand, then rose, and, lifting up her embroidered train, went her way leisurely, as if absorbed in thought. But Seshelma returned into the sea, and, again rowing past Phantasmion, she looked up in his face with the same hideous leer which had chilled his blood before; then diving into the deeper water, she quickly disappeared.

Phantasmion stood for some time gazing on the flood, almost expecting that some new shape would rise out of it. He mused on what had passed, and could not help in some sort connecting it with his heavenly dream. A lady, young and beautiful, was hated and persecuted; powers of earth and sea were leagued against her. He pictured this fair Iarine with the countenance which he had beholden in the vision, and longed to find her and rescue her from peril.

The Prince now bethought him that he was a long way from his royal palace, having fallen on the borders of Rockland, a country adjoining his own dominions; he therefore hastened from the coast, holding up the disabled wing with his hand, and journeyed homeward on foot. After a night's sleep, he repaired to the pomegranate tree, but felt unable to express the imaginations that haunted his mind while Potentilla stood before him. He told the fairy, when she begged to know his pleasure, that he was tired of his butterfly pinions, and wished to try new experiments. "Make my feet," said he, "like those of flies, which climb up the mirrors or walk over the roof of my marble hall; enable me to follow wherever one of those insects can steal along." He had no sooner spoken thus than Potentilla removed the wings she had given him, and fitted to his feet the suckers of flies. This gift pleased Phantasmion well, and he spent the remainder of that day in gliding along the walls and over the vaulted ceilings of his palace, or scaling the pillar-like stems of the loftiest palm trees. Those who witnessed his feats were amazed; but it had been commonly believed that the race of the Palmland kings was under the protection of some mysterious being, and this tale, which had of late years been forgotten, was now recalled to mind with fresh awe and wonder.

Distinguished fantasist Ursula K. Le Guin has maintained that the three greatest adult fantasists of this century are E. R. Eddison, J. R. R. Tolkien, and KENNETH MORRIS. *Morris is the least known, since only two volumes of his work were published commercially during his lifetime, both as children's books. His use of Welsh and Oriental mythologies in his writing is acute and deeply perceptive, but his primary importance is that he resurrected the medieval Celtic fantasy world that has become such a major and prevalent setting for fantasy in this century. Morris devoted his life to the promulgation of theosophy, for decades in California and finally in his native Wales. Much of his short fiction has never been reprinted since its initial appearance in the publications of the Theosophical Society, many of which Morris himself edited, including the second two pieces reprinted here for the first time. A volume of his stories,* The Collected Tales of Kenneth Morris, *edited by Douglas Anderson, is forthcoming.*

3 Tales
BY KENNETH MORRIS

The Sapphire Necklace

(SUGGESTED BY THE COSMIC JOKE OF BEETHOVEN)

Here is the Bringing-in of it: Nothing was more treasured and admired in the Court of the Nooivray of old than a Sapphire Necklace that the princes and regents of the constellations had given the Queen of the Nooivray for her birthday. There were thirteen blue amazing gems in it, that had been mined, cut, polished, and endowed with magical peculiarities in thirteen several stars: to wit, in Altair and Aldebaran, in Vindemiatrix and Fomalhaut, Arcturus and Capella, Sirius and Procyon, Rigel and Betelgeuze, Regulus and Algol and Unukalhai; and their chief peculiarity was that by looking intently into any one of them, you could see in it the destinies of its native star through the age of ages; by reason of which these sapphires were of more value than any others, and the Necklace was without its peer in heaven. So there was grand consternation throughout the galaxies when it was lost.

Here is how the loss happened: A squat little god by the name of Ghuggg came begging to the door of the King of Nooivray's palace at one time; and the one that opened to him went in to get him a bite and a sup and a present, leaving him at the open door. Now he was exceedingly gifted in thiefcraft, so that there wasn't his equal at it in the four quarters of the universe; and no sooner was he left alone there, than his art and his craft and his great gifts stood him in stead, and he procured the Necklace dishonestly, and was away before man or dog could so much as suspect him, let alone pursue and capture. As to where he retired with it, to gloat over his spoils and his cunning: it was to a little, rough, uncouth planet he had in a dark region of space beyond the mountains and the Brink of Things; and there he sat chuckling in the cellar, with the necklace about the place where his neck would have been had he had one; only there was little difference between the head and the body of him, but that the one was uglier than the other—and none could say which that was. He had no light in the cellar, but what came from the sapphires; and that was less than you would think, on account of the heavy grief that had overtaken them, and their shame at the indignity they were suffering. He sat there endeavoring to console them; for he desired them to be at their best.

"Come now," said he; "shame and grief are unbecoming in you; I beseech you to eschew and evitate them religiously! It was your destiny to be rescued by me, that your evolution might be accomplished; rejoice therefore, that that which was to be has indeed befallen!"

But the King of the Nooivray was at a loss; and at a loss were the great barons of his court, the princes and regents of the constellations and stars. So he called them together in council, and held a Gorsedd in a circle of stones near the Pleiades. "Is there any of you has advice to give?" said he. "Such a disaster has not befallen us since Cuthrile king of Iffairn made ice of the universe of old."

"If you would take advice of mine," said the Chieftain of Capricorn, "you would take counsel of the man who saved you then. Merlin Druid you would consult, by my great dominion in heaven!"

"Good advice is that!" said several of them. Then said the King's Heir of Fomalhaut:

"He had a rose-garden eastward of your principality at one time, Lord Capricorn."

"He had," said Capricorn; "and by the splendor of my stars, he has now."

"It is a wonder he was not invited here," said the King of the Nooivray. "Lord Unukalhai, go you with your following upon an embassy to him, if it please you."

So Unukalhai and the stars of the Serpent rode forth, and came to the rose-garden, and to Merlin Druid trimming the roses; and prayed him come with them to the Gorsedd.

"Well, well now," said Merlin Druid; "well, well now! It is the Sapphire Necklace is lost from you, I shouldn't wonder?"

"The Sapphire Necklace it is, and lost from us it is."

"There will be little need for me to come to the Gorsedd," said Merlin. "Were you hearing tell of Gelliwic in Cornwall at any time?"

They consulted together. "We were not," said Unukalhai.

"Or of Caerleon on Usk in Wales?"

"Lord Druid," said Unukalhai, "few will not have heard of Caerleon on Usk."

"There is a man enthroned there by the name of Arthur Emperor," said Merlin. "Go you, if it please you, to him; and he will recover the Necklace for you."

But they doubted they were a sufficient embassy to go to the Emperor Arthur; and returned instead to the Gorsedd, and gave the King of the Nooivray what news they had. "Well, well; we must send to him," said the King; "though it would seem unlikely that a mortal would find what we ourselves are at a loss over."

So then he chose ambassadors to send: Aldebaran, and Fomalhaut, and Unukalhai, with all their retinues. And they set out, and rode through the bluebell woods and the larkspur meads of heaven, and along the margin of the sea; and came at sunset to Caerleon on Usk; and Glewlwyd Gafaelfawr admitted them into the feast and the presence of Arthur. Until dawn they were at meat and mead in the hall there. Then the Emperor said: "I will listen to your message, Lords Princes of the Stars."

They told him what they knew about the Sapphire Necklace. "Is there one of you that has handled it or the jewels it is composed of?" he asked.

"The three of us have," they answered. "Three of the jewels are from the three stars wherein we reign."

"Call Ol the son of Olwydd," said Arthur Emperor. Ol was such a man that seven years before he was born his father's swine were stolen, and when he grew up a man he tracked the swine, and brought them home in seven herds. Very powerful was his olfactory endowment of genius.

"Ol son of Olwydd," said the Emperor; "could you track the jewels as you tracked the swine?"

"Let us get to horse, and away!" said Ol.

And now here is the Story itself: without concealment, understatement, or exaggeration:

So the Arthurians rode away under their lord Arthur with the ambassadors of the King of the Nooivray: along the margin of the sea, and through the larkspur meadows and the bluebell woods of heaven. And they came at last to the foot of mountains higher than any in the world or Wales.

"Ha," said Ol fab Olwydd; "the Sapphire Necklace has been here."

"A marvel if it has," said proud Aldebaran; "not one of the stones was mined in these regions."

"Lord Arthur," said Ol; "if you will take advice of mine you will ride southward with your host through these grim mountains."

"I will do that," said Arthur Emperor.

"Then here will we leave you," said the Lords of the Stars; "and carry the news to the King of the Nooivray in Gorsedd."

So they rode northward over the flowery meadows; but Arthur and his men prepared to follow Ol towards the south.

"Music will be needed for this adventure," said Taliesin Benbardd; he was the Chief Bard and Music-maker of the Universe at that time. "Listen you now," said he; "and let your thoughts and your horses' hoofs keep time to this."

Then he persuaded the notes out of his harp with gentle fingers, so that their thoughts began flowing with the music as they started out. Then he put coercion on the harp as they rode on, so that the mountains were ringing with the music and the beats of the horses' hoofs keeping time with it. So they rode on all day through the mountains that grew grimmer and wilder always, along the edges of great chasms and over torrents that raved world-deep below. When the sun set they came to the Brink of Things. "Over the brink the Necklace has passed," said Ol; "but there is no tracking it by scent farther."

In front lay empty black space, an enormous abysm, wherein there seemed to be nothing. "Is our quest to end here?" asked Glewlwyd Gafaelfawr.

"Oh, no," said Taliesin Benbardd; "the hoofs will keep time to the music still."

"Call Drem, the son of Dremidyd," said Arthur.

Drem was such a man that, when the gnat arose in the morning with the sun, he could see her from Gelliwic in Cornwall as far off as Pen Nant Gofid on the confines of hell; and furthermore, he could easily count the hairs of her beard.

"Drem fab Dremidyd," said Arthur; "do you catch sight of anything beyond there?"

Drem looked forth carefully. "Southward and below there," said he, "there is a blacker blackness moving, ten universes away."

"We will ride forward towards it," said Arthur Fawr.

So they leaped their horses out into the abyss; and by reason of the music of Taliesin Benbardd, empty space was equal to a well-paved road for them, and neither better nor worse; and the beat of the hoofs on the darkness kept time to the music.

"Is that which we seek far away now?" asked Arthur.

"Not so far as it was," said Drem fab Dremidyd. So they rode on, singing now to the music.

Far off in the cellar of his planet Ghuggg caught a rumor of it and trembled. "Eh?" said he; "WHAT'S THAT?" He could hardly induce his ears to listen to more than the beating of his heart. "But my heart beat never to such a rhythm as that," said he. He listened further, and groaned.

"Dear help me better," said he; "I know what it is: it is the harping of the Chief Bard of the Universe; and the men of the Island of the Mighty on the march to it. By the stench of the swamp of bottom-most Annwn, it is that!" said he; and grew pale over what would have been his face, had there been much to distinguish it from the gross rotundity in front of him.

"The music of Taliesin Benbardd it is; and he strongly coercing it from the strings of his harp; and the hoofs of the horses of the Arthurians keeping time to it as they pursue me through the abyss!" He was bewildered and amazed; his bones molten in him with terror. Then he mastered himself, and took courage, and planned his defense.

"Come now," said he; "where is my magic to fortify me against trouble? There is that Drem the son of Dremidyd: his sight will be potent against me unless I take to my magic."

So he took himself to it; and croaked thrice like a frog; and thereupon the blackness the Arthurians rode through became a million times blacker, and even more than that. "Sight is useless here," said Drem fab Dremidyd. "The light I saw by has gone out."

"Call Clust fab Clustfeinad," said the Emperor Arthur. When the ant arose from her nest in the morning, Clust could hear her footsteps from Esgair Oerfel in Ireland as far as to the borders of space; and furthermore, he could hear the thought in her mind before ever she had uttered it.

"Clust fab Clustfeinad," said Arthur, "are you hearing anything from below and beyond there?"

"A frog croaking I heard—if a frog it was; and a man breathing I hear now—if he is a man. Follow you me, if it please you; and I will lead you to him."

So they rode forward after Clust fab Clustfeinad; and Taliesin Benbardd putting fierce, strong, exultant coercion on the harpstrings, and shaking out the music magnanimously through the night; so that tremendous speed was with their horses.

"Is it far away now?" asked Arthur.

"In my deed to heaven and man, it is not far," said Clust. "It is very near at hand."

"Ah," said Arthur then; "the right fore-hoof of Fflamwen my mare struck against hardness; and it seemed to me that the hardness was cracked."

"Cracked it was; and my genius has come back to me," said Ol fab Olwydd. "I smell the Sapphire Necklace; and it is falling down through space below us."

"In my deed it was cracked; and my sight thereby has come back to me," said Drem fab Dremidyd. "I can see the blackness falling away swiftly below, and a blue light shining out through the crack in it, that has the appearance of shining from thirteen bright amazing sapphires within."

"By the ruby in thy ring it cracked, Lord Arthur," said Clust; "and the music sounding out through the crack is like that of the thirteen Arch-flautists of heaven; and even better. Hark you now, if it please you!"

They heard the song of the sapphires, and it was as much as

seventeen times better than Clust had said; and even more than that. It rose out of the crack in Ghuggg's planet that Fflamwen's hoof had made, and soared and floated out through thirteen universes, spreading hope and delight: the sapphires with hope restored to them were appealing to the Arthurians to deliver them.

"Woe is me, the men of Arthur Emperor are upon me!" sighed Ghuggg in his cellar. "The roof is broken by the rude hoofs of their horses; and their intentions are not good." He forgot the empire he desired to found, and longed only for escape. "I must set my planet to spinning and falling, that I may sink into the swamp on the floor of Annwn and be safe from their loathsome clamor and weapons."

He had fallen on the sapphires to hide the light of them; and now set his globe to spinning and whizzing downwards, swifter than the arrow's flight, than the passage of the lightray, than the leaping of thought in the mind of a bard. Towards the swamp at the bottom of things he sped it. But the light of the sapphires shone out through his solid ugliness and through the cracked roof as it fell and as the Arthurians pursued it, their horses diving down towards the depths.

"Their object is theft, and rieving, and violent robbery," sighed Ghuggg; "woe is me, a tenfold curse on all thievers and rievers! The honest may not enjoy their lawful gains for them!" he sighed; and sped his planet the quicker. But the swifter its fall, the swifter were the warsteeds of the Arthurians in pursuit of it; until the apples of gold at the four corners of their saddle-cloths burned and became molten and shone out through space. "Now I am near the swamp!" he chuckled; and then, looking up, moaned in his terror. "Evil on their beards, they are upon me!"

So his planet whirled downwards, obeying his desire. And there was the swamp not ten leagues below him; and a league and more between him and Drych Ail Cibddar the swiftest of the Arthurians. Down and down whirled Ghuggg, gathering impetus; his native stench and corruption awaited him, near at hand.

"Woe is me, how I am oppressed by the foul effluvia arising from it!" sighed Ol fab Olwydd. Every moment the little planet as it fell shone the brighter: the light from the sapphires ever the more impregnating it.

"Now I am saved, and the Necklace with me!" laughed Ghuggg; "in a moment I splash into the fluid!" And as he said it, the forehoofs of Drych Ail Cibddar's horse struck against his roof again.

Now there are sharp rocks on the Floor of Things, jutting out from the filth and slime there; and it was on one of them the planet struck; and what with the swift impact, and the kick of Drych Ail Cibddar's horse, it burst open and was shattered. Out flopped Ghuggg and dived like a frog, the Necklace about his middle, into the corruption. But Drych Ail Cibddar drew rein in time; and in a second the Arthurians were up with him; and there they halted. The swamp was clearly visible now by the light from the sinking sapphires.

And they blazed out the more the deeper they sank in it. The men of the Island of the Mighty, watching presently saw Ghuggg disentangled from them, and float upwards to the surface, charred, dried up and withering away; so that by the time he reached the surface, there was nothing of him to reach it.

"This is a marvel," said Ol fab Olwydd; "the stench is gone, and the air has become sweet and pleasant."

"This is a great marvel," said Drem fab Dremidyd; "for behold you now, the foulness and opacity of it are wasting and clearing; as if it were pure ether below us forevermore."

"In my deed to heaven and man, it is a lovely, bright, astounding marvel!" said Clust son of Clustfeinad; "for music is coming up from the sapphires in the depths like the music of a constellation of noblest stars!"

Arthur looked up and beheld the King of the Nooivray with his court at Gorsedd in the stone circle near the Pleiades; and nothing between but pleasant slopes, wooded and ferny mountains, meadows of cowslips and of gentian.

"King of the Nooivray," he cried, "behold, here is a new constellation of stars; come you now, if it please you, and annex it to the Empire of the Nooivray!"

So those that were in the Gorsedd rode down; and came to where the Arthurians waited; and dismounted there; and the King of the Nooivray embraced the Emperor Arthur; and there was good companionship, warmest friendship, between the men of the Island of the Mighty and the men of the Empire of Heaven. So together they rode down to where the Sapphire Necklace hung, that now was a beautiful constellation of stars: blue, amazing, exquisite islands in infinity. And they annexed them to the Nooivray; and appointed officers of the court to be their rulers and regents. And in this order they rode together from star to star of them, surveying their new dominion, and conversing together pleasantly, and relating to each other the heroic tales of the Island of the Mighty and of the Empire of Heaven; and in this order they sat at feast in the chief palace of the Nwyfre afterwards: that is to say, the Emperor Arthur and the King of the Nooivray; the Blessed Cai and the Regent of Aldebaran; Gwrhyh Gwalstawd Ieithoedd and the King's Heir of Fomalhaut; Greidawl Galldonyd and—

The Regent of the North

The northern winter is altogether ghostly and elemental; there is no friendliness to man to be found in it. There, the snow has its proper habitation; there, in the gaunt valleys of Lapland, in the terrible, lonely desolations, the Frost Giants abide. They are servants of the Regent of the North: smiths, that have the awful mountains for their anvils; and, with cold for flame tempering water into hardness, fashion spears and swords of piercing ice, or raise glittering ramparts about the Pole. All for the dreadful pleasure of doing it! They go about their work silently in the gray darkness; heaven knows what dreams may be haunting them—dreams that no mind could imagine, unless death had already frozen its brain. When the wind wolves come howling down from the Pole, innumerable, unflagging, and insatiable: when the snow drives down, a horde of ghosts wandering senseless, hurrying and hurrying through the night: the giants do their work. They make no sound: they fashion terror, and illimitable terror, and terror. . . . Or—is it indeed only terror that they fashion? . . .

And then spring comes, and the sun rises at last on the world of the North. The snow melts in the valleys; white wisps of cloud float over skies blue as the gentian; over a thousand lakes all turquoise and forget-me-not: waters infinitely calm and clear, infinitely lovely. Then the snow on the mountain dreams dazzling whiteness by day, defiantly glittering against the sun; dreams tenderness, all faint rose and heliotrope and amber, in the evening; blue solemn mystery in the night. Quick with this last mysterious dreaming!—for the nights are hurrying away; they grow shorter always; they slink Poleward, immersed in ghostly preoccupations; by midsummer they have vanished altogether. Then the sun peers incessantly wizardlike over the horizon; the dumb rocks and the waters are invincibly awake, alert, and radiant with some magic instilled into them by the Regent of the North. . . . It is in this spring- and summer-time that you shall see bloom the flowers of Lapland: great pure blossoms in blue and purple and rose and citron, such as are not found elsewhere in the world. The valleys are a dreaming, silent wonder with the myriads there are of them—silent, for the Lapps have followed the reindeer, and the reindeer have followed the snows.

Into this region it was that Halfdan the Aged came, when he was tired of the new ways and faith that had come into the south. The viking days were over forever one could see that. Meek, crozier-bearing men had invaded the realms of Odin and Balder; laying terrible axes of soft words, of chanted prayers and hymns, to the roots of—? All the ancient virtue of the race, said Halfdan the Aged, all the mighty and mystic dreams that had been surging through the Northlands these hundreds of years; sending the brave forth to wonderful deeds and wonderful visions about the seas and coasts of the world. And Inge the king at Upsala, forgetting all things noble and generous, had foresworn Odin and battle-breaking Thor; had foresworn Balder the Beautiful; had welcomed these chanting, canting foreigners, and decreed their faith for his people. So that now nothing remained but a fat, slothful life and the straw-death at the end of it: there should be no more viking expeditions; no more Valhalla; no more Asgard and the Gods. "Faugh!" thought Halfdan Halfdansson, old hero of a hundred raids in the west and south; "this small-souled life for them that can abide it; it is worse than death for a *Man's Son.*"

Not but that his own days of action were over: had been these ten years; had passed with the age of the Vikings. Also his seven sons were in Valhalla long since, and beyond being troubled; they had fallen like men in battle before there was any talk of this Christian heaven and hell; as for his wife, she, royal-hearted woman, had died when the youngest of them was born. So that it would have been easy for him to cut himself adrift from the world and voyage down through pleasant dreams towards death, after the fashion of clean old age. He had already put by, somewhat sadly, the prospect of future expeditions, and was reconciling himself to old age and its illumination, when King Inge went besotted over the foreign faith. From his house, Bravik on the hillside, through whose door the seawinds blew in salt and excellent, he could watch the changes of the Swan-way, and nourish peace upon the music of the sea. Below at the foot of the hill, was the harbor from which his ships used to sail; drawn up on the beach, sheer hulks, still they lay there the *Wild Swan* and the *Dragon,* accustomed to Mediterranean voyagings of old. For his own life, he found no action to regret in it; it had all been heroic doing, clean and honorable and vigorous; and the Gods had had their proper place in it, lighting it mysteriously from within.

But what room was there for dreaming, when the cry *The glory is departed!* rang so insistent? The new order liked him so little, that in place of peace and its accompanying wisdom, the years brought him unease increasingly. With his old skalds about him, to sing to him in the hall in the evenings; with his old and pagan servants, faithful all of them to the past as to himself, he watched the change coming on Sweden with disquietude and disgust; and for the first time in his life, experienced a kind of fear. But it was a pagan and great-hearted fear, and had nought to do with his own fate or future.

He knew the kind of tales these becroziered men from the south were telling, and that were becoming increasingly a substitute for the old valiant stories of the skalds. A man had come to Bravik once, and was welcomed there, who, when the feast was over, and the poets were relating their sagas, had risen in his turn with a story to tell—of a white-faced, agonizing God, who died a felon's death amongst ignoble and unwarlike people. Halfdan had listened to it with growing anger: where was the joy, where the mighty and beautiful forms, the splendid life, of the Divine Ones in this? At the end of it he had called to the stranger:

"Thy tale is a vile one, O foreign skald! Fraught with lies it is, and unwholesome to the hearing."

"Lies it is not, but the truth of truths, O chieftain, and except thou believest, thou shalt suffer the vengeance of God throughout eternity."

"Go!" cried the Viking; and in the one word rang all the outraged ideals that had stood him in stead for sixty years. One does not defend his standpoint, but merely states it. He saw none of the virtues of Christianity, while its crude presentation shocked his religious feelings as profoundly as the blatant negations of atheism shock those of the pious of our own day. And his aspirations had a core of real spirituality in them. The Gods, for these high-souled Pagans, were the fountain of right, the assurance and stability of virtue. Thor, probably, stood for courage, spiritual as well as physical; Odin for a secret and internal wisdom; Balder for a peace that passeth understanding. Things did not end in Berseker fury: the paths of the spirit were open, or had been of old; beyond the hero stood the God; beyond strife, a golden peace founded on the perfection of life. Wars, adventure, and strenuous living were to fashion something divinely calm and grand in the lives of men; that once established, and no possibility of evil left lurking in any human soul. Balder's reign would come something like the glow and afterglow of sunset, or a vast and perfect music enveloping the world— there should be a love as of comrades, as of dear brothers, between all men. But that Peace of Balder and of Odin was separated by all Berserkerism from the peace that is fear or greed. It was a high, perpetual exultation: a heaven into which the meek and weak could not slide passively, but the strong man armed (spiritually) should take it by storm.—And here was negation of the doctrine of the strong man armed; here was proclaiming godhood a thing not robust, joyless, unbeautiful . . . Old Halfdan went moody and depressed for a week after the priest's visit. The serene Balder-mood, into the fulness of which now, in the evening of his life, he had the right to grow naturally had been attacked, and could not be induced to return. A God crucified! . . . his soul cried out for Gods triumphant.

Inge might launch his decrees at Upsala; at Bravik, not the least intention existed of obeying them. With dogged and defiant faith Halfdan performed the rites of the religion of Odin, having dismissed from his house all who hankered after the newly proclaimed orthodoxy. With it all, he was ill at ease: as seeing that Sweden would not long hold a man faithful to her ancient ideals. Tales were brought in, how such and such a pagan chief had suffered the king's vengeance, or had been compelled to profess and call himself Christian. Heaven knew when his own turn might come; Inge would not overlook him forever. Well, there would be no giving in for him no lip profession—a thing not in him to understand. He could swing a battle-ax yet, at the head of his retainers; he could die in his burning house like a Viking's son. That would be something: a blow struck for olden virtue: a beacon of remembrance for Sweden, in the dark days he feared and foresaw. His religious broodings deepened; he strove incessantly to come nearer to the Gods; for although he held it a coward's creed to think They exist to help men, and a brave man's, that men exist to help Them; yet at such a time, he deemed, They might find it worth Their while to turn from vaster wars for a moment, and concern themselves with the fate of Sweden. So he prayed, but his prayer was no petition nor whining after gains; it was a silencing of the mind, a steadfast driving it upward towards heights it had not attained before: eagle altitudes, and sunlight in the windless blue, where no passion comes, and the eternal voices may be heard.

The tide of trouble drew nearer. Presently a messenger came from Inge, with a priest. Halfdan was to install the latter in his house, and learn from him the faith of the Nazarene; was to forgo the Gods, or expect the king's armies. Halfdan sent them back; to say that Inge would be welcome at Bravik: as a friend, as of old; or still more as a foe. Then he dismissed the few women there were in his house, called in his men, and prepared for a siege: thoroughly if fiercely happy at last. But there was no bottom to the king's degeneration, it seemed. After three weeks this came from Upsala: "Halfdan Halfdansson, you are senile; you will die soon, and your false religion will all but die with you. The faith of Christ commands forbearance and forgiveness. You shall die in peace, and suffer hellflame thereafter; I will not trouble with you." *I will not trouble with you.* . . . For a week the old man raged inwardly Inge should not thus triumphantly insult him; he would not die in peace, but lead his fifty against Upsala, and go out fighting. . . . Then the Baldermood came once more; and with it, light and direction vouchsafed him. He would go a-viking.

He summoned his fifty, and proclaimed his intention in the hall. Let who would, stay behind—in a Sweden that at least would let them be. For himself, he would take the Swan-way: he would have delight again of the crisping of blue waves against his prow: he would go under purple sails into the evening, into the mystery, into the aloneness where grandeur is, and it is profitable for souls to be, and there are none to tell heart-sickening tales. . . . There, what should befall him, who could say? Perhaps there would be sweet battle on the Christian coasts; perhaps he would burn and break a church or two, and silence the jangling of the bells that called ignoble races to ignoble prayer. Perhaps there would be battling only with the storm: going out into that vast unstable region the Aesir loved, perhaps they would expend their manhood nobly in war with the shrieking wind, the sweet wild tempest of heaven. At such times the Gods come near, they come very near; they buffet and slay in their love, and out of a wild and viking death, the Valkyrie ride, the Valkyrie ride! . . . There were fifty men in the hall that heard him; there were fifty men that rose and shouted their acclamation; fifty that would take the Swan-way with their lord.

So there came to be noise of ax and hammer in the haven under Bravik: the *Wild Swan* and the *Dragon* being refurbished and made all taut for voyaging. Within a month they set sail. But not southward, and then through Skagerack and Cattegat, out into the waters of Britain and France, as Halfdan had intended. On the first day, a sudden storm overtook them, and singing they plunged into black seas, beneath blind and battling skies. Singing they combatted the wave of the north; they went on, plunging blindly, driven for three days whither they knew not; then, with a certain triumph in their souls, they succumbed, singing, to the gale. They saw the Valkyrie ride through heaven; they gave their bodies to the foam about the rocks, and rose upon the howling winds, clean and joyous of soul at the last.

Halfdan had forgotten Christianity: all thought and memory of it deserted him utterly before the storm had been beating them an hour. In the end it was all pagan, all Viking, exultant lover and fighter of the Gods, that he leaped from his sinking ship in the night, fully armed, into the driving froth and blackness; struggled as long as might be with the overwhelming waters, as befitted his manhood; then lost consciousness, and was buffeted and tossed where the grand elements listed; and thrown at last, unconscious, on the shore.

Certainly he had seen the Valkyrie riding, had heard their warsong above the winds and waves: like the lightning of heaven they had ridden, beautiful and awful beyond any of his old dreaming; why then had they not taken him? This was no Valhalla into which he had come: this dark place smokily lamp-lit; this close air, heavy, it must be said, with stench. And were these the dwarfs, these little figures that moved and chattered unintelligibly in the gloom? . . . Slowly he took in the uncouth surroundings; raising himself, rather painfully, on his elbow from the bed of dry heather on which he was lying. There, on the tent-pole, hung his armor: his helmet with the raven wings; his shield, sword, and battle-ax; these were skins with which he was covered, and of which the walls of the tent were made. He was not dead then? No; it appeared that it was still mortal flesh that he was wearing. He had been thrown on some shore by the waves, and rescued by these quaint, squat people. Ah! he had been driven into the far north, and was among Lapps in the unknown north of the world.

He lay back, exhausted by his bodily and mental effort; and the sigh that broke from him brought the Lapp woman to his side, and the Lapp man after her. They brought him hot broth, and spoke to him, their unknown and liquid tongue, in which no sound unmusical intrudes, was full of gentle kindliness; their words were almost caressing, and full of encouragement and cheer. He had no strength to sit up; the Lapp woman squatted at his head and lifted him in her arms; and while he so leaned and rested the Lapp man fed him, sup by sup; the two of them crooning and chuckling their good will the while. In three days he was on his feet; and convinced that he could not outwear the kindly hospitality of his hosts.

The weeks of the northern spring went by; the flowers of Lapland were abloom in the valley, and old Halfdan wandered daily and brooded amidst the flowers. His mood now had become very inward. He hungered no more after action, nor dwelt in pictures of the past; rather an interiority of the present haunted him: a sweetness, as of dear and near deities, in the crag-reflecting waters, in the fleet cloud-fleeces, in the heather on the hills, and in the white and yellow poppies on the valley-floor. As the summer passed this mood grew deeper: from a prevalent serene peace, it became filled with divine voices almost audibly calling. As for the Lapps, they behaved to him at all times with such tenderness as might be given to a father growing helpless in old age, but loved beyond ordinary standards.

The first frosts were withering the heather; in the valley the flowers had died; the twilight of early winter, a wan iris withering, drooped mournful petals over the world. On the hills all was ghostly whiteness; the Lapps had come south with the winter, and there was a great encampment of them in the valley; it never occurred to Halfdan to wonder why the couple that had saved him had remained during the summer so far from the snows. One day he wandered down to the shore; the sea had already frozen, and the icy leagues of it shone tinted with rose and faint violet and beryl where light from the sun, far and low in the horizon, caught them. Wonderful and beautiful seemed to him the world of the North. There was no taint in the cold, electric air; no memory to make his soul ashamed for his fellow men. The wind blew keen over the ice, blowing back his hair and his beard; it was intense and joyful for him with that Divine life of the Gods that loves and opposes us. He walked out on the ice; something at his feet caught his attention, and he stooped to examine it; it was a spar, belike from the *Wild Swan* or the *Dragon*, the ships he had loved. Then came memory in a flood. All his life had gone from him; the faces familiar of old had vanished; down there, in the south, in the Gothland, all the glory had departed; and there was nothing left for him on earth, but the queer, evil-smelling life in the Lapp tent . . . Yes; there were still the Gods. . . . A strange unrest came upon him; he must away and find the Aesir. . . . He had no plan; only he must find the Bright Ones: must stand in their visible presence, who had been the secret illumination of the best of his life. In mingled longing and exultation he made his way back to the camp.

He found his Lapp friends standing before their tent, and their best reindeer harnessed to an *akja**; they knew, it appeared, that he was to go: and mournfully and unbidden, had made preparation. They brought out his armor, and fondled his hands as they armed him; a crowd gathered about him, all crooning and chuckling their good will, and their sorrow to lose the old man in whose shining eyes, it seemed to them, was much unearthly wisdom. On all sides, evidently, there was full understanding of his purpose, and sad acquiescence; and this did not seem to him strange at all: the Gods were near and real enough to control and arrange all things. He sat down in the *akja*, and took the rein; the Lapps heaped skins about him for warmth; then, waving farewells, amidst an outburst of sorrowful crooning and chuckling, he started. Whither the reindeer might list; whither the mighty Undying Ones might direct.

On, and on, and on. Through ghostly valleys and through the snowstorm, right into the heart of the northern night, the reindeer, never uncertain of the way, drew him. The Balder-mood came to him in the weird darkness; in the cold desolation the bright Gods seemed nearer than ever. Through ghastly passes where the north wind, driving ice particles that stung, came shrieking, boisterous and dismal, down from the Pole to oppose him, on sped the reindeer while the mind of the old Viking was gathered into dreams. —Waiting for him, somewhere beyond, were Those whose presence was a growing glory on the horizon of his soul. . . . The snow-ghosts, wan, innumerable, and silent, came hurrying by; on sped the reindeer, a beautiful beast, heeding never the snow-ghosts over frozen rivers and frozen mountains, through ghostly cold valleys and the snow. Under vast precipices that

* The Lapp sledge of wicker and skin, capable of holding one man sitting with legs stretched out, and guiding the reindeer with a single thong of rein.

towered up, iron and mournful into the night; or along the brink of awful cliffs, with the snowstorm howling below . . . on and on. Who was to measure time on that weird journey? There were no changes of day and night; and Halfdan, wrapped in the warmth of his dreams, hardly would have heeded them if there had been. Now and again the reindeer halted to feed, scraping in the snow for his familiar moss-diet; then on again, and on. It was the beast, or some invisible presence, not the man, who chose the way.

A valley stretched out endlessly before; and afar, afar, a mountain caught on its whiteness some light from heaven, so that amid all the ghostly darkness it shone and shot up, a little dazzling beacon of purity on the rim of the world. The snow had ceased to fall, and no longer the north wind came shrieking to oppose; there was quiet in the valley broken only by the tinkling of the reindeer bells and the scrunch of the falling hoofs on the snow. The white mountain caught the eyes, and at last the mind of the long dreaming Viking; so that he began to note the tinkling of the bells, the sound of the hoofs falling, the desolation before and around. And at last another sound also: long howling out of the mountains on this side and that; long, dreary howling behind, like the cry of ghosts in a nightmare, or the lamentation of demons driven forever through darkness beyond the margin of space. For some time he listened, before waking to knowledge that it was actual sound he listened to; and then for some time longer before it came to him to know whence the sound was. It had drawn nearer by then, much nearer; and peering forth through the glint and gloom, he saw the shadows that were wolves streaming up after him through the valley, and coming down from the mountains; singly, in twos and threes, in multitudes. The reindeer snuffed, tossed its head, and speeded on prodigiously, yet with what gathered on the hillsides, it would be a marvel if he escaped. On came the shadows, until one could see the green fire-sparks of their eyes, behind, to the right and to the left, almost before, and on sped the reindeer, and the white mountain drew nearer.

Then Halfdan the Viking scented war: he remembered his youth and its prowess; he made ready his shield and battle-ax; and thanked the Gods fervently that after all he should go out fighting. The brave reindeer should have what chance it might to escape by its own untrammeled fleetness: so he drew his sword and cut the harness. The beast was away over the snow at twice its former speed; and Halfdan in the *akja* shot forward thirty paces, fell out, and was on his feet in a moment to wait what should come.

A black, shag shadow, the foremost of them, hurled itself howling at his throat—eyes green fire and bared teeth gleaming; the ax swept down, clave its head in mid air, and the howl went out in a rattling groan and sob. No question of failing strength now; old age was a memory—forgotten. The joy of battle came to him, and as the first wolf fell he broke into song:

> *In the bleak of the night and the ghost-held region,*
> *By frozen valley and frozen lake,*
> *A son of the Vikings, breaking his battle,*
> *Doth lovely deeds for Asgard's sake.*
>
> *Odin All-Father, for thee I slew him!*
> *For thee I slew him, bolt-wielding Thor!*
> *Joy to ye now, ye Aesir, Brothers!*
> *That drive the demons forevermore!*

While he sang, another wolf was upon him, and then another and another; and the war-ax that had made play under Mediterranean suns of old, God, how it turned and swept and drove and clave things in the northern night! While they came up one by one, or even in twos, the fight was all in his favor, so he slew as many as a dozen at his singing; then the end began to draw near. They were in a ring about him now; rather fearful of the whirling ax, but closing in. Old age began to tell upon his limbs; he fought on wearying; and the delight of war ebbed from him; his thigh had been snapped at and torn, and he had lost much blood with the wound. Then the ax fell, and he leaned on it for support for a moment, his head bent down over his breast. The war-mood had gone altogether; his mind sped out to the Gods. Of inward time there had been enough, since the ax fell, for the change of mood, for the coming of calm wonder and exaltation; of the time we measure in minutes, enough for the leaping of a wolf. He saw it, and lifted the ax; knowing that nothing could be done. At his left it leaped up; he saw the teeth snap a hand's-breadth from his face. . . . An ax that he knew not, brighter than the lightning, swung; the jaws snapped; the head and the body apart fell to the ground. . . . And there was a wolf leaping on his right, and no chance in the world of his slaying it; and a spear all-glorious suddenly hurtling out of the night, and taking the wolf through the throat, and pinning it dead to the ground. And here was a man, a Viking, gray-bearded, one-eyed, glorious, fighting upon his left; and here was a man, a Viking, young and surpassing beautiful of form and face and mien, doing battle at his right. And he himself was young again, and strong; and knew that against the three of them all the wolves in the world, and all the demons in hell, would have little chance. They fled yelping into the dark; and Halfdan turned to hail those that had fought for him.

And behold, the shining mountain that had seemed so far, shone now near at hand, and for a mountain, it was a palace, exceedingly well-built, lovely with towers and pinnacles and all the fair appurtenances of a king's house. No night nor winter was near it; amidst gardens of eternal sunlight it shone; its portals flung wide, and blithe all things for his entering. And he greeted Odin All-Father, as one might who had done nothing in his life to mar the pleasant friendliness of that greeting. And in like manner he greeted Balder the Beautiful. They linked their arms in his, and in cheerful conversation he passed in with them into the Valhalla.

The Eyeless Dragons:

A CHINESE STORY

Chang Seng-yu was to be the artist; that was why the crowds were so immense. The courts of the Temple of Peace and Joy had been full since dawn; although the sun would undoubtedly be well in heaven before the great Chang would mount the scaffolding and begin to work.

All Nankin had been agog since the word had gone forth that the Emperor desired a dragon painted on either of the two vast wall-surfaces of the Temple; and when it was reported further that Chang Seng-yu was to be the artist, then, indeed, the rejoicing was great. For the grand strokes of his brush were known; and his colors were delicate like the mists of evening on the Yangtse, or clear and lovely like the colors of flowers. Whenever he painted in public, the crowds would gather to watch; and from time to time to applaud the master-strokes, the flashes of daring imagination, the moments when the sparks of creation most visibly flew. And they *knew,* did those crowds of the Chinese Renaissance—some fourteen centuries ago.

They loved Chang Seng-yu for another reason, too, besides his genius and mastery of the brush. He was at least half a *Sennin**: many held that he had drunk the Elixir; that he could rein the flying Dragon, and visit the extremities of the earth, and bestride the hoary crane, to soar above the nine degrees of heaven. Such things were done, in those days. There was a certain power about Chang Seng-yu, that suggested infinite possibilities. One could never tell what might happen, with any picture he might be painting.

A hush in the temple court; the artist has arrived, and with him a little band of disciples, bearing the brushes and pots of color. A quiet, gentle old man, who bows profoundly to the people as he comes in; and greets them with courteous formalities, not unaffectionately, while passing to the door of the Temple. With courteous formalities those spoken to respond, proud of the signal honor done them; for this is a popular hero, be it understood. The tailor and the cobbler have arranged in advance a holiday, and have come now with their families to spend the day in the Temple of Peace and Joy, watching the Master paint: the butcher's apprentice, sent on an errand, can not resist the temptation; the porter, calculating possibilities to a nicety, deems that he may go in, watch so much wall-space covered with sudden life, and then, by hurrying, still arrive in time with his load. For with all these people, painting is poetry made visible, the mysteries of Tao indicated, Magic, the topmost wonder and delight of life. And this being by Chang Seng-yu, will be no ordinary painting—"Ah, in that honorable brush-sweep, one saw the effect of the Elixir!" cried the butcher's apprentice, radiant.

Day by day the crowds gathered in the court, and followed Chang Seng-yu, when he arrived, into the Vast Temple. Day by day the intent silence was broken ever and anon into murmurs, and the murmurs into rippling exclamation. A sweep of the brush, and lo, the jaws of a dragon; and from that the wonderful form grew, perfect at each touch, scale by scale through all the windings of the vast body to the very end of the tail. All in shining yellow that might have been distilled out of the sunset, it gleamed across the great wall: a thing of exquisite curves,

* Adept.

noble lines; flowing, grand, and harmonious; wherein all parts seemed cognate to, and expressive of, the highest perceptions and aspirations of man. To behold it was like hearing the sudden crash of a glorious and awe-inspiring music: the soul of every upright man would at once both bow down and be exalted. The crowd, watching, expected at any moment to see motion quiver through its length; to see it writhe, shake out mighty pinions, break forth from the wall and through the roof, and cleave a way into the blue ether. A little fear mingled with their intense delight: the Master, surely, was dealing in magic.

"Sir," said Lu Chao, "for what reason have you omitted to paint in the honorable eye?"

"Could this sacred Dragon see," answered Chang Seng-yu, "nothing would content his lordship but to seek his home in the playground of the lightnings."

"How is it possible?" said Lu Chao. "The Dragon is beautiful, but it is only a semblance wrought in pigment. How could such a semblance soar into the heavens? The Master is pleased to indulge in humor at the expense of this miserable one."

"Not so, Lu Chao," said the Master. "You have little understanding, as yet, of the mysteries of art."

But Lu Chao doubted, and it was a sorrow to him that Chang Seng-yu should leave his creation incomplete.

The Yellow Dragon was finished, its glorious form covering the upper part of the south wall. The people could hardly forbear to worship; they saw in it Divine Power, the essence of Light-Bringing, the perfect symbol of inspiration, of holy and quickening thought from heaven. "If the Master had not left his creation eyeless," they said, "his lordship would never be content to dwell on earth. Heaven is the right abiding-place for such a one." But Lu Chao went on doubting.

He did not refer to the matter again; but when it came to his turn to hand the brush, newly dipped in the color pot, to Chang Seng-yu, the latter as he looked down would shake his head, and a shadow would pass over his face. "Although of a good disposition, Lu Chao will never be a painter," thought he, sighing.

The scaffolding was removed to the opposite wall, and there, facing the other, a Purple Dragon began to grow. Occasionally the Son of Heaven himself, the Emperor Wu-ti, would visit the temple to inspect the growing work. Then the artist would descend to make obeisance; but Wu-ti, holy man, would have none from the creator of those dragons. "Make your obeisance with me, to these two lordly Messengers of Heaven," said he. "But for what reason has the honorable Master left the eyes to be painted last?"

"Sire," said Chang Seng-yu, "the divine eyes of their lordships will not be painted. There is danger that they would be ill contented with the earth, if they could see to soar into their native empyrean. No man could paint into their eyes such compassion, that they would desire to remain here."

"It is well," said the emperor. "Their soaring aspiration is evident. Let them remain to be the guardians of the Peace and Joy of my People."

Lu Chao heard, but even the Son of Heaven's belief failed to convince him. "It may be as the Master says," thought he; "but such matters are beyond my understanding. How could a semblance wrought of pigment feel aspiration or a desire for the ethereal spaces? It appears to me that the venerable Chang is indulging in humor, when he speaks of painting compassion into their eyes."

The work was drawing to a close, and more and more Lu Chao doubted. It is true that he made progress in painting; and the skill shown in his work was applauded by many. For the day of the Consecration of the Dragons had been appointed in advance; and there was time to spare; and on certain days now the Temple would be closed, and the Master and his disciples would work in the studio. Then Chang Seng-yu, going from one to another, and commenting on the work of each, would shake his head a little sadly over Lu Chao's pictures. "You have skill and perseverance," he would say, "but faith is lacking."

Lu Chao pondered on this, but not with desire to acquire the faith. "Many say that I am making progress," thought he, "and it appears so to me also. The Master, truly, is harsh in his judgments. If I could show him that he is mistaken. . . ." He considered the matter, and thought out his plans.

The Day of Consecration came; the great work was completed. Priests and augurs, sennins and doctors, gathered from all Liang, and from the kingdoms beyond the Yangtse and the Western Mountains. All day long there were sacrifices in the Temple of Peace and Joy, and processions passed through, doing joyful obeisance to the Dragons. At last night came, and the great hall and courts were silent.

The time had come for Lu Chao; now he would prove that the Master had been mistaken: that painted semblances could not shake themselves free from the walls whereon they were painted, and that he himself was making progress unhindered by lack of faith. "It may be that there is Magic," said he, "although I have never seen it. But reason forbids me to believe this."

He took a lantern, a small brush, and such paint as would be needed, and went down through the dark streets towards the Temple. There would be no trouble about obtaining entrance, he knew: should anyone question him, Chang Seng-yu had forgotten something, and had sent him for it. But it was unlikely that he would meet anyone, and he hoped to pass in unseen. "No one will know that I did it," thought he. "It will be understood that the spirits painted in the eyes, displeased that the Master left the work unfinished."

He met no one; succeeded in climbing the gate; found a ladder in the court; placed it against the south wall by the head of the Yellow Dragon; climbed, and prepared to begin. It had been a dark night, but calm, as he came through the city; now, with the first touch of his brush, a peal of thunder, a lightning flash. In his sudden perturbation, the brush dropped, and he must go down after it. Were the genii offended? He hesitated, and had some thought of going home. "But no," said he; "this is fear; this is arrant superstition,"—and mounted the ladder again. The lantern, hung from a rung close to the dragon's head, just threw light on that: a little disk of warm brightness fading into the gloom. It was enough for Lu Chao's purpose. A few brush-strokes; that would be all.

The first, and he was aware of fear. The second, and the wall seemed to him to be taken with unsteadiness. The third, and the sweat broke from his forehead and back, and his hand was trembling violently. He gathered his mind, reasoning with himself; steadied his hand, and put in the last stroke. The Yellow Dragon's eye was painted.

Lu Chao clung to the ladder. By the small light of the lantern he saw the wonderful head turn until it was looking out into the Temple, full face instead of profile. It was the left eye that he had painted; now the two were there, glancing out hither and yonder, proudly, uneasily; flashing fiery rays through the empty darkness. The ladder was shaking, swaying. Suddenly the two amazing eyes were turned full on him, on Lu Chao. A shadow of disgust flitted over them; then they were filled with immeasurable sadness, sorrow deeper than might be borne. The neck drew back; by a supernatural light from the Dragon's eyes, Lu Chao saw it, drawn back and clear out of the wall. A crash, and he saw the immense pinions shaken forth. A horrible swaying of the world; a rending noise, a tearing and a crashing; a blinding flame. . . .

All Nankin was awake, and out in the streets. What the people saw was a Golden Wonder soaring up into the sky: a cometlike glory ascending, till it was lost in the darkness of Heaven.

In the morning the emperor visited the ruins of the Temple of Peace and Joy, and with him went Chang Seng-yu the Master. The north wall alone was standing. The roof had gone up in a single blaze where the fiery wings cleaved it. Of the south wall, only the lower part remained; the rest had fallen. Under the débris they found the ladder, charred and broken, and the crushed body of Lu Chao.

"Ah," said Chang Seng-yu sadly, "he would never have made an artist."

ADVENTURES

Stories of heroes, quests,
battles, in fantastic lands

The first novels of MICHAEL MOORCOCK, *who has been a major force in the evolution of contemporary science fiction, were in imitation of the Martian novels of Edgar Rice Burroughs, heroic science-fantasy adventures. But soon, under the influence of the works of Poul Anderson, especially* The Broken Sword, *and Fritz Leiber's Fahfrd and the Grey Mouser stories, he created the innovative Elric series. Elric is not a barbarian, such as Robert E. Howard's Conan. He is an exile from a superior nonhuman race and is in possession of and possessed by a magic sword that will kill him in the end. In the meanwhile he has some extraordinary experiences. Michael Moorcock has been a motivating spirit of the "New Wave" science fiction of the 1960s, and his major work in SF in the 1970s was the trilogy* Dancers at the End of Time. *In the story herein, Moorcock brings his two series into juxtaposition, putting Elric out of context into the most fantastic SF setting Moorcock has yet created.*

Elric at the End of Time
BY MICHAEL MOORCOCK

1. IN WHICH MRS. PERSSON DETECTS AN ABOVE AVERAGE DEGREE OF CHAOS IN THE MEGAFLOW

Returning from China to London and the Spring of 1936, Una Persson found an unfamiliar quality of pathos in most of the friends she had last seen, as far as she recalled, during the Blitz on her way back from 1970. Then they had been desperately hearty: it was a comfort to understand that the condition was not permanent. Here, at present, Pierrot ruled and she felt she possessed a better grip on her power. This was, she admitted with shame, her favourite moral climate for it encouraged in her an enormously gratifying sense of spiritual superiority: the advantage of having been born, originally, into a later and probably more sophisticated age. The 1960s. Some women, she reflected, were forced to have children in order to enjoy this pleasure.

But she was uneasy, so she reported to the local Time Centre and the bearded, sullen features of Sergeant Alvarez who welcomed her in white, apologising for the fact that he had himself only just that morning left the Lower Devonian and had not had time to change.

"It's the megaflow, as you guessed," he told her, operating toggles to reveal his crazy display systems. "We've lost control."

"We never really had it." She lit a Sherman's and shook her long hair back over the headrest of the swivel chair, opening her military overcoat and loosening her webbing. "Is it worse than usual?"

"Much." He sipped cold coffee from his battered silver mug. "It cuts through every plane we can pick up—a rogue current swerving through the dimensions. Something of a twister."

"Jerry?"

"He's dormant. We checked. But it's like him, certainly. Most probably another aspect."

"Oh, sod." Una straightened her shoulders.

"That's what I thought," said Alvarez. "Someone's going to have to do a spot of rubato." He studied a screen. It was Greek to Una. For a moment a pattern formed. Alvarez made a note. "Yes. It can either be fixed at the nadir or the zenith. It's too late to try anywhere in between. I think it's up to you, Mrs. P."

She got to her feet. "Where's the zenith?"

"The End of Time."

"Well," she said, "that's something."

She opened her bag and made sure of her jar of instant coffee. It was the one thing she couldn't get at the End of Time.

"Sorry," said Alvarez, glad that the expert had been there and that he could remain behind.

"It's just as well," she said. "This period's no good for my moral well-being. I'll be off, then."

"Someone's got to." Alvarez failed to seem sympathetic. "It's Chaos out there."

"You don't have to tell me."

She entered the make-shift chamber and was on her way to the End of Time.

2. IN WHICH THE ETERNAL CHAMPION FINDS HIMSELF AT THE END OF TIME

Elric of Melniboné shook a bone-white fist at the greedy, glaring stars—the eyes of all those men whose souls he had stolen to sustain his own enfeebled body. He looked down. Though it seemed he stood on something solid, there was only more blackness falling away below him. It was as if he hung at the centre of the universe. And here, too, were staring points of yellow light. Was he to be judged?

His half-sentient runesword, Stormbringer, in its scabbard on his left hip, murmured like a nervous dog.

He had been on his way to Imrryr, to his home, to reclaim his kingdom from his cousin Yyrkoon; sailing from the Isle of the Purple Towns where he had guested with Count Smiorgan Baldhead. Magic winds had caught the Filkharian trader as she crossed the unnamed water between the Vilmirian peninsula and the Isle of Melniboné. She had been borne into the Dragon Sea and thence to The Sorcerer's Isle, so-called because that barren place had once been the home of Cran Liret, the Thief of Spells, a wizard infamous for his borrowings, who had, at length, been dispatched by those he sought to rival. But much residual magic had been left behind. Certain spells had come into the keeping of the Krettii, a tribe of near-brutes who had migrated to the island from the region of The Silent Land less than fifty years before. Their shaman, one Grrodd Ybene Eenr, had made unthinking use of devices buried by the dying sorcerer as the spells of his peers sucked life and sanity from them. Elric had dealt with more than one clever wizard, but never with so mindless a power. His battle had been long and exhausting and had required the sacrifice of most of the Filkharians as well as the entire tribe of Krettii. His sorcery had become increasingingly desperate. Sprite fought sprite, devil fell upon devil, in planes both physical and astral, all around the region of The Sorcerer's Isle. Eventually Elric had mounted a massive summoning against the allies of Grrodd Ybene Eenr with the result that the shaman had been at last overwhelmed and his remains scattered in Limbo. But Elric, captured by his own monstrous magickings, had followed his enemy and now he stood in the Void, crying out into appalling silence, hearing his words only in his skull:

"*Arioch! Arioch! Aid me!*"

But his patron Duke of Hell was absent. He could not exist here. He could not, for once, even hear his favourite protégé.

"*Arioch! Repay my loyalty! I have given you blood and souls!*"

He did not breathe. His heart had stopped. All his movements were sluggish.

The eyes looked down at him. They looked up at him. Were they glad? Did they rejoice in his terror?

"*Arioch!*"

He yearned for a reply. He would have wept, but no tears would come. His body was cold; less than dead, yet not alive. A fear was in him greater than any fear he had known before.

"*Oh, Arioch! Aid me!*"

He forced his right hand towards the pulsing pommel of Stormbringer which, alone, still possessed energy. The hilt of the sword was warm to his touch and, as slowly he folded his fingers around it, it seemed to swell in his fist and propel his arm upwards so that he did not draw the sword. Rather the sword forced his limbs into motion. And now it challenged the void, glowing with black fire, singing its high, gleeful battlesong.

"Our destinies are intertwined, Stormbringer," said Elric. "Bring us from this place, or those destinies shall never be fulfilled."

Stormbringer swung like the needle of a compass and Elric's unfeeling arm was wrenched round to go with it. In eight directions the sword swung, as if to the eight points of Chaos. It was questing—like a hound sniffing a trail. Then a yell sounded from within the strange metal of the blade; a distant cry of delight, it seemed to Elric. The sound one would hear if one stood above a valley listening to children playing far below.

Elric knew that Stormbringer had sensed a plane they might reach. Not necessarily their own, but one which would accept them. And, as a drowning mariner must yearn for the most inhospitable rock rather than no rock at all, Elric yearned for that plane.

"*Stormbringer. Take us there.*"

The sword hesitated. It moaned. It was suspicious.

"*Take us there!*" whispered the albino to his runesword.

The sword struck back and forth, up and down, as if it battled invisible enemies. Elric scarcely kept his grip on it. It seemed that Stormbringer was frightened of the world it had detected and sought to drive it back but the act of seeking had in itself set them both in motion. Already Elric could feel himself being drawn through the darkness, towards something he could see very dimly beyond the myriad eyes, as dawn reveals clouds undetected in the night sky.

Elric thought he saw the shapes of crags, pointed and crazy. He thought he saw water, flat and ice-blue. The stars faded and there was snow beneath his feet, mountains all around him, a huge, blazing sun overhead—and above that another landscape, a desert, as a magic mirror might reflect the contrasting character of he who peered into it—a desert, quite as real as the snowy peaks in which he crouched, sword in hand, waiting for one of these landscapes to fade so that he might establish, to a degree, his bearings. Evidently the two planes had intersected.

But the landscape overhead did not fade. He could look up and see sand, mountains, vegetation, a sky which met his own sky at a point half-way along the curve of the huge sun—and blended with it. He looked about him. Snowy peaks in all directions. Above—desert everywhere. He felt dizzy, found that he was staring downward, reaching to cup some of the snow in his hand. It was ordinary snow, though it seemed reluctant to melt in contact with his flesh.

"This is a world of Chaos," he muttered. "It obeys no natural laws." His voice seemed loud, amplified by the peaks, perhaps. "That is why you did not want to come here. This is the world of powerful rivals."

Stormbringer was silent, as if all its energy were spent. But Elric did not sheath the blade. He began to trudge through the snow toward what seemed to be an abyss. Every so often he glanced upward, but the desert overhead had not faded, sun and sky remained the same. He wondered if he walked around the surface of a miniature world. That if he continued to go forward he might eventually reach the point where the two landscapes met. He wondered if this were not some punishment wished upon him by his untrustworthy allies of Chaos. Perhaps he must choose between death in the snow or death in the desert. He reached the edge of the abyss and looked down.

The walls of the abyss fell for all of five feet before reaching a floor of gold and silver squares which stretched for perhaps another seven feet before they reached the far wall, where the landscape continued—snow and crags—uninterrupted.

"This is undoubtedly where Chaos rules," said the Prince of Melniboné. He studied the smooth, chequered floor. It reflected parts of the snowy terrain and the desert world above it. It reflected the crimson-eyed albino who peered down at it, his features drawn in bewilderment and tiredness.

"I am at their mercy," said Elric. "They play with me. But I shall resist them, even as they destroy me." And some of his wild, careless spirit came back to him as he prepared to lower himself onto the chequered floor and cross to the opposite bank.

He was half-way over when he heard a grunting sound in the distance and a beast appeared, its paws slithering uncertainly on the smooth surface, its seven savage eyes glaring in all directions as if it sought the instigator of its terrible indignity.

And, at last, all seven eyes focused on Elric and the beast opened a mouth in which row upon row of thin, vicious teeth were arranged, and uttered a growl of unmistakable resentment.

Elric raised his sword. "Back, creature of Chaos. You threaten the Prince of Melniboné."

The beast was already propelling itself towards him. Elric flung his body to one side, aiming a blow with the sword as he did so, succeeding only in making a thin incision in the monster's heavily muscled hind leg. It shrieked and began to turn.

"Back."

Elric's voice was the brave, thin squeak of a lemming attacked by a hawk. He drove at the thing's snout with Stormbringer. The sword was heavy. It had spent all its energy and there was no more to give. Elric wondered why he, himself, did not weaken. Possibly the laws of nature were entirely abolished in the Realm of Chaos. He struck and drew blood. The beast paused, more in astonishment than fear.

Then it opened its jaws, pushed its back legs against the snowy bank, and shot towards the albino who tried to dodge it, lost his footing, and fell, sprawling backwards, on the gold and silver surface.

3. IN WHICH UNA PERSSON DISCOVERS AN UNEXPECTED SNAG

The gigantic beetle, rainbow carapace glittering, turned as if into the wind, which blew from the distant mountains, its thick, flashing wings beating rapidly as it bore its single passenger over the queer landscape.

On its back Mrs. Persson checked the instruments on her wrist. Ever since Man had begun to travel in time it had become necessary for the League to develop techniques to compensate for the fluctuations and disruptions in the spacetime continua; perpetually monitoring the chronoflow and megaflow. She pursed her lips. She had picked up the signal. She made the semi-sentient beetle swing a degree or two SSE and head directly for the mountains. She was in some sort of enclosed (but vast) environment. These mountains, as well as everything surrounding them, lay in the territory most utilised by the gloomy, natural-born Werther de Goethe, poet and romantic, solitary seeker after truth in a world no longer differentiating between the degrees of reality. He would not remember her, she knew, because, as far as Werther was concerned, they had not met yet. He had not even, if Una were correct, experienced his adventure with Mistress Christia, the Everlasting Concubine. A story on which she had dined out more than once, in duller eras.

The mountains drew closer. From here it was possible to see the entire arrangement (a creation of Werther's very much in character): a desert landscape, a central sun, and, inverted above it, winter mountains. Werther strove to make statements, like so many naïve artists before him, by presenting simple contrasts: The World is Bleak/The World is Cold/Barren Am I As I Grow Old/Tomorrow I Die, Entombed in Cold/For Silver My Poor Soul Was Sold—she remembered he was perhaps the worst poet she had encountered in an eternity of meetings with bad poets. He had taught himself to read and write in old, old English so that he might carve those words on one of his many abandoned tombs (half his time was spent in composing obituaries for himself). Like so many others he seemed to equate self-pity with artistic inspiration. In an earlier age he might have discovered his public and become quite rich (self-pity passing for passion in the popular understanding). Sometimes she regretted the passing of Wheldrake, so long ago, so far away, in a universe bearing scarcely any resemblances to those in which she normally operated.

She brought her wavering mind back to the problem. The beetle dipped and circled over the desert, but there was no sight of her quarry.

She was about to abandon the search when she heard a faint roaring overhead and she looked up to see another characteristic motif of Werther's—a gold and silver chessboard on which, upside down, a monstrous dog-like creature was bearing down on a tiny white-haired man dressed in the most abominable taste Una had seen for some time.

She directed the aircar upwards and then, reversing the machine as she entered the opposing gravity, downwards to where the barbarically costumed swordsman was about to be eaten by the beast.

"Shoo!" cried Una commandingly.

The beast raised a befuddled head.

"Shoo."

It licked lips and returned its seven-eyed gaze to the albino, who was now on his knees, using his large sword to steady himself as he climbed to his feet.

The jaws opened wider and wider. The pale man prepared, shakily, to defend himself.

Una directed the aircar at the beast's unkempt head. The great beetle connected with a loud crack. The monster's eyes widened in dismay. It yelped. It sat on its haunches and began to slide away, its claws making an unpleasant noise on the gold and silver tiles.

Una landed the aircar and gestured for the stranger to enter. She noticed with distaste that he was a somewhat unhealthy looking albino with gaunt features, exaggeratedly large and slanting eyes, ears that were virtually pointed, and glaring, half-mad red pupils.

And yet, undoubtedly, it was her quarry and there was nothing for it but to be polite.

"Do, please, get in," she said. "I am here to rescue you."

"Shaarmraaam torjistoo quellahm vyeearrr," said the stranger in an accent that seemed to Una to be vaguely Scottish.

"Damn," she said, "that's all we need." She had been anxious to approach the albino in private, before one of the denizens of the End of Time could arrive and select him for a menagerie, but now she regretted that Werther or perhaps Lord Jagged were not here, for she realised that she needed one of their translation pills, those tiny tablets which could "engineer" the brain to understand a new language. By a fluke—or perhaps because of her presence here so often—the people at the End of Time currently spoke formal early twentieth-century English.

The albino—who wore a kind of tartan divided kilt, knee-length boots, a blue and white jerkin, a green cloak and a silver breastplate, with a variety of leather belts and metal buckles here and there upon his person—was vehemently refusing her offer of a lift. He raised the sword before him as he backed away, slipped once, reached the bank, scrambled through snow and disappeared behind a rock.

Mrs. Persson sighed and put the car into motion again.

4. IN WHICH THE PRINCE OF MELNIBONÉ ENCOUNTERS FURTHER TERRORS

Xiombarg herself, thought Elric as he slid beneath the snows into the cave. Well, he would have no dealings with the Queen of Chaos; not until he was forced to do so.

The cave was large. In the thin light from the gap above his head he could not see far. He wondered whether to return to the surface or risk going deeper into the cave. There was always the hope that he would find another way out. He was attempting to recall some rune that would aid him, but all he knew depended either upon the aid of elementals who did not exist on this plane, or upon the Lords of Chaos themselves—and they were unlikely to come to his assistance in their own Realm. He was marooned here: the single mouse in a world of cats.

Almost unconsciously he found himself moving downwards, realising that the cave had become a tunnel. He was feeling hungry but, apart from the monster and the woman in the magical carriage, had seen no sign of life. Even the cavern did not seem entirely natural.

It widened; there was phosphorescent light. He realised that the walls were of transparent crystal and, behind the walls, were all manner of artefacts. He saw crowns, sceptres and chains of precious jewels; cabinets of complicated carving; weapons of strangely turned metal; armour, clothing, things whose use he could not guess—and food. There were sweetmeats, fruits, flans and pies, all out of reach.

Elric groaned. This was torment. Perhaps deliberately planned torment. A thousand voices whispered to him in a beautiful, alien language: *"Bie-meee . . . Bie-meee . . ."* the voices murmured. *"Baa-gen baa-gen . . ."*

They seemed to be promising evey delight, if only he could pass through the walls; but they were of transparent quartz, lit from within. He raised Stormbringer, half-tempted to try to break down the barrier, but he knew that even his sword was, at its most powerful, incapable of destroying the magic of Chaos.

He paused, gaping with astonishment at a group of small dogs which looked at him with large brown eyes, tongues lolling, and jumped up at him.

"O, Nee Tubbens!" intoned one of the voices.

"Gods," screamed Elric. "This torture is too much!" He swung his body this way and that, threatening with his sword, but the voices continued to murmur and promise, displaying their riches but never allowing him to touch.

The albino panted. His crimson eyes glared about him. "You would drive me insane, eh? Well, Elric of Melniboné has witnessed more frightful threats than this. You will need to do more if you would destroy his mind!"

And he ran through the whispering passages, looking to neither his right nor his left, until, quite suddenly, he had run into blazing daylight and stood staring down into pale infinity—a blue and endless void.

He looked up. And he screamed.

Overhead were the gentle hills and dales of a rural landscape, with rivers, grazing cattle, woods and cottages. He expected to fall, headlong, but he did not. He was on the brink of the abyss. The cliff-face of red sandstone fell immediately below and then was the tranquil void. He looked back: *"Baa-gen . . . O, Nee Tubbens . . ."*

A bitter smile played about the albino's bloodless lips as, decisively, he sheathed his sword.

"Well, then," he said. "Let them do their worst!"

And, laughing, he launched himself over the brink of the cliff.

5. IN WHICH WERTHER DE GOETHE MAKES A WONDERFUL DISCOVERY

With a gesture of quiet pride, Werther de Goethe indicated his gigantic skull.

"It is very large, Werther," said Mistress Christia, the Everlasting Concubine, turning a power ring to adjust the shade of her eyes so that they perfectly matched the day.

"It is monstrous," said Werther modestly. "It reminds us all of the Inevitable Night."

"Who was that?" enquired golden-haired Gaf the Horse in Tears, at present studying ancient legendry. "Sir Lew Grady?"

"I mean Death," Werther told him, "which overwhelms us all."

"Well, not us," pointed out the Duke of Queens, as usual a trifle literal minded. "Because we're immortal, as you know."

Werther offered him a sad, pitying look and sighed briefly. "Retain your delusions, if you will."

Mistress Christia stroked the gloomy Werther's long, dark locks. "There, there," she said. "We have compensations, Werther."

"Without Death," intoned the Last Romantic, "there is no point to Life."

As usual, they could not follow him, but they nodded gravely and politely.

"The skull," continued Werther, stroking the side of his aircar (which was in the shape of a large flying reptile) to make it circle and head for the left eye-socket, "is a Symbol not only of our Morality, but also of our Fruitless Ambitions."

"Fruit?" Bishop Castle, drowsing at the rear of the vehicle, became interested. His hobby was currently orchards. "Less? My pine-trees, you know, are proving a problem. The apples are much smaller than I was led to believe."

"The skull is lovely," said Mistress Christia with valiant enthusiasm. "Well, now that we have seen it . . ."

"The outward shell," Werther told her. "It is what it hides which is more important. Man's Foolish Yearnings are all encompassed therein. His Greed, his Need for the Impossible, the Heat of his Passions, the Coldness which must Finally Overtake him. Through this eye-socket you will encounter a little invention of my own called The Bargain Basement of the Mind . . ."

He broke off in astonishment.

On the top edge of the eye-socket a tiny figure had emerged.

"What's that?" enquired the Duke of Queens, craning his head back. "A random thought?"

"It is not mine at all!"

The figure launched itself into the sky and seemed to fly, with flailing limbs, towards the sun.

Werther frowned, watching the tiny man disappear. "The gravity field is reversed there," he said absently, "in order to make the most of the paradox, you understand. There is a snowscape, a desert . . ." But he was much more interested in the newcomer. "How do you think he got into my skull?"

"At least he's enjoying himself. He seems to be laughing," Mistress Christia bent an ear towards the thin sound, which grew fainter and fainter at first, but became louder again. "He's coming back."

Werther nodded. "Yes. The field's no longer reversed." He touched a power ring.

The laughter stopped and became a yell of rage. The figure hurtled down on them. It had a sword in one white hand and its red eyes blazed.

Hastily, Werther stroked another ring. The stranger tumbled into the bottom of the aircar and lay there panting, cursing and groaning.

"How wonderful!" cried Werther. "Oh, this is a traveller from some rich, romantic past. Look at him! What else could he be? What a prize!"

The stranger rose to his feet and raised the sword high above his head, defying the amazed and delighted passengers as he screamed at the top of his voice:

Heegeegrowinaz!"

"Good afternoon," said Mistress Christia. She reached in her purse for a translation pill and found one. "I wonder if you would care to swallow this—it's quite harmless . . ."

"*Yakooom, oom glallio,*" said the albino contemptuously.

"Aha," said Mistress Christia. "Well, just as you please."

The Duke of Queens pointed towards the other socket. A huge, whirring beetle came sailing from it. In its back was someone he recognised with pleasure. "Mrs. Persson!"

Una brought her aircar alongside.

"Is he in your charge?" asked Werther with undisguised disappointment. "If so, I could offer you . . ."

"I'm afraid he means a lot to me," she said.

"From your own age?" Mistress Christia also recognised Una. She still offered the translation pill in the palm of her hand. "He seems a mite suspicious of us."

"I'd noticed," said Una. "It would be useful if he would accept the pill. However, if he will not, one of us . . ."

"I would be happy," offered the generous Duke of Queens. He tugged at his green and gold beard. "Werther de Goethe, Mrs. Persson."

"Perhaps I had better," said Una nodding to Werther. The only problem with translation pills was that they did their job so thoroughly. You could speak the language perfectly, but you could speak no other.

Werther was, for once, positive. "Let's all take a pill," he suggested.

Everyone at the End of Time carried translation pills, in case of meeting a visitor from Space or the Past.

Mistress Christia handed hers to Una and found another. They swallowed.

"Creatures of Chaos," said the newcomer with cool dignity, "I demand that you release me. You cannot hold a mortal in this way, not unless he has struck a bargain with you. And no bargain was struck which would bring me to the Realm of Chaos."

"It's actually more orderly than you'd think," said Werther apologetically. "Your first experience, you see, was the world of my skull, which was deliberately muddled. I meant to show that Confusion was the Mind of Man . . ."

"May I introduce Mistress Christia, the Everlasting Concubine," said the Duke of Queens, on his best manners. "This is Mrs. Persson, Bishop Castle, Gaf the Horse in Tears. Werther de Goethe—your unwitting host—and I am the Duke of Queens. We welcome you to our world. Your name, sir . . . ?"

"You must know me, my lord duke," said Elric. "For I am Elric of Melniboné, Emperor by Right of Birth, Inheritor of the Ruby Throne, Bearer of the Actorios, Wielder of the Black Sword . . ."

"Indeed!" said Werther de Goethe. In a whispered aside to Mrs. Persson: "What a marvellous scowl! What a noble sneer!"

"You are an important personage in your world, then?" said Mistress Christia, fluttering the eyelashes she had just extended by half an inch. "Perhaps you would allow me . . ."

"I think he wishes to be returned to his home," said Mrs. Persson hastily.

"Returned?" Werther was astonished. "But the Morphail Effect! It is impossible."

"Not in this case, I think," she said. "For if he is not returned there is no telling the fluctuations which will take place throughout the dimensions . . ."

They could not follow her, but they accepted her tone.

"Aye," said Elric darkly, "return me to my realm, so that I may fulfill my own doom-laden destiny . . ."

Werther looked upon the albino with affectionate delight. "Aha! A fellow spirit! I, too, have a doom-laden destiny."

"I doubt it is as doom-laden as mine." Elric peered moodily back at the skull as the two aircars fled away towards a gentle horizon where exotic trees bloomed.

"Well," said Werther with an effort, "perhaps it is not, though I assure you . . ."

"I have looked upon hell-born horror," said Elric, "and communicated with the very Gods of the Uttermost Darkness. I have seen things which would turn other men's minds to useless jelly . . ."

"Jelly?" interrupted Bishop Castle. "Do you, in your turn, have any expertise with, for instance, blackbird trees?"

"Your words are meaningless," Elric told him, glowering. "Why do you torment me so, my lords? I did not ask to visit your world. I belong in the world of men, in the Young Kingdoms, where I seek my weird. Why, I have but lately experienced adventures . . ."

"I do think we have one of those bores," murmured Bishop Castle to the Duke of Queens, "so common amongst time-travellers. They all believe themselves unique."

But the Duke of Queens refused to be drawn. He had developed a liking for the frowning albino. Gaf the Horse in Tears was also plainly impressed, for he had fashioned his own features into a rough likeness of Elric's. The Prince of Melniboné pretended insouciance, but it was evident to Una that he was frightened. She tried to calm him.

"People here at the End of Time . . ." she began.

"No soft words, my lady." A cynical smile played about the albino's lips. "I know you for that great unholy temptress, Queen of the Swords, Xiombarg herself."

"I assure you, I am as human as you, sir . . ."

"Human? I, human? I am not human, madam—though I be a mortal, 'tis true. I am of older blood, the blood of the Bright Empire itself, the blood of R'lin K'ren A'a which Cran Liret mocked, not understanding what it was he laughed at. Aye, though forced to summon aid from Chaos, I made no bargain to become a slave in your realm . . ."

"I assure you—um—your majesty," said Una, "that we had not meant to insult you and your presence here was no doing of ours. I am, as it happens, a stranger here myself. I came especially to see you, to help you escape . . ."

"Ha!" said the albino. "I have heard such words before. You would lure me into some worse trap than this. Tell me, where is Duke Arioch? He, at least, I owe some allegiance to."

"We have no one of that name," apologised Mistress Christia. She enquired of Gaf, who knew everyone. "No time-traveller?"

"None," Gaf studied Elric's eyes and made a small adjustment to his own. He sat back, satisfied.

Elric shuddered and turned away mumbling.

"You are very welcome here," said Werther. "I cannot tell you how glad I am to meet one as essentially morbid and self-pitying as myself!"

Elric did not seem flattered.

"What can we do to make you feel at home?" asked Mistress Christia. She had changed her hair to a rather glossy blue in the hope, perhaps, that Elric would find it more attractive. "Is there anything you need?"

"Need? Aye. Peace of mind. Knowledge of my true destiny. A quiet place where I can be with Cymoril, whom I love."

"What does this Cymoril look like?" Mistress Christia became just a trifle over-eager.

"She is the most beautiful creature in the universe," said Elric.

"It isn't very much to go on," said Mistress Christia. "If you could imagine a picture, perhaps? There are devices in the old cities which could visualise your thoughts. We could go there. I should be happy to fill in for her, as it were . . ."

"What? You offer me a simulacrum? Do you not think I should

detect such witchery at once? Ah, this is loathsome! Slay me, if you will, or continue the torment. I'll listen no longer!"

They were floating now, between high cliffs. On a ledge far below a group of time-travellers pointed up at them. One waved desperately.

"You've offended him, Mistress Christia," said Werther pettishly. "You don't understand how sensitive he is."

"Yes I do." She was aggrieved. "I was only being sympathetic."

"Sympathy!" Elric rubbed at his long, somewhat pointed jaw. "Ha! What do I want with sympathy?"

"I never heard anyone who wanted it more." Mistress Christia was kind. "You're like a little boy, really, aren't you?"

"Compared to the ancient Lords of Chaos, I am a child, aye. But my blood is old and cold, the blood of decaying Melniboné, as well you know." And with a huge sigh the albino seated himself at the far end of the car and rested his head on his fist. "Well? What is your pleasure, my lords and ladies of Hell?"

"It is your pleasure we are anxious to achieve," Werther told him. "Is there anything at all we can do? Some environment we can manufacture? What are you used to?"

"Used to? I am used to the crack of leathery dragon wings in the sweet, sharp air of the early dawn. I am used to the sound of red battle, the drumming of hooves on bloody earth, the screams of the dying, the yells of the victorious. I am used to warring against demons and monsters, sorcerers and ghouls. I have sailed on magic ships and fought hand to hand with reptilian savages. I have encountered the Jade Man himself. I have fought side by side with the elementals, who are my allies. I have battled black evil . . ."

"Well," said Werther, "that's something to go on, at any rate. I'm sure we can . . ."

"Lord Elric won't be staying," began Una Persson politely. "You see—these fluctuations in the megaflow—not to mention his own destiny . . . He should not be here, at all, Werther."

"Nonsense!" Werther flung a black velvet arm about the stiff shoulders of his new friend. "It is evident that our destinies are one. Lord Elric is as grief-haunted as myself!"

"How can you know what it is to be haunted by grief . . . ?" murmured the albino. His face was half-buried in Werther's generous sleeve.

Mrs. Persson controlled herself. She rose from Werther's aircar and made for her own. "Well," she said, "I must be off. I hope to see you later, everybody."

They sang out their farewells.

Una Persson turned her beetle westward, towards Castle Canaria, the home of her old friend Lord Jagged.

She needed help and advice.

6. IN WHICH ELRIC OF MELNIBONÉ RESISTS THE TEMPTATIONS OF THE CHAOS LORDS

Elric reflected on the subtle way in which laughing Lords of Chaos had captured him. Apparently, he was merely a guest and quite free to wander where he would in their Realm. Actually, he was in their power as much as if they had chained him, for he could not flee this flying dragon and they had already demonstrated their enormous magical gifts in subtle ways, primarily with their shapechanging. Only the one who called himself Werther de Goethe (plainly a leader in the hierarchy of Chaos) still had the face and clothing he had worn when first encountered.

It was evident that this realm obeyed no natural laws, that it was mutable according to the whims of its powerful inhabitants. They could destroy him with a breath and had, subtly enough, given him evidence of that fact. How could he possibly escape such danger? By calling upon the Lords of Law for aid? But he owed them no loyalty and they, doubtless, regarded him as their enemy. But if he were to transfer his allegiance to Law . . .

These thoughts and more continued to engage him, while his captors chatted easily in the ancient High Speech of Melniboné, itself a version of the very language of Chaos. It was one of the other ways in which they revealed themselves for what they were. He fingered his runesword, wondering if it would be possible to slay such a lord and steal his energy, giving himself enough power for a little while to hurl himself back to his own sphere . . .

The one called Lord Werther was leaning over the side of the beast-vessel. "Oh, come and see, Elric. Look!"

Reluctantly, the albino moved to where Werther peered and pointed.

The entire landscape was filled with a monstrous battle. Creatures of all kinds and all combinations tore at one another with huge teeth and claws. Shapeless things slithered and hopped; giants, naked but for helmets and greaves, slashed at these beasts with great broadswords and axes, but were borne down. Flame and black smoke drifted everywhere. There was a smell. The stink of blood?

"What do you miss most?" asked the female. She pressed a soft body against him. He pretended not to be aware of it. He knew what magic flesh could hide on a she-witch.

"I miss peace," said Elric almost to himself, "and I miss war. For in battle I find a kind of peace . . ."

"Very good!" Bishop Castle applauded. "You are beginning to learn our ways. You will soon become one of our best conversationalists."

Elric touched the hilt of Stormbringer, hoping to feel it grow warm and vibrant under his hand, but it was still, impotent in the Realm of Chaos. He uttered a heavy sigh.

"You are an adventurer, then, in your own world?" said the Duke of Queens. He was bluff. He had changed his beard to an ordinary sort of black and was wearing a scarlet costume; quilted doublet and tight-fitting hose, with a blue and white ruff, an elaborately feathered hat on his head. "I, too, am something of a vagabond. As far, of course, as it is possible to be here. A buccaneer, of sorts. That is, my actions are in the main bolder than those of my fellows. More spectacular. Vulgar. Like yourself, sir. I admire your costume."

Elric knew that this Duke of Hell was referring to the fact that he affected the costume of the southern barbarian, that he did not wear the more restrained colours and more cleverly wrought silks and metals of his own folk. He gave tit for tat at this time. He bowed.

"Thank you, sir. Your own clothes rival mine."

"Do you think so?" The hell-lord pretended pleasure. If Elric had not known better, the creature would seem to be swelling with pride.

"Look!" cried Werther again. "Look, Lord Elric—we are attacked."

Elric whirled.

From below were rising oddly-wrought vessels—something like ships, but with huge round wheels at their sides, like the wheels of water-clocks he had seen once in Pikarayd. Coloured smoke issued from chimneys mounted on their decks which swarmed with huge birds dressed in human clothing. The birds had multi-coloured plumage, curved beaks, and they held swords in their claws, while on their heads were strangely shaped black hats on which were blazed skulls with crossed bones beneath.

"Heave to!" squawked the birds. "Or we'll put a shot across your bowels!"

"What can they be?" cried Bishop Castle.

"Parrots," said Werther de Goethe soberly. "Otherwise known as the hawks of the sea. And they mean us no good."

Mistress Christia blinked.

"Don't you mean pirates, dear?"

Elric took a firm grip on his sword. Some of the words the Chaos Lords used were absolutely meaningless to him. But whether the attacking creatures were of their own conception, or whether they were true enemies of his captors, Elric prepared to do bloody battle. His spirits improved. At least here was something substantial to fight.

7. IN WHICH MRS. PERSSON BECOMES ANXIOUS ABOUT THE FUTURE OF THE UNIVERSE

Lord Jagged of Canaria was nowhere to be found. His huge castle, of gold and yellow spires, an embellished replica of Kings Cross station, was populated entirely by his quaint robots, whom Jagged found at once more mysterious and more trustworthy than android or human servants, for they could answer only according to a limited programme.

Una suspected that Jagged was, himself, upon some mission, for he, too, was a member of the League of Temporal Adventurers. But she needed aid. Somehow she had to return Elric to his own dimensions without creating further disruptions in the fabric of Time and Space. The Conjunction was not due yet and, if things got any worse, might never come. So many plans depended on the Conjunction of the Million Spheres that she could not risk its failure. But she could not reveal too much either to Elric or his hosts. As a Guild member she was sworn to the utmost and indeed necessary secrecy. Even here at the End of Time there were certain laws which could be disobeyed only at enormous risk. Words alone were dangerous when they described ideas concerning the nature of Time.

She racked her brains. She considered seeking out Jherek Carnelian, but then remembered that he had scarcely begun to understand his own destiny. Besides, there were certain similarities between Jherek and Elric which she could only sense at present. It would be best to go cautiously there.

She decided that she had no choice. She must return to the Time Centre and see if they could detect Lord Jagged for her.

She brought the necessary co-ordinates together in her mind and concentrated. For a moment all memories, all sense of identity left her.

Sergeant Alvarez was beside himself. His screens were no longer completely without form. Instead, peculiar shapes could be seen in the arrangements of lines. Una thought she saw faces, beasts, landscapes. That had never occurred before. The instruments, at least, had remained sane, even as they recorded insanity.

"It's getting worse," said Alvarez. "You've hardly any Time left. What there is, I've managed to borrow for you. Did you contact the rogue?"

She nodded. "Yes. But getting him to return . . . I want you to find Jagged."

"Jagged? Are you sure?"

"It's our only chance, I think."

Alvarez sighed and bent a tense back over his controls.

8. IN WHICH ELRIC AND WERTHER FIGHT SIDE BY SIDE AGAINST ALMOST OVERWHELMING ODDS

Somewhere, it seemed to Elric, as he parried and thrust at the attacking bird-monsters, rich and rousing music played. It must be a delusion, brought on by battle-madness. Blood and feathers covered the carriage. He saw the one called Christia carried off screaming. Bishop Castle had disappeared. Gaf had gone. Only the three of them, shoulder to shoulder, continued to fight. What was disconcerting to Elric was that Werther and the Duke of Queens bore swords absolutely identical to Stormbringer. Perhaps they were the legendary Brothers of the Black Sword, said to reside in Chaos?

He was forced to admit to himself that he experienced a sense of comradeship with these two, who were braver than most in defending themselves against such dreadful, unlikely monsters—perhaps some creation of their own which had turned against them.

Having captured the Lady Christia, the birds began to return to their own craft.

"We must rescue her!" cried Werther as the flying ships began to retreat. "Quickly! In pursuit!"

"Should we not seek reinforcements?" asked Elric, further impressed by the courage of this Chaos Lord.

"No time!" cried the Duke of Queens. "After them!"

Werther shouted to his vessel. "Follow those ships!"

The vessel did not move.

"It has an enchantment on it," said Werther. "We are stranded! Ah, and I love her so much!"

Elric became suspicious again. Werther had shown no signs, previously, of any affection for the female.

"You loved her?"

"From a distance," Werther explained. "Duke of Queens, what can we do? Those parrots will ransom her savagely and mishandle her objects of virtue!"

"Dastardly poltroons!" roared the huge duke.

Elric could make little sense of this exchange. It dawned on him, then, that he could still hear the rousing music. He looked below. On some sort of dais in the middle of the bizarre landscape a large group of musicians was assembled. They played on, apparently oblivious of what happened above. This was truly a world dominated by Chaos.

Their ship began slowly to fall towards the band. It lurched. Elric gasped and clung to the side as they struck yielding ground and bumped to a halt.

The Duke of Queens, apparently elated, was already scrambling overboard. "There! We can follow on those mounts."

Tethered near the dais was a herd of creatures bearing some slight resemblance to horses but in a variety of dazzling, metallic colours, with horns and bony ridges on their backs. Saddles and bridles of alien workmanship showed that they were domestic beasts, doubtless belonging to the musicians.

"They will want some payment from us, surely," said Elric, as they hurried towards the horses.

"Ah, true!" Werther reached into a purse at his belt and drew forth a handful of jewels. Casually he flung them towards the musicians and climbed into the saddle of the nearest beast. Elric and the Duke of

Queens followed his example. Then Werther, with a whoop, was off in the direction in which the bird-monsters had gone.

The landscape of this world of Chaos changed rapidly as they rode. They galloped through forests of crystalline trees, over fields of glowing flowers, leapt rivers the colour of blood and the consistency of mercury, and their tireless mounts maintained a headlong pace which never faltered. Through clouds of boiling gas which wept, through rain, through snow, through intolerable heat, through shallow lakes in which oddly fashioned fish wriggled and gasped, until at last a range of mountains came in sight.

"There!" panted Werther, pointing with his own runesword. "Their lair. Oh, the fiends! How can we climb such smooth cliffs?"

It was true that the base of the cliffs rose some hundred feet before they became suddenly ragged, like the rotting teeth of the beggars of Nadsokor. They were of dusky, purple obsidian and so smooth as to reflect the faces of the three adventurers who stared at them in despair.

It was Elric who saw the steps cut into the side of the cliff.

"These will take us up some of the way, at least."

"It could be a trap," said the Duke of Queens. He, too, seemed to be relishing the opportunity to take action. Although a Lord of Chaos there was something about him that made Elric respond to a fellow spirit.

"Let them trap us," said Elric laconically. "We have our swords."

With a wild laugh, Werther de Goethe was the first to swing himself from his saddle and run towards the steps, leaping up them almost as if he had the power of flight. Elric and the Duke of Queens followed more slowly.

Their feet slipping in the narrow spaces not meant for mortals to climb, ever aware of the dizzying drop on their left, the three came at last to the top of the cliff and stood clinging to sharp crags, staring across a plain at a crazy castle rising into the clouds before them.

"Their stronghold," said Werther.

"What are these creatures?" Elric asked. "Why do they attack you? Why do they capture the Lady Christia?"

"They nurse an abiding hatred for us," explained the Duke of Queens, and looked expectantly at Werther, who added:

"This was their world before it became ours."

"And before it became theirs," said the Duke of Queens, "it was the world of the Yargtroon."

"The Yargtroon?" Elric frowned.

"They dispossessed the bodiless vampire goat-folk of Kia," explained Werther. "Who, in turn, destroyed—or thought they destroyed—the Grash-Tu-Xem, a race of Old Ones older than any Old Ones except the Elder Old Ones of Ancient Thriss."

"Older even than Chaos?" asked Elric.

"Oh, far older," said Werther.

"It's almost completely collapsed, it's so old," added the Duke of Queens.

Elric was baffled. "Thriss?"

"Chaos," said the duke.

Elric let a thin smile play about his lips. "You still mock me, my lord. The power of Chaos is the greatest there is, only equalled by the power of Law."

"Oh, certainly," agreed the Duke of Queens.

Elric became suspicious again. "Do you play with me, my lord?"

"Well, naturally, we try to please our guests . . ."

Werther interrupted. "Yonder doomy edifice holds the one I love. Somewhere within its walls she is incarcerated, while ghouls taunt at her and devils threaten."

"The bird-monsters . . . ?" began Elric.

"Chimerae," said the Duke of Queens. "You saw only one of the shapes they assume."

Elric understood this. "Aha!"

"But how can we enter it?" Werther spoke almost to himself.

"We must wait until nightfall," said Elric, "and enter under the cover of darkness."

"Nightfall?" Werther brightened.

Suddenly they were in utter darkness.

Somewhere the Duke of Queens lost his footing and fell with a muffled curse.

9. IN WHICH MRS. PERSSON AT LAST MAKES CONTACT WITH HER OLD FRIEND

They stood together beneath the striped awning of the tent while a short distance away armoured men, mounted on armoured horses, jousted, were injured or died. The two members wore appropriate costumes for the period. Lord Jagged looked handsome in his surcoat and mail, but Una Persson merely looked uncomfortable in her wimple and kirtle.

"I can't leave just now," he was saying. "I am laying the foundations for a very important development."

"Which will come to nothing unless Elric is returned," she said.

A knight with a broken lance thundered past, covering them in dust.

"Well played Sir Holger!" called Lord Jagged. "An ancestor of mine, you know," he told her.

"You will not be able to recognise the world of the End of Time when you return, if this is allowed to continue," she said.

"It's always difficult, isn't it?" But he was listening to her now.

"These disruptions could as easily affect us and leave us stranded," she added. "We would lose any freedom we have gained."

He bit into a pomegranate and offered it to her. "You can only get these in this area. Did you know? Impossible to find in England. In the thirteenth century, at any rate. The idea of freedom is such a nebulous one, isn't it? Most of the time when angry people are speaking of 'freedom' what they are actually asking for is much simpler—respect. Do those in authority or those with power ever really respect those who do not have power?" He paused. "Or do they mean 'power' and not 'freedom.' Or are they the same . . . ?"

"Really, Jagged, this is no time for self-indulgence."

He looked about him. "There's little else to do in the Middle East in the thirteenth century, I assure you, except eat pomegranates and philosophise . . ."

"You must come back to the End of Time."

He wiped his handsome chin. "Your urgency," he said, "worries me, Una. These matters should be handled with delicacy—slowly . . ."

"The entire fabric will collapse unless he is returned to his own dimension. He is an important factor in the whole plan."

"Well, yes, I understand that."

"He is, in one sense at least, your protégé"

"I know. But not my responsibility."

"You must help," she said.

There was a loud bang and a crash.

A splinter flew into Mrs. Persson's eye.

"Oh, zounds!" she said.

10. IN WHICH THE CASTLE IS ASSAULTED AND THE PLOT THICKENED

A moon had appeared above the spires of the castle which seemed to Elric to have changed its shape since he had first seen it. He meant to ask his companions for an explanation, but at present they were all sworn to silence as they crept nearer. From within the castle burst light, emanating from guttering brands stuck into brackets on the walls. There was laughter, noise of feasting. Hidden behind a rock they peered through one large window and inspected the scene within.

The entire hall was full of men wearing identical costumes. They had black skull caps, loose white blouses and trousers, black shoes. Their eyebrows were black in dead white faces, even paler than Elric's and they had bright red lips.

"Aha," whispered Werther, "the parrots are celebrating their victory. Soon they will be too drunk to know what is happening to them."

"Parrots?" said Elric. "What is that word?"

"Pierrots, he means," said the Duke of Queens. "Don't you, Werther?" There were evidently certain words which did not translate easily into the High Speech of Melniboné.

"Sshh," said the Last Romantic, "they will capture us and torture us to death if they detect our presence."

They worked their way around the castle. It was guarded at intervals by gigantic warriors whom Elric at first mistook for statues, save that, when he looked closely, he could see them breathing very slowly. They were unarmed, but their fists and feet were disproportionately large and could crush any intruder they detected.

"They are sluggish, by the look of them," said Elric. "If we are quick, we can run beneath them and enter the castle before they realise it. Let me try first. If I succeed, you follow."

Werther clapped his new comrade on the back. "Very well."

Elric waited until the nearest guard halted and spread his huge feet apart, then he dashed forward, scuttling like an insect between the giant's legs and flinging himself through a dimly lit window. He found himself in some sort of storeroom. He had not been seen, though the guard cocked his ear for half a moment before resuming his pace.

Elric looked cautiously out and signalled to his companions. The Duke of Queens waited for the guard to stop again, then he, too, made for the window and joined Elric. He was panting and grinning. "This is wonderful," he said.

Elric admired his spirit. There was no doubt that the guard could crush any of them to a pulp, even if (as still nagged at his brain) this was all some sort of complicated illusion.

Another dash, and Werther was with them.

Cautiously, Elric opened the door of the storeroom. They looked onto a deserted landing. They crossed the landing and looked over a balustrade. They had expected to see another hall, but instead there was a miniature lake on which floated the most beautiful miniature ship, all mother-of-pearl, brass and ebony, with golden sails and silver masts. Surrounding this ship were mermaids and mermen bearing trays of exotic food (reminding Elric how hungry he still was) which they fed to the ship's only passenger, Mistress Christia.

"She is under an enchantment," said Elric. "They beguile her with illusions so that she will not wish to come with us even if we do rescue her. Do you know no counter-spells?"

Werther thought for a moment. Then he shook his head.

"You must be very minor Lords of Chaos," said Elric, biting his lower lip.

From the lake, Mistress Christia giggled and drew one of the mermaids towards her. "Come here, my pretty piscine!"

"Mistress Christia!" hissed Werther de Goethe.

"Oh!" The captive widened her eyes (which were now both large and blue). "At last!"

"You wish to be rescued?" said Elric.

"Rescued? Only by you, most alluring of albinoes!"

Elric hardened his features. "I am not the one who loves you, madam."

"What? I am loved? By whom? By you, Duke of Queens?"

"Sshh," said Elric. "The demons will hear us."

"Oh, of course," said Mistress Christia gravely, and fell silent for a second. "I'll get rid of all this, shall I?"

And she touched one of her rings.

Ship, lake and merfolk were gone. She lay on silken cushions, attended by monkeys.

"Sorcery!" said Elric. "If she has such power, then why—?"

"It is limited," explained Werther. "Merely to such tricks."

"Quite," said Mistress Christia.

Elric glared at them. "You surround me with illusions. You make me think I am aiding you, when really . . ."

"No, no!" cried Werther. "I assure you, Lord Elric, you have our greatest respect—well, mine at least—we are only attempting to—"

There was a roar from the gallery above. Rank upon rank of grinning demons looked down upon them. They were armed to the teeth.

"Hurry!" The Duke of Queens leapt to the cushions and seized Mistress Christia, flinging her over his shoulder. "We can never defeat so many!"

The demons were already rushing down the circular staircase. Elric, still not certain whether his new friends deceived him or not, made a decision. He called to the Duke of Queens. "Get her from the castle. We'll keep them from you for a few moments, at least." He could not help himself. He behaved impulsively.

The Duke of Queens, sword in one hand, Mistress Christia over the other shoulder, ran into a narrow passage. Elric and Werther stood together as the demons rushed down on them. Blade met blade. There was an unbearable shrilling of steel mingled with the cacklings and shrieks of the demons as they gnashed their teeth and rolled their eyes and slashed at the pair with swords, knives and axes. But worst of all was the smell. The dreadful smell of burning flesh which filled the air and threatened to choke Elric. It came from the demons. The smell of Hell. He did his best to cover his nostrils as he fought, certain that the smell must overwhelm him before the swords. Above him was a set of metal rungs fixed into the stones, leading high into a kind of a chimney. As a pause came he pointed upward to Werther, who understood him. For a moment they managed to drive the demons back. Werther jumped onto Elric's shoulders (again displaying a strange lightness) and reached down to haul the albino after him.

While the demons wailed and cackled below, they began to climb the chimney.

They climbed for nearly fifty feet before they found themselves in a small, round room whose windows looked out over the purple crags and, beyond them, to a scene of bleak rocky pavements pitted with holes, like some vast unlikely cheese.

And there, rolling over this relatively flat landscape, in full daylight (for the sun had risen) was the Duke of Queens in a carriage of brass and wood, studded with jewels, and drawn by two bovine creatures which looked to Elric as if they might be the fabulous oxen of mythology who had drawn the warchariot of his ancestors to do battle with the emerging nations of mankind.

Mistress Christia was beside the Duke of Queens. They seemed to be waiting for Elric and Werther.

"It's impossible," said the albino. "We could not get out of this tower, let alone those crags. I wonder how they managed to move so quickly and so far. And where did the chariot itself come from?"

"Stolen, no doubt, from the demons," said Werther. "See, there are wings here." He indicated a heap of feathers in the corner of the room. "We can use those."

"What wizardry is this?" said Elric. "Man cannot fly on bird wings."

"With the appropriate spell he can," said Werther. "I am not that well versed in the magic arts, of course, but let me see . . ." He picked up one set of wings. They were soft and glinted with subtle, rainbow colours. He placed them on Elric's back, murmuring his spell:

> *Oh, for the wings, for the wings of a dove,*
> *To carry me to the one I love . . .*

"There!" He was very pleased with himself. Elric moved his shoulders and his wings began to flap. "Excellent! Off you go, Elric. I'll join you in a moment."

Elric hesitated, then saw the head of the first demon emerging from the hole in the floor. He jumped to the window ledge and leapt into space. The wings sustained him. Against all logic he flew smoothly towards the waiting chariot and behind him, came Werther de Goethe. At the windows of the tower the demons crowded, shaking fists and weapons as their prey escaped them.

Elric landed rather awkwardly beside the chariot and was helped aboard by the Duke of Queens. Werther joined them, dropping expertly amongst them. He removed the wings from the albino's back and nodded to the Duke of Queens who yelled at the oxen, cracking his whip as they began to move.

Mistress Christia flung her arms about Elric's neck. "What courage! What resourcefulness!" she breathed. "Without you, I should now be ruined!"

Elric sheathed Stormbringer. "We all three worked together for your rescue, madam." Gently he removed her arms. Courteously he bowed and leaned against the far side of the chariot as it bumped and hurtled over the peculiar rocky surface.

"Swifter! Swifter!" called the Duke of Queens casting urgent looks backward. "We are followed!"

From the disappearing tower there now poured a host of flying, gibbering things. Once again the creatures had changed shape and had assumed the form of striped, winged cats, all glaring eyes, fangs and extended claws.

The rock became viscous, clogging the wheels of the chariot, as they reached what appeared to be a silvery road, flowing between the high trees of an alien forest already touched by a weird twilight.

The first of the flying cats caught up with them, slashing.

Elric drew Stormbringer and cut back. The beast roared in pain, blood streaming from its severed leg, its wings flapping in Elric's face as it hovered and attempted to snap at the sword.

The chariot rolled faster, through the forest to green fields touched by the moon. The days were short, it seemed, in this part of Chaos. A path stretched skyward. The Duke of Queens drove the chariot straight up it, heading for the moon itself.

The moon grew larger and larger and still the demons pursued them, but they could not fly as fast as the chariot which went so swiftly that sorcery must surely speed it. Now they could only be heard in the darkness behind and the silver moon was huge.

"There!" called Werther. "There is safety!"

On they raced until the moon was reached, the oxen leaping in their traces, galloping over the gleaming surface to where a white palace awaited them.

"Sanctuary," said the Duke of Queens. And he laughed a wild, full laugh of sheer joy.

The palace was like ivory, carved and wrought by a million hands, every inch covered with delicate designs.

Elric wondered. "Where is this place?" he asked. "Does it lie outside the Realm of Chaos?"

Werther seemed non-plussed. "You mean our world?"

"Aye."

"It is still part of our world," said the Duke of Queens.

"Is the palace to your liking?" asked Werther.

"It is lovely."

"A trifle pale for my own taste," said the Last Romantic. "It was Mistress Christia's idea."

"You built this?" the albino turned to the woman. "When?"

"Just now." She seemed surprised.

Elric nodded. "Aha. It is within the power of Chaos to create whatever whims it pleases."

The chariot crossed a white drawbridge and entered a white courtyard. In it grew white flowers. They dismounted and entered a huge hall, white as bone, in which red lights glowed. Again Elric began to suspect mockery, but the faces of the Chaos lords showed only pleasure. He realised that he was dizzy with hunger and weariness, as he had been ever since he had been flung into this terrible world where no shape was constant, no idea permanent.

"Are you hungry?" asked Mistress Christia.

He nodded. And suddenly the room was filled by a long table on which all kinds of food were heaped—and everything, meats and fruits and vegetables, was white.

Elric moved to take the seat she indicated and he put some of the food on a silver plate and he touched it to his lips and he tasted it. It was delicious. Forgetting suspicion, he began to eat heartily, trying not to consider the colourless quality of the meal. Werther and the Duke of Queens also took some food, but it seemed they ate only from politeness. Werther glanced up at the faraway roof. "What a wonderful tomb this would make," he said. "Your imagination improves, Mistress Christia."

"Is this your domain?" asked Elric. "The moon?"

"Oh, no," she said. "It was all made for the occasion."

"Occasion?"

"For your adventure," she said. Then she fell silent.

Elric became grave. "Those demons? They were not your enemies. They belong to you!"

"Belong?" said Mistress Christia. She shook her head.

Elric frowned and pushed back his plate. "I am, however, most certainly your captive." He stood up and paced the white floor. "Will you not return me to my own plane?"

"You would come back almost immediately," said Werther de Goethe. "It is called the Morphail Effect. And if you did not come here, you would yet remain in your own future. It is in the nature of Time."

"This is nonsense," said Elric. "I have left my own realm before and returned—though admittedly memory becomes weak, as with dreams poorly recalled."

"No man can go back in Time," said the Duke of Queens. "Ask Brannart Morphail."

"He, too, is a Lord of Chaos?"

"If you like. He is a colleague."

"Could he not return me to my realm? He sounds a clever being."

"He could not and he would not," said Mistress Christia. "Haven't you enjoyed your experiences here so far?"

"Enjoyed?" Elric was astonished. "Madam, I think . . . Well, what has happened this day is not what we mortals would call 'enjoyment!'"

"But you *seemed* to be enjoying yourself," said the Duke of Queens in some disappointment. "Didn't he, Werther?"

"You were much more cheerful through the whole episode," agreed the Last Romantic. "Particularly when you were fighting the demons."

"As with many time-travellers who suffer from anxieties," said Mistress Christia, "you appeared to relax when you had something immediate to capture your attention . . ."

Elric refused to listen. This was clever Chaos talk, meant to deceive him and take his mind from his chief concern.

"If I was any help to you," he began, "I am, of course . . ."

"He isn't very grateful," Mistress Christia pouted.

Elric felt madness creeping nearer again. He calmed himself.

"I thank you for the food, madam. Now, I would sleep."

"Sleep?" she was disconcerted. "Oh! Of course. Yes. A bedroom?"

"If you have such a thing."

"As many as you like." She moved a stone on one of her rings. The walls seemed to draw back to show bedchamber after bedchamber, in all manner of styles, with beds of every shape and fashion. Elric controlled his temper. He bowed, thanked her, said goodnight to the two lords and made for the nearest bed.

As he closed the door behind him, he thought he heard Werther de Goethe say: "We must try to think of a better entertainment for him when he wakes up."

11. IN WHICH MRS. PERSSON WITNESSES THE FIRST SIGN OF THE MEGAFLOW'S DISINTEGRATION

In Castle Canaria Lord Jagged unrolled his antique charts. He had had them drawn for him by a baffled astrologer in 1590. They were one of his many affectations. At the moment, however, they were of considerably greater use than Alvarez's electronics.

While he used a wrist computer to check his figures, Una Persson looked out of the window of Castle Canaria and wondered who had invented this particular landscape. A green and orange sun cast sickening light over the herds of grazing beasts who resembled, from this distance at any rate, nothing so much as gigantic human hands. In the middle of the scene was raised some kind of building in the shape of a vast helmet, vaguely Greek in conception. Beyond that was a low, grey moon. She turned away.

"I must admit," said Lord Jagged, "that I had not understood the extent . . ."

"Exactly," she said.

"You must forgive me. A certain amount of amnesia—euphoria, perhaps?—always comes over one in these very remote periods."

"Quite."

He looked up from the charts. "We've a few hours at most."

Her smile was thin, her nod barely perceptible.

While she made the most of having told him so, Lord Jagged frowned, turned a power ring and produced an already lit pipe which he placed thoughtfully in his mouth, taking it out again almost immediately. "That wasn't Dunhill Standard Medium." He laid the pipe aside.

There came a loud buzzing noise from the window. The scene outside was disintegrating as if melting on glass. An eerie golden light spread everywhere, flooding from an apex of deeper gold, as if forming a funnel.

"That's a rupture," said Lord Jagged. His voice was tense. He put his arm about her shoulders. "I've never seen anything of the size before."

Rushing towards them along the funnel of light there came an entire city of turrets and towers and minarets in a wide variety of pastel colours. It was set into a saucer-shaped base which was almost certainly several miles in circumference.

For a moment the city seemed to retreat. The golden light faded. The city remained, some distance away, swaying a little as if on a gentle tide, a couple of thousand feet above the ground, the grey moon below it.

"That's what I call megaflow distortion," said Una Persson in that inappropriately facetious tone adopted by those who are deeply frightened.

"I recognise the period." Jagged drew a telescope from his robes. "Second Candlemaker's Empire, mainly based in Arcturus. This is a village by their standards. After all, Earth was merely a rural park during that time." He retreated into academe, his own response to fear.

Una craned her head. "Isn't that some sort of vehicle heading towards the city. From the moon—good heavens, they've spotted it already. Are they going to try to put the whole thing into a menagerie?"

Jagged had the advantage of the telescope. "I think not." He handed her the instrument.

Through it she saw a scarlet and black chariot borne by what seemed to be some form of flying fairground horses. In the chariot, armed to the teeth with lances, bows, spears, swords, axes, morningstars, maces and almost every other barbaric hand-weapon, clad in quasi-mythological armour, were Werther de Goethe, the Duke of Queens and Elric of Melniboné.

"They're attacking it!" she said faintly. "What will happen when the two groups intersect?"

"Three groups," he pointed out. "Untangling that in a few hours is going to be even harder."

"And if we fail?"

He shrugged. "We might just as well give ourselves up to the biggest chronoquake the universe has ever experienced."

"You're exaggerating," she said.
"Why not? Everyone else is."

12. THE ATTACK ON THE CITADEL OF THE SKIES

"Melniboné! Melniboné!" cried the albino as the chariot circled over the spires and turrets of the city. They saw startled faces below. Strange engines were being dragged through the narrow streets.

"Surrender!" Elric demanded.

"I do not think they can understand us," said the Duke of Queens. "What a find, eh? A whole city from the past!"

Werther had been reluctant to embark on an adventure not of his own creation, but Elric, realising that here at last was a chance of escape, had been anxious to begin. The Duke of Queens had, in an instant, aided the albino by producing costumes, weapons, transport. Within minutes of the city's appearance, they had been on their way.

Exactly why Elric wished to attack the city, Werther could not make out, unless it was some test of the Melnibonéan's to see if his companions were true allies or merely pretending to have befriended him. Werther was learning a great deal from Elric, much more than he had ever learned from Mongrove, whose ideas of angst were only marginally less notional than Werther's own.

A broad, flat blue ray beamed from the city. It singed one wheel of the chariot.

"Ha! They make sorcerous weapons," said Elric. "Well, my friends. Let us see you counter with your own power."

Werther obediently imitated the blue ray and sent it back from his fingers, slicing the tops off several towers. The Duke of Queens typically let loose a different coloured ray from each of his extended ten fingers and bored a hole all the way through the bottom of the city so that fields could be seen below. He was pleased with the effect.

"This is the power of the Gods of Chaos!" cried Elric, a familiar elation filling him as the blood of old Melniboné was fired. "Surrender!"

"Why do you want them to surrender?" asked the Duke of Queens in some disappointment.

"Their city evidently has the power to fly through the dimensions.

If I became its lord I can force it to return to my own plane," said Elric reasonably.

"The Morphail Effect . . ." began Werther, but realised he was spoiling the spirit of the game. "Sorry."

The blue ray came again, but puttered out and faded before it reached them.

"Their power is gone!" cried Elric. "Your sorcery defeats them, my lords. Let us land and demand they honour us as their new rulers."

With a sigh, Werther ordered the chariot to set down in the largest square. Here they waited until a few of the citizens began to arrive, cautious and angry, but evidently in no mood to give any further resistance.

Elric addressed them. "It was necessary to attack and conquer you, for I must return to my own Realm, there to fulfill my great destiny. If you will take me to Melniboné, I will demand nothing further from you."

"One of us really ought to take a translation pill." said Werther. "These people probably have no idea where they are."

A meaningless babble came from the citizens. Elric frowned. "They understand not the High Speech," he said. "I will try the Common Tongue." He spoke in a language neither Werther, the Duke of Queens nor the citizens of this settlement could understand.

He began to show signs of frustration. He drew his sword Stormbringer. "By the Black Sword, know that I am Elric, last of the royal line of Melniboné! You must obey me. Is there none here who understands the High Speech?"

Then, from the crowd, stepped a being far taller than the others. He was dressed in robes of dark blue and deepest scarlet and his face was haughty, beautiful and full of evil.

"I speak the High Tongue," he said.

Werther and the Duke of Queens were non-plussed. This was no one they recognised.

Elric gestured. "You are the ruler of the city?"

"Call me that, if you will."

"Your name?"

"I am known by many names. And you know me, Elric of Melniboné, for I am your lord and your friend."

"Ah," said Elric lowering his sword, "this is the greatest deception of them all. I am a fool."

"Merely a mortal," said the newcomer, his voice soft, amused and full of a subtle arrogance. "Are these the renegades who helped you?"

"Renegades?" said Werther. "Who are you, sir?"

"You should know me, rogue lords. You aid a mortal and defy your brothers of Chaos."

"Eh?" said the Duke of Queens. "I haven't got a brother."

The stranger ignored him. "Demigods who thought that by helping this mortal they could threaten the power of the Greater Ones."

"So you did aid me against your own," said Elric. "Oh, my friends!"

"And they shall be punished!"

Werther began: "We regret any damage to your city. After all, you were not invited . . ."

The Duke of Queens was laughing. "Who are you? What disguise is this?"

"Know me for your master." The eyes of the stranger glowed with myriad fires. "Know me for Arioch, Duke of Hell!"

"Arioch!" Elric became filled with a strange joy. "Arioch! I called upon thee and was not answered!"

"I was not in this Realm," said the Duke of Hell. "I was forced to be absent. And while I was gone, fools thought to displace me."

"I really cannot follow all this," said the Duke of Queens. He set aside his mace. "I must confess I become a trifle bored, sir. If you will excuse me."

"You will not escape me." Arioch lifted a languid hand and the Duke of Queens was frozen to the ground, unable to move anything save his eyes.

"You are interfering, sir, with a perfectly—" Werther too was struck dumb and paralysed.

But Elric refused to quail. "Lord Arioch, I have given you blood and souls. You owe me . . ."

"I owe you nothing, Elric of Melniboné. Nothing I do not choose to owe. You are my slave . . ."

"No," said Elric. "I serve you. There are old bonds. But you cannot control me, Lord Arioch, for I have a power within me which you fear. It is the power of my very mortality."

The Duke of Hell shrugged. "You will remain in the Realm of Chaos forever. Your mortality will avail you little here."

"You need me in my own Realm, to be your agent. That, too, I know, Lord Arioch."

The handsome head lowered a fraction as if Arioch considered this. The beautiful lips smiled. "Aye, Elric. It is true that I need you to do my work. For the moment it is impossible for the Lords of Chaos to interfere directly in the world of mortals, for we should threaten our own existence. The rate of entropy would increase beyond even our control. The day has not yet come when Law and Chaos must decide the issue once and for all. But it will come soon enough for you, Elric."

"And my sword will be at your service, Lord Arioch."

"Will it, Elric?"

Elric was surprised by this doubting tone. He had always served Chaos, as his ancestors had. "Why should I turn against you? Law has no attractions for one such as Elric of Melniboné."

The Duke of Hell was silent.

"And there is the bargain," added Elric. "Return me to my own Realm, Lord Arioch, so that I might keep it."

Arioch sighed. "I am reluctant."

"I demand it," bravely said the albino.

"Oho!" Arioch was amused. "Well, mortal, I'll reward your courage and I'll punish your insolence. The reward will be that you are returned from whence you came, before you called on Chaos in your battle with that pathetic wizard. The punishment is that you will recall every incident that occurred since then—but only in your dreams. You will be haunted by the puzzle for the rest of your life—and you will never for a moment be able to express what mystifies you."

Elric smiled. "I am already haunted by a curse of that kind, my lord."

"Be that as it may, I have made my decision."

"I accept it," said the albino, and he sheathed his sword, Stormbringer.

"Then come with me," said Arioch, Duke of Hell. And he drifted forward, took Elric by the arm, and lifted them both high into the sky, floating over distorted scenes, half-formed dream-worlds, the whims of the Lords of Chaos, until they came to a gigantic rock shaped like a skull. And through one of the eye-sockets Lord Arioch bore Elric of Melniboné. And down strange corridors that whispered and displayed all manner of treasures. And up into a landscape, a desert in which grew many strange plants, while overhead could be seen a land of snow and mountains, equally alien. And from his robes Arioch, Duke of Hell produced a wand and he bade Elric to take hold of the wand, which was hot to the touch and glittered, and he placed his own slender hand at the other end, and he murmured words which Elric could not understand and together they began to fade from the landscape, into the darkness of limbo where many eyes accused them, to an island in a grey and storm-tossed sea; an island littered with destruction and with the dead.

Then Arioch, Duke of Hell, laughed a little and vanished, leaving the Prince of Melniboné sprawled amongst corpses and ruins while heavy rain beat down upon him.

And in the scabbard at Elric's side, Stormbringer stirred and murmured once more.

13. IN WHICH THERE IS A SMALL CELEBRATION AT THE END OF TIME

Werther de Goethe and the Duke of Queens blinked their eyes and found that they could move their heads. They stood in a large, pleasant room full of charts and ancient instruments. Mistress Christia was there, too.

Una Persson was smiling as she watched golden light fade from the sky. The city had disappeared, hardly any the worse for its experience. She had managed to save the two friends without a great deal of fuss, for the citizens had still been bewildered by what had happened to them. Because of the megaflow distortion, the Morphail Effect would not manifest itself. They would never understand where they had been or what had actually happened.

"Who on earth was that fellow who turned up?" asked the Duke of Queens. "Some friend of yours, Mrs. Persson? He's certainly no sportsman."

"Oh, I wouldn't agree. You could call him the ultimate sportsman," she said. "I am acquainted with him, as a matter of fact."

"It's not Jagged in disguise is it?" said Mistress Christia who did not really know what had gone on. "This is Jagged's castle—but where is Jagged?"

"You are aware how mysterious he is," Una answered. "I happened to be here when I saw that Werther and the Duke were in trouble in the city and was able to be of help."

Werther scowled (a very good copy of Elric's own scowl). "Well, it isn't good enough."

"It was a jolly adventure while it lasted, you must admit," said the Duke of Queens.

"It wasn't meant to be jolly," said Werther. "It was meant to be significant."

Lord Jagged entered the room. He wore his familiar yellow robes. "How pleasant," he said. "When did all of you arrive?"

"I have been here for some time," Mrs. Persson explained, "but Werther and the Duke of Queens . . ."

"Just got here," explained the duke. "I hope we're not intruding. Only we had a slight mishap and Mrs. Persson was good enough . . ."

"Always delighted," said the insincere lord. "Would you care to see my new—?"

"I'm on my way home," said the Duke of Queens. "I just stopped by. Mrs. Persson will explain."

"I, too," said Werther suspiciously, "am on my way back."

"Very well. Goodbye."

Werther summoned an aircar, a restrained figure of death, in rags with a sickle, who picked the three up in his hand and bore them towards a bleak horizon.

It was only days later, when he went to visit Mongrove to tell him of his adventures and solicit his friend's advice, that Werther realised he was still speaking High Melnibonéan. Some nagging thought remained with him for a long while after that. It concerned Lord Jagged, but he could not quite work out what was involved.

After this incident there were no further disruptions at the End of Time until the beginning of the story concerning Jherek Carnelian and Mrs. Amelia Underwood.

14. IN WHICH ELRIC OF MELNIBONÉ RECOVERS FROM A VARIETY OF ENCHANTMENTS AND BECOMES DETERMINED TO RETURN TO THE DREAMING CITY

Elric was awakened by the rain on his face. Wearily he peered around him. To left and right there were only the dismembered corpses of the dead, the Krettii and the Filkharian sailors destroyed during his battle with the halfbrute who had somehow gained so much sorcerous power. He shook his milk-white hair and he raised crimson eyes to the grey, boiling sky.

It seemed that Arioch had aided him, after all. The sorcerer was destroyed and he, Elric, remained alive. He recalled the sweet, bantering tones of his patron demon. Familiar tones, yet he could not remember what the words had been.

He dragged himself over the dead and waded through the shallows towards the Filkharian ship which still had some of its crew. They were, by now, anxious to head out into open sea again rather than face any more terrors on Sorcerer's Isle.

He was determined to see Cymoril, whom he loved, to regain his throne from Yyrkoon, his cousin . . .

15. IN WHICH A BRIEF REUNION TAKES PLACE AT THE TIME CENTRE

With the manuscript of Colonel Pyat's rather dangerous volume of memoirs safely back in her briefcase, Una Persson decided it was the right moment to check into the Time Centre. Alvarez should be on duty again and his instruments should be registering any minor imbalances resulting from the episode concerning the gloomy albino.

Alvarez was not alone. Lord Jagged was there, in a disreputable Norfolk jacket and smoking a battered briar. He had evidently been holidaying in Victorian England. He was pleased to see her.

Alvarez ran his gear through all functions. "Sweet and neat," he said. "It hasn't been as good since I don't know when. We've you to thank for that, Mrs. P."

She was modest.

"Certainly not. Jagged was the one. Your disguise was wonderful, Jagged. How did you manage to imitate that character so thoroughly? It convinced Elric. He really thought you were whatever it was—a Chaos Duke?"

Jagged waved a modest hand.

"I mean," said Una, "it's almost as if you *were* this fellow 'Arioch' . . ."

But Lord Jagged only puffed on his pipe and smiled a secret and superior smile.

WILLIAM MORRIS *was one of the most dynamic Victorian "Renaissance Men," an artist who sought to bring back the beauty and power of medieval art to the contemporary world. He wrote a pastoral utopian novel,* News from Nowhere *(1891), translated Norse sagas into English poetry, designed books at his marvelous Kelmscott Press in Hammersmith, England, even designed the Morris chair and created wallpaper designs. His contributions to the emergence of fantasy for adults were numerous and significant, focusing on heroic fantasies of marvelous feats.* The Well at the World's End *(1896) is his most important fantasy novel, but "Lindenborg Pool" (1856), an early work in his career, shows evidence that Morris, as has often been noted, is one of the great forefathers of Sword and Sorcery/Heroic Fantasy.*

Lindenborg Pool
BY WILLIAM MORRIS

I read once in lazy humour Thorpe's "Northern Mythology," on a cold May night when the north wind was blowing; in lazy humour, but when I came to the tale that is here amplified there was something in it that fixed my attention and made me think of it; and whether I would or no, my thoughts ran in this way, as here follows.

So I felt obliged to write, and wrote accordingly, and by the time I had done the grey light filled all my room; so I put out my candles, and went to bed, not without fear and trembling, for the morning twilight is so strange and lonely. This is what I wrote.

Yes, on that dark night, with that wild unsteady north wind howling, though it was Maytime, it was doubtless dismal enough in the forest, where the boughs clashed eerily, and where, as the wanderer in that place hurried along, strange forms half showed themselves to him, the more fearful because half seen in that way: dismal enough doubtless on wide moors where the great wind had it all its own way: dismal on the rivers creeping on and on between the marshlands, creeping through the willows, the water trickling through the locks, sounding faintly in the gusts of the wind.

Yet surely nowhere so dismal as by the side of that still pool.

I threw myself down on the ground there, utterly exhausted with my struggle against the wind, and with bearing the fathoms and fathoms of the heavily-leaded plumb-line that lay beside me.

Fierce as the wind was, it could not raise the leaden waters of that fearful pool, defended as they were by the steep banks of dripping yellow clay, striped horribly here and there with ghastly uncertain green and blue.

They said no man could fathom it; and yet all round the edges of it grew a rank crop of dreary reeds and segs, some round, some flat, but none ever flowering as other things flowered, never dying and being renewed, but always the same stiff array of unbroken reeds and segs, some round, some flat. Hard by me were two trees leafless and ugly, made, it seemed, only for the wind to go through with a wild sough on such nights as these; and for a mile from that place were no other trees.

True, I could not see all this at that time, then, in the dark night, but I knew well that it was all there; for much had I studied this pool in the day-time, trying to learn the secret of it; many hours I had spent there, happy with a kind of happiness, because forgetful of the past. And even now, could I not hear the wind going through those trees, as it never went through any trees before or since? could I not see gleams of the dismal moor? could I not hear those reeds just taken by the wind, knocking against each other, the flat ones scraping all along the round ones? Could I not hear, moreover, the slow trickling of the land-springs through the clay banks?

The cold, chill horror of the place was too much for me; I had never been there by night before, nobody had for quite a long time, and now to come on such a night! If there had been any moon, the place would have looked more as it did by day; besides, the moon shining on water is always so beautiful, on any water even: if it had been starlight, one could have looked at the stars and thought of the time when those fields were fertile and beautiful (for such a time was, I am sure), when the cowslips grew among the grass, and when there was promise of yellow-waving corn stained with poppies; that time which the stars had seen, but which we had never seen, which even they would never see again—past time!

Ah! what was that which touched my shoulder?—Yes, I see, only a dead leaf.—Yes, to be here on this eighth of May too of all nights in the year, the night of that awful day when ten years ago I slew him, not undeservedly, God knows, yet how dreadful it was!—Another leaf! and another!—Strange, those trees have been dead this hundred years, I should think. How sharp the wind is too, just as if I were moving along and meeting it;—why, I *am* moving! what then, I am not there after all; where am I then? there are the trees; no, they are freshly-planted oak saplings, the very ones that those withered last-year's leaves were blown on me from.

I have been dreaming then, and am on my road to the lake: but what a young wood! I must have lost my way; I never saw all this before. Well—I will walk on stoutly.

May the Lord help my senses! I am *riding!*—on a mule; a bell tinkles somewhere on him; the wind blows something about with a flapping sound: something? in Heaven's name, what? *My* long black robes.—Why—when I left my house I was clad in serviceable broadcloth of the nineteenth century.

I shall go mad—I am mad—I am gone to the Devil—I have lost my identity; who knows in what place, in what age of the world I am living now? Yet I will be calm; I have seen all these things before, in pictures surely, or something like them. I am resigned, since it is no worse than that. I am a priest then, in the dim, far-off thirteenth century, riding, about midnight I should say, to carry the blessed sacrament to some dying man.

Soon I found that I was not alone; a man was riding close to me on a horse; he was fantastically dressed, more so than usual for that time, being striped all over in vertical stripes of yellow and green, with quaint birds like exaggerated storks in different attitudes counterchanged on the stripes; all this I saw by the lantern he carried, in the light of which his debauched black eyes qu:te flashed. On he went, unsteadily rolling, very drunk, though it was the thirteenth century, but being plainly used to that, he sat his horse fairly well.

I watched him in my proper nineteenth-century character, with insatiable curiosity and intense amusement; but as a quiet priest of a long-past age, with contempt and disgust enough, not unmixed with fear and anxiety.

He roared out snatches of doggrel verse as he went along, drinking songs, hunting songs, robbing songs, lust-songs, in a voice that sounded far and far above the roaring of the wind, though that was high, and rolled along the dark road that his lantern cast spikes of light along ever so far, making the devils grin: and meanwhile I, the priest, glanced from him wrathfully every now and then to That which I carried very reverently in my hand, and my blood curdled with shame and indignation; but being a shrewd priest, I knew well enough that a sermon would be utterly thrown away on a man who was drunk every day in the year, and, more especially, very drunk then. So I held my peace, saying only under my breath:

"Dixit insipiens in corde suo, Non est Deus. Corrupti sunt et abominabiles facti sunt in studiis suis; non est qui faciat bonum, non est usque ad unum: sepulchrum patens est guttur eorum; linguis suis dolose agebant, venenum aspidum sub labiis eorum. Dominum non invocaverunt; illic trepidaverunt timore, ubi non erat timor. Quis dabit ex Sion salutare Israel?"

and so I went on, thinking too at times about the man who was dying and whom I was soon to see: he had been a bold bad plundering baron, but was said lately to have altered his way of life, having seen a miracle or some such thing; he had departed to keep a tournament near his castle lately, but had been brought back sore wounded, so this drunken servant, with some difficulty and much unseasonable merriment, had made me understand, and now lay at the point of death, brought about by unskilful tending and such like. Then I thought of his face—a bad face, very bad, retreating forehead, small twinkling eyes, projecting lower jaw; and such a voice, too, he had! like the grunt of a boar mostly.

Now don't you think it strange that this face should be the same, actually the same as the face of my enemy, slain that very day ten years ago? I did not hate him, either that man or the baron, but I wanted to see as little of him as possible, and I hoped that the ceremony would soon be over, and that I should be at liberty again.

And so with these thoughts and many others, but all thought strangely double, we went along, the varlet being too drunk to take much notice of me, only once, as he was singing some doggrel, like this, I think, making allowances for change of language and so forth:

"*The Duke went to Treves
On the first of November;
His wife stay'd at Bonn—
Let me see, I remember;*

> "*When the Duke came back
> To look for his wife,
> We came from Cologne,
> And took the Duke's life;*
>
> "*We hung him mid high
> Between spire and pavement,
> From their mouths dropp'd the cabbage
> Of the carles in amazement.*"

'Boo—hoo! Church-rat! Church-mouse! Hilloa, Priest! have you brought the pyx, eh?"

From some cause or other he seemed to think this an excellent joke, for he almost shrieked with laughter as we went along; but by this time we had reached the castle. Challenge, and counter-challenge, and we passed the outermost gate and began to go through some of the courts, in which stood lime trees here and there, growing green tenderly with that Maytime, though the north wind bit so keenly.

How strange again! as I went farther, there seemed no doubt of it; here in the aftertime came that pool, how I knew not; but in the few moments that we were riding from the outer gate to the castle-porch I thought so intensely over the probable cause for the existence of that pool, that (how strange!) I could almost have thought I was back again listening to the oozing of the land-springs through the high clay banks there. I was wakened from that, before it grew too strong, by the glare of many torches, and, dismounting, found myself in the midst of some twenty attendants, with flushed faces and wildly sparkling eyes, which they were vainly trying to soften to due solemnity; mock solemnity I had almost said, for they did not seem to think it necessary to appear really solemn, and had difficulty enough apparently in not prolonging indefinitely the shout of laughter with which they had at first greeted me. "Take the holy Father to my Lord," said one at last, "and we will go with him."

So they led me up the stairs into the gorgeously-furnished chamber; the light from the heavy waxen candles was pleasant to my eyes after the glare and twisted red smoke of the pine-torches; but all the essences scattered about the chamber were not enough to conquer the fiery breath of those about me.

I put on the alb and stole they brought me, and, before I went up to the sick man, looked round on those that were in the rooms; for the rooms opened one into the other by many doors, across some of which hung gorgeous tapestry; all the rooms seemed to have many people, for some stood at these doors, and some passed to and fro, swinging aside the heavy hangings; once several people at once, seemingly quite by accident, drew aside almost all the veils from the doors, and showed an endless perspective of gorgeousness.

And at these things my heart fainted for horror. "Had not the Jews of late," thought I, the priest, "been very much in the habit of crucifying children in mockery of the Holiest, holding gorgeous feasts while they beheld the poor innocents die? these men are Atheists, you are in a trap, yet quit yourself like a man."

"Ah, sharp one," thought I, the author, "where are you at last? try to pray as a test.—Well, well, these things are strangely like devils.—O man, you have talked about bravery often, now is your time to practise it: once for all trust in God, or I fear you are lost."

Moreover it increased my horror that there was no appearance of a woman in all these rooms; and yet was there not? there, those things —I looked more intently; yes, no doubt they were women, but all dressed like men;—what a ghastly place!

"O man! do your duty," my angel said; then in spite of the bloodshot eyes of man and woman there, in spite of their bold looks, they quailed before me.

I stepped up to the bedside, where under the velvet coverlid lay the dying man, his small sparkling eyes only (but dulled now by coming death) showing above the swathings. I was about to kneel down by the bedside to confess him, when one of those—things—called out (now they had just been whispering and sniggering together, but the priest in his righteous, brave scorn would not look at them; the humbled author, half fearful, half trustful, dared not): so one called out:

"Sir Priest, for three days our master has spoken no articulate word; you must pass over all particulars; ask for a sign only."

Such a strange ghastly suspicion flashed across me just then; but I choked it, and asked the dying man if he repented of his sins, and if he believed all that was necessary to salvation, and, if so, to make a sign, if he were able: the man moved a little and groaned; so I took it for a sign, as he was clearly incapable either of speaking or moving, and accordingly began the service for the administration of the sacraments; and as I began, those behind me and through all the rooms (I know it was through all of them) began to move about, in a bewildering dance-like motion, mazy and intricate; yes, and presently music struck up through all those rooms, music and singing, lively and gay; many of the tunes I had heard before (in the nineteenth century); I could have sworn to half a dozen of the polkas.

The rooms grew fuller and fuller of people; they passed thick and fast between the rooms, and the hangings were continually rustling; one fat old man with a big belly crept under the bed where I was, and wheezed and chuckled there, laughing and talking to one who stooped down and lifted up the hangings to look at him.

Still more and more people talking and singing and laughing and twirling about, till my brain went round and round, and I scarce knew what I did; yet, somehow, I could not leave off; I dared not even look over my shoulder, fearing lest I should see something so horrible as to make me die.

So I got on with the service, and at last took the Pyx, and took thereout the sacred wafer, whereupon was a deep silence through all those rooms, which troubled me, I think, more than all which had gone before, for I knew well it did not mean reverence.

I held it up, that which I counted so holy, when lo! great laughter, echoing like thunder-claps through all the rooms, not dulled by the veiling hangings, for they were all the raised up together, and, with a slow upheaval of the rich clothes among which he lay, with a sound that was half snarl, half grunt, with helpless body swathed in bedclothes, a huge *swine* that I had been shriving tore from me the Holy Thing, deeply scoring my hand as he did so with tusk and tooth, so that the red blood ran quick on to the floor.

Therewithal he rolled down on to the floor, and lay there helplessly, only able to roll to and fro, because of the swathings.

Then right madly skirled the intolerable laughter, rising to shrieks that were fearfuller than any scream of agony I ever heard; the hundreds of people through all those grand rooms danced and wheeled about me, shrieking, hemming me in with interlaced arms, the women loosing their long hair and thrusting forward their horribly-grinning unsexed faces toward me till I felt their hot breath.

Oh! how I hated them all! almost hated all mankind for their sakes; how I longed to get right quit of all men; among whom, as it seemed, all sacredest things even were made a mock of. I looked about me fiercely, I sprang forward, and clutched a sword from the gilded belt of one of those who stood near me; with savage blows that threw the blood about the gilded walls and their hangings right over the heads of those—things—I cleared myself from them, and tore down the great stairs madly, yet could not, as in a dream, go fast enough, because of my passion.

I was out in the courtyard, among the lime trees soon, the north wind blowing freshly on my heated forehead in that dawn. The outer gate was locked and bolted; I stooped and raised a great stone and sent it at the lock with all my strength, and I was stronger than ten men then; iron and oak gave way before it, and through the ragged splinters I tore in reckless fury, like a wild horse through a hazel hedge.

And no one had pursued me. I knelt down on the dear green turf outside, and thanked God with streaming eyes for my deliverance, praying Him forgiveness for my unwilling share in that night's mockery.

Then I arose and turned to go, but even as I did so I heard a roar as if the world were coming in two, and looking toward the castle, saw, not a castle, but a great cloud of white lime dust swaying this way and that in the gusts of the wind.

Then while the east grew bright there arose a hissing, gurgling noise, that swelled into the roar and wash of many waters, and by then the sun had risen a deep black lake lay before my feet.

And this is how I tried to fathom the Lindenborg Pool.

Next to Edgar Rice Burroughs, A. MERRITT was the great fantasist of the pulp magazines in the early part of the twentieth century. He wrote a series of novels, including The Ship of Ishtar and Burn, Witch, Burn, and others that made him a widely read, immensely popular author; but his first and most famous novel was The Moon Pool, expanded from his 1918 novella and its sequel, The Conquest of the Moon Pool. *This kind of pulp fantasy is the source of such contemporary off-shoots as the current Indiana Jones movies. Several of Merritt's stories were made into films in the 1930s. You can also see the aggressive blend of what we now call science fiction with the fantasy, using scientists and professionals to heighten the contrast between the scientific present and the magical past, mysterious and wonderful and very dangerous.*

The Moon Pool
BY A. MERRITT

1. THE THROCKMARTIN MYSTERY

I am breaking a long silence to clear the name of Dr. David Throckmartin and to lift the shadow of scandal from that of his wife and of Dr. Charles Stanton, his assistant. That I have not found the courage to do so before, all men who are jealous of their scientific reputations will understand when they have read the facts entrusted to me alone.

I shall first recapitulate what has actually been known of the Throckmartin expedition to the island of Ponape in the Carolines—the Throckmartin Mystery, as it is called.

Dr. Throckmartin set forth, you will recall, to make some observations of Nan-Matal, that extraordinary group of island ruins, remains of a high and prehistoric civilization, that are clustered along the vast shore of Ponape. With him went his wife to whom he had been wedded less than half a year. The daughter of Professor Frazier-Smith, she was as deeply interested and almost as well informed as he upon these relics of a vanished race that titanically strew certain islands of the Pacific and form the basis for the theory of a submerged Pacific continent.

Mrs. Throckmartin, it will be recalled, was much younger, fifteen years at least, than her husband. Dr. Charles Stanton, who accompanied them as Dr. Throckmartin's assistant, was about her age. These three and a Swedish woman, Thora Helversen, who had been Edith Throckmartin's nurse in babyhood and who was entirely devoted to her, made up the expedition.

Dr. Throckmartin planned to spend a year among the ruins, not only of Ponape, but of Lele—the twin centers of that colossal riddle of humanity whose answer has its roots in immeasurable antiquity; a weird flower of man-made civilization that blossomed ages before the seeds of Egypt were sown; of whose arts we know little and of whose science and secret knowledge of nature nothing.

He carried with him complete equipment for his work and gathered at Ponape a dozen or so natives for laborers. They went straight to Metalanim harbor and set up their camp on the island called Uschen-Tau in the group known as the Nan-Matal. You will remember that these islands are entirely uninhabited and are shunned by the people on the main island.

Three months later Dr. Throckmartin appeared at Port Moresby, Papua. He came on a schooner manned by Solomon Islanders and commanded by a Chinese half-breed captain. He reported that he was on his way to Melbourne for additional scientific equipment and whites to help him in his excavations, saying that the superstition of the natives made their aid negligible. He went immediately on board the steamer *Southern Queen* which was sailing that same morning. Three nights later he disappeared from the *Southern Queen* and it was officially reported that he had met death either by being swept overboard or by casting himself into the sea.

A relief-boat sent with the news to Ponape found the Throckmartin camp on the island Uschen-Tau and a smaller camp on the island called Nan-Tanach. All the equipment, clothing, supplies were intact. But of Mrs. Throckmartin, of Dr. Stanton, or of Thora Helversen they could find not a single trace!

The natives who had been employed by the archeologist were questioned. They said that the ruins were the abode of great spirits— *ani*— who were particularly powerful when the moon was at the full. On these nights all the islanders were doubly careful to give the ruins wide berth. Upon being employed, they had demanded leave from the day before full moon until it was on the wane and this had been granted them by Dr. Throckmartin. Thrice they had left the expedition alone on these nights. On their third return they had found the four white people gone and they "knew that the *ani* had eaten them." They were afraid and had fled.

That was all.

The Chinese half caste was found and reluctantly testified at last that he had picked Dr. Throckmartin up from a small boat about fifty miles off Ponape. The scientist had seemed half mad, but he had given the seaman a large sum of money to bring him to Port Moresby and to say, if questioned, that he had boarded the boat at Ponape harbor.

That is all that has been known to anyone of the fate of the Throckmartin expedition.

Why, you will ask, do I break silence now; and how came I in possession of the facts I am about to set forth?

To the first I answer: I was at the Geographical Club recently and I overheard two members talking. They mentioned the name of Throckmartin and I became an eavesdropper. One said:

"Of course what probably happened was that Throckmartin killed them all. It's a dangerous thing for a man to marry a woman so much younger than himself and then throw her into the necessarily close company of exploration with a man as young and as agreeable as Stanton was. The inevitable happened, no doubt. Throckmartin discovered; avenged himself. Then followed remorse and suicide."

"Throckmartin didn't seem to be that kind," said the other thoughtfully.

"No, he didn't," agreed the first.

"Isn't there another story?" went on the second speaker. "Something about Mrs. Throckmartin running away with Stanton and taking the woman, Thora, with her? Somebody told me they had been recognized in Singapore recently."

"You can take your pick of the two stories," replied the other man. "It's one or the other I suppose."

It was neither one nor the other of them. I know—and I will answer now the second question—because I was with Throckmartin when he—vanished. I know what he told me and I know what my own eyes saw. Incredible, abnormal, against all the known facts of our science as it was, I testify to it. And it is my intention, after this is published, to sail to Ponape, to go to the Nan-Matal and to the islet beneath whose frowning walls dwells the mystery that Throckmartin sought and found—and that at the last sought and found Throckmartin!

I will leave behind me a copy of the map of the islands that he gave me. Also his sketch of the great courtyard of Nan-Tanach, the location of the moon door, his indication of the probable location of the moon pool and the passage to it and his approximation of the position of the shining globes. If I do not return and there are any with enough belief, scientific curiosity and courage to follow, these will furnish a plain trail.

I will now proceed straightforwardly with my narrative.

For six months I had been on the d'Entrecasteaux Islands gathering data for the concluding chapters of my book upon "Flora of the Volcanic Islands of the South Pacific." The day before, I had reached Port Moresby and had seen my specimens safely stored on board the *Southern Queen*. As I sat on the upper deck that morning I thought, with homesick mind, of the long leagues between me and Melbourne and the longer ones between Melbourne and New York.

It was one of Papua's yellow mornings, when she shows herself in her most somber, most baleful mood. The sky was a smoldering ocher. Over the island brooded a spirit sullen, implacable and alien; filled with the threat of latent, malefic forces waiting to be unleashed. It seemed an emanation from the untamed, sinister heart of Papua herself—sinister even when she smiles. And now and then, on the wind, came a breath from unexplored jungles, filled with unfamiliar odors, mysterious, and menacing.

It is on such mornings that Papua speaks to you of her immemorial ancientness and of her power. I am not unduly imaginative but it is a mood that makes me shrink—I mention it because it bears directly upon Dr. Throckmartin's fate. Nor is the mood Papua's alone. I have felt it in New Guinea, in Australia, in the Solomons and in the Carolines. But it is in Papua that it seems most articulate. It is as though she said: "I am the ancient of days; I have seen the earth in the throes of its shaping; I am the primeval; I have seen races born and die and, lo, in my breast are secrets that would blast you by the telling, you pale babes of a puling age. You and I ought not be in the same world; yet I am and I shall be! Never will you fathom me and you I hate though I tolerate! I tolerate—but how long?"

And then I seem to see a giant paw that reaches from Papua toward the outer world, stretching and sheathing monstrous claws.

All feel this mood of hers. Her own people have it woven in them, part of their web and woof; flashing into light unexpectedly like a soul from another universe; masking itself as swiftly.

I fought against Papua as every white man must on one of her yellow mornings. And as I fought I saw a tall figure come striding down the pier. Behind him came a Kapa-Kapa boy swinging a new valise. There was something familiar about the tall man. As he reached the gangplank he looked up straight into my eyes, stared at me for a moment and waved his hand. It was Dr. Throckmartin!

Coincident with my recognition of him there came a shock of surprise that was definitely—unpleasant. It was Throckmartin—but there was something disturbingly different about him and the man I had known so well and had bidden farewell less than a year before. He was then, as you know, just turned forty, lithe, erect, muscular; the face of a student and of a seeker. His controlling expression was one of enthusiasm, of intellectual keenness, of—what shall I say—expectant search. His ever eagerly questioning brain had stamped itself upon his face.

I sought in my mind for an explanation of that which I had felt on the flash of his greeting. Hurrying down to the lower deck I found him with the purser. As I spoke he turned and held out to me an eager hand —and then I saw what the change was that had come over him!

He knew, of course, by my face the uncontrollable shock that my closer look had given me. His eyes filled and he turned briskly to the purser; then hurried off to his stateroom, leaving me standing, half dazed.

At the stair he half turned.

"Oh, Goodwin," he said. "I'd like to see you later. Just now—there's something I must write before we start—"

He went up swiftly.

" 'E looks rather queer—eh?" said the purser. "Know 'im well, sir? Seems to 'ave given you quite a start, sir."

I made some reply and went slowly to my chair. I tried to analyze what it was that had disturbed me so; what profound change in Throckmartin that had so shaken me. Now it came to me. It was as though the man had suffered some terrific soul searing shock of rapture and horror combined; some soul cataclysm that in its climax had remolded his face deep from within, setting on it the seal of wedded joy and fear. As though indeed ecstasy supernal and terror infernal had once come to him hand in hand, taken possession of him, looked out of his eyes and, departing, left behind upon him ineradicably their shadow.

Alternately I looked out over the port and paced about the deck, striving to read the riddle; to banish it from my mind. And all the time still over Papua brooded its baleful spirit of ancient evil, unfathomable, not to be understood; nor had it lifted when the *Southern Queen* lifted anchor and steamed out into the gulf.

2. DOWN THE MOON PATH

I watched with relief the shores sink down behind us; welcomed the touch of the free sea wind. We seemed to be drawing away from something malefic; something that lurked within the island spell I have described, and the thought crept into my mind, spoke—whispered rather—from Throckmartin's face.

I had hoped—and within the hope was an inexplicable shrinking, an unexpressed dread—that I would meet Throckmartin at lunch. He did not come down and I was sensible of a distinct relief within my disappointment. All that afternoon I lounged about uneasily but still he kept to his cabin. Nor did he appear at dinner.

Dusk and night fell swiftly. I was warm and went back to my deckchair. The *Southern Queen* was rolling to a disquieting swell and I had the place to myself.

Over the heavens was a canopy of cloud, glowing faintly and testifying to the moon riding behind it. There was much phosphorescence. Now and then, before the ship and at the sides, arose those strange little swirls of mist that steam up from the Southern Ocean like the breath of sea monsters, whirl for a moment and disappear. I lighted a cigarette and tried once more to banish Throckmartin's face from my mind.

Suddenly the deck door opened and through it came Throckmartin himself. He paused uncertainly, looked up at the sky with a curiously eager, intent gaze, hesitated, then closed the door behind him.

"Throckmartin," I called. "Come sit with me. It's Goodwin."

Immediately he made his way to me, sitting beside me with a gasp of relief that I noted curiously. His hand touched mine and gripped it with tenseness that hurt. His hand was icelike. I puffed up my cigarette and by its glow scanned him closely. He was watching a large swirl of the mist that was passing before the ship. The phosphorescence beneath it illumined it with a fitful opalescence. I saw fear in his eyes. The swirl passed; he sighed; his grip relaxed and he sank back.

"Throckmartin," I said, wasting no time in preliminaries. "What's wrong? Can I help you?"

He was silent.

"Is your wife all right and what are you doing here when I heard you had gone to the Carolines for a year?" I went on.

I felt his body grow tense again. He did not speak for a moment and then:

"I'm going to Melbourne, Goodwin," he said. "I need a few things —need them urgently. And more men—white men."

His voice was low; preoccupied. It was as though the brain that dictated the words did so perfunctorily, half impatiently; aloof, watching, strained to catch the first hint of approach of something dreaded.

"You are making progress then?" I asked. It was a banal question, put forth in a blind effort to claim his attention.

"Progress?" he repeated. "Progress—"

He stopped abruptly; rose from his chair, gazed intently toward the north. I followed his gaze. Far, far away the moon had broken through the clouds. Almost on the horizon, you could see the faint luminescence of it upon the quiet sea. The distant patch of light quivered and shook. The clouds thickened again and it was gone. The ship raced southward, swiftly.

Throckmartin dropped into his chair. He lighted a cigarette with a hand that trembled. The flash of the match fell on his face and I noted with a queer thrill of apprehension that its unfamiliar expression had deepened; become curiously intensified as though a faint acid had passed over it, etching its lines faintly deeper.

"It's the full moon tonight, isn't it?" he asked, palpably with studied inconsequence.

"The first night of full moon," I answered. He was silent again. I sat silent too, waiting for him to make up his mind to speak. He turned to me as though he had made a sudden resolution.

"Goodwin," he said. "I do need help. If ever man needed it, I do. Goodwin—can you imagine yourself in another world, alien, unfamiliar, a world of terror, whose unknown joy is its greatest terror of all; you all alone there; a stranger! As such a man would need help, so I need—"

He paused abruptly and arose to his feet stiffly; the cigarette dropped from his fingers. I saw that the moon had again broken through the clouds, and this time much nearer. Not a mile away was the patch of light that it threw upon the waves. Back of it, to the rim of the sea was a lane of moonlight; it was a gleaming gigantic serpent racing over the rim of the world straight and surely toward the ship.

Throckmartin gazed at it as though turned to stone. He stiffened to it as a pointer does to a hidden covey. To me from him pulsed a thrill of terror—but terror tinged with an unfamiliar, an infernal joy. It came to me and passed away—leaving me trembling with its shock of bitter sweet.

He bent forward, all his soul in his eyes. The moon path swept closer, closer still. It was now less than half a mile away. From it the ship fled; almost it came to me, as though pursued. Down upon it, swift and straight, a radiant torrent cleaving the waves, raced the moon stream. And then—

"Good God!" breathed Throckmartin, and if ever the words were a prayer and an invocation they were.

And then, for the first time—I saw—*it!*

The moon path, as I have said, stretched to the horizon and was bordered by darkness. It was as though the clouds above had been parted to form a lane—drawn aside like curtains or as the waters of the Red Sea were held back to let the hosts of Israel through. On each side of the stream was the black shadow cast by the folds of the high canopies. And straight as a road between the opaque walls gleamed, shimmered and danced the shining, racing, rapids of moonlight.

Far, it seemed immeasurably far, along this stream of silver fire I sensed, rather than saw, something coming. It drew into sight as a deeper glow within the light. On and on it sped toward us—an opalescent mistiness that swept on with the suggestion of some winged creature in darting flight. Dimly there crept into my mind memory of the Dyak legend of the winged messenger of Buddha—the Akla bird whose feathers are woven of the moon rays, whose heart is a living opal, whose wings in flight echo the crystal clear music of the white stars— but whose beak is of frozen flame and shreds the souls of the unbelievers. Still it sped on, and now there came to me sweet, insistent tinklings —like a pizzicati on violins of glass, crystalline, as purest, clearest glass transformed to sound. And again the myth of the Akla bird came to me.

But now it was close to the end of the white path; close up to the barrier of darkness still between the ship and the sparkling head of the moon stream. And now it beat up against the barrier as a bird against the bars of its cage. And I knew that this was no mist born of sea and air. It whirled with shimmering plumes, with swirls of lacy light, with spirals of living vapor. It held within it odd, unfamiliar gleams as of shifting mother-of-pearl. Coruscations and glittering atoms drifted through it as though it drew them from the rays that bathed it.

Nearer and nearer it came, borne on the sparkling waves, and less and less grew the protecting wall of shadow between it and us. The crystalline sounds were louder—rhythmic as music from another planet.

Now I saw that within the mistiness was a core, a nucleus of intenser light—veined, opaline, effulgent, intensely alive. And above it, tangled in the plumes and spirals that throbbed and whirled were seven glowing lights.

Through all the incessant but strangely ordered movement of the —*thing*—these lights held firm and steady. They were seven—like seven little moons. One was of a pearly pink, one of delicate nacreous blue, one of lambent saffron, one of the emerald you see in the shallow waters of tropic isles; a deathly white; a ghostly amethyst; and one of the silver that is seen only when the flying fish leap beneath the moon. There they shone—these seven little varicolored orbs within the opaline mistiness of whatever it was that, poised and expectant, waited to be drawn to us on the light filled waves.

The tinkling music was louder still. It pierced the ears with a shower of tiny lances; it made the heart beat jubilantly—and checked it dolorously. It closed your throat with a throb of rapture and gripped it tight like the hand of infinite sorrow!

Came to me now a murmuring cry, stilling the crystal clear notes, it was articulate—but as though from something utterly foreign to this world. The ear took the cry and translated with conscious labor into the sounds of earth. And even as it compassed, the brain shrank from it irresistibly and simultaneously it seemed, reached toward it with irresistible eagerness.

"Av-o-lo-ha! Av-o-lo-ha!" So the cry seemed to throb.

The grip of Throckmartin's hand relaxed. He walked stiffly toward the front of the deck, straight toward the vision, now but a few yards away from the bow. I ran toward him and gripped him—and fell back.

For now his face had lost all human semblance. Utter agony and utter ecstasy—there they were side by side, not resisting each other; unholy inhuman companions blending into a look that none of God's creatures should wear—and deep, deep as his soul! A devil and a god dwelling harmoniously side by side! So must Satan, newly fallen, still divine, seeing heaven and contemplating hell, have looked.

And then—swiftly the moon path faded! The clouds swept over the sky as though a hand had drawn them together. Up from the south came a roaring squall. As the moon vanished what I had seen vanished with it—blotted out as an image on a magic lantern; the tinkling ceased abruptly—leaving a silence like that which follows an abrupt and stupendous thunder clap. There was nothing about us but silence and blackness!

Through me there passed a great trembling as one who had stood on the very verge of the gulf wherein the men of the Louisades say lurks the fisher of the souls-of men, and has been plucked back by sheerest chance.

Throckmartin passed an arm around me.

"It is as I thought," he said. In his voice was a new note; of the calm certainty that has swept aside a waiting terror of the unknown. "Now I know! Come with me to my cabin, old friend. For now that you too have seen I can tell you"—he hesitated—"what it was you saw," he ended.

As we passed through the door we came face to face with the ship's first officer. Throckmartin turned quickly, but not soon enough for the mate not to see and stare with amazement. His eyes turned questioningly to me.

With a strong effort of will Throckmartin composed his face into at least a semblance of normality.

"Are we going to have much of a storm?" he asked.

"Yes," said the mate. Then the seaman, getting the better of his curiosity, added, profanely: "We'll probably have it all the way to Melbourne."

Throckmartin straightened as though with a new thought. He gripped the officer's sleeve eagerly.

"You mean at least cloudy weather—for"—he hesitated—"for the next three nights, say?"

"And for three more," replied the mate.

"Thank God!" cried Throckmartin, and I think I never heard such relief and hope as was in his voice.

The sailor stood amazed. "Thank God?" he repeated. "Thank—what d'ye mean?"

But Throckmartin was moving onward to his cabin. I started to follow. The first officer stopped me.

"Your friend," he said, "is he ill?"

"The sea!" I answered hurriedly. "He's not used to it. I am going to look after him."

I saw doubt and disbelief in the seaman's eyes but I hurried on. For I knew now that Throckmartin was ill indeed—but that it was a sickness neither the ship's doctor nor any other could heal.

3. "DEAD! ALL DEAD!"

Throckmartin was sitting on the side of his berth as I entered. He had taken off his coat. He was leaning over, face in hands.

"Lock the door," he said quietly, not raising his head. "Close the portholes and draw the curtains—and—have you an electric flash in your pocket—a good, strong one?"

He glanced at the small pocket flash I handed him and clicked it on. "Not big enough I'm afraid," he said. "And after all"—he hesitated —"it's only a theory."

"What's only a theory?" I asked in astonishment.

"Thinking of it as a weapon against—what you saw," he said, with a wry smile.

"Throckmartin," I cried. "What was it? Did I really see—that thing—there in the moon path? Did I really hear—"

"This for instance," he interrupted.

Softly he whispered: "Av-o-lo-ha!" With the murmur I seemed to hear again the crystalline unearthly music; an echo of it, faint, sinister, mocking, jubilant.

"Throckmartin," I said. "What was it? What are you flying from, man? Where is your wife—and Stanton?"

"Dead!" he said monotonously. "Dead! All dead!" Then as I recoiled in horror—"All dead. Edith, Stanton, Thora—dead—or worse. And Edith in the moon pool—with them—drawn by what you saw on the moon path—and that wants me—and that has put its brand upon me—and pursues me."

With a vicious movement he ripped open his shirt.

"Look at this," he said. I gazed. Around his chest, an inch above his heart, the skin was white as pearl. The whiteness was sharply defined against the healthy tint of the body. He turned and I saw it ran around his back. It circled him. The band made a perfect cincture about two inches wide.

"Burn it!" he said, and offered me his cigarette. I drew back. He gestured—peremptorily. I pressed the glowing end of the cigarette into the ribbon of white flesh. He did not flinch nor was there odor of burning nor, as I drew the little cylinder away, any mark upon the whiteness.

"Feel it!" he commanded again. I placed my fingers upon the band. It was cold—like frozen marble.

He handed me a small penknife.

"Cut!" he ordered. This time, my scientific interest fully aroused, I did so without reluctance. The blade cut into flesh. I waited for the blood to come. None appeared. I drew out the knife and thrust it in again, fully a quarter of an inch deep. I might have been cutting paper so far as any evidence followed that what I was piercing was human skin and muscle.

Another thought came to me and I drew back, revolted.

"Throckmartin," I whispered. "Not leprosy!"

"Nothing so easy," he said. "Look again and find the places you cut."

I looked, as he bade me, and in the white ring there was not a single mark. Where I had pressed the blade there was no trace. It was as though the skin had parted to make way for the blade and closed.

Throckmartin arose and drew his shirt about him.

"Two things you have seen," he said. "*It*—and its mark—the seal it placed on me that gives it, I think, the power to follow me. Seeing, you must believe my story. Goodwin, I tell you again that my wife is dead—or worse—I do not know; the prey of—what you saw; so, too, is Stanton; so Thora. How—" He stopped for a moment. Then continued:

"And I am going to Melbourne for the things to empty its den and its shrine; for dynamite to destroy it and its lair—if anything made on earth will destroy it; and for white men with courage to use them. Perhaps—perhaps after you have heard, you will be one of these men?"

He looked at me a bit wistfully. "And now—do not interrupt me, I beg of you, till I am through—for"—he smiled wanly—"the mate may be wrong. And if he is"—he arose and paced twice about the room—"if he is I may not have time to tell you."

"Throckmartin," I answered, "I have no closed mind. Tell me—and if I can I will help."

He took my hand and pressed it.

"Goodwin," he began, "if I have seemed to take the death of my wife lightly—or rather"—his face contorted—"or rather—if I have seemed to pass it by as something not of first importance to me—believe me it is not so. If the rope is long enough—if what the mate says is so—if there is cloudy weather until the moon begins to wane—I can conquer—that I know. But if it does not—if the dweller in the moon pool gets me—then must you or some one avenge my wife—and me—and Stanton. Yet I cannot believe that God would let a thing like that conquer! But why did He then let it take my Edith? And why does He allow it to exist? Are there things stronger than God, do you think, Goodwin?"

He turned to me feverishly. I hesitated.

"I do not know just how you define God," I said. "If you mean the will to know, working through science—"

He waved me aside impatiently.

"Science," he said. "What is our science against—that? Or against the science of whatever cursed, vanished race that made it—or made the way for it to enter this world of ours?"

With an effort he regained control of himself.

"Goodwin," he said, "do you know at all of the ruins on the Carolines; the cyclopean, megolithic cities and harbors of Ponape and Lele, of Kusaie, of Ruk and Hogolu, and a score of other islets there? Particularly, do you know of the Nan-Matal and Metalanim?"

"Of the Metalanim I have heard and seen photographs," I said. "They call it don't they, the Lost Venice of the Pacific?"

"Look at this map," said Throckmartin. He handed me the map. "That," he went on, "is Christian's map of Metalanim harbor and the Nan-Matal. Do you see the rectangles marked Nan-Tanach?"

"Yes," I said.

"There," he said, "under those walls is the moon pool and the seven gleaming lights that raise the dweller in the pool and the altar and shrine of the dweller. And there in the moon pool with it lie Edith and Stanton and Thora."

"The dweller in the moon pool?" I repeated half-incredulously.

"The thing you saw," said Throckmartin solemnly.

A solid sheet of rain swept the ports, and the *Southern Queen* began to roll on the rising swells. Throckmartin drew another deep breath of relief, and drawing aside a curtain peered out into the night. Its blackness seemed to reassure him. At any rate, when he sat again he was calm.

"There are no more wonderful ruins in the world than those of the island Venice of Metalanim on the east shore of Ponape," he said almost casually. "They take in some fifty islets and cover with their intersecting canals and lagoons about twelve square miles. Who built them? None knows! When were they built? Ages before the memory of present man, that is sure. Ten thousand, twenty thousand, a hundred thousand years ago—the last more likely.

"All these islets, Goodwin, are squared, and their shores are frowning sea-walls of gigantic basalt blocks hewn and put in place by the hands of ancient man. Each inner water-front is faced with a terrace of those basalt blocks which stand out six feet above the shallow canals that meander between them. On the islets behind these walls are cyclopean and time-shattered fortresses, palaces, terraces, pyramids; immense courtyards, strewn with ruins—and all so old that they seem to wither the eyes of those who look on them.

"There has been a great subsidence. You can stand out of Metalanim harbor for three miles and look down upon the tops of similar monolithic structures and walls twenty feet below you in the water.

"And all about, strung on their canals, are the bulwarked islets with their enigmatic giant walls peering through the dense growths of mangroves—dead, deserted for incalculable ages; shunned by those who live near.

"You as a botanist are familiar with the evidence that a vast shadowy continent existed in the Pacific—a continent that was not rent asunder by volcanic forces as was that legendary one of Atlantis in the Eastern Ocean. My work in Java, in Papua, and in the Ladrones had set my mind upon this Pacific lost land. Just as the Azores are believed to be the last high peaks of Atlantis, so evidence came to me steadily that Ponape and Lele and their basalt bulwarked islets were the last points of the slowly sunken western land clinging still to the sunlight, and had been the last refuge and sacred places of the rulers of that race which had lost their immemorial home under the rising waters of the Pacific.

"I believed that under these ruins I might find the evidence of what I sought. Time and again I had encountered legends of subterranean networks beneath the Nan-Matal, of passages running back into the main island itself; basalt corridors that followed the lines of the shallow canals and ran under them to islet after islet, linking them in mysterious chains.

"My—my wife and I had talked before we were married of making this our great work. After the honeymoon we prepared for the expedition. It was to be my monument. Stanton was as enthusiastic as ourselves. We sailed, as you know, last May in fulfilment of our dreams.

"At Ponape we selected, not without difficulty, workmen to help us—diggers. I had to make extraordinary inducements before I could get together my force. Their beliefs are gloomy, these Ponapeans. They people their swamps, their forests, their mountains and shores with malignant spirits—*ani* they call them. And they are afraid—bitterly afraid of the isles of ruins and what they think the ruins hide. I do not wonder—now! For their fear has come down to them, through the ages, from the people 'before their fathers,' as they call them, who, they say, made these mighty spirits their slaves and messengers.

"When they were told where they were to go, and how long we expected to stay, they murmured. Those who, at last, were tempted made what I thought then merely a superstitious proviso that they were to be allowed to go away on the three nights of the full moon. If only I had heeded them and gone, too!"

He stopped and again over his face the lines etched deep.

"We passed," he went on, "into Metalanim harbor. Off to our left —a mile away arose a massive quadrangle. Its walls were all of forty feet high and hundreds of feet on each side. As we passed it our natives grew very silent; watched it furtively, fearfully. I knew it for the ruins that are called Nan-Tanach, the 'place of frowning walls.' And at the silence of my men I recalled what Christian had written of this place; of how he had come upon its 'ancient platforms and tetragonal enclosures of stonework; its wonder of tortuous alleyways and labyrinth of shallow canals; grim masses of stonework peering out from behind verdant screens; cyclopean barricades. And now, when we had turned into its ghostly shadows, straightaway the merriment of our guides was hushed and conversation died down to whispers. For we were close to Nan-Tanach—the place of lofty walls, the most remarkable of all the Metalanim ruins." He arose and stood over me.

"Nan-Tanach, Goodwin," he said solemnly—"a place where merriment is hushed indeed and words are stifled; Nan-Tanach—where the moon pool lies hidden—lies hidden behind the moon rock, but sends its diabolic soul out—even through the prisoning stone." He raised clenched hands. "Oh, Heaven," he breathed, "grant me that I may blast it from earth!"

He was silent for a little time.

"Of course I wanted to pitch our camp there," he began again quietly, "but I soon gave up that idea. The natives were panic-stricken —threatened to turn back. 'No,' they said, 'too great *ani* there. We go to any other place—but not there.' Although, even then, I felt that the secret of the place was in Nan-Tanach, I found it necessary to give in. The laborers were essential to the success of the expedition, and I told myself that after a little time had passed and I had persuaded them that there was nothing anywhere that could molest them, we would move our tents to it. We finally picked for our base the islet called Uschen-Tau—you see it here—" He pointed to the map. "It was close to the isle of desire, but far enough away from it to satisfy our men. There was an excellent camping-place there and a spring of fresh water. It offered, besides, an excellent field for preliminary work before attacking the larger ruins. We pitched out tents, and in a couple of days the work was in full swing."

4. THE MOON ROCK

"I do not intend to tell you now," Throckmartin continued, "the results of the next two weeks, Goodwin, nor of what we found. Later— if I am allowed I will lay all that before you. It is sufficient to say that at the end of those two weeks I had found confirmation of many of my theories, and we were well under way to solve a mystery of humanity's youth—so we thought. But enough. I must hurry on to the first stirrings of the inexplicable thing that was in store for us.

"The place, for all its decay and desolation, had not infected us with any touch of morbidity—that is not Edith, Stanton or myself. My wife was happy—never had she been happier. Stanton and she, while engrossed in the work as much as I, were of the same age, and they frankly enjoyed the companionship that only youth can give youth. I was glad—never jealous.

"But Thora was very unhappy. She was a Swede, as you know, and in her blood ran the beliefs and superstitions of the Northland—some of them so strangely akin to those of this far southern land; beliefs of spirits of mountain and forest and water—werewolves and beings malign. From the first she showed a curious sensitivity to what, I suppose, may be called the 'influences' of the place. She said it 'smelled' of ghosts and warlocks.

"I laughed at her then—but now I believe that this sensitivity of what we call primitive people is perhaps only a clearer perception of the unknown which we, who deny the unknown, have lost.

"A prey to these fears, Thora always followed my wife about like a shadow; carried with her always a little sharp hand-ax, and although we twitted her about the futility of chopping fantoms with such a weapon she would not relinquish it.

"Two weeks slipped by, and at their end the spokesman for our natives came to us. The next night was the full of the moon, he said. He reminded me of my promise. They would go back to their village next morning; they would return after the third night, as at that time the power of the *ani* would begin to wane with the moon. They left us sundry charms for our 'protection,' and solemnly cautioned us to keep as far away as possible from Nan-Tanach during their absence—although their leader politely informed us that, no doubt, we were stronger than the spirits. Half-exasperated, half-amused I watched them go.

"No work could be done without them, of course, so we decided to spend the days of their absence junketing about the southern islets of the group. Under the moon the ruins were inexpressibly weird and beautiful. We marked down several spots for subsequent exploration, and on the morning of the third day set forth along the east face of the breakwater for our camp on Uschen-Tau, planning to have everything in readiness for the return of our men the next day.

"We landed just before dusk, tired and ready for our cots. It was only a little after ten o'clock when Edith awakened me.

" 'Listen! she said. 'Lean over with your ear close to the ground!' I did so, and seemed to hear, far, far below, as though coming up from great distances, a faint chanting. It gathered strength, died down, ended; began, gathered volume, faded away into silence.

" 'It's the waves rolling on rocks somewhere,' I said. 'We're probably over some ledge of rock that carries the sound.'

" 'It's the first time I've heard it,' replied my wife doubtfully. We listened again. Then through the dim rhythms, deep beneath us, another sound came. It drifted across the lagoon that lay between us and Nan-Tanach in little tinkling waves. It was music—of a sort; I won't describe the strange effect it had upon me. You've felt it—"

"You mean on the deck?" I asked. Throckmartin nodded.

"I went to the flap of the tent," he continued, "and peered out. As I did so Stanton lifted his flap and walked out into the moonlight, looking over to the other islet and listening. I called to him.

" 'That's the queerest sound!' he said. He listened again. 'Crystalline! Like little notes of translucent glass. Like the bells of crystal on the sistrums of Isis at Dendarah Temple,' he added half-dreamily. We gazed intently at the island. Suddenly, on the gigantic sea-wall, moving slowly, rhythmically, we saw a little group of lights. Stanton laughed.

" 'The beggars!' he exclaimed. 'That's why they wanted to get away, is it? Don't you see, Dave, it's some sort of a festival—rites of some kind that they hold during the full moon! That's why they were so eager to have us *keep* away, too.'

"I felt a curious sense of relief, although I had not been sensible of any oppression. The explanation seemed good. It explained the tinkling music and also the chanting—worshipers, no doubt, in the ruins—their voices carried along passages I now knew honeycombed the whole Nan-Matal.

" 'Let's slip over,' suggested Stanton—but I would not.

" 'They're a difficult lot as it is,' I said. 'If we break into one of their religious ceremonies they'll probably never forgive us. Let's keep out of any family party where we haven't been invited.'

" 'That's so,' agreed Stanton.

"The strange tinkling music, if music it can be called, rose and fell, rose and fell—now laden with sorrow, now filled with joy.

" 'There's something—something very unsettling about it,' said Edith at last soberly. 'I wonder what they make those sounds with. They frighten me half to death, and, at the same time, they make me feel as though some enormous rapture was just around the corner.'

"I had noted this effect, too, although I had said nothing of it. And at the same time there came to me a clear perception that the chanting which had preceded it had seemed to come from a vast multitude—thousands more than the place we were contemplating could possibly have held. Of course, I thought, this might be due to some acoustic property of the basalt; an amplification of sound by some gigantic sounding-board of rock; still—

" 'It's devilish uncanny!' broke in Stanton, answering my thought.

"And as he spoke the flap of Thora's tent was raised and out into the moonlight strode the old Swede. She was the great Norse type—tall, deep-breasted, molded on the old Viking lines. Her sixty years had slipped from her. She looked like some ancient priestess of Odin." He hesitated. "She knew," he said slowly, "something more far-seeing than my science had given her sight. She warned me—she warned me! Fools and mad that we are to pass such things by without heed!" He brushed a hand over his eyes.

"She stood there," he went on. "Her eyes were wide, brilliant, staring. She thrust her head forward toward Nan-Tanach, regarding the moving lights; she listened. Suddenly she raised her arms and made a curious gesture to the moon. It was—an archaic—movement; she seemed to drag it from remote antiquity—yet in it was a strange suggestion of power. Twice she repeated this gesture and—the tinkling died away! She turned to us.

" 'Go!' she said, and her voice seemed to come from far distances. 'Go from here—and quickly! Go while you may. They have called—' She pointed to the islet. 'They know you are here. They wait.' Her eyes widened further. 'It is there,' she wailed. 'It beckons—the—the—'

"She fell at Edith's feet, and as she fell over the lagoon came again the tinklings, now with a quicker note of jubilance—almost of triumph.

"We ran to Thora, Stanton and I, and picked her up. Her head rolled and her face, eyes closed, turned as though drawn full into the moonlight. I felt in my heart a throb of unfamiliar fear—for her face had changed again. Stamped upon it was a look of mingled transport and horror—alien, terrifying, strangely revolting. It was"—he thrust his face close to my eyes—"what you see in mine!"

For a dozen heart-beats I stared at him, fascinated; then he sank back again into the half-shadow of the berth.

"I managed to hide her face from Edith," he went on. "I thought she had suffered some sort of a nervous seizure. We carried her into her tent. Once within the unholy mask dropped from her, and she was again only the kindly, rugged old woman. I watched her throughout the night. The sounds from Nan-Tanach continued until about an hour before moonset. In the morning Thora awoke, none the worse, apparently. She had had bad dreams, she said. She could not remember what they were—except that they had warned her of danger. She was oddly sullen, and I noted that throughout the morning her gaze returned again half-fascinatedly, half-wonderingly to the neighboring isles.

"That afternoon the natives returned. They were so exuberant in their apparent relief to find us well and intact that Stanton's suspicions of them were confirmed. He slyly told their leader that 'from the noise they had made on Nan-Tanach the night before they must have thoroughly enjoyed themselves.'

"I think I never saw such stark terror as the Ponapean manifested at the remark! Stanton himself was so plainly startled that he tried to pass it over as a jest. He met poor success! The men seemed panic-stricken, and for a time I thought they were about to abandon us—but they did not. They pitched their camp at the western side of the island —out of sight of Nan-Tanach. I noticed that they built large fires, and whenever I awoke that night I heard their voices in slow, minor chant —one of their song 'charms,' I thought drowsily, against evil *ani*. I heard nothing else; the place of frowning walls was wrapped in silence —no lights showed. The next morning the men were quiet, a little depressed, but as the hours wore on they regained their spirits, and soon life at the camp was going on just as it had before.

"You will understand, Goodwin, how the occurrences I have related would excite the scientific curiosity. We rejected immediately, of course, any explanation admitting the supernatural. Why not? Except the curiously disquieting effects of the tinkling music and Thora's behavior there was nothing to warrant any such fantastic theories—even if our minds had been the kind to harbor them.

"We came to the conclusion that there must be a passageway between Ponape and Nan-Tanach, known to the natives—and used by them during their rites. Ceremonies were probably held in great vaults or caverns beneath the ruins.

"We decided at last that on the next departure of our laborers we would set forth immediately to Nan-Tanach. We would investigate during the day, and at evening my wife and Thora would go back to camp, leaving Stanton and me to spend the night on the island, observing from some safe hiding-place what might occur.

"The moon waned; appeared crescent in the west; waxed slowly toward the full. Before the men left us they literally prayed us to accompany them. Their importunities only made us more eager to see what it was that, we were now convinced, they wanted to conceal from us. At least that was true of Stanton and myself. It was not true of Edith. She was thoughtful, abstracted—reluctant. Thora, on the other hand, showed an unusual restlessness, almost an eagerness to go. Goodwin"—he paused—"Goodwin, I know now that the poison was working in Thora—and that women have perceptions that we men lack—forebodings, sensings. I wish to Heaven I had known it then—Edith!" he cried suddenly. "Edith—come back to me! Forgive me!"

I stretched the decanter out to him. He drank deeply. Soon he had regained control of himself.

"When the men were out of sight around the turn of the harbor," he went on, "we took our boat and made straight for Nan-Tanach. Soon its mighty sea-wall towered above us. We passed through the water-gate with its gigantic hewn prisms of basalt and landed beside a half-submerged pier. In front of us stretched a series of giant steps leading into a vast court strewn with fragments of fallen pillars. In the center of the court, beyond the shattered pillars, rose another terrace of basalt blocks, concealing, I knew, still another enclosure.

"And now, Goodwin, for the better understanding of what follows and to guide you, should I—not be able—to accompany you when you go there, listen carefully to my description of this place: Nan-Tanach is literally three rectangles. The first rectangle is the sea-wall, built up of monoliths. Gigantic steps lead up from the landing of the sea-gate through the entrance to the courtyard.

"This courtyard is surrounded by another, inner basalt wall.

"Within the courtyard is the second enclosure. Its terrace, of the same basalt as the outer walls, is about twenty feet high. Entrance is gained to it by many breaches which time has made in its stonework. This is the inner court, the heart of Nan-Tanach! There lies the great central vault with which is associated the one name of living being that has come to us out of the mists of the past. The natives say it was the treasure-house of Chau-te-leur, a mighty king who reigned long 'before their fathers.' As Chau is the ancient Ponapean word both for sun and king, the name means 'place of the sun king.'

"And opposite this place of the sun king is the moon rock that hides the moon pool.

"It was Stanton who first found what I call the moon rock. We had been inspecting the inner courtyard; Edith and Thora were getting together our lunch. I forgot to say that we had previously gone all over the islet and had found not a trace of living thing. I came out of the vault of Chau-te-leur to find Stanton before a part of the terrace studying it wonderingly.

" 'What do you make of this?' he asked me as I came up. He pointed to the wall. I followed his finger and saw a slab of stone about fifteen feet high and ten wide. At first all I noticed was the exquisite nicety with which its edges joined the blocks about it. Then I realized that its color was subtly different—tinged with gray and of a smooth, peculiar—deadness.

" 'Looks more like calcite than basalt,' I said. I touched it and withdrew my hand quickly, for at the contact every nerve in my arm tingled as though a shock of frozen electricity had passed through it. It was not cold as we know cold that I felt. It was a chill force—the phrase I have used—frozen electricity—describes it better than anything else. Stanton looked at me oddly.

" 'So you felt it, too,' he said. 'I was wondering whether I was developing hallucinations like Thora. Notice, by the way, that the blocks beside it are quite warm beneath the sun.'

"I felt them and touched the grayish stone again. The same faint shock ran through my hand—a tingling chill that had in it a suggestion of substance, of force. We examined the slab more closely. Its edges were cut as though by an engraver of jewels. They fitted against the neighboring blocks in almost a hair-line. Its base, we saw, was slightly curved, and fitted as closely as top and sides upon the huge stones on which it rested. And then we noted that these stones had been hollowed to follow the line of the gray stone's foot. There was a semicircular depression running from one side of the slab to the other. It was as though the gray rock stood in the center of a shallow cup—revealing half, covering half. Something about this hollow attracted me. I reached down and felt it. Goodwin, although the balance of the stones that formed it, like all the stones of the courtyard, were rough and age-worn—this was as smooth, as even surfaced as though it just left the hands of the polisher.

" 'It's a door!' exclaimed Stanton. 'It swings around in that little cup. That's what make the hollow so smooth.'

" 'Maybe you're right,' I replied. 'But how the devil can we open it?'

"We went over the slab again—pressing upon its edges, thrusting against its sides. During one of those efforts I happened to look up—and cried out. For a foot above and on each side of the corner of the gray rock's lintel I had seen a slight convexity, visible only from the angle at which my gaze struck it. These bosses on the basalt were circular, eighteen inches in diameter, as we learned later, and at the center extended two inches only beyond the face of the terrace. Unless one looked directly up at them while leaning against the moon rock—for this slab, Goodwin, *is* the moon rock—they were invisible. And none would dare stand there!

"We carried with us a small scaling-ladder, and up this I went. The bosses were apparently nothing more than chiseled curvatures in the stone. I laid my hand on the one I was examining, and drew it back so sharply I almost threw myself from the ladder. In my palm, at the base of my thumb, I had felt the same shock that I had in touching the slab below. I put my hand back. The impression came from a spot not more than an inch wide. I went carefully over the entire convexity, and six times more the chill ran through my arm. There were, Goodwin, seven circles an inch wide in the curved place, each of which communicated the precise sensation I have described. The convexity on the opposite side of the slab gave precisely the same results. But no amount of touching or of pressing these spots singly or in any combination gave the slightest promise of motion to the slab itself.

" 'And yet—they're what open it,' said Stanton positively.

" 'Why do you say that?' I asked.

" 'I—don't know,' he answered hesitating. 'But something tells me so. Throck,' he went on half earnestly, half laughingly, 'the purely scientific part of me is fighting the purely human part of me. The scientific part is urging me to find some way to get that slab either down or open. The human part is just as strongly urging me to do nothing of the sort and get away while I can!'

"He laughed again—shamefacedly.

" 'Which will it be?' he asked—and I thought that in his tone the human side of him was ascendant.

" 'It will probably stay as it is—unless we blow it to bits,' I said.

" 'I thought of that,' he answered, 'and—I wouldn't dare,' he added somberly enough. And even as I had spoken there came to me the same feeling that he had expressed. It was as though something passed out of the gray rock that struck my heart as a hand strikes an impious lip. We turned away—uneasily, and faced Thora coming through a breach in the terrace.

" 'Miss Edith wants you quick,' she began—and stopped. I saw her eyes go past me and widen. She was looking at the gray rock. Her body grew suddenly rigid; she took a few stiff steps forward and ran straight to it. We saw her cast herself upon its breast, hands and face pressed against it; heard her scream as though her very soul was being drawn from her—and watched her fall at its foot. As we picked her up I saw steal from her face the look I had observed when I first heard the crystal music of Nan-Tanach—that unhuman mingling of opposites!"

5. AV-O-LO-HA

"We carried Thora back, down to where Edith was waiting. We told her what had happened and what we had found. She listened gravely, and as we finished Thora sighed and opened her eyes.

" 'I would like to see the stone,' she said. 'Charles, you stay here with Thora.' We passed through the outer court silently—and stood before the rock. She touched it, drew back her hand as I had; thrust it forward again resolutely and held it there. She seemed to be listening. Then she turned to me.

" 'David,' said my wife, and the wistfulness in her voice hurt me— 'David, would you be very, very disappointed if we went from here— without trying to find out any more about it—would you?'

"Goodwin, I never wanted anything so much in my life as I wanted to learn what that rock concealed. You will understand—the cumulative curiosity that all the happenings had caused; the certainty that before me was an entrance to a place that, while known to the natives—for I still clung to that theory—was utterly unknown to any man of my race; that within, ready for my finding, was the answer to the stupendous riddle of these islands and a lost chapter in the history of humanity. There before me—and was I asked to turn away, leaving it unread!

"Nevertheless, I tried to master my desire, and I answered— 'Edith, not a bit if you want us to do it.'

"She read my struggle in my eyes. She looked at me searchingly for a moment and then turned back toward the gray rock. I saw a shiver pass through her. I felt a tinge of remorse and pity!

" 'Edith,' I exclaimed, 'we'll go!'

"She looked at me hard. 'Science is a jealous mistress,' she quoted. 'No, after all it may be just fancy. At any rate, you can't run away. No! But, Dave, I'm going to stay too!'

" 'You are not!' I exclaimed. 'You're going back to the camp with Thora. Stanton and I will be all right.'

" 'I'm going to stay,' she repeated. And there was no changing her decision. As we neared the others she laid a hand on my arm.

" 'Dave,' she said, 'If there should be something—well—inexplicable tonight—something that seems—too dangerous—will you promise to go back to our own islet tomorrow, or, while we can, and wait until the natives return?'

"I promised eagerly—for the desire to stay and see what came with the night was like a fire within me.

"And would to Heaven I had not waited another moment, Goodwin; would to Heaven I had gathered them all together then and sailed back on the instant through the mangroves to Uschen-Tau!

"We found Thora on her feet again and singularly composed. She claimed to have no more recollection of what had happened after she had spoken to Stanton and to me in front of the gray rock than she had after the seizure on Uschen-Tau. She grew sullen under our questioning, precisely as she had before. But to my astonishment, when she heard of our arrangements for the night, she betrayed a febrile excitement that had in it something of exultance.

"We had picked a place about five hundred feet away from the steps leading into the outer court.

"We settled down just before dusk to wait for whatever might come. I was nearest the giant steps; next to me Edith; then Thora, and last Stanton. Each of us had with us automatic pistols, and all, except Thora, had rifles.

"Night fell. After a time the eastern sky began to lighten, and we knew that the moon was rising; grew lighter still, and the orb peeped over the sea; swam suddenly into full sight. Edith gripped my hand, for, as though the full emergence into the heavens had been a signal, we heard begin beneath us the deep chanting. It came from illimitable depths.

"The moon poured her rays down upon us, and I saw Stanton

start. On the instant I caught the sound that had roused him. It came from the inner enclosure. It was like a long, soft sighing. It was not human; seemed in some way—mechanical. I glanced at Edith and then at Thora. My wife was intently listening. Thora sat, as she had since we had placed ourselves, elbows on knees, her hands covering her face.

"And then suddenly from the moonlight flooding us there came to me a great drowsiness. Sleep seemed to drip from the rays and fall upon my eyes, closing them—closing them inexorably. I felt Edith's hand relax in mine, and under my own heavy lids saw her nodding. I saw Stanton's head fall upon his breast and his body sway drunkenly. I tried to rise—to fight against the profound desire for slumber that pressed in on me.

"And as I fought I saw Thora raise her head as though listening; saw her rise and turn her face toward the gateway. For a moment she gazed, and my drugged eyes seemed to perceive within it a deeper, stronger radiance. Thora looked at us. There was infinite despair in her face—and expectancy. I tried again to rise—and a surge of sleep rushed over me. Dimly, as I sank within it, I heard a crystalline chiming; raised my lids once more with a supreme effort, saw Thora, bathed in light, standing at the top of the stairs, and then—sleep took me for its very own—swept me into the very heart of oblivion!

"Dawn was breaking when I wakened. Recollection rushed back on me and I thrust a panic-stricken hand out toward Edith; touched her and felt my heart give a great leap of thankfulness. She stirred, sat up, rubbing dazed eyes. I glanced toward Stanton. He lay on his side, back toward us, head in arms.

"Edith looked at me laughingly. 'Heavens! What sleep!' she said. Memory came to her. Her face paled. 'What happened?' she whispered. 'What made us sleep like that?' She looked over to Stanton, sprang to her feet, ran to him, shook him. He turned over with a mighty yawn, and I saw relief lighten her face as it had lightened my heart.

"Stanton raised himself stiffly. He looked at us. 'What's the matter?' he exclaimed. 'You look as though you've seen ghosts!'

"Edith caught my hands. 'Where's Thora?' she cried. Before I could answer she ran out into the open calling: 'Thora! Thora!'

"Stanton stared at me. 'Taken!' was all I could say. Together we went to my wife, now standing beside the great stone steps, looking up fearfully at the gateway into the terraces. There I told them what I had seen before sleep had drowned me. And together then we ran up the stairs, through the court and up to the gray rock.

"The gray rock was closed as it had been the day before, nor was there trace of its having opened. No trace! Even as I thought this Edith dropped to her knees before it and reached toward something lying at its foot. It was a little piece of gray silk. I knew it for part of the kerchief Thora wore about her hair. Edith took the fragment; hesitated. I saw then that it had been *cut* from the kerchief as though by a razor-edge; I saw, too, that a few threads ran from it—down toward the base of the slab; ran to the base of the gray rock and—under it! The gray rock was a door! And it had opened and Thora had passed through it!

"I think, Goodwin, that for the next few minutes we all were a little insane. We beat upon that diabolic entrance with our hands, with stones and clubs. At last reason came back to us. Stanton set forth for the camp to bring back blasting powder and tools. While he was gone Edith and I searched the whole islet for any other clue. We found not a trace of Thora nor any indication of any living being save ourselves. We went back to the gateway to find Stanton returned.

"Goodwin, during the next two hours we tried every way in our power to force entrance through the slab. The rock within effective blasting radius of the cursed door resisted our drills. We tried explosions at the base of the slab with charges covered by rock. They made not the slightest impression on the surface beneath, expending their force, of course, upon the slighter resistance of their coverings.

"Afternoon found us hopeless, so far as breaking through the rock was concerned. Night was coming on and before it came we would have to decide our course of action. I wanted to go to Ponape for help. But Edith objected that this would take hours and after we had reached there it would be impossible to persuade our men to return with us that night, if at all. What then was left? Clearly only one of two choices: to go back to our camp and wait for our men to return and on their return try to persuade them to go with us to Nan-Tanach. But this would mean the abandonment of Thora for at least two days. We could not do it; it would have been too cowardly.

"The other choice was to wait where we were for night to come; to wait for the rock to open as it had the night before, and to make a sortie through it for Thora before it could close again. With the sun had come confidence; at least a shattering of the mephitic mists of superstition with which the strangeness of the things that had befallen us had clouded for a time our minds. In that brilliant light there seemed no place for fantoms.

"The evidence that the slab had opened was unmistakable, but might not Thora simply have *found* it open through some mechanism, still working after ages, and dependent for its action upon laws of physics unknown to us upon the full light of the moon? The assertion of the natives that the *ani* had greatest power at this time might be a far-flung reflection of knowledge which had found ways to use forces contained in moonlight, as we have found ways to utilize the forces in the sun's rays. If so, Thora was probably behind the slab, sending out prayers to us for help.

"But how explain the sleep that had descended upon us? Might it not have been some emanation from plants or gaseous emanations from the island itself? Such things were far from uncommon, we agreed. In some way, the period of their greatest activity might coincide with the period of the moon, but if this were so why had not Thora also slept?

"As dusk fell we looked over our weapons. Edith was an excellent shot with both rifle and pistol. With the idea that the impulse toward sleep was the result either of emanations such as I have described or man made, we constructed rough-and-ready but effective neutralizers, which we placed over our mouths and nostrils. We had decided that my wife was to remain in the hollow spot. Stanton would take up a station on the far side of the stairway and I would place myself opposite him on the side near Edith. The place I picked out was less than five hundred feet from her, and I could reassure myself now as to her safety, as I looked down upon the hollow wherein she crouched. As the phenomena had previously synchronized with the rising of the moon, we had no reason to think they would occur any earlier this night.

"A faint glow in the sky heralded the moon. I kissed Edith, and Stanton and I took our places. The moon dawn increased rapidly; the disk swam up, and in a moment it seemed was shining in full radiance upon ruins and sea.

"As it rose there came as on the night before the curious little sighing sound from the inner terrace. I saw Stanton straighten up and stare intently through the gateway, rifle ready. Even at the distance he was from me, I discerned amazement in his eyes. The moonlight within the gateway thickened, grew stronger. I watched his amazement grow into sheer wonder.

"I arose.

"'Stanton, what do you see?' I called cautiously. He waved a silencing hand. I turned my head to look at Edith. A shock ran through me. She lay upon her side. Her face was turned full toward the moon. She was in deepest sleep!

"As I turned again to call to Stanton, my eyes swept the head of the steps and stopped fascinated. For the moonlight had thickened more. It seemed to be—curdled—there; and through it ran little gleams and veins of shimmering white fire. A languor passed through me. It was not the ineffable drowsiness of the preceding night. It was a sapping of all will to move. I tore my eyes away and forced them upon Stanton. I tried to call out to him. I had not the will to make my lips move! I had struggled against this paralysis and as I did so I felt through me a sharp shock. It was like a blow. And with it came utter inability to make a single motion. Goodwin, I could not even move my eyes!

"I saw Stanton leap upon the steps and move toward the gateway. As he did so the light in the courtyard grew dazzlingly brilliant. Through it rained tiny tinklings that set the heart to racing with pure joy and stilled it with terror.

"And now for the first time I heard that cry *'Av-o-lo-ha! Av-o-lo-ha!'* the cry you heard on deck. It murmured with the strange effect of a sound only partly in our own space—as though it were part of a fuller phrase passing through from another dimension and losing much as it came; infinitely caressing, infinitely cruel!

"On Stanton's face I saw come the look I dreaded—and yet knew would appear; that mingled expression of delight and fear. The two lay side by side as they had on Thora, but were intensified. He walked on up the stairs; disappeared beyond the range of my fixed gaze. Again I heard the murmur—*'Av-o-lo-ha!'* There was triumph in it now and triumph in the storm of tinklings that swept over it.

"For another heart-beat there was silence. Then a louder burst of sound and ringing through it Stanton's voice from the courtyard—a great cry—a scream—filled with ecstasy insupportable and horror unimaginable! And again there was silence. I strove to burst the invisible bonds that held me. I could not. Even my eyelids were fixed. Within them my eyes, dry and aching, burned.

"Then, Goodwin—I first saw the inexplicable! The crystalline music swelled. Where I sat I could take in the gateway and its basalt portals, rough and broken, rising to the top of the wall forty feet above, shattered, ruined portals—unclimbable. From this gateway an intenser light began to flow. It grew, it gushed, and into it, into my sight, walked Stanton.

"Stanton! But—Goodwin! What a vision!" He ceased. I waited—waited.

6. INTO THE MOON POOL

"Goodwin," Throckmartin said at last, "I can describe him only as a thing of living light. He radiated light; was filled with light; overflowed with it. Around him was a shining cloud that whirled through and around him in radiant swirls, shimmering tentacles, luminescent, coruscating spirals.

"I saw his face. It shone with a rapture too great to be borne by living men, and was shadowed with insuperable misery. It was as though his face had been remolded by the hand of God and the hand of Satan, working together and in harmony. You have seen it on my face. But you have never seen it in the degree that Stanton bore it. The eyes were wide open and fixed, as though upon some inward vision of hell and heaven! He walked like the corpse of a man damned who carried within him an angel of light.

"The music swelled again. I heard again the murmuring—*'Av-o-lo-ha!'* Stanton turned, facing the ragged side of the portal. And then I saw that the light that filled and surrounded him had a nucleus, a core —something shiftingly human shaped—that dissolved and changed, gathered itself, whirled through and beyond him and back again. And as this shining nucleus passed through him Stanton's whole body pulsed with light. As the luminescence moved, there moved with it, still and serene always, seven tiny globes of light like seven little moons.

"So much I saw and then swiftly Stanton seemed to be lifted—levitated—up the unscalable wall and to its top. The glow faded from the moonlight, the tinkling music grew fainter. I tried again to move. The spell still held me fast. The tears were running down now from my rigid lids and brought relief to my tortured eyes.

"I have said my gaze was fixed. It was. But from the side, peripherally, it took in a part of the far wall of the outer enclosure. Ages seemed to pass and I saw a radiance stealing along it. Soon there came into sight the figure that was Stanton. Far away he was—on the gigantic wall. But still I could see the shining spirals whirling jubilantly around and through him; felt rather than saw his tranced face beneath the seven lights. A swirl of crystal notes, and he had passed. And all the time, as though from some opened well of light, the courtyard gleamed and sent out silver fires that dimmed the moon-rays, yet seemed strangely to be a part of them.

"Ten times he passed before me so. The luminescence came with the music; swam for a while along the man-made cliff of basalt and passed away. Between times eternities rolled and still I crouched there, a helpless thing of stone with eyes that would not close!

"At last the moon neared the horizon. There came a louder burst of sound; the second, and last, cry of Stanton, like an echo of the first! Again the soft sigh from the inner terrace. Then—utter silence. The light faded; the moon was setting and with a rush life and power to move returned to me, I made a leap for the steps, rushed up them, through the gateway and straight to the gray rock. It was closed—as I knew it would be. But did I dream it or did I hear, echoing through it as though from vast distances a triumphant shouting—*'Av-o-lo-ha! Av-o-lo-ha!'*?

"I remembered Edith. I ran back to her. At my touch she wakened; looked at me wonderingly; raised herself on a hand.

" 'Dave!' she said, 'I slept—after all.' She saw the despair on my face and leaped to her feet. 'Dave!' she cried. 'What is it? Where's Charles?'

"I lighted a fire before I spoke. Then I told her. And for the balance of that night we sat before the flames, arms around each other —like two frightened children."

Suddenly Throckmartin held his hands out to me appealingly.

"Goodwin, old friend!" he cried. "Don't look at me as though I were mad. It's truth, absolute truth. Wait—" I comforted him as well as I could. After a little time he took up his story.

"Never," he said, "did man welcome the sun as we did that morning. As soon as it was light we went back to the courtyard. The basalt walls whereon I had seen Stanton were black and silent. The terraces were as they had been. The gray slab was in its place. In the shallow hollow at its base was—nothing. Nothing—nothing was there anywhere on the islet of Stanton—not a trace, not a sign on Nan-Tanach to show that he had ever lived.

"What were we to do? Precisely the same arguments that had kept us there the night before held good now—and doubly good. We could not abandon these two; could not go as long as there was the faintest hope of finding them—and yet for love of each other how could we remain? I loved my wife, Goodwin—how much I never knew until that day; and she loved me as deeply.

" 'It takes only one each night,' she said. 'Beloved, let it take me.'

"I wept, Goodwin. We both wept.

" 'We will meet it together,' she said. And it was thus at last that we arranged it."

"That took great courage indeed, Throckmartin," I interrupted. He looked at me eagerly.

"You do believe then?" he exclaimed.

"I believe," I said. He pressed my hand with a grip that nearly crushed it.

"Now," he told me, "I do not fear. If I—fail, you will prepare and carry on the work."

I promised. And—Heaven forgive me—that was three years ago.

"It did take courage," he went on, again quietly. "More than courage. For we knew it was renunciation. Each of us in our hearts felt that one of us would not be there to see the sun rise. And each of us prayed that the death, if death it was, would not come first to the other.

"We talked it all over carefully, bringing to bear all our power of analysis and habit of calm, scientific thought. We considered minutely the time element in the phenomena. Although the deep chanting began at the very moment of moonrise, fully five minutes had passed between its full lifting and the strange sighing sound from the inner terrace. I went back in memory over the happenings of the night before. At least fifteen minutes had intervened between the first heralding sigh and the intensification of the moonlight in the courtyard. And this glow grew for at least ten minutes more before the first burst of the crystal notes.

"The sighing sound—of what had it reminded me? Of course—of a door revolving and swishing softly along its base.

" 'Edith!' I cried. 'I think I have it! The gray rock opens five minutes after upon the moonrise. But whoever or whatever it is that comes through it must wait until the moon has risen higher, or else it must come from a distance. The thing to do is not to wait for it, but to surprise it before it passes out the door. We will go into the inner court early. You will take your rifle and pistol and hide yourself where you can command the opening—if the slab does open. The instant it moves I will enter. It's our best chance, Edith. I think it's our only one.'

"My wife demurred strongly. She wanted to go with me. But I convinced her that it was better for her to stand guard without, prepared to help me if I were forced from what lay behind the rock again into the open.

"The day passed too swiftly. In the face of what we feared our love seemed stronger than ever. Was it the flare of the spark before extinguishment? I wondered. We prepared and ate a good dinner. We tried to keep our minds from anything but scientific aspect of the phenomena. We agreed that whatever it was its cause must be human, and that we must keep that fact in mind every second. But what kind of men could create such prodigies? We thrilled at the thought of finding perhaps the remnants of a vanished race, living perhaps in cities over whose rocky skies the Pacific rolled; exercising there the lost wisdom of the half-gods of earth's youth.

"At the half-hour before moonrise we two went into the inner courtyard. I took my place at the side of the gray rock. Edith crouched behind a broken pillar twenty feet away, slipped her rifle-barrel over it so that it would cover the opening.

"The minutes crept by. The courtyard was very quiet. The darkness lessened and through the breaches of the terrace I watched the far sky softly lighten. With the first pale flush the stillness became intensified. It deepened—became unbearably—expectant. The moon rose, showed the quarter, the half, then swam up into full sight like a great bubble.

"Its rays fell upon the wall before me and suddenly upon the convexities I have described seven little circles of light sprang out. They gleamed, glimmered, grew brighter—shone. The gigantic slab before me turned as though on a pivot, sighing softly as it moved.

"For a moment I gasped in amazement. It was like a conjurer's trick. And the moving slab I noticed was also glowing, becoming opalescent like the little shining circles above.

"Only for a second I gazed and then with a word to Edith flung myself through the opening which the slab had uncovered. Before me was a platform and from the platform steps led downward into a smooth corridor. This passage was not dark, it glowed with the same faint silvery radiance as the door. Down it I raced. As I ran, plainer than ever before, I heard the chanting. The passage turned abruptly, passed parallel to the walls of the outer courtyard and then once more led abruptly downward. Still I ran, and as I ran I looked at the watch on my wrist. Less than three minutes had elapsed.

"The passage ended. Before me was a high vaulted arch. For a moment I paused. It seemed to open into space; a space filled with lambent, coruscating, many-colored mist whose brightness grew even as I watched. I passed through the arch and stopped in sheer awe!

"In front of me was a pool. It was circular, perhaps twenty feet wide. Around it ran a low, softly curved lip of glimmering silvery stone. Its water was palest blue. The pool with its silvery rim was like a great blue eye staring upward.

"Upon it streamed seven shafts of radiance. They poured down upon the blue eye like cylindrical torrents; they were like shining pillars of light rising from a sapphire floor.

"One was the tender pink of the pearl; one of the aurora's green; a third a deathly white; the fourth the blue in mother-of-pearl; a shimmering column of pale amber; a beam of amethyst; a shaft of molten silver. Such are the colors of the seven lights that stream upon the moon pool. I drew closer, awestricken. The shafts did not illumine the depths. They played upon the surface and seemed there to diffuse, to melt into it. The pool drank them!

"Through the water tiny gleams of phosphorescence began to dart, sparkles and coruscations of pale incandescence. And far, far below I sensed a movement a shifting glow as of something slowly rising.

"I looked upward, following the radiant pillars to their source. Far above were seven shining globes, and it was from these that the rays poured. Even as I watched their brightness grew. They were like seven moons set high in some caverned heaven. Slowly their splendor increased, and with it the splendor of the seven beams streaming from them. It came to me that they were crystals of some unknown kind set in the roof of the moon pool's vault and that their light was drawn from the moon shining high above them. They were wonderful, those lights—and what must have been the knowledge of those who set them there!

"Brighter and brighter they grew as the moon climbed higher, sending its full radiance down through them. I tore my gaze away and stared at the pool. It had grown milky, opalescent. The rays gushing into it seemed to be filling it; it was alive with sparklings, scintillations, glimmerings. And the luminescence I had seen rising from its depths was larger, nearer!

"A swirl of mist floated up from its surface. It drifted within the embrace of the rosy beam and hung there for a moment. The beam seemed to embrace it, sending through it little shining corpuscles, tiny rosy spiralings. The mist absorbed the rays, was strengthened by it, gained substance. Another swirl sprang into the amber shaft, clung and fed there, moved swiftly toward the first and mingled with it. And now other swirls arose, here and there, too fast to be counted, hung poised in the embrace of the light streams; flashed and pulsed into each other.

"Thicker and thicker still they arose until the surface of the pool was a pulsating pillar of opalescent mist; steadily growing stronger; drawing within it life from the seven beams falling upon it; drawing to it from below the darting, red atoms of the pool. Into its center was passing the luminescence I had sensed rising from the far depths. And the center glowed, throbbed—began to send out questing swirls and tendrils.

"There forming before me was *that* which had walked with Stanton, which had taken Thora—the thing I had come to find!

"With the shock or realization my brain sprang into action. My hand fell to my pistol and I fired shot after shot into its radiance. The place rang with the explosions and there came to me a sense of unforgivable profanation. Devilish as I knew it to be, that chamber of the moon pool seemed also—in some way—holy. As though a god and a demon dwelt there, inextricably commingled.

"As I shot the pillar wavered; the water grew more disturbed. The mist swayed and shook; gathered itself again. I slipped a second clip into the automatic and, another idea coming to me, took careful aim at one of the globes in the roof. From thence I knew came the force that shaped the dweller in the pool. From the pouring rays came its strength. If I could destroy them I could check its forming. I fired again and again. If I hit the globes I did no damage. The little motes in their beams danced with the motes in the mist, troubled. That was all.

"Up from the pool like little bells, like bubbles of crystal notes rose the tinklings. Their notes were higher, had lost their sweetness, were angry, as it were, with themselves.

"And then out from the inexplicable, hovering over the pool, swept a shining swirl. It caught me above the heart; wrapped itself around me. I felt an icy coldness and then there rushed over me a mingled ecstasy and horror. Every atom of me quivered with delight and at the same time shrank with despair. There was nothing loathsome in it. But it was as though the icy soul of evil and the fiery soul of good had stepped together within me. The pistol dropped from my hand.

"So I stood while the pool gleamed and sparkled; the streams of light grew more intense and the mist glowed and strengthened. I saw that its shining core had shape—but a shape that my eyes and brain could not define. It was as though a being of another sphere should assume what it might of human semblance, but was not able to conceal that what human eyes saw was but a part of it. It was neither man nor woman; it was unearthly and androgynous. Even as I found its human semblance it changed. And still the mingled rapture and terror held me. Only in a little corner of my brain dwelt something untouched; something that held itself apart and watched. Was it the soul? I have never believed—and yet—

"Over the head of the misty body there sprang suddenly out seven little lights. Each was the color of the beam beneath which it rested. I knew now that the dweller was—complete!

"And then—behind me I heard a scream. It was Edith's voice. It came to me that she had heard the shots and followed me. I felt every faculty concentrate into a mighty effort. I wrenched myself free from the gripping tentacle and it swept back. I turned to catch Edith, and as I did so slipped—fell. As I dropped I saw the radiant shape above the pool leap swiftly for me!

"There was the rush past me and as the dweller paused, straight into it raced Edith, arms outstretched to shield me from it!"

He trembled.

"She threw herself squarely within its diabolic splendor," he whispered. "She stopped and reeled as though she had encountered solidity. And as she faltered it wrapped its shining self around her. The crystal tinklings burst forth jubilantly. The light filled her, ran through and around her as it had with Stanton and I saw drop upon her face—the look. From the pillar came the murmur—*'Av-o-lo-ha!'* The vault echoed it.

" 'Edith!' I cried. 'Edith!' I was in agony. She must have heard me, even through the—thing. I saw her try to free herself. Her rush had taken her to the very verge of the moon pool. She tottered; and in an instant—she fell—with the radiance still holding her, still swirling and winding around and through her—into the moon pool! She sank, Goodwin, and with her went—the dweller!

"I dragged myself to the brink. Far down I saw a shining, many-colored nebulous cloud descending; caught a glimpse of Edith's face, disappearing; her eyes stared up to me filled with supernal ecstasy and horror. And—vanished!

"I looked about me stupidly. The seven globes still poured their radiance upon the pool. It was pale-blue again. Its sparklings and coruscations were gone. From far below there came a muffled outburst of triumphant chanting!

" 'Edith!' I cried again. 'Edith, come back to me!' And then a darkness fell upon me. I remember running back through the shimmering corridors and out into the courtyard. Reason had left me. When it returned I was far out at sea in our boat wholly estranged from civilization. A day later I was picked up by the schooner in which I came to Port Moresby.

"I have formed a plan; you must hear it, Goodwin—" He fell upon his berth. I bent over him. Exhaustion and the relief of telling his story had been too much for him. He slept like the dead.

7. THE DWELLER COMES

All that night I watched over him. When dawn broke I went to my room to get a little sleep myself. But my slumber was haunted.

The next day the storm was unabated. Throckmartin came to me at lunch. He looked better. His strange expression had waned. He had regained much of his old alertness.

"Come to my cabin," he said. There, he stripped his shirt from him. "Something is happening," he said. "The mark is smaller." It was as he said.

"I'm escaping," he whispered jubilantly. "Just let me get to Melbourne safely, and then we'll see who'll win! For, Goodwin, I'm not at all sure that Edith is dead—as we know death—nor that the others are. There was something outside experience there—some great mystery."

And all that day he talked to me of his plans.

"There's a natural explanation, of course," he said. "My theory is that the moon rock is of some composition sensitive to the action of moon rays; somewhat as the metal selenium is to sun rays. There is a powerful quality in moonlight, as both science and legends can attest. We know of its effect upon the mentality, the nervous system, even upon certain diseases.

"The moon slab is of some material that reacts to moonlight. The circles over the top are, without doubt, its operating agency. When the light strikes them they release the mechanism that opens the slab, just as you can open doors with sunlight by an ingenious arrangement of selenium-cells. Apparently it takes the strength of the full moon to do this. We will first try a concentration of the rays of the *nearly* full moon upon these circles to see whether that will open the rock. If it does we will be able to investigate the pool without interruption from—from— what emanates.

"Look, here on the chart are their locations. I have made this in duplicate for you in the event of something happening to me."

He worked upon the chart a little more.

"Here," he said, "is where I believe the seven great globes to be. They are probably hidden somewhere in the ruins of the islet called Tau, where they can catch the first moon rays. I have calculated that when I entered I went so far this way—here is the turn; so far this way, took this other turn and ran down this long, curving corridor to the hall of the moon pool. That ought to make lights, at least approximately, here." He pointed.

"They are certainly cleverly concealed, but they must be open to the air to get the light. They should not be too hard to find. They must be found." He hesitated again. "I suppose it would be safer to destroy them, for it is clearly through them that the phenomenon of the pool is manifested; and yet, to destroy so wonderful a thing! Perhaps the better way would be to have some men up by them, and if it were necessary, to protect those below, to destroy them on signal. Or they might simply be covered. That would neutralize them. To destroy them—" He hesitated again. "No, the phenomenon is too important to be destroyed without fullest investigation." His face clouded again. "But it is *not* human; it can't be," he muttered. He turned to me and laughed. "The old conflict between science and too frail human credulity!" he said.

Again—"We need half a dozen diving-suits. The pool must be entered and searched to its depths. That will indeed take courage, yet in the time of the new moon it should be safe, or perhaps better after the dweller is destroyed or made safe."

We went over plans, accepted them, rejected them, and still the storm raged—and all that day and all that night.

I hurry to the end. That afternoon there came a steady lightening of the clouds which Throckmartin watched with deep uneasiness. Toward dusk they broke away suddenly and soon the sky was clear. The stars came twinkling out.

"It will be tonight," Throckmartin said to me. "Goodwin, friend, stand by me. Tonight it will come, and I must fight."

I could say nothing. About an hour before moonrise we went to his cabin. We fastened the port-holes tightly and turned on the lights. Throckmartin had some queer theory that the electric rays would be a bar to his pursuer. I don't know why. A little later he complained of increasing sleepiness.

"But it's just weariness," he said. "Not at all like that other drowsiness. It's an hour till moonrise still," he yawned at last. "Wake me up a good fifteen minutes before."

He lay upon the berth. I sat thinking. I came to myself with a start. What time was it? I looked at my watch and jumped to the port-hole. It was full moonlight; the orb had been up for fully half an hour. I strode over to Throckmartin and shook him by the shoulder.

"Up, quick, man!" I cried. He rose sleepily. His shirt fell open at the neck and I looked, in amazement, at the white band around his chest. Even under the electric light it shone softly, as though little flecks of light were in it.

Throckmartin seemed only half-awake. He looked down at his breast, saw the glowing cincture, and smiled.

"Oh, yes," he said drowsily, "it's coming—to take me back to Edith! Well, I'm glad."

"Throckmartin!" I cried. "Wake up! Fight!"

"Fight!" he said. "No use; keep the maps; come after us."

He went to the port and drowsily drew aside the curtain. The moon traced a broad path of light straight to the ship. Under its rays the band around his chest gleamed brighter and brighter; shot forth little rays; seemed to move.

He peered out intently and, suddenly, before I could stop him, threw open the port. I saw a glimmering presence moving swiftly along the moon path toward us, skimming over the waters.

And with it raced little crystal tinklings and far off I heard a long-drawn murmuring cry.

On the instant the lights went out in the cabin, evidently throughout the ship, for I heard shouting above. I sprang back into a corner and crouched there. At the port-hole was a radiance; swirls and spirals of living white cold fire. It poured into the cabin and it was filled with dancing motes of light, and over the radiant core of it shone seven little lights like tiny moons. It gathered Throckmartin to it. Light pulsed through and from him. I saw his skin turn to a translucent, shimmering whiteness like illumined porcelain. His face became unrecognizable, inhuman with the monstrous twin expressions. So he stood for a moment. The pillar of light seemed to hesitate and the seven lights to contemplate me. I shrank further down into the corner. I saw Throckmartin drawn to the port. The room filled with murmuring. I fainted.

When I awakened the lights were burning again.

But of Throckmartin there was no trace!

There are some things that we are bound to regret all our lives. I suppose I was unbalanced by what I had seen. I could not think clearly. But there came to me the sheer impossibility of telling the ship's officers what I had seen; what Throckmartin had told me. They would accuse me, I felt, of his murder. At neither appearance of the phenomenon had any save our two selves witnessed it. I was certain of this because they would surely have discussed it. Why none had seen it I do not know.

The next morning when Throckmartin's absence was noted, I merely said that I had left him early in the evening. It occurred to no one to doubt me, or to question me further. His strangeness had caused much comment; all had thought him half-mad. And so it was officially reported that he had fallen or jumped from the ship during the failure of the lights, the cause of which was another mystery of that night.

Afterward, the same inhibition held me back from making his and my story known to my fellow scientists.

But this inhibition is suddenly dead, and I am not sure that its death is not a summons from Throckmartin.

And now I am going to Nan-Tanach to make amends for my cowardice by seeking out the dweller. So sure am I that all I have written here is absolutely true.

In the following story by Edward John Moreton Drax Plunkett, LORD DUNSANY, *a boy takes up the sword that once belonged to the hero Welleran and defends the beautiful city of Merimna. Dunsany, who began writing at the turn of the twentieth century, was one of the founders of adult fantasy. Using myth, the Bible, history, fairy tales, and folk tales as his inspiration, he created a series of heroic worlds entirely his own, peopled with warriors and creatures both good and evil. Along with William Morris, he established a high or Mandarin style for otherworldly fantasy: ornate, complex, perhaps even mannered. But whereas Morris' style is archaic, Dunsany's is biblical, pure, and original. Lord Dunsany and Kenneth Morris were nearly exact Celtic contemporaries, but whereas Morris revived the ancient settings of his forebears, Dunsany chose to invent new possibilities.*

The Sword of Welleran
BY LORD DUNSANY

Where the great plain of Tarphet runs up, as the sea in estuaries, among the Cyresian mountains, there stood long since the city of Merimna well-nigh among the shadows of the crags. I have never seen a city in the world so beautiful as Merimna seemed to me when first I dreamed of it. It was a marvel of spires and figures of bronze, and marble fountains, and trophies of fabulous wars, and broad streets given over wholly to the Beautiful. Right through the centre of the city there went an avenue fifty strides in width, and along each side of it stood likenesses in bronze of the Kings of all the countries that the people of Merimna had ever known. At the end of that avenue was a colossal chariot with three bronze horses driven by the winged figure of Fame, and behind her in the chariot the huge form of Welleran, Merimna's ancient hero, standing with extended sword. So urgent was the mien and attitude of Fame, and so swift the pose of the horses, that you had sworn that the chariot was instantly upon you, and that its dust already veiled the faces of the Kings. And in the city was a mighty hall wherein were stored the trophies of Merimna's heroes. Sculptured it was and domed, the glory of the art of masons a long while dead, and on the summit of the dome the image of Rollory sat gazing across the Cyresian mountains toward the wide lands beyond, the lands that knew his sword. And beside Rollory, like an old nurse, the figure of Victory sat, hammering into a golden wreath of laurels for his head the crowns of fallen Kings.

Such was Merimna, a city of sculptured Victories and warriors of bronze. Yet in the time of which I write the art of war had been forgotten in Merimna, and the people almost slept. To and fro and up and down they would walk through the marble streets, gazing at memorials of the things achieved by their country's swords in the hands of those that long ago had loved Merimna well. Almost they slept, and dreamed of Welleran, Soorenard, Mommolek, Rollory, Akanax, and young Iraine. Of the lands beyond the mountains that lay all round about them they knew nothing, save that they were the theatre of the terrible deeds of Welleran, that he had done with his sword. Long since these lands had fallen back into the possession of the nations that had been scourged by Merimna's armies. Nothing now remained to Merimna's men save their inviolate city and the glory of the remembrance of their ancient fame. At night they would place sentinels far out in the desert, but these always slept at their posts dreaming of Rollory, and three times every night a guard would march around the city clad in purple, bearing lights and singing songs of Welleran. Always the guard went unarmed, but as the sound of their song went echoing across the plain towards the looming mountains, the desert robbers would hear the name of Welleran and steal away to their haunts. Often dawn would come across the plain, shimmering marvellously upon Merimna's spires, abashing all the stars, and find the guard still singing songs of Welleran, and would change the colour of their purple robes and pale the lights they bore. But the guard would go back leaving the ramparts safe, and one by one the sentinels in the plain would awake from dreaming of Rollory and shuffle back into the city quite cold. Then something of the menace would pass away from the faces of the Cyresian mountains, that from the north and the west and the south lowered upon Merimna, and clear in the morning the statues and the pillars would arise in the old inviolate city. You would wonder that an unarmed guard and sentinels that slept could defend a city that was stored with all the glories of art, that was rich in gold and bronze, a haughty city that had erst oppressed its neighbours, whose people had forgotten the art of war. Now this is the reason that, though all her other lands had long been taken from her, Merimna's city was safe. A strange thing was believed or feared by the fierce tribes beyond the mountains, and it was credited among them that at certain stations round Merimna's ramparts there still rode Welleran, Soorenard, Mommolek, Rollory, Akanax, and young Iraine. Yet it was close on a hundred years since Iraine, the youngest of Merimna's heroes, fought his last battle with the tribes.

Sometimes indeed there arose among the tribes young men who doubted and said: "How may a man for ever escape death?"

But graver men answered them: "Hear us, ye whose wisdom has discerned so much, and discern for us how a man may escape death when two score horsemen assail him with their swords, all of them sworn to kill him, and all of them sworn upon their country's gods; as often Welleran hath. Or discern for us how two men alone may enter a walled city by night, and bring away from it that city's king, as did Soorenard and Mommolek. Surely men that have escaped so many swords and so many sleety arrows shall escape the years and Time."

And the young men were humbled and became silent. Still, the suspicion grew. And often when the sun set on the Cyresian mountains, men in Merimna discerned the forms of savage tribesmen black against the light, peering towards the city.

All knew in Merimna that the figures round the ramparts were only statues of stone, yet even there a hope lingered among a few that some day their old heroes would come again, for certainly none had ever seen them die. Now it had been the wont of these six warriors of old, as each received his last wound and knew it to be mortal, to ride away to a certain deep ravine and cast his body in, as somewhere I have read great elephants do, hiding their bones away from lesser beasts. It was a ravine steep and narrow even at the ends, a great cleft into which no man could come by any path. There rode Welleran alone, panting hard; and there later rode Soorenard and Mommolek, Mommolek with a mortal wound upon him not to return, but Soorenard was unwounded and rode back alone from leaving his dear friend resting among the mighty bones of Welleran. And there rode Soorenard, when his day was come, with Rollory and Akanax, and Rollory rode in the middle and Soorenard and Akanax on either side. And the long ride was a hard and weary thing for Soorenard and Akanax, for they both had mortal wounds; but the long ride was easy for Rollory, for he was dead. So the bones of these five heroes whitened in an enemy's land, and very still they were, though they had troubled cities, and none knew where they lay saving only Iraine, the young captain, who was but twenty-five when Mommolek, Rollory and Akanax rode away. And among them were strewn their saddles and their bridles, and all the accoutrements of their horses, lest any man should ever find them afterwards and say in some foreign city: "Lo! the bridles or the saddles of Merimna's captains, taken in war," but their beloved trusty horses they turned free.

Forty years afterwards, in the hour of a great victory, his last wound came upon Iraine, and the wound was terrible and would not close. And Iraine was the last of the captains, and rode away alone. It was a long way to the dark ravine, and Iraine feared that he would never come to the resting-place of the old heroes, and he urged his horse on swiftly, and clung to the saddle with his hands. And often as he rode he fell asleep, and dreamed of earlier days, and of the times when he first rode forth to the great wars of Welleran, and of the time when Welleran first spake to him, and of the faces of Welleran's comrades when they led charges in the battle. And ever as he awoke a great longing arose in his soul as it hovered on his body's brink, a longing to lie among the bones of the old heroes. At last when he saw the dark ravine making a scar across the plain, the soul of Iraine slipped out through his great wound and spread its wings, and pain departed from the poor hacked body and, still urging his horse forward, Iraine died. But the old true horse cantered on till suddenly he saw before him the dark ravine and put his forefeet out on the very edge of it and stopped. Then the body of Iraine came toppling forward over the right shoulder of the horse, and his bones mingle and rest as the years go by with the bones of Merimna's heroes.

Now there was a little boy in Merimna named Rold. I saw him first, I, the dreamer, that sit before my fire asleep, I saw him first as his mother led him through the great hall where stand the trophies of Merimna's heroes. He was five years old, and they stood before the great glass casket wherein lay the sword of Welleran, and his mother said: "The sword of Welleran." And Rold said: "What should a man do with the sword of Welleran?" And his mother answered: "Men look at the sword and remember Welleran." And they went on and stood before the great red cloak of Welleran, and the child said: "Why did Welleran wear this great red cloak?" And his mother answered: "It was the way of Welleran."

When Rold was a little older he stole out of his mother's house quite in the middle of the night when all the world was still, and Merimna asleep dreaming of Welleran, Soorenard, Mommolek, Rollory, Akanax, and young Iraine. And he went down to the ramparts to hear the purple guard go by singing of Welleran. And the purple guard came by with lights, all singing in the stillness, and dark shapes out in the desert turned and fled. And Rold went back again to his mother's house with a great yearning towards the name of Welleran, such as men feel for very holy things.

And in time Rold grew to know the pathway all round the ramparts, and the six equestrian statues that were there guarding Merimna still. These statues were not like other statues, they were so cunningly wrought of many-coloured marbles that none might be quite sure until very close that they were not living men. There was a horse of dappled marble, the horse of Akanax. The horse of Rollory was of alabaster, pure white, his armour was wrought out of a stone that shone, and his horseman's cloak was made of a blue stone, very precious. He looked northward.

But the marble horse of Welleran was pure black, and there sat Welleran upon him looking solemnly westwards. His horse it was whose cold neck Rold most loved to stroke, and it was Welleran whom the watchers at sunset on the mountains the most clearly saw as they peered towards the city. And Rold loved the red nostrils of the great black horse and his rider's jasper cloak.

Now beyond the Cyresians the suspicion grew that Merimna's heroes were dead, and a plan was devised that a man should go by night and come close to the figures upon the ramparts and see whether they were Welleran, Soorenard, Mommolek, Rollory, Akanax, and young Iraine. And all were agreed upon the plan, and many names were mentioned of those who should go, and the plan matured for many years. It was during these years that watchers clustered often at sunset upon the mountains but came no nearer. Finally, a better plan was made, and it was decided that two men who had been by chance condemned to death should be given a pardon if they went down into the plain by night and discovered whether or not Merimna's heroes lived. At first the two prisoners dared not go, but after a while one of them, Seejar, said to his companion, Sajar-Ho: "See now, when the King's axeman smites a man upon the neck that man dies."

And the other said that this was so. Then said Seejar: "And even though Welleran smite a man with his sword no more befalleth him than death."

Then Sajar-Ho thought for a while. Presently he said: "Yet the eye of the King's axeman might err at the moment of his stroke or his arm fail him, and the eye of Welleran hath never erred nor his arm failed. It were better to bide here."

Then said Seejar: "Maybe that Welleran is dead and that some other holds his place upon the ramparts, or even a statue of stone."

But Sajar-Ho made answer: "How can Welleran be dead when he even escaped from two score horsemen with swords that were sworn to slay him, and all sworn upon our country's gods?"

And Seejar said: "This story his father told my grandfather concerning Welleran. On the day that the fight was lost on the plains of Kurlistan he saw a dying horse near to the river, and the horse looked piteously toward the water but could not reach it. And the father of my grandfather saw Welleran go down to the river's brink and bring water from it with his own hand and give it to the horse. Now we are in as sore a plight as was that horse, and as near to death; it may be that Welleran will pity us, while the King's axeman cannot because of the commands of the King."

Then said Sajar-Ho: "Thou wast ever a cunning arguer. Thou broughtest us into this trouble with thy cunning and thy devices, we will see if thou canst bring us out of it. We will go."

So news was brought to the King that the two prisoners would go down to Merimna.

That evening the watchers led them to the mountain's edge, and Seejar and Sajar-Ho went down towards the plain by the way of a deep ravine, and the watchers watched them go. Presently their figures were wholly hid in the dusk. Then night came up, huge and holy, out of waste marshes to the eastwards and low lands and the sea; and the angels that watched over all men through the day closed their great eyes and slept, and the angels that watched over all men through the night awoke and ruffled their deep blue feathers and stood up and watched. But the plain became a thing of mystery filled with fears. So the two spies went down the deep ravine, and coming to the plain sped stealthily across it. Soon they came to the line of sentinels asleep upon the sand, and one stirred in his sleep calling on Rollory, and a great dread seized upon the spies and they whispered "Rollory lives," but they remembered the King's axeman and went on. And next they came to the great bronze statue of Fear, carved by some sculptor of the old glorious years in the attitude of flight towards the mountains, calling to her children as she fled. And the children of Fear were carved in the likeness of armies of all the trans-Cyresian tribes with their backs towards Merimna, flocking after Fear. And from where he sat on his horse behind the ramparts the sword of Welleran was stretched out over their heads as ever it was wont. And the two spies kneeled down in the sand and kissed the huge bronze foot of the statue of Fear, saying: "O Fear, Fear." And as they knelt they saw lights far off along the ramparts coming nearer and nearer, and heard men singing of Welleran. And the purple guard came nearer and went by with their lights, and passed on into the distance round the ramparts still singing of Welleran. And all the while the two spies clung to the foot of the statue, muttering: "O Fear, Fear." But when they could hear the name of Welleran no more they arose and came to the ramparts and climbed over them and came at once upon the figure of Welleran, and they bowed low to the ground, and Seejar said: "O Welleran, we came to see whether thou didst yet live." And for a long while they waited with their faces to the earth. At last Seejar looked up towards Welleran's terrible sword, and it was still stretched out pointing to the carved armies that followed after Fear. And Seejar bowed to the ground again and touched the horse's hoof, and it seemed cold to him. And he moved his hand higher and touched the leg of the horse, and it seemed quite cold. At last he touched Welleran's foot, and the armour on it seemed hard and stiff. Then as Welleran moved not and spake not, Seejar climbed up at last and touched his hand, the terrible hand of Welleran, and it was marble. Then Seejar laughed aloud, and he and Sajar-Ho sped down the empty pathway and found Rollory, and he was marble too. Then they climbed down over the ramparts and went back across the plain, walking contemptuously past the figure of Fear, and heard the guard returning round the ramparts for the third time, singing of Welleran; and Seejar said: "Ay, you may sing of Welleran, but Welleran is dead and a doom is on your city."

And they passed on and found the sentinel still restless in the night and calling on Rollory. And Sajar-Ho muttered: "Ay, you may call on Rollory, but Rollory is dead and naught can save your city."

And the two spies went back alive to their mountains again, and as they reached them the first ray of the sun came up red over the desert behind Merimna and lit Merimna's spires. It was the hour when the purple guard were wont to go back into the city with their tapers pale and their robes a brighter colour, when the cold sentinels came shuffling in from dreaming in the desert; it was the hour when the desert robbers hid themselves away, going back to their mountain caves; it was the hour when gauze-winged insects are born that only live for a day; it was the hour when men die that are condemned to death; and in this hour a great peril, new and terrible, arose for Merimna and Merimna knew it not.

Then Seejar turning said: "See how red the dawn is and how red the spires of Merimna. They are angry with Merimna in Paradise and they bode its doom."

So the two spies went back and brought the news to their King, and for a few days the Kings of those countries were gathering their armies together; and one evening the armies of four Kings were massed together at the top of the deep ravine, all crouching below the summit waiting for the sun to set. All wore resolute and fearless faces, yet inwardly every man was praying to his gods, unto each one in turn.

Then the sun set, and it was the hour when the bats and the dark creatures are abroad and the lions come down from their lairs, and the desert robbers go into the plains again, and fevers rise up winged and hot out of chill marshes, and it was the hour when safety leaves the thrones of Kings, the hour when dynasties change. But in the desert the purple guard came swinging out of Merimna with their lights to sing of Welleran, and the sentinels lay down to sleep.

Now into Paradise no sorrow may ever come, but may only beat like rain against its crystal walls, yet the souls of Merimna's heroes were half aware of some sorrow far away as some sleeper feels that some one is chilled and cold yet knows not in his sleep that it is he. And they fretted a little in their starry home. Then unseen there drifted earthward across the setting sun the souls of Welleran, Soorenard, Mommolek, Rollory, Akanax, and young Iraine. Already when they reached Merimna's ramparts it was just dark, already the armies of the four Kings had begun to move, jingling, down the deep ravine. But when the six warriors saw their city again, so little changed after so many years, they looked towards her with a longing that was nearer to tears than any that their souls had known before, crying to her:

"O Merimna, our city: Merimna, our walled city.

"How beautiful thou art with all thy spires, Merimna. For thee we left the earth, its kingdoms and little flowers, for thee we have come away for awhile from Paradise.

"It is very difficult to draw away from the face of God—it is like a warm fire, it is like dear sleep, it is like a great anthem, yet there is a stillness all about it, a stillness full of lights.

"We have left Paradise for awhile for thee, Merimna.

"Many women have we loved, Merimna, but only one city.

"Behold now all the people dream, all our loved people. How beautiful are dreams! In dreams the dead may live, even the long dead and the very silent. Thy lights are all sunk low, they have all gone out, no sound is in thy streets. Hush! Thou art like a maiden that shutteth up her eyes and is asleep, that draweth her breath softly and is quite still, being at ease and untroubled.

"Behold now the battlements, the old battlements. Do men defend them still as we defended them? They are worn a little, the battlements," and drifting nearer they peered anxiously. "It is not by the hand of man that they are worn, our battlements. Only the years have done it and indomitable Time. Thy battlements are like the girdle of a maiden, a girdle that is round about her. See now the dew upon them, they are like a jewelled girdle.

"Thou art in great danger, Merimna, because thou art so beautiful. Must thou perish to-night because we no more defend thee, because we cry out and none hear us, as the bruised lilies cry out and none have known their voices?"

Thus spake those strong-voiced, battle-ordering captains, calling to their dear city, and their voices came no louder than the whispers of little bats that drift across the twilight in the evening. Then the purple guard came near, going round the ramparts for the first time in the night, and the old warriors called to them, "Merimna is in danger! Already her enemies gather in the darkness." But their voices were never heard because they were only wandering ghosts. And the guard went by and passed unheeding away, still singing of Welleran.

Then said Welleran to his comrades: "Our hands can hold swords no more, our voices cannot be heard, we are stalwart men no longer. We are but dreams, let us go among dreams. Go all of you, and thou too, young Iraine, and trouble the dreams of all the men that sleep, and urge them to take the old swords of their grandsires that hang upon the walls, and to gather at the mouth of the ravine; and I will find a leader and make him take my sword."

Then they passed up over the ramparts and into their dear city. And the wind blew about, this way and that, as he went, the soul of Welleran who had upon his day withstood the charges of tempestuous armies. And the souls of his comrades, and with them young Iraine, passed up into the city and troubled the dreams of every man who slept, and to every man the souls said in their dreams: "It is hot and still in the city. Go out now into the desert, into the cool under the mountains, but take with thee the old sword that hangs upon the wall for fear of the desert robbers."

And the god of that city sent up a fever over it, and the fever brooded over it and the streets were hot; and all that slept awoke from dreaming that it would be cool and pleasant where the breezes came down the ravine out of the mountains; and they took the old swords that their grandsires had, according to their dreams, for fear of the desert robbers. And in and out of dreams passed the souls of Welleran's comrades, and with them young Iraine, in great haste as the night wore on; and one by one they troubled the dreams of all Merimna's men and caused them to arise and go out armed, all save the purple guard who, heedless of danger, sang of Welleran still, for waking men cannot hear the souls of the dead.

But Welleran drifted over the roofs of the city till he came to the form of Rold lying fast asleep. Now Rold was grown strong and was eighteen years of age, and he was fair of hair and tall like Welleran, and the soul of Welleran hovered over him and went into his dreams as a butterfly flits through trellis-work into a garden of flowers, and the soul of Welleran said to Rold in his dreams: "Thou wouldst go and see again the sword of Welleran, the great curved sword of Welleran. Thou wouldst go and look at it in the night with the moonlight shining upon it."

And the longing of Rold in his dreams to see the sword caused him to walk still sleeping from his mother's house to the hall wherein were the trophies of the heroes. And the soul of Welleran urging the dreams of Rold caused him to pause before the great red cloak, and there the soul said among the dreams: "Thou art cold in the night; fling now a cloak around thee."

And Rold drew round about him the huge red cloak of Welleran. Then Rold's dreams took him to the sword, and the soul said to the dreams: "Thou hast a longing to hold the sword of Welleran: take up the sword in thy hand."

But Rold said: "What should a man do with the sword of Welleran?"

And the soul of the old captain said to the dreamer: "It is a good sword to hold: take up the sword of Welleran."

And Rold, still sleeping and speaking aloud, said: "It is not lawful; none may touch the sword."

And Rold turned to go. Then a great and terrible cry arose in the soul of Welleran, all the more bitter for that he could not utter it, and it went round and round his soul finding no utterance, like a cry evoked long since by some murderous deed in some old haunted chamber that whispers through the ages heard by none.

And the soul of Welleran cried out to the dreams of Rold: "Thy knees are tied! Thou are fallen in a marsh! Thou canst not move."

And the dreams of Rold said to him: "Thy knees are tied, thou are fallen in a marsh," and Rold stood still before the sword. Then the soul of the warrior wailed among Rold's dreams, as Rold stood before the sword.

"Welleran is crying for his sword, his wonderful curved sword. Poor Welleran, that once fought for Merimna, is crying for his sword in the night. Thou wouldst not keep Welleran without his beautiful sword when he is dead and cannot come for it, poor Welleran who fought for Merimna."

And Rold broke the glass casket with his hand and took the sword, the great curved sword of Welleran; and the soul of the warrior said among Rold's dreams: "Welleran is waiting in the deep ravine that runs into the mountains, crying for his sword."

And Rold went down through the city and climbed over the ramparts, and walked with his eyes wide open but still sleeping over the desert to the mountains.

Already a great multitude of Merimna's citizens were gathered in the desert before the deep ravine with old swords in their hands, and Rold passed through them as he slept holding the sword of Welleran, and the people cried in amaze to one another as he passed: "Rold hath the sword of Welleran!"

And Rold came to the mouth of the ravine, and there the voices of the people woke him. And Rold knew nothing that he had done in his sleep, and looked in amazement at the sword in his hand and said: "What art thou, thou beautiful thing? Lights shimmer in thee, thou art restless. It is the sword of Welleran, the curved sword of Welleran!"

And Rold kissed the hilt of it, and it was salt upon his lips with the battle-sweat of Welleran. And Rold said: "What should a man do with the sword of Welleran?"

And all the people wondered at Rold as he sat there with the sword in his hand muttering, "What should a man do with the sword of Welleran?"

Presently there came to the ears of Rold the noise of a jingling up in the ravine, and all the people, the people that knew naught of war, heard the jingling coming nearer in the night; for the four armies were moving on Merimna and not yet expecting an enemy. And Rold gripped upon the hilt of the great curved sword, and the sword seemed to lift a little. And a new thought came into the hearts of Merimna's people as they gripped their grandsires' swords. Nearer and nearer came the heedless armies of the four Kings, and old ancestral memories began to arise in the minds of Merimna's people in the desert with their swords in their hands sitting behind Rold. And all the sentinels were awake holding their spears, for Rollory had put their dreams to flight, Rollory that once could put to flight armies and now was but a dream struggling with other dreams.

And now the armies had come very near. Suddenly Rold leaped up, crying: "Welleran! And the sword of Welleran!" And the savage, lusting sword that had thirsted for a hundred years went up with the hand of Rold and swept through a tribesman's ribs. And with the warm blood all about it there came a joy into the curved soul of that mighty sword, like to the joy of a swimmer coming up dripping out of warm seas after living for long in a dry land. When they saw the red cloak and that terrible sword a cry ran through the tribal armies, "Welleran lives!" And there arose the sounds of the exulting of victorious men, and the panting of those that fled, and the sword singing softly to itself as it whirled dripping through the air. And the last that I saw of the battle as it poured into the depth and darkness of the ravine was the sword of Welleran sweeping up and falling, gleaming blue in the moonlight whenever it arose and afterwards gleaming red, and so disappearing into the darkness.

But in the dawn Merimna's men came back, and the sun arising to give new life to the world, shone instead upon the hideous things that the sword of Welleran had done. And Rold said: "O sword, sword! How horrible thou art! Thou art a terrible thing to have come among men. How many eyes shall look upon gardens no more because of thee? How many fields must go empty that might have been fair with cottages, white cottages with children all about them? How many valleys must go desolate that might have nursed warm hamlets, because thou hast slain long since the men that might have built them? I hear the wind crying against thee, thou sword! It comes from the empty valleys. It comes over the bare fields. There are children's voices in it. They were never born. Death brings an end to crying for those that had life once, but these must cry for ever. O sword! sword! why did the gods send thee among men?" And the tears of Rold fell down upon the proud sword but could not wash it clean.

And now that the ardour of battle had passed away, the spirits of Merimna's people began to gloom a little, like their leader's, with their fatigue and with the cold of the morning; and they looked at the sword of Welleran in Rold's hand and said: "Not any more, not any more for ever will Welleran now return, for his sword is in the hand of another. Now we know indeed that he is dead. O Welleran, thou wast our sun and moon and all our stars. Now is the sun fallen down and the moon broken, and all the stars are scattered as the diamonds of a necklace that is snapped off one who is slain by violence."

Thus wept the people of Merimna in the hour of their great victory, for men have strange moods, while beside them their old inviolate city slumbered safe. But back from the ramparts and beyond the mountains and over the lands that they had conquered of old, beyond the world and back again to Paradise, went the souls of Welleran, Soorenard, Mommolek, Rollory, Akanax, and young Iraine.

Set in an alternate present in which the "degaussing of cold-iron" caused a burst of magical innovation parallel with our own industrial revolution, POUL ANDERSON'S *"Operation Afreet" is a fantasy story with science fiction sensibilities. Werewolves, genies, and basilisks all have their military applications. In this fantasy universe, magic works, but it is handled with the same pragmatism with which we handle technology. This is the structure of the universe of many fine fantasy stories that have been influenced by Robert A. Heinlein's famous* Magic, Inc, *including "Operation Afreet," James E. Gunn's "Sine of the Magus," and Larry Niven's* The Magic Goes Away. *Magic is just another technology, but one that allows us wonderful adventures. Poul Anderson, a leading SF writer for four decades now, began his career as a novelist in the 1950s with the fantasy classic,* The Broken Sword.

Operation Afreet
BY POUL ANDERSON

I

It was sheer bad luck, or maybe their Intelligence was better than we knew, but the last raid, breaking past our air defenses, had spattered the Weather Corps tent from here to hell. Supply problems being what they were, we couldn't get replacements for weeks, and meanwhile the enemy had control of the weather. Our only surviving Corpsman, Major Jackson, had to save what was left of his elementals to protect us against thunderbolts; so otherwise we took whatever they chose to throw at us. At the moment, it was rain.

There's nothing so discouraging as a steady week of cold rain. The ground turns liquid and runs up into your boots, which get so heavy you can barely lift them. Your uniform is a drenched rag around your shivering skin, the rations are soggy, the rifles have to have extra care, and always the rain drums down on your helmet till you hear it in dreams. You'll never forget that endless gray washing and beating; ten years later a rainstorm will make you feel depressed.

The one consolation, I thought, was that they couldn't very well attack us from the air while it went on. Doubtless they'd yank the cloud cover away when they were ready to strafe us, but our broomsticks could scramble as fast as their carpets could arrive. Meanwhile, we slogged ahead, a whole division of us with auxiliaries—the 45th, the Lightning Busters, pride of the United States Army, turned into a wet misery of men and dragons hunting through the Oregon hills for the invader.

I made a slow way through the camp. Water ran off tents and gurgled in slit trenches. Our sentries were, of course, wearing Tarnkappen, but I could see their footprints form in the mud and hear the boots squelch and the tired monotonous cursing.

I passed by the Air Force strip; they were bivouacked with us, to give support as needed. A couple of men stood on guard outside the knockdown hangar, not bothering with invisibility. Their blue uniforms were as mucked and bedraggled as my OD's, but they had shaved and their insignia—the winged broomstick and the anti-Evil Eye beads—were polished. They saluted me, and I returned the gesture idly. *Esprit de corps,* wild blue yonder, nuts.

Beyond was the armor. The boys had erected portable shelters for their beasts, so I only saw steam rising out of the cracks and caught the rank reptile smell. Dragons hate rain, and their drivers were having a hell of a time controlling them.

Nearby lay Petrological Warfare, with a pen full of hooded basilisks writhing and hissing and striking out with their crowned heads at the men feeding them. Personally, I doubted the practicality of that whole corps. You have to get a basilisk quite close to a man, and looking straight at him, for petrifaction; and the aluminum-foil suit and helmet you must wear to deflect the influence of your pets is an invitation to snipers. Then, too, when human carbon is turned to silicon, you have a radioactive isotope, and maybe get such a dose of radiation yourself that the medics have to give you St. John's Wort plucked from a graveyard in the dark of the moon.

So, in case you didn't know, cremation hasn't simply died out as a custom; it's become illegal under the National Defense Act. We have to have plenty of old-fashioned cemeteries. Thus does the age of science pare down our liberties.

I went on past the engineers, who were directing a gang of zombies carving another drainage ditch, and on to General Vanbrugh's big tent. When the guard saw my Tetragramaton insigne, for the Intelligence Corps, and the bars on my shoulders, he saluted and let me in. I came to a halt before the desk and brought my own hand up.

"Captain Matuchek reporting, sir," I said.

Vanbrugh looked at me from beneath shaggy gray brows. He was a large man with a face like weathered rock, 103 percent Regular Army, but we liked him as well as you can like a buck general. "At ease," he said. "Sit down. This'll take a while."

I found a folding chair and lowered myself into it. Two others were already seated whom I didn't know. One was a plump man with a round red face and a fluffy white beard, a major bearing the crystal-ball emblem of the Signal Corps. The other was a young woman. In spite of my weariness, I blinked and looked twice at her. She was worth it—a tall green-eyed redhead with straight high-cheeked features and a figure too good for the WAC clothes or any other. Captain's bars, Cavalry spider . . . or Sleipnir, if you want to be official about it.

"Major Harrigan," grumbled the general. "Captain Graylock. Captain Matuchek. Let's get down to business."

He spread a map out before us. I leaned over and looked at it. Positions were indicated, ours and the enemy's. They still held the Pacific seaboard from Alaska halfway down through Oregon, though that was considerable improvement from a year ago, when the Battle of the Mississippi had turned the tide.

"Now then," said Vanbrugh, "I'll tell you the overall situation. This is a dangerous mission, you don't have to volunteer, but I want you to know how important it is."

What I knew, just then, was that I'd been told to volunteer or else. That was the Army, at least in a major war like this, and in principle I couldn't object. I'd been a reasonably contented Hollywood actor when the Saracen Caliphate attacked us. I wanted to go back to more of the same, but that meant finishing the war.

"You can see we're driving them back," said the general, "and the occupied countries are primed and cocked to revolt as soon as they get a fighting chance. The British have been organizing the underground and arming them while readying for a cross-Channel jump. The Russians are set to advance from the north. But we have to give the enemy a decisive blow, break this whole front and roll 'em up. That'll be the signal. If we succeed, the war will be over this year. Otherwise it might drag on for another three."

I knew it. The whole Army knew it. Official word hadn't been passed yet, but somehow you feel when a big push is impending.

His stumpy finger traced along the map. "The 9th Armored Division is here, the 12th Broomborne here, the 14th Cavalry here, the Salamanders here where we know they've concentrated their firebreathers. The Marines are ready to establish a beachhead and retake Seattle, now that the Navy's bred enough Krakens. One good goose, and we'll have 'em running."

Major Harrigan snuffled into his beard and stared gloomily at a crystal ball. It was clouded and vague; the enemy had been jamming our crystals till they were no use whatsoever, though naturally we'd retaliated. Captain Graylock tapped impatiently on the desk with a perfectly manicured nail. She was so clean and crisp and efficient, I decided I didn't like her looks after all. Not while I had three days' beard bristling from my chin.

"But apparently something's gone wrong, sir," I ventured.

"Correct, damn it," said Vanbrugh. "In Trollburg."

I nodded. The Saracens held that town: a key position, sitting as it did on U.S. Highway 20 and guarding the approach to Salem and Portland.

"I take it we're supposed to seize Trollburg, sir," I murmured.

Vanbrugh scowled. "That's the job for the 45th," he grunted. "If we muff it, the enemy can sally out against the 9th, cut them off, and throw the whole operation akilter. But now Major Harrigan and Captain Graylock come from the 14th to tell me the Trollburg garrison has an afreet."

I whistled, and a chill crawled along my spine. The Caliphate had exploited the Powers recklessly—that was one reason why the rest of the Moslem world regarded them as heretics and hated them as much as we did—but I never thought they'd go as far as breaking Solomon's seal. An afreet getting out of hand could destroy more than anybody cared to estimate.

"I hope they haven't but one," I whispered.

"No, they don't," said the Graylock woman. Her voice was low and could have been pleasant if it weren't so brisk. "They've been dredging the Red Sea in hopes of finding another Solly bottle, but this seems to be the last one left."

"Bad enough," I said. The effort to keep my tone steady helped calm me down. "How'd you find out?"

"We're with the 14th," said Graylock unnecessarily. Her Cavalry badge had surprised me, however. Normally, the only recruits the

Army can dig up to ride unicorns are picklefaced schoolteachers and the like.

"I'm simply a liaison officer," said Major Harrigan in haste. "I go by broomstick myself." I grinned at that. No American male, unless he's in holy orders, likes to admit he's qualified to control a unicorn. He saw me and flushed angrily.

Graylock went on, as if dictating. She kept her tone flat, though little else. "We had the luck to capture a bimbashi in a commando attack. I questioned him."

"They're pretty close-mouthed, those noble sons of . . . um . . . the desert," I said. I'd bent the Geneva Convention myself, occasionally, but didn't relish the idea of breaking it completely—even if the enemy had no such scruples.

"Oh, we practiced no brutality," said Graylock. "We housed him and fed him very well. But the moment a bite of food was in his throat, I'd turn it into pork. He broke pretty fast, and spilled everything he knew."

I had to laugh aloud, and Vanbrugh himself chuckled; but she sat perfectly deadpan. Organic-organic transformation, which merely shuffles molecules around without changing atoms, has no radiation hazards but naturally requires a good knowledge of chemistry. That's the real reason the average dogface hates the technical corps: pure envy of a man who can turn K rations into steak and French fries. The quartermasters have enough trouble conjuring up the rations themselves, without branching into fancy dishes.

"Okay, you learned they have an afreet in Trollburg," said the general. "What about their strength otherwise?"

"A small division, sir. You can take the place handily, if that demon can be immobilized," said Harrigan.

"Yes. I know." Vanbrugh swiveled his eyes around to me. "Well, Captain, are you game? If you can carry the stunt off, it'll mean a Silver Star at least—pardon me, a Bronze."

"Uh—" I paused, fumbling after words. I was more interested in promotion and ultimate discharge, but that might follow too. Nevertheless . . . quite apart from my own neck, there was a practical objection. "Sir, I don't know a damn thing about the job. I nearly flunked Demonology 1 in college."

"That'll be my part," said Graylock.

"You!" I picked my jaw off the floor again, but couldn't find anything else to say.

"I was head witch of the Arcane Agency in New York before the war," she said coldly. Now I knew where she got that personality: the typical big-city career girl. I can't stand them. "I know as much about handling demons as anyone on this coast. Your task will be to escort me safely to the place and back."

"Yeah," I said weakly. "Yeah, that's all."

Vanbrugh cleared his throat. He didn't like sending a woman on such a mission, but time was too short for him to have any choice. "Captain Matuchek is one of the best werewolves in the business," he complimented me.

Ave, Caesar, morituri te salutant, I thought. No, that isn't what I mean, but never mind. I can figure out a better phrasing at my leisure after I'm dead.

I wasn't afraid, exactly. Besides the spell laid on me to prevent that, I had reason to believe my personal chances were no worse than those of any infantryman headed into a firefight. Nor would Vanbrugh sacrifice personnel on a mission he himself considered hopeless. But I did feel less optimistic about the prospects than he.

"I think two adepts can get past their guards," the general proceeded. "From then on, you'll have to improvise. If you can put that monster out of action, we attack at noon tomorrow." Grimly: "If I haven't got word to that effect by dawn, we'll have to regroup, start retreating, and save what we can. Okay, here's a geodetic survey map of the town and approaches—"

He didn't waste time asking me if I had really volunteered.

II

I guided Captain Graylock back to the tent I shared with two brother officers. Darkness was creeping across the long chill slant of rain. We plodded through the muck in silence until we were under canvas. My tentmates were out on picket duty, so we had the place to ourselves. I lit the saint-elmo and sat down on the sodden plank floor.

"Have a chair," I said, pointing to our one camp stool. It was an animated job we'd bought in San Francisco: not especially bright, but it would carry our duffel and come when called. It shifted uneasily at the unfamiliar weight, then went back to sleep.

Graylock took out a pack of Wings and raised her brows. I nodded my thanks, and the cigaret flapped over to my mouth. Personally, I smoke Luckies in the field: self-striking tobacco is convenient when your matches may be wet. When I was a civilian and could afford it, my brand was Philip Morris, because the little red-coated smoke sprite can also mix you a drink.

We puffed for a bit in silence, listening to the rain. "Well," I said at last, "I suppose you have transportation."

"My personal broomstick," she said. "I don't like this GI Willys. Give me a Cadillac anytime. I've souped it up, too."

"And you have your grimoires and powders and whatnot?"

"Just some chalk. No material agency is much use against a powerful demon."

"Yeah? What about the sealing wax on the Solly bottle?"

"It isn't the wax that holds an afreet in, but the seal. The spells are symbolic; in fact, it's believed their effect is purely psychosomatic." She hollowed the flat planes of her cheeks, sucking in smoke, and I saw what a good bony structure she had. "We may have a chance to test that theory tonight."

"Well, then, you'll want a light pistol loaded with silver slugs; they have weres of their own, you know. I'll take a grease gun and a forty-five and a few grenades."

"How about a squirter?"

I frowned. The notion of using holy water as a weapon has always struck me as blasphemous, though the chaplain said it was permissible against Low World critters. "No good to us," I said. "The Moslems don't have that ritual, so of course they don't use any beings that can be controlled by it. Let's see, I'll want my Polaroid flash too. And that's about it."

Ike Abrams stuck his big nose in the tent flap. "Would you and the lady captain like some eats, sir?" he asked.

"Why, sure," I said. Inwardly, I thought: Hate to spend my last night on Midgard standing in a chow line. When he had gone, I explained to the girl: "Ike's only a private, but we were friends in Hollywood—he was a prop man when I played in *Call of the Wild* and *Silver Chief*—and he's kind of appointed himself my orderly. He'll bring us some food here."

"You know," she remarked, "that's one good thing about the technological age. Did you know there used to be widespread anti-Semitism in this country? Not just among a few Johannine cranks; no, among ordinary respectable citizens."

"Fact?"

"Fact. Especially a false belief that Jews were cowards and never found in the front lines. Now, when religion forbids most of them to originate spells, and the Orthodox don't use goetics at all, the proportion of them who serve as dogfaces and Rangers is simply too high to ignore."

I myself had gotten tired of comic-strip supermen and pulp-magazine heroes having such monotonously Yiddish names—don't Anglo-Saxons belong to our culture too?—but she'd made a good point. And it showed she was a trifle more than a money machine. A bare trifle.

"What'd you do in civilian life?" I asked, chiefly to drown out the incessant noise of the rain.

"I told you," she snapped, irritable again. "I was with the Arcane Agency. Advertising, public relations, and so on."

"Oh, well," I said. "Hollywood is at least as phony, so I shouldn't sneer."

I couldn't help it, however. Those Madison Avenue characters gave me a pain in the rear end. Using the good Art to puff some self-important nobody, or to sell a product whose main virtue is its total similarity to other brands of the same. The SPCA has cracked down on training nixies to make fountains spell out words, or cramming young salamanders into glass tubes to light up Broadway, but I can still think of better uses for slick paper than trumpeting Ma Chère perfume. Which is actually a love potion anyway, though you know what postal regulations are.

"You don't understand," she said. "It's part of our economy—part of our whole society. Do you think the average backyard warlock is capable of repairing, oh, say a lawn sprinkler? Hell, no! He'd probably let loose the water elementals and flood half a township if it weren't for the inhibitory spells. And we, Arcane, undertook the campaign to convince the Hydros they had to respect our symbols. I told you it's psychosomatic when you're dealing with these really potent beings. For that job, I had to go down in an aqualung!"

I stared at her with more respect. Ever since mankind found how to degauss the ruinous effects of cold iron, and the goetic age began, the world had needed some pretty bold people. Apparently she was one of them.

Abrams brought in two plates of rations. He looked wistful, and I would have invited him to join us except that our mission was secret and we had to thresh out the details.

Captain Graylock 'chanted the coffee into martinis—not quite dry enough—and the dog food into steaks—a turn too well done; but you can't expect the finer sensibilities in a woman, and it was the best chow I'd had in a month. She relaxed a bit over the brandy, and I learned that her repellent crispness was simply armor against the slick types she dealt with, and we found out that our first names were Steven and Virginia. But then dusk had become dark outside, and we must be going.

III

You may think it was sheer lunacy, sending two people, one of them a woman, into an enemy division on a task like this. It would seem to call for a Ranger brigade, at least. But present-day science had transformed war as well as industry, medicine, and ordinary life. Our mission was desperate in any event, and we wouldn't have gained enough by numbers to make reinforcements worthwhile.

You see, while practically anyone can learn a few simple cantrips, to operate a presensitized broomstick or vacuum cleaner or turret lathe or whatever, only a small minority of the human race can qualify as adepts. Besides years of study and practice, that takes inborn talent. It's kind of like therianthropy: if you're one of the rare persons with chromosomes for that, you can change into your characteristic animal almost by instinct; otherwise you need a transformation performed on you by powerful outside forces.

My scientific friends tell me that the Art involves regarding the universe as a set of Cantorian infinities. Within any given class, the part is equal to the whole and so on. One good witch could do all the runing we were likely to need; a larger party would simply be more liable to detection, and would risk valuable personnel. So Vanbrugh had very rightly sent us two alone.

The trouble with sound military principles is that sometimes you personally get caught in them.

Virginia and I turned our backs on each other while we changed clothes. She got into an outfit of slacks and combat jacket, I into the elastic knit garment which would fit me as well in wolf-shape. We put on our helmets, hung our equipment around us, and turned about. Even in the baggy green battle garb she looked good.

"Well," I said tonelessly, "shall we go?"

I wasn't afraid, of course. Every recruit is immunized against fear when they put the geas on him. But I didn't like the prospect.

"The sooner the better, I suppose," she answered. Stepping to the entrance, she whistled.

Her stick swooped down and landed just outside. It had been stripped of the fancy chrome, but was still a neat job. The foam-rubber seats had good shock absorbers and well-designed back rests, unlike Army transport. Her familiar was a gigantic tomcat, black as a furry midnight, with two malevolent yellow eyes. He arched his back and spat indignantly. The weatherproofing spell kept rain off him, but he didn't like this damp air.

Virginia chucked him under the chin. "Oh, so, Svartalf," she murmured. "Good cat, rare sprite, prince of darkness, if we outlive this night you shall sleep on cloudy cushions and lap cream from a golden bowl." He cocked his ears and raced his motor.

I climbed into the rear seat, snugged my feet in the stirrups, and leaned back. The girl mounted in front of me and crooned to the stick. It swished upward, the ground fell away and the camp was hidden in gloom. Both of us had been given witch-sight—infrared vision, actually —so we didn't need lights.

When we got above the clouds, we saw a giant vault of stars overhead and a swirling dim whiteness below. I also glimpsed a couple of P-56's circling on patrol, fast jobs with six brooms each to lift their weight of armor and machine guns. We left them behind and streaked northward. I rested the BAR on my lap and sat listening to the air whine past. Underneath us, in the rough-edged murk of the hills, I spied occasional flashes, an artillery duel. So far no one had been able to cast a spell fast enough to turn or implode a shell. I'd heard rumors that General Electric was developing a gadget which could recite the formula in microseconds, but meanwhile the big guns went on talking.

Trollburg was a mere few miles from our position. I saw it as a vague sprawling mass, blacked out against our cannon and bombers. It would have been nice to have an atomic weapon just then, but as long as the Tibetans keep those antinuclear warfare prayer wheels turning, such thoughts must remain merely science-fictional. I felt my belly muscles tighten. The cat bottled out his tail and swore. Virginia sent the broomstick slanting down.

We landed in a clump of trees and she turned to me. "Their outposts must be somewhere near," she whispered. "I didn't dare try landing on a rooftop; we could have been seen too easily. We'll have to go in from here."

I nodded. "Okay. Gimme a minute."

I turned the flash on myself. How hard to believe that transforming had depended on a bright full moon till only ten years ago! Then Wiener showed that the process was simply one of polarized light of the right wavelengths, triggering the pineal gland, and the Polaroid Corporation made another million dollars or so from its WereWish Lens. It's not easy to keep up with this fearful and wonderful age we live in, but I wouldn't trade.

The usual rippling, twisting sensations, the brief drunken dizziness and half-ecstatic pain, went through me. Atoms reshuffled into whole new molecules, nerves grew some endings and lost others, bone was briefly fluid and muscles like stretched rubber. Then I stabilized, shook myself, stuck my tail out the flap of the skin-tight pants, and nuzzled Virginia's hand.

She stroked my neck, behind the helmet. "Good boy," she whispered. "Go get 'em."

I turned and faded into the brush.

A lot of writers have tried to describe how it feels to be were, and every one of them has failed, because human language doesn't have the words. My vision was no longer acute, the stars were blurred above me and the world took on a colorless flatness. But I heard with a clarity that made the night almost a roar, way into the supersonic; and a universe of smells roiled in my nostrils, wet grass and teeming dirt, the hot sweet little odor of a scampering field mouse, the clean tang of oil and guns, a faint harshness of smoke— Poor stupefied humanity, half-dead to such earthy glories!

The psychological part is the hardest to convey. I was a wolf, with a wolf's nerves and glands and instincts, a wolf's sharp but limited intelligence. I had a man's memories and a man's purposes, but they were unreal, dreamlike. I must make an effort of trained will to hold to them and not go hallooing off after the nearest jackrabbit. No wonder weres had a bad name in the old days, before they themselves understood the mental changes involved and got the right habits drilled into them from babyhood.

I weigh a hundred and eighty pounds, and the conservation of mass holds good like any other law of nature, so I was a pretty big wolf. But it was easy to flow through the bushes and meadows and gullies, another drifting shadow. I was almost inside the town when I caught a near smell of man.

I flattened, the gray fur bristling along my spine, and waited. The sentry came by. He was a tall bearded fellow with gold earrings that glimmered wanly under the stars. The turban wrapped around his helmet bulked monstrous against the Milky Way.

I let him go and followed his path until I saw the next one. They were placed around Trollburg, each pacing a hundred-yard arc and meeting his opposite number at either end of it. No simple task to—

Something murmured in my ears. I crouched. One of their aircraft ghosted overhead. I saw two men and a couple of machine guns squatting on top of the carpet. It circled low and lazily, above the ring of sentries. Trollburg was well guarded.

Somehow, Virginia and I had to get through that picket. I wished the transformation had left me with full human reasoning powers. My wolf-impulse was simply to jump on the nearest man, but that would bring the whole garrison down on my hairy ears.

Wait—maybe that was what was needed!

I loped back to the thicket. The Svartalf cat scratched at me and zoomed up a tree. Virginia Graylock started, her pistol sprang into her hand, then she relaxed and laughed a bit nervously. I could work the flash hung about my neck, even as I was, but it went more quickly with her fingers.

"Well?" she asked when I was human again. "What'd you find out?"

I described the situation, and saw her frown and bite her lip. It was really too shapely a lip for such purposes. "Not so good," she reflected. "I was afraid of something like this."

"Look," I said, "can you locate that afreet in a hurry?"

"Oh, yes. I've studied at Congo U. and did quite well at witch-smelling. What of it?"

"If I attack one of those guards, and make a racket doing it, their main attention will be turned that way. You should have an even chance to fly across the line unobserved, and once you're in the town your Tarnkappe—"

She shook her red head. "I didn't bring one. Their detection systems are as good as ours. Invisibility is actually obsolete."

"Mmm—yeah, I suppose you're right. Well, anyhow, you can take advantage of the darkness to get to the afreet house. From there on, you'll have to play by ear."

"I suspected we'd have to do something like this," she replied. With a softness that astonished me: "But Steve, that's a long chance for you to take."

"Not unless they hit me with silver, and most of their cartridges are plain lead. They use a tracer principle like us; every tenth round is argent. I've got a ninety percent probability of getting home free."

"You're a liar," she said. "But a brave liar."

I wasn't brave at all. It's inspiring to think of Valley Forge, or the Alamo, or San Juan Hill, or Casablanca where our outnumbered Army stopped three Panther divisions of von Ogerhaus' Afrika Korps—but only when you're safe and comfortable yourself. Down underneath the antipanic geas, a cold knot was in my guts. Still, I couldn't see any other way to do the job, and failure to attempt it would mean court-martial.

"I'll run their legs off once they start chasing me," I told her. "When I've shaken 'em, I'll try to circle back and join you."

"Okay." Suddenly she rose on tiptoe and kissed me. The impact was explosive.

I stood for a moment, looking at her. "What are you doing Saturday night?" I asked, a mite shakily.

She laughed. "Don't get ideas, Steve. I'm in the Cavalry."

"Yeah, but the war won't last forever." I grinned at her, a reckless fighting grin that made her eyes linger. Acting experience is often useful.

We settled the details as well as we could. She herself had no soft touch: the afreet would be well guarded, and was plenty dangerous in itself. The chances of us both seeing daylight were nothing to feel complacent about.

I turned back to wolf-shape and licked her hand. She rumpled my fur. I slipped off into the darkness.

I had chosen a sentry well off the highway, across which there would surely be barriers. A man could be seen to either side of my victim, tramping slowly back and forth. I glided behind a stump near the middle of his beat and waited for him.

When he came, I sprang. I caught a dark brief vision of eyes and teeth in the bearded face, I heard him yelp and smelled the upward spurt of his fear, then we shocked together. He went down on his back, threshing, and I snapped for the throat. My jaws closed on his arm, and blood was hot and salty on my tongue.

He screamed again. I sensed the call going down the line. The two nearest Saracens ran to help. I tore out the gullet of the first man and bunched myself for a leap at the next.

He fired. The bullet went through me in a jag of pain and the impact sent me staggering. But he didn't know how to deal with a were. He should have dropped on one knee and fired steadily till he got to the silver bullet; if necessary, he should have fended me off, even pinned me with his bayonet, while he shot. This one kept running toward me, calling on the Allah of his heretical sect.

My tissues knitted as I plunged to meet him. I got past the bayonet and gun muzzle, hitting him hard enough to knock the weapon loose but not to bowl him over. He braced his legs, grabbed my neck, and hung on.

I swung my left hind leg back of his ankle and shoved. He fell with me on top, the position an infighting werewolf always tries for. My head swiveled; I gashed open his arm and broke his grip.

Before I could settle the business, three others had piled on me. Their trench scimitars went up and down, in between my ribs and out again. Lousy training they'd had. I snapped my way free of the heap—half a dozen by then—and broke loose.

Through sweat and blood I caught the faintest whiff of Chanel No. 5, and something in me laughed. Virginia had sped past the confusion, riding her stick a foot above ground, and was inside Trollburg. My next task was to lead a chase and not stop a silver slug while doing so.

I howled, to taunt the men spilling from outlying houses, and let them have a good look at me before making off across the fields. My pace was easy, not to lose them at once; I relied on zigzags to keep me unpunctured. They followed, stumbling and shouting.

As far as they knew, this had been a mere commando raid. Their pickets would have re-formed and the whole garrison been alerted. But surely none except a few chosen officers knew about the afreet, and none of those knew we'd acquired the information. So they had no way of telling what we really planned. Maybe we *would* pull this operation off—

Something swooped overhead, one of their damned carpets. It rushed down on me like a hawk, guns spitting. I made for the nearest patch of woods.

Into the trees! Given half a break, I could—

They didn't give it. I heard a bounding behind me, caught the acrid smell and whimpered. A weretiger could go as fast as I.

For a moment I remembered an old guide I'd had in Alaska, and wished to blazes he were here. He was a were-Kodiak bear. Then I whirled and met the tiger before he could pounce.

He was a big one, five hundred pounds at least. His eyes smoldered above the great fangs, and he lifted a paw that could crack my spine like a dry twig. I rushed in, snapping, and danced back before he could strike.

Part of me heard the enemy, blundering around in the underbrush trying to find us. The tiger leaped. I evaded him and bolted for the nearest thicket. Maybe I could go where he couldn't. He ramped through the woods behind me, roaring.

I saw a narrow space between a pair of giant oaks, too small for him, and hurried that way. But it was too small for me also. In the half second that I was stuck, he caught up. The lights exploded and went out.

IV

I was nowhere and nowhen. My very body had departed from me, or I from it. How could I think of infinite eternal dark and cold and emptiness when I had no senses? How could I despair when I was nothing but a point in spacetime? . . . No, not even that, for there was nothing else, nothing to find or love or hate or fear or be related to in any way whatsoever. The dead were less alone than I, for I was all which existed.

This was my despair.

But on the instant, or after a quadrillion years, or both or neither, I came to know otherwise. I was under the regard of the Solipsist. Helpless in unconsciousness, I could but share that egotism so ultimate that it would yield no room even to hope. I swirled in the tides and storms of thoughts too remote, too alien, too vast for me to take in save as I might brokenly hear the polar ocean while it drowned me.

—danger, this one—he and those two—somehow they can be a terrible danger—not now (scornfully) *when they merely help complete the ruin of a plan already bungled into wreck—no, later, when the next plan is ripening, the great one of which this war was naught but an early leaf—something about them warns thinly of danger—could I only scan more clearly into time!—they must be diverted, destroyed, somehow dealt with before their potential has grown—but I cannot originate anything yet—maybe they will be slain by the normal chances of war—if not, I must remember them and try later—now I have too much else to do, saving those seeds I planted in the world—the birds of the enemy fly thick across my fields, hungry crows and eagles to guard them—*(with ever wilder hate) *my snares shall take you yet, birds—and the One Who loosed you!*

So huge was the force of that final malevolence that I was cast free.

V

I opened my eyes. For a while I was aware entirely of the horror. Physical misery rescued me, driving those memories back to where half-forgotten nightmares dwell. The thought flitted by me that shock must have made me briefly delirious.

A natural therianthrope in his beast shape isn't quite as invulnerable as most people believe. Aside from things like silver—biochemical poisons to a metabolism in that semifluid state—damage which stops a vital organ will stop life; amputations are permanent unless a surgeon is near to sew the part back on before its cells die; and so on and so on, no pun intended. We are a hardy sort, however. I'd taken a blow that probably broke my neck. The spinal cord not being totally severed, the damage had healed at standard therio speed.

The trouble was, they'd arrived and used my flash to make me human before the incidental hurts had quite gone away. My head drummed and I retched.

"Get up." Someone stuck a boot in my ribs.

I lurched erect. They'd removed my gear, including the flash. A score of them trained their guns on me. Tiger Boy stood close. In man-shape he was almost seven feet tall and monstrously fat. Squinting through the headache, I saw he wore the insignia of an emir—which was a military rank these days rather than a title, but pretty important nevertheless.

"Come," he said. He led the way, and I was hustled along behind.

I saw their carpets in the sky and heard the howling of their own weres looking for spoor of other Americans. I was still too groggy to care very much.

We entered the town, its pavement sounding hollow under the boots, and went toward the center. Trollburg wasn't big, maybe five thousand population once. Most of the streets were empty. I saw a few Saracen troops, antiaircraft guns poking into the sky, a dragon lumbering past with flames flickering around its jaws and cannon projecting from the armored howdah. No trace of the civilians, but I knew what had happened to them. The attractive young women were in the officers' harems, the rest dead or locked away pending shipment to the slave markets.

By the time we got to the hotel where the enemy headquartered, my aches had subsided and my brain was clear. That was a mixed blessing under the circumstances. I was taken upstairs to a suite and told to stand before a table. The emir sat down behind it, half a dozen guards lined the walls, and a young pasha of Intelligence seated himself nearby.

The emir's big face turned to that one, and he spoke a few words—I suppose to the effect of "I'll handle this, you take notes." He looked back at me. His eyes were the pale tigergreen.

"Now then," he said in good English, "we shall have some questions. Identify yourself, please."

I told him mechanically that I was called Sherrinford Mycroft, Captain, AUS, and gave him my serial number.

"That is not your real name, is it?" he asked.

"Of course not!" I replied. "I know the Geneva Convention, and you're not going to cast name-spells on me. Sherrinford Mycroft is my official johnsmith."

"The Caliphate has not subscribed to the Geneva Convention," said the emir quietly, "and stringent measures are sometimes necessary in a jehad. What was the purpose of this raid?"

"I am not required to answer that," I said. Silence would have served the same end, delay to gain time for Virginia, but not as well.

"You may be persuaded to do so," he said.

If this had been a movie, I'd have told him I was picking daisies, and kept on wisecracking while they brought out the thumbscrews. In practice it would have fallen a little flat.

"All right," I said. "I was scouting."

"A single one of you?"

"A few others. I hope they got away." That might keep his boys busy hunting for a while.

"You lie," he said dispassionately.

"I can't help it if you don't believe me." I shrugged.

His eyes narrowed. "I shall soon know if you speak truth," he said. "If not, may Eblis have mercy on you."

I couldn't help it, I jerked where I stood and sweat pearled out on my skin. The emir laughed. He had an unpleasant laugh, a sort of whining growl deep in his fat throat, like a tiger playing with its kill.

"Think over your decision," he advised, and turned to some papers on the table.

It grew most quiet in that room. The guards stood as if cast in bronze. The young shavetail dozed beneath his turban. Behind the emir's back, a window looked out on a blankness of night. The sole sounds were the loud ticking of a clock and the rustle of papers. They seemed to deepen the silence.

I was tired, my head ached, my mouth tasted foul and thirsty. The sheer physical weariness of having to stand was meant to help wear me down. It occurred to me that the emir must be getting scared of us, to take this much trouble with a lone prisoner. That was kudos for the American cause, but small consolation to me.

My eyes flickered, studying the tableau. There wasn't much to see, standard hotel furnishings. The emir had cluttered his desk with a number of objects: a crystal ball useless because of our own jamming, a fine cut-glass bowl looted from somebody's house, a set of nice crystal wineglasses, a cigar humidor of quartz glass, a decanter full of what looked like good Scotch. I guess he just liked crystal.

He helped himself to a cigar, waving his hand to make the humidor open and a Havana fly into his mouth and light itself. As the minutes crawled by, an ashtray soared up from time to time to receive from him. I guessed that everything he had was 'chanted so it would rise and move easily. A man that fat, paying the price of being a really big werebeast, needed such conveniences.

It was very quiet. The light glared down on us. It was somehow hideously wrong to see a good ordinary GE saint-elmo shining on those turbaned heads.

I began to get the forlorn glimmerings of an idea. How to put it into effect I didn't yet know, but just to pass the time I began composing some spells.

Maybe half an hour had passed, though it seemed more like half a century, when the door opened and a fennec, the small fox of the African desert, trotted in. The emir looked up as it went into a closet, to find darkness to use its flash. The fellow who came out was, naturally, a dwarf barely one foot high. He prostrated himself and spoke rapidly in a high thready voice.

"So." The emir's chins turned slowly around to me. "The report is that no trace was found of other tracks than yours. You have lied."

"Didn't I tell you?" I asked. My throat felt stiff and strange. "We used owls and bats. I was the lone wolf."

"Be still," he said tonelessly. "I know as well as you that the only werebats are vampires, and that vampires are—what you say—4-F in all armies."

That was true. Every so often, some armchair general asks why we don't raise a force of Draculas. The answer is routine: they're too light and flimsy; they can't endure sunshine; if they don't get a steady blood ration they're apt to turn on their comrades; and you can't possibly use them around Italian troops. I swore at myself, but my mind had been too numb to think straight.

"I believe you are concealing something," went on the emir. He gestured at his glasses and decanter, which supplied him with a shot of Scotch, and sipped judiciously. The Caliphate sect was also heretical with respect to strong drink; they maintained that while the Prophet forbade wine, he said nothing about beer, gin, whisky, brandy, rum, or akvavit.

"We shall have to use stronger measures," the emir said at last. "I was hoping to avoid them." He nodded at his guards.

Two held my arms. The pasha worked me over. He was good at that. The werefennec watched avidly, the emir puffed his cigar and went on with his paperwork. After a long few minutes, he gave an order. They let me go, and even set forth a chair for me, which I needed badly.

I sat breathing hard. The emir regarded me with a certain gentleness. "I regret this," he said. "It is not enjoyable." Oddly, I believed him. "Let us hope you will be reasonable before we have to inflict permanent injuries. Meanwhile, would you like a cigar?"

The old third degree procedure. Knock a man around for a while, then show him kindness. You'd be surprised how often that makes him blubber and break.

"We desire information about your troops and their plans," said the emir. "If you will cooperate and accept the true faith, you can have an honored position with us. We like good men in the Caliphate." He smiled. "After the war, you could select your harem out of Hollywood if you desired."

"And if I don't squeal—" I murmured.

He spread his hands. "You will have no further wish for a harem. The choice is yours."

"Let me think," I begged. "This isn't easy."

"Please do," he answered urbanely, and returned to his papers.

I sat as relaxed as possible, drawing the smoke into my throat and letting strength flow back. The Army geas could be broken by their technicians only if I gave my free consent, and I didn't want to. I considered the window behind the emir. It was a two-story drop to the street.

Most likely, I'd just get myself killed. But that was preferable to any other offer I'd had.

I went over the spells I'd haywired. A real technician has to know at least one arcane language—Latin, Greek, classical Arabic, Sanskrit, Old Norse, or the like—for the standard reasons of sympathetic science. Paranatural phenomena are not strongly influenced by ordinary speech. But except for the usual tag-ends of incantations, the minimum to operate the gadgets of daily life, I was no scholar.

However, I knew one slightly esoteric dialect quite well. I didn't know if it would work, but I could try.

My muscles tautened as I moved. It was a shuddersome effort to be casual. I knocked the end of ash off my cigar. As I lifted the thing again, it collected some ash from the emir's.

I got the rhyme straight in my mind, put the cigar to my lips, and subvocalized the spell.

"Ashes-way of the urningbay,
upward-way ownay eturningray,

*as-way the arksspay do yflay,
ikestray imhay in the eye-way!"*

I closed my right eye and brought the glowing cigar end almost against the lid.

The emir's El Fumo leaped up and ground itself into *his* right eye. He screamed and fell backward. I soared to my feet. I'd marked the werefennec, and one stride brought me over to him. I broke his vile little neck with a backhanded cuff and yanked off the flash that hung from it.

The guards howled and plunged for me. I went over the table and down on top of the emir, snatching his decanter en route. He clawed at me, wild with pain, I saw the ghastliness in his eye socket, and meanwhile I was hanging on to the vessel and shouting:

*"Ingthay of ystalcray,
ebay a istralmay!
As-way I-way owthray,
yflay ouyay osay!"*

As I finished, I broke free and hurled the decanter at the guards. It was lousy poetics, and might not have worked if the fat man hadn't already sensitized his stuff. As it was, the ball, the ashtray, the bowl, the glasses, the humidor, and the windowpanes all took off after the decanter. The air was full of flying glass.

I didn't stay to watch the results, but went out that window like an exorcised devil. I landed in a ball on the sidewalk, bounced up, and began running.

VI

Soldiers were around. Bullets sleeted after me. I set a record reaching the nearest alley. My witch-sight showed me a broken window, and I wriggled through that. Crouching beneath the sill, I heard the pursuit go by.

This was the back room of a looted grocery store, plenty dark for my purposes. I hung the flash around my neck, turned it on myself, and made the changeover. They'd return in a minute, and I didn't want to be vulnerable to lead.

Wolf, I snuffled around after another exit. A rear door stood half open. I slipped through into a courtyard full of ancient packing cases. They made a good hideout. I lay there, striving to control my lupine nature which wanted to pant, while they swarmed through the area.

When they were gone again, I tried to consider my situation. The temptation was to hightail out of this poor, damned place. I could probably make it, and had technically fulfilled my share of the mission. But the job wasn't really complete, and Virginia was alone with the afreet—if she still lived—and—

When I tried to recall her, the image came as a she-wolf and a furry aroma. I shook my head angrily. Weariness and desperation were submerging my reason and letting the animal instincts take over. I'd better do whatever had to be done fast.

I cast about. The town smells were confusing, but I caught the faintest sulfurous whiff and trotted cautiously in that direction. I kept to the shadows, and was seen twice but not challenged. They must have supposed I was one of theirs. The brimstone reek grew stronger.

They kept the afreet in the courthouse, a good solid building. I went through the small park in front of it, snuffed the wind carefully, and dashed over street and steps. Four enemy soldiers sprawled on top, throats cut open, and the broomstick was parked by the door. It had a twelve-inch switchblade in the handle, and Virginia had used it like a flying lance.

The man side of me, which had been entertaining stray romantic thoughts, backed up in a cold sweat; but the wolf grinned. I poked at the door. She'd 'chanted the lock open and left it that way. I stuck my nose in, and almost had it clawed off before Svartalf recognized me. He jerked his tail curtly, and I passed by and across the lobby. The stinging smell was coming from upstairs. I followed it through a thick darkness.

Light glowed in a second-floor office. I thrust the door ajar and peered in. Virginia was there. She had drawn the curtains and lit the elmos to see by. She was still busy with her precautions, started a little on spying me but went on with the chant. I parked my shaggy behind near the door and watched.

She'd chalked the usual figure, same as the Pentagon in Washington, and a Star of David inside that. The Solly bottle was at the center. It didn't look impressive, an old flask of hard-baked clay with its hollow handle bent over and returning inside—merely a Klein bottle, with Solomon's seal in red wax at the mouth. She'd loosened her hair, and it floated in a ruddy cloud about the pale beautiful face.

The wolf of me wondered why we didn't just make off with this crock of It. The man reminded him that undoubtedly the emir had taken precautions and would have sympathetic means to uncork it from afar. We had to put the demon out of action . . . somehow . . . but nobody on our side knew a great deal about his race.

Virginia finished her spell, drew the bung, and sprang outside the pentacle as smoke boiled from the flask. She almost didn't make it, the afreet came out in such a hurry. I stuck my tail between my legs and snarled. She was scared, too, trying hard not to show that but I caught the adrenalin odor.

The afreet must bend almost double under the ceiling. He was a monstrous gray thing, nude, more or less anthropoid but with wings and horns and long ears, a mouthful of fangs and eyes like hot embers. His assets were strength, speed, and physical near-invulnerability. Turned loose, he could break any attack of Vanbrugh's, and inflict frightful casualties on the most well-dug-in defense. Controlling him afterward, before he laid the countryside waste, would be a problem. But why should the Saracens care? They'd have exacted a geas from him, that he remain their ally, as the price of his freedom.

He roared something in Arabic. Smoke swirled from his mouth. Virginia looked tiny under those half-unfurled bat membranes. Her voice was less cool than she would have preferred: "Speak English, Marid. Or are you too ignorant?"

The demon huffed indignantly. "O spawn of a thousand baboons!" My eardrums flinched from the volume. "O thou white and gutless infidel thing, which I could break with my least finger, come in to me if thou darest!"

I was frightened, less by the chance of his breaking loose than by the racket he was making. It could be heard for a quarter mile.

"Be still, accursed of God!" Virginia answered. That shook him a smidgen. Like most of the hell-breed, he was allergic to holy names, though only seriously so under conditions that we couldn't reproduce here. She stood hands on hips, head tilted, to meet the gaze that smoldered down upon her. "Suleiman bin-Daoud, on whom be peace, didn't jug you for nothing, I see. Back to your prison and never come forth again, lest the anger of Heaven smite you!"

The afreet fleered. "Know that Suleiman the Wise is dead these three thousand years," he retorted. "Long and long have I brooded in my narrow cell, I who once raged free through earth and sky and will now at last be released to work my vengeance on the puny sons of Adam." He shoved at the invisible barrier, but one of that type has a rated strength of several million p.s.i. It would hold firm—till some adept dissolved it. "O thou shameless unveiled harlot with hair of hell, know that I am Rashid the Mighty, the glorious in power, the smiter of rocs! Come in here and fight like a man!"

I moved close to the girl, my hackles raised. The hand that touched my head was cold. "Paranoid type," she whispered. "A lot of these harmful Low Worlders are psycho. Stupid, though. Trickery's our single chance. I don't have any spells to compel him directly. But—" Aloud, to him, she said: "Shut up, Rashid, and listen to me. I also am of your race, and to be respected as such."

"Thou?" He hooted with fake laughter. "Thou of the Marid race? Why, thou fish-faced antling, if thou'dst come in here I'd show thee thou'rt not even fit to—" The rest was graphic but not for any gentlewere to repeat.

"No, hear me," said the girl. "Look and hearken well." She made signs and uttered a formula. I recognized the self-geas against telling a falsehood in the particular conversation. Our courts still haven't adopted it—Fifth Amendment—but I'd seen it used in trials abroad.

The demon recognized it too. I imagine the Saracen adept who pumped a knowledge of English into him, to make him effective in this war, had added other bits of information about the modern world. He grew more quiet and attentive.

Virginia intoned impressively: "I can speak nothing to you except the truth. Do you agree that the name is the thing?"

"Y-y-yes," the afreet rumbled. "That is common knowledge."

I scented her relief. First hurdle passed! He had *not* been educated in scientific goetics. Though the name is, of course, in sympathy with the object, which is the principle of nymic spells and the like—nevertheless, only in this century has Korzybski demonstrated that the word and its referent are not identical.

"Very well," she said. "My name is Ginny."

He started in astonishment. "Art thou indeed?"

"Yes. Now will you listen to me? I came to offer you advice, as one jinni to another. I have powers of my own, you know, albeit I employ them in the service of Allah, the Omnipotent, the Omniscient, the Compassionate."

He glowered, but supposing her to be one of his species, he was ready to put on a crude show of courtesy. She couldn't be lying about her advice. It did not occur to him that she hadn't said the counsel would be good.

"Go on, then, if thou wilst," he growled. "Knowest thou that tomorrow I fare forth to destroy the infidel host?" He got caught up in his dreams of glory. "Aye, well will I rip them, and trample them, and break and gut and flay them. Well will they learn the power of Rashid the bright-winged, the fiery, the merciless, the wise, the . . ."

Virginia waited out his adjectives, then said gently: "But Rashid, why must you wreak harm? You earn nothing thereby except hate."

A whine crept into his bass. "Aye, thou speakest sooth. The whole world hates me. Everybody conspires against me. Had he not had the aid of traitors, Suleiman had never locked me away. All which I have sought to do has been thwarted by envious ill-wishers— Aye, but tomorrow comes the day of reckoning!"

Virginia lit a cigaret with a steady hand and blew smoke at him. "How can you trust the emir and his cohorts?" she asked. "He too is your enemy. He only wants to make a cat's-paw of you. Afterward, back in the bottle!"

"Why . . . why . . ." The afreet swelled till the spacewarp barrier creaked. Lighting crackled from his nostrils. It hadn't occurred to him before; his race isn't bright; but of course a trained psychologist would understand how to follow out paranoid logic.

"Have you not known enmity throughout your long days?" continued Virginia quickly. "Think back, Rashid. Was not the very first thing you remember the cruel act of a spitefully envious world?"

"Aye—it was." The maned head nodded, and the voice dropped very low. "On the day I was hatched . . . aye, my mother's wingtip smote me so I reeled."

"Perhaps that was accidental," said Virginia.

"Nay. Ever she favored my older brother—the lout!"

Virginia sat down cross-legged. "Tell me about it," she urged. Her tone dripped sympathy.

I felt a lessening of the great forces that surged within the barrier. The afreet squatted on his hams, eyes half-shut, going back down a memory trail of millennia. Virginia guided him, a hint here and there. I didn't know what she was driving at, surely you couldn't psychoanalyze the monster in half a night, but—

"—Aye, and I was scarce turned three centuries when I fell into a pit my foes must have dug for me."

"Surely you could fly out of it," she murmured.

The afreet's eyes rolled. His face twisted into still more gruesome furrows. "It was a pit, I say!"

"Not by any chance a lake?" she inquired.

"Nay!" His wings thundered. "No such damnable thing . . . 'twas dark, and wet, but—nay, not wet either, a cold which burned . . ."

I saw dimly that the girl had a lead. She dropped long lashes to hide the sudden gleam in her gaze. Even as a wolf, I could realize what a shock it must have been to an aerial demon, nearly drowning, his fires hissing into steam, and how he must ever after deny to himself that it had happened. But what use could she make of—

Svartalf the cat streaked in and skidded to a halt. Every hair on him stood straight, and his eyes blistered me. He spat something and went out again with me in his van.

Down in the lobby I heard voices. Looking through the door, I saw a few soldiers milling about. They'd come by, perhaps to investigate the noise, seen the dead guards, and now they must have sent after reinforcements.

Whatever Ginny was trying to do, she needed time for it. I went out that door in one gray leap and tangled with the Saracens. We boiled into a clamorous pile. I was almost pinned flat by their numbers, but kept my jaws free and used them. Then Svartalf rode that broomstick above the fight, stabbing.

We carried a few of their weapons back into the lobby in our jaws, and sat down to wait. I figured I'd do better to remain wolf and be immune to most things than have the convenience of hands. Svartalf regarded a tommy gun thoughtfully, propped it along a wall, and crouched over it.

I was in no hurry. Every minute we were left alone, or held off the coming attack, was a minute gained for Ginny. I laid my head on my forepaws and dozed off. Much too soon I heard hobnails rattle on pavement.

The detachment must have been a good hundred. I saw their dark mass, and the gleam of starlight off their weapons. They hovered for a while around the squad we'd liquidated. Abruptly they whooped and charged up the steps.

Svartalf braced himself and worked the tommy gun. The recoil sent him skating back across the lobby, swearing, but he got a couple. I met the rest in the doorway.

Slash, snap, leap in, leap out, rip them and gash them and howl in their faces! They were jammed together in the entrance, slow and clumsy. After a brief whirl of teeth they retreated. They left half a dozen dead and wounded.

I peered through the glass in the door and saw my friend the emir. He had a bandage over his eye, but lumbered around exhorting his men with more energy than I'd expected. Groups of them broke from the main bunch and ran to either side. They'd be coming in the windows and the other doors.

I whined as I realized we'd left the broomstick outside. There could be no escape now, not even for Ginny. The protest became a snarl when I heard glass breaking and rifles blowing off locks.

That Svartalf was a smart cat. He found the tommy gun again and somehow, clumsy though paws are, managed to shoot out the lights. He and I retreated to the stairway.

They came at us in the dark, blind as most men are. I let them fumble around, and the first one who groped to the stairs was killed quietly. The second had time to yell. The whole gang of them crowded after him.

They couldn't shoot in the gloom and press without potting their own people. Excited to mindlessness, they attacked me with scimitars, which I didn't object to. Svartalf raked their legs and I tore them apart —whick, snap, clash, Allah Akbar and teeth in the night!

The stair was narrow enough for me to hold, and their own casualties hampered them, but the sheer weight of a hundred brave men forced me back a tread at a time. Otherwise one could have tackled me and a dozen more have piled on top. As things were, we gave the houris a few fresh customers for every foot we lost.

I have no clear memory of the fight. You seldom do. But it must have been about twenty minutes before they fell back at an angry growl. The emir himself stood at the foot of the stairs, lashing his tail and rippling his gorgeously striped hide.

I shook myself wearily and braced my feet for the last round. The one-eyed tiger climbed slowly toward us. Svartalf spat. Suddenly he zipped down the banister past the larger cat and disappeared in the gloom. Well, he had his own neck to think about—

We were almost nose to nose when the emir lifted a paw full of swords and brought it down. I dodged somehow and flew for his throat. All I got was a mouthful of baggy skin, but I hung on and tried to work my way inward.

He roared and shook his head till I swung like a bell clapper. I shut my eyes and clamped on tight. He raked my ribs with those long claws. I skipped away but kept my teeth where they were. Lunging, he fell on me. His jaws clashed shut. Pain jagged through my tail. I let go to howl.

He pinned me down with one paw, raising the other to break my spine. Somehow, crazed with the hurt, I writhed free and struck upward. His remaining eye was glaring at me, and I bit it out of his head.

He screamed! A sweep of one paw sent me kiting up to slam against the banister. I lay with the wind knocked from me while the blind tiger rolled over in his agony. The beast drowned the man, and he went down the stairs and wrought havoc among his own soldiers.

A broomstick whizzed above the melee. Good old Svartalf! He'd only gone to fetch our transportation. I saw him ride toward the door of the afreet, and rose groggily to meet the next wave of Saracens.

They were still trying to control their boss. I gulped for breath and stood watching and smelling and listening. My tail seemed ablaze. Half of it was gone.

A tommy gun began stuttering. I heard blood rattle in the emir's lungs. He was hard to kill. *That's the end of you, Steve Matuchek,* thought the man of me. *They'll do what they should have done in the first place, stand beneath you and sweep you with their fire, every tenth round argent.*

The emir fell and lay gasping out his life. I waited for his men to collect their wits and remember me.

Ginny appeared on the landing, astride the broomstick. Her voice seemed to come from very far away. "Steve! Quick! Here!"

I shook my head dazedly, trying to understand. I was too tired, too canine. She stuck her fingers in her mouth and whistled. That fetched me.

She slung me across her lap and hung on tight as Svartalf piloted the stick. A gun fired blindly from below. We went out a second-story window and into the sky.

A carpet swooped near. Svartalf arched his back and poured on the Power. That Cadillac had legs! We left the enemy sitting there, and I passed out.

VII

When I came to, I was prone on a cot in a hospital tent. Daylight was bright outside; the earth lay wet and steaming. A medic looked around as I groaned. "Hello, hero," he said. "Better stay in that position for a while. How're you feeling?"

I waited till full consciousness returned before I accepted a cup of bouillon. "How am I?" I whispered; they'd humanized me, of course.

"Not too bad, considering. You had some infection of your wounds—a staphylococcus that can switch species for a human or canine host—but we cleaned the bugs out with a new antibiotic technique. Otherwise, loss of blood, shock, and plain old exhaustion. You should be fine in a week or two."

I lay thinking, my mind draggy, most of my attention on how delicious the bouillon tasted. A field hospital can't lug around the equipment to stick pins in model bacteria. Often it doesn't even have the enlarged anatomical dummies on which the surgeon can do a sympathetic operation. "What technique do you mean?" I asked.

"One of our boys has the Evil Eye. He looks at the germs through a microscope."

I didn't inquire further, knowing that *Reader's Digest* would be waxing lyrical about it in a few months. Something else nagged at me. "The attack . . . have they begun?"

"The— Oh. That! That was two days ago, Rin-Tin-Tin. You've been kept under asphodel. We mopped 'em up along the entire line. Last I heard, they were across the Washington border and still running."

I sighed and went back to sleep. Even the noise as the medic dictated a report to his typewriter couldn't hold me awake.

Ginny came in the next day, with Svartalf riding her shoulder. Sunlight striking through the tent flap turned her hair to hot copper. "Hello, Captain Matuchek," she said. "I came to see how you were, soon as I could get leave."

I raised myself on my elbows, and whistled at the cigaret she offered. When it was between my lips, I said slowly: "Come off it, Ginny. We didn't exactly go on a date that night, but I think we're properly introduced."

"Yes." She sat down on the cot and stroked my hair. That felt good. Svartalf purred at me, and I wished I could respond.

"How about the afreet?" I asked after a while.

"Still in his bottle." She grinned. "I doubt if anybody'll ever be able to get him out again, assuming anybody would want to."

"But what did you *do?*"

"A simple application of Papa Freud's principles. If it's ever written up, I'll have every Jungian in the country on my neck, but it worked. I got him to spinning out his memories and illusions, and soon found he had a hydrophobic complex—which is fear of water, Rover, not rabies—"

"You can call me Rover," I growled, "but if you call me Fido, gives a paddling."

She didn't ask why I assumed I'd be sufficiently close in future for such laying on of hands. That encouraged me. Indeed, she blushed, but went on: "Having gotten the key to his personality, I found it simple to play on his phobia. I pointed out how common a substance water is and how difficult total dehydration is. He got more and more scared. When I showed him that all animal tissue, including his own, is about eighty percent water, that was that. He crept back into his bottle and went catatonic."

After a moment, she added thoughtfully: "I'd like to have him for my mantelpiece, but I suppose he'll wind up in the Smithsonian. So I'll simply write a little treatise on the military uses of psychiatry."

"Aren't bombs and dragons and elfshot gruesome enough?" I demanded with a shudder.

Poor simple elementals! They think they're fiendish, but ought to take lessons from the human race.

As for me, I could imagine certain drawbacks to getting hitched with a witch, but— "C'mere, youse."

She did.

I don't have many souvenirs of the war. It was an ugly time and best forgotten. But one keepsake will always be with me, in spite of the plastic surgeons' best efforts. As a wolf, I've got a stumpy tail, and as a man I don't like to sit down in wet weather.

That's a hell of a thing to receive a Purple Heart for.